CREEPY HOLLOW

BOOKS 7, 8, 9

EMERSON'S STORY

GLASS FAERIE

SHADOW FAERIE

REBEL FAERIE

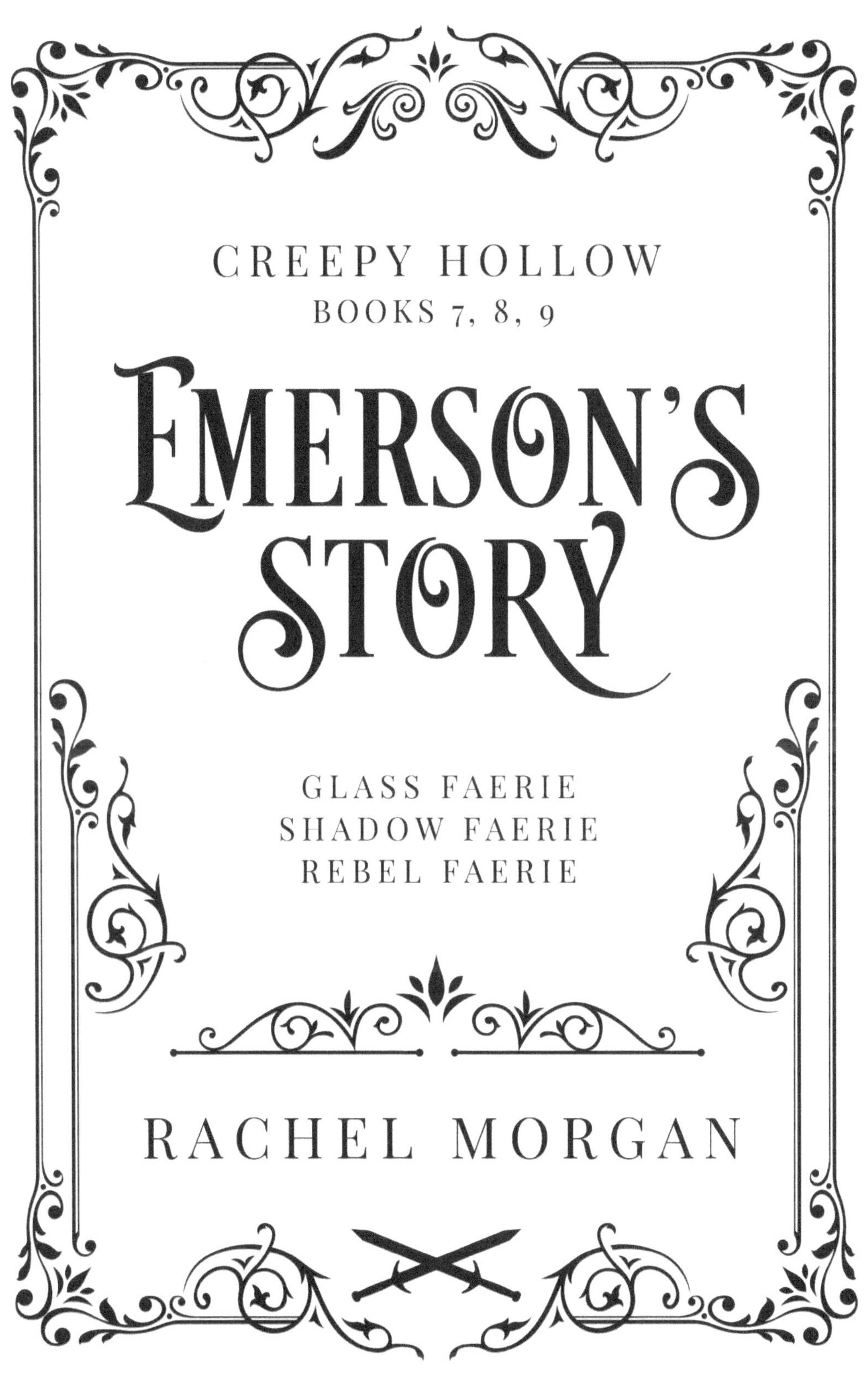

CREEPY HOLLOW

BOOKS 7, 8, 9

EMERSON'S STORY

GLASS FAERIE
SHADOW FAERIE
REBEL FAERIE

RACHEL MORGAN

Emerson's Story
Creepy Hollow Books 7, 8, 9

Glass Faerie, Copyright © 2017 Rachel Morgan
Shadow Faerie, Copyright © 2017 Rachel Morgan
Rebel Faerie, Copyright © 2017 Rachel Morgan

This Edition Published in 2024

ISBN 978-1-998988-09-9

www.rachel-morgan.com

GLASS FAERIE

PART I

CHAPTER 1

In the dirty alley between Tygo's Diner and the abandoned library, the stench of rotting garbage provokes my gag reflex. I focus on breathing through my mouth as I remove the crumpled brown paper package from my messenger bag and hold it up. "You know the price, Slade." I wave the package at him. "Take it or leave it."

Slade raises an eyebrow. He breathes out a painfully long sigh before turning to the wad of notes in his hand. He flicks lazily through them, counting out the right amount. But instead of handing the money over, he leans one shoulder against the wall and watches me with a smirk. "You drive a hard bargain, Emerson Clarke."

"Stop being an idiot. The price is exactly the same as last time. Do you want it or not?"

"Course I want it. Lighten up, Em." He shrugs, his shoulder rubbing against the giant yellow X graffitied across the bricks. "Just trying to make this exchange more entertaining."

I shove the bag against his chest and remove the cash from his hand. "I don't need any more entertainment in my life."

"Hey, you seriously need to chill out," he calls after me as I turn away.

"Thanks for the advice." I don't bother to look over my shoulder at him as I stride away, my sneakers crunching against the damp, dirty ground. I'm almost at the end of the alley when the back door of Tygo's Diner swings open. I dodge out of the way to avoid being hit in the face. "Jeez, Marty."

"Oh, great, you're still here." He holds a trash bag out toward me. "You forgot this one."

I consider telling him my shift ended five minutes ago, but it isn't worth the argument. I press my lips together, push Slade's money into my jeans pocket, and take the bag. Marty lets the door slam shut without another word. Grumbling beneath my breath, I walk the few steps back toward the dumpster. Slade, still slouching at the other end of the alley, ignores me as I hold my breath, lift the dumpster lid, and heft the trash bag up and over the edge.

I'm about to lower the lid when I hear rustling from within the dumpster. *Just a rat*, I tell myself, knowing I should close the lid. But that part of my brain that always wants to know if the things I see and hear are actually real keeps my arm frozen in place. The scratching, rustling sound moves up the side of the dumpster. A scaly arm appears, clawing its way over the edge with blue talons and glowing yellow liquid dripping from—

I drop the lid and jump back, swearing out loud.

"Scared of something, Em?" Slade sniggers as he walks past me.

"No," I snap back. But as he rounds the corner and disappears, I swallow, my heart thudding way too fast. I peek around the side of the dumpster, looking for a half-squashed reptilian arm protruding from beneath the lid. But there's nothing there. "Overactive imagination," I mutter to myself as I hurry away, which is the same lie I always use.

I feel easier once I'm out on the main street. Hooking my thumb beneath the strap of my messenger bag, I slow my steps, no longer feeling as though I'm running from something. My fear evaporates as I remind myself that with Slade's money added to my savings, I finally have enough for a bus trip.

"Hey, Em!"

I swing around in the direction of the shout and find Val perched atop the wall surrounding Stanmeade Elementary School. "Hey." I wave at her as I change direction and cross the grassy area outside the school. I dump my bag on the ground, then run straight at the wall. My right foot strikes the bricks and launches me upward. With my palms flat on top of the wall, it's easy to pull my legs up.

"Nice one," Val says as I walk deftly along the top of the wall toward her.

"Thanks." I sit beside her and dust my hands on my jeans. "It's an easy wall, though. Not as high as some of the others we've tried."

"I know. Hey, check this out." She pushes her dark frizzy hair out of her face and holds her phone in front of me. "Latest Top Ten video from ParkourForLife."

Looking past the crack on Val's cellphone screen, I watch a guy leap from one building, somersault through the air, and land on the next building, followed by nine more spectacular moves. "Awesome," I murmur. "I'd love to be able to do all that."

"Totally," Val agrees. "I kinda feel like we'll have to go somewhere else to stretch our skills though. The urban playground here is just too limiting."

"The urban playground?" I repeat with a laugh.

"Yeah. People call it that, right?"

"Um …"

"Well, I call it that." She spreads her arms out, almost smacking me in the face with her elbow. "I present to you the Stanmeade urban playground. It's ugly, but it's where we started."

I shake my head, still smiling. "You got the ugly part right. And the limiting part. We know this place and its obstacles too well now."

"Yeah. Anyway, how was your shift?"

I shrug. "Slightly above average. I sold another one of Chelsea's homemade concoctions. Slade Murphy again."

"Again? Ooh, do tell. What secret recurring ailment is Slade Murphy suffering from? Anything super embarrassing we should warn his girlfriend about?"

"It was actually for his girlfriend. A contraceptive tea of some sort."

Val tilts her head back and laughs. "Well, let's hope that works."

"I guess it must be working, since this is the second pack I sold him. Anyway, that's not important." I pull my sleeves down to cover my thumbs. "What's important is that I've finally saved enough for another bus ride."

Val straightens. "To visit your mom?"

"Yes, obviously."

"Cool," she says, though her voice lacks enthusiasm.

"What?"

"It's just …" She shifts a little. "Are you sure you want to do that? It really upset you last time you visited her."

I chew on my lower lip before answering. "I know, but I'm hoping it'll be different this time. She might be better. Besides, it'll be worth it to get out of this place for a little bit. I'm counting the days until I don't have to share a house with pain-in-the-ass people anymore."

"I hear ya," Val says, her curls bouncing as she nods. I know she doesn't entirely mean it, though. Our family situations are both tough, but in completely different ways. While I'm stuck with an aunt who hates me and a prima donna cousin, Val has four younger siblings her mom expects her to help take care of. And I know Val loves them, despite all her complaining. So in a few months' time when we're finally done with school, I have a feeling I'll be leaving on my own.

"Hey! Get off there!" We look over our shoulders into the school yard where Mrs. Pringleton is shaking her bony finger at us.

"But we're not doing anything wrong," Val shouts back.

Her gnarled hands form fists, and the pink birthmarks across one side of her face turn pinker. "I'm calling the police if you don't get off there in the next ten seconds!"

"Cool," Val says. "Tell Uncle Pete I say hi."

"Val." I nudge her arm while trying to keep from laughing. "Let's not give the old woman a heart attack, okay? We can climb right back up once she leaves."

"Fiiiiine." Val shuffles her butt to the edge of the wall and jumps down. I follow a moment later. "I guess I should go home to the mini monsters anyway," she adds. "But I'm giving myself another five minutes of freedom first." She sits on the grass and crosses her legs.

"Fine by me." I remain standing but lean back against the wall and play with the edge of my sleeve. "You're probably already in trouble for being late, so what's an extra five minutes?"

"Exactly."

A car rumbles by, and on the other side of the road I notice a person who wasn't there a minute ago. A guy with an annoyingly familiar swagger to his step. "Wonderful," I mutter. "What's Dash doing back here?"

"Hmm?" Val looks up. "Oh. Probably going to the party."

"What party?"

She twists her head to the side and looks up at me. "You know, the one at the Mason farmhouse."

"I didn't know, actually. Is Jade's older brother home again?"

"Yeah. Supposedly looking after Jade and the other Mason kid while their parents are away."

"And instead he's throwing another party," I say with a sigh.

"Yeah. Lucky for us lowly high-schoolers."

"Sure. If that's your thing." I look back across the road at Dash. As always, he's highlighted his honey-blond hair with streaks of bright green. All I can do is shake my head at the odd color combination. "His hair is so weird. I don't know how they let him get away with it at whatever preppy school he goes to."

"You don't know how they let him get away with amazing hair?" Val asks with a laugh.

"No, I mean the color."

She laughs harder and shakes her head. "I don't know what you could possibly find offensive about that boy's beautiful hair, but okay. I won't argue with you."

I look down at her with a frown. "Beautiful hair? Really?"

She shrugs. "What can I say? I find him attractive."

I groan and look up once more, and Dash chooses that moment to glance across the street, give us a charming grin, and wink. "Seriously?" I mutter. "Who the hell winks at people?"

"Dash, apparently, although probably only at you." Val smacks my ankle. "You know he loves to irritate you. Anyway, you should come to the party. If Dash came all the way home for it, you know it's gonna be good."

"Please. Dash is probably bored out of his mind at whatever uptight, snooty private school he goes to. No doubt he jumps at the chance to go to *any* party."

"So … does that mean you'll come?"

I shake my head as I watch Dash continue on down the street. "Not my scene, Val. You know that."

"You know you can still come to parties even if you don't want to drink, right?"

"So I can stand there totally sober and watch the rest of you get hammered? No thanks."

"Or you could just have a *little* bit." She pats my sneaker. "You need to chill out more, Em."

I fold my arms across my chest. "Remember how my uncle died of alcohol poisoning? And how my mom tried to drown out her delusions by drinking? Yeah. I'm trying to avoid situations like that."

Val is quiet as she gets to her feet. "Come on, Em. You know that's never going to happen to you."

I blink away the memory of that scaly, glowing arm reaching out of the dumpster. "Okay, here's a reason for you: Dash is going to be at that party, and I don't feel like ruining my night."

"Okay, okay, I get it. You're not coming to the party." She loops an arm around my neck and hugs me. "Try to have a good evening anyway."

"Thanks. I'll see you tomorrow."

We head in different directions, Val walking around the back of the school to cut across the field, while I continue along the road. Long shadows stretch across the pavement, and the washed-out orangey brown haze of sunset fills the sky. I turn just after the post office—

—and see a figure in a silver hooded cloak standing in the middle of the road. In front of him or her is a man with pointed ears. The cloaked figure touches the man, and the man becomes a solid statue of gleaming, faceted crystal.

With a gasp, I duck back behind the building, my heart thundering. I press my back against the warm brick wall and slap both hands over my eyes. I count to ten while forcing myself to breathe slowly. "There's nothing there," I whisper to myself. I start counting again, and this time I keep going. I reach eighty before I'm brave enough to lower my hands from my face. Slowly, I peek around the edge of the building—and of course, there's no sign that a hooded figure and a person made of crystal were ever there. *Because they weren't*, I tell myself. I press my back against the wall once more. "You didn't see anything," I whisper. "There was nothing there. You didn't see anything strange. You are not losing your mind."

But as I hurry along the main road, choosing to take the longer route home, I can't help thinking of all the times weird things like this have happened. The unidentifiable creature sitting on the park swing one day. That man with the pointed ears who came to the diner one afternoon. And that time I looked in the bathroom mirror and for just a moment, my hair was blue. "I'm not losing my mind," I repeat quietly, almost desperately. This is probably related to something I saw on TV. Or something I read. My brain is processing something fictional and regurgitating it more vividly than I expected. This is what people mean when they talk about an overactive imagination, right? "Yeah, that must be it," I murmur. "That must be it."

It must be *anything* except the obvious: that I'm turning out just like my mother.

I try to keep my gaze focused on the ground at my feet the rest of the way home, not wanting to see anything I shouldn't be seeing. It's a much longer journey than if I'd used the street I was supposed to use. The street the cloaked figure was on. It's dark by the time I reach our driveway, and I almost run up it and around the side of Chelsea's house. I'm never this eager to get home, but I've somehow convinced myself that I'll be safe once I get inside. I let myself in through the kitchen door and take a moment to breathe as the door clicks shut behind me.

A boiling pot containing something that smells like it could be pasta sits on the stove. Through the open door that leads to the garage salon, I hear Chelsea and Georgia chatting. My earlier fear begins to seem silly in comparison to the ordinariness around me.

I cross the kitchen without calling hello to Chelsea and Georgia. They won't particularly care that I'm home, and I don't particularly care to greet them. Instead, I head straight for my bedroom, removing the money from my pocket as I go. I force my door open, shoving it past yet another box of Chelsea's salon supplies that seems to have found its way into this room since this morning. I let my messenger bag slip off my shoulder and onto the bed, my focus now on counting out my commission from the money Slade paid me. The rest, of course, goes to dear Aunt Chelsea. She's the one who makes the weird herbal remedies.

I pull my ice cream tub of toiletries off the shelf above my bed and look inside it for the resealable plastic bag I keep my savings in. I'll count it all now and make sure I have enough, then buy a bus ticket tomorrow. I riffle through the various bottles, my fingers feeling for the crumpled plastic bag.

It's gone.

My stomach drops as I empty the tub's contents onto my bed, just to be sure. I spread everything out, but the little zipper bag definitely isn't there. My skin grows cold, then hot. That was months and *months* of savings, all so that I could visit Mom, and now it's *gone*?

My hands become fists as I storm out of the room and head straight for the salon. I find Georgia lounging in one of the chairs, staring at herself in the mirror as she combs her hand through her sleek blonde hair. On the opposite side of the room, Chelsea stocks the shelves with more of her homemade herbal products.

"Where's my money?" I demand.

Georgia jumps in fright and almost slips out of her chair, but Chelsea is still for a moment before turning to face me. "*Your* money, Emerson?" she says. "I think you mean *my* money."

"Excuse me?"

"You've been stealing from me for months."

"*Stealing* from—I have never stolen a single thing from you. I always give you exactly what you're due and only keep the percentage I'm allowed. You know that."

"Right." Chelsea crosses her arms and nods. "And then you go back to my bedroom afterwards and steal whatever you want. Money's been going missing from my purse for months now. At first I thought I was imagining it, that it must be my mistake, but then I started keeping track of exactly how much was there." She gives me a triumphant smile, as if she's done something wonderfully clever. "And you know what I discovered? Small amounts of money started to disappear every week or so. And look where I found it." She digs in her pocket and pulls out a plastic bag. *My* plastic bag.

"That is my hard-earned savings," I tell her, feeling a knot of nausea forming in my stomach. "That is not yours."

"Don't lie to me. I know how you girls spend money. As if it grows on trees and you have no responsibilities in the world. What I want to know is where is the rest of it?" She shakes the bag in the air between us. "Because you've taken way more than what's left here."

"I didn't steal from you!" I shout. I glance at Georgia, who's watching the two of us with a small smile. My anger increases a level as I point at her. "You want to know where your money's been going? *That's* where you should be looking."

"Don't you dare pin this on Georgia. She would never steal from me."

"Well it isn't me, so that doesn't leave anyone else, does it."

Chelsea lets out an incredulous laugh. "I cannot believe you, Emerson. After everything I've done for you. I work so hard to take care of both of you, and this is how you repay me? You steal from me and then you run all over town doing that useless parkour nonsense."

"Everything?" I repeat. "Did you say after *everything* you've done for me?" Normally I'd keep my mouth shut. I'd bite down my anger and let her try to convince herself how amazingly charitable she is. But not this time. Not when she's taken my one chance at visiting Mom. "You mean giving me Georgia's second-hand clothing, making me sleep in what is essentially your storeroom for *five years*, and using me as your live-in maid?"

"I gave you a home," she shouts. "You should be grateful for the roof over your head. What would have happened to you if there'd been no one to take you in after they locked your mother up? Your father sure as hell didn't want you. He seems to be covering all your mother's medical bills in that fancy faraway hospital, but is he interested in supporting you? Nope. I've never even met the man."

Chelsea's used this tack before to try to hurt me, but it never works. I couldn't care less about my father or the fact that he has no interest in me. I don't even know what he looks like. "Please," I say between clenched teeth. "Just give me back my money."

"You're not getting this money back, Emerson. End of story." Chelsea tucks the plastic bag back into her pocket and turns to her shelves of herbal garbage. Georgia pushes herself out of her chair and leaves the room. I stand there feeling sick, my body shaking, finally realizing that the hope I've been holding onto for months—the hope of finally visiting Mom again—is gone. And I can't even blame Chelsea for it. Not entirely. Not when someone else is responsible for this mess.

I stride out of the salon and head for Georgia's room. She's sitting on her bed with a magazine, smiling sweetly, knowingly.

"It was you," I say, taking a few steps into her room. "You told her where my money was."

She lowers the magazine. "What could you possibly need all that money for, Em? You know we need it to keep the household running. How could you be so selfish?"

"How could *you* be so selfish stealing from your own mother?"

"I *need* things," she says. "Things you don't need. Things you wouldn't understand, and Mom doesn't seem to understand either."

I glare at her for another few moments, my anger so intense I could *scream*. But it would do no good. I still have to get through another few months here, and so I clamp my mouth shut, turn around, and aim for the door.

But that's when I see it: Hanging from a knob on the wardrobe, the tag still attached to the hem, is a brand new dress. "*This* is the stuff you need?" I demand, grabbing the hanger, spinning around, and shaking the dress at her.

"Yes." She sits a little straighter, as if I've finally got her attention now that I'm threatening her clothing. "I have a boyfriend and a social life and a future. That kind of stuff doesn't come for free. You have to look good if you want to—"

I fling the dress at her, and she yelps as it hits the side of her head. "You bought a *dress*?" I yell. "I've been saving for almost a year so I could visit my mother, and you took that away from me for a *DRESS*?"

Something flashes across the room. Light and heat and the sound of a sizzle. It vanishes as Georgia falls back against the pillows with a scream.

Fear cracks through my anger, drenching me in goosebumps. I rush over to Georgia. "What's wrong? What happened?"

She shoves me away with one hand, the other covering her cheek. "What the hell did you do to me?" she gasps, her eyes wider than I've ever seen them.

"I didn't do—"

"You threw something at me! Like a firecracker or something. You freak, what is *wrong* with—"

"I didn't throw anything!"

"Get off her!" Chelsea's hands wrap around my shoulders and tug me backward.

In the quiet that follows, all I hear is my heavy breathing and Georgia's whimpering. She lowers her hand, revealing blood seeping from a shallow gash across her cheek. She glares at me with renewed hatred. "Oh, my poor baby," Chelsea gasps, grabbing a tissue from the box on the nightstand. She drops onto the bed beside Georgia and presses the tissue against her cheek before turning her scowl toward me. "I can't do this anymore, Em. You have never shown any gratitude for the sacrifices I've had to make for you. You've stolen from me, and now you've physically assaulted

Georgia. The police can deal with you."

"The *police?*"

She stands and brushes past me. "You're not my problem anymore." I follow her into the kitchen where she picks up her phone from the table. When she taps a few numbers and brings the phone to her ear, I realize she isn't joking.

Fear dissolves my anger. "Chelsea, wait. I'm sorry. Georgia provoked me, but I shouldn't have lost my temper like that. It won't happen again. You don't have to bring the cops into this. Please." I feel sick having to beg her, having to plead with this woman who's made me scrub toilets, do Georgia's laundry, lie to the various men she's always stringing along, and then demand my gratitude for the privilege of doing all these things for her. But it's only for a few more months. Then I'll be eighteen, school will be done, and I can make a plan to get out of here. But if the police get involved, who knows where I'll end up.

"No," Chelsea says. "I can't believe you're making me do this, but I have no choice now. I have to protect my daughter."

"Chelsea, please. Protect her from what?" I step closer, clasping my hands together beneath my chin. "I swear I'll never—"

"You're going to end up as crazy as your mother," she snaps, "and I don't want you in this house when that happens."

I reel back as if she slapped me.

"Hello?" she says into the phone, turning away from me. "Yes, um, please can you send someone to—"

I bolt past her toward the back door.

"Hey, get back here!" she yells as I tug the door open and run.

But I don't go back. And I don't stop running.

CHAPTER 2

I RACE ACROSS THE BACKYARD, SCALE THE NEIGHBOR'S FENCE, AND EASILY VAULT THE low wall on the other side of their garden. I have no plan other than to get as far away from home as possible before the cops show up. My sneakers slam pavements and my body launches across several more obstacles before I realize I'm heading for Val's house. I get about halfway there when I remember she won't be home. I'm not sure what time that party was supposed to start, but things generally get going pretty early around here. It's not like there's much else to do. Besides, Val's house is probably the first place Chelsea will send the cops.

I slow my steps and place my hands on my hips as I catch my breath. My heart is thrumming, my body almost vibrating. I force myself to take a long, slow breath. "What the hell are you doing?" I mutter to myself. Maybe I shouldn't have run. Maybe I should have stayed and explained myself. What's the worst that could have happened?

You're going to end up as crazy as your mother.

If the cops believe Chelsea—if someone performs some kind of medical test on me and her words turn out to be *true*—then the worst that could happen isn't a physical assault charge. It isn't juvy or community service or whatever the local law enforcement decides is a suitable punishment for me. No, the worst thing would be ending up in a facility just like my mother's. Locked away to keep me from hurting others. Drugged to keep me from seeing things that aren't there.

Basically, my worst nightmare would come true.

I find myself running again, this time toward Jade Mason's place on the outskirts of town. It's further away than I remember, and I'm breathless by the time I get there. I slow down near the bottom of the long driveway so I'm not a sweaty, panting mess when I reach the party.

Outside the Masons' house, I find people milling around beside a bonfire and others sitting on the porch. Music reaches my ears. Not seeing Val anywhere outside, I run up the porch steps and into the house.

"Yo, Em, you made it this time." Eric, the idiot who sits next to me in English class, nods at me from where he's leaning against the hallway wall with some of his friends. "Hey, did you bring any of that herbal stuff your aunt sells?" He makes a few thrusting motions with his pelvis while his friends laugh. "You know how it gets me—"

"Is Val here?" I ask.

"Yeah, that way." He jerks his head toward the living room at the other end of the hallway. "Want a drink first?"

I walk past him without answering, letting the howls and boos from his friends mingle with the thumping background music. In the dim, smoky living room, Dash is standing just inside the doorway, commanding an audience of several girls. His eyebrows twitch momentarily into a frown when he sees me, but it only lasts a moment. Then he shakes his head and smirks.

Ignoring him, I walk into the room and spot Val on a couch with a bunch of our classmates. She has a cup in each hand. "Val!" I hurry over to her.

"Hey, you came." She beams at me as she shuffles over and nods her head toward the open spot on the couch. "Come sit here."

"No, I'm—can I talk to you?"

She must hear the urgency in my voice—or perhaps see it on my face—because she pushes herself to her feet immediately. "Something wrong?" she asks, walking with me to the edge of the room. We stop beside a window. My body still feels like it's humming, so I shake my hands, roll my shoulders, and force myself to breathe out slowly. Val frowns. "Em, what is it?"

"Chelsea found my stash of money. She freaked out and accused me of stealing from her."

"What? No way. You would never *steal* from her."

"Of course I wouldn't. It was obviously Georgia, but there's no point in telling Chelsea that. She would never believe her little angel capable of stealing. And then … I—I lost my temper, and Georgia and I were fighting, and I scratched her face." I can't tell Val it wasn't me. I can't tell her that something strange and inexplicable happened in that room. She'd probably look at me the same way Chelsea did in the kitchen. *You're going to end up as crazy as your mother.* "And then she said she can't deal with me anymore and called the cops."

"Seriously?" Val looks at me as if she may not have heard correctly. "Chelsea called the cops because you scratched Georgia? That's ridiculous."

"I know. But …" I look around. "Is your cousin here? Lexi? If I can talk to her, then she can explain to her dad what actually happened, and he can tell the other cops, and then they won't take me away."

"Take you away?" Val starts laughing. "Em, you need to chill. Uncle Pete isn't going to take this seriously. He knows you're not, like, an actual criminal. Maybe he'll make you pick up litter in the park or something, just to keep Chelsea happy, but he isn't going to *take you away*."

Suddenly I wonder if I'm being as silly as Val seems to think. It was just a scratch, after all. Well, a bit more than a scratch, but hardly life-threatening. "You think?" I run a hand through my hair, not willing to relax just yet.

"Yeah, come on. This is a small town. We all know each other. People don't get locked up for something this stupid."

"I guess."

"What do you mean you *guess?*" She smiles and nudges me with one hand still grasping a cup. Cold liquid sloshes over the edge and splashes my arm. "Obviously I'm right about this. So just relax. Have fun. Get a drink."

I sigh, trying to breathe out my panic and not fully succeeding. "You remember that this kind of setting isn't exactly my idea of fun, right?"

"I know. But Jade's brother's friend Marcus is gonna be here soon, and I need backup. You know I get weird when I'm left alone with a hot guy. Please stay."

I don't exactly *want* to stay, but it's probably the best option. Chelsea wasn't joking about pressing charges—or attempting to, at least—but she'll probably calm down if I give her a bit of space for the night. "Yeah, okay."

"Yay." Val grins. "Here, have a drink." She holds one of her cups out toward me, then rolls her eyes at my raised eyebrow. "It's non-alcoholic, I promise. Gotta stay hydrated, remember? Alcoholic—" she lifts the other cup "—and non-alcoholic."

I hesitate, but I'm thirsty after working in the diner's kitchen all afternoon, taking the extra-long route home, and then running across town to get here. I realize it's been hours since I drank anything. "Thanks." I survey the room over the top of the cup as I take a gulp, expecting something sweet and fizzy. But the drink burns like fire all the way down my throat. I cough and splutter and shove the cup back toward Val.

"What's wrong?"

"Val, this is awful," I manage to say. "What's in it?"

With a confused expression, she takes the cup from me and sips. Then she raises the other cup, sniffs, and tastes it. "Hmm." Her frown deepens. "I guess they both have alcohol. I must have finished the soda already." She shrugs. "Oh well. At least you only had a little."

"Val!"

"What? I'm sorry. I didn't do it on purpose. And one sip isn't going to kill you."

I cough again, trying to rid my throat of the burning sensation. "It was a bit more than a sip," I mutter.

Val downs the remainder of one cup, then leaves it on the windowsill and grasps my hand. As she tugs me behind her, I hope we're headed back to the couch I found her on. Instead, she pulls me into the next room where too many people are squished together, nodding their heads in time to the beat and yelling to each other over the music.

Val leans into me and says, "Ooh, Marcus is here already. See him over there in the corner? And you can snuggle up to that guy he's with. Maybe we'll both end up with someone by the end of the night, and then we'll go double-dating and get married and live happily ever after."

I shake my head at Val's ridiculous daydreams. "Right, and then they'll cheat on us, and we'll both end up alone like our moms."

"Hey!" Val smacks my arm, but her smile jumps back into place as she pulls me across the room toward Marcus and his friend. The friend's name is Trent, and sure, he's not bad to look at, but I'm way too distracted to enjoy his company. I lean against the wall, playing with the hairband around my wrist and occasionally nodding so the three of them think I'm paying attention to their conversation. Instead, my thoughts are far away, flitting continuously between Chelsea's words—*you're going to end up as crazy as your mother*—the cloaked person I imagined on the street, and the unexplained gash across Georgia's cheek. Around and around my thoughts go, until nothing seems to make sense anymore.

I become aware that my body is still humming. Probably Val's awful drink. *That doesn't make sense*, my thoughts whisper at the back of my mind, but I've never drunk alcohol before, so how would I know? Maybe everyone starts to feel strange after one giant sip.

Val is looking at me, smiling and speaking, and I try to follow what she's saying, but I can't seem to focus anymore. Her words slip in one side of my head and out the other, and the room is somehow ... *tilting* just the slightest. I look at the floor, but it seems normal. This feeling in my head isn't normal, though. This hazy semi-awareness. The sensation that I'm cocooned in something soft that dampens the *thump, thump, thump* of the music and the sound of Val's voice. Perhaps I should be concerned, but I can't find the part of me that cares. The part of me that wants to fall into this soft cocoon and sleep is taking over.

I remember the couch in the next room. "I'm just … gonna …" I point to the door and start moving toward it. I've never had to concentrate on walking upright, but it's strangely difficult right now. The floor keeps wanting to move up toward me.

The couch is packed with people. They wouldn't like it if I lay down on them, so I manage to maneuver my way out of the room and into the hallway. I drag my hand along the wall, keeping myself upright as I make my way to the front door. The air outside is cooler, fresher. I stand on the porch for a while, leaning against the railing and breathing in deeply until I notice the air isn't that fresh after all. It smells like smoke.

I need to get home. I need to walk and breathe and leave this weird haziness behind. I need to *sleep*. Everything will be clearer when I wake up in the morning.

The porch stairs are a challenge, but I manage to navigate them. I'm relieved to be on the grass and moving away from the house and the people, but the cotton-wool stuffiness in my brain seems to follow me.

"Hey, there you are." Val appears at my side. "Are you leaving already?"

"Whatareyou … doingoutside?" I pause, open my mouth wider, and focus intently on not slurring my next words. "You should be in there with your hot guy."

"Ugh, no, I just said the dumbest thing ever. Marcus looked at me like I was a kid. *So* embarrassing. I swear, I wish the earth had just split open and swallowed me whole."

"So what?" I mumble, my voice resonating oddly in my ears as I sway on the spot. "Then let the earth split open and swallow you whole."

A tremor rumbles beneath our feet. "What was that?" Val asks.

With a grinding screech, a jagged tear zigzags across the garden, tearing the earth open. Terror shreds through some of the cotton wool in my head, making everything a little clearer. I smother a scream and stumble backward.

But Val slips at the edge of the crack and slides into it.

"Val!" I fall onto my knees and scramble closer. She's clinging to the edge, screaming. I can't see how deep the crack is, but suddenly it begins narrowing. As I grab onto Val's arms, dark earth closes in around her body. "Stop!" I gasp. "Stop, please stop! Help!" I give her arms a desperate tug, lose my grip on her, and fall backwards.

And darkness envelops everything.

whacks my head repeatedly with a hammer. When I finally manage to unglue my
eyelids and blink several times, I squint at my blurry bedroom, trying to remember
how I got home and into bed.

Except this isn't my bedroom.

Alarm rushes through me, clearing the haze and causing my head to pound even
more. Nausea crawls up my throat as recent events flood my brain. The blood on
Georgia's face—Chelsea calling the cops—the party—an earthquake splitting the
ground open and—*what the hell happened last night?* That last bit can't have been real.
There must have been something weird in Val's drink.

My pulse thumps in my ears as I take in the unfamiliar bedroom and its stylish
furnishings. On the other side of the room, someone opens the door and walks in.
"Oh, you're awake," he says. "Morning."

"*Dash?* Where am … Did you *abduct* me? What the actual fu—"

"Whoa, hold on there, Miss Potty Mouth." He picks up a chair and moves it
closer to the bed. "Mom's nearby. She doesn't appreciate language like that."

I gape at him. "This is your house?" I had no idea rooms this nice existed in the
crummy little town of Stanmeade. "What the hell am I doing here?"

"Well," he says as he drops into the chair, "I had to rescue you from the mess
you made."

"The mess I made?" I press my hands over my face so I don't have to look at
him. The pounding ache behind my eyes intensifies and the nausea threatens to
overwhelm me. "What was in that drink?" I mumble.

"Nothing sinister," he says lightly. "Faeries don't respond well to the alcohol humans manufacture, that's all. I guess you've managed to stay away from it until now, otherwise you'd be familiar with the hangover effects."

I lower my hands and push the duvet back. "You know what, Dash? You can make fun of me all you want. I don't care, especially considering 'faerie' is probably the weakest taunt you've ever come up with." I stand, my feet sinking into the plush carpet. "Just let me out of here so I can get home."

Dash rises. "That's going to be a little difficult."

I place my hands on my hips and give him my fiercest glare—which probably isn't that fierce, given my current state. "You're not seriously going to try and stop me, are you?"

"No, I'm not going to stop you from doing anything. I just need to explain a few things first. Well, a lot of things, actually. So you should probably sit down."

"I don't think so." I push past him, glancing at the mirror over the dresser, and— "What the—" I gasp, almost tripping over my own feet. I grip the edge of the dresser and stare for several horrified moments at the strands of bright color mixed in with my dark brown hair.

"Em?"

"My hair is blue!" I screech. I swing around, regretting it immediately when the room keeps spinning despite the fact that I've come to a stop.

"Oh. Yeah. I forgot you couldn't see that before."

"*Why is my hair blue?*"

He sighs. "You were born that way."

My voice is slow and shaky as I say, "I was not born with blue hair."

"You were. You just haven't been able to see it until now. It's … well, it's a faerie trait. You're a magical being, but your magic is kind of … faulty. Sometimes it's there—like the first time you saw me when I was actually hidden by a glamour— but most of the time it isn't. Well," he adds with a frown, "until last night when it exploded all over everything. It hasn't disappeared since then, so I have a feeling it's here to stay now."

Silence fills the room for several seconds, until I become aware of the fact that my mouth is hanging open. "You're insane," I whisper.

"I'm not insane. I'm just not doing this part particularly well, it would seem. Which isn't entirely my fault, I'd like to point out, seeing as you're already strongly biased against me."

"My strong bias exists for excellent reasons!" I yell. "Which now include the fact that you *dyed parts of my hair blue!*"

He blinks. "You need to get past the hair thing. It doesn't come close to being the biggest revelation of the day."

"This is complete crap." I turn and head for the door—but he gets there first and blocks the way with his body.

"You need to hear me out, Em. You're going to be horribly confused if you don't let me explain everything."

I swivel around and head for the opposite side of the room, to the glass double doors through which I can make out a balcony. I don't particularly want to climb down the side of the building in my current state, but I'll do it if it's the only way out of this room. I tug the doors open, hurry outside, and freeze.

In the expansive garden below, which is washed in the pale light of dawn, the trees and rose bushes are glowing. Not due to artificial lighting, but as if the luminescence emanates from within the plants themselves. Blueish white roses, and luminous purple leaves. Silver water trickles over the rocks in the water feature at the garden's center, where two tiny creatures that look like winged horses are drinking.

"Get me out of here," I whisper. My hands rise to squeeze the sides of my face, as if this is a terrible dream I can force myself to wake from. "Take me back home."

Above the thudding of my pulse in my ears, I hear Dash's footsteps moving closer. "I can't. Aside from all the things I still have to explain, you also need to tell me exactly what you did last night."

"Take me back."

"Emerson, you can't hide from this. I know you didn't expect everything to change, but now it has, so—"

"Take me back!" I yell, grasping his T-shirt in both my hands and tugging him closer. "I want to wake up. In my own bedroom. Far away from you and your—"

"Fine!" He removes my fists from his clothing. "If you insist on being so difficult. If you insist on ignoring what's right in front of your eyes." He holds his hand up, palm facing the bedroom, and something pen-shaped flies through the air—*through the freaking air*—and into his grasp. The blood drains from my face as my brain rejects what I'm seeing. Pinpricks of light slide across my vision as Dash writes on the wall beside the balcony door. His hand encircles my wrist and tugs me forward into the wall—*into* the wall—and when everything vanishes into darkness, I'm so relieved because I know the nightmare is coming to an end. I know I'll wake up soon.

"Happy now?" Dash says.

The darkness melts away, and I'm standing on the road a few houses down from Chelsea's. The kid from next door rides down the driveway on his older brother's battered bicycle. "Morning, Em," he says as he rides past, lifting his hand to wave at me, then returning it swiftly to the handlebars as he wobbles.

I blink. Without looking back, I start walking. Quickly, almost at a run, as my brain works furiously to come up with a logical explanation for what just happened. This is some kind of super vivid dream. Or maybe it *was* a vivid dream, and I've just woken up—on the street? Barefoot? I falter and throw a glance over my shoulder, but Dash is nowhere to be seen. Obviously, because I was never with him. I've been *dreaming*. Flip, there must have been something seriously weird in Val's drink last night. Something more than just alcohol.

I come to a sudden halt as an image of Val tumbling into a crack in the earth flashes across my vision. "That never happened," I whisper to myself. "Val is fine." I press my hands over my face, breathing in slowly and pushing aside the single thought that keeps trying to force its way to the front of my mind: *I'm mentally ill, just like my mother.*

I shake my head and hurry up the driveway, feeling for my phone as I go. It isn't in any of my pockets, though. Did I leave it at the party last night? I push the back door open and walk into the kitchen.

"Emerson!"

I flinch and look up. Chelsea rises from the table and takes a few fumbling steps backward, knocking a box of cereal off the counter in the process. Val's Uncle Pete, his uniform buttons straining against the bulge of his stomach, gets to his feet. He keeps his wary gaze on me as Chelsea asks, "Where have you been?"

"Uh …" That's a good question, actually. One I wish I knew the answer to. "I knew you were pissed off," I explain carefully, "and I didn't want to make things worse, so I stayed away. And I'm *so* sorry about fighting with Georgia. But you know we argue all the time." My gaze flits to Pete before returning to Chelsea. "It isn't something you need to get the cops involved for."

I expect her to shout at me like she did last night, but her grip on the counter tightens as she swallows and looks at Pete. His fingers twitch, his right hand clenching and unclenching. "What happened at the Masons' house last night, Emerson?"

"The—the Masons' house?"

"Don't pretend you know nothing," Chelsea says, a slight wobble evident in her voice. "We've heard all about it. We saw the video."

"What video? What are you talking about?"

Pete moves forward, places his cell phone on the table, and pushes it toward me. I take a step closer and look down at the grainy, shaky footage of a bonfire and people laughing. The fire moves out of view as the person holding the camera turns and almost bumps into Val. After a quick apology, Val walks away. More laughter, someone shouts, "Emerson's drunk," and then the camera follows Val. It gets close enough to pick up her voice as she says, "I swear, I wish the earth had just split open and swallowed me whole."

My blood chills. I watch myself swaying, eyes half-closed. "So what? Then let the earth split open and swallow you whole."

I know what's coming before I see it. Goosebumps race across my skin as the footage wobbles again, then focuses on the ground. The earth rips itself open in one grinding, shuddering zigzag. Val slips and disappears. I hear screams and shouting, and then the video cuts off.

My brain wants to reject what I've just seen, but it can't. *It happened*, I say silently to myself. *It actually happened.*

Chelsea begins swearing repeatedly beneath her breath, and for some reason, Dash's voice resonates in my head: *Mom's nearby. She doesn't appreciate language like that.*

"What the hell was that?" Pete asks, his voice a whisper now.

I open my mouth, but I can't come up with an answer.

"Holy heck, it's like having flipping *Carrie* living under my own roof," Chelsea wails. "You have to take her away, Pete. Please just get her out of here."

"Wait! I … I didn't do that. It must have been a coincidence. An earthquake happened at the same time I was talking. You don't think I could actually *make* that happen, do you?" I'm trying to convince myself as much as them. "And what about Val? Did she—"

"You don't need to worry about Val," Pete says. "But you do need to come with me."

"Are you kidding? You—I mean—didn't you see what else was happening there? Illegal underage drinking? You should be dealing with *that*, not this weird earthquake coincidence."

"Don't try to change the subject, Em." Slowly, as if approaching a dangerous animal, Pete comes toward me. I take a quick step backwards, moving beyond his reach. He frowns and hesitates. "Em, please. We don't need to make this unpleasant. We just want to get you somewhere safe so you don't hurt anyone."

"But I'm not going to hurt anyone, I swear."

Another two policemen move from the hallway into the kitchen, and I realize they must have been waiting there the whole time. They're backup. Because I'm supposedly too dangerous for one cop to handle. I shake my head, barely able to believe this is happening, as I inch further away from them.

A pause.

No one speaks.

Then all three policemen lunge toward me. Chelsea screams, chairs are knocked aside, and moments later I'm being dragged outside. Rough paving grazes my feet, and pain shoots through my shoulders as my arms are almost yanked from their sockets.

"LET GO!" I yell.

Their hands spring away from me so fast that the momentum swings the three men around and dumps them on the ground. "What the hell?" Pete groans. He pushes himself onto his knees and dives for my legs.

I jump backwards out of reach. "Get away from me!"

As if kicked with superhuman strength, Pete slides across the grass, through the door, and into the kitchen table. Chelsea shrieks again. At the sound of a crackle, I look down and see sparks—*sparks?*—whizzing around my hands. Icy terror drenches me.

"Time to go," a voice says behind me. Something grips my arm, and before I have time to tear myself away, I'm pulled into darkness, a silent scream on my lips.

CHAPTER 4

The darkness evaporates to reveal Dash at my side and a garden bathed in the golden glow of sunrise. The same garden I saw from the balcony minutes ago. I shove Dash away from me, drop onto my knees, and throw up on the grass.

"Lovely," he says when I'm done. "Thank goodness I didn't take you back inside the house."

"What happened to … to Val?" I gasp, trying to swallow down the urge to throw up again and failing.

When my retching finally ends, Dash says, "She's fine. One of my teammates got her out of the ground. She's already forgotten the whole thing."

"How could she have …" My words trail off as I look up and see one of those miniature winged horses soaring through the air behind Dash. I climb slowly to my feet and look around. The roses and leaves are still faintly glowing, but their luminescence is less obvious now with the sun's golden light filtering through the trees. The little horse lands in a shallow part of the rock pool and begins frolicking, tossing droplets of silver water about as it plays. Wherever the water lands, a silver mushroom pops up.

My brain keeps repeating the same message: I must be dreaming. This is *not possible*. I've gone off the deep end and entirely lost my mind. But I don't think my imagination is capable of coming up with this kind of fantastical detail. And everything seems so *real*. The fresh scent of flowers, the prickle of grass beneath my feet. The sour taste of puke in my mouth.

"Explain," I whisper. "Make this make sense."

Dash folds his arms over his chest. "Okay then. Once upon a time there lived a little girl whose name was—"

I cut him off with a glare. "Don't turn my life into some fairytale crap. Just give me the facts." Something bright flies from the tip of my tongue, and my immediate thought is that I must be so angry I'm actually spitting saliva. But no. It's a spark of light. The same kind that crackled around my hands after Pete was somehow thrown away from me. Fear slithers down my spine as I clamp my mouth shut.

"Okay, here are the bare-bone facts," Dash says. "Magic is real, and it exists in a realm that overlaps with the world you grew up in. Fae live on this side; humans and all the other non-magical creatures you recognize live on the other side. I'm a faerie, like you. I'm also a guardian, which means I'm trained to fight dark magic, dangerous fae, that sort of thing. The day you and I first met, I had an assignment on your side of the veil."

"The day you ruined everything," I murmur, remembering my mother wailing, covering her head with her hands, shouting about things that weren't real.

Dash looks annoyed that I've interrupted his story. "You have *got* to stop hating me for that. You know they would have taken her away anyway. Maybe not that day, but soon afterwards. She wasn't in her right mind—"

"Don't you dare talk about her."

"*Anyway*," he continues loudly, "nobody was supposed to see me, but you did. And with that color in your hair, I knew you were a faerie. But then it kind of flickered and was gone, and you couldn't see me anymore. It was as if everything magical about you was suddenly bottled up, inaccessible. Once we were done with the assignment, I mentioned you in my Guild report, and they—"

"Your Guild report?" I say with a snort. "You were like twelve. Does this Guild of yours breed child soldiers or something?"

"No. We're not soldiers, and by the time training is done, we're not children anymore. And I was thirteen, not twelve. I'd just begun my training. It was a group assignment, but we were all in different areas of the park, and I was the only one who had any interaction with you. So yes, I reported it afterwards. Faeries with dodgy magic who think they're human shouldn't be ignored."

"Oh, right, because I'm probably a danger to society or something like that," I say with a roll of my eyes.

"Potentially, yes." Dash's tone is deadly serious, and an image of the ground ripping open comes immediately to mind. I wrap my arms around myself and look away. "I don't know if the Guild investigated you at all," Dash continues, "because it was none of my business. I got on with my training, and it was about six months later when you showed up near another one of my assignments. Then a few months later you were there again."

"I remember seeing you," I murmur. "I figured you must live somewhere near Stanmeade. I thought it was weird, since it's so far away from where I first saw you. In that park near where Mom and I used to live. But I was so mad at you that I didn't focus too much on it being a weird coincidence."

"Well, the Guild didn't think it was a coincidence. They thought something else might be going on. That maybe your weird on-off magic was causing problems, or attracting trouble-makers or something, and that's how I ended up with three assignments near you. But they couldn't find any connection, and someone on the Council said you should be left alone. That the Guild shouldn't interfere with you unless there was evidence that your magic really was breaking free and causing trouble. But the rest of the Council wanted someone to keep tabs on you, just in case. They complained about it being a waste of time and resources for a trained guardian to do it, though, so I volunteered." His mouth pulls up one side in a half-grin. "We were encouraged to take on extra projects outside of training. It looks good on the resume. Shows initiative or something."

I throw my hands up. "Wonderful. You're my flipping babysitter."

"Uh, I think detective might be a more accurate comparison."

"Stalker, maybe?"

"I mean, it was like this ongoing puzzle, trying to figure out what was wrong with you and how you ended up in that awful little human town."

"Perhaps mad scientist would be more fitting. Highly offensive mad scientist."

He folds his arms over his chest. "I think we should stop the comparisons. You clearly don't understand the importance of what I do."

"And you clearly think far too highly of yourself. But then, I've always known that, haven't I."

"I think, Emerson," he says with an annoying smirk, "that we should focus on the great many things you *haven't* always known."

His words bring home the seriousness of the situation. I try to tell myself yet again that I'm dreaming or high or drunk, but it's a weak lie I have no hope of believing. I shut my eyes and press my fingers against my temples. "So I'm not crazy after all," I murmur. "The strange things I've seen—creatures that shouldn't exist—they've actually been real."

"Yes. Well, unless you really are seeing things that aren't—"

"Wait. Wait, wait, wait." I open my eyes, step closer, and grasp his T-shirt as hope comes to life inside me. "Does this mean my mother was never crazy either?

The voices, the hallucinations … her mind didn't make them up? They were actually there? Because, I mean, if I have this … *magic*—" it still sounds so odd to apply the word to myself "—then she must have it too."

"Actually," Dash says carefully, removing my fists from his T-shirt, "the Guild sent someone to Tranquil Hills to check on your mother after the third time you showed up near an assignment. They couldn't sense any magic in her."

"So … she's …"

"Yes. I'm sorry. She's always been sick."

I turn away, not wanting him to see the crushing disappointment. I remind myself not to be surprised, though. Of course it was too much to hope that Mom might actually be sane. That's the way life works, right? You hope for something, and then life kicks you in the face and laughs at you.

I clear my throat. "So it must have been my father then. The loser I don't know at all. He must have been—you know—like me."

"Well …"

When Dash doesn't finish, I turn back to look at him. "Well what?"

He screws up his face, then says, "Please don't hit me."

Dread stirs in the pit of my stomach. "Why would I hit you?"

"Because … Okay, look. You're not a halfling. We know that for sure. You're a faerie, and that means you must have had two faerie parents. So … therefore … the woman locked up in Tranquil Hills Psychiatric Hospital isn't your mother."

I stare at him, unable to speak. His words seem to echo around my head. *Isn't your mother … isn't your mother … isn't your mother.*

"Silence?" Dash says eventually. "I guess that's better than screaming and hitting and telling me I must be—"

"Shut up."

How can Mom not be my mom? For some reason, this is harder to comprehend than anything else. She's my *mother*. She raised me. Everything was great until her crazy moments started becoming a little harder to hide. Everything went to hell soon after that, but before, when she was normal, life was good. It was just me and her against the world. We were a team.

I bend over, my hands pressing against my knees, and breathe deeply. "It can't be true," I manage to say past the nausea. "There must be some other explanation. Something you people have missed. I don't know what, but … something."

"Emerson …"

"I think I might be sick again."

Dash pats my back briefly. "Well, at least we're outside."

"What am I supposed to do?"

"There's a very effective tonic for nausea. We can go inside and get some."

"With my *life*, you idiot." I straighten. "Everything is completely screwed up. I'm a magical freak, my aunt wants to get me locked up somewhere far away, my mother is apparently not my mother, and—and these damn spark things won't get off me!" I shake my hands as flickers of light dance about them once more. "Not to mention there's video footage of the whole disaster at the Masons' farm. It's probably online already, and soon the entire world will know that I'm—"

"Hey, calm down. The world isn't going to know anything. Do you honestly think this is the first time we've dealt with something like this? Of course it isn't. We're not amateurs. Most people's memories of last night had been altered by this morning, although we missed a few who still need to be dealt with, including whoever took that phone to the cops. But that footage will have vanished within the next few hours, I can promise you that." He gives me a reassuring smile. "No one will remember that you were involved, and the top story on the news will be about the unexpected earthquake that ripped through Stanmeade." He tilts his head. "Speaking of which, can you tell me what actually happened? Why did the ground tear open like that?"

"*Why?*" I stare at him. "Because apparently I have magic that suddenly decided to—and I quote—explode all over everything. Those were your words, right?"

"Yes, but I thought I heard you say something before it happened, and that's not—"

He cuts himself off as he looks over my shoulder. I swivel around and see a young woman walking toward us. "Well," Dash mutters. "That was terrible timing."

"Oh, because our alone time is up now?" I return my gaze to him. "Boohoo. I'm devastated."

His eyes narrow slightly. "You should be. There's something very important we need to—"

"Dash, we gotta go," the woman says as she reaches us. "One of the Guild Councilors is waiting to see the girl."

I'd like to point out that 'the girl' has a name, but I'm more concerned by what this woman just said. "A Councilor? Why?"

"Because you're a faerie who's been living in the human world," Dash says as the woman bends down and writes on the grass with a pen, "and now that your magic has appeared, you have no idea how to use it. There are protocols in place for this kind of situation."

"Protocols?" That sounds far too clinical for my liking.

"Yes, of course. They'll put you into their special program for people like you. Other fae who, for whatever reason, grew up in the human world without knowing how to use their magic. They're mostly younger fae, but every now and then someone older turns up, like you. It'll be fun."

No it won't. It doesn't sound fun at all. I don't want to meet strange people and learn how to become a member of their stupid magic club. I want to get back to my real life and pretend none of this happened. Or perhaps hide in a corner and fall apart because Mom isn't even my—

Don't go there, I instruct myself. I don't fall apart in front of other people. Especially not Dash.

"Shall we get going then?" he asks, gesturing to the ground where a dark hole has appeared beside the kneeling woman. A dark hole not of earth or rock, but of … *nothing*. My brain tells me I should be shocked, but I think I'm beyond that point now. Nothing seems impossible anymore.

"Em? Ready to go?"

Ready to go? Such a simple, ordinary question. The kind of thing Val might say when she arrives at my place before school. Or Chelsea might say to Georgia when they're on their way to the shops. Or Mom used to say, with her hand reaching out for mine, when we'd finished playing at the park in the afternoon and had to walk home.

Mom.

An image of her flashes before my eyes again. A little house, wild roses in the garden, number twenty-nine on the old wooden gate. Mom pruning the bushes, and a young version of me dancing around her and singing while our new puppy chases butterflies. Mom who isn't my Mom. My heart cracks a little. I shove the pain aside. *Later*, I tell myself. *Deal with that later. Fall apart later.*

I take a deep breath that sounds as shaky as I feel. "Yeah. Let's go. Just … can you get me that anti-nausea tonic first?"

CHAPTER 5

Dash runs into his house to fetch the anti-nausea tonic, leaving me alone with his guardian colleague who makes it clear with her long sighs and deep frowns that she's annoyed by this waste of time. The hole she opened in the ground closes up, and she stands there with her arms folded over her chest, staring past me.

Fortunately, Dash doesn't take long to return. He hands me a small bottle made of brown glass. It's suspiciously similar to the bottles Chelsea packages her herbal remedies in. I remove the lid and sniff the contents. "Jeez, Em, it isn't poisonous," Dash says. "Just drink it."

I'm feeling horrible enough that I'm willing to risk the possibility of Dash playing a trick on me, so I tip the little bottle back over my mouth. The liquid doesn't taste like anything, but I instantly begin to feel better.

"Great," says the woman who's been giving her face a good workout by switching between sickly sweet smiles for Dash and irritated frowns directed at me. "Can we get moving?"

"Yes. And let's open an upright doorway instead of one on the ground," Dash says. "It'll be easier for Em to walk into and out the other side, considering she doesn't have much experience with faerie paths." He removes a pen and starts writing in the air. "If I could just … get it to …"

"Dash, this is a waste of—"

"Ah, there we go. Easy peasy." He gives the woman a dazzling smile, but I'm distracted by the growing patch of darkness appearing in mid-air. It spreads rapidly until it's roughly the size and shape of a door. It must be the same thing as the hole the woman opened in the ground. The same thing that appeared on the balcony earlier when Dash took me back home.

"Is that … some kind of teleportation hole?"

"Faerie paths," Dash says, holding his hand out to me. "Although they're not really paths at all. It's this dark empty space that exists somewhere outside of our world and yours, and it can be accessed by opening magical doorways. All you have to do is think of your destination or say the name of the place you want to go to. So much easier than cars and planes."

Easier, perhaps, but far more foreboding. Reluctantly, I take Dash's hand and walk forward. On his other side, the woman happily loops her arm through his. I look over my shoulder as the edges of the doorway spread toward each other, closing the gap, and then we're in complete and utter darkness. "Can people get stuck inside here?" I whisper as we walk forward, which is an odd thing to do when I can't feel anything beneath my feet.

"No. I've never heard of anyone getting stuck. Although I think, if you know the right magic, you can stay here for longer than usual. I've heard of people hiding inside the faerie paths if they're trying to get away from someone."

"Stop thinking," the woman mutters. "I'm trying to direct the paths, and they're not going anywhere with all our thoughts tugging in different directions."

I clamp my mouth shut and try to *not think*, but light appears up ahead before I've figured out if I'm doing it correctly. We walk forward into a small room, sparsely furnished with a mirror, a sideboard displaying painted plates, and a rug covering the wooden floorboards. I pull my hand free of Dash's and step away from him. "This is your Guild?" I was expecting something bigger and more … magical.

"Nope. This an old house in a deserted area beside a tropical beach."

I turn my withering gaze back to him. "Why is it always so hard to get a straight answer out of you?"

"He's telling the truth," the woman says, rushing to Dash's defense. I notice she hasn't bothered to introduce herself, so I decide not to bother either.

"The Guild can be a little intimidating," Dash explains, wandering over to the sideboard. "It's enormous and busy, with loads of people around at this time of day. Faeries, mainly, but other fae as well. Sometimes criminals are brought in, or stray magic escapes from the training section of the Guild. And the fact that you can't see *any* of it from the outside, and then you walk through a grand entrance that transforms itself from a tree, and you're greeted by all this sudden activity … well, it can be overwhelming at first." He flips the plate over and examines the back before returning it to its stand. "So we take fae who are new to our world to this halfway house first."

"Oh. Okay." My brain catches hold of what is probably the least important piece of information I've heard all day. "So … if we really are near a beach, then the ocean must be close by?"

Dash gives me a quizzical look. "Not too far from here."

The fact that I might get to see the ocean for the first time is far easier to focus on than anything else right now. I walk to the nearest window and look out, but all I see is a forest of palm trees.

"I need to get back," the woman says as I try to peer between the trees. "No message on the plate?"

"Nothing yet," Dash says.

"Well, she'll be here soon, I'm sure. She sounded in a hurry when she sent me to fetch you. Anyway, I hope it doesn't take too long to hand the girl over. I know your team has far more exciting stuff going on at the moment."

I look around in time to see her brush her hand from Dash's shoulder down to his elbow. With a half-smile, she turns away, and I resume my examination of the landscape outside, muttering, "Seriously?" under my breath. She doesn't look that much older than us, but surely there are plenty of guys in this world who are both more age-appropriate and more mature than Dash.

"Thanks," he says. Then: "Em, what are you looking for? Actually, never mind. That isn't important."

I give up on my search for the ocean and fold my arms as I walk back toward him. "Of course not. Nothing could possibly be as important as whatever it is you're about to tell me, right?"

"Right," he says, but the front door opens at that moment, and in walks a short blonde girl with orange stripes in her hair and fiery orange eyes to match.

"Oh, Dash, you're here." She gives him a bright smile.

"Uh, yes. I am. Why are you here?"

"Just checking you made it." Her eyes slide to me. "Is this Emerson?"

Dash lets out a sigh. "Yes. Em, this is Jewel. She's a member of my team at the Guild."

Jewel? They have weird hair and eyes *and* weird names? "Hi," I say uncertainly.

"Hey." Jewel gives me a smile that's way too friendly considering we just met. "Oh, hang on." She slips her hand into one of her pockets and removes what I first assume to be a phone because of the shape, but turns out to be semi-transparent and orange-gold in color. She looks at the surface, and I do a double take as tiny gold words melt into view.

"Is that a Guild-wide memo?" Dash asks. "I think my amber just pinged as well."

"Yes." As Jewel peers more closely at the honey-colored rectangle, I notice dark swirling patterns tattooed on the inside of her wrists. "A Griffin attack on a small village near Twiggled Horn. Five dead."

"Five dead from a Griffin attack? They don't normally kill people."

"Yeah, well, they're dangerous outlaws, so what do you expect." Jewel swipes her hand across the amber thing, and the words disappear.

"Griffin?" I ask. "Like the mythical creature?" Nothing would surprise me at this point.

"No," Dash says. "Although yes, griffins do exist. But in this case we're talking about people with extra magic. Abilities most normal fae don't posses. Griffin Abilities. You'll learn about them soon enough." His expression darkens. "They're pretty much a law unto themselves."

Jewel rolls her eyes before giving me a sweet smile. "Dash doesn't always explain things particularly well. These dangerous fae used to live out in the open, doing whatever they pleased, without anyone knowing they were different. But it's hard to hide a Griffin Ability these days. Testing is mandatory. The Guild just wants to keep an eye on them—understandably—but they're always going on about how they're discriminated against. So in recent years, those who managed to get away from the Guild without being tagged have banded together. Formed some kind of secret organization. And now they take out their Guild-directed anger on innocent people just to get attention."

"Unacceptable," Dash mutters.

"Exactly. So you can understand why the Guild wants to keep a record of all Griffin Gifted, right? They need to be held accountable for their actions."

She seems to be waiting for me to respond. I consider telling her I don't give a crap about faerie outlaws and politics, but decide to change the subject instead. "What's the orange rectangle thing?"

"Oh. This?" Jewel holds up the honey-colored device.

"Amber," Dash says. "Faerie cell phone."

Behind him, one of the plates on the sideboard emits an abrupt shriek. I let out an involuntary gasp and take a hurried step backward. "What the fu—"

"Seriously?" Dash says, interrupting me mid-curse. He picks up the plate and turns it over. "The situation really doesn't warrant that kind of language, Em."

I gape at him as my pattering heart rate returns slowly to normal. "You're kidding, right? What's the big deal with the no-swearing thing? I don't see any little kids around, unless you'd like to count yourself in that category."

"Very funny," he deadpans, looking up from the plate. "And if you'd had your mouth cleaned out with soap spells as many times as I have, you'd understand my automatic response to bad language. Super unpleasant spell, that one. The taste hangs around for hours afterwards."

I stare at him. "I'm trying to figure out if you're joking."

"Nope. My mother's always been deadly serious about the no-swearing policy in our household. Anyway, the Councilor's on her way. Message on the plate said she just left the Guild."

"That was the sound of a *message?*"

"It isn't supposed to shriek like that," Jewel says. "I think the notification spell is faulty."

The front door swings open, revealing a smartly dressed woman. "Oh, wonderful, you're here. I didn't have time to check with surveillance. Shall we go through to the sitting room?" Without waiting for an answer, she strides past us and opens the door beside the sideboard.

"Councilor Waterfield," Dash whispers as he takes my arm and steers me around toward the door.

I expected her to be older, being a member of this special faerie Council or whatever it is, but she probably hasn't hit thirty yet. I'm also starting to wonder if this world consists of any men, or if it's just Dash and all the females that fawn over him. I pull my arm free of his grip, muttering that I'm perfectly capable of walking into the next room without assistance.

The sitting room is pretty, with antique furniture and a large bay window on one side. I think I might be able to see something beige in color through the trees that could be a strip of sand, but Councilor Waterfield invites me to sit before I can take a closer look out the window. I choose one of the single armchairs so I don't have to sit right next to Dash or the Councilor. She sits with her back to the window, and Dash takes the armchair beside mine. I clasp my hands tightly together in my lap, feeling suddenly nervous.

"Emerson," the woman says. "I'm Councilor Waterfield. First of all, welcome to the magical realm. I trust Dash has explained the basics to you?"

"I have," Dash says before I can answer. "Only the very basics, though. She has a lot more to learn." He flashes a grin in my direction, which I wish I could scratch right off. He's enjoying this way too much.

"So, Emerson." The Councilor opens a bag at her feet and pulls out a larger version of the amber thing Jewel was using. Before she tilts it upward to face her, I see gold lettering appear across its surface. "We've been tracking you for the last … five years? Is that correct?" She looks up from her magical device.

"Yes," Dash answers once more. "Em was twelve when we began tracking her."

"So that makes you seventeen now."

"If math is the same in this world as it is in mine," I say, "then yes."

Her smile tightens somewhat. "Numbers are numbers, Emerson, no matter which side of the veil you happen to be on. And *this side* is your side. You'll need to start referring to it as such."

"Of course," I say, when all I want to do is scream that I only just found out about the existence of this side, so give me a damn break!

Councilor Waterfield leans back, making herself more comfortable. "In case Dash didn't tell you, I'm the Guild representative for Chevalier House, which is where you'll be staying for a while. It's a school for people like you. People who've been brought up with humans and might have had access to their magic but haven't had anyone to teach them how to use it, or perhaps their magic has only just appeared, and because of some mishap or other, we've now become aware of their existence."

"What makes it suddenly appear?" I ask. "Why was my magic inaccessible before? Or—why did it come and go? Dash said it was kind of … faulty."

She purses her lips before answering. "To be honest, I don't know. If you were a halfling, it would make more sense. Their magic is highly unpredictable and can sometimes present itself later in life. But faeries … Well, I don't know. I suppose it happens every now and then."

"Wonderful. So I'm a freak even by this world's standards."

"You're not a freak, Emerson. After you've spent some time at Chevalier House, you'll be able to fit in with the rest of our world just fine."

"So basically you're sending me to magical etiquette school?"

She breathes out through her nose. I think her patience is beginning to wear thin. "It's far more than that. They'll teach you about your magic, about our world. They'll assist with the logistics of merging your old life with your new one. Whether you should return home or stay here, what story your family will believe while you're away, what you should tell your family if you decide to return home. Things like that."

I cross my arms tightly against my chest. "You should probably know that you needn't bother coming up with a story for my aunt. She'll assume I've run away, she'll be glad, and that'll be the end of it."

Councilor Waterfield looks down at her device, pausing for a moment as she reads something. "It appears that's the story she was given, actually. A guardian glamoured as a policeman has informed your aunt that you ran away. He told her that a security camera caught you getting onto a bus. Police attempted to find you on the other side, but you somehow slipped away without being noticed. They're still on the lookout for you. Your friends have been told the same story."

"But that's a lie." I sit forward. "I don't want my friends thinking I ran away."

"Well, Emerson, I'm afraid you don't really have a choice. Once you've spent some time at Chevalier House and can safely return to the human world, you can come up with a good excuse for why you ran away. We can have one of our guardians glamoured as a policeman say he or she tracked you down, if that story works for you. I'm sure you can make your friends understand."

I slump back in my chair. This woman doesn't understand, and neither will Val. She'll see right through me if I try to lie.

"Now, as I was saying," Councilor Waterfield continues, examining her device again. "All footage of last night's earthquake incident has been located and destroyed so that no one knows you were connected, and memories have been altered. An expensive cover-up—not all magic is free or cheap, you know—but we can't have humans running around spreading stories about what you did. And if you do decide to return to your old life, you can do so safely without anyone knowing what happened."

"So … so that's it? I have to go to this school for a little bit, and then I can return to my world?"

"Yes." She slides her amber device back into her bag. "Dash will take you there now."

"Um, who pays for this school?" I ask, angling my body away from Dash as I ask. Pointless, since he can still hear me, but I'd rather not see his expression if I have to admit to Councilor Waterfield that I have absolutely no money.

"It's funded by the Guild," she says. "The program is considered part of security. It's dangerous having fae running around with magic they can't control. Far better to have you educated so you can safely re-enter society, on this side of the veil or the other side. Now." She stands and picks up her bag. "Someone will arrive here shortly to run a few tests on you before you leave for Chevalier House."

"Tests?" I shrink back against the cushions. "What tests?"

"Oh, nothing scary. Just standard procedure. To test for Griffin Abilities, magic levels, that sort of thing."

"I don't want any tests. Don't I have the right to refuse things like—"

"Perhaps," Dash says as he stands, "we could do the tests in a few days after Em has settled into Chevalier House. She's been through a lot already. And with her … history. Her mother …" He lowers his voice, as if whispering that one word—*mother*—instead of speaking it out loud means it won't bring up all the shock, confusion and hurt I felt earlier. I stamp down the pain as Dash continues. "I assume you remember everything from my previous reports, Councilor, so you'll understand that the concept of 'running tests' has negative connotations to her." He places his hands respectfully behind his back. As his sleeves pull up slightly, I notice the same tattoo on his wrists that I saw on Jewel's arms.

Councilor Waterfield clicks her tongue. "Fine. I'll send someone to Chevalier House at the end of the week to do the tests there."

That doesn't sound much better, but hopefully I'll be out of Chevalier House by then. We leave the sitting room and find Jewel still hanging around near the front door. She looks up from her amber, her eyes wide. "Big news," she says. "Like, *huge*. Someone's made a breakthrough with a spell for the veil. The Guild thinks they'll finally be able to seal the tear over Velazar Island. There's a meeting in twenty minutes so they can tell us more about it."

"Correct," Councilor Waterfield says, hurrying past Jewel. "That's why I was late getting here. We received the news just this morning. Now, if you'll excuse me, I need to get back before the meeting begins." She holds a pen up to the front door, and after a few scribbled words, a dark opening appears. Even though I expected it this time, it's still horribly unnatural so see a hole of nothingness taking shape and then disappearing after swallowing a person.

"This is so exciting," Jewel says once the Councilor is gone. "Are you coming?"

Dash shakes his head. "I'm escorting Em to Chevalier House now."

"Oh, but this is important. Bring her with, and you can take her to Chevalier afterwards."

"No need," Dash says with an easy smile. "I'm sure you'll tell me all about it later. And I doubt Em wants to sit through a Guild meeting after everything she's been through in the last few hours."

Jewel's smile slips for just a second, before stretching wide once again. "You're always so thoughtful, Dash. Going the extra mile with your assignments." She leans in and gives him a hug and a quick kiss on the cheek. "See you later."

I wait until she's gone before saying, "I see you don't mind pissing off your girlfriend."

"Girlfriend? Jewel?" He laughs. "We're just friends. Wait, why did you say she's angry? She wasn't angry."

I slowly shake my head. "You're such an idiot."

He grins. "For once, dear Emerson, you are almost right. I was *almost* an idiot earlier." His gaze moves past me and up, scanning the ceiling briefly. "Fortunately, I was saved just in time."

I can't help glancing up as well, but I see nothing except a few cobwebs and a spider. Apparently those aren't unique to the human world.

At the sound of the front door opening, I look past Dash. On the doorstep stands a man with pointed ears and spiked black hair. *This is normal now*, I remind myself as my eyes refuse to move from those abnormally tapered ears. *Totally normal.*

"Emerson?" he enquires. I nod. "The professor is expecting you."

CHAPTER 6

WE ARRIVE AT AN EMBELLISHED METAL GATE SEPARATING US FROM A GARDEN OF manicured maroon grass and bushes adorned in the colors of autumn. A chilly breeze raises goosebumps along the exposed part of my arms. "Is this anywhere near the house we were just in?" I ask. It doesn't feel like it, but with the faerie trails—faerie paths?—making travel so quick, it's impossible to tell.

"No," Dash says. "We're in a completely different part of the world in the foothills of a mountain range."

I peer between the metal-shaped leaves of the gate, and on the other side of the enormous house, I see snow-capped mountain peaks. The elf—I assume the pointed ears means he's an elf—opens the gate and lets us into the garden. We walk along the paved path, up the few steps to the front door, and inside. A crackling fire and a cozy atmosphere greets us in the large open entrance hall of Chevalier House.

"I'll get the professor," the elf says, heading toward the stairs.

I cross the room, my feet sinking into the thick rug as I look around. A table stands in the middle of the room, with a beautifully painted vase at its center filled with flowers I don't recognize. Richly embroidered curtains frame the windows, and painted portraits in gilded frames decorate the walls. I think about staying here, even for just a few days, and I can't quite believe it. It's a million times fancier than any other house I've ever lived in. "Of course it is," I mutter, shaking my head.

"What?" Dash asks.

"The Guild, your parents' home, this place … I guess when you live in a world of magic, everyone can have whatever fancy, schmancy house they like."

"Well, not really." Dash pushes his hands into his pockets. "Most faeries live in regular tree houses. That's how we lived until Mom got lucky with her fashion design and clothes casting. She won an award, and then this celebrity hired her to make a dress for some important event. Word started spreading about her work, and she ended up with more high-society clients. Even some of the Seelies—the fae royalty—have worn her dresses. So, yeah." He shrugs. "Now we have a fancy, schmancy house."

"Interesting. Must have been hard for you whenever you were in my world, having to pretend you lived in some crappy part of Stanmeade."

"So hard," he jokes, though his voice lacks humor.

"No wonder you still live at home with your parents. Why rush to move out and be independent when you can lounge around in a mansion for years?"

He doesn't respond, and I continue to examine the portraits on the wall. In the corner of my vision, I see someone walk into the room and out another door, but I ignore whoever it is. "So, you and Jewel aren't together, but you have matching tattoos," I say to cover the growing silence. Silence leaves space for thoughts of Mom to sneak in, and I'm not ready to deal with that. "Seems pretty serious to me. I mean, there's no going back from that, right?"

"Matching tattoos? Oh." Dash starts laughing. "You mean these?" He holds his hands up, displaying his tattooed wrists, then doubles over as laughter consumes him. I fold my arms and pointedly ignore him until he's recovered enough to say, "These are guardian markings. We get them once we've graduated."

"Wow, you actually managed to graduate? How surprising."

"Yep." He smiles proudly. "Less than a year ago."

I can't help rolling my eyes before turning back to the portrait of a young woman. I read the ridiculous name on the polished bronze plaque beneath the painting: Azure Plumehof. Seriously? Azure, Dash, Jewel ... Don't these magical people know anything about normal names? My gaze slides to the date below the name, which tells me this painting is over three hundred years old. Flip. I wonder if the house is also that old.

I hear laughter behind me and look over my shoulder to see a young boy grinning while Dash writes on the boy's arm with the same pen he uses to open magic doorways. I make out a spark of light before the boy says, "Thanks, Dash!" and runs off.

I look away, pretending to examine the crystal-embellished tassels hanging from one of the curtain tie-backs. "Will they give me one of those magic pens here?"

"What magic pens?" Dash asks.

"You know." I glance back at him, nodding toward the pen in his hand. "The pens you guys use to open doorways."

"Oh." Dash snickers. "That isn't a pen. It's a stylus."

"It looks like a pen. And from what I've seen, it acts like a pen."

"Well, it isn't. It has no ink. It's essentially just a stick that channels magic."

"So … it's a magic wand?"

"Pretty much. And you'll have to prove you can safely use your magic before you'll get one."

"Fine," I mutter, crossing my arms and wandering over to the table. I lean closer to the vase and examine the oddly shaped flowers.

"Dash, Emerson!" exclaims a female voice from the direction of the stairs. "How lovely to see the two of you."

I straighten and step back as a woman with pink in her blonde hair and miniature banana earrings dangling from her ears descends the stairs. A woman I'd guess to be in her twenties, maybe early thirties. The same woman, I realize with a lurch, from the portrait. "Emerson," she says as reaches the bottom of the stairs. "So lovely to meet you. I'm Professor Azure Plumehof, but please call me Azzy." She holds her hand toward me. I stare at it, then back up at her face.

"Azure Plumehof?" I look over my shoulder at the portrait, then back. "You can't be. The woman in that painting would be over three hundred years old. She'd be a shriveled-up old prune."

Azzy laughs as she lowers her hand, apparently unperturbed that I didn't bother to shake it. "Dash didn't explain that part?"

"I guess it didn't come up," Dash says. "She was too fixated on the fact that her hair is blue."

I glance down at the pastel blue strands hanging over my shoulder that I'd somehow managed to forget about. With a blink, I return my attention to the most recent earth-shattering revelation. "Wait. You're telling me you people are immortal or something?"

"Is that so hard to believe," Dash asks, "given every other so-called 'impossible' thing you've discovered so far this morning?"

"It's—just—"

"We're not immortal, dear," Azzy says with a brief frown in Dash's direction. She clasps her hands together over her layers of loose, floaty clothing. "We live several centuries, which is a far cry from immortality."

"Several … centuries …" I murmur.

"Don't worry," Azzy says, smiling kindly. "We'll give you plenty of time to absorb all this new information. That's why Chevalier House exists—to give you a safe place to learn more about yourself and the world you're now part of. There will be history lessons, magic lessons—all the basics that young faeries learn in junior school—and interviews so you can give us information that will assist in finding your real family."

"My—what?" *Real* family? I hadn't given the idea a moment's thought.

"But we can begin all that tomorrow. For now, let me show you to your room. I'm sure you've had a trying day so far, and you probably need to rest. You'll find everything you could possibly need in your room: clothes, toiletries, makeup—if that's your thing. If you need something else that I've forgotten, or if the clothes are the wrong size, just let me know." She pauses, as if she might be expecting me to say something, but I'm a bit too overwhelmed to form words. "And if your brain is too fired up for you to rest right now," she continues, "you can explore the house and the gardens. Meet the other fae who are staying with us at the moment."

"And if you need me," Dash adds, "just tell Azzy. She knows how to get hold of me."

I blink. "Need *you*?" Now there's a ridiculous notion. "You don't have to babysit me anymore, Dash. I can get through the rest of this without you."

"I'm sure you can. Just tell Azzy everything that happened last night, okay?" He exchanges a glance with Azzy, then returns his gaze to me. "Everything. So she can help you."

I frown at him. "Obviously. What did you think I was gonna do? Pretend the whole thing didn't happen? I've tried that already, and it didn't make any of this craziness go away."

"We'll have a good chat, don't worry," Azzy says, patting Dash's arm before taking my hand and steering me toward the stairs. "Let's get you settled in, Em. Can I call you Em, or do you prefer Emerson?"

"She likes Emmy," Dash tells her. I twist my head over my shoulder and imagine sparks flying out of my eyes straight at him. Unfortunately, magic doesn't seem to work that way, and I'm left simply glaring at his smiling face. "Have fun," he says with a small wave before turning and heading for the door. And despite the fact that I want to slap him—despite telling him I don't need him—I have the sudden panicked urge to call out, "Wait, don't leave me here!" Because even though I've always hated him, he's the last tie to my normal life, and he's about to disappear through that door.

But I swallow my panic and don't say a word. I face forward and let Azzy lead me up the stairs. Because I've survived everything life has ever thrown at me *on my own*, and this will be no different.

CHAPTER 7

She isn't your mother.

This piece of information keeps knocking on the inside of my brain, and now that I'm alone, nothing I do can distract me from it. I examine every part of my bedroom—almost as nice as the guest room in Dash's parents' house—but fluffed-up pillows, a luxuriously soft carpet, and a four-poster bed can't keep the image of a mother who isn't my mother from branding itself onto the inside of my mind.

I open the wardrobe and discover, upon finding a mirror there, that I look terrible. My skin is pale, and my eyelids are smudged with dark makeup. I pick up some clean clothes from one of the shelves and, after peering both ways down the hall to make sure I'm not about to bump into anyone, I cross to the bathroom Azzy pointed out. What I find there is enough to startle me out of my upsetting thoughts for a time. I expected a bath or shower, but instead I find a small pool surrounded by pebbles and filled with steaming, scented water. It's the most inviting thing I've seen in ages, and I'm more than happy to push aside every thought racing through my head, strip out of my dirty clothes, and sink into the hot water.

But even this distraction doesn't last long. So after dressing myself in clean clothes that somehow fit perfectly, I leave my room. I wander around the house, through a library lined with books from floor to ceiling, into a dining room with a long rectangular table at its center, and across a kitchen larger than Chelsea's house. I explore the garden, ignoring every person—every fae … being … *thing*—I come across.

But my thoughts keep going back to Mom. I try to hold onto the picture of her I've always had, to the place she's always held in my life. The place and title of *mother*. But the idea is beginning to crumble as questions start sneaking in through the cracks of my defenses: How did she end up with me? Who do I really belong to? Why didn't she ever tell me? Who the hell am I if I'm not her daughter? And despite the fact that it fills me with guilt, I try to imagine what my 'real' mother might be like. But my imagination comes up blank. I can't picture anyone except the woman I grew up with.

When I realize I've been standing motionless in front of the same weird polka-dot plant for several minutes, staring unseeingly past it, I decide I'm done with real life for today. I can deal with all my questions, doubts, confusions, and *magic* tomorrow. I return to my room, drag the curtains closed, climb into bed, and do my best to fall asleep. When Azzy knocks on my door and says something about dinner, I pull the duvet over my head and ignore her.

"Everyone, this is Emerson," Azzy says the following morning after introducing the other seven people in the library: a faerie, an elf, and five half somethings. "Remember how uncertain you felt about everything when you first arrived here? That's how Em feels right now. So remember to do your best to welcome her."

Everyone looks at me. I slide a little lower in my chair. If I knew how to open that gap I opened in the earth the other night, I'd be tempted to do it again right now and crawl into it.

"Well then," Azzy continues. "You can get better acquainted over lunch. For now, you all need to get back to whatever you're working on at the moment. Em, you'll be with me."

I stand along with everyone else. Two of my fellow weirdos move to a table together and chat quietly as they open several enormous textbooks. The rest leave the library through the door that leads into the garden.

"So, Em," Azzy says, ushering me over to another table. "As I'm sure you've realized, this isn't like an ordinary school. We never know when someone will arrive, and everyone has a different story. Some fae have no previous knowledge of the magic world at all, like you, while others have had some exposure to magic, but haven't formally been taught anything. So as you can see, we need to tailor our lessons and training to each individual."

"Um, yes," I say after a pause, since it seems she's waiting for a sign that I'm listening to her.

"So we're going to begin with a little bit of history about this world. Momentous occasions from the past, as well as more recent events that have played an important role in shaping our world."

"Fun." I try not to sound bored, but I can tell I'm not doing a very good job. What happened to learning about actual magic?

"It is fun. Especially since I'm going to get some of the other students to explain things to you."

"What?"

Azzy gives me a knowing smile. "I thought that might get you to pay attention."

"So … that part was a joke?"

"Oh, no, I was being entirely serious. This way you don't have to listen to me droning on for hours. I've found it to be a wonderful way of learning. It helps the students who've been here longer to remember what they've learned, it teaches *you* the most important facts, and you'll get to know each other in the process. I'll supervise, of course, to make sure they don't tell you a bunch of nonsense, but essentially it will all be a discussion."

Wonderful. So this is what I have to look forward to every day that I'm here. "So, um, when will I learn how to do some actual magic? I thought that was all I needed to know. Control the magic, then I can leave."

She smiles. "We'll start this afternoon with something easy. After you've told me exactly what happened the other night when you accidentally used magic."

I sigh as I get up and follow her to the table with the other two fae. "Why does everyone want me to tell them exactly what happened? Isn't every detail of the whole event written up in some boring Guild report somewhere?"

"I'm sure it is, but it can't hurt to explain it again. Now, you sit here with George and Aldo—" she pulls a chair out for me as the two boys look up "—and I'm going to get my tea."

I ease myself into the chair, my gaze moving warily between the two boys. "Hi," says the younger one, who looks about ten years old. "I'm George. This is Aldo."

"Okay, let me see if I remember this correctly. You're a faerie," I say, pointing to Aldo, "and you're a halfling?" My gaze moves to George.

"Yep." George nods and smiles.

I remember Dash mentioned the word halfling and saying I couldn't be one, but he didn't explain any more than that. "So what exactly is a halfling? Someone only half magical?"

"Not exactly," Aldo says. He looks a little older, fourteen or fifteen perhaps. Although age doesn't seem to make sense in this world, so I could be totally wrong.

"It means two different parents. So a faerie and an elf, for example. Or a human and a faerie, even though fae laws say interaction with humans is wrong."

"That's what I am," George says, sticking his hand into the air as if volunteering to answer a question. "Faerie dad plus human mom. Dad says he got bored with this world, so he went adventuring in the other one. He met my mom and he hasn't come back here since. He thought I barely had any magic when I was little, but it started increasing after I turned ten last year. Things got a little out of hand last month when I accidentally set our shed on fire with enchanted flames that couldn't be put out with water. I was sent here after that."

"Wow. Almost as dramatic as my story," I say. "So how do you tell the difference between faeries and halflings? Someone told me I'm definitely a faerie, but what if he was wrong?"

"No, you're definitely a faerie," Aldo says. "It's easy to tell because faeries have a color."

"A color?"

"You haven't noticed?" He leans forward and rests his elbows on the table. "You have blue in your hair and eyes. I have red. That guardian who brought you here has green. Azzy has pink, although she prefers to call it cerise."

"It is cerise," Azzy says as she walks back into the library and comes toward our table with a teacup and saucer floating through the air beside her. She takes a seat. "Now, Em, have you thought of your first question?"

I clear my throat and force myself to look away from the levitating teacup. "Oh, I thought they were just going to tell me stuff."

"But how will they know what to tell you if you don't ask a question?"

I raise an eyebrow. This style of teaching seems questionable, but I'm no expert, so I probably shouldn't point that out. "Um … let's see …" What do I want to know? I want to know if it's absolutely certain that Mom isn't my mom. I want to know how I ended up living with her. I want to know how I'm supposed to look at life and myself when I'm suddenly not the person I've always thought I was. I want to know if it's possible to have an identity crisis at the age of seventeen.

But I'm not going to ask any of those questions, of course. They're far too personal, and these kids won't know the answers anyway. "Um, well, Dash explained the faerie paths, but is that the only way to get to the other world? What if someone doesn't have one of those stylus things?" What worries me is that *I* don't have one of those stylus things, and I need a way to get out of here if things end up going badly.

"Ooh, okay, I've got this," George says, his hand shooting into the air again.

"So there are gaps here and there in the veil between the two worlds, and fae can get through those gaps. I don't remember exactly where they are, though, or where they came from. I think they've always existed. Oh, and there's the tear in the veil over Velazar Island," he adds. "That's not natural, though. It shouldn't exist. Some witches created it years ago."

I glance at Azzy. "That sounds like it might have been an important event."

"It was," she says, looking pleased. I can tell what she's thinking: this group learning thing is working out just as she planned. "Can you tell us more about that event, Aldo?"

"Uh, sure, okay." He taps his stylus on the desk. "Well, there was this guy called Draven. Okay, wait, let's backtrack a bit." He frowns, then continues. "It was about, um, twenty-eight years ago when one of the Unseelie princes was trying to take over his mother's court. Instead, he and the Unseelie Queen were both killed by Draven, who was this insanely powerful halfling, and Draven ended up taking over the Unseelie Court. There was lots of fighting and brainwashing and stuff, and eventually Draven was killed. At least, that's what everyone thought."

"Dun, dun, duuuuun," George says in dramatic tones, making Azzy chuckle.

"Ten years later, the Seelie princess who'd been in prison all that time for helping Draven—because he was actually her son—"

"*Super* complicated," George adds.

"Yeah, so the Seelie princess found out that Draven was actually still alive and in hiding," Aldo continues, "and she betrayed him and handed him over to the Guild in exchange for her freedom."

"She wasn't the best mother," Azzy says with a shake of her head.

"Then the princess killed her mother and sister so she could claim the Seelie crown. So that kinda backfired on the Guild—because, you know, the Guild and the Seelie Court work together, so they lost their queen and got a horrible new one. And then it turned out that the Seelie princess was working with some witches, and they wanted to rule over the human world too. They decided it shouldn't be separate from this world anymore. So they used an ancient spell and horrible dark magic to tear through the veil, but what ended up happening was that as the hole tore wider and wider, it started consuming both worlds."

"I don't think they knew that would happen," George says.

"No, obviously not. Anyway, Draven ended up at the scene—probably to get revenge on his mother—and he was killed. For real this time. There was more fighting, and somehow the hole in the veil stopped getting bigger."

"The monument," Azzy prompts.

"Right. There was an ancient monument from the mer kingdom, and when the tear in the veil tried to pass it, the monument's magic was strong enough to hold the tear in place and keep it from getting any bigger. So now it's just there, this giant hole in the veil over Velazar Island—"

"Which is a *floating* island," George adds with a grin. "Well, two islands now, because there was a prison on the other side so the Guild chopped the island in half after the veil thing happened."

"And guardians are stationed by the hole at all times," Aldo continues, "hiding it with a glamour and making sure no one gets close enough to touch the monument."

"So there's no way to close it?" I ask.

"Scholars have been working on it ever since," Azzy says. "And I hear there's finally been a breakthrough, actually."

I vaguely remember Jewel saying something yesterday about a spell for a veil. "I think I heard about that. The Guild had a meeting about it yesterday."

"Yes, so that's quite exciting." Azzy smiles at us before picking up her teacup. "Anyway, are you keeping up so far, Em?"

"I think so. Not sure I totally understand the Seelie and Unseelie thing, though."

"Oh, the different courts." Azzy nods toward Aldo before taking another sip of her tea.

"Um, the courts rule over different parts of our world," Aldo says. "The Guild and the Seelie Court work together to kind of maintain order and peace and keep the world running. They decide on laws, and they prohibit magic that involves hurting other people. Unseelies tend to keep to themselves. They also like to ignore laws and use whatever dark magic they feel like, and the Seelie Court can't always do anything about it. I think." He looks to Azzy for confirmation.

"Essentially, yes. It's a complicated balance."

"So what happened to the Seelie princess?" I ask. "The one who killed her mother and sister and was working with the witches? The Guild didn't allow her to continue ruling, did they?"

Azzy shakes her head and places her teacup on its saucer. "No. After the veil-tearing spell, the death penalty was reinstated, and Princess Angelica—who I suppose was actually Queen Angelica at that point—was sentenced to death."

My eyes widen. "Wow. So who was left to take over the court?"

"Her sister's son. So currently we have a king in both courts. King Idrind in the Seelie Court, who is quite a young king, and King Savyon in the Unseelie Court, who's been ruling ever since Draven's first 'death.'"

More weird names, I think to myself. Out loud, I say, "This is all very interesting, but it doesn't help me get my own magic under control. That's all I really need to know, right?"

"If you decide to stay in this world," Azzy says, "then you need to know how it works."

"But I won't be staying here."

She smiles. "No need to make that decision now."

"I'm pretty sure I've already made the decision."

Azzy laughs. "Okay, okay. That's absolutely fine, but I'm still required by the Guild to teach you some history. But I promise we'll get to the actual magic straight after lunch, okay? Now." She leans forward and watches me intently with her dark pink eyes. "Have you been told anything about Griffin Abilities?"

I remember Dash mentioning them yesterday. "Um … faerie superpowers?"

"Kinda, yes," Aldo says. He looks at Azzy.

"Well, go ahead," she says to him. "Tell Em all about them."

I sit back in my chair, and the rest of the morning passes by with explanations of what Griffin Abilities are (additional, unnatural magical abilities), where they originally came from (metal discs containing the magic of a super powerful halfling from centuries ago), and how they're passed on these days since the discs are all gone (when two Griffin Gifted have a child, although sometimes the child will come out normal).

After a few more rounds of questions and answers, Azzy finally lets us break for lunch. I stand and stretch, and am about to follow Aldo and George when I notice Aldo's stylus on the table amongst the books. After a brief glance around the room to make sure no one's watching me, I casually reach forward and pick it up. I lift my T-shirt and stick it into the waistband of my jeans, then hurry out.

The stylus digs into my chest the whole time I'm sitting at lunch, and I'm afraid it's going to suddenly open a doorway on my body or set me on fire or cast some other spell of its own accord. But I manage to make it through lunch in one piece.

Straight afterwards, Azzy tells me to put a sweater on over my T-shirt and meet her outside. "Ready to learn some magic?" she asks when I find her near a statue of a centaur pointing a bow and arrow at the sky.

It's probably the strangest question I've ever been asked. I can still barely believe magic itself exists, let alone that I have the ability to play around with it. I swallow and roll my shoulders in an attempt to relax. "Probably not, but let's go for it."

CHAPTER 8

"So how does this work?" I ask as we stand in the garden some distance away from the other students. "I say some magic words and something happens?"

"Is that what happened the other night when you accidentally used magic?" Azzy asks.

"Um, no, those were just normal words. My friend Val was embarrassed about something she'd said to a guy, and she made a comment about wishing the earth would open up and swallow her whole. So I said …" I swallow and wrap a few strands of hair around my forefinger, ashamed of the state I was in that night. "I was kind of out of it, because I'd had a little bit of alcohol, and apparently that isn't good for faeries, so I … I don't know, exactly, but I said something like, 'So what? Then just let the earth swallow you whole.' And then … it happened."

"I see." Azzy nods slowly.

"Was it to do with my thoughts? Was I perhaps picturing it, and my magic appeared at the same time, so that made it actually happen?"

"You know, Em, I'm not sure. Strange things can happen when a person's magic first reveals itself after being dormant for years. But I'm going to try and find out for you, okay?" She gives me a smile that seems less enthusiastic than previously. "And it's probably best that you don't mention exactly what you did to anyone else. Not until I can find out more."

"Oh. Why—"

"In the meantime," she says before I can ask my question, "let's start with the basics. Magic exists around you and inside you. In order to get it to *do* something, you need to draw it out from within you and either release it in some form, or channel it through a stylus. A lot of our magic works that way, by writing the words to a specific spell onto something, while channeling magic through the stylus."

Part of my brain is still stuck wondering why I'm supposed to keep what happened the other night a secret, so I take a few moments to process Azzy's words. "Um, okay, so once I can channel it, can I do anything I want with it?"

"No, we have limitations, of course. Drawing upon that power tires us out, just like exercising would tire you out. If you reach the point where you have almost nothing left, then you need to rest, to regain your magical strength." She walks slowly back and forth as she speaks, her loose clothing fluttering around her. "And there are limitations to exactly what you can do. You can't just snap your fingers and have a pile of gold sitting in front of you, or a rainbow arcing across the entire sky."

"Okay. But superpowered faeries can do things like that?"

"Yes. Griffin Abilities allow people to do magic that no one should be able to do. But we'll get to the specifics of what's possible and what isn't later," she adds with a wave of her hand. "The first thing I want you to practice is the part where you actually draw upon your own magic. It will initially seem like something you have to focus intently on every time, but it will soon become instinctual. Then you'll find that you can do it automatically without even thinking about it."

"Like driving a car?"

"Well, I don't have any personal experience in that area, but yes, I suppose it's like driving a car." She stops pacing and holds her hands out palm-up in front of her. "Once you've drawn power out of yourself, if you're not channeling it through something, you can simply hold it in your hands. It will appear as a sort of glowing, swirling mass that can then be transformed into other things." As she speaks, a roughly spherical shape of light takes form above her hands, sparking this way and that like energy struggling to break free. "For now," she says, "I just want you to focus on getting to the point where you're holding it."

I swallow, then blink as Azzy's magic vanishes and she lowers her hands to her sides. "Um, okay. Should I close my eyes?"

"If that will help you focus, then yes."

My eyelids slide closed, and I concentrate on picturing a deep, hidden place inside me. I have to rid my mind of unhelpful images of intestines and other organs, but eventually I get there.

"Can you feel it yet?" Azzy asks quietly. "Humming, thrumming, vibrating. Find it, and imagine gathering some of it up in your hands and pulling it free."

I picture myself doing as she says, hoping that in reality it isn't as slippery and difficult to hold onto as I'm imagining it to be.

"There it is," she whispers.

I open my eyes, and I'm so startled to see the glowing mass hovering about my hands that I gasp and step backwards, whipping my hands away from the magic. It fizzles into nothing.

Azzy laughs. "Well done, that was good."

A breathy laugh escapes me. "I actually did it."

"You did. Now for the next challenge: can you do it again?"

I hold my hands out once more and close my eyes. I expect it to be easier the second time, but when I open my eyes, I find nothing above my palms. So I try again, taking my time, feeling for that faint humming that never used to be part of me. I tug and coax, but once again, I find my hands empty.

"Patience," Azzy murmurs. "Don't get frustrated with yourself."

I repeat the process, but I can't seem to clear my mind as easily anymore. The cold air distracts me. The chirping of insects fills my ears. I shake my arms out, breathe deeply several times, and try yet again.

Nothing.

"Ugh, this sucks! Why is it so hard?"

Azzy, standing patiently to one side, folds her arms. "Because today is the first time you've tried doing it. It will take lots of practice before it becomes easy."

"But I need to know how to do this *now*."

"Em, you need to go easy on yourself," she says with a laugh. "You have to learn everything a faerie child would spend the whole of junior school learning, and that isn't going to happen in an afternoon. Even if you're smart and dedicated, it will still take several months to—"

"*Months?*" I repeat, icy shock racing through me. "What are you talking about? I can't be here for *months*."

"Why not? Is there something important you need to get back to? I was under the impression the Guild had sorted out your story with your human relatives and friends. No one is expecting you back on that side of the veil any time soon."

"That doesn't make a—what about—there's my *mother*!" I stammer. "And I have a plan. I need to finish school and move closer to her and get a job that pays better. Then I can actually help her. How am I supposed to finish school if I'm *here* for months? I'm only supposed to be here for—I don't know—a week or two."

"I'm sorry, Em." Azzy's brow furrows in confusion. "I don't know who told you that, but this is definitely going to take longer than a week or two."

"I ... just ... I can't do this." I back away from her.

"Em, wait—"

"I'm going to my room."

"Emerson, please be mature about this," Azzy calls after me. "Let's just have a chat instead of you rushing off to hide from it all."

I don't look back. I run past the statues and into the house—and straight past the stairs that lead up to the bedrooms. I tug the front door open and keep running. Along the path and out the gate. I have no idea where I'm going, of course, but I need to get away from this place. I dart between trees, around bushes, and over rocks. I may not be good at magic, but I'm good at running. So I run and run and run, and eventually I trip over something and slide halfway down a steep part of the forest. I scramble up and brush my scratched and dirty hands against my jeans, allowing myself to catch my breath.

I'm far from the house now, so I pull Aldo's stylus free from my jeans. I hold it like a pen and rest my hand against the nearest tree. I've seen this spell several times now, so I should be able to remember the words. I try to focus and reach for whatever magic exists inside me while writing out the words I witnessed both Dash and Jewel writing. They spoke some foreign words as well, so I take a stab at repeating what I remember hearing.

It's hopeless. I've either got the writing wrong, or the spoken words wrong, or I'm not channeling enough magic through the stylus. Probably a combination of all three. I spin around and throw the stylus onto the ground. After a moment's pause, I drop down beside it. I cross my legs and arms and breath out a huff of air. This is so stupid. What am I supposed to do now? Keep walking until I find one of those natural openings between the two worlds? And how would I know it if I saw it? No, that's a stupid plan. Especially if there aren't many of those openings. I could be hundreds or even thousands of miles away from one. What I'll have to do instead is keep walking until I come across a person who can take me to the human world. Chevalier House can't be too far from civilization, right?

I force myself to keep moving, trying not to think of the fact that I could be completely wrong. As I walk and walk and walk, the light overhead slowly grows dim. By the time night starts to close in and I haven't yet come across any sign of either a person or civilization, genuine fear gathers at the edge of my mind. I run my hands roughly up and down my arms, trying to keep warm, but it does little good.

Then I hear something. The repetitive rustle of footsteps on leaves. Relief and uncertainty crash into me at the same time, freezing me to the spot for several moments. Then I regain my senses and slip behind the nearest tree, peeking out in the direction of the sound. In this world, it's definitely safer to check things out before waving hello.

The being that eventually comes into view looks like a man. His face is in shadow, and he wears a long black coat that reaches below his knees. When I see it isn't some form of monster, I almost step out from behind the tree and call for him. But something holds me back. A shift in the air. A feeling of unease. I notice movement across the forest floor, as if insects and tiny creatures are scuttling away from him. The sense that something here is *wrong* engulfs me.

I crouch down amongst the tree roots, covering my head with my hands and trying to curl myself into as small a ball as possible. *Please, please, please don't see me,* I chant silently. Eventually, his footsteps fade to nothing. I allow myself to breathe out long and slow before standing and peering tentatively around the tree. I take a few steps.

And a dark shape leaps out at me.

CHAPTER 9

I go down with a scream, the creature on top of me. Leathery wings flap around me, and a snarling mouth snaps at my face. I fight back with fists and elbows and knees. With a great heave, I manage to kick it off me. It leaps again—but something bright and glittering flashes through the darkness. The monster screeches as a golden blade slashes back and forth, forcing it further away from me. It swipes one wing at the man holding the blade, then darts to the side and flaps away.

The man turns around—and I see that it's Dash.

I scramble up and back away until I feel the rough surface of a tree trunk behind me. I lean against it, not trusting my own legs to keep me upright. Breathless, I ask, "How … how did you find me?"

"Does it matter?" Dash takes a step toward me.

"Yes. Here I am trying to get back to my normal life, and my stalkerish babysitter shows up out of the blue."

He lets go of his knife, and it simply … disappears. "I think you're probably supposed to be thanking your stalkerish babysitter right now."

I push away from the tree and increase the distance between us. "I'm not thanking you for anything. All you want to do is drag me back to that stupid school."

Instead of reminding me that he's just saved my life, he says, "Bad first day?"

"Of course it was bad. This place—this world—isn't for me. I don't belong here. Why doesn't anyone understand that?"

"We do understand. That's what Chevalier House is for."

"You're not listening to me. I don't. Want. To be here. Okay? I don't want to have weird lessons with strangers, I don't care about the history of this world, and I don't want any of this magic. I just want OUT."

Confusion crosses Dash's features. "But … isn't this better than what you had before?"

"No! I don't want this!" I yell. I begin pacing, flinging my arms wildly about as I go, not caring that random sparks are escaping my fingers and burning the leaves on the ground. "Two days ago, my life was the same old crap it's always been. Now I'm magical, I'm in a foreign world, my mom isn't my mom, and basically I don't have a f—" I cut myself off before finishing. "I don't have an *effing* clue who I am or what's going on. I just want to go back to my plan where I finish school, move far away from Chelsea, and figure out how to get Mom out of that hospital. And yes, I'm well aware that it was a crappy life, but it was *my* life and I knew what to do with it."

Dash's forehead remains creased. "But you can still do all that. I mean, not exactly like that, but once you've got the magic side of things under control, you can go back to normal life. In fact, magic will *help* you with normal life, if you're discreet about it. So you shouldn't be trying to turn your back on it."

I pause, staring into the darkness and seeing nothing as my brain ticks quickly through something I hadn't considered until now. I turn slowly and face Dash. "Can magic heal my mom?"

He hesitates, his mouth open, then closes it and slowly shakes his head. "She isn't magical. It would be too risky to use magic on her body, especially on her mind. We don't know if it would damage her and make things worse."

I throw my hands up. "Then what the hell is the point in having these stupid powers? How are they supposed to help me?"

"Um, because of everything else you can do with magic?"

I fold my arms over my chest. "Can I walk through the faerie paths straight into her hospital room and take her back through them to somewhere else?"

"Well, no, you can't take her anywhere through the paths because humans can't travel that way. But *you* can go anywhere. You could visit her right now. I mean," he adds quickly, "if you thought that was a good idea."

I hesitate. Clearly Dash doesn't think it's a good idea to visit her right now, and he's probably right. I want to, of course. I want nothing more. But I don't want to go with him. I don't want him to see my mother in her current state, and I don't want him to see *me* and my reaction when I see her like that. I need to learn this faerie paths thing so I can travel there on my own. "Okay, so I can't rescue her from the hospital that way," I say. "But I could conceal myself with magic, right? And I could use magic to distract everyone while I get Mom out of the building, and magic could adjust the paperwork so everyone thinks she was properly discharged. And magic could put my name into the school system to say that I graduated, and it could help me get some money to set up a simple life somewhere and keep Mom safe. Right?"

"Yes, exactly. See? Magic is good for something. Although," he adds with a frown, "I'm not saying I advocate you doing any of those things. We're not supposed to mess around with human lives and, like, use magic to illegally get hold of money."

"You're also not saying that you would stop me."

"I'm saying …" Dash scratches his head. "I'm saying you should go back to Chevalier House and continue learning how to safely use your magic. We can consider all options after that."

I nod slowly. "Right."

He hesitates, watching me with narrowed eyes. "You're thinking about doing all those illegal things, aren't you?"

"I'm thinking about going back to Chevalier House." Which is the truth, actually, seeing as magic has suddenly become the best way to dig myself out of my crappy life and give Mom a better future than the one she's currently facing.

Dash sighs. "Well, your motives may be questionable, but if they'll get you back into Chevalier House tonight, then I've done my job."

"Great. Well done. Should we get going then?" I turn around, and something that looks like a winged lizard leaps off a branch and flies right at me. "Holy sh—"

"Sherbet," Dash says, catching the tiny creature. "Holy sherbet. That's what she was gonna say, little guy. No need to get upset."

"Holy *sherbet*," I snap. "What the hell is that thing?"

Before my eyes, the creature begins to change form. One moment it's some kind of reptile, and the next it's a kitten. "Ah, looks like a shapeshifter," Dash says. "Formattra is the official name, I think. These little guys are quite rare. I wonder how he ended up here."

"Shapeshifters? Terrific. Are werewolves real too?"

"Well, you do get higher fae who are shapeshifters, but I think they transform into other people, not animals. You know, like another faerie transforming to look like me."

"Because who wouldn't want to look like you, right?"

"Exactly." The creature stretches out and sniffs me. I scuttle backwards out of its reach. "Hey, come on, he likes you," Dash says. "Don't you want a pet?"

"No. I don't like pets."

Dash laughs. "Impossible. Why don't you like pets?"

"They die, and it's sad." *Or they run away and never come back.*

"That is definitely not a good enough reason."

"Fine. I'll soon be leaving, and who will take care of him then? Is that a good enough reason?"

The creature flickers between several forms so quickly I can't tell what it is until it becomes a kitten again. "He's just a baby, Em," Dash says, scratching the kitten's head. "He needs someone to take care of him."

I tilt my head to the side. "You said they're very rare, didn't you? So can I sell him for lots of money?"

Dash's face falls. He hugs the creature to his chest and covers its ears. "That's a terrible thing to say, Em. Don't listen to her, little guy," he whispers. "She didn't mean that."

"Ugh, seriously?" My hands clench into fists. "Can we go now? You said I need to get back to the house, and now you're wasting time out here with this weird shapeshifting thing."

He watches me, his mouth open as if he wants to say something. Then he shakes his head. "Yeah, okay. Let's go." As he raises his stylus to write a doorway, the shapeshifting creature leaps away and disappears into the darkness. Dash extends his hand to me, and I reluctantly take it. Whoever came up with the physical contact rule for faerie path traveling obviously didn't take into account the possibility that some people might never want to hold hands.

When the darkness disappears to reveal dim light, we're standing outside the Chevalier House gate. "You could have just taken us straight into the house, you know."

"I couldn't, actually," Dash says as he pushes the gate open. "The faerie paths don't open inside the house or anywhere in the garden."

I swing the gate shut behind us. "That's weird. Why?"

"Security measure. It's like that for most private properties. Only the owners can open doorways inside the house itself."

"Kind of a stupid security measure if anyone can just open the gate."

"The gate won't open for just anyone, though," Dash says as we follow the path up to the house. "If you've walked through it in the company of someone who lives here—like the elf who brought us here yesterday—then you've been granted magical access to pass through the gate."

I allow a long sigh to pass my lips. "That all seems unnecessarily complicated. People should just use padlocks and keys."

Dash chuckles. "Such a human thing to say."

"Bite me," I mutter.

We walk into Chevalier House's entrance hall and find Dash's BFF teammate Jewel waiting for us. "Oh, you found her," Jewel says, a smile lighting up her face. "Well done."

"Are you also part of the babysitting team?" I ask.

She frowns. "What do you mean? I was with Dash when Azzy sent the message to say you'd run. I offered to help look for you."

"How nice of you," I say flatly.

Dash nudges me with his elbow, and I take a step away from him so he can't do it again. Azzy hurries into the room then. "Emerson." She places her hands on her hips and gives me a stern look. "Running away wasn't necessary. I hope you know that we aren't going to force you to stay here against your will. If you're completely certain you're not interested in this world, we can send you back to the Guild and they can give you one of those devices that block all magic."

"Device?" I ask.

"It's a ring or bangle or something. I'm not sure what form they're using these days. It's something that can't be removed, and it will block your magic entirely."

"Oh. I didn't know that was an option." But as Dash pointed out, magic can help me to help Mom. Especially since the kind of job I could get as a high school graduate wouldn't pay nearly as much as the kind of job I could get if I whipped up an enchanted version of some higher qualification. If I want to be better equipped to help Mom, then I need to stick around a bit longer. "I'm sorry, Azzy," I force myself to say. "I'm here to learn now. I won't run again."

"Wonderful. Now, why don't you two stay for dinner?" Azzy asks Jewel and Dash. "Or do you have important cases to deal with?"

"Our team's done for the day," Jewel says. She links arms with Dash. "We'd love to stay for dinner."

"Wonderful," Azzy says, wrapping an arm around Dash's shoulders and squeezing them briefly.

"Yeah, really wonderful," I mutter. "I'm just gonna … clean up, I guess."

"Of course," Azzy says, nodding toward one of the doors leading off the entrance hall. "Try not to confuse it with the front door, Em. We wouldn't want you getting lost outside again."

I consider rolling my eyes, but it's too much effort. "I think I can manage."

When I'm done splashing water on my face and combing my fingers through my hair—which surprises me, yet again, with its bright blue strands—I leave the bathroom and find Jewel waiting alone in the entrance hall. She pushes away from the table. I glance around, but it's definitely me she's walking toward. "Um, hi?"

She smiles, and it seems almost genuine. "Look, I really don't want to do the whole teenage, mean-girl thing, since I know we're all practically adults around here, but I do just want to point out that Dash isn't exactly available."

I decide to play dumb. "Available for what?"

She rolls her eyes. "You know, a relationship."

"Oh." I fold my arms. "Why is that?"

"Well, look, it's not official yet, but we kind of have a thing going."

"A thing? Really? I never would have guessed that, given the way he tries to charm every female he comes across."

Jewel's smile slips a little. "Yeah, I know he's dated a bunch of girls, but none of those relationships have lasted long, and I know exactly why."

I feign intense interest. "You do?"

"Yes, it's obvious: he's searching for the right person. And he's so close to discovering that it's me, so I just don't want anything to ruin that for us now."

"Oh, wow, it's you? How do you know that?"

"Because so much of our lives have been spent together. We trained together. We grew up together. We even played together as babies. We're meant to be."

I blink. "That's the dumbest thing I've ever heard."

"Hey!"

"Who cares if you played together as babies? I doubt either of you can remember it."

"That doesn't matter! It means we have a *history*," she snaps, all trace of her sweet smile gone. "And if we have a history, we'll have a stronger future."

"Really? 'Cause Dash and I have a history too, and it's only ever made me dislike him."

"Yes, because you have the *wrong* history. We have the *right* history, so—"

"Jewel?" I pause to make sure she's listening. "You can have him. I'm not interested."

"Oh. Really?"

"Really. I have other priorities right now." I walk past her and head for the dining room, where loud chatter and mouthwatering aromas fill the air. At the long rectangular table sit the seven other students currently attending Chevalier House, as well as a few fae I've seen walking around. Teachers, perhaps, and the man with his hand on Azzy's wrist, chuckling as he leans closer to say something only she can hear, must be her husband or partner or something of that nature.

"Emerson! You missed something exciting while you were gone," George tells me as I take a seat.

"Oh, what did I miss?"

"Another new person arrived."

"And that counts as exciting?" I pull the nearest platter of food closer and begin dishing roasted vegetables onto my plate. They smell a thousand times more delicious than anything Chelsea's ever cooked.

"That's two new people in two days," Azzy says from the head of the table. "That doesn't happen often here."

"And she's old like you," George adds.

I lower the serving spoon. "Excuse me?"

"Oh, gosh, as old as Emerson?" Dash's eyes widen. "That's seriously old."

George, sitting beside Dash across the table from me, chews his lip as his brow furrows. "Oh, I thought … But isn't Azzy the one who's super old? And Emerson is, like, your age?" he says to Dash.

"Okay, and *this*," I say, pointing my fork for emphasis, "is why it's so flipping confusing having people who are a bazillion years old looking like they're in their twenties."

Dash shrugs. "We can't help it if we have magic running through our systems, keeping us young and beautiful."

"I know, it's so great, right?" Jewel says as she hurries into the dining room and selects the only available seat on Dash's side of the table.

"Bazillion? I'm only three hundred and four," says the man sitting beside Azzy. "I'm Paul, by the way," he adds with a smile in my direction. "Azzy's husband."

"Hi." I return his smile, pleased to discover that at least some fae have normal names. After tasting some of my food and trying not to moan out loud at how amazing it is, I ask, "So where's the other new girl?"

"She wasn't feeling so well," Azzy says. "Had a traumatizing few days. I gave her something to eat when she arrived just before dinner, and she's sleeping now. The two of you can begin lessons together tomorrow."

"Great." I'm less than thrilled about sharing lessons with someone else—what if she slows me down?—but since I've decided to commit myself fully to the Chevalier House program, I should probably be polite to everyone living here.

I turn my attention back to my food, piling a few more delicacies onto my plate when I think no one's looking. Dash catches my eye, though. I return his smirk with a glare. Spoiled brat probably has a live-in chef at home. No doubt he eats like this all the time.

At the end of the meal, the dishes rise up of their own accord and fly out of the dining room toward the kitchen. I try not to act too surprised, but I can't help pressing myself back against my chair in fright when my plate first rises into the air. I excuse myself soon afterwards and leave the dining room; all this chatter and activity over dinner isn't something I'm used to. I'd rather get to bed early so I can focus properly on all this magic stuff tomorrow.

"Em?"

I turn on the bottom step leading up to the bedrooms and look back.

"It's good that you came back," Dash says, wandering into the entrance hall. "When you're kicking butt at all your lessons in a few weeks' time, let me know so I can gloat about being the one who talked you into staying."

The only response I give him is another glare.

"Hey, come on, I'm just joking."

"You know, I've been trying to figure out why so many people like you when you're actually such a jackass."

He shrugs. "Probably because no one else is under the impression that I ruined their lives, so they're able to see me for who I really am."

"Which is what, exactly?"

"Friendly guy, charming smile, not half-bad to look at."

"I'm surprised they can see anything past that gigantic head of yours."

He frowns and raises a hand to his head. "What's wrong with my—"

"I meant your ego, dumb-ass."

"Hey, I said not half-bad. That should only give me a half-sized ego, right?"

"On you, that's more than big enough," I say as I turn and head up the stairs.

"Good night, Emmy," he calls after me.

"Shut up," I grumble beneath my breath.

I reach my door, push it open—and jump backward at the sight of a tiger sitting on my bed. The tiger flickers and morphs into an owl, then a crow, and then a kitten. Relief courses through me, followed quickly by irritation. "No," I say. "No, no, no. This isn't happening. You were supposed to stay out there in the forest." The kitten blinks. "I'm giving you to Dash. He can take care of you." I scoop the kitten up and hurry back along the hall.

At the top of the stairs, I stop. Azzy and Dash are standing close together in the entrance hall below, Dash looking uncharacteristically serious. "We have until the end of the week," he says quietly, "so there's no immediate rush. But we'll get a plan in place, probably for the day after tomorrow."

"Good. And make sure it looks like an accident."

"Of course."

I bite my lip, shrinking back into the shadows, knowing instinctively that I wasn't supposed to hear whatever they were talking about. Before I can decide what to do about the shapeshifting animal, Dash pulls the front door open and leaves. Azzy walks back to the dining room, her lightweight, oversized top floating behind her.

"What on earth?" I whisper to the kitten. An instant later, it becomes a bunny. "Fine. Dash is gone, so you're on your own." I place the bunny on the stairs, then hurry back to my room, my mind already racing through explanations for what Dash and Azzy could have been talking about. Perhaps it wasn't anything sinister at all. *Make sure it looks like an accident.* That doesn't sound good, though. But whatever it is, I won't be getting involved. I've survived this long by keeping my nose out of other people's business, and that isn't about to change.

After visiting the steaming hot pool in the bathroom—the best thing about this house aside from the food—I climb into bed and tap the lamp to turn it off. It's powered by magic, of course—electricity doesn't seem to exist in this world—and Azzy told me to lightly tap it with my finger to turn it on and off. So far, it seems to be working.

I settle down against the pillows, finding it easier to drift off tonight than last night. I'm almost asleep when a sound—a gentle tap at the door—rouses me. So quiet I wonder if I might have imagined it. I sit up, watching the door through the dim grey light from the window and waiting. When the knock comes a second time, I know I'm not imagining it. "Yes?" I call through the darkness. My door opens slowly, revealing the silhouette of a female figure. "Who's there?" I ask, nerves fluttering suddenly in my stomach.

"Are you Emerson?" she asks. "The other new girl?"

"Um, yes." I lean over and turn on my lamp as she slips inside and shuts the door. She hurries across the room and drops onto the edge of my bed. I scoot backwards, putting a little more distance between us as I take in her appearance: a creased robe the same color as the one I found hanging in my wardrobe, pale skin, and eyes a deep blueish purple. It's the same color that runs through her dark hair, which, if I remember my lessons correctly, mean she's a faerie, not some other kind of fae.

"Please help me," she whispers, her eyes wide. "It isn't safe here. We need to leave."

PART II

CHAPTER 10

"Um ... what?" I ask, utterly confused. "What are you talking about? And who are you?"

"I'm Aurora. I just got here this evening. The professor told me there was another new girl, and I thought that since you haven't got too deep into their program yet, and they haven't brainwashed you, or whatever it is that happens here, we can get away together."

"Brainwash? Where'd you get that from?"

"Because I—I may not know how to use my magic at all, but I did grow up in this world, and I know things. I've heard things. About this place." She inches a little closer. "People disappear from here sometimes. Like, they just vanish without a trace soon after their training begins. And it's made to look like Chevalier House has nothing to do with it, but how can it not? People come in here, and they never leave. They just disappear. And I don't want that to happen to me. I just got my freedom, and I don't want to lose it."

If I could move any further away from this girl, I would, but I'm already backed up against the wall. "So, you're saying ... they *kill* some of the people who come in here?"

"I don't know. Maybe." She tugs at the silky belt of her robe, pulling it tighter. "Or maybe it's something worse. Maybe they're prisoners somewhere. Maybe they're being experimented on."

"Do you have any proof of that?"

"Of course not, but that doesn't make it untrue."

Given what I overheard between Dash and Azzy earlier, I'm almost inclined to believe this girl, but her wide, terror-filled eyes remind me all too much of Mom.

Mom looking desperate and afraid, speaking about equally irrational things. "Look, Aurora. I don't mean to be unfriendly, but I don't want to get involved in whatever you're talking about. You have your issues, and I have mine. Let's just get through this Magic 101 thing, and we can both go our separate ways."

She draws back, hurt filling her eyes. "You don't believe me? You seriously want to take your chances with these people you've only just met, instead of considering that I might be telling you the truth? That you and I might never get the chance to go our separate ways if something happens to us before then?"

I think again of Dash and Azzy's quiet conversation. "Okay," I say slowly. "It's true that I don't know the people here at all, but I don't know you either. You could be making this up."

She takes a deep breath. "What do you want to know? I'll … I'll tell you everything. When you understand how horrendous my life's been up until now, you'll understand why I don't ever want to be a prisoner again. I'll do anything to get out of here."

I raise my eyebrows at the word 'prisoner,' but I'm still not ready to believe this girl. If there are insane people in my world, there must be insane people in this one too. "Why don't we leave this until the morning?"

"No! Just let me explain myself. How will you know if you can trust me until you've heard what I have to say? How do you know you can trust *them*?"

I consider shouting out for Azzy, but Aurora's right. I *don't* know if I can trust anyone here. What if Chevalier House and this program is all an elaborate ruse to gather untrained magical beings? I don't know why anyone would do that, but I don't know much about this world, so there could be a reason. "Fine. Tell me what you want to tell me."

"Okay. So, I was brought up by witches—"

"Witches?" I give her a doubtful look. "Like on broomsticks? Nobody's said anything to me about witches. Are they even real?"

Her eyes narrow. "You've been in this world for all of five minutes, and you've already decided you know more than I do?"

"I just—"

"No, they don't have anything to do with broomsticks. I don't even know what that means."

"Oh. You've never been in my world?"

"The non-magic realm? No, never. Why would they have taken me there? I've spent most of my life locked up in their home. The only things I know are the things

I've heard them talk about, and the things I've read in their books. I don't know how I ended up living in a house with witches, because they never bothered to tell me. They … they treated me like their servant." She pulls her knees up and wraps her arms around them. "They never taught me how to use my magic, because that would have made me stronger. I could have used it against them. They caught me reading about Chevalier House once, when I was trying to figure out an escape plan and where I would go if I ever got away. They laughed and said that even if I managed to run away from them, Chevalier House wouldn't do me any good. Fae disappear from here all the time."

"If that were true, surely the Guild would know about it. They would have shut down the program by now." It can't be true. I need it to not be true. I need Azzy to teach me everything about magic so I can get back to my own world and help Mom.

"Unless the Guild's in on it too," Aurora says in conspiratorial tones.

"So if Chevalier House is dangerous, why did you come here?"

"I didn't *choose* to come here." She returns her feet to the floor and leans closer to me. "I finally managed to get away from the witches after months of careful planning. I was all on my own until a guardian caught me stealing food. That's how I ended up at the Guild, and they're the ones who sent me here."

I sigh. "You know this all sounds ridiculous, right? And the only thing you've got to go on is what a bunch of witches have told you. Obviously they'd want you to believe that Chevalier House can't help you. They didn't want you running away."

"Okay, so *maybe* they were lying. But are you willing to take that risk? Do you even *want* to be here?"

"Actually, yes. I do. I realized today that magic can help me far more than anything I've ever learned in my own world, and I need to know how to use it before returning home."

"If they ever allow you to return home," Aurora points out.

"Fine. What exactly are you suggesting then? That we run away together?"

"Yes. Everything's locked up now—I already checked downstairs—but we can wait for a chance tomorrow and run together. Then we can figure out what to do once we're free."

"No," I say flatly. "I'm sorry, but no. I tried that today and it didn't work. I have a different plan now, and it doesn't include running away with someone I just met."

"You're being so naive," she whispers with a fearful shake of her head.

"Am I? I don't trust you, and I don't trust them, so who am I going to go with? Obviously the side that's most likely to help me. And right now, that looks like

Chevalier House. If something weird's going on, I'll figure it out soon enough and then I'll run. But for now, I'm staying put." I shove aside the tiny voice that says Aurora might be right. That the strange conversation I overheard is evidence enough. Because I *need* this program to work. Now that I've realized how much magic can do for me in my own world, I'm clinging to it as if it's my only hope for a better life.

Aurora swallows, then breathes out slowly. She tucks a few strands of hair behind her ear, leaning away from me. "Okay. I'm—I'm sorry I bothered you with this." She slides off my bed and stands. "I'll … um … I guess you're right. We should each be looking out for ourselves."

I nod, since I'm not sure what else to do or say.

"Okay, well … good night." She turns and hurries out of my room.

"So weird," I murmur as I tap the lamp, plunging the room into darkness once more. I keep telling myself I've made the right decision, but I can't help turning her words over and over in my mind, and it's a long time before I fall asleep.

CHAPTER 11

"It's lovely that the two of you arrived at the same time and can learn together," Azzy says to Aurora and me as the two of us sit side by side at a library table the following morning. "It doesn't often happen that way."

Aurora says nothing, so I decide to say nothing too. I doubt either of us thinks there's anything 'lovely' about this situation. In fact, I'm surprised she's still here. She seemed so desperate last night; I thought she'd have found a way to escape the house while the rest of us were sleeping. But she was sitting at the dining room table when I got there this morning, frowning at her plate. She didn't look up once during breakfast.

"Right, then," Azzy says. "I'm going to explain glamours this morning, and after that we'll move outside to try some basic magic before lunch. No need to run away this time, Em," she adds with a chuckle. I sense Aurora's eyes on me, and I make a determined effort not to meet her gaze. "Then perhaps later, Em," Azzy says, "you can give me any information you think might be helpful in finding your real family. And you too, Aurora."

Icy apprehension shoots through my veins. I've been trying to ignore the idea that I have another family out there somewhere. It makes me sick every time I remember Mom isn't actually my mother. "Um …"

"Unless you don't want to, of course," Azzy adds quickly.

"I'm interested," Aurora says, which is surprising enough to make me look her way. I wonder what game she's playing, or if she might possibly be serious. Perhaps she hopes to discover something useful about her family before fleeing Chevalier House.

"Azzy?" I look around as Paul walks into the library. "I've just received the

71

guardians' report." He waves a rolled-up piece of paper. "They didn't find anything suspicious."

"Suspicious about what?" Aldo asks. He's reading alone at another table in the library while George works on some practical skills outside. "Did something happen?"

"The security enchantments picked up something outside our gate in the early evening yesterday," Paul explains. "The Guild was alerted, and a couple of guardians came to check things out. They told us they didn't find anything, but they left someone stationed out there for the night anyway."

"Do you think … maybe … it was the Griffin rebels?" Aldo says. "They hate the Guild, so they would hate us too, right?"

"I'm sure it was nothing," Azzy says with a smile. "And Paul," she adds in a low voice, though we can all still hear her, "I don't think it's necessary to scare the students."

"But we have a right to know what's going on, don't we?" Aldo protests. "If there's a threat, we should know about it."

"Nothing is going on," Azzy assures him. "The Griffin rebels have absolutely no reason to attack us. We have nothing to do with them."

I look over at Aurora. Her violet eyes meet mine, and her eyebrows rise the tiniest bit, as if to say, *See? I told you something's going on here.*

"Enough about that," Azzy says, clapping her hands together. "Aurora, do you know what a glamour is?"

Startled, Aurora swings back to face Azzy. "Not really. The witches didn't tell me anything about them."

The next hour passes with Azzy explaining glamours of all types, from the simple kind I'm supposed to be able to cast over myself without even thinking about it, to the immensely complex kind that conceal buildings inside trees so they're hidden from view. I realize that this is probably what Dash was referring to when he spoke about tree houses, and it's impossible to wrap my mind around the concept. A whole house full of space hidden inside one tree trunk? *How the freaking heck?*

"Magic makes the impossible possible," Azzy says, which doesn't seem like much of an explanation to me.

Something tickles my ankle. I look down, twitching involuntarily when I see a grasshopper clinging to the bottom of my jeans. I'm about to swat it away when it flickers, drops to the floor, seems to kind of bulge out, and becomes a frog. "Seriously?" I whisper. "Leave me alone."

"Em?" Azzy asks, pausing in the middle of a description of exactly what happened to one of the Guilds years ago when its glamour magic was destroyed. "Everything okay?"

"Uh, yes. Just a frog."

"Oh, it must have hopped in from outside. I'm sure it'll find its way back out. Now, shall we try some magic?"

Excitement pulses through me as we follow Azzy into the garden. *Be patient,* I instruct myself. *Don't get frustrated. You can do this.* We stop near a three-tiered fountain. I rub my hands up and down my arms. "It's a little cold to practice outside, isn't it?"

"Yeah," Aurora murmurs. No doubt she's feeling it worse than I am. I've at least got jeans on; she's wearing a long skirt and open sandals.

"Nonsense." Azzy turns to face us. "As long as the fountain hasn't iced over, it isn't too cold. Besides, the low temperature will help motivate you to learn how to keep yourself warm with magic."

"If we don't freeze to death first," I mutter.

"Young people," Azzy mutters as she flicks her hand toward a bench on the other side of the fountain. "Always so dramatic." A retort rises to my tongue, but it freezes there as I watch the bench slide around the fountain and come to a halt behind Azzy. She sits, folds her hands together on her knees, and looks at us. "I'd like you to start by drawing magic from your core. Aurora, you said you're already familiar with how to do this?"

"Um, yes. I practiced on my own whenever I wasn't being watched."

"Wonderful. Em, you've got some catching up to do."

"Yay," I mutter. "I always love it when teachers pit students against each other to try get them to perform better."

Azzy sits a little straighter and brushes something non-existent off her sleeve. "I'm sure I have no idea what you're talking about."

"Can we just get on with this?" Aurora asks quietly. I look over and see that she's already holding a glowing sphere of magic above her palms.

Gritting my teeth, I close my eyes and repeat Azzy's instructions from yesterday. I have to stop and refocus three times before I produce a visible mass of magic, but after I've done it once, I can repeat it several times without a problem. "Okay," I say, almost giddy with elation as I hold my own power in my hands. "What's next?"

"Fire," Azzy says with a gleam in her eyes. She pulls a scrap of paper from the folds of her loose clothing and draws something on it with her stylus, using the bench to press against. Almost immediately, three long, slender candles push their way up out of the paper.

"How did you—"

"That's a lesson for another day." She stands. "Here's a candle for each of you. Now that you can call on your magic at will, I want you to shape it into a flame." She holds the third candle up in front of her face. "Some spells require written words, and some require spoken words. Some require both, or a specific movement of the hands. What we're going to do now requires a spoken word only—and of course, the subconscious nudging of your magic toward the candle."

She makes it sound easy, this 'subconscious nudging,' but I'm guessing it's one of those things that takes loads of practice and effort before it becomes instinctive.

"Repeat after me," Azzy says. She utters a strange word I've never heard before, then blows gently at the candle. A flame flickers to life.

Aurora starts practicing, and of course she gets it right on her third try. I, however, blow again and again and nothing happens. I try different ways of speaking the magical word, changing the emphasis from the first syllable to the last, but it makes no difference.

"Stop," Azzy says eventually. "I don't think you're sending any magic toward the candle at all. Don't forget that part. Pull on your magic, speak the word, and then imagine blowing that power out of your mouth and straight at the candle.

I do as she says. And nothing happens.

My patience snaps. I throw the candle onto the grass. "I don't understand. I managed to rip the ground apart without even trying, and now I can't even light a candle."

"That was different—"

"I *know* it was different. It was easy and it was English. This is … just … stupid words that don't make sense."

"Em," Azzy says, and her voice carries a warning tone.

"No, seriously. The other night I just said something and it happened."

"Emerson."

"Why can't I just keep doing that?" I bend and scoop the candle up. Holding it high, I say, "Candle, start burning." Nothing happens. "Start burning!" I shout. Still nothing. I swing around and point at the tree. "Fall over!" Nothing. I face the fountain. "Break into a hundred pieces and put yourself back together!" A shiver ripples up my spine, and I realize those last words sounded oddly distant and yet weirdly resonant at the same time.

The fountain vibrates. Cracks form across the tiers and splinter rapidly outwards.

A pause.

Silence.

Then the entire fountain explodes.

Aurora screams as water and pieces of stone fly outward. Suddenly, we're both flat on the ground. I force my head up to see what's happening. The stone pieces freeze, reverse, and fly straight back to their starting point, all joining together perfectly. I suck in a breath as the last crack vanishes, returning the fountain to its exact original form.

More silence.

Then Aurora scoots backward across the ground. "That's not normal," she gasps. "That is *so* not normal."

"I did it," I murmur. "I used magic."

"That wasn't magic," Azzy whispers.

I twist around to look at her. "What do you mean?"

Slowly she shakes her head. "Not normal magic. Not the kind of magic the rest of us have."

I look past her and find Paul and the remainder of the students standing a few feet away, their expressions all frozen in shock. "I'll get hold of the Guild," Paul says quietly.

"Why?" I push myself onto my feet. "What did I do? What's wrong?"

Aurora stands, and Azzy looks between the two of us. "You're lucky I got you both onto the ground so quickly. You might have been badly hurt otherwise."

"Answer me," I say to her, and again, that strange ripple rushes up my spine.

Azzy jolts. Abruptly, and almost robotically, she says, "I've never seen magic like that before. No faerie should be able to do what you just did. I suspect you have a Griffin Ability. Paul's contacting the Guild now, and they'll probably send someone here immediately to test you. What happens next is up to them." Her voice cuts off abruptly, and she slaps a hand over her mouth as if to stop anymore words tumbling out. Then she breathes out slowly and lowers her hand. "Don't do that again. Don't speak again."

"But I—"

"Emerson," she interrupts. "Your voice is dangerous. Please don't speak again until a Guild member is here."

A chill races across my skin, followed by a flush of heat. Anxiety tightens my stomach. This is all going wrong. I'm supposed to learn magic and then go home. I'm not supposed to be in trouble with the Guild. I'm not supposed to be one of those dangerous superpowered faeries everyone seems to hate.

"Come, let's go inside." Azzy takes my arm and leads me toward the house. I think about fighting her, about pushing her away and running, but I'm overcome by exhaustion all of a sudden. My arms hang weakly at my sides, and a wave of dizziness passes through me. It's gone by the time we reach the entrance hall, but I still feel too drained to think about running anywhere.

Azzy ushers everyone out of the room, then hurries off to another part of the house, leaving me alone in the entrance hall with Paul. He stands with his arms crossed firmly over his chest, not once removing his eyes from me. Azzy reappears a minute or two later with a mug in her hand. "You're tired, I know," she says quietly. "This will help you regain your strength." Paul frowns, but he doesn't stop Azzy from handing the mug to me.

I take a hesitant sip, then keep drinking until the thick, chocolatey liquid is finished. It's sweet and warm and comforting, and I begin feeling stronger almost immediately. I place the mug on the table and look at Azzy. "There must be a mistake, right? I can't possibly have one of those Griffin Ability things. What happened out there … that was just uncontrolled magic or something. Right?"

"You shouldn't be speaking," Paul says.

"Because I have a *dangerous voice*? That's absurd. I'm sure there's another explanation for—"

"Em, stop," Azzy says. "Please. I think it's safer if you say nothing."

At that moment, the front door of Chevalier House swings open and two figures stride in. A woman I don't recognize, and—

"Dash," I say the moment I see him. It's weird, but I'm actually relieved he's here.

"Emerson," the woman says, staring me down with eyes that appear to be almost bronze in color. She's dressed in a well-tailored pants suit, and her hair is pulled back tightly in a bun. I can't figure out her expression. It definitely isn't a smile, but it isn't fear or wariness or anger. "I'm Head Councilor Ashlow. Why didn't you tell us you could perform unnatural magic?"

I throw my hands up, because this is becoming too much now. "You're kidding, right? *All* magic is unnatural to me! I only just discovered it exists! How was I supposed to know that saying something and then having it happen is considered unusual in this world?"

"Not just unusual. Impossible."

"Well … exactly. How was I supposed to know that?"

She breathes out sharply and extends her closed hand toward me. Her fingers uncurl to reveal a bright green pill sitting on her palm. "Councilor Waterfield should have tested you the first day you arrived in this world. She shouldn't have let *you*—" she pins her gaze on Dash for a moment "—talk her out of it."

Dash frowns. "I hope you're not suggesting I intentionally kept this information from you, Councilor Ashlow. I had no idea Griffin magic was involved."

"I'm not sure what to think right now." She looks at me again. "Take the pill, Emerson."

Something tells me that disobeying isn't an option, so I take the pill and place it on my tongue. It dissolves quickly. Dash's eyes rove over me, his expression darkening. I look down at myself, and my heart misses a beat or two when I see my body glowing faintly green. "So it's true," Dash says. "She's one of them."

"And you didn't know?"

"Of course not. I would have reported it immediately if I suspected she had a Griffin Ability. It's my job to protect our world from people like her." He almost spits out that last word, and for a moment I consider spitting right back at him. But then he wraps his iron-like grip around my upper arm and begins steering me toward the door, and my hatred of him is quickly replaced by ice-cold fear.

"What are you—but I haven't done anything wrong. I'm not one of those Griffin rebels. I don't want to attack people. Surely you can't hold me responsible for crimes I've never committed, or crimes that you think I *might* possibly commit in the future."

"We can, actually," Councilor Ashlow says as we reach the door. "Our laws state that the world needs to be protected from people like you. In some cases, that means tagging and tracking you. Knowing your whereabouts and activities at all times. In extreme cases, it means limiting your freedom. The Council will need to meet to discuss your case, but I'm in no doubt, Emerson, that they will find it extreme indeed. I'm sorry." She doesn't look sorry, though. If anything, she seems excited by the fact that she's just apprehended another Griffin Gifted faerie.

"But … this … how did it even happen?" I ask, trying to stall, trying to come up with a way out of this. "Those magical discs … no, that can't be right. They haven't been around for years. So—"

"Both your parents must have been Griffin Gifted," Councilor Ashlow says. "That's the only explanation."

"Wait," I say as she opens the door. "Wait, please. What does limiting my freedom mean?"

"It means you'll be kept somewhere," Dash answers, forcing me out onto the top step.

"Kept?"

"Yes, like a safe house kind of thing."

I stop walking and manage to tug my arm free of his grip. "So a prison."

Dash looks back at me. "It isn't like that, Em. No one wants you to be a prisoner. It's just that you're dangerous, so you can't be set loose, either in this world or the human one. Surely you understand that."

I force back the ache in my throat and the tears pricking behind my eyes. I clench my teeth together and say, "You're enjoying this, aren't you. It's probably the best entertainment you've had in ages. You've never liked me, and now you get to see me locked up. You're doing to me what you did to my mother."

His eyes narrow and he opens his mouth, but Councilor Ashlow interrupts with a groan. "All this unnecessary drama. Just get on with it." She pulls the door shut and heads past us down the stairs. Dash tugs me against his side and forces me to follow her.

"Firstly," he says quietly, "you're the one who doesn't like me. And secondly, this has nothing to do with anyone liking anyone else. You're a threat, so we have to take precautions. That's it."

"But I'm not a threat!" My emotions are dangerously close to the surface all of a sudden, and I take a moment to swallow them down. "I mean, not intentionally. I didn't choose to be this way. This isn't fair."

He's quiet for so long that I assume he's now ignoring me. But as we walk out of the gate and find Councilor Ashlow opening a faerie paths doorway, he says, "Life isn't fair, Em. You already know that."

Councilor Ashlow looks back at us as the dark hole in the air grows larger. "Hurry up," she says. "We need to get to the Guild."

Dash's grip on my arm tightens, but he walks forward without hesitation. "Don't think about anything," he says as we step into the darkness. "It'll confuse the faerie paths, and that won't end well for any of us."

I struggle to quiet my racing thoughts, but I must somehow manage to do a good enough job, because soon, light materializes ahead of us. We walk into a small room where a man in a uniform behind an elaborately carved wooden desk greets us. I remember Dash saying something about a grand entrance transforming from a tree, but he must have been referring to a different part of the Guild because the only impressive thing in this room is the desk.

"This way," Councilor Ashlow says, gesturing to an open door on our right. Dash pushes me through it, and my mouth drops open at the site of an enormous foyer with a wide, sweeping staircase on the opposite side and glittering chandelier lights hanging here and there. My darting eyes take in men and women in dark clothing, hair of every color, gleaming white floors and twirling patterns etched into the walls—before an alarm begins shrieking in my ears.

"It's okay," Councilor Ashlow says, holding a hand up to halt the people who race toward her. "We're already aware of the Griffin Ability. I'm taking her to the detainment area now."

Get out, my brain says as my panicked thoughts return in full force. *Get out of here!* But I don't know how. What did I do the other day when the cops were trying to take me away? I must have used my Griffin Ability, but I have no idea how.

I sense Dash watching me. "I'm going to let go of you now," he says. "Can you behave?"

I nod as his grip loosens and his arm slides away from mine. Then I shove him as hard as I can and run.

CHAPTER 12

I trip over my own feet—or over something invisible, since I swear I've never been that clumsy—and hit the floor on my side. My so-called useless parkour practice kicks in, and I continue rolling. Onto my stomach, my hands push against the floor, and I spring up onto my feet. I catch a glimpse of Dash sprawled on the floor with guardians tumbling over him before I take off in the opposite direction, repeating "Get away from me, get away from me!" in the desperate hope that my Griffin Ability will appear and give my words actual power. In my haste to get back to the room we entered through, I can't tell if my voice is any different, but I keep repeating the words anyway. And either it's working, or these guardians are even worse than the Stanmeade cops, because they're falling all over each other.

I rush into the entrance hall just as someone runs out—and I crash right into her. The force slams me backward, but she lunges forward and grabs my arm, pulling me upright. "Aurora?" I gasp as she pulls me into the room. "What are you doing here?"

"Trying to help you!"

Glittering rope lashes out at me and snaps around my arm, tugging me out of Aurora's grasp and onto the floor. I scrabble uselessly at the glossy surface before looking up at the guard who greeted us a minute ago. He's standing on the desk now, dragging me swiftly toward him. "Get away!" I yell, hoping it will work. Invisible power knocks him through the open door and into the foyer, yanking me sharply to the side as the rope grows taut.

Light flashes, severing the rope and leaving a small piece attached to my arm. I look up and find Aurora with a stylus in her hand. "Get up!" She rushes to the wall and writes on it. "Come on!"

I look toward the foyer, where guardians are racing toward us, flashes of magic escaping their hands. I jump up and lurch toward Aurora and the growing darkness behind her. "You can use a stylus?" I gasp as I take her hand.

"Don't think of anything," she instructs as she pushes me ahead of her into the faerie paths. "And don't let go."

"I thought you didn't know—" My words cut off as Aurora's hand is torn free of mine. I swing around to see what's happening and find two guardians hauling her backward.

"Emerson!" she shrieks, one hand reaching out for me.

I hesitate, conflicting parts of my brain screaming *Save her!* and *Save yourself!* And in that moment, the darkness of the faerie paths closes around me. I try to remember what I'm supposed to do now, what I'm supposed to focus on or say, but then I'm falling backward through the darkness. I land hard on the ground as tangled trees and overgrown bushes take form around me. I groan and cough and try to suck in air as I sit up. I have no idea where the faerie paths have dumped me. For a moment, I wonder if I might have been lucky enough to end up back in the normal world, but as two minuscule people-shaped beings with wings flit past me, my hope dies. "Brilliant," I mutter as I climb to my feet, leaves rustling beneath my shoes.

I look around, but Aurora is nowhere to be seen. Guilt mingles with my relief at having escaped. I should have tried to pull her back into the paths. The only reason she was there was to help me. I press my fingers against my temples and try to convince myself that nothing bad will happen to her. It's not like she's Griffin Gifted. They'll just send her back to Chevalier House, and once she's finished training, she'll be free. Although, now that I think about it, does she even need training? Last night she said she didn't know how to use her magic, but she had no problem cutting the rope around my arm or opening a faerie paths doorway.

I lift my right arm and frown at the sparkling piece of rope still attached to it. I try to undo the knot or loosen it enough to pull my hand free, but it won't budge. So after one last glance around the forest, I pick a direction and start moving. The air is warmer here than in the garden we were training in this morning, which tells me I'm probably nowhere near Chevalier House. Unfortunately, that might mean I'm right next to whichever tree conceals the Guild, so I'd better get away from the area as quickly as possible.

I start running, swerving between trees, launching my body easily over giant tree roots, and giving a wide berth to an exotic bush with large, blood-red thorns. I throw the occasional glance over my shoulder, but nothing seems to be following me. Eventually, I slow to a quick walk. Something tickles the side of my neck, and I swat at my skin, afraid that some dangerous magical insect is biting me. A screech rips through the air right beside my ear. I leap away, letting out my own startled yelp and spinning around to face whatever's attacking me. A fluffy bird that might be an owl flaps as it descends clumsily toward the forest floor, morphing into a kitten as it reaches the ground. Sad, high-pitched mews fill the air.

"Holy sh … sherbet." I rub my ear as the adrenaline rush subsides. "You nearly deafened me. What are you doing here, you weird little thing? You're supposed to be back at Chevalier House." The kitten flashes between several unrecognizable forms before settling as a fox cub. It walks over to me and begins nuzzling my ankle. I step away and fold my arms over my chest. It looks up with wide, pleading eyes.

And I give in.

"Fine. You can stay with me. But I'm not giving you a name. It'll all be downhill from there." I tuck the soft, furry creature beneath my arm and continue walking.

And almost fall over in fright when someone steps out of the air in front of me. "*Dash?*" I stumble backward, the shapeshifting creature transforming into something tiny as it leaps away from me. "How did you find me?"

"Doesn't matter. We—" The space ripples beside him. He steps hastily away, raising his hand. A knife appears in his grip as he places himself between me and whatever threat we're about to face.

"Oh, you found her," Jewel says, walking out of the darkness. "Well done."

"Jewel?" Dash says. The knife vanishes as he lets go of it. "How did you—Why are you here?"

Hurt flashes briefly across her face as I carefully inch away from the two of them. "Just trying to help," she says. "You still have that tracking spell on your amber from the other night in the spider tunnels."

"Right." Dash retrieves his amber, drags his finger across the surface in a series of weird patterns, then shoves it back into his pocket. "Don't need that anymore."

"What's the big deal? I thought you needed help finding her."

"No big deal. I can handle it, that's all." He grabs my wrist before I can move too far away and twists it behind my back.

"Can you really handle it?" I ask in taunting tones as he ties my hands together. "It didn't seem like it back at the Guild. Are you guardians always so useless?"

Dash comes back around to stand in front of me, his expression showing genuine amusement. "No. They're not."

Huh. Maybe my Griffin Ability worked after all. "Ropes, untie," I instruct.

Nothing happens. Dash quirks an eyebrow, then starts laughing.

"What's she doing?" Jewel asks.

"My guess is she's trying to make her Griffin Ability work."

"Oh." Jewel's brow puckers. "Maybe we should tape her mouth shut."

"Nah, she doesn't have the first clue how to use her Griffin Ability."

Heat rises to my face. "I'm gonna strangle you with this rope when I finally get it off. Rather that than end up a prisoner for the rest of my life."

"As I've already explained," Dash says slowly, "you won't be a prisoner. You just won't have the same level of freedom as everyone else."

I blink, unable to believe he's this stupid. "Are you listening to yourself? Do you know what the definition of prisoner is?"

"Em, it isn't that bad, I promise. Look, I know you're worrying about your mother—"

"Don't you dare bring her up right—"

"—but I'm sure the Guild will let you visit her under supervision. And our researchers are working all the time on trying to find a way to remove Griffin Abilities. That could happen soon, and then you'll be free again. Please try to understand." He throws a quick glance at Jewel before returning his gaze to me. "We're trying to keep the rest of the world safe, and this is unfortunately one of the precautions we have to take."

"Come on, Dash, you're wasting time," Jewel complains. "We need to get her back to the Guild." She pulls her stylus out and raises it.

"Don't," I say, and when I feel that odd tingle spreading rapidly throughout my body and my voice echoing oddly in my ears, I rush to add, "Don't open a doorway! Neither of you open a doorway!"

The rush of strangeness passes, and Jewel frowns at me over her shoulder. Then she presses her stylus against a tree and opens her mouth. After appearing to struggle for several seconds, she says, "I—I can't do it. I can't say the words."

Dash swings around to face me. "Oh, *come on*. You did not just do that."

I let out a shaky laugh. "I think I did, actually."

"Now none of us can go anywhere."

I nod slowly as I take in a deep breath. "Good."

"Undo what you just did," Jewel says, pointing her stylus at me.

"No way. Even if I wanted to, I have no idea how this Griffin Ability thing works."

Dash lets out a long sigh. "Oh well. Time to walk, I guess."

"Dash!" Jewel exclaims. "How are you not seriously pissed off right now?"

He shrugs. "We've been through worse. You know that. A *lot* worse." He starts walking. After several moments, the rope pulls taut between us and I'm forced to follow him. "Try to keep up, Emmy. Wouldn't want to get yourself eaten by some kind of dark, sinister creature." Despite his nonchalance, I notice the way his fists clench periodically at his sides. He's definitely angry with me. No doubt he's already in trouble for letting me get away from the Guild. Hopefully he'll wind up suspended or, even better, fired. If he's going to continue to ruin my life, I can ruin his too.

"We're near the edge of the forest, right?" Jewel says. "On the side with the waterfall?" Dash nods, and Jewel scribbles something onto her amber. "Okay, Councilor Ashlow and a bunch of guardians will meet us there in a few minutes.

"Good." Dash writes something on his amber too, then adds, "Do you want to run ahead and meet them?"

"Yeah, okay." Jewel takes off through the trees, and the moment she's out of sight, Dash stops.

"Okay. We don't have much time. You—"

The air ripples so close I almost feel it move. A dark hole opens up, and a child tumbles out and crashes into me. "Oh, oops, sorry," he mumbles, pushing himself away from me and staggering backward.

"Are you flipping kidding me?" Dash demands. "What the heck are you doing here, Jack?"

The boy, who can't be more than ten, gives Dash a wide smile. "I wanted to be part of the mission. I listened to where everyone was going, but … I don't know. Where is everyone?"

"Jack, you need to go home immediately. Your parents are—" Dash looks up at the sound of crunching leaves up ahead. "Hide," he whispers, shoving the boy behind the nearest tree and dragging me forward once more.

"Dash, hurry up," Jewel calls as she comes into view. "They're waiting for us."

"Coming," Dash says before muttering something else under his breath. I keep my questions to myself as my mind races to figure out what's going on. Dash is afraid of something, and there must be a way I can use that to my advantage.

We catch up to Jewel, and after walking another minute or so, we reach the edge of the forest. The trees thin out and come to an end. A short distance away, on a grassy patch of open space, Head Councilor Ashlow and several guardians are waiting for us. A stream runs past them and disappears over the edge of what must be a very high cliff, since I can't hear the water hitting the bottom.

"Well done for finding her, Dash," Councilor Ashlow says. "Although the fact that you haven't gagged her makes me question your intelligence."

"It was a fluke that she managed to use her Griffin Ability on us," Dash says. "I'm confident it won't happen again soon. But I'll gag her now to be safe." He brings me to a halt in front of the Councilor, but a collective murmur racing abruptly through the group distracts him before he can tie anything over my mouth. We both turn, and I see another group of people walking out of the trees. I assume at first that these are more guardians, but the sudden flash of glittering weapons all around me proves my assumption wrong.

"Well, well," Councilor Ashlow says. "The Unseelies have decided to show their faces."

"And why wouldn't we?" A man says, walking forward. I sense a change in the atmosphere—something I can't quite explain—and I wonder if that's how the Councilor knows these faeries are with the Unseelie Court. "A particularly interesting Griffin Ability has come to light," he continues. "We thought we should take a closer look."

"No need. We have everything under control."

"Of course you do. You probably plan to hand this girl over to the Seelie Court to be used as their own personal weapon."

Councilor Ashlow smiles. "What we plan to do with her is none of your business."

"It is our business when she could turn out to be one of the most powerful weapons in existence. What's to stop you from using her against us?"

"I suppose you'll have to trust that we like to keep the laws we make, unlike the members of your court."

"Trust?" He laughs. "I don't think so."

"Well, at the risk of sounding petty," Councilor Ashlow says, "we found her first. So we certainly won't be handing her over to you."

"Of course not. And I suppose you wouldn't like it if we took her from you by force."

"You could try, but I doubt you'd be successful."

The man's expression becomes thoughtful. "Since we can't come to a mutually beneficial arrangement, perhaps neither of us should possess this weapon. Perhaps she should be killed."

Perhaps WHAT? My heart rate kicks up notch.

"The only way we'll be killing her," Councilor Ashlow says, "is if *you* get your dirty talons on her." She looks around at her guardians, lowering her voice as she adds, "Don't let that happen. If it does—if it looks like they might get away with her—you have my permission to kill the girl."

"What?" I gasp, finally finding my voice. "That can't be legal."

"Yes, Councilor," Dash says, along with his fellow guardians.

I tug and twist and try to face him. "Are you kidding me? Are you really such a monster?"

Dash doesn't move, but his eyes dart around the clearing, between the trees and up to the canopy tops. "Sometimes," he mutters as the Unseelies advance on us, "we have to be monsters to protect the rest of the world." He tugs me backward as his companions spring forward.

Shouts and grunts and the clash of blades soon fill the air, along with a confusing mix of sparks, wind, glass shards and cackling birds. I wriggle and kick and yell, "Get away from me!" But it doesn't work this time. I try to focus on the core of magic deep inside me, just as Azzy instructed, but it makes not difference. Dash's hands remain firmly attached to me.

Two of the Unseelie faeries break through the line of guardians and come racing for us. "Stop them!" Dash yells, backing further away toward the edge of the cliff. One is tackled to the ground. The other launches forward. Dash spins me out of the way. "I'm sorry about this," he says. And then he shoves me clear off the edge of the cliff.

CHAPTER 13

I barely hear my scream as I plummet toward my death. Foamy water and jagged rocks rise rapidly to meet me. Faster, faster, faster—

Then my body decelerates abruptly and a dark shadow swoops below me as I come almost, almost, *almost* to a halt. Then I'm tumbling out of the air and into a pair of strong arms, and someone's saying, "Don't worry, I've got you." I land clumsily on the back of a creature with wings and find myself sandwiched between it and whoever it was that caught me. An arm wraps around my stomach. I squeeze my eyes shut and cling more tightly to that arm than anything I've ever held onto. I don't care who or what it is. I don't care if it's an Unseelie faerie or a guardian who wants to lock me up or some kind of new being I've never met. My brain cares about only one fact right now: I'm not falling anymore.

We begin moving upward. It's a jerky, flapping motion, but at least it's up and not down. I don't open my eyes. I don't want to see anything. Up and up, sideways, and up some more, and all the while I silently repeat, *Don't let go, don't let go, don't let go.* Then we plummet downward, and an involuntary gasp escapes me. But it's over, and we're landing amongst the trees, and that strong pair of arms is pulling me off the winged creature. "She's fine," he says to someone as he deposits me on the ground. "We were almost too late, but she's fine."

My legs are shaking so badly they can't hold me up. I land on my butt, blinking and gasping and taking in the people around me in disjointed snapshot moments. Three faeries. *Blink.* A man, dark blue, bending closer to me with concern on his face. *Blink.* A woman, purple, saying something I can't hear. *Blink.* Another woman, watching something through the trees, hair of actual gold sliding over her shoulder. Dark tattoos weave across her arms and reach up the side of her neck.

"Emerson? Emerson!" I refocus on the woman who's now crouching beside me. The one with wide eyes of vibrant purple who somehow knows my name. "Can you hear me?"

I try to speak, but words won't seem to come out of my mouth. Every time I blink, I see water, rocks and death rushing full-speed toward me.

"You're safe now," she says, her hand reaching toward me. I jerk away, my body still shaking uncontrollably. 'Safe' doesn't mean a thing to me anymore. Her companion may have saved my life, but didn't Dash save my life too? And a day later he tried to kill me.

"Vi, they're coming this way," the golden haired one says. "No time to get the gargoyle back into the paths. Can you keep Emerson quiet while they pass?"

The woman in front of me nods. "Emerson," she says, leaning a tiny bit closer, but not attempting to touch me again. "We're all going to turn invisible now. It's nothing to freak out about. Just an illusion to hide us while the guardians pass. But we need to keep quiet, okay? Completely quiet."

I nod jerkily, despite the fact that her warning isn't necessary. Even if my brain was capable of manufacturing words right now, I wouldn't make a sound while anyone from the Guild runs by. Not after they so readily tried to dispose of me. A moment later, all three faeries vanish. I look down—and manage to hold back my squeak of terror when I find that my body is gone. I know she said 'invisible,' but I didn't realize I wouldn't be able to see myself either. I thought ... I don't know what I thought.

At the sound of hurried footsteps, I look up. I almost scramble backward when I see the guardians running straight for us, but they swerve and continue running past. "... might not have been this way," Councilor Ashlow is saying to the rest of her guardians, "but we have to check. Especially if the rest of the team can't find her body. And find out who that cloaked person was. It didn't look like he or she was with the Unseelies."

We wait in silence for at least a minute after the guardians pass. Then: "I think that's fine, Calla," the guy who caught me says. The three of them reappear. When I look down, I'm relieved to see my own body once more. I'm not shaking as much as when we first landed, so I push myself up onto my feet. I still feel weak in the wake of more adrenaline than my body's ever produced in one go, but at least I can stand now.

"Sorry about the dramatic rescue," the man says, reaching over and patting the leathery winged creature I haven't looked at properly until now. Ridged horns curve out of its head, and fangs protrude from its wide mouth. "We ran out of time to get a better plan in place. Vi, can you open a doorway? We should get going."

"I—I'm not—um—" I cut myself off when it becomes clear I can't utter more than a few stammering words. I hate sounding so weak and confused. It isn't me. I'm *stronger* than this, dammit, but everyone has a limit to what they can endure without completely breaking down, and I think I'm fast approaching mine. I swallow and breathe in deeply before trying again. "I'm not … I'm not going anywhere with you. Thank you for saving me, but I don't know who you are."

"Right, sorry," the man says. "I'm Ryn, and this is Violet." He gestures to the woman with the dark purple hair. With a nod toward the tattooed, golden haired woman, he adds, "And that's Calla."

"You can trust us," Violet says. "We know everyone's been after you since you arrived in this world, and we can keep you safe."

I press my hands over my eyes and suck in a shaky breath. "I don't trust you," I whisper, finding myself dangerously close to tears. "I don't trust anyone. Everybody wants to lock me up or kill me."

"Emerson." I lower my hands and find Violet right in front of me, staring intently into my eyes. "You *can* trust us. You know why? Because we're exactly like you."

I shake my head. "What do you mean?"

"We're all Griffin Gifted."

CHAPTER 14

"Crap." I stumble backward in my haste to put some distance between me and these faeries. "You guys are part of that Griffin rebel movement, aren't you."

"Yes." Confusion crosses Violet's face. "Which is a good thing. It means we're on your side."

"But ... you're the bad guys."

"Uh, no we're not," Calla says.

"That's what the Guild—what everyone in this world—says."

"Of course that's what the Guild says. They don't trust us. They want to track our every move or lock us up so we can't use our 'dangerous' magic without supervision. They just tried to do the same thing to you."

I hesitate, because she's right, of course. "They ... they said you attack people."

Ryn's expression darkens. "Is that what they're telling people now?"

"They'll twist any story to their advantage," Violet says. "They want people to be afraid of us."

Calla's head whips around. "Guys, I think they're coming back this way."

"On it," Ryn says, already raising a stylus and scribbling invisible words in the air.

"Are you coming?" Violet asks. "Please, you can trust us."

I swallow. Perhaps this is all a lie and I'm being tricked yet again, but I don't exactly have anyone else to turn to. "Can you help me?" I ask. "With ... everything?"

She takes my hand and squeezes it. "That's what we do."

Hot air dances across my skin as the darkness of the faerie paths evaporates around us. My feet sink into soft sand. I turn slowly on the spot, squinting against the harsh light as my eyes take in the same scenery on all sides: rolling sand dunes that go on and on, seemingly forever. "You guys live in a desert?"

Calla smiles. "Yep. You wouldn't think to look for us out here, would you?"

"I guess not," I say, keeping the rest of my thoughts to myself. My thoughts of how unpleasant it must be to live amidst all this sand and heat.

"This way," Ryn says, nodding to his right and leading the gargoyle by its reins. I have no idea how he knows which direction to go in since every sand dune looks the same to me. We've barely taken a few steps, though, when the faint outline of something dome-shaped comes into view. I blink a few times, but the outline only grows stronger. I'm afraid to ask if I'm imagining things, so I keep my mouth shut. But a minute or so later when the dome is right in front of us and I can make out the hazy shapes of trees and buildings within, I figure it must be real.

"This," Violet says, "is our oasis. An enchanted piece of land beneath a dome of magic. And once you've passed through the dome layer—" she takes my hand and pulls me through after her "—you now have a spell placed upon you that means you can never speak about this place. Even if you're questioned under the influence of truth potion, you won't be able to say a thing. Which means everyone here will always be safe."

The air is immediately cooler, and the fresh scent of plants fills my nostrils. I'm aware of a small smile on my lips as I slowly look around. Grass and bushes and streams, fountains and flowers and a few small buildings, plus a number of enormous trees with houses built into the upper branches. "Actual tree houses," I murmur. "Not the glamoured type I learned about this morning."

"Yes," Violet says. "I lived on Kaleidos for a little while, and they have tree houses like these. I really liked them, so I suggested we do the same thing here."

"And we spent years before this living in glamoured trees or Underground or inside mountains," Calla adds, "so when the Guild forced us to run and we had to make a new home somewhere, we decided we didn't want to live in concealed houses anymore. The outer dome keeps us hidden, so our actual houses don't have to be hidden."

"It's really cool." I push away the thought that if I could just get Mom safely into the magic world, she and I could happily live here for the rest of our lives. She'd love the gardens, the fountains, the flowers. But I don't know if that's possible, so I'll leave my dreams for another day. Another time, when I've figured out if I can really trust these people. "What do you guys do here?" I ask, watching Ryn hand the gargoyle reins to a bald man with eyes that don't look normal.

"We rescue Griffin Gifted and hide them from the Guild," he says, turning back to me. "We also help people in other ways. Basically, we do what the Guild does, but on a smaller scale."

"It's also non-official and illegal," Calla says. "So, you know, that's another reason the Guild doesn't like us."

"Oops," says a small voice behind us. We all turn, and there stands the boy who appeared in the forest before Dash dragged me out to the edge of the cliff. "I was hoping I'd get home before you."

After a pause filled with shocked silence, Violet walks forward, takes hold of the boy's shoulders, and makes sure her face is right in front of his before asking, "Where have you been?"

"Um …"

"Did you leave the oasis?"

He blinks. "Maybe. I just … wanted to help with the rescue mission."

"Jack Linden Larkenwood," she says, "you're grounded." She straightens and lets go of him. "For the next decade."

"What?"

"For the next *century*."

"Mom!" Jack lets out a dramatic groan and turns to Ryn. "Da-ad," he whines.

Ryn folds his arms. "Do you want me to add another decade?"

"Ugh, you guys ruin everything!"

"No, ruining things is what you did when you decided to disobey the rules and leave the oasis," Violet says. "Now please give me whoever's stylus you decided to steal."

Jack mumbles something too quiet for anyone to hear before handing over a stylus, crossing his arms, and sticking his lower lip out. Calla covers her mouth to hide a smile before turning away. Looking past her, I see the bald man walking back toward us. When he reaches Calla's side, I realize why his eyes look strange: his pupils are vertical instead of round.

"Lord Sedon wants to arrange a meeting with the two of you," he says to Ryn and Violet. "He's on hold on one of the mirrors."

"Great, we'll come speak to him now," Ryn says.

"Is Chase back yet?" Calla asks.

"No," the bald man says. "You missed a mirror call from him earlier, though."

"Oh, I'll see if I can get hold of him now." She hurries away.

"Jack," Violet says, "please take Emerson to one of the empty rooms and then show her around a bit while Dad and I do some work."

"Will you un-ground me if I do that?"

"No. You'll do it because you want to be friendly and welcoming to Emerson."

"Fine," he groans.

"Great. Emerson, we'll see you a little later," Violet says. "We can meet for …" She hesitates, then laughs. "Sorry, it always takes a moment to readjust when traveling between time zones. It's afternoon here, isn't it, so we can meet for sundowners by the hammocks."

"That sounds …" Like the kind of vacation I've only ever dreamed about. "That sounds nice."

I watch the two of them walk away. When they're out of earshot, Jack turns to me and grins. "I actually am friendly and welcoming."

"Okay. Good to know."

"Come, you can choose a room."

I walk with him, slowing my pace to match is short stride. "Who set up this whole place?"

"Dad and Uncle Chase. They said it took them like a year to get all the right enchantments in place. But that was before I was born, so obviously I don't remember any of it."

"Who's Chase?"

"Aunt Calla's husband."

I nod. "So … are your dad and Chase the ones in charge?"

"I guess. But so are Mom and Aunt Calla. And Uncle Gaius. Although he's not really my uncle, he's just Uncle Chase's friend since forever, and he doesn't come out of his house much anymore, since he's sick. I think they're all in charge. Well, they set the rules, and I get in trouble with all of them if I break them, so they must all be in charge."

We reach the base of one of the giant trees. Steps have been carved into it, starting from the bottom and curving around the side of the trunk as they climb higher. Jack leads me up, moving as quickly as his short legs will take him. "How old are you, Jack?"

He drags his hand along the trunk as we climb. "I'm eight and a half. How old are you?"

"Seventeen. Eighteen in a few months."

"Did you go to school where you're from? 'Cause you can do that here. I have lessons with the other kids who live here, and mostly it's fun. You can join us if you want, although you'll probably be with Junie because you're older."

I sigh and say, "No, I'd probably be with you." *In fact*, I add silently, *if there's a class lower than yours, that's probably where I belong.*

"So this is our house," Jack says as we reach the first large structure built into the branches. "It's got more rooms, like a kitchen and lounge and stuff, and then higher up are just bedrooms and bathing rooms for new people. Then if they stay and they want other rooms, Merrick just adds them on."

I stop for a moment and look up at the smaller wooden structures built above us. "I probably shouldn't ask about how bathrooms work all the way up there. I mean, I guess magic takes care of all the … plumbing?"

Jack shrugs. "I don't know. I guess." He continues moving up, and I follow him, grateful for all the physical activity Val and I have done over the past couple of years in our quest to teach ourselves parkour.

"Looks like you have to be quite fit to live here," I comment. "It's a long way up if you forget something when you leave your house in the morning."

"I know!" Jack exclaims. "And I haven't learned how to boost myself with magic yet, so it takes like forever. Mom and Dad can get up here in seconds if they have to. It's so unfair."

"Well, you'll probably be able to do that soon, right? I mean, you know how to do the faerie paths thing." I'm still particularly interested in that spell. The sooner I learn it, the sooner I'll feel more in control of my situation.

"Oh, yeah, the faerie paths. I'm not supposed to know that one yet. But I've always paid attention when Mom and Dad do it. I'm a fast learner." He looks back at me with a proud smile, then increases his pace a little, as if spurred on by his own words. "Okay," he says a little breathlessly after we've passed four smaller tree houses. "This one's empty. Or you can go higher if you want. There are another three that are empty. Merrick always adds more on when he has time."

"This one's fine." I place my hands on my hips and look around as I give myself a few moments to catch my breath. The branches up here are wide enough to walk along without having any balance issues. Good thing I'm not afraid of heights, though. The distance from here to the ground is enough to cause some serious damage to anyone who might freak out and slip.

"Okay, come see," Jack says. He skips along the branch and pushes the door open. I follow him into a bedroom, plainly furnished with nothing more than a bed, a wardrobe and a chair in the corner. It's still nicer than the room I've always slept in at Chelsea's house, though. At least I don't have to climb over boxes of hair products and share my shelves with tiny bottles of strange concoctions.

"Is that a bathroom?" I ask, pointing to a closed door on the other side of the room.

"Yeah. So this is just the basic stuff they put in all the rooms. It's kinda boring, so you can change whatever you want. You can even change the shape of the room, if you'd like something different. Merrick will do it. He's an architect faerie. And Junie—she's an elf—is a designer. So if you tell her what you want your bed to look like, she can easily change it. Or, like, if you want that chair to be a swing hanging from the ceiling, she can do that too. She did that in my room, but then I fell off one night when I was supposed to be sleeping, not playing, so Mom and Dad made her change it to an armchair, which isn't nearly as fun. But Junie made it dragon-shaped, so I guess it's not that bad."

I smile at this outburst of information. "Sounds cool." I walk to the window, and my smile stretches a little wider at the sight of the orchard, the river, and the sun going down in the distance. I've never imagined having a view like this from my own bedroom. *And you still don't*, a small voice reminds me. This isn't really my bedroom, and I probably won't be here for long. Nothing this amazing could ever last.

"The wardrobe's empty now," Jack says, "but Mom will put some clothes in it later. Dash's mom is a clothes caster, and she sends *tons* of clothes here. Some of them are weird, and Mom hides those ones, but most are normal. Oh, where did that come from?" I swing around and look to where he's pointing. In the corner, sitting on the chair, is a kitten.

I cross the room with a sigh. "This little guy is a shapeshifting creature that keeps following me everywhere. I thought he ran away when Dash found me in the forest, but he must have just shifted into something really small and climbed into one of my pockets or something." The creature shifts rapidly back and forth between two forms I can't identify, like an old TV flickering between channels. Then it settles as a kitten again.

"Cool, he's just like Filigree!" Jack says.

"Filigree?"

"Yeah, Mom's pet. He doesn't shift much anymore 'cause he's super old and Mom says he doesn't have the energy now, but he used to change into all kinds of things. He was even a dragon once, but then he slept for like three days solid after that 'cause it used so much of his magic." Jack crouches in front of the chair. "What's this one's name?"

"He doesn't have one."

"Ah, can I name him please?" Jack begs, his eyes widening in delight as he looks over his shoulder at me.

"Sure. He'll probably end up staying here anyway. It's not like he's *mine*. He just seems to like following me." A strange twist, given that my first pet had the opposite reaction and ran away after only a few days.

"Yay." Jack scoops the kitten up and cradles it against his chest. "I shall name him …" Jack squeezes his eyes shut as he thinks. "Bandit. His name will be Bandit."

I nod slowly. "Sounds cool."

We walk back down all the stairs—my legs getting a good workout in the process—and Jack shows me around the rest of the dome, pointing out a greenhouse, a school, a vegetable garden and orchard, an outdoor gym area, and a building that apparently contains a laboratory and some other 'out-of-bounds' places Jack doesn't know much about. "It's stuff to do with their work and how they help people. That's all I know."

"There's a lot here," I say as we stop beside a narrow river with a swan-shaped boat floating near the bank. "It's bigger than I first thought."

"It was smaller when I was little," Jack says, "but Merrick keeps adding onto it. He gets bored when he isn't helping Mom and Dad with cases. Anyway, come see the playground." He grabs my hand and tugs me away from the river. "I kept it till last 'cause it's my favorite place here. The swing is amazing. You have to try it."

The playground turns out to be filled with the same kind of equipment I'd expect to find in my world. The swing, too, looks pretty much normal. "It doesn't just go backwards and forward," Jack says when I ask what's so special about it. "See, you strap yourself in, and the swing goes all the way around. As many times as you want."

"Wow, okay. That is cool. It's enchanted, I assume?"

"Yeah, obviously. Do you want to have a go?"

"Uh, maybe another time. It's just … this is a lot. I'm still getting used to all the magical stuff."

"Oh, right, sorry. You're from the other world. I remember now. So what do you do for fun there?"

"Oh. Um …" I push my hands into my back pockets. "Well, I hang out with my friend Val. We taught ourselves this thing called parkour. It's kind of like a sport. You use whatever environment you're in—like buildings, walls, stairs, whatever—as an obstacle course. There's lots of jumping and running and climbing. And falling, but falling the right way. Like landing on your shoulder and rolling and standing up."

"Okay. Is it fun?"

"Yeah. You have to be creative about getting from point A to point B. It's like an art, actually. The art of rapid movement despite obstacles. An ordinary person might take the stairs out of a building and then walk along the road to wherever they're going. Instead, we'd figure out how to jump or climb down, and then vault over walls and through gardens to get to the destination the quickest way possible."

"Cool. Can you teach me?"

"Uh, sure. If you can teach me how to open the faerie paths."

"Okay." He wraps an arm around one of the swing's chains. "But we'd have to use someone's stylus. Without them knowing. And ... I don't really wanna get grounded again."

"Right. Yeah. You should stay out of trouble." Those last few words come out sounding unexpectedly deep and resonant, and that same strange shiver from earlier ripples up my spine and across my arms.

"What was that?" Jack asks, pulling his head back as he eyes me with suspicion. "You sounded weird."

"Um ..." I'm not sure if he knows about my Griffin Ability. "Probably just some escaping magic. I don't really know how to use it yet." He nods slowly while I look around for something else to talk about. "So where are the hammocks? I think I'm probably supposed to meet your parents there soon."

"This way," he says, taking off in another direction. I hurry after him, grateful for the lasting effects of the chocolate energy drink Azzy gave me before letting the Guild take me away. I probably would have passed out from exhaustion long ago without it.

Jack leads me to a collection of hammocks strung between trees near a round, open-sided pavilion. Large couches sit beneath the pavilion's decorative roof. "I think I'll wait over there," I tell him.

"Cool. I'm going to find some food for Bandit."

I watch him wandering away until a familiar voice behind me says, "Hey, you got here safely."

I spin around, my heart thundering in my chest. "Dash." I jerk away from his outstretched hand. "He's found us!" I yell. "The Guild's found us!"

CHAPTER 15

"Whoa, hey, calm down." Dash blinks, confused. "I'm on your side. How have you not figured that out yet?"

"It's okay, Emerson," Violet says, running up to me. "He's telling the truth. He's on our side."

"How can he possibly be on our side?" Anger rushes hotly through my veins, escaping in violent sparks that shoot away from me and aim straight for Dash's face.

"Ow!" He ducks and bats the magic away with both hands. "What the heck, Em?"

"You tried to imprison me! And then you pushed me off the edge of a cliff!"

"Jeez, Em, I'm the only reason you got away from the Guild. You never would have escaped without my help." He straightens as my magic stops attacking him. "You don't think guardians are normally that clumsy, do you? And the cliff …" He shrugs, looking a little sheepish. "Well, we ran out of time, so I had to improvise. But I knew Ryn and Vi were out there. I knew someone would catch you."

"*You knew someone would catch me?*" I repeat in disbelief. "I almost died!"

"But you didn't. You're fine. And now you're safe, which was the plan from the very beginning."

"What plan?"

"You know, to get you here to the Griffin rebels."

"Wait." I blink and hold my hands up. "You knew all along that I had a Griffin Ability, and you didn't say anything to me?"

Dash's eyes flick toward Violet before returning to me. "Well, we weren't certain. That's why I kept trying to get you to tell me exactly what happened that night at the party, but you weren't interested in talking about it."

"Are you kidding? If it was so important—if having a Griffin Ability is so dangerous—you could have forced the information out of me. Told me, 'Em, this isn't normal magic. You could be in danger because of it. You have to tell me what happened, for your own safety.'" I throw my hands up in complete exasperation. "Did you consider that option, Dash?"

He folds his arms over his chest, his expression growing stormier by the second. "Perhaps you don't clearly remember the occasion on which you completely freaked out and ran away from Chevalier House, but you weren't exactly in the mood to be forced into anything. And forgive me, but I kinda thought you had enough to deal with at that moment, having just found out about, you know, *everything* else. I thought I was being *kind* not dumping another horrible revelation on your shoulders. And I figured Azzy would get the truth out of you soon enough—which she had already done, actually. I didn't know it, but she'd already contacted Ryn by the time I got you back to Chevalier House. We just didn't manage to get you safely away before you revealed to everyone what you can do."

"Hang on. Azzy's in on this whole thing? That's what the two of you were whispering about last night?"

"You heard that?"

"Yes, Prof Azzy's on our side too," Violet says.

"Then why the hell did Paul call the Guild to come get me?"

"Because Azzy is the only one who's in on this," she explains. "Paul isn't. He's firmly on the Guild's side, just like everyone else working at Chevalier House, so his automatic response was to contact them."

"Okay fine. Fine!" I face Dash again. "But you still didn't explain a damn thing to me after I accidentally revealed my ability. If your Griffin friends were planning to come and rescue me, why didn't you just tell me?"

"I tried, Em, but we weren't alone for long enough after that. I couldn't say anything with other guardians around. If the Guild gets even the tiniest hint that I'm not entirely on their side, things would turn out very badly."

"Looking after your own skin, I see," I mutter.

"Emerson—"

"Not just my skin," Dash snaps, interrupting Violet before she can get any further. "I'm looking out for everyone else who lives here. Protective magic might keep me from being able to tell the Guild about this place if I were ever questioned, but I know far more than that. I know what Azzy's doing and about all the people who come in and out of here. Can you imagine what would happen if the Guild got that information out of me?"

"Then why bother working at the Guild if it's such a gigantic risk?"

"Hello! Because Vi and Ryn and everyone else here need people on the inside. They wouldn't know what's going on otherwise. They wouldn't have known about you, or about what the Guild was planning to do with you."

"It's true," Violet says. "The information Dash gives us about the Guild is extremely valuable. And aside from that, he *wants* to be a guardian. He wants to help people. He shouldn't have to walk away from that just because he's connected to us."

I cross my arms tightly over my chest, wanting to say that other people have to give up their dreams all the time, so what makes Dash so special that he gets to keep his? But my childish, petty thoughts aren't helpful, so I manage to remain quiet.

Violet's gaze shifts between the two of us. "Should we … perhaps … sit down?" she suggests after several more moments of silence have passed.

With a terse nod, I follow her up the pavilion steps. I wait for Dash to sit so I can choose a spot far away from him, but he nods at me to sit first. Idiot. Is he pretending to have good manners or something? I take a seat on a blue-and-white-striped couch and hug one of the fluffy white cushions against my stomach. Dash has the decency not to sit right next to me. "So, are we okay now?" he asks. "You and me?"

I shrug. "As okay as we ever were, I guess."

"Cool. So you still don't like me, but at least you don't believe I wanted to kill you."

I nod. "Pretty much."

"Great," Violet says, waving to Ryn as he walks toward the pavilion with a tray of glasses floating in the air beside him. "As long as the two of you don't want to kill each other, everything should be fine."

"Dash," Ryn says as reaches us. "Thanks for helping out with the rescue." He shakes Dash's hand, as if pushing me off a cliff was some great accomplishment. "I know Emerson wasn't too pleased about the way it happened, but you had to keep your cover somehow."

"Thanks. It's good to know that *some* people appreciate my sacrifice." He gives me a pointed look.

"Yeah, whatever. *Such* a sacrifice, I'm sure. And you guys can stop calling me Emerson," I add. "Em is fine."

"Or Emmy," Dash says.

I clench my teeth together. "I will hurt you."

"I will hurt you," he mimics in a high-pitched voice.

Violet sighs and lowers herself onto one of the couches. "Were we ever this immature?"

"Of course not," Ryn says, taking a seat opposite her. "Well, you might have been, but I'm sure I wasn't."

She laughs. "That is definitely not true."

"Dash, I heard you had a small problem getting here," Ryn says, neatly changing the subject. "Calla said she got a message from you asking her to go meet you somewhere and bring you back here."

"Uh, yeah." Dash turns his gaze to me. "So, I have a small problem."

"And why is that my problem?"

"Because it's your fault. I can't use the faerie paths anymore. It's impossible for me to travel anywhere if I'm alone."

"Aaaaand I still don't see how that's my problem."

"Em, come on. It's your Griffin Ability that did this to me. You need to fix it."

"I don't know how. And even if I did, wouldn't that look suspicious to the Guild? I'm supposed to be dead, right, so how could I fix your faerie paths problem?"

"I don't know. I guess I could say the effects of your magic wore off."

"And when Jewel still can't use the faerie paths? That's going to look seriously suspicious, Dash."

"She has a point," Ryn says.

"Just try it, Em. Try right now. Say, 'You can open doorways to the faerie paths.' And if it works, then we can get you to sneak up on Jewel while she's sleeping and do the same to her."

"That's really creepy, Dash."

"Just try!"

I lean back, cross my arms, and say, "You can open doorways to the faerie paths."

He sighs. "Perhaps you could put a little effort into it?"

"Who says it works that way?"

"I don't know, but it certainly didn't work the way you just said it. Your voice didn't go all … weird."

I uncross my arms and fiddle absently with the sleeve of my sweater. "Weird how? What does my voice sound like when it happens?"

"Sort of … deeper. A little distorted. And kind of … not like an echo, but it was as if I could hear it in the air all around me."

I nod slowly. "It kinda sounded like that to me too."

"Do you want to try again?" Violet asks. "Focusing this time, instead of just saying the words."

Since it isn't Dash asking, I agree to try again. I try several more times, even closing my eyes and focusing intently on pulling out that power from deep inside me as I tell Dash he's allowed to open doorways to faerie paths. But just like at the edge of the cliff, nothing happens. My voice remains normal.

Eventually I slump back against the couch and hug the fluffy cushion closer to my chest. "See? Can't do it."

"Well, no need to stress about it," Violet says. "We can definitely help you."

"Really?"

"Yes. And in the meantime, Dash will just have to figure out another way to get around."

"Ugh, seriously? I'm going to have to be *taken* everywhere like a child," Dash complains.

"Good thing you work in teams at the Guild," Ryn says. "One of your teammates should be happy to help you and Jewel, right?"

"It's still extremely limiting."

"Poor you," I say without a shred of sympathy.

His eyes narrow as he looks at me. "You're enjoying this."

I shrug. "You pushed me off a cliff."

"Is that going to be your comeback for everything?"

"Probably. I feel like it's never gonna get old."

"So," Violet says loudly. "Would anyone like a drink?" She gestures to the tray of glasses Ryn brought with him, which is sitting on a small round table beside his chair.

"Okay," I say, pointing to one containing alternating layers of green and pink. "As long as it has no alcohol manufactured by humans."

"No alcohol at all," Ryn assures me as he hands over the glass. "Dash? Would you like something?"

"Nah, I'm actually gonna go say hi to Gaius if he's awake. Haven't seen him in a while. And I'm sure your conversation with Emmy—" he winks at me as he stands "—will be more pleasant if I'm not around."

"Finally," I mutter as Dash walks away. "He doesn't hang out here often, does he?"

Violet shakes her head and pushes her hair back away from her face. "Not too often."

"Thank goodness for—Oh. Those marks on your wrist." My eyes follow her arm as she lowers it. "They're the same as the ones Dash has. Isn't that supposed to mean you're a guardian?"

"Yes."

"But … you have a Griffin Ability, so … oh, was this before they came up with a way to test for Griffin Abilities? Sorry, the age thing is confusing. You look so young but you could be a hundred years old for all I know."

"Not quite," she says with a laugh.

"Not even close, actually," Ryn adds.

"But yes, I was a guardian. Ryn, Calla and I were all guardians before we were outlaws. Well, Calla never actually had the chance to graduate, but Ryn and I did. We worked for the Guild for a number of years without anyone knowing we were Griffin Gifted. Then the Guild developed a way to test for Griffin Abilities, and we were revealed as 'traitors' along with all the other Griffin Gifted. We ran before the Guild could deactivate our marks, though, so we still have access to our guardian weapons. You may have seen them? Gold and sparkly. They appear when we need them and disappear when we let go."

I nod, picturing the fight at the edge of the cliff. "Are those guardian-specific?"

"Yes. Only guardians have access to weapons like that."

"So now you basically do what you did before, but without the Guild's approval? So … you're like vigilantes?"

Her smile is wry. "Pretty much. Not something we ever planned to be, but the Guild kinda forced us into it. Especially since their system doesn't function as well as it's supposed to."

"What do you mean?"

"They work with Seers. Fae who have an ability to glimpse the future. They See things that will go wrong, and the Guild sends guardians to prevent those things from happening. The problem is, there are too many of those visions. There are never enough guardians to deal with them all, so the visions that are deemed less important are thrown out. We have a Guild contact, however, who gathers those up and gets them to us as quickly as possible. We deal with anything that hasn't already happened."

"Cool." I lapse into silence, thinking through everything she's explained. Then I remember that I'm holding a drink, so I take a sip. It tastes like a mixture of pine needles and something fruity, which isn't a bad combination. I wait for Ryn or Violet to ask me a question, but it seems they might be waiting for me to steer the conversation. Either that or they're having their own silent conversation with their eyes.

"Anyway," I say eventually, "what do you guys want to chat about? My Griffin

Ability? The fact that I can't perform even the most basic magic? The fact that my mom isn't my mom?" Violet raises both eyebrows, and I inwardly curse myself for letting that last one slip out. "Griffin Ability," I say hurriedly. "Let's go with that one."

"Uh, yes," she says. "I'm very interested to hear more about your Griffin Ability. I've never come across anyone who can speak things into being. That's incredible."

"You mean dangerous, right? That's what everyone else seems to think."

"Dangerous, yes, if you can't control it. But we're all dangerous if we can't control our magic. And you've only just discovered yours, so of course you don't know what to do with it yet. But we'll do whatever we can to help you, I promise."

I chew on my lip and slowly shake my head. "Perhaps I should stop speaking altogether, because I never know when something I say is going to come out as a magical command. Also …" I place my glass on the floor before pressing my hands together. "There's a possibility Jack is never going to be in trouble again."

Ryn tilts his head. "What did you say to him?"

"I think my exact words were, 'You should stay out of trouble.' And my Griffin Ability randomly switched on at that moment. So … I'm not really sure what kind of effect that's going to have on him."

Violet bursts out laughing. "Well, I'm looking forward to seeing the results of that one."

"Yeah, but what if I'd said something different? Something bad?"

Ryn pushes a hand through his hair. "Yes, there are definitely risks as long as you don't know when the ability will kick in. But completely muting yourself isn't practical. Perhaps just think about everything you want to say before you say it, and make sure it isn't a command or instruction."

My shoulders slump. "That sounds even less practical. I'm sure it would be easier to tape my mouth closed than to tell myself I have to think about every word before it leaves my mouth."

"It won't be a problem for long," Violet says. "We can start working on it tomorrow. Well, the next day, I suppose. You'll need to go to the lab tomorrow so Ana can take a sample of your magic. The elixir to stimulate your Griffin Ability should then be ready the day afterwards."

"Lab?" Cold, hard fear takes shape in the pit of my stomach. "I—that's—I'm not very—"

"Of course, I'm sorry. Dash mentioned you have a fear of all things medical. But don't worry. There are no needles or anything. It's just a simple spell, and you won't feel a thing."

I pluck at the hairs of the fluffy cushion, unable to get rid of my frown. I hate that Dash has been talking about me to these people. What else has he told them?

"Seriously, Em, it isn't a big deal," Ryn says. "We need to take a sample of your magic so we can create an elixir that will stimulate your Griffin Ability. Once you get used to what it feels like having that particular part of your magic switched on, you can hopefully figure out how to do it without the aid of the elixir. It needs to be specific to your magic, though, which is why we need the sample."

I lick my lips, reach forward for the drink at my feet, and take a long gulp. "Okay," I say after I've set it down again. "I guess that makes sense." That doesn't mean Ryn and Violet aren't lying to me, though. They might intend to use my magic for something else.

Violet leans forward, her amber now clasped between her hands. "Do you want to tell us anything about your mom?"

Suddenly, this feels like an interrogation. "Um …"

"What's her name? What hospital is she at?"

I scratch at a dirty mark on my jeans. "Daniela Clarke. And she's at Tranquil Hills Psychiatric Hospital. It's … well, the setting is tranquil. The inside isn't."

Vi nods and scribbles something onto her amber with a stylus.

"What are you writing down? Are you telling someone? Dash said those amber things are like cell phones, so are you messaging someone?"

"Em, calm down," Ryn says. "She's taking notes, that's all."

Violet sits back. "I know Dash told you that it isn't possible for your mom to be your biological mother. That must have been a huge shock for you to find out."

I nod but say nothing.

"I'm really sorry, Em. It's a lot to take in all at once, I know. Finding out that you're not who you thought you were and that you might have a whole new family somewhere out there. Do you want us to try find out more about them?"

I shake my head. "My mom's my only family. I don't need to know about anyone else."

"Okay. Just let us know if you change your mind."

"Yeah." I won't be changing my mind.

"Em, you don't have to freak out." It's Ryn who leans forward this time, watching me intently. "I'm serious. We only want to help you. If you really don't want us to take a sample of your magic, we're not going to force you. And if you don't want to talk about your mother, that's fine. We won't mention her again. We want you to feel safe here, that's all. We're hiding from the Guild just like you are. We understand what it's like to be hunted. We understand what it's like to want nothing more than a safe place to call home."

I realize I've been holding my breath while he's been speaking, and I slowly let it out. I think I believe him. I *think* I do. The only problem is … "This isn't ever going to be my home," I say carefully, hoping they understand I don't mean to offend them. "I have a life somewhere else. And a mother who needs me. I need to get back to that world when my magic is no longer a danger to everyone around me."

Ryn nods. "Then that's what we'll help you do."

CHAPTER 16

I spend an hour or two that evening in my room with Junie, the elf Jack mentioned earlier, trying not to stare at her ears while she creates linen for the bed and curtains for the windows, and changes the chair from a hard wooden thing into a soft armchair with flower-patterned fabric. Bandit takes an immediate liking to the new armchair and promptly curls up on it and falls asleep. Junie asks if I want anything else, and when I ask about getting a clock so I won't be late for breakfast in the morning—no more cell phone alarm to wake me up—Junie paints the time onto my wall. A minute later, when the number magically increases by one digit, I suck in a breath. Even after several days in this world, magic continues to surprise me.

While the room is more rustic than the one I had at Chevalier House, I prefer this one. When I'm finally left alone, I spend a while at the window, staring at the tiny lights in the trees and the millions of stars visible through the dome layer. But eventually my eyelids become too heavy, and I climb into bed.

I sleep better than expected, waking to the sound of singing coming from the direction of the painted numbers on my wall. After using the pool in my little garden-themed en-suite bathroom, I head down the many stairs on the outside of the tree to Violet and Ryn's house. I tap on the half-open door before pushing it open and walking into what appears to be their kitchen. The scent of something baking fills the air.

"Oh, morning, Em," Violet says, smiling at me over her shoulder. She's standing at a counter where the contents of a jug seems to be stirring itself, and a knife is neatly slicing through an apple. Her hand hovers above three mugs, and though I can't see inside them, I assume something magical is going on. "You can take a seat at the table," she says. "Coffee?"

"Oh, thank goodness. I was worried coffee might not exist in this world."

She laughs, picks up the three mugs, and carries them to the table. The jug carries on stirring itself behind her. "It isn't quite the same as the coffee you're probably used to, but hopefully you'll like it."

Jack runs into the kitchen, shouting, "Morning, Em! Did you bring Bandit with you?"

"Jack, please," Violet says. "You don't have to be so loud indoors."

"Sorry," Jack whispers with a mischievous grin as Ryn walks into the room behind him.

"Hey, Em," he says to me. Then to Violet: "Sorry, I got distracted. I was going to finish the coffee."

"All under control," Violet tells him. She gives him a quick kiss as he slips his arm around her waist. "Can you get the muffins out?"

"So did you bring Bandit?" Jack asks again, climbing onto a chair.

"Actually, he went back to sleep after I got up. He's probably still upstairs in my room."

"Oh." Jack deflates, then perks up when his mother places a small glass of something brown in front of him. "Ooh, chocolate, chocolate, chocolate."

"Hey, can I join you guys for breakfast?" The question comes from the direction of the door, and it's Calla who's peering around it. "Chase isn't back yet."

"Of course." Violet motions to one of the empty chairs. "Are you worried about him?"

"No, I'm sure he's fine. Things sometimes take longer than he expects, that's all. Hey, Em," she adds with a wave in my direction. "Ooh, are those muffins?" She slips quickly into a chair, rubbing her hands together as Ryn places a plate of steaming muffins in the center of the table. Violet adds a plate of sliced fruit beside it—at least half of which I don't recognize—while I try to remember if Chelsea, Georgia and I have ever eaten anything that doesn't come out of a cereal box at breakfast time. I don't know how to bake, and I doubt they do either.

"Something to drink?" Violet says to Calla.

"No, don't worry. I'll help myself to something in a minute."

Violet joins the table, and Jack proceeds to tell Calla all about Bandit, the 'new Filigree,' while everyone helps themselves to food. He then turns his attention to me and gives me a detailed outline of what Bandit's diet should include and how many times a day I should feed him. "I can help you, if you want," he adds.

"Thanks. You can actually keep him if you—" Violet cuts me off with a quick and vigorous shake of her head. I backpedal quickly. "I mean, um, you can keep visiting him. As much as you like. And I'm sure he'd love it if you bring him food." I risk a glance in Violet's direction, hoping I've successfully fixed my blunder. She smiles and gives me a brief nod.

Beside her, Calla mutters something and lowers her amber onto the table beside her plate. "Everything okay?" Violet asks.

"That was a message from Perry. He says there was an attack at a faerie boarding school last night, and another one at that village near Twiggled Horn. That's the second one at that particular village this week. Something bad is going on out there."

"I think I heard about that," I say, at which Calla looks across at me in surprise. "Well, the first one," I add. "Not the one that just happened. I only remember because the name of the place is so strange."

"It's the name of an oddly shaped mountain," Ryn says. "What did you hear about the first attack?"

I try to recall the details Jewel passed on to Dash when she received the message. "They said five people were killed, I think. Oh, and they said it was a Griffin attack. I remember now. That was the first time I heard about Griffin Abilities."

Calla's mouth drops open. "What? That's one of the stories the Guild is spreading around? But we were nowhere near Twiggled Horn. And we don't kill people. Ugh, the Guild makes me so mad sometimes. I can't believe they pinned that on us."

Her amber buzzes briefly across the table again. She picks it up and reads it. "Oh, brilliant." Her hands fall to her lap in exasperation. "The Guild's official message is that no one has claimed responsibility for these recent attacks, but they have reason to believe they were carried out by Griffin rebels."

I watch Violet's hands clench tightly around her knife and fork. Ryn's expression darkens. "Such lies," he grinds out between his teeth. "They know it isn't us, so they'd damn well better be doing whatever they can behind the scenes to figure out who's really responsible."

"Sounds just as messed up as our law enforcement system," I mutter.

"Dad," Jack says uncertainly. "I thought we weren't supposed to say 'damn.'"

A small smile breaks past Ryn's frown. He reaches across and ruffles Jack's hair. "You're right. Thanks for reminding me."

"Yeah, I guess we shouldn't let this get to us," Calla says, pushing her amber away and selecting another muffin. "The Guild's been spreading lies about us for ages. This is hardly any different."

"True," Violet says. "Although they definitely need to find out who's behind this."

"Hopefully they can manage without our help," Ryn says with a superior smile that reminds me, just for a moment, of Dash.

Calla's amber shivers yet again. She frowns at the latest message. "Perry says there's something extra weird about the way these fae were killed. Says I should meet him so he can explain properly." She stands. "I guess I'd better get going. Oh, but I want some of that chocolate cinnamon stuff Jack loves so much first." She hurries to the counter.

"Morning, everyone."

We all look toward the door. At the sight of Dash, I suppress a groan. "Dash?" Violet says. "Can you use the faerie paths again?"

"No, but I have other friends here who are happy to help me out."

"Don't you have a job you should be at right now?" Calla asks.

"Yeah, I'm heading to work in a few minutes. Just stopped by to say hi."

Calla places a hand on her hip. Behind her, the jug that was stirring itself with a spoon earlier pours some of its contents into a glass. "You stopped by to 'say hi?' Why don't I believe you?"

"I don't know. I'm a friendly guy. I'm not sure why you'd doubt my desire to wish everyone a good morning."

She shakes her head as she picks up the glass and moves toward him. "Well, good morning, then. And goodbye. I'm heading out now."

"Stay alive," Dash calls cheerfully after her as she leaves.

"Stay alive?" I repeat. "Is that a common greeting around here?"

Violet throws a quick glance at Jack before quietly saying, "It's a common sentiment, even if we don't always say it out loud."

Dash walks into the kitchen. "How nice of you to welcome Em to the oasis with baked goods." He leans past Violet and grabs a blueberry muffin. "I approve."

"Dash," I say, deciding to be civil. "Do you know what happened to Aurora after I got away from the Guild yesterday?"

He leans his hip against the table. "Aurora?"

"The other new girl from Chevalier House. The one who showed up at the Guild and helped me escape. Guardians got hold of her before she could get into the faerie paths with me."

"Oh yeah." Dash chews and swallows. "They put her in a detainment cell for a few hours. Then they sent her back to Chevalier House after questioning her."

Guilt twists in my gut. "Questioning her?"

"They wanted to know why she'd come to help you. As far as they knew, there was no connection between the two of you."

"There wasn't—isn't," I say. "I have no idea why she came to help me."

"Who is this girl?" Ryn asks.

"She arrived at Chevalier House the day before yesterday. She seemed super suspicious of the whole setup. She said she'd heard that people disappear from there sometimes—which I suppose makes sense now that I know Azzy helps Griffin Gifted people."

"Do you think this girl also has a Griffin Ability?" Violet asks.

I lift my shoulders. "No idea. I suppose Azzy will let you know soon enough if she does. Anyway, what's weird is that she was supposedly a slave to a bunch of witches who never taught her how to use magic. But she somehow got to the Guild on her own, used magic to cut my ropes, and opened a way to the faerie paths."

Ryn considers my words. "Maybe she picked up some basic magic skills around the witches. Although," he adds with a frown, "witches don't travel through faerie paths."

"So witches are real? That part wasn't made up?"

Ryn exchanges a look with Violet. "Witches are very real." He pushes against the table and stands. "I'll contact Azzy now. She can tell me if there's anything we need to be suspicious about."

We start clearing up then, partly with the use of magic and partly—at least for Jack and me—by hand. He and I are drying the dishes washed by one of Violet's spells when I realize Dash and Violet have gone into the next room. I think I hear my name mentioned, and my anger flares up immediately. Hasn't Dash told these people enough about me and my personal life already?

"… can help her, right?" Dash is saying. "Come on, you can find anyone."

"No I can't, and I don't want you telling her that. You know how it works. I need to touch something that belongs to—"

"To her parents, right. I've thought about that. *She* belongs to her parents. So just touch her, and you'll be able to find them."

"Dash, she hasn't belonged to her birth parents for a very long time," Violet says. "That isn't going to work. Besides, she's not interested in finding them."

"Exactly," I say, loud enough to startle them both. They look around with guilty expressions. "So thank you, Dash, for sticking your nose where it doesn't belong, but as you can see, I don't want your help."

He opens his mouth as if to argue, but then he sighs and raises his hands in surrender. "Sorry. I thought I was helping. I'll stay out of it."

"Probably best," Violet says quietly.

"Cool, well, I guess I'll head to work then." He raises his hand and makes a fist, holding it in the air in front of Violet as he grins at her. "Have a good day saving lives."

She rolls her eyes and bumps his fist with hers. "You too." She watches him leave, then turns to me. "I'm sorry about that. I hope you know I wasn't going to do anything without your permission."

I nod hesitantly, wanting to believe her. "What were you guys talking about? Being able to find someone … Is that your Griffin Ability?"

She nods. "Yes. I can find people. If I know the person I'm looking for, it's easy. The connection's already there. If I don't, then I need to be holding something that belongs to that person."

"That's so weird," I murmur. *No less weird than being able to speak things into being*, a tiny voice reminds me. "Hang on," I add as something occurs to me. "Is that how Dash found me yesterday after I escaped the Guild? And the other night when I ran away from Chevalier House? Did you tell him where I was?"

She nods, looking guilty once again. "Azzy sent a message to say you'd run. I searched for you, then told Dash where to find you."

"That's …" I shake my head. "I … I don't even know how to feel about that."

"Like your privacy's been violated?"

"Kind of, I guess. Like I can never truly hide anywhere, even if I want to."

She nods. "I know. I hate making people feel like that. I only do it when it's necessary. In your case, we were worried for your safety."

"Wait, how did it work if you didn't have anything that belongs to me?"

She closes her eyes for a moment and rubs the back of her neck. "Now you're really going to think we violated your privacy." She opens her eyes. "I have a hairband that belongs to you. Dash took it off your wrist the night he brought you home after you passed out at that party. He figured we might need to find you at some point."

I cross my arms and stare at the floor. "Yeah. This is all very weird."

"I should probably tell you about Ryn too. Get all the weirdness out of the way in one go."

"Oh dear. That doesn't sound good."

"And just so you know, none of these abilities are a secret. We don't want people to think we're hiding things from them, so we're very open with those who live here."

"Okay, so what can Ryn do?"

"He can sense your emotions."

I blink. "That's … not cool. At all. What if I don't want him knowing what I'm feeling?"

She shrugs. "Try to not feel what you're feeling?"

"Is that even possible?"

"Not really. Trust me, I have years of experience in this area." She looks briefly over her shoulder as Jack calls for her. Something about a book he can't find. "Anyway," she says, turning back to me. "It isn't such a big deal. Most of the time, people's emotions are evident in their expressions and actions. Ryn's ability just makes him a little more intuitive than most, that's all."

I bite my lip and frown some more at the rug on the floor. Perhaps she's right, but that doesn't make me feel any more comfortable about being around him.

"I'm sorry, Em. I know this is all quite overwhelming. There's plenty more I want to explain, but I need to help Jack get ready for school, and then I've got some work things to deal with. I thought you could take today easy—just look around, hang out in the hammocks, practice whatever Azzy taught you before you left Chevalier—and tonight we can talk about the best way to teach you everything you need to know, including your Griffin Ability."

Fabulous. Sounds like you've got everything perfectly worked out. I push my sarcastic, bitter thoughts aside. "Okay. I guess that's a plan. And … can I ask one more thing?" Now's probably the best time, while she's still feeling guilty about using her Griffin Ability on me. I swallow and peel my gaze from the floor. "Can you take me to visit my mother?"

CHAPTER 17

"It's been almost a year since I saw her," I rush on, suddenly feeling like I need to convince Violet this is a good idea. "I saved up—I was going to take a bus—and then my aunt found my stash and took it. And then everything went to sh—I mean, um, everything got messed up."

"Almost a year?" Violet repeats with raised eyebrows. "Em, that's horrible. I'm so sorry. I can't imagine how hard it is to be separated from her for so long."

"But now I don't have to be, right? Traveling through the faerie paths is quick and easy. But I can't do it myself yet, so I need someone's help."

Her expression becomes conflicted, and I can sense that tiny voice inside me getting ready to yell, *See? I knew it! They don't really want to help you.* "I understand how desperate you must be to see her," Violet says carefully, "but you have to understand that it will be risky. The Guild knows all about her. They probably already have someone watching to see if you'll go there."

"Wait, seriously?" I hadn't considered that. "You really think someone's hanging out at Tranquil Hills just in case I show up?"

"Yes. Your power is valuable to the Guild. They'll want to get it back if they can."

"But they think I'm dead."

"Do they? You might not know this yet, but it's hard to kill a faerie, Em. Our magic can help us survive a great many things that would kill a human. If the Guild doesn't find your body, they'll assume you survived somehow."

"Mom! I still can't find the book," Jack shouts from somewhere in the house.

"Just keep looking," she calls over her shoulder.

"This is bad." I can't keep still so I start pacing. "So the Guild is probably watching my mom. Do you think they'd hurt her? You know, try to use her against me?"

"I highly doubt it. I know they seem like it, but they're not the bad guys."

"Really?" My voice is laced with sarcasm. "They certainly seemed like the bad guys when they were trying to kill me yesterday. And if my magic is so valuable to them, why would they think twice about threatening a sick human woman who means nothing to them?"

"Em, one of the major purposes of the Guild is to *protect* humans. They don't mean—"

"And what about the Unseelies? They somehow knew about me and my Griffin Ability, so they probably know about Mom too. Won't they try to take her? That's villain move number one, right? Use a person's loved ones against them. They've probably taken her al—"

"Em, calm down." Violet grips my upper arms and gives them a reassuring squeeze. "We're one step ahead of you. I already sent someone last night to check that your mother's okay. That's why I asked you the name of the hospital yesterday. He reported back that she's fine. He couldn't go into her room in case someone was watching, but he saw her from a distance."

"Oh. Okay." My rising doubts shrink back down. "Thank you." I tuck my hair behind one ear as she lets go of me and steps back. "So, can I visit her? I mean, I know someone from the Guild might be watching, but I can disguise myself. I'll be really careful."

I expect her to argue about it not being safe—that's what grown-ups do, right?—but instead she nods. "Yes, we can help you do that, but like I said, it will be dangerous. If your mother has no other family or friends that regularly visit her, then the Guild will expect that anyone going to see her now is associated with you. So even if Calla creates an illusion that makes you appear entirely different, the Guild will likely be suspicious. That's her Griffin Ability, by the way. Casting illusions."

"Wow. Oh yes, she made us invisible yesterday."

"That's right."

"Can she make me appear invisible to everyone except my mother?"

"She can, although it tires her out much faster to project an illusion onto some while keeping it from others. So as long as you understand that you may have to get out of there on short notice, we can make this work."

I nod fervently. "I can do that. A short visit is better than nothing."

"Okay. Later, then? Calla's schedule's full for the day, but she'll be able to take you late this afternoon."

"Thank you." Excited anticipation rushes suddenly through me. I'm going to see her. I'm actually going to see Mom.

Jack appears in the doorway, hefting a heavy book. "Look, Mom, I found it."

Violet claps her hands together. "See? I knew you could do it. Come on, let's get you to school."

Late in the afternoon, when I'm tired of practicing pulling magic out of myself, and my brain is almost bursting with all the things I want to talk to Mom about, I wait for Calla in the pavilion. As people I don't know wander past, I slide a little lower on one of the couches and avoid making eye contact. I watch Jack running by in the company of several children. They slow near the hammocks and jostle as they try to decide who gets which one. Jack tries to jump onto one, but it ends up flipping over and depositing him on his stomach on the ground. I stand quickly, unsure if I should run over to check he's okay, but he pushes himself up a moment later, laughing along with his friends.

"Hey, it's Emerson!" he shouts suddenly, grinning and pointing my way. They all start running toward me, which I find a little alarming. "Emerson," Jack says when he reaches the pavilion. "Remember you were saying you know how to fall the right way?"

I stare down awkwardly at five young faces. "Fall?"

"Yeah, when you and your friend do that park stuff."

"Oh, parkour. Yes."

"So can you teach me how to fall out of a hammock the right way? So that I look cool?"

I can't help laughing at that. "I'm sorry, Jack. I don't know if there's *any* way to fall out of a hammock that looks cool."

"See?" says a girl whose eyes have vertical pupils like the guy I saw yesterday when I arrived here. "Such a dumb idea."

"Hey, don't be such a witch," another boy says.

She gasps. "That is *so mean.*"

"You can't talk about witches in front of Jack, remember?" a second girl says.

"It's fine," Jack tells them with a dramatic sigh. "It's just my mom and dad and Aunt Calla who don't like talking about witches."

"Why not?" I ask, wondering what terrible blunder I made when I spoke about Aurora and witches earlier today.

"They killed my sister," Jack says, so matter-of-factly that at first I wonder if he's making a terrible joke. But the other four children nod, their expressions serious.

"That's—oh my goodness. That's horrible. I'm so sorry, Jack."

"Yeah." He looks down. "I didn't know her. It happened a long time ago, way before I was born."

"Hey there, guys." Calla jogs up to the pavilion steps. "What happened way before you were born, Jack?"

"Nothing." He gives her a wide smile. "We're gonna go back to the hammocks." He runs away, followed closely by his friends.

"Okay then," Calla says, watching them for a moment. "So." She turns to me. "Ready to go?"

I suck in a deep breath, trying to figure out how to answer her. She probably doesn't realize what a loaded question that is. "Yes," I say eventually, despite the fact that I doubt I'll ever feel ready.

"We need to leave from outside the oasis," she says. "And I want to talk to Ryn quickly before we go."

"Okay." I fall into step beside her as we leave the pavilion behind. "Are there a lot of people living here?" I ask, glancing up at a faerie couple walking hand in hand in the other direction.

"Yes, quite a few. Most end up leaving if we can help them live safely somewhere else, but there are individuals and families who decide to stay. We now have over a hundred fae who call this place home."

"All Griffin Gifted?"

"Not all, but mostly, yes."

"Okay here's something I don't understand: How are there so many fae who ended up with Griffin Abilities? I was told it started with magical discs someone created long ago, but weren't there only six of them? I know they were passed around to various people, but seriously? How did those discs get into the hands of so many?"

Calla pushes her gleaming gold hair over her shoulder. "It may seem like a lot, but the number is small in comparison to the population of our world."

"Okay, sure, but still. All these people from six discs of magic?"

"Think about the fact that those discs were around for centuries. They granted power, which means others coveted them, which means they were frequently stolen. Add to that the fact that two Griffin Gifted can possibly pass on Griffin magic to their offspring, and you wind up with even more of us."

"I suppose when you take into account the fact that you guys live so long, it makes more sense. I'm still having trouble accepting that part. Or at least, applying it to myself. I can't imagine still being alive in a few hundred years time." And I can't imagine how I'm supposed to deal with all my human friends and family growing old and dying while I still look like a twenty-year-old. "Is Jack Griffin Gifted?" I ask, forcing my mind in a less depressing direction.

"No, thank goodness. If he wants to leave here one day and join the rest of the world, he can do so without having to hide a secret ability."

"Good afternoon, ladies."

I slow to a halt as Dash waves and walks toward us. "Ugh, really?" is all I can bring myself to say.

"Interesting to see you back here so soon," Calla comments. "The Guild definitely isn't working you hard enough."

He shrugs. "They tell us to take our first year easy."

"They do not." She eyes him suspiciously. "What are you really doing here?"

"I was updating Vi on something earlier and she mentioned that you're taking Em to see her mom. I thought—"

"You're not coming with," I tell him.

"Hey, I just thought you guys could do with some extra protection. You'll be focused on your mom, and Calla will be focused on whatever illusion she's using to cover you. Don't you think you need a third person to keep an eye on things? In case a doctor or another guardian shows up?"

"No."

"Actually," Calla says, "that's a perfectly sensible plan. But I was going to ask Ryn to come with us."

"Ryn's out with Vi at the moment. I was just up there looking for them." He nods toward one of the giant trees. "And everyone else who's mission-approved is busy." He grins. "Looks like it's a good thing I showed up."

I manage to keep myself from groaning out loud. "Fine. Whatever. Just stay away from my mother. She doesn't need you ruining her life any further."

Calla frowns, opens her mouth, then appears to think better of whatever she was going to say. "Okay then. Let's go."

Once we're out in the desert, Calla opens a doorway to the faerie paths and tells me to focus firmly on picturing the outside of the hospital. Though complete darkness surrounds me, I shut my eyes anyway, imagining the high walls, the security gate, the discreetly small sign with the hospital's name on it, and mountain peaks in the distance.

"Well done," Calla says.

I open my eyes and look across an empty street at the exact scene I just pictured. "That's amazing," I murmur.

Dash raises the hood of his jacket and pulls it over his head. "What?" he asks when I give him an odd look. "I don't want my face showing up on any Guild surveillance orbs."

"Surveillance what? And you're going to be invisible, aren't you?"

"Invisible to people, yes. Not to bugs. I don't know if they're watching, but it's good to be careful."

"Am I supposed to know what you're talking about?" At that moment, a shiver sends goosebumps racing up my back and into my hair. "Oh—um—you can—" I grab Dash's arm, in case my ability has any doubt who I'm talking to. "You can open doorways to the faerie paths," I blurt out.

Dash stares at me with wide eyes. Calla looks equally startled. "Well that came outta nowhere," she says.

Dash quickly removes a stylus from inside his jacket and crouches down. He writes on the tar, muttering those words I still can't clearly make out. Darkness appears, spreading rapidly into a large hole leading to the faerie paths. "Yes! Finally! Thanks, Em." He rises and puts his stylus away. "Now we'll have to come up with a way for you to fix Jewel as well."

"That was pretty darn cool," Calla says.

"Yeah. When I'm saying something useful."

"True. Okay, let's focus on the hospital again. Do you remember anything about what the inside looks like?"

"Yes, I remember the waiting area. But I don't remember where Mom's room is. It's been a while since I was here."

"Not a problem," she says. "The guy who checked things out for us last night said she's in room twenty-six. I'm sure we can find it. All you need to do is picture the waiting room so we can safely get inside." She opens another faerie paths doorway.

"Wait," I say before we step into the darkness. "Are you absolutely sure we'll be invisible on the other side?"

"Yes. I'm focusing on invisibility. You're focusing on the waiting room. Dash, you're emptying your mind." She gives him a half-smile. "Should be easy."

"That's why I'm here, right?" he says without missing a beat. "Empty-minded muscle."

I shake my head, link arms with both of them, and walk forward. I squeeze my eyes shut and picture the waiting room. The rows of chairs, the hard-angled reception desk, the confusing abstract paintings, and the tall monochrome flower pots. I smell it before I see it: detergent and something sour. As if someone threw up in here recently.

I look down, and instead of seeing my body, I see the polished floor. I cling more tightly to Calla and Dash. "Okay," I whisper. I look around, the memory of my last visit coming back to me. "We need to get through that door on the right. The one that looks like it requires an ID tag."

"I guess we'll need to go through the paths again," Calla says.

One of the women behind the main desk looks up, frowning in our direction. "Move quietly," Calla instructs, her whisper barely audible now. I feel a tug pulling me to my left. Calla leads us around the corner to an alcove with another few chairs and a window onto the garden. When we're out of view of the desk, we suddenly become visible again. "Quickly," she says, opening a doorway. We hurry into it. Moments later, we're on the other side of the security door.

We head along the corridor, arms still linked so we don't lose each other. Bright sunlight streams in through the windows, illuminating more canvases of colorful art. The gardens themselves, visible through the windows, are neatly manicured. From here, I can see a group of patients sitting on the lawn in a circle. Tranquil Hills is pretty and serene, but that's part of what makes my skin crawl whenever I'm here. It's like icing on a cake that has worms crawling through it. Perfume sprayed over rotting garbage. Nothing can hide the true nature of this place.

We pass silently through an open living area where people sit in twos or threes at small tables playing board games or card games. They're all watched by nurses around the room. This is where Mom was the first time I came to visit. We sat here together and played Go Fish while Chelsea waited for me in the reception area, refusing to see her 'crazy sister.' A shiver races across my skin at the memory. "Okay, Em?" Calla whispers.

"Yeah."

We enter another corridor on the other side of the room. Fewer windows and less light. Closed doors lining the right hand side. "Okay, here's a number twenty," Calla says. "I guess we just keep going and we'll find twenty-six."

My heart leaps, pounding faster with every step we take. Nervousness makes me nauseous and light-headed. I still can't believe I'm about to see her. "There it is," I whisper as a door with a number twenty-six on it comes into view.

"I haven't seen anyone suspicious yet," Dash says. "Anyone I recognize from the

Guild, I mean."

"Can I go in?" I ask, stopping outside the door.

"Yes," Calla says letting go of me. On my other side, Dash moves away. "We'll keep watch out here, and I'll make sure you appear invisible to anyone who walks past."

I swallow. If I could see my hand, I'd probably find it shaking. I fumble a moment with the door handle—misjudging the distance and bumping the door with my invisible knuckles—before finding it and wrapping my hand around it. I push down, take a deep breath, and slowly open the door. Too scared to take a step forward, I peer inside.

The room is empty.

My head pounds as disappointment and relief collide. "Where is she?"

I sense movement beside me, then hear Dash's voice: "Perhaps she's eating a meal. Or having some kind of social time. Or a bathroom break. Is she usually restricted to her room, or does she only come back here to sleep?"

"I don't know." My words come out harsher than I intended. "I haven't been here in a long time."

"We'll just have to wait," Calla says. "It's okay. I'm only projecting one illusion right now, and it's a simple one, so it isn't too tiring."

"Okay. Thank you." One of them bumps into me as I move to the side, and after a moment of shuffling, we're all leaning against the wall beside door number twenty-six. There's no way I'm waiting inside that room on my own. The corridor will do just fine. As the seconds tick by, my anxiety begins to rise again. Up and up, my insides twisting tighter and tighter.

"You aren't going to say anything to her about magic, are you?" Dash asks eventually, breaking the silence.

"Firstly," I tell him, "you don't get to tell me what I should speak to my mother about. And secondly, no. I'm not so stupid that I'm going to tell her I'm a faerie with magic. I don't even know if I'm going to tell her I know she isn't my real mother. There are dozens of things I *want* to say, and I probably won't end up saying any of them because I don't want to freak her out."

Like last time.

We're quiet for a minute or two as someone in the company of a nurse walks slowly past us and into one of the other bedrooms. The nurse leaves soon afterwards.

"Vi told me it's been a long time since you saw her," Calla says once we're alone again. "You can probably talk to her about whatever's happened in your normal life up until a few days ago. Stuff you did at school. Updates on your friends."

"All the parkour skills you and Val have learned," Dash adds.

Val. Val who's probably confused and angry that I ran away and left her behind.

"Yeah, maybe," I say. "But also ... well, I like to chat to her about the good old days." I stare past the blank wall ahead of me and picture Mom as she used to be, smiling and happy. "I think she likes remembering our pretty garden, and the little house we lived in, and the ornaments she collected. I've often imagined taking her back there one day. Returning to the simple, happy life we used to have. It always seemed impossible, but now with magic ..." I trail off, coming back to the present with a jolt and remembering who I'm with: Dash, who doesn't deserve to know my private thoughts and wishes, and Calla, who probably wouldn't approve of any of the things I plan to do with my magic once I know how to use it.

"With magic?" she prompts.

"Nothing. Wait, is that ... Oh, heck, I think that's her." Two people are walking toward us. A nurse and a woman with dark messy hair, not quite as tall as I remember, and dressed in sweatpants and a hoodie. My heart rate rockets upward and my conflicting emotions reach a peak. I think I might throw up right here. But I manage to breathe through it as Mom walks closer. *It's her!* my mind shrieks as she passes me and goes into her room. *It's really, really her!* She's right here, after so many months. I'll finally be able to speak to her, hug her, let her know I think of her every single day and that she won't have to be here for much longer.

The nurse stops in the doorway. "Just lie down and I'm sure it'll pass soon," she says to Mom. Her voice lacks feeling, as if the words mean nothing to her. Or, I wonder briefly, as if she's spoken those same words a hundred times before. "You know you can call one of us if you start feeling any worse."

Mom gives her a distant smile and a nod.

The nurse closes the door and walks away.

I take another dizzying few breaths before moving forward and grasping the handle. As I push the door open, I suddenly become visible again. Mom looks up. She blinks and frowns. A smile spreads rapidly across my face, turning into a laugh. "Mom." I walk into the room—

—and an alarm begins blaring.

CHAPTER 18

Mom screams and scrambles backward across her bed. Calla and Dash, visible now, rush into the room. Calla goes immediately to the wall and scribbles across it. "We have to go," she calls to me.

"What? I don't under—"

"It's a Guild alarm. It was set for you."

"But I only just … Mom, it's okay, it's me." I ignore Calla and Dash and approach Mom cautiously. "Everything's fine, Mom. Don't worry about the alarm." I reach for her, but she shrinks back, slapping wildly at my hands. "It's okay, it's just me," I say desperately. "It's Emmy. Your daughter. I came to—"

"Em, we gotta go." Dash takes my arm and pulls me toward the faerie paths.

"No!" I wrench my arm free. "I need to get her!"

"What? No, we can't take her with us."

"I won't leave without her!"

"You can't take her through the paths, Em!" Calla shouts above the alarm.

"Then we go out the front door with her!" I shout back.

"And then what? We'd have to find somewhere safe for her in this world. Someone who knows how to care for her. And what about her medication, her treatment?"

"The medication makes her worse!" I gesture to Mom, now hiding under her blankets, curled up and wailing, rocking back and forth.

Movement in the corridor draws my gaze away. Dash throws his hand out, and the door slams itself shut. He runs to it and begins drawing big glowing patterns across it. "This won't hold them for long," he says as the door shudders beneath an assault from the other side.

"Em, we will come back for her," Calla says firmly. "I promise. But we're not taking her anywhere until we have a solid plan." She reaches for my hand. "Dash, stay here and keep watch. Make sure no one does anything to—Actually, no. You go with Em. I'll stay. You can't risk your cover, and I can more easily hide myself."

"Got it." Dash grabs my arm as Calla pushes us both toward the gaping hole leading to the faerie paths.

"Mom." The word is a half-whisper, half-sob as I throw one last look over my shoulder before the darkness consumes us. I stumble through it, Dash pulling me along, until soft orange light appears ahead of us. I breathe in the rapidly cooling evening air of the desert as sand shifts beneath my feet. I pull away from Dash.

"Em ..." He reaches for me, but I smack his hand away.

"Don't touch me." His hands fall to his sides while I wrap mine tightly around my body. I need to hold myself together.

Quietly, Dash says, "She didn't recognize you, did she."

Thanks, Dash, I want to yell. *THANK YOU FOR POINTING THAT OUT!* Instead I bite my lip until the tears recede. There's no point in screaming at him. He doesn't know about the nerve he's struck. He doesn't know that the last time I visited Mom, she ended up cowering in the corner of her room and screaming about the stranger—me. He doesn't know that several nurses had to hold her down while I left the room in tears, and he doesn't know how desperately I hoped this time would be different.

"Emerson—"

"Don't."

"I'm sorry I did this to you." His tone is pleading, and his hands are clasped tightly together beneath his chin.

"What?"

"I'm sorry! She's in that hospital because of me. I've always denied it, and some logical, defensive part of my brain still argues that she would have been institutionalized at some point anyway, and that you can't really blame me, but ... you can. It was my fault. On that day, in that moment, she went completely over the edge because of me. And ... I'm sorry."

I blink, look down at the sand, then back up at him. "What do you expect me to say to that?"

"I ... I don't know. I just needed you to know how sorry I am."

"Why? It doesn't change anything."

"It might change how much you hate me."

I shake my head. "Get over yourself, Dash. This isn't about you." I turn away, looking for the faint outline of the dome. It's almost invisible, but I manage to spot it. I start trudging across the sand, picturing the hidden world within the dome. Lush vegetation, twinkling bugs, and the gentle scent of flowers. A peaceful scene contrasting starkly with the repeating memory of a bare white room and Mom screaming while scrambling away from me.

Again.

Again.

Again.

I frown and blink and look away, desperate to push the image from my mind. The tension in my chest eases the moment I pass through the magic layer and into the oasis. I hate that I'm glad to be back here. It feels like a betrayal to Mom. I shouldn't enjoy a single moment of this sanctuary while she's trapped between four blank walls. Trapped inside her own mind.

"Em, wait," Dash calls as I stride away from him. "We're going to get her out. We couldn't do it today, but that doesn't mean it won't happen. We'll give her a better life somehow, I promise."

"Thanks," I answer, not looking back at him, "but you shouldn't make promises you don't know how to keep."

I don't come out of my room that evening to join anyone for dinner, but I hear Violet and Ryn outside my door, speaking quietly to one another. Calla joins them at some point. I press my ear against the door long enough to hear her say that Mom is okay and the guardians who were waiting for me didn't do anything to her after I left. Then I move back to the bed.

The Guild knows I was there. They'll probably increase the number of guardians hanging around, and if I try to visit again, it'll be even more likely that I'll be caught. Not that I have much hope of convincing Calla to take me back. She and her companions are probably regretting offering to help me. I could have got her caught. Ruined Dash's cover. Maybe the three of them are standing out there trying to come up with a kind way of telling me they can't do anything more for Mom. And it's not like I'd blame them. They don't owe me anything. They'll probably forget about me as soon as the next desperate person arrives at the oasis.

Which suits me just fine, since I'm used to taking care of things on my own.

CHAPTER 19

That image of Mom screaming, wild terror in her eyes, floods my mind first thing the next morning. I make a conscious effort to focus on something else: My Griffin Ability. I need to learn how to use it. Last night could have turned out so differently if I'd been able to calm Mom down with just a few words. If I'd been able to tell that magical alarm to turn itself off. I need to get past my fear of all things medical and hand over a sample of my magic. I need that elixir.

Mom. Cowering. Her mouth open in a silent scream.

I shove the memory aside yet again and turn over—and find Bandit snuggled beside me in kitten form. I'm about to push him away from me, but he looks so darn cute curled up with his nose tucked beneath one paw. And it's oddly comforting to realize I haven't been alone all night. I reach out and stroke two fingers from his head down his back, hoping he doesn't turn out to be just like the puppy that ran away.

My stomach grumbles. I wonder if Violet's breakfast invitation was only for yesterday morning, or if it extends for as many mornings as I'm here. Hopefully the latter, since I have no food in this room. I get dressed and check the enchanted numbers on my wall—I'm later than yesterday morning—before hurrying down the stairs, one hand trailing against the tree trunk to steady me if I trip over an uneven step. I slow down before reaching Ryn and Violet's door. It's open, which is a good sign, and the heavenly aromas wafting through the door start my stomach grumbling again, but I'm still not sure if I'm welcome here a second time. Especially after freaking out at the hospital yesterday and putting Calla and Dash at risk.

I move a little closer and see Violet, Jack and Calla at the table. Jack straightens, jumps off his chair, and runs toward me. "I'm sorry, Emerson!" He wraps his arms around my middle and squeezes tight.

"Oh, um, okay." I pat his back awkwardly. "What are you sorry for?"

"I don't know. Mom and Dad were talking about you this morning and they sounded worried, and when I asked Mom what was wrong, she said you probably just need a big hug."

"Jack," Violet scolds, rising from her chair and then standing there hesitantly. Color appears in her cheeks. "You should ask before you do things like that. Some people don't like to be hugged by people they don't know well."

Confusion crosses Jack's face as he pulls back. "But Em knows me. We walked around the whole oasis together."

"It's fine," I say hurriedly, leaning down and hugging him quickly, despite the growing awkwardness. I'd prefer to keep my personal space to myself, but I don't want to hurt Jack's feelings.

"Would you like to join us?" Violet asks, gesturing to the table and still looking somewhat embarrassed.

"Yes, thank you. I wasn't sure if, um …" I shove my hands awkwardly into my back pockets as I hover near the table. "Well, I know you invited me yesterday, but I wasn't sure if that was just a first-day thing, like for everyone who's new, or—"

"Oh, that was for every morning while you're here," she says with a smile, sitting again.

"Yeah, we don't want you to starve all the way up there in the top of the tree," Calla adds.

I pull a chair out and take a seat. "Do you cook amazing breakfasts every morning?"

"Dad actually made the pancakes," Jack tells me before helping himself to another one.

"And no, we don't do breakfasts like this every morning," Violet says. "But when things are less busy and we have time, then we do."

I help myself to two pancakes and reach for a small jug of what looks like syrup, but could very possibly be an exotic magical alternative. I prepare myself for the possibility of it tasting very different. Ryn walks into the house as I finish drizzling it over my pancakes.

"Okay, everything's sorted," he says as he joins us at the table. "Em, we're going to get your mom out of hospital today, if it's all right with you."

"I—yes. Of course that's all right with me." I pause with a fork and a piece of pancake in the air in front of me and shake my head, giving myself a moment to take in the news. "Today? Already? That's amazing."

Ryn laughs. "Yes, today."

"I mean, I know Calla said we'd go back for her, but … I just figured that would take a while. I'm sure you have plenty of other priorities, and my mom's just … a human stuck in a hospital."

Ryn lowers the mug he just picked up and looks directly at me. "She's your mother. That makes her a priority. And if she's been stuck in that hospital for years, then it clearly isn't doing anything to help her. We were talking about getting her out as soon as possible, and then Dash called last night to tell me it had to be today and that he plans to help. So today it is. Everything's been planned."

"You know, I'm seriously starting to wonder if the Guild is going to fire Dash soon. He's spending more time on cases for us these days than the job he's paid to do."

"Don't worry about him," Violet says, reaching for a glass of something green. "He works a lot harder than you think."

"Works hard?" Calla snorts. "You think so? That boy is far too chilled. He's probably sitting back and letting his team do all the work."

"Just like he does with the ladies," Jack says.

Violet chokes on her drink. "Excuse me?" She sets her glass down. "What exactly are you talking about, young man?"

"That's what he said to me," Jack tells her, his tone defensive. Then he deepens his voice, probably in an attempt to impersonate Dash. "I just sit back, and the ladies come flocking."

Violet blinks at Jack while Calla bursts out laughing. Ryn tries to keep the smile off his face as he clears his throat and says, "I hope you realize, Jack, that that's not the way to find the right girl."

Jack screws up his face and reaches for another pancake. "I'm not looking for any girl."

"Good," Violet says as I chew and wait patiently for a moment to ask for more details about Mom's rescue plan. "And when you do, you'll find out it takes a lot more effort than just sitting back and waiting." She looks across the table at Ryn, her frown replaced by a small smile.

Ryn winks at her. "Like glow-bug asses in the sky."

Violet flicks her fingers, and a spark bounces off Ryn's shoulder. "Don't say ass," she whispers.

"Mom and Dad said ass!" Jack shouts gleefully.

Violet rolls her eyes and Calla starts laughing again. I smile and wait for the laughter to die down before saying, "So, uh, what's the plan for getting my mom out of Tranquil Hills?"

"Right, sorry," Ryn says. He takes a sip from his mug, then continues. "Calla and Dash will go into the hospital and retrieve her. Dash doesn't have a Griffin Ability, so he won't set off the alarm the Guild put on her room. He'll need to sedate her so she doesn't put up a fight. Obviously not with magic, so he'll use something herbal that doesn't contain any magical elements. Then they'll use an illusion of invisibility and carry her through the building and out the main door."

"And the door that requires an ID tag?" I ask.

"They'll wait for someone to go through and then follow them before the door closes. Same with the main gate. Vi and I will be waiting for them outside, mainly as backup in case anything goes wrong. Then, since we can't get your mom through the paths, we'll need to drive to one of the natural openings between this world and that one."

"You can drive?" I ask, doubt very much evident in my voice.

"No, but one of our Guild contacts has a sister—a halfling with no magic—who's always lived in that world. She's agreed to drive us. So we'll meet her down the road from the hospital, and we've calculated it'll take about five days to get to the nearest opening."

"Five *days*? Surely you can't keep her sedated the entire time?"

"No. I assumed you'd want to travel in the car with her. When she wakes up, you can explain everything to her so she doesn't panic."

I hesitate, not wanting to have to explain what happened last night. The fact that my own mother didn't recognize me.

"I know," he says gently. "Calla told me what happened. You're worried she still won't recognize you. But we were hoping it might have been the stress of the alarm going off, and two other unfamiliar people in her room. It will hopefully be easier once she's away from the hospital."

"She ..." I swallow and push my hand through my hair. "She didn't recognize me last time either. When I went almost a year ago. I hoped last night would be different, but it was just as bad."

"Perhaps something in her medication confuses her," Calla says. "You said yourself that the medication makes her worse."

"It's just that after she moved there, she always seemed a bit ... spaced out. We played a card game the first time I visited, and her responses were so slow."

"Well, we'll take it as it comes," Ryn says. "Two of us will always be with you in the car. Not necessarily Vi or Calla or I, but two people from the team. Possibly people you haven't met yet, but they're all a hundred percent trustworthy. We'll swap out every few hours over the five days. If your mom panics, someone will be there to help you calm her down."

"And when we get to this world? Then what?"

"There's a healing institute we plan to take her to. White Cedars. It's private, has nothing to do with the Guild. We've sent people there before, and the Guild's never known anything about it. Hopefully someone there can figure out if it's possible to help your mom."

I lean forward. "Do you think there's a chance? Dash said we can't use magic on her because she's human. Was he wrong?"

"He wasn't, but our healers don't always work with magic. I don't know their methods in detail, but we may as well ask them to try. Nothing in your world has worked so far."

I nod vigorously. "Yes. I agree. Thank you."

"Sure. Shall we enjoy the pancakes now before they get too cold?"

"I've had three," Jack announces.

"Little piggy," Calla tells him.

I cut into my second pancake—and out of the blue, that tingle I'm becoming familiar with rushes up my spine, into my hair and down to my fingertips. I grasp for something harmless to say, to test this thing, and blurt out, "Pass the syrup."

There's a beat of silence, and then four hands reach out simultaneously, knocking into each other and toppling the syrup jug onto its side. Together, in a fumbling, sticky mess, the four of them slide the fallen jug across the table to rest in front of my plate.

Calla is the first to snatch her hand away. "What was that? Was that your Griffin Ability?"

"Wow, that was weird," Violet says, pulling her hand back.

"Mom, what's going on? What just happened?" Jack holds his sticky hand up in front of his face. Violet reaches for a cloth and passes it to him.

"I'm sorry," I say in a small voice. "I suddenly felt it coming on, and I wanted to test it, and I tried to think of something silly and safe. I didn't think it would make a mess."

"It's fine," Violet says. "Not a big deal."

I look at Ryn, because he's the only one who hasn't said anything yet. "You think it's a big deal, don't you."

"Not the mess," he says. "The Griffin Ability. The power to make other people do things with just a simple command. That's a big deal."

"Yeah. I know." Using my fork, I push a piece of pancake around my plate, no longer interested in eating it. I half expect Ryn to give me that clichéd line about great power and great responsibility, but he doesn't, which makes me like him a little more. "So, I should probably go to that laboratory you mentioned and hand over a sample of my magic."

"I'll take you after breakfast," Violet says. Then she briefly explains my Griffin Ability to Jack—"That's so cool!" is his response—and the atmosphere around the table slowly returns to normal after that.

"I need to finish a few things before we get going," Ryn says, standing. He clears a few items from the table and gets a cleaning spell going in the sink. "I'll be in the mountain if you need me. Otherwise, we'll meet at the base of the tree at eleven?" He glances at Violet and Calla, then at me.

"Sure," I say. It's not like my schedule is full.

"Oh, hey." Ryn stops to greet someone in the doorway. "I didn't know you were back. How'd it go?"

"Uncle Chase!" Jack shouts.

Calla pushes her chair back immediately and runs to the door. The man standing there pulls her into a hug. "Oh, you know how it is," he says to Ryn over her shoulder. "Things got a little complicated, but it all worked out in the end."

"Great. Looking forward to hearing more about it. I need to get to the mountain now, but Calla can fill you in on what's happening today." As he leaves, the man in the doorway gives Calla a quick kiss and says something in a voice too low for the rest of us to hear.

She nods, then turns around and gestures to me. "This is Emerson. Em, this is Chase." I walk a little closer as she introduces me. "Remember the girl Dash was keeping an eye on for the Guild? Her magic finally kicked in properly and it turns out she's Griffin Gifted."

"Welcome to the club," Chase says, reaching forward with a tattooed arm to shake my hand. He pauses, gripping my hand for a moment too long as his eyes dart quickly across the room before returning to me.

"What?" I pull my hand back quickly. "Please don't tell me you can read minds or something, because I'm not sure I can handle that. Having someone feel all my emotions is weird enough."

His expression relaxes into a smile. "No. Nothing to do with minds. I have a knack for controlling the weather."

"Really? That's weird."

"It's come in useful at times. What's yours?"

"I say things and then they happen."

"She told the earth to split open and it did," Calla adds.

Chase's brow rises. "Impressive. You must be at the top of the Guild's most-wanted list right now."

I nod. "Pretty much."

"Okay, we need to get to the lab," Violet says. She sweeps her hand through the air past the table, then ducks as the remaining dishes fly into the sink. "Jack, please dry the dishes when the spell's finished washing them, and make sure you're ready for school by the time I get back."

"Aah, Mom, but I wanted to introduce Em to Filigree. She hasn't met him yet."

"Em needs to come with me, and Filigree's being a grumpy old sloth right now. It isn't the best time."

With a downcast expression, Jack walks to the sink and reaches for a dish cloth. "Here, I'll help you," Calla says. "Don't be grumpy like Filigree."

As Violet and I walk out and head down the stairs, I ask, "Is there a mountain somewhere inside this dome that I've missed?"

"A mountain? No. Why would—Oh." She chuckles. "Because of what Ryn said on his way out. No, that's just what we call the building that has the rooms we meet in to plan and discuss missions and Seer visions and everything else. The lab's there too. Chase used to run things from a mountain, back when Ryn and I were still at the Guild. Then we all ended up here, and some of the people he worked with previously started calling that building the mountain. It's silly, I know, but the name stuck."

I put my hand out and run it along the tree as we descend. "Silly, but it makes an interesting story, at least." We pass a person with greenish scaled skin walking up the stairs, and Violet introduces me quickly before we continue. At the bottom of the tree, I push my hands into my back pockets. "Can I ask you something more serious?"

"Yes, of course."

It's an awkward subject, but less awkward—hopefully—than if I'd asked at the breakfast table. "Um, how do I earn my keep here?"

Her smile turns bemused. "Earn your keep? You don't have to earn your keep, Em."

"But, I mean, nothing in life is free, right? Everything costs something. So if I'm not contributing, then how does that work?"

She shakes her head. "Don't you worry about that. We have paying clients. They help us keep things running."

"Really? That's it? I don't have to pay anything?"

"Nope, not a thing," she says with a laugh. "If you decide to stay here, then we can find a way for you to contribute. If you end up leaving, then just consider this all a gift. Either way, you don't need to worry about it now."

Stay here … with Mom. Didn't I wish for that the moment I first walked into the oasis? I shove the thought aside quickly, not wanting to somehow jinx the possibility.

"Can I ask you something now?" she says.

"Yeah, okay."

"What's up with you and Dash?"

My internal defenses go up immediately. "What do you mean?"

"Well, he's been talking about you for years—this not-so-human girl he's been keeping tabs on for the Guild—but he failed to mention that you … dislike him? Hate him? Hold a grudge against him?"

"Can I tick all of the above?"

She laughs. "How interesting. Most girls seem to fall all over him trying to get his attention."

"I've noticed. And I've never understood why."

"So what unforgivable thing did he do to you?"

I look at her. "You said he's spoken about me. Didn't he tell you what happened with my mom?"

She nods. "He saved her life, didn't he?"

"Saved? More like ruined."

Surprise colors her expression. "Oh. What happened?"

"Well, it's because of him that my mother was taken away to a psychiatric hospital."

Still looking completely lost, she says, "Um … how?"

I raise my eyes to the treetops and let out a frustrated sound. "Okay. Dash obviously never gave you the whole story, so here it is."

CHAPTER 20

"I was twelve, almost thirteen," I tell her. "One of my friends had a birthday party at the park. Mom had been okay for a little while. She had episodes sometimes, but at least they all happened when she was at home. No one knew about them. Anyway, the party was going well. I was happy, Mom was interacting with people.

"Then Dash showed up out of nowhere. I'd never met him before. Didn't know who he was. And suddenly he started running toward us for no reason, launched himself right over the table, and crashed directly into Mom. I was standing near her, and he managed to knock us both down at the same time. I got up and started yelling at him. That's when Mom lost it." I wrap my arms around myself and focus on the river as we walk alongside it. "I realize now that she couldn't see him. That she thought I was yelling at nothing. Or maybe she saw something I didn't. One of the imaginary people always out to get her. Maybe that's who she thought I was yelling at, I don't know. Anyway, she ended up completely freaking out. She was cowering on the ground, sobbing and rocking, wailing about someone coming to get her and her daughter. Everyone in the park was watching her—and me. Dash had somehow vanished by then.

"Some of the other grown-ups in the park tried to help her. Tried to figure out what was going on. But she screamed at them to get away. To stop trying to hurt her. And then she started scratching at herself, trying to get something invisible off her skin. Someone must have called an ambulance, because the next thing I knew, paramedics were strapping her to a gurney—I guess to stop her from hurting herself—and carrying her away. I was allowed in the back of the ambulance with her, and that was the last time I saw my friends. I still remember the looks on their faces just before the ambulance doors slammed shut. The fear, the confusion. The whispers to one another.

"I went to live with Chelsea after that, and unlike before with the previous episodes, Mom never got better. It was like the incident in the park was the trigger that sent her off the edge completely. I don't know. Maybe it would have happened anyway because of something else, or maybe she would have stayed the same if there had been no incident that day.

"Then I saw Dash a few months later in Stanmeade. I thought it was a cruel coincidence that we ended up living in the same crummy part of the world. I had no idea, obviously, that he was there because of some magical assignment, or that he later hung around because he was keeping an eye on me. All I knew was that I hated him for ruining my life and my mother's life. It could have been so different if not for what happened in the park."

Violet touches my shoulder, and I realize we've come to a standstill beside the river. "I'm so sorry. It must have been traumatizing to see your mother like that."

I nod slowly, breathing in a long breath and exhaling all the memories. At least, that's what I'm trying to do. It doesn't seem to be working.

"But didn't Dash tell you why he was in the park that day?" she asks. "I realize he couldn't tell you as long as you didn't know anything about magic and our world, but has he told you in the past few days?"

"Something about an assignment? A group assignment, I think. He didn't give me details."

"He and some of his fellow trainees were there because a Seer had a vision of that park. A vision of several trolls running through and injuring people. Humans wouldn't have been able to see the trolls, of course, so I suppose it would have appeared as a tremor, with people falling and getting hurt. The assignment was given to a group of first years and their mentor because the Guild didn't think it was a serious threat. The trainees were meant to divert the trolls. They almost succeeded, but one got away. Dash saw it heading for your mother. If you don't remember seeing it, then perhaps it was behind you. Anyway, Dash knocked you and your mom out of the way, and his mentor chased after the rogue troll. Then you got up and confronted Dash, who was so shocked that you could actually see him that he couldn't come up with an explanation." She chuckles. "I remember him telling us about it in great detail. He said it was the most exciting assignment he'd had so far."

I take a few moments to absorb this information before responding. "So … you're saying … he actually *saved* my mom?" This is a difficult concept for my brain to wrap itself around, given that I've spent years blaming Dash for putting Mom in a mental institution.

"Yes. I mean, she would have been badly injured otherwise, or worse. Humans have been killed by trolls before. So it's a good thing he got her out of the way. What happened afterwards, though, was horrible. I'm not trying to diminish that in any way."

I shake my head slowly. "No. I know." I cross my arms, then drop them to my sides, then start pacing along the bank as confusion and frustration tangle around each other. "Why didn't he tell me this?"

"I'm not sure."

"Ugh, now I have to be *grateful* to him. How am I supposed to do that?"

"Uh … I don't know."

I stop, let out a huff, and say, "Sorry, let's keep moving. I know we're supposed to be at the lab now."

"Yeah, okay." We continue walking, and eventually Violet says, "Thanks for telling me what happened. I know it can't have been easy."

I nod. Then, since I don't seem to have left my frustration behind just yet, I blurt out, "What is it about him that makes so many females fawn all over him? I mean sure, he's good-looking, but that doesn't make up for being a gigantic asshat most of the time. And yes, I realize that he's now an asshat who saved my mom, but he's still an asshat."

A snort-laugh escapes her. "Asshat?"

"Yes."

She sighs. "If you've only ever hated him, then you've never had a chance to see the side of him everyone else sees."

"Which is?"

"He's friendly and charming, and he has a way of paying attention to people and showing an interest in their lives that makes them feel … special, I suppose. It's just part of his personality, but some girls read too much into it. They like it when a handsome guy pays attention to them—even if he's a few years younger, which, you'll soon find out, doesn't mean much when you live for centuries—and they end up wanting more than Dash ever intended to give."

"Okay, all I'm hearing is that he uses his charm to manipulate people, and then he acts like he has no idea what's going on when they want more from him."

Violet smiles and shakes her head. "I've known him since he was born, so I'm probably biased in the other direction, but I'm pretty sure he isn't manipulative. I've seen that he's respectful toward his parents, that he's honest, that he's extremely hardworking when he thinks no one's watching." She rolls her eyes. "Granted, he can be a little too full of himself at times, but on the whole, he's a good guy. He genuinely cares about people. He likes to put them at ease, make them laugh. And that's why they end up liking him and enjoying his company."

"Well, you're right that I haven't seen that side of him."

Violet directs me toward a bridge. "Perhaps you'll get a chance to see that side of him now."

I almost say, *I certainly hope not*, but I realize that sounds a little too negative. We cross over the river and head for a large building on the other side. It looks like the kind of ordinary house one would see in a nice neighborhood in the human world. We walk up the steps and onto the porch, and Violet opens the door. The first room we pass is taken up mostly by a long rectangular table and chairs, but the wide bay window and the plants spread across the windowsill give it more of a homey feel than a boardroom feel. The rest of the doors we pass are closed—I remember Jack saying something about out-of-bounds areas—until we reach the end of the passage, where the last door is ajar.

Violet pushes it open and gestures for me to walk in. My first thought is of the labs at school, but this is a far more interesting version. The counters around the edge of the room are covered in jars with colorful liquids and oddly shaped ingredients, laboratory equipment like test tubes, beakers and burners, all interspersed with scattered cogs, levers, pipes, and gadgets I don't recognize. The three parallel workbenches across the center of the room are slightly tidier, with flames, bubbling beakers, and steaming pots indicating live experiments in progress. Except they're probably not experiments, now that I think about it. They're probably … potions?

"Oh, hey there." A woman comes sliding toward us on a wheeled chair. Except it isn't a wheeled chair, I realize when she stops in front of us. The chair has no legs at all, and it's floating in midair. The woman, who has pointed ears and an interesting hairstyle of thin braids twisted around each other and piled on top of her head, stands and places her hands on her hips. "You're Emerson, right?"

"Yes. Um, I'm supposed to give you a sample of my magic?"

"Yes, for the Griffin Ability elixir."

"This is Ana, by the way," Violet adds.

"Right, yes. I'm Ana." She walks to one of the shelves and removes an empty glass sphere. "It's pretty simple," she says, returning to me. "Hold the orb in your hands, I'll recite the incantation, and by the end of it, some of your magic will have been drawn out of you and into the orb."

"Does it hurt?" I ask.

"No, but you'll feel a kind of tug. The important thing is not to resist."

I nod. "All right."

"Just relax. Seriously, this isn't a big deal. Close your eyes and chill."

I do as she suggests, blocking out the beakers and gadgets and the glass ball in my hands. The words she begins chanting are foreign, so I have no idea what she's saying. As she slowly repeats them, I begin to feel the tug she spoke about. A strange, slow pull in the region of my chest. I try not to resist. I think I might even be leaning forward a little.

"Okay, all done," Ana says.

I straighten and open my eyes. The orb is filled with the same glowing, sparkling mass that appeared in my hands when Azzy taught me how to access my magic. "Cool," I murmur.

"I should have the elixir done by tomorrow," Ana says, taking the orb from me. "So what's your Griffin Ability?"

I scoop my hair back, twist it, and pull it over my shoulder. "Sometimes, when I say something, it actually happens. Like if I told you to drop that glass ball on the floor, you'd have no choice but to do it. And if I told the river outside to dry up … well, I think it would dry up."

Ana's eyes widen. She nods slowly. "Hectic. That's a big one."

"Yeah. I discovered as much. Now I need to know how to control it so I'm not a danger to everyone. Honestly, though, I'd be happy if you guys could just get rid of it." I frown. "That isn't an option, is it?"

Ana's gaze flicks to Violet for a moment before returning to me. "It used to be, but Gaius isn't well anymore. His Griffin Ability is that he can remove and transfer others' abilities. He did it many times, for those who didn't want to be Griffin Gifted. And slowly, he started getting sick." She moves to the other side of the room and places the glass orb in a box. "He didn't connect it to his Griffin Ability until a few years ago," she continues, walking back to us. "He started realizing then that each time he removed another one, it made him sicker. He's very weak now. Doesn't often come out of his house. This lab—all the inventions and the potions—used to be his." Her eyes slide across the counters and shelves. "He taught me everything."

"And we're very grateful you stepped up," Violet says.

"Yeah, yeah. Okay, go away now. You people keep giving me too much to do." She plops back onto her chair and glides away.

"Thanks, Ana," Violet calls after her.

On the way back to the tree, we talk about what kind of lessons I need in order to learn all the ordinary magic I still know nothing about. I joke that I might not need to learn anything if I can just get my Griffin Ability right. And then I wonder, as Violet continues talking through a plan for my magical education, if there might be some truth to my joke. If I can make things happen with a simple verbal command, shouldn't that be enough?

When we get back to the base of the tree, Calla and Ryn are already waiting for us. "Ready for the rescue mission?"

CHAPTER 21

"OKAY, THIS IS FAIRLY STRAIGHTFORWARD," RYN SAYS AS THE FIVE OF US STAND hidden amongst the trees a good distance down the road from the entrance to Tranquil Hills Psychiatric Hospital. "We'll wait until Perry and his sister get here. Em, you'll stay with them. Calla and Dash will go into the hospital, and Vi and I will wait outside near the entrance. If anything goes wrong and you're followed out by guardians, we'll be ready to fight. That shouldn't happen, though, since you'll be invisible."

"Is she in her room now?" Calla asks.

Ryn produces something that looks like a small round mirror. "Yes. Still in her room."

"What's that?" I ask, leaning closer.

"I left a spider in her room yesterday," Calla says. "Not an actual spider," she adds quickly. "It's a little enchanted surveillance device. It didn't look like the guardians were going to do anything to your mom when I left yesterday, but I thought we should keep an eye on her anyway."

"The Guild probably has some of their own in there," Dash says, "in addition to that Griffin Ability detector."

"Anyway, the spider is linked to the mirror," Calla says, handing it to me so I can take a closer look. "So when the charm is on, we can see into your mom's room."

A jolt passes through me as I look down at Mom sitting on her bed, paging through a magazine. She seems so normal. So completely different from yesterday. Her head jerks up suddenly, her gaze pointing across the room at the door. It doesn't open though. She stares at it for a while, hugging the magazine to her chest. Then her lips move, saying something we can't hear, before she returns to reading the magazine.

In the awkward silence that follows, I hand the mirror back to Ryn, then turn to face Dash. "Please don't scare her."

"I won't, I promise. She won't even see me."

"How are you sedating her?"

"Calla's going to make me appear as one of the nurses, and I'll take her a drink."

"And if that doesn't work?"

He flips his hood up over his head. "Then we'll figure something else out. Don't worry, Em. Everything will be fine."

At the sound of a car slowing down on the road, I turn and peer through the trees. "Is that them?"

The car comes to a stop. Ryn holds a hand up for us to be quiet as the front passenger door opens and a tall guy with green in his hair climbs out. "Yes, that's Perry. And that must be Hannah," he adds as a woman gets out the other side of the car. We walk toward them, and Perry waves when we come into view.

The introductions are quick, then Calla says, "Right, let's get this done."

"Okay, Vi and I will be waiting near the entrance," Ryn says, raising his amber and glancing at it. He frowns.

"What is it?" Vi asks.

"Message from Azzy. The girl who tried to help Em escape, Aurora, disappeared from Chevalier House this morning. Azzy assumes she ran away."

"Not surprising," I say. "Aurora spoke about running away the night she got there. She wanted me to go with her."

"Interesting." Ryn pushes the amber into a pocket. "Anyway, we can wonder about that later. Let's get moving."

Calla and Dash disappear through one doorway, then Ryn and Vi head through another one to wait further up the road near the hospital entrance. Perry bids them a cheery farewell, then turns to me with interest. "So. You're Em."

"Yes. I am. You, uh, might have seen me when a whole bunch of guardians chased me through the Guild foyer."

"I missed that, unfortunately, but I've heard all about your magnificent Griffin Ability."

"Magnificent, huh? Well, I'd offer to give you a demonstration, but I don't really know how. This thing seems to switch on and off by itself."

"Probably best not to try it," Hannah says, placing her hands on the roof of the car and resting her chin on them. "Things could get scary."

I lean against the car and face her. "So you grew up knowing about magic, but you don't have any magic yourself?"

"Yeah. Kinda the opposite of your experience."

"I used to go visit her and show her all the spells I'd learned," Perry says.

"And I'd show him my computer and the Internet and the best shows on TV. It was fun."

We chat for a while about their respective childhoods, but nothing can distract me from the fact that time is ticking by and Calla and Dash haven't returned yet. "Do you think everything's okay?" I blurt out eventually, interrupting Perry in the middle of a description of his first time using a TV remote. "They're taking a while. I thought they'd be out by now."

"I'm sure everything's fine," he says. "And if it isn't, Vi and Ryn would have gone in to help them."

I push my hair back, then start winding some of it around and around my finger. "I hate this. Just … waiting and not knowing."

"Do you want to play a game?" Perry asks. "I'm sure we can come up with—"

"Wait. I hear something." Something like feet slapping against tar. I walk into the road and try to see further up the hill past the curve. So far, no one's come into view. I can definitely hear them, though. I clench my hands together and press them against my chin as I hold my breath, barely blinking.

Then I see them. All four of them running, Ryn and Dash easily carrying Mom between them. I take off up the hill to meet them. "Yes, glass," Calla pants when I reach them. "Or crystal, I don't know."

"But who the hell was it?" Violet asks.

"I don't know!"

"Is Mom okay?" I ask, running faster now to keep up with them.

"It was that hooded, cloaked person who showed up with the Unseelies by the cliff," Dash says. "I'm sure of it."

"She's bleeding!" I gasp, noticing the trail of blood running down Mom's arm. "Why is she bleeding?"

"She's fine," Dash says.

"She's cut!"

"She's *fine*, Em. Why aren't you in the car? Perry, Hannah," he shouts. "Get in the car."

"Who are you running from?" Perry shouts back.

"Get in the car!" four voices yell at the same time.

He tugs the driver's door open, pushes Hannah inside, then runs around to the other side.

"What the hell happened?" I ask as we reach the car.

"Someone got there before us," Calla pants. She pulls open one of the back doors. "But I think we—"

"Everybody, stop."

I whirl around. On the other side of the road, stepping out from the shadows, is a figure in a silver hooded cloak.

CHAPTER 22

"YOU HAVE SOMETHING I WANT," THE FIGURE SAYS, AND THOUGH HER FACE IS HIDDEN in shadow, the pitch of her voice tells me she's a woman. As her cloak billows around her, a memory flashes to the front of my mind: A person in a silver cloak just like this one, standing in a road in Stanmeade and turning a man into a solid crystalline statue.

"Shield," Violet whispers, and in unison, she and Calla raise their hands. Something almost invisible shimmers in the air in front of us. At once, the woman raises her hand. Glass shards, jagged and deadly, fly straight at us. Instinctively, my arm flies up to protect my face. But the glass stops, embedded in the invisible layer that hangs in the air in front of us.

I look behind us, hoping the guys have got Mom into the car by now, but their hands are in the air as well, and Mom is draped over Ryn's shoulder. Perry rushes around the car to join them, while Ryn swears under his breath. "Why isn't it working?"

I whip my head back around to see that the woman has increased her assault on us—and some of the glass shards are twisting their way through the shield. The first piece slices free on this side and flies straight for my face.

Perry's hand strikes out, diverting the glass to the side before it reaches us. In the car, Hannah is screaming.

"Be ready when the shield goes down," Violet shouts. "You know the drill."

Glass shoots past me and sinks into the metal part of the car door. Hannah's screams intensify. Then the air is filled with the screech of tires as the car reverses rapidly. The hooded woman sweeps her hand toward it, and a blizzard of broken glass flies from her fingers.

"No!" Perry yells, throwing his hand out. Not toward the woman, but toward the car. It spins out of the way, and the glass embeds itself into several trees. Frenzied revving fills the air, and then the car is speeding away.

"Attack!" Violet yells.

The woman, striding confidently toward us with her hand already raised, is tossed into the air. She spins, flies sideways, and drops onto the ground on the other side of the road. Sick with horror, I take a few hurried steps backwards to where Mom's lying on the ground. Ryn must have put her down so he could fight. I look up and see him crossing the road with Violet. Calla falls into step with them.

The woman rolls onto her side and extends her hand. Glass pieces skitter across the tar toward us. Ryn sweeps them aside with a wave of his hand, but I drop onto my knees in front of Mom, shielding her just in case. Dash hovers hesitantly at my side, and Perry hurries across the road to join the others.

The woman pushes herself up.

"Don't let her touch you," Calla says. "Do *not* let her touch you." A shimmering shield appears. On the other side, the woman lifts both hands above her head and, with an unearthly scream, releases a spray of glittering glass into the air. It shreds through the tops of the trees and rains down around her.

"Magic …"

My heart almost stops at the sound of that one quiet word. I look down. Mom's eyes are half open. She's staring across the road, but not at the woman or the falling glass or the sparkling guardian weapons now visible. She's looking at her own outstretched hand—where glowing sparks are drifting lazily around her fingers.

I pull back in fright. "What the actual freak?" I whisper. I blink several times, but the magic is still there. My heart thunders and my mind races. "You have magic. We can use the paths." I clear my voice and shout, "We can use the paths!"

Dash looks down. "No, your mom can't—"

"We can. She can." I jump to my feet, taking Mom's arm and trying to pull her up. "Open a doorway quickly."

"But she—"

"Open it!" I struggle to get Mom into a sitting position, but as soon as I let go of her, she falls back down again. She must still be partly sedated. "Help me." I call to Dash as he writes a doorway spell onto the road. A dark hole grows beside him as he reaches for Mom's other arm.

"Are you sure about this?"

"Yes, I saw her—" I cry out as a sharp pain slices across the side of my neck.

"Crud." Dash throws a look over his shoulder. "The glass is getting through again. Are you—"

"I'm fine," I say with one hand pressed against my neck. "Get Mom into the paths."

Together we pull her to the edge of the opening, and just before we fall into it, I see Dash look across the road one last time. I know he's worried about the others, but as selfish as it is, I care only about Mom right now. I lean into the darkness, tugging Mom and Dash with me.

"I don't know where we're going," I say as silence presses against my ears and Mom becomes weightless beside me.

"I've got it," Dash says, and seconds later we drop onto grass. I stumble as Mom's sudden weight drags me down, and all three of us end up on the ground. A quick glance around at the night sky above us and the unfamiliar building nearby tells me I'm in a new place. "This is the healing institute," Dash says. "White Cedars. You'll be safe here. I need to go back." He pushes himself quickly to his feet. "They might need help."

I nod, propping Mom up against my side. "Yeah. Be careful."

He lifts his stylus, but the air ripples nearby, and Violet, Ryn, Calla and Perry run onto the grass a moment later. "Oh, you're all right," Dash says, his expression brightening. "Thank goodness."

And then suddenly we're all talking over each other:

"Is your mom okay?"

"Yes, she—"

"What happened to that woman?"

"She got away. Fled the moment she saw you were gone."

"*Why the faerie paths?*" Violet asks, her eyes wide with worry. "How did you know she'd survive?"

"She has magic," I say, and finally everyone stops talking. "She woke up, and I saw it in her hand, sparking around her fingers." My lips stretch into a wide smile. "She is my mother after all."

PART III

CHAPTER 23

EVERY STARTLING REVELATION OVER THE PAST SEVERAL DAYS HAS GIVEN ME EMOTIONAL whiplash—and this one is both the worst and best. I had just begun to accept the fact that Mom wasn't my real mother, and suddenly that truth has been flipped on its head entirely. It sends my brain spinning once more. It leaves me wanting to sob with relief.

But I don't have a moment for that, because soon after we arrive on the grass outside White Cedars Healing Institute, several faeries come rushing out to help us. Mom is barely conscious, so they carry her quickly inside. Someone cleans the blood on my neck and tells me the cut will be totally healed within the hour, and then they disappear, along with Mom, into a room I'm not allowed to be in.

The rest of us end up in a waiting room that reminds me more of a spa than a hospital, with its gentle lighting, herbal scents, and plants that seem to form part of the building itself. Not that I've ever been to a spa, but I've seen movies.

"That was the same woman who appeared just before you guys rescued Em," Dash says, pacing across the wooden floor. "By the cliff, when the guardians and Unseelies were fighting. I mean, I didn't see her face, but that silver cloak looked the same, and there were glass shards flying about that day. I assumed they were part of someone's offensive magic, but it must have been this woman."

"Did you see what she did in the hospital?" Calla says. "Before we got Em's mom out?"

"Yes."

"She touched one of the nurses and he transformed instantly into a frozen glass structure. One touch, and that was it. Then she pushed him over, and he shattered into a million pieces."

Violet sucks in a quiet gasp and covers her mouth with her hand.

Perry looks up. "That's what happened at that boarding school and the village by Twiggled Horn. Those attacks I told you about."

"I know," Calla says. "That's what I thought of the moment I saw it."

"Plus several more incidents from the past few months," Perry adds. "Cases of missing fae where the only thing left behind was shattered glass. We couldn't understand what those were all about until eyewitness explained what happened in that village a few days ago."

"And then you realized those people weren't missing after all," Ryn says, his voice grim. "They *were* the shattered glass."

"Yeah."

"What's the connection between all the attacks?" Violet asks.

"It may be a coincidence," Perry says, "but the only connection so far is that most of those who've been killed either worked at the Guild in the past, or were related in some way to Guild employees, either past or present. But again, it could be a coincidence, since some of the deaths were fae unrelated to the Guild in any way."

"They could have been collateral damage," Violet says.

Perry inclines his head. "Possibly."

"So either this woman in the silver cloak is the one carrying out these attacks," Calla says, "or there's a group of fae who all dress the same and attack with the same magic."

"That can't be," Violet says with a frown. "This must be a Griffin Ability, right?"

"Must be," Ryn says. "Any faerie can transform things into glass, and our magic itself can be shaped into glass if we choose, but to transform living beings? That shouldn't be possible. At least, not by any spell I've heard of. It must be a Griffin Ability."

"I think I've seen her before," I say, finally speaking up. "The same day my magic revealed itself. The day of the party, when I accidentally used my Griffin Ability. I was heading home, and I saw a cloaked person touch a man, and he turned into crystal or glass or something."

Dash brings his endless pacing to a halt. "You didn't mention that before."

"Well, to be honest, I didn't believe my eyes. I had no idea magic existed yet. I thought I was, you know, starting to lose my mind like Mom. So ... I just ignored it. I ducked behind a building, and when I looked again, it was all gone. And so much has happened since then that I didn't remember it until now, when she appeared on the other side of the road. I didn't notice her the day the Guild and the Unseelies were fighting over me." I give Dash a pointed look. "Guess I was preoccupied with the fear that I was about to be killed."

He rolls his eyes and looks away. Perry gets to his feet. "Well, uh, I'm going to check on Hannah."

"Did she get away safely?" I ask.

"She did," Perry says, not meeting my eyes. "I went to find her while the healers were getting your mom into a room. I … I'm sorry she panicked and fled. She's never been in a situation like that before."

"It's okay," Ryn says quietly. "We don't blame her."

I chew on my lower lip, deciding not to comment. I was horrified when I watched what I thought was Mom's only safe escape route speed into the distance. But I get why Hannah did it. She was looking out for herself—a skill I've been honing for years.

After Perry leaves, Violet turns to Ryn. "I think we need to get home too. Check on Jack, make sure those other Seer visions were dealt with." She looks at me. "We'll come back a bit later and keep you company."

"I'll stay here with Em now," Calla says.

"Oh, I don't mind waiting on my own," I tell them. "Seriously. Calla, your husband just came back from … somewhere. Wouldn't you rather be with him?"

"Sure, but I can see him later."

"No, it's fine, really. I'm happy on my own, and I know you've all got stuff to do." Violet and Ryn exchange a glance. "Seriously," I repeat.

"Okay," Violet says, "but we'll be back a bit later." She leaves through the faerie paths with Ryn and Calla. I look at Dash, expecting him to leave through another faerie paths doorway, but he walks to a chair a few seats away from me and sits. He shifts his body to face mine.

"Seriously, Dash. I don't mind waiting on my own."

"How's your neck?" he asks. "It looks almost better from over here."

I'd forgotten about the cut, actually. I place my fingers gingerly against the area. There's no pain, and a raised line of skin tells me a scar has already formed. "Holy crap. It healed so quickly. I thought they were exaggerating when they said it would be better within the hour."

Dash smiles. "And you know the scar will heal too, right? That will also be gone within the hour."

"That's amazing."

"Also …" He leans forward on his knees. "I'm sorry the rescue plan for your mom turned into such a mess. The rest of us deal with that kind of magical confrontation all the time, but for you and Hannah, it must have been scary. Things could have gone badly wrong."

"But they didn't. Everything worked out in the end." I smile, which seems easier now than it's been in a long time. "I'm just so happy Mom's out of that hospital. I'm happy we're in the same world again, and that all that stuff about her not being my mom was just a nightmare."

He nods. "Yeah. Hopefully."

My smile slips a little. "What do you mean *hopefully*? She's my mother. How could she not be?"

"Well, I just mean … you look like a faerie and she doesn't, so how does that work?"

"But I didn't look like a faerie either before my magic broke out, right? You said you couldn't always see my blue hair. So obviously Mom is the same."

"Yeah …" He shakes his head. "I still don't understand why it happened that way for you. Faeries don't grow up with blocked or inaccessible magic. Halflings do, sometimes, but you're not a halfling."

"Okay, so maybe Mom and I are some strange type of faerie you've never come across before. That could be possible, right?"

He lifts one shoulder in a slow, uncertain shrug. "I guess."

"What other explanation is there? Actually, never mind. In this world, there are probably a whole host of strange, complicated explanations involving different kinds of magic. And I don't care to know any of them."

Dash looks down at his hands, then quietly says, "I'm not trying to make you upset again. And whether she's biologically related to you or not doesn't change who she is to you. I just thought you would want to know the truth about the situation, whatever it happens to be."

I lean back, pull my legs up, and wrap my arms around them. "You think I might want to know the truth? That's interesting, considering you never told me what really happened in the park that day."

A frown pulls at his features, but he doesn't look up at me. "What do you mean?"

"You know what I'm talking about." My arms tighten around my legs. "You saved my mother's life. There was something else there that day. Something I didn't see because you knocked us both out of the way. Something that might have … killed her."

Dash slowly leans back, rubbing one hand along the side of his neck. "Who told you?"

"Violet."

He nods, but says nothing.

"So? Why didn't you tell me? I realize you couldn't explain it before, but since everything happened in the past few days, you still haven't told me."

"Because … I mean … how would that conversation have gone? You would have said, 'You ruined my mother's life.' Then I would have said, 'Actually, I saved it.' And then you would have told me, 'Spending the rest of her days in a mental hospital is *not* the same as saving her life.' Then we'd probably argue some more, and you'd still hate me."

I'm quiet for a moment, because I have to admit there's a strong likelihood things would have gone that way. "Maybe. Or maybe I'd hate you less. Or … I don't know. Maybe I'd be grateful she's still alive. I *am* grateful she's still alive. There's a chance, at least, for her to get better. But you've known all this time that you actually helped her that day, and instead of letting me in on that little secret, you allowed me to blame you for landing her in hospital."

"Wait." He straightens a little. "Are you *angry* with me?"

"Yes!"

"But I thought we just established that I actually saved your mom's life."

"Yes, so now I have to be grateful to you. Which sucks because I don't like you. So the whole thing just … pisses me off!"

He stares at me another moment, then doubles over with laughter.

"Oh, fantastic. This is all just hilarious, is it?"

"You have to admit," he says between breaths, "that it is."

"I don't have to admit anything." I cross my arms, but there's a smile tugging at my lips, and I'm finding it impossibly hard to fight it. So I give in and let it stretch across my face. I think a small laugh might even escape me.

Eventually when we're quiet again and I'm staring at my hands, I lace my fingers together and slowly let out a long breath. It frustrates me that I have to be grateful to him, but that doesn't change the fact that I *am* grateful to him. "Thank you for saving her," I say, and though my voice is small, I know he hears it.

"You're welcome, Em." He looks over at me and grins. "See? We can be mature. Isn't it nice?"

My smile is back again. "I guess it isn't *completely* overrated."

He stands and pushes his hands into his pockets. "Do you want to go find something to drink? Or eat?"

"Hospital cafeteria food? No thanks."

"This isn't your world, remember? The vast selection of hot drinks available in this world is mind-blowing."

"Mind-blowing? Really?" I place my hands on the arms of the chair and push myself up. "One would think I've had enough mind-blowing experiences in the past few days, but I guess not. Let's go find a hot drink."

"Great. It's a date."

"It is most definitely not a date."

"You know what I mean," he says as we walk out of the waiting area.

"No, I know what *I* mean, and I'm making sure that you also know what I mean."

"Miss Clarke?" Just outside the waiting room, a healer stops in front of us. "Can I speak with you?"

I can't help the dread that begins to form in the pit of my stomach. "Yes. Definitely. Is my mom okay?"

"Shall we sit?" She gestures to the chairs behind us.

"Why?" Panic rises rapidly into my throat. "Do you have something bad to tell me?"

She smiles. "Not at all. It's just more comfortable."

"Oh. Right. Of course."

We return to the waiting area, and as the three of us sit, she asks, "Are you happy for us to talk in front of the gentleman, or would you prefer to speak alone with me?"

My brain stumbles over the word 'gentleman'—Dash? A gentleman? Ha!—before getting to the actual question. "Um ..."

"That's okay. I'll wait outside while you guys talk," Dash says, saving me from having to answer.

"Is she awake?" I ask the healer once Dash is gone. "Can I talk to her?"

"She isn't awake, unfortunately. She became very upset and confused after we brought her in, and we ended up having to sedate her again. We ran a few tests then, which revealed that even though we can't sense any magic in her, she is in fact a faerie. She also tested positive for a Griffin Ability."

I pull my head back in surprise. But then I tell myself that this makes complete sense. If she is indeed my mother, then obviously she has a Griffin Ability.

"This is a somewhat baffling case," the healer continues. "We haven't encountered anything quite like it before, so if you tell us everything you know about her, including the mental illness you mentioned when we brought her in earlier, then we'll do everything we can to figure out what's going on."

CHAPTER 24

Switching time zones so often is messing with my mind. I feel like it should be the middle of the night by the time I leave the healing institute with Dash—because it *is* the middle of the night there—but it's early evening when we reach the oasis. Violet and Ryn are preparing dinner while Jack sits at the kitchen table doing homework.

"She's a faerie," I announce to them as I walk in. "She's a faerie with a Griffin Ability, but they can't sense her magic, and she doesn't *look* like a faerie, and she's currently too confused and upset to explain anything to anyone, so … yeah. That's the situation."

"And the plot thickens," Dash says, rubbing his hands together.

"Dash!" I punch his arm. "This is my *life*, not some mystery novel."

"Jeez, sorry, I know." He walks into the kitchen and looks over Jack's shoulder at whatever he's working on. "It is a mystery, though. You and your mom both are."

"A mystery we're happy to help you solve," Ryn says, looking across the kitchen at me, "if you'd like our help."

"I'd definitely like to solve it. Where should we start?"

"With whatever you can remember from before she ended up at Tranquil Hills," Ryn says.

Violet leaves a wooden spoon stirring a pot and steps away from the stove. "Dinner will still be a while, so why don't we sit in the living room and start solving this puzzle?"

"Awesome," Dash says. "You guys sit. I'll get drinks. I know my way around this kitchen."

Jack gathers his books and follows Ryn, Vi and me into the next room. He spreads his work out on the floor and carries on. "Have you noticed Dash hanging out here a lot more than usual?" Ryn says to Violet.

"I have." She looks at me. "I can think of only one reason for that."

I raise an eyebrow. "I hope you're not suggesting it's because of me. Because that's the most absurd answer you could possibly have come up with."

"From where I'm sitting, it looks like the only answer."

I pull my legs up and cross them beneath me. "In the unlikely event that you happen to be right, I'm sure it's only because it's a brand new challenge for him to be around a girl who has zero romantic interest in him."

Violet laughs. "You could be right. That would definitely be a new experience for him."

"Actually," Dash says from the doorway, "I'm hanging around more than usual because I've been following Em's case for longer than anyone else, and I'm extremely curious to get to the bottom of all this mystery."

"Hey!" Violet flicks her hand. A cushion flies across the room and knocks Dash against the side of his head. "Eavesdropping is rude. I know your parents taught you that." With a laugh, he disappears back to the kitchen.

"Hey, look," Jack says. "Filigree and Bandit are playing." I follow the direction of his pointing pen and see two animals: a squirrel sitting beneath one of the side tables, and a kitten bouncing back and forth in front of it, swiping at the air with its paws, then leaping away. The squirrel blinks and remains motionless. "Well, Bandit's playing," Jack corrects. "Filigree's being a grumpy squirrel."

"Cute," I say. "Although I hope Bandit doesn't irritate Filigree too much."

"Don't worry about it," Violet says. "Filigree needs to learn to chill out a bit. He's getting too uptight in his old age."

"Okay, have we begun solving the mystery yet?" Dash asks, coming into the living room with a drink in each hand and another two floating beside him. They're all blue, and I'm certain I've never tasted whatever's inside them.

"I don't know how we're supposed to solve anything," I tell them. "I just had this conversation with the healer, and nothing useful came up. She asked me about my childhood and my father, but I don't know a thing about him except that he's supposedly been paying for Mom's hospital bills. And I can't remember anything strange from my childhood. Unless you count Mom's delusions, but those didn't have anything to do with—Well, now I wonder." I lean back and stare at the opposite wall with a frown. "Maybe they weren't delusions after all. Maybe she could see things I couldn't see because my magic was blocked. But she didn't ever look any different—

her hair, I mean—so doesn't that mean her magic was always blocked too?"

"I would think so," Violet says, absently playing with a lock of her purple hair.

"When she had these delusions," Ryn asks, "did she seem rational? As if she was speaking normally to someone who just happened to be invisible?"

I slowly shake my head. "No. She didn't seem rational to me at all. She usually ended up in a highly panicked state."

"Hmm, okay."

"Do you remember any friends of hers that we could possibly try to track down?" Dash asks. "If any of them turn out to be magical, we can question them. I mean, in case your mom is still confused for a while and can't explain things herself."

I shake my head. "Not really. There was just … well, I wouldn't classify her as a friend because she and Mom always fought whenever she came over, but I guess they must have been friends at some point."

"What was her name?"

"Um … I just remember …" I push my hand through my hair. "Line."

"Line? That's not a name."

"I know, but that's all I remember. It was a long time ago, okay. I would hear them shouting at each other through the wall, and I remember Mom saying "line" a lot."

"That's weird," Dash says.

"What did this friend look like?" Violet asks.

"I don't know. I never saw her. Mom would always say, 'My friend's coming over now. You need to go to your room.' And then she'd close me in my bedroom, and soon after that I'd hear them arguing."

"Doesn't sound like much of a friend," Dash says.

"What did they argue about?" Ryn asks.

I sigh. "I don't know. I couldn't hear much. I tried to just ignore them and play with my dolls." I twist my hair around my finger, feeling awkward beneath all these questions. "See? I told you I can't remember anything useful."

"When your mother was taken to hospital and you were sent to live with your aunt," Ryn says, "what happened to all the things in your house?"

"Uh … I don't know, actually. I think my dad must have cleared stuff out, and then a few weeks after I got to Chelsea's, some boxes arrived. Chelsea opened one or two, then closed them back up and put them away somewhere. Probably my bedroom, since that's where she likes to store stuff."

"Then that's where we start looking," Ryn says. "Do you want to go take a look tomorrow morning before you go back to White Cedars?"

"I can go with you," Dash volunteers immediately.

"Of course you can," I say, "because apparently you never have to do any work for the Guild anymore."

He shrugs. "Work is flexible. Plenty of time in the field. They'll think I'm working on one of the many other ongoing cases we have."

"Just don't blame me when you get yourself fired, okay?"

He places a hand over his heart. "Your concern is so touching, Em."

I turn to Violet. "Can you teach me that cushion throwing thing?"

"Ooh, I'll do it!" Jack sweeps his hand wildly through the air, and four different cushions soar off their seats and pummel Dash's head.

"Hey, stop, I surrender!"

"More cushions!" I cry, urging Jack on. And soon Dash is buried beneath almost every cushion in the living room. Bandit leaps on top of the pile, and even Filigree comes over to check things out. By the time we move to the kitchen for dinner, my stomach and cheeks are aching, and I realize I've laughed more in the past few hours than I have in ages.

CHAPTER 25

"It feels a lot longer than five or six days since I was here," I say to Dash as we stand in the back parking lot of Stanmeade Elementary School. "And I don't know if I'm doing this glamour thing correctly." Violet gave me a lesson last night, and another one this morning, but I'm still not really sure what I'm doing.

"Unfortunately we'll only know if it isn't working if a human looks over and sees you," Dash says, "and by then it'll be too late."

"It would have helped if you'd brought us out of the faerie paths a little closer to Chelsea's house. Like in her backyard, perhaps."

"Okay, so here's something you may not know yet, Em," he says, leaning against a car and facing me. "It takes a lot of focus to land in exactly the right spot when using the faerie paths, and the further away the destination is, the more focus in requires, so—"

"So we do this step by step. Got it. We first come to the edge of Stanmeade, then we go to Chelsea's house."

"Right."

"Oh, careful. Don't let Mrs. Pringleton see you." I pull him down between two cars as Mrs. Pringleton steps out of the back door. She raises a cigarette to her lips and lights it.

"I have a functioning glamour, remember," Dash says. "You don't need to worry about anyone seeing me." He peers around the edge of the car. "Ah, the splotchy faced teacher. I've always been afraid of her, and I never even went to school here."

"Don't be rude. It's a birthmark or something."

"Right, sorry. Can't be rude about things like that."

"Exactly." I rub my left shoulder through my T-shirt. At the sound of a faint ping, Dash reaches for his amber. "What's up?" I ask as his eyes scan the surface.

"Just another Guild-wide memo updating us on the spell that's supposed to fix the veil. Finished testing … everything looks good … still setting a date and organizing a ceremony for the actual closing of the tear." He sighs. "I don't know why they want to waste time with a ceremony. They should just send a few people out there and fix the darn thing. That hole's been in the sky almost as long as I've been alive."

"Then I suppose another few days or weeks won't make much difference."

"Yeah, but it's a waste of resources." Dash puts his amber away. "Guardians have to be there at all times, making sure people from our side don't interfere with the monument that keeps the hole from getting bigger. And on the other side, they have to make sure it's glamoured and humans don't accidentally walk into it. Anyway, is the scary teacher finished her cigarette yet?"

I peek around the car. "Nope. I don't know how many cigarettes she's planning to smoke, and I don't trust my glamour, so can we open a doorway here on the ground?" I gesture to the space between the two cars.

"Yeah, okay." Dash presses his stylus to the ground.

"Wait, can I try again?" I ask before he writes anything.

"Oh. Yeah, sure. Just don't get frustrated if it still doesn't work." He hands me his stylus while I remove a folded up note from my back pocket. "This stuff takes time to get right."

"Yeah, yeah. Everyone keeps saying that." I hold the paper in one hand and copy the letters onto the ground, speaking the other few words I've now memorized, and trying to imagine magic streaming out of my core, down my arm, and into the stylus. A thrill races through me as the words I've written begin to glow, but when they fade away, nothing happens. "Fine. You do it." I hand the stylus back to Dash.

"You almost got it," he says. "Maybe you just didn't release enough magic through the stylus. That part will become automatic soon, and then this spell will be easy."

"Yeah, whatever. Just open the doorway."

Dash writes the words, and this time, a dark gap into the faerie paths spreads across the ground. "Are you taking us inside the house now?" Dash asks before we climb into the paths. "Remember to focus on exactly the right room if you don't want to land up in front of Chelsea."

"Bedroom. Right. Chelsea will be in her salon all day, so if we stay in my room with the door locked, we should be fine. She always has music playing, so I doubt she'll hear anything."

"With the door locked, huh?" He waggles his eyebrows. "That must be against the rules."

"Idiot," I mutter with a shake of my head. "Chelsea never bothered with rules like that. I doubt she would have cared if I ever had a guy in my bedroom."

"Oh, so you've never—"

"Just get into the faerie paths."

With a snicker, he slips into the darkness, pulling me in after him. I direct all my focus on picturing the inside of my bedroom. The single bed, the desk that used to be a part of Chelsea's salon, the boxes piled up against the wall. When light touches my eyelids, I open them and see the scene I pictured. The darkness melts away as I take a step forward into the room. "Hmm," Dash says, looking around. "It's—"

"Don't."

"I was going to say cozy."

"No you weren't. Okay, these are all the boxes." I gesture to the left side of the room. "It's mostly Chelsea's stuff, but Mom's boxes must be under there somewhere. I don't remember Chelsea ever getting rid of them."

Dash walks to the desk and picks up a photo frame with a picture of Val and me sticking our tongues out at the camera. Val's metal tongue ring is visible, and I've got a heart-shaped candy sitting on my tongue—because my fear of needles meant piercings were *one* thing we would never do together.

"I really miss her," I say quietly. "And I think she's probably seriously mad at me for leaving. Hopefully I'll be able to come back soon and explain things to her. Not the magical things, obviously, but something else. Something I still need to come up with."

"Whatever you eventually tell her," Dash says, returning the frame to the desk, "I'm sure she'll forgive you. She's your best friend."

"Yeah. She's pretty awesome." I start lifting Chelsea's boxes off the top of the collection. "Although she told me she finds you attractive, so her judgement is questionable."

"Interesting." Dash's lips spread into a crooked smile. "You know, she's pretty cute too."

I roll my eyes. "What about Jewel?"

He stands beside me and begins moving boxes with magic from one side of the room onto my bed. "What about her?"

"Don't you have … you know, a thing?"

A box pauses in mid-air. "What thing?"

"Like, you guys are together or something. Or you will be soon."

"What? No, I told you before. We're just friends." The boxes continue their journey across the room. I glance at each one that passes, making sure we're still moving Chelsea's stuff. "She likes this other guy," Dash adds. "Um, Sean something-or-other. He graduated a year ahead of us. I'm sure she used to pine after him."

"She was probably doing that thing girls do where they pretend to like someone else to try and make the guy they're actually interested in jealous."

"Oh. Are you sure? Because normally girls just come out and tell me they like me."

"Of course." I sigh and fold my arms. "I forgot who I was talking to. Oh, wait, stop. I think that's one of Mom's boxes." The box that was about to add itself to my bed, the box with an orange star-shaped sticker on the side, changes direction and lands at our feet instead. "Look for other boxes that have stickers like this," I tell Dash as I move to the desk and grab a pair of scissors from a drawer. I crouch down, slice through the tape, and bend the cardboard flaps back. CDs and DVDs look up at me. Useless entertainment from the past. "Okay, this one looks boring. You can start with that." I move to the second box that just arrived at my side.

"The boring box. Thanks."

I look up. "You pushed me off a cliff."

"Ah, we're back to that, are we?"

"Never gets old."

Two boxes bump into each other, tumble out of the air, and land on Dash's foot. "Aaaaah ffffffuzzbuckling hamster balls!"

A loud snort of laughter escapes me. I slap my hand over my mouth before saying, "Are you kidding? You finally feel like swearing and you come up with fuzzbuckling hamster balls?"

"Shut up," he says through gritted teeth.

"Shh." I twist my head around and look toward the bedroom door. Somewhere beyond it, someone is talking. I jump up, move quietly to the door, and lean closer.

"… probably just something in the kitchen," Chelsea is saying. "Like the broom over there. It's always falling over."

I wait, and when I don't hear her voice again, I assume she's gone back into her salon. "All clear," I say to Dash. "Just don't drop any more boxes."

"I think I've found them all." He gestures to the small collection of boxes with colored stickers.

"Great." I sit on the floor beside my second open box, and Dash sits opposite me. "Seriously, though," I say as if the interruption never happened, "Jewel seemed really into you. Maybe you should think about it."

"Uh …" He shuffles through the CDs and DVDs before pushing the box away and pulling another one closer. "Maybe. Maybe not. We grew up together, so I know almost everything about her. We've been through good times and bad. We actually went to our graduation ball together, although just as friends." He removes some books, clothes and an old ice cream container from the second box. I look through Mom's jewelry collection. "In many ways, she probably is perfect for me," he continues. "If we were another two people, maybe we would be. But for me … I just don't think of her like that. She's more like a sister. She's always there, and she's fun to hang out with, and sometimes she's super annoying, but I still love her." He shrugs. "But like a—"

"—sister," I finish, closing the jewelry box, reaching past some old pictures of Mom and me, and moving on to a folder containing a whole bunch of pamphlets. "Right. Just don't tell Jewel that, okay? I mean, you should definitely tell her you don't feel the same way about her, but you should not use the words, 'I think of you as a sister.'"

"Why?"

"It's a cliché. She'll hate it. Just … use other words."

He nudges my knee with his shoe as a smile grows on his lips. "Look at you being all sympathetic toward someone you don't like. Some might even think you have a heart."

"Of course I have a heart, dumb-ass."

"Yeah, I know," he says quietly, returning the books and clothes to the box. "You wouldn't have hated me so much all these years if you didn't have a heart."

"I'm not sure that makes sense, but okay."

"You know, because of your mom. You hated me because you cared so much about her."

I swallow and look down at all the pamphlets on my lap. They're information and maps for a whole load of different tourist destinations around the country, which is unhelpful, so I shove them back into the folder.

"Looks like she wanted to travel," Dash says, nodding to the folder as he opens the ice cream container. "Oh, what's all this?" He holds up a tiny glass teddy bear clutching a glass heart. Then a miniature china doll and an angel made of dried grass.

"Just ornaments. Mom liked collecting pretty things."

"They're … kinda ugly."

"Well, yeah, to you and me maybe. But she obviously thought all those little things were pretty."

"To each his own, I guess. Well, her own in this case." He packs the ice cream container away. "Hey, what time is it? Vi was gonna meet us here, wasn't she?"

"Um …" I look up at the old-fashioned alarm clock beside the bed. "It's a little after nine."

"Okay. That's about ten at the oasis, I think. Her meeting should be finished soon." He pulls another box forward. "Have I mentioned how nice it is talking to you without the heat of your hatred trying to burn through me? I always wondered what it would be like. You know, just to be friends."

"It is nice, I guess. Kind of a relief, actually. It was tiring always having to be angry around you. And it's nice when you're serious sometimes instead of always joking around."

"Really? You like it when I'm serious? Isn't that … boring?"

"No, not if it's real." I look up at him. "Sometimes, Dash, the situation calls for seriousness. In that case, it really isn't helpful when you joke around."

His gaze moves away from mine, settling on all the boxes on the bed. "I know I joke a lot. But that's because life really sucks sometimes, and joking about it is better than succumbing to dark, depressing thoughts. And joking makes people—most people—laugh, so it's worth it."

"Wait. Did you just say life sucks? Because that I don't believe. Your life is a freaking cakewalk compared to mine."

He leans back on his hands. "Okay firstly, I've never heard of that comparison, but walking on a giant cake sounds amazing, so we should try that sometime. And secondly …" He pauses. "You know what I do for a living, right? I mean, it isn't the safest job in the world."

"Yeah, okay. So?"

"So people have died. People I care about."

I blink, unable to look away from those very green—and suddenly very serious—eyes. "Oh."

"Yeah." He reaches forward and digs into the box in front of him. "We all know, going in, that the life of a guardian is high-risk, but that doesn't stop it from being horrendously shocking and painful when …" He pulls out a file and places it on his lap. "Well, when a classmate or someone who's trained you for years ends up killed."

I press my hands together in my lap. "I'm really sorry."

"It happens," he says lightly. "I'm not the only one. Vi lost her mother when she was very young. Jewel's uncle was killed a few years ago." He flips the file open. "Oh, finally. This looks like something useful."

I crawl around the boxes and sit beside Dash, grateful for the distraction. He pages past old school certificates from the same school I went to before I moved here, health insurance forms, bank account information, and something related to the purchase of a car. "Who's Macy Clarke?" he asks. "I thought your mom's name was Daniela."

"Oh, she was Macy growing up, but she didn't like that name. She changed it to Daniela when I was very young. Legally changed it, I mean. So all these later documents like bank accounts say Daniela, not Macy."

"That's weird."

"I suppose. But none of these pages are useful," I add, my shoulders slumping in disappointment. "What are we hoping to find anyway?"

"I don't know. A birth certificate, or something related to a school or institution from my world, perhaps."

I notice a lump beneath the next page. I reach across Dash and turn the page quickly, but it's just another ornament that tumbles out. A flower made of pink glass or crystal. "These things are everywhere," I grumble, picking it up and dropping it into one of the boxes.

The next page is a photo of two teen girls who, I realize when I take a closer look, are Mom and Chelsea. "Oh my goodness," I whisper. "What if Chelsea and Georgia are just like Mom and me? I didn't think of that until now."

"I'd like to say no because I've never sensed the tiniest hint of magic in either of them, but I'm not sure about anything anymore." He turns to the next page: a lease agreement from fifteen years ago. "What about family?" he asks. "Grandparents? Aunts, uncles, cousins?"

"No grandparents. I think there might be some other cousins. Mom's cousins, I mean, not mine. But I've never met—" My head snaps up as I notice movement near the door. My automatic thought is that Chelsea is somehow opening my locked door, but it's the spreading darkness of a faerie paths doorway that I see. A figure with vibrant purple hair jumps out of the paths and into my bedroom.

"Finally," Aurora says with a smile. "It's about time you showed up here."

CHAPTER 26

Dash is on his feet a second later, magic crackling around his fingers. "What are you—" He jerks forward, his eyes slide shut, and he collapses on the floor beside the boxes. Behind him is an unfamiliar young man.

I scramble away until my back hits the edge of the desk before pushing myself up. "Aurora, what the hell is this?"

"We should go," she says to the other faerie. She moves toward me. I launch forward and grab hold of Dash just as something tugs my T-shirt and something else wraps around my arm.

Bright light flares and blinds me, blotting everything out in sudden, brilliant white. When the whiteness fades and I'm able to see again, I find myself in an entirely different place. A garden with flowers and hedges, but the colors are muted and the light is dim. The edges of the scene seem smudged and hazy, like a dream where only a few details are clear. Everywhere I look, I see wisps of black smoke detaching themselves from the environment and disappearing. "Where are we? How did we get here? And what did you do to Dash?"

Aurora looks down at Dash with a disapproving expression. "That's annoying. I was hoping to leave him behind."

"What did you do to him?" I demand.

"Stunner spell," the guy says. Streaks of burgundy color the waves of his black hair. "Don't worry, he'll be fine later. Why don't we sit?" He gestures to a bench behind him.

"Why don't we *sit*? No! I'm not sitting."

"Okay. We'll sit. You can remain standing if you'd prefer that." As if we're stuck inside some ludicrous theatrical work, the two of them sit in unison. "I know that was an unpleasant first impression," he says, "so perhaps we can start again. I'm Roarke. Crown Prince of the Unseelie Court." He gestures to Aurora. "I believe you've met my sister."

Crown Prince.

Unseelie Court.

Sister.

I hear the words, but my brain takes a while to process them. "U-unseelie Court?" I repeat eventually.

"Yes."

"So you …" I look at Aurora. "You're … a princess. Of the Unseelie Court."

"Yes."

I'm standing here with a prince and princess. A magical prince and princess. In a weirdly grayish scene where shadow-like smoke rises continuously from everything. If I hadn't already encountered so much strangeness in the past few days, I'd be convinced this was a dream.

"A member of our court was at that party when you split the earth open," Roarke says. "Who knows how he found his way there, but that's beside the point. He told my father what he saw, and about the words you spoke just before it happened. Dad said it must be a Griffin Ability and that we needed to get you to our court before the Guild found out about it. We didn't realize that this one—" he looks down at Dash "—was a guardian. You ended up at the Guild a whole lot faster than we anticipated. We thought we were too late, but then they sent you to Chevalier House instead."

"And that's where I came in," Aurora says. "I showed up at the Guild, gave them my made-up story, and off to Chevalier House I went."

"Why even bother with all that crap?" I ask, throwing my hands up. "Your father is a *king*. Why couldn't he just storm into Chevalier House and take me himself?"

Roarke sighs. "Emerson, don't you know anything about protective magic?"

"No, I do not. I didn't grow up here, remember?"

"My father did actually visit Chevalier House himself, but he couldn't get onto the property. And he didn't want to upset the Guild by attacking the protective enchantments. He didn't want a whole bunch of guardians descending upon us, demanding we return you. Things would have become messy. So he sent Aurora instead."

I turn my gaze to her. "Poor little Aurora. A slave for a bunch of witches. Such a traumatizing experience." I let out a bitter laugh. "And all of that was a lie."

"Not *all* of it," she says sheepishly. "My name wasn't a lie. And I do actually have a history with witches. I lived with one when I was very little—before she got tired of me and dumped me at the Unseelie Court. Then Dad decided to adopt me, so that's how I ended up a member of the Unseelie royal family." She smiles at Roarke before her gaze shifts back to me. "But the story about being a slave ... well, Dad said that was a case the Guild dealt with a few years ago. Witches with faerie slaves. It sounded like a good story to me."

"Well it didn't work. So what was your grand plan after I refused to run away with you?"

She crosses one leg neatly over the other and leans back against the bench. "I figured I'd try to get close to you. I thought maybe if you got to know me a little better, you'd trust me. I'm really not as bad as you're probably thinking right now." Her violet eyes sparkle with mirth. Faerie color seems to be the only true color in this oddly muted scene. "I knew I only had a few days to convince you, though. Once the Guild tested you for a Griffin Ability, we'd be out of time."

"I guess you didn't count on me giving away my Griffin Ability all on my own. Sorry to ruin your Plan B."

Aurora shrugs. "I improvised. Went back to the Guild and tried to get you out. Which would have worked, by the way—" she gives me a pointed look "—if you hadn't let those guardians get their hands on me."

"I hope you're not expecting me to apologize."

"No, although you could thank me for helping you escape."

I cross my arms and stare at her. If gratitude is what she wants, she'll be waiting a long time.

"Unfortunately you disappeared after the encounter at the edge of Creepy Hollow," Roarke says, continuing the story, "so we had to make another plan."

"You didn't presume me dead?"

"No, of course not. We know about the Griffin rebels. We assumed they rescued you. We also assumed you'd go back to your hometown at some point, so I've been waiting for you there."

"Well, you guys certainly worked hard to get your hands on me. I guess I should be flattered."

"You're not surprised, are you?" he asks, a crease marring his brow. "Bringing things into being simply by speaking them is an extraordinary power. I don't think anyone's ever been able to do that. Obviously we'd do anything to get you on our side."

"Terrific. Well here I am, so I guess that makes you guys the winners.

Congratulations."

Aurora gives me a puzzled look. "We *want* you Emerson. Isn't it nice to be wanted?"

"No! I don't want anyone else to want me." I screw my eyes shut, clench my fists, and reach for my magic. "You don't want me, you don't want me," I repeat over and over, hoping desperately that my Griffin Ability will kick in.

"It's not working," Aurora says, raising her voice a little to speak over me. "We still want you."

I open my eyes, but my hands remain fists. "You want to imprison me, manipulate me, force me to speak horrible, evil things into being. Does that sound about right?"

"Actually, Emerson," Roarke says as he stands. "I'd like to marry you."

An indefinite amount of time passes in silence, with only the sound of my pulse throbbing in my ears. Then I blink. "Say that again."

"I would like to marry you."

I step back, raising my hands. If my eyebrows could climb any higher, I think they'd be in my hair. "You know what? I don't generally use words like this, but I feel they're appropriate in this situation: you're crazy, Roarke. Bonkers. Loony. Completely nuts and one hundred percent unhinged. *I am not marrying you.*"

He tilts his head a fraction to the side. "No one's been able to help your mother yet, have they?"

A shiver that has nothing to do with my Griffin Ability raises the hairs on my arms. "What do you know about my mother?"

"I know her mind is sick. And I know that your friends can't help her."

"You don't know that. Maybe they can help her."

He shakes his head. "They don't know what made her the way she is."

"And you do?"

His lips stretch slowly into a smile. "I do. And I know the magic required to heal her."

"I assume you're not going to tell me."

"Not unless you marry me, no."

"I'm not marrying you!" I yell. "It's—I don't even know where to begin with how utterly insane that is. It's not happening."

"It isn't insane. It makes a lot of sense, actually. In the history of your world— the human world—royal marriages were often used to solidify alliances between countries. This is a similar concept. We would like to ally ourselves with a source of great power, so—"

"So you want to marry it. Wow. That has got to be the least romantic proposal anyone in either world has ever been presented with."

His mouth quirks in amusement. "Nobody said this was about romance, Emerson."

"I'm not marrying you! You could be, like, five hundred years old."

"I'm twenty-one."

"It's still not happening."

"Then your mother will never be healed."

I shake my head. "I don't believe you. I don't think you know what's wrong with her. You'd say anything to get me to do what you want. To get me to stay here in this creepy Unseelie Court."

Aurora speaks up. "Oh, this isn't the Unseelie Court."

"Then where are we?"

"Agree to marry me," Roarke says, "and you'll find out."

"NO!"

A quiet mumble catches my attention. I look down at Dash. His hand twitches, his leg moves a little, and he mumbles again. "That can't have been a very strong stunner spell, Roarke," Aurora says. She rises and moves to stand beside him. "We should take him back. I don't want him waking up here."

"We can take them both back," Roarke says. "I think this conversation is over. For now, at least."

I look back and forth between the two of them. "Wait. Am I missing something? You're not forcing me to go with you to … I don't know, your palace or wherever?"

"No."

"But … I don't understand. You said your father wants my Griffin Ability."

"He does," Roarke says. "And so do I. But he and I have slightly different views on how, exactly, to possess that power. He's happy to force you into doing his will. To keep you as a prisoner. I, on the other hand, would prefer it if you willingly became a member of our court. Our family."

I wonder again if this guy is genuinely insane. "Why would I ever come willingly?"

As if it's the simplest answer in the world, he says, "To save your mother."

"Come on, Roarke," Aurora says. "Let's go."

"I'd like you to keep this, Emerson," Roarke says, holding out the smallest mirror I've ever seen. It's round and would fit easily into the palm of my hand. "A simple touch of magic, and it will contact me. If you change your mind, you can let me know."

I stare at the mirror without taking it. "I won't be changing my mind."

"Well, if you won't take it …" He steps closer, grips my shoulder so I can't move away, and slips the mirror into the left front pocket of my jeans. He's so close now. So close and so damn sure of himself. He'll have no idea what's hit him when I bring my knee right up into his—

"What's going on?" Dash asks. He sits up, blinks, then jumps quickly to his feet.

"It's okay." I hurry to his side before he can attack anyone. I wouldn't mind seeing Roarke flat on the ground, but right now it's probably more important to get out of here. "These friendly people were just about to let us go," I say to Dash. "I'll explain everything when we get back."

"Roarke? Aurora?" a deep voice calls from beyond the hedge on our right.

"Dammit," Roarke mutters. "Go that way," he says to us, pointing in the other direction. "Hide."

I don't need to be told twice. I grab Dash's arm, and together we run. Past hedges and rose bushes and through the rising wisps of smoke. The garden is endless, with the same features repeating over and over and the edges of my vision remaining hazy. Eventually, Dash tugs me to a stop. Shadow-black smoke dances and curls around us. He swats at it. "You have a *lot* of explaining to do, Em," he pants. "But let's get the hell out of here first." He pats his jacket, finds his stylus, and bends down to write on the ground.

Nothing happens.

"What the fffffudge-pixie? Why isn't it working?"

"What the *what*? Okay, when we're done panicking, we're going to have a serious conversation about your extremely weird curse words."

"Em! Why can't I open the faerie paths?"

"I—I don't know. We didn't actually get here through the faerie paths. There was a bright flash, and then we arrived."

"That's very strange." Dash turns slowly, looking around. "I don't even know if we're in our world."

Something moves against one of the hedges. An unnatural shape, twisting and stretching and pulling away from the leaves. "Dash." Sick terror coalesces in my stomach. I reach for his hand and grip it tightly. "What is that?"

I hear his intake of breath the moment he sees it. "What the …" His hand tightens around mine. He pulls me closer against his side. The ghostly shape—a being so black it could be made of the darkness of the faerie paths—billows and shifts and dives toward us.

Dash's hand flies up. Bright sparks shoot away from him, heading straight for the shadow creature. Unfortunately, the magic passes right through the shifting darkness and out the other side, as if this being is made of nothing.

"Run!" We take off again, faster than before, weaving and dodging through this endless, smoke-mist garden. I throw a look over my shoulder, and the creature is high in the air, bigger and closer. Then it swoops down, becoming a twisting snake-like thing gliding over the grass in pursuit of us. "Crap oh crap oh crap," I gasp, looking forward and forcing my legs to move faster. "Wait, is that a door?" Off to the left, in the center of another hedge, I see an open arched doorway and light beyond it.

"Yes." Dash swerves toward it. "Dammit, this place makes no sense."

"I know, just run!" My feet slam the grass. My arms pump against the air. We're almost there when an icy coldness slithers over my shoulder. I jerk away as a desperate scream breaks free from my throat. We hurtle through the doorway and Dash swings his arm around, slamming the door shut with a burst of magic and bringing us to a skidding halt on a polished wooden floor.

I spin around, facing the door while backing away from it. My chest heaves as I catch my breath. My heart slams repeatedly against the inside of my ribcage. "Are you okay?" Dash pants. My hand is still clamped tightly around his, and there's no chance in hell of me letting go right now. He feels like my only anchor in this nightmarish world that could lift me up and whip me away at any moment.

"I ... I think so. Are you okay?"

"I don't know," he says. "I'm starting to wonder if I'm still unconscious and stuck in a dream."

"A nightmare is more like it." When the door remains firmly closed, I risk moving my eyes away from it. I look up, but there's nothing above us. At least, if there is a ceiling, it's so high up I can't see it. The wooden floor and the wall on either side of the arched door extend forever on both sides. I turn to look behind me—and realize there's a large opening in the air. "Dash." I point to the piece of land and the ocean beyond it. "Do you see that?"

Dash steps around me, not letting go of my hand. He leans forward, staring intently. "That's ... Holy shizmonkey. That's Velazar Island. The part with the monument. You can see the monument at the bottom edge there. Em, this ..." His eyes trace around the whole of the opening. "This is the tear in the veil."

It makes no sense to me at all that we've ended up here, but if that's our world on the other side of this hole, then ... "Can we get through it?"

"I hope so." He pulls me forward. We reach the opening, and when nothing holds us back, we keep going. One foot onto the monument. Then another. I let go of Dash's hand as he jumps down. I quickly follow him.

With two feet safely on the ground in a world of genuine color and bright, midday sun, I look out at the ocean. Vast and magnificent. Waves surging forward. More powerful and awe-inspiring than I could have imagined.

"Okay *that* makes no sense," Dash says.

I look back to see what he's talking about. On the other side of the gaping hole in the air, instead of an arched door and a polished floor, I see a field and blue sky. "But … that isn't where we just came from."

"No," Dash murmurs. "We were somewhere else entirely. Somewhere … I don't know. In between here and there?"

"Hey! What are you doing here?" A spark of magic whizzes past us. Two guardians come running out from behind the monument. I duck down and twist out of the way as Dash opens a doorway to the faerie paths. I dive into it with him, clearing my mind and trusting him to take us somewhere safe.

CHAPTER 27

"Why are we in Chelsea's backyard?" I ask the moment the darkness clears and I find myself on crunchy, half-dead grass.

"We need that last box," Dash says. "The one with the files. We might still find something useful in there. We can take it back to the oasis and *then*—" he runs a hand through his hair "—then we can try to figure out what the heck we just ran from and where we were."

"And what an Unseelie prince and princess have to do with any of it."

Dash's mouth drops open. "Did you say—"

"I did."

"Wow. So that's why she tried to help you escape from the Guild. She wanted to take you to the Unseelies. Wait, but why did they let you go so easily now?"

I sigh. "I'll explain later."

"Hey, there you guys are," a familiar voice says. Violet walks around the side of the house toward us. "I got here a few minutes ago and found a bit of a mess in the bedroom with all those boxes. I tried to find both of you, and for some reason my Griffin Ability came up with nothing, which was a little alarming. So I'm glad to see you're safe."

"You couldn't find us?" Dash asks. He looks at me. "We can add that to the list of seriously weird things about that creepy garden."

Violet stops in front of us. "What are you talking about? Where were you?"

"We can explain back at the oasis," I tell her. "We just want to get one of those boxes from inside and take it with us."

"Okay," she says slowly. Concern tightens her features, but then she breathes in, appearing to shake it off. "Em, look what I've got." She holds up a vial with a cork stopper. "Ana gave it to me this morning. Ready to start testing that Griffin Ability?"

A flare of excitement lights up inside me. "Yes. Definitely."

Dash steps away. "I'll go get the—" He stops, frowning as he looks around at the fence. Something rustles beyond it, followed by the muted sound of footsteps on grass. "Was someone watching us?" he asks. He walks past me, pulls himself up into the spindly tree in the corner of the garden, and looks over the fence. "Well, if someone was watching us, they're gone now."

"We're glamoured anyway," Violet says as Dash jumps down, "so it doesn't matter."

"You guys might be," I say, "but I'm probably not. I doubt my glamour's working. I probably look like I'm standing here talking to myself." Which, I realize, will convince anyone watching me that I've finally gone off the deep end just like everyone in Stanmeade thought I would.

"Let's get that box," Violet says. "We can go inside through the paths. I think your aunt is in the kitchen making coffee or tea or something."

"Ah, lovely, you're still here."

I whip back around at the sound of the voice. It's her, the woman in the silver cloak, hurrying out of the faerie paths and into Chelsea's backyard. The vial of elixir slips from Violet's fingers as she sweeps her hands up and around. A slight ripple in the air confirms that a shield has formed around us. "Who are you?" she asks. Beside her, Dash reaches into the air. A glittering sword appears in one hand, and a whip in the other.

The woman lowers her hood, revealing a black mask covering most of her face. All I see are her lips and eyes. "You can call me Ada," she says. "And then you can hand Em over."

"Not happening," Violet says.

Then, as if this situation needed an additional complication, the back door swings open and Chelsea comes running out. "Emerson, where the hell have you been?" she shouts. Her narrowed eyes stare only at me, which confirms my suspicion that I'm the only one here without a glamour. Then abruptly, her expression changes. Her eyes widen, watching me with a mixture of fear and confusion. As if she knows she's supposed to be afraid of me now but can't remember why. She takes a few careful steps back. Her eyes dart down to the phone in her hand as she begins tapping the screen. "Just … stay calm, okay? I don't want any trouble."

"Oh, what a waste of time," Ada says. In a few quick strides, she's in front of Chelsea. She touches her shoulder—

"No!" Violet shouts. She drops the shield.

—and Chelsea becomes a statue of glass. A bow and arrow blaze into existence in Violet's outstretched arms. Ada raises her leg and kicks Chelsea. Then she twists out of the way, the arrow zooms past her, and Chelsea strikes the ground, shattering into countless glass shards.

I gasp and push both hands into my hair. "That didn't just happen," I whisper.

The back door bangs again, and this time it's Georgia running out. "Mom!" she screams.

"Stop!" Violet yells as Ada turns to Georgia. Violet lunges forward just as Dash's whip lashes out. The whip encircles Ada's wrist and Violet leaps onto her back. The two of them tumble to the ground, but it's too late. Glass rushes up Georgia's body, solidifying her into a statue almost instantly.

"Vi, watch out!" Dash yells, running to Violet's aid. Violet rolls away from Ada and jumps to her feet. Ada swings her leg around, knocking Georgia to the ground. She shatters apart just like her mother.

I tug at my hair, swearing repeatedly, guilt and terror threatening to consume me, because I know *this is all happening because of me*. Ada dodges Violet and Dash's magic and spins around. Her fingertips graze Violet's arm before flashing out and striking Dash's hand.

"No, no, NO!" I yell, but again, it's too late. Glass consumes them, turning them to motionless, faceted statues. Ada raises her leg. "Stop! Just stop! I'll do whatever you want!"

She pauses. Lowers her foot to the ground. "You know it's too late for them, right? There's no coming back from this."

I drop onto my knees, my shaking legs no longer able to hold me up. "What do you want? My Griffin Ability? That's fine. I'll go with you. I—I don't know how to make it work, but I'll try. Just please, don't kill them."

She barks out a laugh. "I think they're dead already, Em."

"Tell me what you want from me," I beg.

Ada steps away from Violet and Dash, which leaves me almost wilting with relief. *It's hard to kill a faerie*, Violet told me. *Our magic can help us survive a great many things that would kill a human.* I can still see her and Dash. They're solid glass, but they're still there. As long as they aren't shattered into a million pieces, there's hope for them.

"You know," Ada says, facing me with her hands on her hips, "I always wondered if you might have a Griffin Ability hiding within you. And if you did, I wondered if it might ever make itself known, or if it would remain blocked forever, along with the rest of your magic." She tilts her head to the side, examining me. "You don't know how to use it though, do you. You would have stopped me already if you did."

It takes a few moments for the full meaning of her words to sink in. "You … wait. You know who I am?"

"I've known you almost as long as you've been alive, Em. That's why I was here a few days ago, checking in with someone. The someone who's been watching you for me. Imagine if I'd come a few hours later," she adds with a wicked grin. "That someone would have had a *far* more interesting update for me."

This is getting freakier by the second. "Someone's been—Who? Was it that man you killed? The one I saw you turn to glass?"

"No, no. That was just someone who followed me here. Someone who thought he could ambush and kill me." She chuckles. "It didn't take much effort to get rid of him."

I shudder at how easily she speaks about killing people. "Then who? And how do you know me? Who—*what* am I? And what the hell do you want from me?"

She gives me a pitying smile as she moves closer. "I know all this attention has probably gone to your head, so it might come as a surprise to hear that I don't actually want *you*."

"Y-you don't?"

"No. At least not yet. I want your mother."

Your mother.

A chill races across my skin. I swallow past the nausea rising up my throat. "Why? That makes no sense."

"It doesn't have to make sense to you, Em. Just tell me where she is."

I slowly shake my head. "You can't have her."

Ada crouches down in front of me. "Would you prefer to watch this town become consumed by broken glass? Would you like to watch your friends fracture and shatter and die?"

"Of course I don't want that."

"Then you simply need to tell me where your mother is. I'm not going to hurt her. Well, perhaps I should rephrase that. I'm not going to *kill* her. I'm just going to do something a little bit … irreversible."

My face is wet with all the tears I don't usually allow to fall. "I can't."

"Yes you can."

"I can't, I can't," I wail, covering my face with my hands. "How can you ask me to do this? She's my *mother*. I love her more than anything."

"Then you have left me no choice."

I lower my hands to see her leaning forward. She presses her fingers into the earth. "What are you doing?"

She doesn't answer. Where her fingers meet the earth, glass begins spreading slowly outwards. Blades of grass harden, fracture, and break apart. I jump up and back away from the encroaching splinters. Meanwhile, Ada has moved to the side of the house. She flattens her palm against the wall, and glass spreads out around her hand.

"Wait, please stop. You don't have to do this."

"You're forcing me to do this, Em. As long as you don't tell me what I want to know, this magic will keep spreading, and it will fracture everything in its path. This town will soon be nothing but shattered glass."

I look desperately around. The glass inches closer to Violet and Dash. If it reaches them, they'll shatter apart. I won't get a chance to see if they're still alive beneath their hardened glass shells. I let out a wordless cry, covering my face again. This all comes down to one impossible choice: who do I save? Mom? Or Violet, Dash and the rest of Stanmeade? "Don't make me choose," I moan. I peek through my fingers. The glass shards have almost reached Violet. They're barely a foot away from the edge of her boot.

Inching closer.

And closer.

And I can't give up my own mother, but what about *all these people who are going to die*?

"Okay stop! I'll tell you." Misery and self-loathing crack my heart open. "She's at White Cedars. Just make it stop, please!"

"White Cedars," Ada repeats. "Thank you, dear Em." She walks past me to the fence and opens a doorway to the faerie paths.

"Wait. You need to stop the glass."

"To be honest, Em, I've never liked this town. I always felt a little sorry for you having to live here."

"What? No! Are you seriously going to destroy an entire town and everyone in it?"

"I don't know. I guess we'll see how far the magic gets." She walks into the paths and looks back over her shoulder. "You can run and save yourself, or sit here and let the glass crack you apart like everyone else. It's your choice. Personally, I'd prefer it if you save yourself. I might one day have a use for you if you get that ability under control." She laughs. "And how deliciously ironic it would be if you were the one who helped me see the revenge plan through."

With a burst of anger, I launch myself after her. If I can get into the paths—if I can get to Mom before Ada does—

But the darkness closes up. The fence reappears, and I crash into it. Pain flares through my shoulder, my arm, and I slide down to the ground, groaning out loud. I clutch my shoulder while thoughts of how utterly useless I am beat against the inside of my head. I possess a power that people would kill to get their hands on, but I can't—

The vial.

The elixir that will stimulate my Griffin Ability.

I jump up, leap across the patches of glass, and search for the vial Violet dropped. It must be on the grass somewhere. And once I've taken this elixir, my ability will *stay* on, right? Then I can yell out more than one command.

The creaking, screeching sound of the house beginning to fall apart startles me. I look across at Violet. The glass has almost reached her boot. "No," I whisper. My eyes return to their desperate search of the ground as my brain plays through all the things I need to shout out.

Daniela Clarke, you are invisible. No one can find you or hurt you or kill you.

Glass, reverse your magic. Stop moving, stop shattering, stop killing.

Violet and Dash, you are not made of glass. Return to your original forms.

Finally, I spot the vial. It's near the base of the tree Dash climbed, pieces of glass just about touching it. I jump over more glass, race toward it, drop down, reach for it—but Ada's magic has touched it. Shards stab into it, splintering and crushing it, and I dare not touch it for fear that her magic will spread into me.

The elixir is gone.

A great sob rips through my chest. I stand and step back, watching the unstoppable glass magic. It's reached Violet's boot now, splintering along the front edge. I can't save her, and I can't save Mom. As more tears course down my cheeks, I squeeze my eyes shut. I open my mouth and pour all the pain from the last five years into one aching scream. I scream until I can't breathe anymore.

And then—hope.

I sense that shiver, that brief pulse of power rushing through me, and I have a split second to decide: save Mom—or save everyone here. My words come tumbling out in a desperate rush. "Glass magic, you have no power! Reverse, vanish, return everything and everyone to the way they were before and restore all—" The deep reverberation in my voice is gone by the time I reach the word 'restore,' but I think I uttered enough of the command.

I look around, holding my breath, waiting for my power to take effect.

The glass stops moving. Slowly, it sinks into the ground, leaving the lawn as it was before. Pieces of Chelsea and Georgia rush back together and, as utterly impossible as it seems, my aunt and cousin begin moving, groaning, sitting up. The broken side of the house pieces itself back together like a demolition scene in reverse. And Violet and Dash—

They gasp for air, sucking in great deep breaths of it as the glass vanishes from around their bodies. "Oh thank goodness." I rush across the yard toward them.

"What just—"

"Take me to White Cedars! Please, it's urgent. Ada went there to get Mom."

Violet turns swiftly to the wall and writes against it. "Dash, get back to the oasis. Tell Ryn and Chase what's happened. I'll take Em." I grasp her hand and rush into the darkness with her.

We're still running when we come out the other side on the lawn in front of White Cedars Healing Institute.

"I know where her room is," I say as we race past the reception area, healers shouting after us. Along the corridor, turn, another corridor. I run into her room, past a pile of glass on the floor, and tug the curtain back. "She's still here," I say, relief flooding my body. "She's here, but …" I look at the floor, at the sharp glass pieces. "But Ada was here too. Mom?" I turn back to her and shake her arm. "Mom, wake up." But she doesn't stir, and I can't help hearing Ada's voice in my head: *I'm just going to do something a little bit … irreversible.*

Healers rush in then, and we're forced to wait outside. They confirm that Mom's still alive, but that's all they say before they shut Mom's door and one of them leads us back to the waiting area. Last night, I found the gentle lighting, soft chairs and herbal scents comforting, but none of it helps today. Nothing can comfort me when I'm convinced there's something terribly wrong with Mom.

"Tell me what happened after Dash and I were turned to glass," Violet says gently. Her words remind me abruptly that just minutes ago she was essentially dead. She was a non-moving, non-breathing statue, all because she got involved with me and my mother. But instead of freaking out about it, she's now comforting *me*.

I push my guilt down and tell her everything. The glass spreading everywhere, the vial of elixir breaking, Ada forcing me to choose between Mom and everyone else. "I failed," I whisper to her when I'm done.

She wraps both arms around me and hugs me tightly, which only intensifies my guilt. "You saved a whole town full of people, Em." She pulls back and looks intently at me. "Your cousin and aunt should be—*were*—dead. Your magic saved them. That isn't a failure. That's …"

A scary kind of power, I think to myself. Out loud, I say, "But I failed my mother."

Violet, of course, tries to convince me otherwise, but I know the truth. I gave my own mother up to a magical being who wanted to hurt her in some way. After all my promises that I'd make a better life for the two of us. And that means I failed her.

Finally, one of the healers returns to the waiting area. "Is she alive?" I ask immediately, jumping to my feet.

"Yes." The healer, a petite woman with a long braid hanging over one shoulder, gestures for me to sit. "But she appears to be in a deep state of unconsciousness."

"How? Why? What happened to her?"

"We're not certain. The healer who was in the room at the time was attacked and …" She takes a deep breath. "Well, we've all read about the glass faerie in the news. And you saw what was on the floor."

I nod, realizing that this woman obviously knew the healer Ada killed. "I know. I'm sorry. But isn't there any way you can figure out what happened to her? What would put her into a coma so quickly?"

"There are several possibilities. We've tested for all of them and have ruled them all out."

"Okay, so?" I prompt. "Now what?"

"Well …" The healer looks from me to Violet and back again. "Since there isn't anything else we can do for her at the moment, we'd like to suggest that she might be more comfortable—and safer—if she stayed at home. If she ever wakes up, you can bring her back."

"*If* she ever wakes up? Did you just say *if?*"

"Thank you," Violet rushes to say before the healer can respond. "That sounds like a good idea. I think it would be safer for her to stay with us than to remain here."

The healer nods and stands. "I'll organize the paperwork."

Once she's left the room, Violet says, "Em, we will fix this. You can try using your Griffin Ability and tell her to wake up. If that doesn't work, we'll find something else. I don't know how, but we will. We'll do all the research we can, and when we eventually discover the spell that put her into a coma, we'll be able to get her out of it."

"And if her mind is still sick when she wakes up?"

"Then we'll figure that out too." Her fingers wrap around my hand and squeeze it. She smiles. "Everything will be okay in the end."

I manage to return the smile, because I've realized there is another way for Mom to be okay in the end. A backup plan. A plan Violet would never approve of …

CHAPTER 28

Several hours later, I finish tucking Mom into bed in a room of her own at the oasis. I smooth her dark hair back off her forehead, then sit in the chair beside the bed for a while, thinking of all the questions I haven't been able to ask her yet. And all the new questions that have been added to my mental list since this morning. Who is Ada, and how does she know Mom? Why did she want to put Mom into a permanent coma?

Something a little bit … irreversible.

I push the memory of Ada's words away. I don't want to accept that Mom will never wake up, but it's hard to ignore the facts: Ana prepared more elixir for me this afternoon, and it stimulated my Griffin Ability long enough to tell Mom to wake up—but she didn't respond. It seems that my magical, resonating voice, which had the power to piece two people back together and bring them to life today, somehow cannot wake my mother.

Something a little bit … irreversible.

If the healers don't know what kind of magic has put Mom into a permanent sleep, then it must be something completely different. Something more sinister. Something that those who ignore laws and play around with dark magic might know about.

And that's where the backup plan comes in.

I stand and walk to the box in the corner of the room. The box Dash went back for while I was at the healing institute with Mom. I was hopeful it might still contain something useful, but a quick look earlier through the remaining files revealed nothing.

I open the box, push my hand down past the files, and feel for the pink crystal flower I dropped in here. After finding it, I cross the room and leave it on the bedside table. It's so small it looks ridiculous sitting there on its own, but I know Mom would like the fact that it's there.

After watching her a little while longer, I kiss her cheek and leave the room, closing the door gently behind me.

"Come see, come see!" Jack grabs my hand as I head downstairs. "Merrick and Junie added more stuff inside the dome while you were gone." He tugs me all the way down to the bottom of the tree.

"Ah, there she is," Dash says as I step onto the grass. "How are you doing?"

I shrug. "Okay, I guess. You?"

"Feeling better now that I'm no longer a glass statue."

"You know," I say to him, "glass statues are far quieter and less annoying than certain people."

"Ah, come on, you would have missed me if I hadn't made it."

I allow myself a smile. "Maybe."

"Well, anyway, I think you're going to like the latest addition to the oasis."

"Don't tell her!" Jack says. "She has to see first otherwise it ruins the surprise."

The three of us walk together, the conversation remaining light as Jack tells us what he's currently learning at school. I notice Dash sneaking the occasional glance my way, probably trying to figure out if I really am okay.

"Okay, wait," Jack says. "Stop here." We're almost past the orchard, which is illuminated this evening with tiny golden glow-bugs and pink-orange light. "We should blindfold her."

I raise an eyebrow. "Did you blindfold everyone who's come to see this new addition?"

"Yes. Okay, not everyone," Jack admits. "But some people."

"How about if I just close my eyes?"

Jack tilts his head to the side. "Will you promise not to open them?"

"Yes. But you have to promise not to let me trip over anything."

"Yes, of course." He loops his arm through mine, and I close my eyes.

"No peeking," Dash says.

After another minute or so of walking, Jack brings me to a halt. I can smell and hear something that makes me suspicious, but I can't possibly be right. "Okay, you ready?" Jack says. "Open your eyes."

So I do. Goosebumps race across my skin at the sight of the pale stretch of sand and the gentle sunset-colored waves tumbling onto it.

"Isn't it awesome?" Jack says. "We have a beach!"

I blink against the sheen of moisture forming over my eyes. "It's amazing." He takes off across the sand, leaps into the shallow waves, and kicks water into the air.

Dash pushes his hands into his pockets. "Merrick was talking a few days ago about what to add next, and I remembered you looking out the window at the halfway house and asking about the ocean. So I told him it would be cool to have a beach and a little piece of the ocean here."

I bite my lip to get my silly emotions under control, then say, "Today was the first time I saw it in real life. On the island. And that was only for a moment, so it's amazing to have it right here."

"Oh. Really?" Dash faces me. "So that's why you were asking about it that day. We should go see the real thing then. I can take you right now, if you want. Just gotta make sure we aren't ambushed by anyone else who wants to get their evil talons into you."

"No," I say with a smile. "This is perfect for now."

"Hey," a voice calls behind us. Ryn walks onto the sand, followed by Violet and a floating basket. "What do you think of our little bit of the sea?"

"I love it," I tell him.

"We thought we'd have a beach picnic for dinner," Violet says, gesturing to the floating basket. It lands neatly on the sand, and the folded blanket on top rises and spreads itself out beside the basket. We sit while Violet unpacks the food and Jack continues jumping and splashing in the water. Calla and Chase join us a few minutes later, spreading their own blanket next to ours.

We eat our picnic dinner as the sun slowly disappears. At some point, Bandit and Filigree crawl out of the picnic basket in mouse form and wait patiently for some food. Well, Filigree waits patiently; Bandit does a lot of jumping around in between his waiting.

When it's almost too dark to see, floating lanterns appear all the way along the beach. Though I notice each of the adults watching me at some point throughout the evening, no one asks any questions about earlier or proposes any wild theories about Mom or the mysterious glass faerie Ada. It's as if there's an unspoken agreement that tonight isn't for rehashing the day's events. Tonight is for enjoying the beach, appreciating delicious fruits and snacks I've never tasted before, chasing Jack along the sand, and coming up with ideas for what to add next to the oasis.

I soak it all in, knowing this evening is both a first and a last for me.

"Em!" Jack drops down beside me some time after our meal. "Did I tell you about the new dance we learned this morning?"

"Um, I think you told me about everything else you learned today. I'm not sure you mentioned a dance. Do you have regular dance classes here?"

"We all learn the traditional faerie dances when we're in junior school," Dash explains. "Vi and Ryn didn't want the kids who live here to miss out, so dancing is included in the lessons."

"Can I teach you?" Jack asks me. "Then you can practice with me."

"Oh. Um, okay." Dancing isn't my thing, but I suppose I'll give it a go if it'll make Jack happy. I walk with him a few paces away from the blankets, then face him and take hold of his hands.

"Okay, so you step forward like this. Yes, with that foot first. And then you step back. And our hands come together like this."

"Okay."

"So we repeat that four times, and then we turn around each other like this."

Somewhere behind me, music begins playing. Curious to know where it's coming from, I look over my shoulder and see Ryn urging a glass ball into the air. Colorful lights inside the ball flicker in time to the music, which tells me that's where the music must be coming from. "Amazing," I murmur. "What is that?"

"Em, you're not concentrating," Jack complains.

"Right, sorry."

He demonstrates the next move for me, but I'm finding it hard to keep up. "You know, I hate to say it, Jack, but I think the kind of dancing we do in the human world—where we just sway from side to side—is a whole lot easier. See, you put your arms around my waist—" I move his arms into place "—and I put my arms around your shoulders, and we sway."

"That's super boring. And you're too tall."

"True, but I'm too tall for your dance too."

"You just need a taller partner," Dash says, moving to my side and holding his hand out toward me.

"Oh. No. Thank you. I'm not really into dancing. And … um … I was going to go to bed now anyway."

"So early?" he asks. "Come on, just until the end of the song. We can do your boring swaying thing." He gives me his charming smile, and I see a hint of the Dash all those girls fall over themselves for.

"Fine. Just don't stand on my toes."

"With boring swaying, my dear Emerson, I doubt that will be a problem."

I put my hands around his neck. His arms slide around my waist and pull me closer. I rest my chin on his shoulder, which feels a bit strange, but also kinda nice. We step slowly from side to side, a little more than just a swaying motion, but way simpler than whatever Jack was trying to teach me.

"Em," Dash says quietly. "Emmy. I'm really sorry. About your mom. But at least she's here now. And we'll find a way to heal her. We will. I've been looking out for you ever since I screwed up all those years ago, and I won't stop now. Whatever I can do to help, I'll do it. She'll get better, and you can both stay here, and the two of you will finally have the life you've always promised her."

My eyes travel across the scene, and my heart breaks as I realize that everything I've ever wanted is right here—and that I will never have it. Tears prick my eyes, my throat aches, and suddenly I can't speak. I bite my lip, harder and harder until the tears recede and I can breathe again.

When the song is over, I don't leave immediately. I sit with everyone for a while longer. I laugh at Dash's terrible jokes and smile at Jack's antics. Then I head back to the giant trees along with everyone else. I cheerfully say goodnight and climb up to my room as if nothing is different. As if my chest isn't aching. As if I haven't just said goodbye.

CHAPTER 29

I open the wardrobe, and instead of reaching for pajamas, I pull out the warmest jacket I can find. I don't know how cold it is where I'm going, so it's best to be prepared. "Sorry, Bandit," I say to the wolf cub sleeping on the chair in the corner, "but you won't be coming with me this time. It's safer for you to stay here."

I remove my T-shirt and grab a clean one off the top of the pile—just as I hear footsteps outside my door. "Hey, Em." It's Calla's voice. The door clicks open. "I wanted to ask you if—Oh, I'm sorry."

"No, it's fine," I say with a nervous laugh, turning away as I fumble with the T-shirt.

"I'm sorry, I should have knocked."

"No, no. It's my fault for getting changed without closing the door properly. I didn't think." I pull the T-shirt over my head before turning to face her. But instead of a smile, I find her staring at me, her face devoid of color. "What's wrong? Are you okay?" She can't possibly know what I'm about to do, can she?

"I …" Her hand grasps the doorframe, and she grips it tightly, as if it's the only thing keeping her upright.

"Calla?" I take an uncertain step toward her.

She closes her eyes, shakes her head, and lets out a faint laugh. "I'm sorry." She opens her eyes, blinks, and gives me a half-smile. "I must have had more to drink than I thought. Just a dizzy moment. That's all."

"Um, okay."

"Anyway." She clears her throat. "I just, uh, came up here to ask you if you want to go running around the edge of the oasis with us early in the morning."

"Oh. Actually, I think I'd rather sleep in tomorrow. It's been, you know … quite a day."

She nods, still looking at me a little oddly. "Yeah. Definitely."

"Um, okay. Well, goodnight."

"Night. Hey, Em?" I look up. "That's a pretty tattoo on your shoulder. I didn't notice it before."

"Oh, it isn't a tattoo. Needles freak me out." I reach up and touch my left shoulder. "It's actually a birthmark. My clothes usually cover it, so that's probably why you haven't seen it before."

She nods, gripping the door again, and I start to wonder if whatever she's drunk tonight might have had its origin in the human realm. "How interesting," she says faintly. "It looks just like a flower."

"Yes, it does." I frown. "Are you sure you're okay?"

"Definitely." She smiles. "Sleep tight, okay?"

I nod, feeling guilty for lying to her. "You too."

She closes the door. Bandit, watching curiously from the chair, lowers his head and watches me through half-closed eyes. Once I'm sure Calla's gone, I slip my hand into my left front pocket and take out the mirror.

I feel bad for stealing a stylus from Ryn and Vi's kitchen, but I don't have much of a choice since I don't have my own. I don't pass anyone on my way down the stairs, or when I'm walking across the grass. It's almost too easy to slip through the dome layer and into the desert.

I write the faerie paths spell into the sand several times without it working. I don't lose my patience, though. Seeing the words glow this morning gave me confidence that I'm almost there with this faerie paths thing. I try yet again—and excitement races through me at the sight of a dark space opening up. I slide into it, whispering the name I was given.

I'm greeted on the other side by the scene I was told to expect: a natural rock pool in a forest clearing with beams of afternoon light shining through the nearby trees.

"Emerson," a voice says from behind me. "I was a little surprised to hear back from you so soon. You seemed adamant you wouldn't be changing your mind."

I turn to face Roarke. "Circumstances change. I've decided I might be willing to believe that you can help my mother."

He folds his arms across his chest. "Interesting."

"There's just one thing. I'm going to require proof before I accept your proposal. Proof that you know what's wrong with my mother and can fix her."

"That might be difficult," he says, "considering I won't be telling you anything until after we're married."

"But she needs help now. I'll … sign a contract or something. A contract saying that I agree to marry you if you can first heal her."

"A contract?" He laughs. "The kind of contract you're referring to doesn't mean much in this world. What if I heal your mother, and then you decide not to follow through?"

"What if I marry you and then you decide not to heal my mother?"

A hint of amusement touches his lips. "I suppose one of us is going to have to learn to trust the other."

"Well then. I look forward to earning your trust." Because I certainly don't plan to marry this Unseelie Prince without first seeing my mother healthy. "Did you bring the magical device you spoke about?"

"Yes." Roarke reaches inside his long coat and produces a small coin-shaped item. He steps closer and brushes aside the hair behind my ear. It's unsettling having him stand so close, but I pretend it doesn't bother me. He presses the coin to the skin behind my ear, and when he pulls his hand away, the coin remains. I raise my fingers and gently touch it, making sure it doesn't move. "You're certain no one will be able to find me while I'm wearing this? I don't want anyone … interfering with our arrangement."

"Completely certain. The Unseelie Court has been making use of items like this for a very long time."

I let out a slow breath. "Okay then. I guess I'm ready to go with you."

SHADOW FAERIE

PART I

PROLOGUE
DASH

Dash had been at his desk at the Creepy Hollow Guild for less than ten minutes when his amber, sitting beside the goblin abduction report he was working on, shivered and emitted a chirp. Glowing gold words rose to the surface of the rectangular device. Recognizing Violet's handwriting, Dash quickly pulled the amber closer. His eyes darted up to check who might have been standing close enough to his desk to have seen the message. The open office area was filled with the bustle of morning activity: a junior guardian team returning from a night mission; two trainees delivering scrolls; and his own teammate, Jewel, hard at work on something. It was highly unlikely any of these people would know who the message on Dash's amber was from, but it still made him nervous corresponding with Griffin rebels while beneath the Guild's own roof.

He leaned back in his chair, schooling his expression into one of nonchalance, and read the message: *Do you know where Em is? I can't find her.* Ice chilled Dash's veins as he struggled to keep his expression neutral. If Vi couldn't find someone, that meant serious trouble. Thanks to her Griffin Ability, she should be able to find anyone who wasn't concealed by some form of magic. Em's Griffin Ability, however, was a whole new story. Was she playing around with it? Testing whether she could hide herself? Dash reached across his desk, grabbed his stylus, and wrote a quick response on his amber. *No. Are you sure she left? Check orbs.*

Vi's reply came seconds later: *Checking now.*

I'm on my way over, Dash scribbled as he pushed away from his desk and stood.

"Leaving already?" Jewel asked. Dash looked up as she stood and walked around her desk. "You only just got here."

"I need to check on something. One of the witness reports from the goblin abduction case. A few details are missing." Dash cringed internally, hating having to lie to one of his best friends. "I'll get one of the guards downstairs to open a doorway for me," he added quickly. Like Jewel, he wasn't supposed to be able to open doorways to the faerie paths anymore. An annoyance Em's Griffin Ability was responsible for. Em had since reversed the magic's effect on Dash, but Jewel didn't know that. The only thing Jewel knew was that Em had escaped the Guild's clutches and disappeared.

"Do you need me to go with you?" Jewel asked.

"No, don't worry. It'll be quick." He gave her a smile, which he suspected looking nothing like his usual easygoing grin.

"Okay. Hey, is everything all right?" Jewel caught his arm before he could turn away. "You're not normally so serious first thing in the morning." Her hand lingered a moment too long on his arm, and the conversation he'd had with Em came to mind. She'd pointed out that Jewel clearly wanted to be more than just his friend, a fact Dash had somehow been oblivious to until this moment. How had he missed it? And why had Jewel never said anything to him about her feelings for him? She must have exceptional control over them. He hadn't noticed any random magical outbursts.

Not important right now, Dash reminded himself. "Yes, everything's fine. I'm just … more tired than usual." That, at least, was the truth. He'd been up late the night before talking with Chase, discussing when to return to Tranquil Hills Psychiatric Hospital to examine whatever records were on file for Em's mother. With unknown magic preventing her from waking up, she wasn't in a position to explain why she and her daughter had lived for so long in the non-magic world, masquerading as human. Hopefully Em's father could provide some answers instead. Em said she knew nothing about him, but if he was the one who'd been paying Daniela Clarke's medical bills, the hospital must surely have his name and contact details.

"Okay. See you later then." Jewel returned to her chair.

Dash should have left then—he *wanted* to leave—but he couldn't ignore Jewel's desire to be more than friends now that he knew about it. "Hey, do you want to hang out this evening?" he asked before he could change his mind. "We should … talk." It would no doubt turn into the most awkward conversation they'd ever had, but he needed to do it. It wasn't fair of him to allow Jewel to continue hoping for something that would never happen.

"Yeah, okay. Great."

"Cool." Dash hurried down the Guild's main staircase, across the foyer, and into the room with bare walls used for accessing the faerie paths. "Do you mind opening a doorway for me?" he asked the woman standing guard just inside the door.

"Still haven't found that Griffin Gifted girl, huh?"

"Nope."

"I hope you do," the woman replied as she walked to the wall and raised her stylus. "I heard she's a dangerous one."

"Yeah," Dash muttered. "Extremely dangerous. I plan to find her."

The woman stepped back as part of the wall pulled away to reveal the darkness of the faerie paths beyond. Dash walked forward. Once the light had vanished behind him, he focused his thoughts on the oasis hidden in the middle of a desert thousands of miles away.

Minutes later, he hurried up the porch steps of the little white house on one side of the oasis, past a few closed doors, and into the surveillance room. A row of glass orbs lined three of the four walls, and within each orb was a miniature form of a different part of the oasis. Magic connected each orb to the enchanted bugs that flew around outside, displaying everything the bugs saw. Vi was bent over, staring intently into one of the orbs, while Calla and Chase sat in front of another one. "What can you see?" Dash asked, not bothering with a greeting.

"Oh, Dash, hey," Vi said as she turned to face him. "The orbs show that Em left during the night. Just beyond the dome layer, she opened a doorway to the paths and went through it."

"She must have taken someone's stylus."

"Yes. There was one missing from our kitchen this morning."

"I just don't understand," Calla said, her finger swiping repeatedly across the orb in front of her as she moved backwards in time through the scenes it displayed. "Why would she leave?"

Vi shook her head as she shrugged. "Any number of reasons, I suppose. Maybe she wanted to see one of her old friends. Or maybe she remembered something that could help her mother. What's far more worrying is the fact that I can't find her. What could possibly be shielding her?"

"Nothing good," Chase muttered.

"Dash, you never told me what happened when I couldn't find you and Em yesterday," Vi continued. "Remember, when I came to meet the two of you at her aunt's house?"

"Oh yes." Dash cursed inwardly—with the kind of words his mother wouldn't approve of—at having forgotten, yet again, to mention that strange place and the people who had taken him and Em there. "I don't know where we were, but it was weird. Everything seemed drained of color, and parts of it were sort of … smudged. Unclear or unformed. And we couldn't access the faerie paths. We ended up running from some shadowy creature I've never seen before, and somehow we found ourselves near the tear in the veil. But not on the human side, and not on the fae side. Somewhere … I don't know. Maybe it wasn't even real. Maybe it was some kind of hallucination. Anyway," he continued with a deep breath, "we were there because of the Unseelies. The prince and princess."

"Seriously?" Chase looked away from the orb he'd been examining.

"Yes. That girl who was at Chevalier House for a few days—Aurora—is actually the Unseelie princess."

"So that's what she was doing at Chevalier House," a new voice said from the doorway. Dash looked around and saw Ryn standing there. "Aurora wanted Em to run away with her. She was obviously planning to take Em back to the Unseelie Court."

"You didn't think to mention any of this last night?" Calla said to Dash, an accusatory edge to her voice.

"To be honest, I didn't think of it at all. Em said she was going to tell me what happened later—since I was, uh, stunned and unconscious for part of the time—but then that glass faerie showed up, and we almost died, and then we raced off to get Em's mom, and … I didn't think of the Unseelies again until late last night when I got home."

"Great, so we have no idea what they told Em," Calla said, crossing her arms and frowning at the floor.

Dash said nothing. It was unlike Calla to be so ticked off at him, but he couldn't blame her. He was furious with himself for not asking Em about that strange shadowy world last night. She'd seemed distant and unhappy, and, like an idiot, he'd tried to distract her with dancing. What the hell was wrong with him? How could he just *forget* that two members of the Unseelie royal family had transported Em to a strange place and then mysteriously let her go?

"So …" Vi rubbed her temples. "The fact that we can't find Em now might have something to do with the Unseelies."

"Unless she herself doesn't want to be found," Chase said. "She left voluntarily. She might have used her Griffin Ability to shield herself somehow."

"Whatever her reason for leaving, she must be planning to come back," Ryn said, walking into the room and taking a closer look at one of the orbs. "Her mother is still here, after all."

Dash shook his head. "She may have left of her own accord, but what if the Unseelies got hold of her once she was out there? They let her go yesterday, but they definitely still want her. They might be holding her against her will now."

"So what do we do?" Vi asked. "Wait to see if she comes back? And if so, how long do we wait?"

"She has to come back," Calla murmured, chewing on her thumbnail as she stared unseeingly at the floor. "She has to."

Ryn looked across the room. "What's wrong?"

Calla lowered her hand and frowned at her brother. "Don't do that."

"Hey, I'm not *trying* to feel what you're feeling," Ryn said, holding his hands up in defense, "but your anxiety is just about giving me a panic attack. I've been trying to ignore it but it's practically assaulting me."

"Anxiety?" Chase moved closer to her. "About what?"

"Jeez, people," Calla exclaimed. "I'm just preoccupied with another case. Everything's fine. Can we focus on how we're going to figure out where Em is? Just in case she *is* someone's prisoner now?"

"I have some Unseelie contacts," Chase said. "I'll see what I can find out."

"Good. I'm getting back to work on other stuff then," Calla said. She crossed the room and left without a word, leaving several moments of awkward silence in her wake. With a frown, Chase followed her.

Dash cleared his throat. "The Guild also has Unseelie contacts. I'll ask if anyone knows anything. And I'll question our Seelie contacts as well. It's possible they found Em but haven't informed the Guild yet."

"Thanks," Vi said.

"Let us know as soon as you discover anything," Ryn added.

"Of course." Dash turned and strode out of the room, already reaching into his pocket for his amber and stylus so he could contact the Guild's Unseelie liaison. He paused near the front door as he wrote a quick message enquiring whether the liaison had received any news regarding a Griffin Gifted girl.

"… something going on?"

At the sound of voices, Dash leaned to the side and peered out the window. Calla paced back and forth across the porch. "She has to come back, Chase. She has to."

"Okay, seriously." Chase caught her arm and pulled her to a halt. "Tell me what's going on."

Dash knew he shouldn't be eavesdropping, but if it was something about Em ...

Calla took a deep breath. "I saw something. Last night. When I went up to ask Em if she wanted to join us this morning. It made me hope that maybe ... somehow ..." She shook her head. "I mean, I know it's crazy to even think it. My brain is still playing through everything that happened back then and how it could even be possible. But if it's true ..." She grabbed the front of Chase's T-shirt in both fists. "Chase, if it's true, then we *have* to make sure Em comes back."

Chase took Calla's hands in both of his. "You're not making any sense. What did you see?"

"You can't tell anyone, okay? Not until I know if it's true. I don't want to be responsible for any more broken hearts."

"Broken hearts? When did you—"

She leaned closer to Chase and whispered, her words too quiet now for Dash to hear through the window. He watched as Chase's brow furrowed further. "Not possible," he said as Calla stepped back. "Or ... is it? When I first saw her, I thought ..."

"Thought what?"

Chase's gaze became unfocused as he stared over Calla's shoulder for several moments, clearly lost in thought. A small smile stretched his lips as he returned his attention to her. "I think you could be right."

Her answering smile lit up her face. "I think so too. But I don't know for certain, and I refuse to get excited until we confirm this. I know someone who can tell us beyond a doubt, but I don't know where he is. You need to help me find him."

"Vi can help if she has ..." Chase's words trailed off as he shook his head. "But you don't want her to know."

"No. Not yet." Calla took his arm and pulled him down the stairs with her. "We first need to find out if it's true." Her voice grew fainter as she and Chase headed away from the house, leaving Dash with more questions and no answers. He had his own mystery to solve, though. *Where are you, Em?* he wondered silently as he opened the door and stepped onto the porch.

His amber shivered in his hand, and he stopped to read the Unseelie liaison's reply: *No recent info from the Unseelies. Nothing interesting anyway.* Of course not. The Unseelies would never *choose* to inform the Guild if they happened to be in possession of a powerful Griffin Gifted girl. But Dash had to check, just in case the liaison had heard something. Now he'd have to contact the Seelie liaison. After that, it would be time to move on to unofficial channels. "Somehow, Em," he muttered as he strode away. "Somehow, I'll find you."

CHAPTER 1

Things I never imagined: One, escaping the miserable town of Stanmeade long before I ever dreamed it possible. Two, becoming almost-friends with the guy I hated for years. Three, climbing the outside of a faerie palace tower with a stolen stylus in my pocket so I can hide at the top and open a faerie paths doorway with magic. Oh yeah. And I never imagined using words like 'palace tower,' 'faerie paths' and 'magic' without sounding like an inpatient at a mental institution. But that was before I discovered I'm a faerie, and that a hidden world of magic exists alongside the one I grew up in. That was before I landed at the top of everyone's most-wanted list for possessing a unique and dangerous faerie superpower. And that was before I took the biggest risk of my life and agreed to marry a faerie prince of the Unseelie Court in the hope of saving my mother.

So yes. I imagine things now that most people from my old life would consider impossible. Like a dark hole of nothingness materializing across the gold-veined marble walls at the top of the tower I've climbed. I needed to get away from the watchful eyes of the palace guards, and this turret forming the highest point of the Unseelie Palace seemed like a good spot. Unfortunately, the spell I've been whispering and the words I've written repeatedly across the wall seem to be producing nothing.

I heave a frustrated sigh and clench my fingers around the jewel-encrusted stylus. I stole it from Aurora's room yesterday. Only the best of the best for a princess, so I doubt there's anything wrong with it. Which means … perhaps my magic is the problem? I place the stylus on the turret floor and cup my hands together, then breathe out slowly and feel for the core of power within me. Almost instantly, a roughly spherical shape of white glitter and wispy fragments hover above my hand. It seems almost easy to produce magic now, after having practiced so much in the past few days. No need to squeeze my eyes shut, furrow my brow, and imagine dragging the magic out of myself like a mouse tugging on a truck.

So if my magic and the stylus aren't the problem, and the spell itself is correct—which I'm certain it is, given I used it to leave the oasis—that leaves only one answer: the faerie paths are not accessible from this tower.

"Dammit," I whisper. I shove the stylus back into my pocket and stare out across the endless lands of perfect summer. Brilliant green lawns, flowers in every color, enchanted water features surrounded by shrubs clipped into ornamental shapes, and various areas for entertaining: a pergola here, a gazebo there, the queen's bower off to the right beyond that little bridge. And just beyond the palace grounds, the turrets of manor houses belonging to Unseelie nobles rise above the trees.

And almost none of it, according to Aurora, accessible via the faerie paths. No one leaves this palace and no one arrives except through the main entrance. "It's not as though you *need* to go anywhere else now," she told me when I asked about the faerie paths. "Just relax and enjoy your brand new palace life."

Relax? I don't think so. If *almost* no part of this palace and its grounds can be accessed by the faerie paths, that means there must be some areas where doorways can be opened. And if I'm hoping to escape once I've learned everything I need to know from Prince Roarke, then I have to find at least one of those areas. If I can't, I'm going to have to get creative with my Griffin Ability. And that will require figuring out how to actually use it.

"My lady?"

My body tenses at the sound of the unexpected voice. I whip around, my heart already thrashing in my chest. But it's only Clarina, the handmaid Aurora 'gifted' to me upon my arrival. She stands beside the ruby-studded gold trapdoor. The *open* trapdoor I'm certain was locked until now because I found my way to the other side of it yesterday afternoon and couldn't get through it. I wouldn't have bothered opening one of the lower windows and scaling the wall otherwise. I clear my throat and clasp my hands together. "Um, yes?"

"Her Highness, Princess Aurora, sent me to fetch you," Clarina says, her eyes fixed on the floor near my feet. I've told her not to worry about averting her gaze when speaking to me, but it's made no difference. Just like when I told her I'm no 'lady' and she doesn't have to refer to me as such. "But how else will I show you respect, my lady?" she asked. "I can't simply call you by your name." I told her that of course she could, but that didn't go down well either.

"How did she know I was up here?" I ask.

"One of her guards saw you from a window."

I wipe my hands on my jeans. "Did, uh, did it sound to you like Aurora—Miss—Her Highness—" Darn these stupid titles. "Did it sound like she was angry with me for being up here?"

"No, my lady," Clarina says. "She was concerned, but not angry. She reminded her guards that you're welcome to explore your new home, but that they're also supposed to keep you alive."

"Right. Cool. That's what I thought. I mean, about the exploring part." Aurora gave me a brief tour when I arrived three days ago, then told me I could go pretty much wherever I wanted, other than people's private suites or chambers or whatever she called them. Since then, I've wandered all over the palace under the guise of curiosity, doing my best to pretend I'm at ease in a home as vast and opulent as this palace. I attempt to ignore the guards who watch me and the court members who smile politely before whispering to one another. And I try not to shiver when the atmosphere shifts, as it does occasionally, into something cold and unsettling.

"Uh, well, I guess we'd better go then," I say, realizing that Clarina is waiting for me to speak. She nods and steps onto the staircase below the trapdoor. I follow her down, flinching when the trapdoor bangs shut of its own accord behind me. Together we descend the spiral staircase all the way to the ground floor of the palace and into a vast column-lined hallway. Its black marble floors are polished to a glassy shine and the precious stones embedded in the ceiling reflect the enchanted lamps burning on pedestals between each column. The rest of the palace is much like this: gleaming black edges, gold embellishments, and glittering gems. Rooms large enough to get lost in, and furnishings so lavish I'd probably vomit if I knew what they cost.

It's impossible to imagine ever being at home here.

We climb more stairs, cross more hallways, and pass more fae dressed like they belong on the set of a period drama. They all give me curious glances as I pass. Unlike Clarina and Noraya—Aurora's other handmaid—none of these people know who I am. They have no idea I've agreed to marry their prince. How could they possibly suspect that he and I have anything to do with each other when Roarke's been gone since the moment he dumped me here in his sister's care? Aurora said he'd return this morning, but I've seen nothing of him. I'm starting to wonder if he's planning to avoid me until the day of our wedding—whenever that may be.

Finally, Clarina and I reach the wing housing the royal family's quarters. I've never been far enough into it to see the rooms belonging to the king and queen themselves, but I've passed Roarke's suite, and I've been into Aurora's every day since

I arrived here. I look over my shoulder at the door leading into Roarke's rooms as I pass. The door is closed and no guards stand outside it, which I take to mean that Roarke isn't inside.

"Darn," I mutter, quietly enough that Clarina won't hear me. A frown pulls at my brow as I face forward again. And then that strange feeling of unease, that inexplicable sense of *wrongness*, pervades my senses. As if cold, rotting fingers are about to reach from the shadows to clamp around the back of my neck. A flicker of a shadow scurries across the edge of my vision, but when I look over my shoulder again, it's gone. And so is that sense of discomfort.

"Lady Emerson?" Clarina says. I look ahead and see her waiting with one hand resting against Aurora's door. "Is everything all right?"

"Um, yes. I'm fine." Perhaps I keep imagining that odd feeling. Perhaps that's what homesickness feels like. Maybe, as unlikely as it seems, I'm actually missing the rundown home I lived in with Chelsea and Georgia. *No way*, I think to myself, almost laughing out loud at the farfetched thought. I may miss my best friend Val, and all the fun we had together, and the freeing feeling of not being hunted down by various members of the fae realm, but I certainly don't miss that horrible little house and my spiteful aunt and cousin.

Clarina opens the door to Aurora's suite and stands aside to let me walk in. She bobs into a quick curtsey as I pass, then closes the door behind me. I hear her feet tap away across the polished marble floor outside. On the other side of the sitting room, which is decorated in muted tones and floral fabrics, Princess Aurora, adopted daughter of the Unseelie King and Queen, sits at a small round table. Laid out in front of her is a variety of food, a teapot and two teacups. She leans back in her chair and surveys me. "Really, Em? Climbing the outside of the east tower? Are you *trying* to scandalize the entire court? If you wanted to see the view from the top so badly, you could have just asked someone to unlock the trapdoor instead of risking your life."

I cross the room and stop beside the chair on the opposite side of the table from her. "Well, you know. It was earlyish. I didn't want to bother anyone. And besides, there was hardly any risk involved. I can handle a simple wall. Those great big marble bricks have gaps between them that are perfect for hand- and footholds."

Aurora tucks her hair—black and blueish purple—behind one ear and reaches forward for her teacup. "And if you'd slipped? Aside from the enormous trouble I'd be in with Roarke and my father if you fell and got yourself killed, it just isn't appropriate to go around climbing walls." She gives me a pointed look over the top of her teacup. "You know, given your future position in this palace."

I choose to ignore her reference to the fact that I'm supposed to be a princess soon and cross my arms over my chest. I begin pacing to and from the window. "Where's Roarke? You said he'd be back by now, but I didn't see anyone standing guard outside his rooms, so I assume he isn't in there."

"He and Dad must have been delayed, that's all. They have important business to deal with at the moment. You can't expect them to rush back simply because you're desperate to see your betrothed." She smirks. I stick my tongue out at her. She throws a strawberry at me, then laughs when I dodge and continue walking. "They'll be back soon, I'm sure. And please stop pacing. You're making me nervous." She waves to the chair opposite hers. "Sit down. Have you had breakfast yet?"

"No." I drop into the chair with my arms still crossed. "I was too busy taking risks and climbing walls, remember?"

"You should choose breakfast next time." With a neat twist of her hand, a plate of butterfly-shaped pastries rises on its own and moves toward me. She'd no doubt be pleased if I used magic to lift one of the pastries and move it to my own plate, but that kind of thing seems like laziness to me. And I don't think I could do it without knocking the whole plate over.

"You know why I want to see Roarke," I say to her after placing a pastry on my plate—with my own perfectly functional hand. "He and I have an agreement, and he's done nothing to fulfill his part yet." Agreement. Such a simple word. It doesn't carry nearly as much weight as the word 'marriage.'

"Of course he hasn't fulfilled his part yet. I hope you know he doesn't plan to give you any information on how to get your mother out of her enchanted coma or fix her mental illness until *after* the union ceremony."

"Yes," I say quietly, still staring at my plate. "I do know that." What I also know is that I don't intend for that ceremony to ever happen. Everyone needs to *think* it will happen, but I plan to find out everything I need to know before the marriage takes place. Of course, I have no idea how I'm going to do that yet, but being in possession of a powerful Griffin Ability—speaking things into existence—can't hurt. If I can use it at just the right moment in just the right way, I should be able to get out of here alive with all the information I need. I clear my throat and add, "I know, but he needs to prove himself to me. He needs to tell me *something* so I'll know he isn't just lying to get me to marry him."

"My dear brother would never do something like that," Aurora says, directing a few more items of food onto her plate.

I don't know her well enough yet to know if she's joking or if she really believes that. Either way, I'm not willing to trust Roarke. I need my own plan, and that involves gaining control of my Griffin Ability. I break off a piece of pastry and stare at it for a moment or two before saying, "Since climbing tower walls isn't appropriate, perhaps my time would be better spent practicing my Griffin Ability. With the elixir, I mean, not just waiting for the random moments when my magic chooses to switch itself on."

She shakes her head and finishes swallowing another mouthful of her tea. "I'm sorry, Em, but I was told not to give it to you until Roarke and my father return. Here, have some citrullamyn." Several segments of a fruit that looks like a blood-red version of an orange fly in an arc from her plate onto my mine.

"Uh, thanks." I slowly chew one while trying to figure out what I can say to change Aurora's mind. I need that elixir in order to stimulate my Griffin Ability. The first vial I had was crushed to pieces during my encounter with Ada—the supremely nasty faerie who almost destroyed the whole of Stanmeade with her glass magic— but one of the Griffin rebels made more elixir so I could try to wake Mom from her enchanted coma. It didn't work, but at least I had some of the elixir left. I brought it with me, planning to secretly consume tiny amounts in the hope of gaining control of my Griffin Ability without the Unseelies knowing. But I was searched before entering the palace. A guard discovered the elixir, and Aurora confiscated it. Roarke, who didn't seem interested in spending more than a few minutes with his betrothed, had already left by that point.

"But Aurora," I say to her in my most reasonable voice, "I'm no use to your family if I can't figure out how to control my Griffin Ability. That's the only reason Roarke's marrying me, remember? So I need that elixir to help me learn how to use it."

"Yes, but you don't need to learn *right this moment*. You can practice under supervision when Roarke and Dad return."

I look her squarely in the eyes. "Don't they trust you to supervise me? Do they think you can't handle me?"

She tilts her head back and laughs. "Oh, my dear Em. If you're going to try to manipulate me, you'll have to be a lot more subtle about it. That was a terrible attempt."

I slide lower in my chair with a defeated sigh. "This is all such a waste of time," I mutter. "Mom's still stuck in some kind of evil, magic-induced coma, and I'm getting absolutely nowhere in figuring out how to help her."

"You're not wasting time. You're learning how to use everyday magic and how to live as one of us," Aurora says. "Speaking of which, please sit up straight. My mother would have heart palpitations if she saw you slouching like that."

Aurora's mother. The Unseelie Queen herself. I had dinner with her and Aurora on my first night here, with servants waiting on us the entire evening, filling our goblets with oddly colored drinks and our plates with food even better than the food Azzy cooked back at Chevalier House. I found it difficult to enjoy anything, though, given the anxiety cramping my stomach and making my fingers shake. It wasn't as though Queen Amrath was cruel or unfriendly. She was over-the-top polite, in fact, but I knew she was watching me the entire time. Sizing me up. Waiting for me to prove myself completely unworthy of marrying her son. With every awkward moment that passed, I reminded myself of my highly valuable Griffin Ability. *That'll keep you alive and safe*, I kept telling myself. *They want your power more than they want a well-mannered princess.*

"Em?" Aurora says. "Are you listening to me?"

I clear my throat and push myself up so I'm sitting straighter. I force my shoulders back. "Sorry. What did you say?"

"I said we need to have a talk about what you're wearing, and also that you should try the honeystar tea. It's quite invigorating. Noraya, come pour some tea for Emerson."

Noraya, who was standing so still by the bedroom door that I didn't notice her there, moves closer to the table. With a brief wave of her hand, the teapot rises into the air. "Oh, don't worry," I say quickly, sitting forward. "I can pour the tea."

"Let her do it, Em," Aurora says.

"But it's just tea," I argue as the teapot tilts over my cup and dark steaming liquid streams from its spout. "I can pour it myself." Not with magic, since that would probably result in tea splashing all over the table, but my own two hands would do the job just fine.

"It doesn't matter whether you *can* do it or not," Aurora tells me. "What matters is that when you're a member of the royal family, it's proper for servants to wait on you."

"I'm not a member of the royal family yet." *And I hopefully never will be.*

"It's also proper for you to wear court-appropriate clothing," Aurora adds as Noraya steps away from the table, "and those—" she eyes my jeans and T-shirt with disapproval "—are not appropriate. Clarina and I will have to have another chat. She clearly hasn't understood her instructions."

"What? No, it isn't Clarina's fault. She gives me a new dress every morning, just as you told her to, but I don't want to wear any of them. They're ridiculous. Hundreds of layers of fabric with corsets and feathers and jewels and … stuff. It isn't me." The jeans, T-shirt and hoodie I've been wearing for the past few days are the clothes I had on when I arrived here. I hang them over a chair in my bedroom every night, and every morning I find them folded and clean, on the same chair.

Aurora arches an eyebrow. "Ridiculous?" she repeats. I realize I may have offended her, given the long skirt, tight bodice and bell-shaped sleeves of the dress she's wearing. "I'm afraid it doesn't matter what you or anyone else thinks, since that's the way my mother and father wish the members of their court to dress."

"Well, your parents have a seriously outdated sense of fashion. Everyone looks like they're playing dress-up or getting ready to shoot a steampunk film."

Her expression grows serious. "I wouldn't say things like that if I were you." She lowers her voice, leans closer, and adds, "My father has eyes and ears everywhere, and he wouldn't appreciate comments like that."

A chill creeps across my skin. Seems I haven't been imagining the feeling of being watched. I wrap my arms around myself, feeling naked despite the fact that I'm dressed. "Even in the bedrooms?"

"Well." Aurora leans back. "Perhaps only ears in the bedrooms."

"That's just … wrong," I whisper.

She laughs, and again I can't tell if she's joking about all of this. "Only if you have something to hide," she says. She bites into another unidentifiable fruit and watches me as she chews and swallows. "Now tell me: how are you coming along with the magic I've taught you so far? Can you move things yet? Try to lift your plate and move it around in the air."

"Uh …" I begin twisting a strand of hair around my forefinger. "Are you sure that's a good idea? What if I drop it?"

"Then Noraya will gather up the broken pieces and throw them away. No big deal."

My gaze slips down to the hair wrapped around my finger. I'm almost used to the bright blue color mixed in with the dark brown. It's part of what marks me as a faerie. As someone who belongs in this world. Slowly, I lower my hand. "Yeah, okay. I'll try."

Drawing magic from deep inside me is easy now, but sending it toward the plate, coaxing it around and beneath and telling it to *lift something up*, is a different story. Ever so slowly, with my hands clenched in my lap and my eyes just about boring holes into the plate, it begins to rise. It wobbles slightly, and the half-eaten pastry and pieces of red citrus slide to one side. I try to right it, end up overcompensating, and the whole plate flips over. The food lands on the table with several soft thumps, and the plate remains suspended upside down in the air. It shudders and sways before I imagine my magic lowering it carefully. It drops the final few inches, landing neatly on top of my breakfast.

Aurora claps her hands. "Well, that was entertaining. Hardly perfect, but it's a good start."

"I guess." I turn the plate over and begin cleaning up my mess.

"Em, you could barely do anything when you arrived here a few days ago. This is an achievement. Oh, and I have some more books for you." She gestures over her shoulder, and a pile of books on the low table between the couches rises into the air before dropping down again, the individual books smacking loudly into each other as they land. "You can carry them out with magic when we're finished here."

"Sure." I try not to work out how long it will take me to get back to my own rooms if I have to magically transport a pile of books the entire way there. Hopefully I can convince one of the guards who surreptitiously follow me around at a distance to help me once I'm out of Aurora's sight.

As I get back to eating my mess of a breakfast, the door opens and Clarina slips into the room. She moves silently to stand beside Noraya and, after a moment's pause, begins whispering to her.

"What's going on?" Aurora asks loudly, not bothering to look around at them.

Clarina falls silent, her wide eyes darting across the room toward her mistress. From across the room, I see her throat bob as she swallows.

"Clarina." Aurora pushes her plate away and turns in her chair to face the two handmaids. "Part of your job is to *report* secrets to me, not to whisper them in my vicinity. Now tell me what's going on."

Clarina bobs her head. "Yes, Your Highness. I apologize. It's just that … it's so horrible."

"What's so horrible? What happened?"

"One of the guards …" Clarina's eyes shift to Noraya, whose chin shudders as she stares at the floor. Clarina clears her throat and returns her gaze to Aurora. "One of the guards was found dead in the garden," she says in a shaky voice. "Grey and wrinkled and dead."

CHAPTER 2

I pace across the sitting room of my suite—smaller than Aurora's, but no less luxurious—waiting for someone to come and tell me what's going on. Aurora sent me back here in the company of several guards immediately after Clarina's creepy words about someone grey, wrinkled, and dead in the garden, but I've received no news since then. I walk onto my balcony and look down yet again, but I still can't see anything interesting. This death must have happened on the other side of the palace.

I wander inside again, between the armchairs and around the table. I sit at the writing desk and try to read one of the books I'm supposed to be studying, but I can't focus. Thoughts of Mom and all the Griffin rebels I ran away from keep slipping through the cracks of my concentration. Guilt over vanishing with no explanation. Sadness at having to leave Bandit behind. I'm even starting to miss Dash, of all people. And then there's the avalanche of questions: Who am I? Who is Mom? How did we come to live in the human realm with our magic blocked? Just to name a few …

I abandon the book and end up lying on the divan, watching the glow-bugs that are fixed to the ceiling, and slowly lifting and lowering cushions with magic. It requires my full attention to get this simple maneuver right, which means there's no room in my mind for questions and distracting thoughts.

Without warning, the main door to my suite is thrown open. My two levitating cushions land on my chest and tumble to the floor. I push myself up hurriedly, twisting around to face the door, and find Aurora striding into the room. Someone pulls the door shut behind her as I stand and ask, "Is everything okay? Did you find out what happened?"

"I don't know what happened, but I've spoken to the people who found the dead guard." She walks onto the balcony. I follow her out into the warm mid-morning sunshine. "I saw him, Em. It was …" She sucks in a breath and shakes her head. "Horrifying. The color in his hair was completely gone, and his face …" She turns away and rests her hands on the balcony railing. "His skin was sagging and wrinkled. It was just awful. That doesn't happen to our kind, Em. That *doesn't happen*. Not naturally anyway. And this means that—" She cuts herself off, her fingers tightening on the balustrade.

"Means what? That this guard was attacked with magic?" I mentally kick myself for that unimpressive feat of deduction. *Obviously* this guard was attacked with magic.

"Yes. Something like that." Aurora shakes her head and returns her gaze to me. "Anyway, I received a message from Roarke. He said we shouldn't speak of it to anyone. Only a few people know what the guard looked like, and we don't want everyone finding out and getting scared."

I can't help raising my eyebrows. "You think the rest of this palace doesn't already know? Someone must have told Clarina, and surely Clarina and Noraya have told others by now."

"They won't have told a soul. Clarina and Noraya have been with me forever—well, Noraya's been here forever, and Clarina's been with me for at least three years—so they know how to keep their mouths shut. Clarina was with one of my mother's handmaids when she saw the dead guard, and she came straight here afterwards. A few other guards have seen him, but they've also been told to keep quiet."

I lean against the balustrade and stare across the garden. In the distance, two large birds soar across the sky. At least, I assume they're birds. Their wings seem a little too big for their bodies, though. "Does anyone know who did it?" I ask, looking away from the flying creatures. "I mean, if it's impossible to sneak into this palace, then it must be a guest or someone who lives here."

Aurora exhales and plasters a fake smile onto her face. "We mustn't speak of it anymore, Em. Forget about it now."

"Forget? That's unlikely. Don't you want to know more?"

"No. Roarke and my father will take care of it when they return. Which should be just before dinner, apparently."

"Oh." My unease shifts into something more positive. "That's great."

"Yes. Now, what other magic was I showing you yesterday?" She rubs her hands together and walks back inside. "You practiced moving things, and there was also …"

"Fire," I remind her. "Well, tiny flames. So I don't accidentally burn the palace down."

"Yes, that's right. Have you made any improvement?"

I snap my fingers together and open my hand, palm-up, hoping the spell has become instinctual enough for a flame to appear automatically above my hand. My palm, however, remains empty. "Um … apparently not."

"Yes, well, you're not even trying." She sits primly at the edge of the divan. "You need to focus. You're not at the point yet where it happens automatically. Now, try again."

I grumble beneath my breath before lowering my hands to my sides, closing my eyes, and telling myself to relax. I need to be able to release magic, then focus fully on the moment when it's ready to shift from something raw and formless into anything else. At that point, I have to mentally shape it into a flame before it disappears. And all this, apparently, will happen almost instantly once I've done it enough times. I've just about reached a relaxed mental state when a tap on the other side of the door interrupts my concentration.

"Enter," Aurora calls out.

Noraya walks in and hurries to Aurora's side. She bends and whispers something before straightening.

Aurora rises with a sigh. "Of course. I'll come now. Sorry, Em, but my mother would like to see me. You should carry on practicing, though. And get started on reading those books. You have a lot to learn if you're going to fit in here."

I watch her leave before dropping into an armchair and slumping back against the gold-embroidered cushions. Then I force myself to sit up straight and focus on producing a flame. I have no intention of fitting in here—not in the long run—but I need to at least pretend I'm planning to see this union through. Besides, I'll probably need to use magic to get myself out of here. I may as well take this opportunity to learn as much as I can.

After trying repeatedly to produce a flame and succeeding about fifty percent of the time, I settle down with the smallest book from the pile Aurora gave me this morning. It's a collection of basic spells that reads as though it was written for a first grader. Perfect. As embarrassing as it is, this is exactly the kind of thing I need.

Once I've successfully managed to shrink a cushion to about half of its size, then enlarge it, and then return it to normal, I pick up a different book and settle into an armchair. It contains accounts of history even older than the history I learned at Chevalier House. The initial dividing of the courts, and the very first Seelie and Unseelie families. I haven't got very far when I hear a faint scratching sound. I lower the book and look around, trying to figure out where the scratching is coming from, but whatever it was has stopped. With a frown, I return to reading.

But the scratching begins again. From the direction of the desk, perhaps? I stand slowly, wondering what exactly I'll do if I tug open one of the drawers and a nasty magical creature pounces out at me. For some reason, my imagination conjures up an image of a disembodied hand, which doesn't help my pattering heart rate at all.

Three sharp taps at the door cause the book to slip from my fingers. I close my eyes for a moment and breathe out shakily, almost laughing at myself for becoming so jumpy. "Come in," I call as I bend to pick up the book.

"Your lunch, Lady Emerson," Clarina says from the doorway.

I straighten, leave the book on the armchair, and push my hair out of my face. "Right. Thanks." I've eaten lunch with Aurora each day since I arrived here, but she obviously has other matters to attend to today. Clarina carries the tray of food to the table near the balcony doors while I edge closer to the desk on the other side of the room. Feeling silly now for having been afraid of a simple scratching sound, but still a little wary of what might have been causing it, I yank open the drawer on the left and quickly stand back. The stolen stylus rolls toward the back of the drawer—and nothing jumps out at me. I push the drawer closed and open the one on the right. It's filled with the blank scrolls that were on top of the first pile of books Aurora gathered for me.

"Is everything all right, Lady Emerson?" Clarina asks.

My cheeks flush as I look over my shoulder at her. "Yes, sorry. I thought I heard something, but ..." I turn back and peer into the drawer. "But there's nothing here."

"There are many small creatures living in the gardens here," Clarina tells me. "Some of them come inside on occasion. Most of them are harmless."

"Most?" I repeat.

She smiles faintly at the floor, but doesn't elaborate. "Do you need anything else, my lady?"

I pick up the history book on my way to the table. "I don't think so. This looks amazing." She bobs her head and walks back toward the door.

"Clarina?" I ask as I lower myself into a chair.

She stops and looks around, her eyes meeting mine for only a moment before focusing on the floor. "Yes, Lady Emerson?"

"What makes you an Unseelie faerie?"

She hesitates before answering. "What do you mean?"

"*Are* you even an Unseelie faerie? Is everyone who lives and works in the palace considered Unseelie?"

She frowns at the floor. "Yes, I believe so, my lady."

"What makes you different from someone who isn't Unseelie? I'm trying to remember what I was told when I first arrived in this world, but it wasn't much. I think someone said the magic here is slightly different? Something about dark magic?"

"Any magic they don't agree with they call dark magic."

"They?"

"Those who are not Unseelie. Some of our magic is the same as theirs," she explains. "Like the power that resides naturally within all of us, or the power we absorb from the elements or the plants. But they don't like it when we take power from other living beings—lesser beings—and they don't like some of the procedures involved in certain spells. So that's where the divide comes in. I think," she adds, folding her hands together demurely in front of her.

My eyes graze over the spread of food on the table. It's far more than I could ever eat in one meal. I wish I could ask Clarina to sit down and eat with me while I ask her more questions, but I know she'd never agree to that. "What counts as a lesser being?" I ask.

Again, she looks confused. "Well, everything that isn't a faerie, of course."

A chill raises the hairs on my arms, despite the warm breeze wafting in through the open balcony doors. "Do, um, do you do that often? Take power from other living beings?"

"No, my lady. I haven't ever needed to. I've been healed before by spells that were specifically Unseelie, but I personally haven't absorbed raw power from another being."

"Okay. I see." I'm not sure what else to say, aside from telling her that taking someone else's power sounds downright creepy and just plain wrong.

"Do you have any other questions, my lady?"

"Uh … not right now."

She turns, then adds, "You don't need to be disturbed by all this, my lady. It's unfamiliar to you, I know, but it isn't wrong. It's just different. And, well, I've always been told that we shouldn't be afraid of something just because it's different."

"Um, yes, that's true. Thank you, Clarina." I give her a smile that fades the moment the door closes behind her. I know I shouldn't be afraid of something simply because it's different, but if it's different *and* it's hurting someone, that's not okay. Perhaps I've misunderstood it, though. Perhaps this 'taking power' thing isn't nearly as ominous as it sounds. It may only be a little bit of power, not enough to kill someone. And perhaps they only take it from beings that are willing.

I help myself to some food, reopen the book, and continue reading. After only a few minutes, a subdued thump comes from the direction of my bedroom. I lower the sandwich that was halfway toward my mouth and slot a fork between the pages of the book to keep my place. I silently lift a knife and rise from the chair to face the half-open bedroom door.

And then I spend far too long frozen in place, wondering whether I should investigate on my own or risk looking stupid by asking a guard to go into my bedroom and hunt down the mysterious *thing* that hasn't made another sound since that first thump. I decide in the end to risk looking foolish. Better than getting chomped by one of the *non*-harmless creatures from outside—or by whatever it was that killed that guard this morning.

I open the main door, stick my head out, and find two women in guard uniforms standing just outside. They spend at least twenty minutes searching every inch of my bedroom while I pretend to read. And when they leave, having found no hint of a threat, I'm almost certain I see one rolling her eyes at the other.

CHAPTER 3

"Has your Griffin Ability appeared again?" Aurora asks that evening as we retire to the couches in her private sitting room. It's late, dinner is over, and Roarke still isn't back. Asking when he'll return is useless, so I've given up, but I still find myself burning with frustration every time I picture Mom permanently asleep. My hands want to curl into fists whenever I think of all the minutes, hours, and days passing by.

"I felt it in my sleep last night," I tell her, removing a cushion from behind my back and hugging it to my chest. Better to squeeze the cushion than to continuously dig my nails into my palms. "It woke me up. By the time I figured out what was happening, the moment had passed. I didn't manage to get a single word out before the magic was gone."

"What would you have said?"

I shake my head as I watch the dancing flames in the fireplace. Given that it's summer here, I wouldn't have thought it necessary to light a fire at night, but the room feels pleasantly warm and cozy. "I don't know. I was half asleep and trying to think of something, but the feeling was gone before I'd come up with any command."

She watches me for some time, while I continue to stare past her at the flames. "Do you really think the elixir is going to help you?"

I focus on her, my mood lifting instantly. Could she possibly be thinking of giving the elixir back to me? "Of course it helps. It turns the ability on so I can use it."

"Yes, I know, but you said the point of the elixir is to somehow teach you to use and control the ability on your own. It's supposed to help you recognize what your Griffin magic feels like, right? So that you can call on that magic at will without the help of the elixir?"

"Yes, something like that."

"But you already know what it feels like."

I look down at my arms wrapped around the cushion. "Yes, I do."

"So then why—"

"Why can't I do it on my own?" I sigh, my excitement dissipating. She isn't going to give me that elixir. "I don't know. I've tried. I imagine the feeling. I picture pulling magic from deep inside me, but nothing ever happens. Maybe if I had that elixir, I could—"

"No," she says. "I'm not giving you something that will become a crutch, especially since there isn't a lot of it, and once it's gone, we don't know how to make more. Not to mention what a bad idea it is to give you something that will immediately switch on a dangerous ability you could then use against me."

"Aurora, I would never—"

"Yeah, yeah." She rolls her eyes. "You're going to be part of my family soon, so I'd like to be able to trust you, but we're not there yet. No, the reason I'm bringing this up is because I've been thinking about how your ability might work." She tilts her head to the side and stares thoughtfully across the room at the curtains concealing the balcony doors. "Perhaps, because it's such a powerful ability, it needs to sort of … replenish itself. That would explain why you can't use it all the time."

"Okay. Maybe. Do some kinds of magic work that way?"

"Well, all magic works that way, actually." She shifts her position, folds one leg neatly over the other, and faces me. "It's just that we hardly ever use it all up in one go, so we don't realize that it's constantly replenishing. If you do something that's particularly strenuous on your magic, like lifting something very heavy and holding it in the air for a long time, then you'll eventually tire yourself out. Magically, I mean. Then you need to rest while your magic restores itself."

"Like replenishing energy if you do something that's physically exhausting?" I ask.

"Yes. So I wonder if maybe your Griffin Ability works in a similar way, but in quick bursts rather than slowly over a long period of time."

I nod. "That sounds like it could make sense. It always feels as though it comes over me in a sudden rush, gets used up immediately with whatever I happen to say at the time, and then it's gone."

"Or it ends up released into your surroundings with no purpose if you don't say anything at all." She taps her chin and purses her lips. "Hmm. I wonder if you could hang on to it and use it at a later time instead of having to release it whenever it's replenished.

"Uh … I could try that?" I suggest, having no idea how I would actually 'hang on' to this elusive power of mine.

"Anyway, this is all speculation at this point," Aurora continues. "We need to gather some actual evidence. Take note of exactly when it happens. The day and time. And keep track of other things, like whether you've used an unusually large amount of your normal magic on something else. Because we don't know whether your normal magic has any effect on your Griffin magic, or if the two are independent of each other."

I nod as she speaks. "Basically, we want to figure out if we can predict when it will happen."

"Yes. You're going to have to be very thorough, Em. Record every detail that could possibly influence your Griffin Ability."

"Yeah, definitely." I frown as my mind races back over all the times I've given a magical command, trying to force the events into a pattern that makes sense. I end up shaking my head. "Maybe we're wrong. There was one time when I used it twice within a few minutes. So the replenishing theory wouldn't make sense then."

"Well, perhaps you didn't use it all up with the first thing you said. Perhaps you *can* hang onto some of it, but you didn't realize that's what you were doing. That's why you had some left over for a second command, but then after that it was all used up."

I chew on my lower lip before answering. "Yeah. Maybe."

"Or perhaps your magic is still settling," Aurora suggests. "That's what happens to halflings if their magic appears later in life. It often comes and goes for a while before becoming consistently present. Maybe, once a little more time has passed, your Griffin Ability will appear at regular intervals."

I push one hand through my hair. "So many possibilities and unknowns."

"That's why you need to start documenting everything. That's the only way we'll learn if my theory is correct or not."

I stand and drop the cushion onto the couch. I wander over to the fireplace and lift the silver candlestick holder from the mantelpiece. I practiced lighting the candle repeatedly before dinner, and I managed to produce a flame with almost every attempt. I snap my fingers beside the wick—and a flame ignites it.

"Well done." Aurora claps her hands in delight. "Okay. Now that you've got that one right, what shall I teach you next?"

Instead of answering her, I ask, "Is this what you do every night? Eat dinner alone in your room? Or do you have family dinners when everyone's home?"

If she's confused by my change of subject, she doesn't show it. "Well, it's always different," she says with a shrug. "Sometimes we use one of the smaller dining rooms and have dinner with just the four of us. Sometimes extended family members join us. Sometimes we entertain guests, or my mother will entertain her friends, or I'll entertain some of the young ladies of the court. If I'm tired of everyone, then I eat alone here." She cocks her head. "Why do you ask?"

"I'm just trying to picture what your normal life is like. Clarina told me you have ladies-in-waiting, but you sent them away on holiday. And I haven't seen you interact with anyone other than your mother and a handful of servants and guards, so—"

"So you're wondering if I'm a miserable loner?" she asks with one raised eyebrow.

"No. I'm wondering if you're trying to hide me from everyone else who lives here."

Several moments pass before she answers. "I wouldn't call it *hiding*, but I suppose that's essentially what it is. People are going to ask questions about you, Em. They're already asking questions about this strange friend of mine who doesn't look like she belongs here. It's easier if we don't put ourselves in a position where we have to answer anyone until the right time."

"And the right time will be ... ?"

"When you and Roarke make an official announcement about your engagement. No one will question your presence here then. They wouldn't dare."

The words 'official announcement' send a chill through me. Then, despite the fact that I'm standing beside the fire, the chill seems to become real. Goosebumps rise across my skin, and cold air whispers across the back of my neck. I look over my shoulder, but despite the distinct feeling that someone is watching me, I don't see anyone else in the room.

With a quiet click, the door opens. My gaze darts toward it. It swings slowly open, and into the room walks Roarke. Sharp angles, dark hair perfectly in place, and eyes the color of red wine. His intense gaze sweeps across the room before landing on me. His lips curl into half a smile as a flush heats my skin.

"Oh, look at that." Aurora clasps her hands together beneath her chin. "She's thrilled to see you, Roarke."

"Indeed." As the door closes itself behind Roarke, he walks slowly toward me, hands behind his back. "If only she was thrilled for the right reasons and not because she's been desperate to interrogate me since the moment she arrived here."

I swallow before speaking. "I'm glad you haven't forgotten why I'm here."

He stops in front of me, close enough that I have to look up to meet his eyes.

I knew he was tall, of course, but I'd forgotten the way his commanding presence makes him seem even taller. I won't step back, though. I refuse to be intimidated by the guy I'm supposed to be marrying soon, regardless of the fact that I have no intention of actually going through with the union.

Roarke's smile stretches a little wider, and from behind his back, he produces a rose. A gold, delicately fashioned rose with a ruby at the center of its solid gold petals. "My lady," he murmurs, bowing slightly as he hands the rose to me. I hesitate, then take it from him. He leans farther forward, his face suddenly way too close to mine, and his lips briefly graze my cheek. A cold shiver skitters across my skin and down my neck. "My apologies for taking so long to return. My father and I don't often have to deal with matters personally, but this was one of those occasions. We thought it best to stay where we were until the job was done."

"Uh … okay. Thanks for that cryptic explanation."

"Soon, my love, you'll be part of the family. You'll know all our secrets."

"Your *love*? Really?" I place the gold rose on the mantelpiece and cross my arms over my chest. "I think it's a little soon for that, Roarke."

Roarke looks at Aurora with a quiet chuckle. "Have you been teaching her how to play hard to get?"

Aurora stretches out across the couch, straightening the layers of her skirt over her legs. "Nope. It appears she knows how to do that on her own."

I almost make a comment about how this is all a game to them, but since I'm hoping to beat them at it and get out of here alive, I should probably play along. "How about we get to know each other a little better before you start throwing the words 'my love' around? You haven't even taken me on a date yet."

"A date? Well, I hope you have something a little smarter to wear than that—" he gestures to my jeans and hoodie "—if you're planning to go on a date with a prince. And speaking of clothing, have you not been given more appropriate attire?"

"I have, but I prefer to wear the kind of clothes I'm comfortable in."

"Refused," Aurora says from across the room. "She flat-out refused to wear any of the dresses."

I breathe out sharply through my nose. "Those dresses look like they're from another century. I know this is a palace full of royals, but can't you move with the times in the clothing department? The rest of the fae world seems to wear pretty much the same kind of clothes people wear in my world."

"*This* is your world, Em," Aurora reminds me. "And if you bothered to take a closer look inside your wardrobe, I think you'd find that the outfits hanging there are of the latest fashion. Formal fae fashion, which may not be familiar to you, but still. Only the very latest designs."

"You're right," I tell her, moving away from Roarke to lean against an armchair. "I'm not familiar with formal fae fashion."

"Enough about clothing," Roarke says. He turns to face me, pushing his hands into the pockets of his long coat, which is covered in finely detailed silver embroidery and is no doubt the latest in 'formal fae fashion.' "Tell me, my love—" He cuts himself off. "Apologies," he adds with a slight dip of his head. "Please tell me, my *lady*, what you think of your new home."

"Since you've seen the inside of my previous home, I assume you can figure out my feelings toward this one."

"You love it?" he asks. "You're in complete awe? You're unendingly grateful you get to spend the rest of your life here?"

"Not exactly. It is beautiful, I'll give you that. Not quite what I expected, but definitely beautiful."

"Ah, now I'm intrigued." He lifts the gold rose from the mantelpiece and twirls it between his fingers. "What were you expecting?"

I lift my shoulders in a slow shrug as I try to put my initial expectations into words. "I don't know. You Unseelies are meant to be the evil bad guys, right? So I was expecting something … colder. Darker. A dead forest surrounding your palace, or perpetual winter or something. But, you know, everything's sunny and warm and alive." *Outside, at least*, I add silently. I say nothing about the cold, oppressive feeling that sometimes presses on my shoulders when I'm inside the palace. The chill I can sense in the air right now.

Roarke tilts his head to the side. "You haven't looked outside at night, have you."

I cast my mind back to the three nights I've spent here so far. Each evening when I've returned to my room, the curtains have been drawn, the enchanted lamps lit, and the small pool in my forest-themed bathroom has been filled with steaming hot water and scented bubbles. "No, I don't think I have."

He walks past me, places the gold rose on the table Aurora and I normally eat at, and waves his hand past the curtains. As they open themselves, he turns back and extends his hand toward me. "Let me show you something."

Reluctantly, I place my hand in his. He opens the balcony doors and leads me outside. I suck in a breath at the unexpectedly frigid air. Then, as I reach the balcony railing and look down, my lips part in amazement at the sight of the glittering winter wonderland covering the entire palace grounds. "Wow," I whisper.

"My mother likes summer," Roarke says, "but my father likes winter. Her magic controls the day, and his controls the night."

My eyes trail across the snow-covered topiary, the frozen fountains, and the icicles hanging from the fingertips of the nearest statue. "That must be very confusing for all the plants and creatures residing in these gardens."

"Fortunately for them, they're magical too. They can handle it."

A shiver courses through me, and Roarke shrugs free of his coat. "What a gentleman," I say drily as he places it over my shoulders. "Although I would have expected there to be a spell that prevents people from getting cold."

"There is. But my magic levels are a little low at present." Standing closer to me now, he reaches up and tucks my hair behind my right ear. I stiffen immediately, staring somewhere in the region of his neck instead of into his eyes, but as his fingers brush the small coin-shaped piece of metal attached to the skin behind my ear, I relax a little. He isn't trying to be intimate; he's checking if the concealment device is still there.

"Worried I might have taken it off?" I ask, pleased to hear that my voice is steady.

"Not particularly. You don't know the magic required to remove it."

"But you're checking anyway. Just in case."

"Of course. I'd be foolish not to check. You might have found someone in this palace willing to remove it for you, or your Griffin Ability might have come alive long enough for you to instruct this device to remove itself."

"And why would I do that?"

"Second thoughts about our agreement. Guilt, perhaps." He leans sideways against the balustrade, entirely comfortable in the chilly night air. "Have you begun to feel guilty yet, Emerson?"

Begun? Guilt has been eating at me since before I even got here. I gave up my mother's hidden location to a dangerous faerie who then put her into a magical coma. I ran from the people who helped me and asked for nothing in return. I abandoned my best friend without so much as a goodbye. None of this, however, is Roarke's business. So I clear my throat and ask, "Why would I be feeling guilty? I agreed to this arrangement in order to help someone. I shouldn't have to feel guilty about that."

"True, but perhaps you've become afraid since you arrived here. Perhaps you want your friends—the Griffin rebels?—to know where you are after all."

I haven't confirmed Roarke's suspicion that it was the Griffin rebels who rescued me the day I ran from both the Guild and the Unseelies and fell from the edge of a cliff. He's asked where I was hiding out, but even if I wanted to, I couldn't tell him about that enchanted safe place. When in the company of others, I'm unable to even think of it, let alone speak the name of the place or its location. Instead, a blank space appears in my mind, presumably part of the protective spell that helps to keep that place safe. My memory of it always returns when I'm alone, but it's still disconcerting every time it completely vanishes from my mind.

Refusing to look away from Roarke's gaze, I say, "I'm not afraid, and I have not changed my mind. The last thing I want is my friends showing up here. Why would I risk them ruining our agreement before you've had a chance to follow through with your part?"

His smile is slow and careful. "Good. I'm glad to hear it."

"Which reminds me," I add. "You still need to prove that you actually have useful information that can help my mother. You can't expect me to marry you without some assurance that you're telling the truth."

"Are you saying you're not fully committed to our intended union?"

"I am," I say fiercely, hoping the lie doesn't show on my face, "but only if you're fully committed to completely healing my mother. I want to be able to trust you, Roarke. Please give me a reason to."

"Hmm." Roarke narrows his eyes as if considering my request. "Let's see. You—"

"Emerson Clarke?"

I look toward the balcony doors at the sound of an unfamiliar male voice. In the doorway stands a guard I don't recognize. "Yes?" I ask.

"The Unseelie King wishes to meet you."

CHAPTER 4

THE JOURNEY THROUGH THE PALACE TO MEET THE KING FEELS BOTH TORTUROUSLY long and frighteningly quick. It's enough time for me to get myself completely worked up, but not nearly enough time to calm down and prepare myself.

"My father isn't as kind as I am," Roarke tells me as we stride across glossy marble hallways with two uniformed faeries ahead of us and two behind. "He wants to keep you no matter what. Daughter-in-law or prisoner."

Wonderful. That doesn't make me want to throw up at all.

"I won't let that happen, of course," Roarke adds, "but it would be better if you don't make any joking comments about changing your mind or not being certain about the union. Things might get … unpleasant."

"I've already told you I'm not changing my mind." In my effort to mask my fear, my words come out louder than I intended. "I'm here, aren't I?" I continue in a lower voice. "And *I* came to *you*. Doesn't that prove how serious I am about this arrangement?"

"All I'm saying is that he doesn't appreciate jokes or sarcasm, so it's in your best interests to be polite. And you should probably remove my coat. You look very strange in it."

I slip Roarke's coat off and hand it back to him. "Perhaps it's in his best interests to be polite too, given how valuable my Griffin Ability is to him. If he makes me his prisoner, I'll never give him what he wants."

I try very hard to believe my own words, but Roarke's raised eyebrows and pitying expression make it impossible. As we stop outside an oversized, ornately carved door, he faces me. "You won't need to *give* him anything, Emerson. He'll take whatever he wants."

A guard opens the door. The unnatural chill in the air intensifies, and the doorway itself seems to stretch wider like a giant mouth preparing to swallow me whole. I smell damp earth and rotting leaves. My heart pounds faster as images of slimy creatures, skulls, and beetles flash across my mind.

Then I blink away the imagined images and find that the doorway hasn't changed at all, and the room it opens onto isn't a dark mouth but a large office. Roarke takes my arm and steers me forward, since my feet have forgotten how to move on their own. "Remember, I'm on your side," he whispers to me. "Prove to my father that you're willing to work with us, and I'll make sure you're never forced into anything."

I don't answer, my attention focused instead on the interior of the king's office. To the right is a table large enough for at least a dozen people to sit around. Oddly, though, whatever's on top of the table appears blurred when I try to look too closely at it. My gaze swings to the left—and I'm even more startled by what I see there: no wall encloses the office on that side. Instead, it extends into an underground cavern made of rough rock and illuminated by pale light.

"Leave us."

The deep voice brings my attention to the desk straight ahead of us. The surface is as polished as every other slab of marble that fills this palace. On the other side, a tall chair that appears to be made of the same rough rock as the cavern faces away from us. The chair remains motionless as the guards leave the room and close the door. Then, despite the fact that it must weigh a ton, the chair turns smoothly to face us.

King Savyon looks nothing like his son. His white-blond hair is streaked with black. His eyes are dark holes that bore into me. Without speaking, he places one hand on top of the other on the desk in front of him. Gold rings set with multi-colored gems glitter on every finger.

"Father, this is Emerson Clarke," Roarke says. I swallow and force myself to stand straighter. I'm pretty sure this is one of those situations where I'm not supposed to show fear, but I think I'm about to fail miserably.

The king stands, walks around to the front of his desk, and folds his arms across his chest. His eyes travel all the way down my body and up again, his gaze like a cold, creeping finger stroking along my skin. His expressionless gaze lingers on my hoodie, then travels slowly up to my face, where he holds my gaze for several terrifying moments. Despite my determination not to be intimidated, I almost wilt with relief the moment his eyes release me and move to Roarke. I wrap my arms tightly around my body and stare at the floor just in front of my feet.

"Well," King Savyon says, his voice a deep rumble I can almost feel in my own chest. "She's a far cry from the woman I hoped you'd one day unite with, Roarke. She's barely fit to be a servant in this court, let alone a princess."

"Really, Father?" Roarke drawls. "That's the nicest thing you have to say?"

"What do you expect when you present me with such a dismal prospect for a daughter-in-law?"

"I can assure you, Father, that her Griffin Ability more than makes up for what she lacks in other areas."

Those black eyes settle on me once more. "I certainly hope so. I'd like to see a demonstration now."

I open my mouth, my eyes darting between the two of them. I'm unsure if I'm allowed to speak, but they need to know that I can't perform on demand. "Don't worry, Emerson," Roarke says before I can say anything. He reaches inside his coat and produces a small vial. "I have your precious elixir right here. Yokshin, our inventions master, has been examining it, but there's plenty left for you to use."

Crap. This is so not what I planned to use the elixir for. I'm supposed to be alone with Roarke when he gives it to me so I can instruct him to tell me everything he knows about Mom and how to fix her. That isn't going to work right now unless I can give an instruction to the king at the same time. To remain frozen in place, perhaps. So he can't interfere. As Roarke turns to face me, thoughts race wildly through my head. Am I brave enough to do this? If I don't do it now, will I get another chance? And if I do command him now, how will I get past all the guards on my way out? Command them as well? Will there be enough time to give Roarke, his father, and all the palace guards an instruction before my Griffin Ability runs out?

"The compulsion potion first," the king says. "Then the Griffin potion."

"Of course," Roarke says, removing another small bottle from within his coat.

"The—what?" I ask.

"Compulsion potion," Roarke repeats, removing the lid. "It's exactly what it sounds like. You can be compelled to do certain things while under the influence of this potion. It's just to make sure you behave while using your Griffin Ability. We wouldn't want you doing something silly or irrational." He laughs. "Like telling us all to kill ourselves or something."

All hope withers. "So—so you're going to force me to say something?"

"This is just a precaution, Emerson. My father doesn't know yet if he can trust you."

He hands the bottle to me, and because I know I have absolutely no choice in the matter, I lift it to my lips. "How much?" I ask before tipping it back.

"Just a sip."

The potion tastes like something familiar, but I can't identify it. I hand the bottle back to Roarke, just as I realize that this compulsion thing sounds very much like the Griffin Ability everyone in this world has been trying to get their hands on. *My Griffin Ability.* "Wait—but—if you have such a thing as a compulsion potion, then what's the big deal about my Griffin Ability? You can already tell people to do things and they'll do them. You don't need—" I realize what I'm saying too late. *You don't need me.* Not something I should be pointing out when my Griffin Ability is the only leverage I have.

"We can force people to take a potion and then compel them to say or do certain things," Roarke explains. "That isn't the same as telling the ground to split apart and then watching it happen a moment later." He places the Griffin Ability elixir in my hand and steps back to stand beside his father. Now that they're next to each other, I can see the faint resemblance between them despite their dramatic differences in hair and eye color. "Emerson," Roarke says. "Don't you think it would be fun if it started raining in here?"

Though it's an odd suggestion, I find that I agree with him. It would be the most marvelous thing in the world if it started raining right here in this room. "Yes," I tell him.

"Then you should take a sip of that elixir and make it rain."

He's right. That's exactly what I should do. So I remove the stopper from the vial and pour a few drops onto my tongue. Then I wait for that familiar tingle, that sense that the Griffin magic hidden somewhere within me is rushing suddenly to the surface. I look up at the ceiling and say, "Start raining."

And it does.

I'm drenched within seconds, gasping and tensing my shoulders against the icy water. Roarke and the king remain completely dry, as if invisible umbrellas shield them from the downpour. "Tell it to stop," Roarke calls out over the roar of raindrops.

I can't sense if there's any Griffin power left simmering at the surface of my magic, and it's impossible to hear my voice above the noise. But when I tell the rain to stop, I feel the words resonating in my head the way they do when my Griffin Ability comes alive, and I know it's worked.

"Very good," the king says as I stand there shivering. He looks at Roarke. "Is Yokshin able to recreate the elixir? If not, and the Griffin Ability is random, the girl won't be as useful to us as I'd hoped."

"He's uncertain about recreating it, but in Aurora's last message to me before we returned, she said she's been working on some theories as to how the ability might work. She thinks it may become more predictable."

The king nods. "Well then. Are you sure you want to go through with this union? It would be simpler to deal with the girl as a prisoner."

"Yes, I'm sure. I don't want her to be a prisoner." Roarke looks at me as though considering a purchase he's about to make. "I actually quite like her. And Mother and Aurora can train her in the ways of the court. After some time, it'll feel as though she's always belonged here. She'll become one of us. She'll be happy to help us out whenever we have need of her Griffin Ability. We won't even have to force her. Right, Emerson?"

"Yes," I answer.

A distant howl echoes through the cavern.

"Good," the king says again, paying no attention to the howl. "Until then, Roarke, you will give her a compulsion potion every day and tell her exactly what to say if and when her Griffin Ability appears." All hope I had of using my Griffin Ability on Roarke slips away like ash through my fingers. "And you, Miss Clarke." The king takes a step toward to me, which is about a thousand times closer than I'd like him to be. "Find out if Aurora's theory—whatever it may be—is correct. Do everything you can to learn how your Griffin Ability works. You'll be far more useful to us that way, and useful people are less likely to end up dead."

"Father," Roarke says with a roll of his eyes. "That's not helpful. She doesn't understand your sense of humor yet."

The king's expression doesn't change one bit. Either he's *very* good at keeping a straight face, or that wasn't a joke.

Another howl pierces the silence, louder this time. The king doesn't look toward the cavern, so neither do I. Whatever creature or person is making that sound, I don't want to know.

"We will announce the union at your mother's birthday celebration in two weeks," the king says to Roarke. "You have until then to decide when the union ceremony will take place."

A third howl morphs into sobs, shouts and the sounds of a struggle. Finally, the king looks toward the cavern, and though I don't want to, I follow his gaze. Two Unseelie guards are dragging a man across the cavern's uneven floor. As the man struggles, one of the guards shoots a spark of magic into his side, and the man twists away and howls in agony.

I look at Roarke, begging with my eyes for us to leave right now. But he's watching the struggling man with an unreadable expression.

"Ah, you found him," the king says. "This is the last one, I presume?"

"Yes, Your Grace."

"Very good." As the two guards step away from the man, King Savyon raises his hand. The man, who looked for a moment as if he was about to run, swallows and closes his eyes. The king clenches his hand tightly around the air and turns his fist abruptly to the side. Across the room, at the edge of the cavern, the man's head does the same, bending almost parallel to his shoulder. *Too far*, my mind shrieks. *Too far, TOO FAR!*

Then a sickening crack. The man's cry cuts off. The king jerks his hand upward. The man's head is ripped entirely off his body, and both parts fall to the floor, spurting blood everywhere.

A strangled gasp escapes me. My hand flies up to cover my mouth. I squeeze my eyes shut, but there's no way I'll ever be able to unsee that.

As if from a distance, I hear the king's voice. "That will be all, Roarke. Take the girl back to her quarters."

A hand latches onto my arm. I blink and force my eyes away from the dead body as Roarke pulls me toward the door. He opens it and lets me walk ahead of him. "And Roarke," the king adds. "See to it that someone burns those hideous clothes she's wearing. I don't understand why it hasn't been done already."

"She refused to part with them, apparently."

I dare to look back at the king. He doesn't sigh. He doesn't smile. He barely moves as he says, "The clothes will be burned. It's up to Miss Clarke whether she's still in them when that happens."

The door swings slowly toward us. The moment it clicks shut, I start running.

CHAPTER 5

I run all the way back to my bedroom, tug the door open, and slam it shut. I take a few unsteady steps into the room, barely seeing my surroundings. All I see is a man's neck flipping to the side, and blood squirting from—

I turn, blinking, as if I can somehow look away from the memory. Still breathing heavily from the run, I push my fingers through my hair. What the hell was I thinking coming to this place? That I'd actually be able to get away with the answers I need because I have a powerful Griffin Ability I can use against people? A Griffin Ability I can't call upon at will, and which can be used to fulfill someone else's purposes due to a potion I didn't know existed. What a miserable joke. I should have guessed, though, that something like this would happen. There's so much I don't know about this world and its magic, but what I *should* have known was what an idiot idea it was to put myself in the midst of a bunch of powerful, dark magic-wielding faeries.

From somewhere behind me, a soft thump reaches my ears. I freeze. I know I should run. I should pull the door open and keep running until this palace is far behind me. But fear sticks my feet to the floor. Ever so slowly, I twist around and look over my shoulder. Across the room on the round table, sitting beside the tray of tea and macarons Clarina must have left here not long ago, is a small owl. As I watch, the owl seems to collapse in on itself. An instant later, a black kitten sits in its place.

"Bandit?" I whisper in disbelief. I turn fully to face the shapeshifting creature. It flicks its right ear in response. Without a moment's pause, I race across the room and scoop him into my arms, tears burning my eyes. "I don't know how you got here or where you've been hiding or if you're the one who's been making strange noises in my suite," I whisper, "but I'm so, so, so glad to see you." I thought I left him sleeping in my room when I snuck away from the oasis, but he must have shifted into something smaller and climbed into one of my pockets. Wouldn't be the first time. "Please don't leave me," I mumble into his fur, my words running together. "Please don't leave me here alone. I'm sorry about the things I said when you first showed up. That I don't like pets and that maybe I could sell you. I swear I didn't mean any of that. I had a puppy once, but it ran away and never came back, and Mom and I searched, but we couldn't find it and I cried for days." I suck in a long breath and lower my arms enough to look down at him sitting in them. He looks back up with perfectly adorable kitten eyes. "I know you're magical, but you probably don't understand a word I'm saying, do you?" He tilts his head to the side, looking for all the world as if he's trying to figure out what I'm saying. "Yeah," I whisper, pulling him to my chest again. "So just don't disappear, okay? This place is *not safe*. Not for either of us. If you'd seen what I just—"

"Emerson?" Roarke's voice on the other side of the door sends a jolt through me. I have no idea how he'll feel about the idea of a shapeshifting pet showing up here, so I hurry into the bedroom and place Bandit on the bed. "Stay here," I whisper to him before pulling the bedroom door closed. With limbs that are still shaking, I cross the sitting room and open the main door just wide enough to peek through the gap at Roarke.

"Are you all right?" he asks.

Another brief flash of spraying blood and ripping flesh crosses my mind. I swallow, flattening one hand on the doorframe and the other on the back of the door. *Pull yourself together*, I silently instruct. *You chose to come here. You chose this option to help Mom. Now make it work.* "Yes, thank you. I'll be fine. It was just a little bit of a shock, that's all. Seeing … that." I doubt it's necessary to elaborate on exactly what I'm referring to.

"Can I come in?" he asks.

"Uh … okay."

We sit side by side on the divan with a respectable amount of space between us. I risk a glance at the closed door separating us from the bedroom. Hopefully Bandit's intelligent enough to know he needs to remain hidden. "I'm sorry you had to see that," Roarke says. "I know it must have seemed brutal and cruel, but it didn't happen for no reason. That man disobeyed the king, and the consequence was death."

I breathe out slowly. Since Roarke seems to be waiting for a response, I say, "Okay."

"I just wanted to explain because I don't want you to be afraid to live here. That man was a criminal. He and several others stole from my father. He deserved death. But for those of us who play by the rules, life here is good."

For those of us who play by the rules. Roarke's reassurances only increase my fear.

I'm not planning to play by the rules. I'm planning to steal knowledge and then run for my life. "I know," I say quietly. "I understand. Like I said, it was just a shock. I've only been here a few days, and everything is very … different. I'm still getting used to it." I swallow. "I think it might help to put me at ease if I knew for certain that I could trust you. If you could tell me a few things—about Mom—then I'd know you can truly help me."

He leans back on one hand and surveys me as his serious expression turns to amusement. "You're actually not as bad at this as Aurora made out. Still fairly transparent, but I'm impressed you're trying."

I narrow my eyes at him. "Trying what?"

"To twist this situation to your advantage." He cocks his head to the side. "I'm curious. Did that scene with my father actually upset you, or is your entire reaction a ruse so you can try to manipulate some information out of me?"

My mouth drops open of its own accord. I close it quickly and grit my teeth together as I respond. "Of course I was upset by it. It was *horrible*." I lean away from him. "Were you motivated by any genuine concern when you decided to come to my room, or is this part of whatever game *you're* playing?"

He smiles again, but it's softer this time. "I'm sorry. It seems the two of us are still figuring each other out. And yes, my concern for you was genuine. I'm not so cruel that it means nothing to me to see you upset. We might be about to form one of the least romantic unions in history, but that doesn't mean I'm not going to at least *try* to care for you."

I fold my arms over my chest, hugging myself tighter than usual. "Well, in the unlikely event that you're telling the truth, thank you for *trying*."

He examines me for another few moments. "What can I say to convince you I'm being truthful?"

"You could start with—"

"Shall I tell you about the little house you grew up in? Number twenty-nine Phipton Way. Shall I tell you about the wild roses your mother loved to tend in the garden? Or about the friend who used to visit sometimes? The one who always ended up arguing with your mother. The one you never actually met, because you were always told to go to your room. Or what about the time your mom showed up to fetch you from school an hour early and stood outside the fence speaking to things that weren't there? Would telling you about these things be enough to prove to you that I know more about your mother than anyone who's tried to help you so far?"

A shiver slithers up my spine. "How do you know these things?"

His eyebrows pinch together slightly. "You still don't get it, do you. You don't understand how valuable you are. When I heard about your Griffin Ability, I made it my priority to learn everything I could about you. I tracked down your aunt, then your mother, and then the one person who connected Daniela and Emerson Clarke to this world."

"What person?"

"The person who knows who you are. The person who made your mother the way she is."

My heart thunders dangerously fast. "Tell me."

He simply shakes his head. "All will be revealed after our union."

I shake my head, grinding the words out between my teeth. "And you want me to believe you're not cruel."

"I'm not," he says quietly. "It's just that you're not the only person who wants something. I want something too, and I don't trust that you'll give it to me unless I withhold information from you."

"I *will* go through with this union."

"Really? That's honestly what you're planning to do?"

Dammit. Is there some kind of magic going on here that tells him I'm lying? Is that compulsion potion still at work? But he hasn't specifically *compelled* me to tell the truth. "Yes," I say to him, willing myself to believe it's the truth. "That's what I'm planning to do."

"And yet you haven't asked for any details of how I'm going to fulfill my side of the agreement once the union's taken place. How exactly will your mother be woken and healed? Will I teach you the spells and let you go to her? Will I insist on doing it myself? What will happen to your mother once she's well?"

Crap. He's got me there. "I have plenty of questions for you, Roarke, but you haven't exactly been around for me to ask them. You've only been back a few hours, and we didn't have much time to talk before your father wanted to see me."

"True. Well then, do you want to ask how things will work after the union?"

I tilt my chin up. "How are things going to work after the union?"

He sighs. "Why are you so resistant? I understand that it's not ideal marrying someone you only just met, but it's not as though you're getting a disappointingly average life out of this deal. I'm offering you *everything*. A beautiful home, a powerful family, wealth beyond all imagining. And don't tell me you don't want any of that because *everyone* wants that. And there isn't anything wrong with wanting it. You'll be one of the lucky few who gets to have it all."

"You're right," I say quietly, unfolding my arms and placing my hands in my lap. "I'm very lucky."

"So once we're married, I'll go to your mother and—"

"No," I interrupt. "You—I'll go. I'll get her and bring her back here." I pause. "You wouldn't keep me from doing that, would you? From going to get her? I mean, obviously I'd come back."

"Obviously," he repeats. "But that doesn't mean my father would be happy with you leaving. If you don't want me to fetch your mother, and you're not allowed to fetch her either, then you can contact whoever it is that's keeping her safe and arrange a meeting. At a neutral location, one that your 'friends' don't need to worry about me discovering. I'll send some people to fetch your mother. My most trusted men."

I consider his suggestion. "Fine. If that's the only way."

"Once she's here, I'll wake her. I'll heal her mind. Then she can tell you the truth about everything. You can finally have all your questions answered. She can stay here too, and you can finally stop worrying about her. Stop fighting, stop struggling. Life will be good for you, Emerson."

"Sounds perfect."

"Does it? I know you're fond of sarcasm, so forgive me for doubting you."

I roll my eyes. "Obviously it isn't *perfect*, but it's as close to perfect as life could ever possibly be, so if marrying you is the only way to get there, then I'll do it."

"Really?"

"Yes."

He leans forward and takes hold of one of my hands. He stares intently into my eyes, and though I don't feel any different, I can't help wondering if he's trying to use some kind of magical discernment spell I know nothing about. "Are you lying to me, Emerson?"

I shake my head, willing myself not to look away from him. "I am not lying. My mother is the most important person in the world to me. I would do anything to make her better." And I realize as I finish speaking that I'm telling the truth. I *would* do anything for her—and that includes marrying a prince I barely know. So if there's no way out of this, if it proves impossible to get the information I need from Roarke before the wedding, then I'll do this. I'll marry him. And Mom will finally be the happy, healthy mother I remember.

And then …

One day, no matter how far in the future, no matter how long it takes me to figure out exactly how to do it, I'll get the two of us out of here.

CHAPTER 6

 Aurora calls to me from across the terrace as I swing beneath my dance partner's arm, spin around, step-step-step behind him, and return to our starting position. After clapping briefly, Aurora adds, "You only messed up once this time."

"What?" I step away from the young man who's been filling in as my partner. Aurora's cousin or second cousin or something along those lines. My husband-to-be is, apparently, too important or busy for this kind of thing. "I thought I got it all right."

"No, the part in the beginning straight after you touch palms? You turned the wrong way."

I roll my eyes. "Do you really think anyone's going to notice?"

"Yes. In a ballroom full of dancing couples, when everyone else turns one way and you turn the other, it will most certainly be noticeable."

"Fine. I assume you're going to tell me to do it again?" I've been practicing for hours already, but I know Aurora won't be happy until I've got it completely right.

"Yes," she says with a nod.

So I face my partner and try not to sigh too loudly as we begin again. At least my outfit is fairly easy to move in. After my terrifying meeting with the king, I set aside my stubbornness and took a closer look at my wardrobe—and discovered I didn't detest the clothes as much as I expected I would. They weren't all puffy dresses, I was pleased to see. More like combinations of pants and fitted, coat-like dresses, some with long, embellished sleeves and high necks, others with no sleeves and full-length gloves. As the days have passed, I've come to appreciate the rich details and exotic styles worn by the members of the Unseelie Court. And the more I think about it, the more sense it makes that in a world filled with magic and enchantment, the clothing would be anything but ordinary.

Or perhaps I'm simply getting used to being here, which is a terrifying thought.

We do the dance three more times before Aurora finally lets us stop. Her cousin, who looked like he might stab himself if forced to spin me around one more time, bolts before Aurora can pin another boring task on him. "Noraya, we'll take refreshments now," she says, waving past me to where her handmaid is waiting in the doorway to the library.

I join Aurora on the other side of the terrace and lower myself into the swinging seat beside her. It hangs by nothing more than a single vine, and I'm a little wary of placing my entire weight into the hollow hemisphere. But Aurora keeps telling me not to doubt magic, and her seat's been perfectly fine so far. After a few moments, I relax back against the cushions and lift my feet so I can swing gently back and forth. I look out at the garden, but there isn't much happening. The library terrace is on a quieter side of the palace.

"So, now that I can dance without messing up," I say to Aurora, swinging my seat to face hers, "can we do something more exciting this afternoon? Like archery? I was starting to get slightly less than terrible at our last lesson. Or I could show you more parkour moves. You could actually try some of them this time instead of just watching me."

She laughs and shakes her head at my apparent silliness. "You don't think that was it for the dance lessons, do you? You've learned one dance, Em. Now you need to learn the rest of them. And we only have three days until Mother's birthday ball."

My feet drop onto the floor. "Seriously? I have to learn every dance?"

"Yes. It'll be bad enough when people discover that the princess-to-be is someone who's spent her entire life in the human realm and knew nothing of this world until a few weeks ago. If they don't see you using magic or dancing every kind of dance, it'll be even worse."

"Wait, you want me to use magic at the ball? In front of people?"

"Of course." She moves her hand in a circle, and her seat begins to slowly spin. "That should be fine, shouldn't it? You can handle the basics now."

"Yes, I just didn't realize it was expected, that's all. I'll try not to forget."

"That's the thing, Emerson." Her voice reaches me from the other side of her hemisphere seat. "You need to get to the point where you don't have to remind yourself. It should become an automatic part of your daily life, used even for the simplest of tasks."

"Sounds a little bit like laziness to me."

"You know what's lazy?" She brings her seat to a halt once she's facing me again and plays absently with the pendant around her neck: a silver oval shape with a black stone at its center. "Sitting in front of a glossy screen and mindlessly watching moving pictures."

I give her my least impressed look. "Are you referring to TV and movies? Because that isn't laziness. It's entertainment, and it's part of—"

"Part of human life. Just as magic is part of faerie life. It's part of *your* life now, Em, so get used to it."

"So many things to get used to," I muse, staring out across the garden again.

"Yes, like beautiful clothes, exotic holidays, lavish parties and being waited on for the rest of your life."

"I was referring more to this world and its politics and geography and history and creatures and … *everything*," I say quietly. "It's all so different from the life I grew up in."

"True," she says. "That's why you should focus on the frivolous stuff instead. It's a lot easier to get used to. The rest will follow in time."

I nod, despite the fact that I don't agree with her. I can't tell her that I'm still determined to find a way out of all this. Even now, after endless lessons in magic, etiquette and dancing, after lengthy discussions of union ceremony details, I still can't imagine this wedding actually taking place. I know I'm probably in denial. I know it's unlikely Roarke will tell me anything else about my mother until we're married. But I won't give up until the moment that union ceremony begins.

Noraya returns then with two tall glasses floating in front of her. She's so good at this levitating thing that she doesn't even need to use her hands. They remain neatly clasped behind her back as she walks forward, eyes pointed firmly ahead instead of watching the floating glasses. "Lemonade, Your Highness," she says as she reaches us.

I push myself forward and stand as one of the glasses moves toward Aurora. I wrap my hand around the other one. "Thanks, Noraya." She risks a glance at me, smiles, then looks hurriedly away.

"You need to get over that," Aurora says to me once Noraya has walked back to the library doorway. "There's nothing wrong with being waited on."

I settle carefully into my seat without spilling any of my drink. "I don't like lounging back and being handed things. It just seems … rude."

"It's rude to keep her from doing her job properly."

"Well, anyway, she smiled at me, so I don't think she minded."

Aurora lowers her glass and blinks. "She smiled at you?"

"I mean, not *at* me," I add hastily, not wanting to get Noraya in trouble. "Not in an impolite way. Um, anyway, I wanted to ask you about dresses for your mother's birthday ball. I assume you'll tell me what I'm supposed to wear? I don't think I can be trusted to pick out the right kind of dress."

Aurora narrows her eyes at the abrupt shift in subject, but she lets it slide. "Yes. Mother and I had three dresses made for you. We'll decide which one to go with once we know what Roarke will be wearing."

"Right. Of course. Because it would be *dreadful* if the colors clashed or something."

She rolls her eyes and nudges my knee with her shoe. "It would be dreadful. The two of you need to look like the perfect match."

"Which is silly, because we're never going to *be* the perfect match. We don't even—Oh." I sit forward slightly. "My Griffin Ability. I can sense it coming on." In the time that I've been here, I've become more attuned to the way my magic feels. Being forced to keep endless records of the ordinary magic I use each day, how much I eat, how tired or energized I feel, and exactly when my Griffin Ability appears has made me far more aware of every tiny change in my magic.

"Ah, that's just about the same time as the past few mornings, right?" Aurora says. "A little before lunch time?"

"Yes. And I used a lot more of my normal magic than usual last night trying to melt that fountain, so we can probably say for sure now that ordinary magic levels don't have much influence on my Griffin magic."

"Excellent. Don't forget to add that to your notebook. I think we have a reasonably good idea of how your ability works now, but you should probably continue keeping track of it for another few weeks. Just so we can be certain."

I didn't think my Griffin Ability made any sense when it first revealed itself, but perhaps, as Aurora suggested, it was still 'settling' during my first few days in this world. Since then, my excessive record-keeping has revealed a fairly regular pattern: My Griffin Ability appears twice a day, approximately twelve hours apart, give or take an hour or two. And in between those times, there's nothing I can do—aside from taking the elixir, which is now depleted—that will make it appear. Which means it's likely that Aurora's replenishing theory is correct.

I lower my glass of lemonade and sit at the edge of my seat. I close my eyes and try to predict the exact moment just before I get that tingling sensation racing up my spine. "I picture it kind of a like a volcano getting ready to erupt," I murmur. "Pressure builds up deep inside me, and then suddenly it all rushes to the surface, ready to explode."

"What did Roarke compel you to say this time?" Aurora asks.

Just as the king instructed, Roarke gives me a compulsion potion every day—well, twice a day now that we've figured out the pattern—and tells me exactly what to say when my Griffin Ability is ready for use. "He compelled me to try and preserve the power, if possible. If not, then I'm supposed to tell every yellow rose in the garden to become blue."

"Ugh, what a stupid command. He really needs to come up with some more interesting uses for your magic. Anyway, I'm glad he's letting you practice trying to hold it back. You need to learn to master this, Em."

"Yeah." I clench my hands together and clamp my mouth shut as the Griffin magic ripples through me, demanding to be released. *Hold it back, hold it back, hold it back*, I silently instruct myself. And when I'm certain the magic is about to rip itself free of me, forcing me to speak the instruction Roarke gave me, it just … doesn't. Slowly, it starts to feel like less effort to hold it back. I open my eyes, my hands relaxing in my lap. "I think I did it," I say with a smile. "I can still feel the power there, like a weird humming just beneath my skin. I wonder how long I can—"

Power rushes out of me, turning my voice deeper and more resonant. "Every yellow rose in the garden will become blue," I say.

Aurora sits forward a little, looking past me. After a moment, she says, "It worked. I can only see a few yellow rose bushes from here, but they just turned blue."

I slump back against my cushions, sending my seat into jerky, swinging motion. "Crap, that was barely a minute."

"Well, perhaps you got excited too soon." Aurora leans back and takes a sip of her lemonade. "Try for longer next time before you tell me you 'did it.' All you need is practice."

"Wonderful. Another thing to practice," I say with a sigh.

"Tell Roarke to compel you to actually hold it back, not just to *try*. And none of this 'If you can't, then this is what you'll say.' He's basically giving you permission to fail."

"Mm." I'm waiting for the day Roarke is busy enough to forget to compel me. That's the day I'll make sure I'm with him at exactly the right moment. I'll command him to write down every spell required to wake and heal my mother. Then if anything's left of my Griffin Ability, I'll use it to get myself out of here.

"Don't you want to finish your lemonade?" Aurora asks, lifting my glass from the ground with a simple wave of her hand. "You need to remain hydrated if you're going to survive the rest of the day's dancing lessons."

I take the glass from the air and down the remainder of the lemonade. "You're going to have to find another willing member of your court to be my partner," I remind her, "and your cousin's probably already told everyone to avoid me and my terrible dancing, so—Oh. That's an idea."

"What?"

"Do you think it would work if I used my Griffin Ability to tell myself that I can dance every faerie dance perfectly?"

"Uh …" Aurora's expression becomes thoughtful. "Hmm. I wonder. I mean, how does your Griffin magic work in the first place? Does it obey your exact words, or your intention behind the words? Does it work according to what you're picturing in your head when you command something? In which case, the dancing thing wouldn't work because you don't know—and therefore can't picture—all the steps in the other dances. And another thing," she adds, tapping the side of her glass with her fingernails. "If you tell me to do something, but the way I understand your command isn't the same way you meant it, whose intention will the magic obey? Yours or mine?"

I tilt my head back against the cushions. "I have no idea, but I'm starting to wish this Griffin Ability came with an instruction manual."

"Experimentation, Em. That's all it requires."

"Sure, but it's frustrating when I have to wait half a day between every new experiment."

"Unless you can hang onto your power and use little bits at a time."

"Maybe." I turn my seat to face the library doors as footsteps tap across the terrace.

"Your Highness," Clarina says as she reaches us. "My lady," she adds, directing her words toward me before turning back to Aurora. "Phillyp is ready for your lesson."

"Oh, wonderful." Aurora hands her glass of half-finished lemonade to Clarina before standing.

"And your mother just sent a message to say she'd like to discuss some of the details for the ball with you."

"Mother always has fabulously bad timing, doesn't she," Aurora says with a sigh. "She'll just have to wait."

"Of course, Your Highness. Shall I tell her the usual?"

"Yes. Tell her I'm in the middle of my archery lesson. I'll come straight to her as soon as I'm done."

Clarina nods once. "And shall I escort Lady Emerson back to her chambers?"

"Um … no, actually. Em can come with me this time." Aurora gives me a wicked grin. "I trust you now to keep my secrets."

After a quick curtsey, Clarina leaves. "Goodness," I say. "I'm shocked to discover that the perfect princess is keeping secrets from her own mother."

She gives my arm a playful smack. "No you're not. Besides, it isn't a big deal. It's just something my mother doesn't approve of." Instead of going back inside, she steps off the terrace onto the grass.

"Your mother doesn't approve of you doing archery either," I point out as I follow her, "but she hasn't stopped you from taking lessons."

"Yes, well, I told her it was either archery or magical combat, and there was no way she'd ever allow her little princess to learn magical combat."

"Which is what, exactly?" I bend as both a silver butterfly and a lizard with wings—one chasing the other—flit too close to my head.

"You know how you draw on your power, and in its most basic form, it's just raw power held in your hands?" Aurora says.

"Yes." That was the very lesson I received from Azzy at Chevaliar House.

"Well, all you do is throw that magic at someone. I mean, there's more to it than that. Those who are trained in magical combat will often transform their magic into other things. Stones or blades or flocks of birds with sharp pecking beaks. Something that can more easily take down an opponent than just a mass of sparks. But your mind has to be so quick. You have to be able to mentally shape your magic just like that." She snaps her fingers. "Over and over, while also protecting yourself."

I look around as we move further away from the palace. This part of the garden is unfamiliar to me, and all I can see up ahead is a thicket of trees. "So the queen didn't want you learning this skill?"

"No. It isn't very princess-like. We have guards to fight for us if necessary. She agreed to archery instead because all it entails is shooting arrows at inanimate objects that don't shoot back at me."

"Far more civilized," I comment. "But that clearly wasn't daring enough for you, so you had to try something else."

"Yep."

"Something your mother most certainly wouldn't approve of."

"Exactly."

"And that is?"

A grin stretches her lips as we reach the trees. "Dragon riding."

CHAPTER 7

My steps come to a halt. "Wait." I hold a hand up. "Wait, wait, wait. You guys have *dragons?*"

"Yes." Aurora turns back to look at me. "Haven't you seen them flying around occasionally?"

"Well … I've seen *something* in the sky. I assumed they were overgrown birds, or some kind of flying creature I haven't met yet."

She dissolves into giggles. "Overgrown birds? Seriously?"

"I've only seen them from a distance," I say defensively. "It was difficult to judge their size."

"Well, you're about to see them up close."

I blink. My feet still don't move. "Holy crap," I whisper.

"What? You're not afraid, are you?"

"No. I mean, maybe. Probably. I'm just having one of those moments where I wonder if I'm actually dreaming. We're talking about *dragons*, Aurora. I grew up thinking they only existed in fiction, and now I'm about to *see* one? My brain has absolutely no clue how to react to that."

"Come on." She takes my arm and pulls me forward. "Your brain has another minute or two to figure things out. The dragon enclosures are just on the other side of these trees."

"Dragons," I murmur. "You have dragons. Actual dragons."

"We used to have gargoyles too," she adds. "Well, by 'we' I mean the previous generation of royals. Gargoyles aren't as big as dragons, but just as scary, so I've heard. They used to stand guard on top of the palace, but they all disappeared a few decades ago."

"Really?" I think of the creature Ryn was riding when he saved me from plummeting to my death off the edge of a cliff. I'm pretty sure that was a gargoyle.

"Yeah, my father had been king for a few years, and the gargoyles never seemed to like him. One day they all just flew away, and no one's seen them since."

"How odd," I say slowly. I won't be mentioning to Aurora that I was rescued by a Griffin rebel on the back of a gargoyle, but I can't help wondering if it's one of the gargoyles that used to live here.

We step out beyond the trees, but I don't see any dragons yet. Or enclosures, for that matter. I look up, but there's nothing in the sky either. "You'll have to look down," Aurora tells me. "Over there."

My heart thumps faster as we approach the edge of a pit dug into the ground. Gradually, as the rim all the way around comes into view, I'm able to make out the sheer size of this hole. The other side is several sports fields away. We stop about a foot from the edge, and I look down at a lush, jungle-like environment. For a moment, I struggle to make out any kind of creature amidst the trees and colorful plants, but then something moves. A thick, scale-covered neck. A gargantuan head, rising and twisting slowly to face us until it's almost level with the top of the pit.

"Em," Aurora says, "meet Imperia."

The dragon's body shimmers blue-green and purple as she moves, and the massive spikes running along her back are reddish pink. Her tail, ending in a green arrow-head shape, whips around, easily knocking down a row of shrubs. Then she becomes still, angles her head a little to the side, and watches me with eyes glowing like fiery orange embers.

"She's beautiful, isn't she?" Aurora says.

My mouth is open, my tongue is dry, and my feet are rooted to the spot—despite the fact that a very insistent voice at the back of my mind is screaming for me to run for my life. "Incredible," I whisper.

"Each pit belongs to a different dragon. Imperia's always preferred a tropical environment, but the next pit is filled with ice. And the one furthest away—which would take us quite some time to walk to—is deep enough to contain a mountain."

"Wow. And can they, uh, fly out of their pits whenever they want?" My legs finally remember how to work, and I take a shaky step backward as Imperia lifts her head a little higher.

"No, there's an invisible shield layer over the top. The dragons aren't allowed out unless they're with a rider."

"Okay." I swallow. "And I notice there aren't any walls around these pits. Would the shield layer catch someone if they fell?"

Aurora appears unconcerned as she says, "No."

"But … then …"

"If someone's stupid enough to fall into a dragon pit, then they deserve to be eaten. But Imperia probably wouldn't do that. Not to anyone she knows, at least. She's really quite friendly. So." She turns to face me. "Do you want to ride her?"

I'm not sure how long my mouth is open before I finally mange to reply. "I … actually … do."

Aurora beams at me. "I like you even more now." She bends down and runs her hand along the grass. As she straightens, a line of gold forms a perfect ring around us. Without warning, the ground shudders. The circular piece of earth we're standing on becomes separate from the ground around it and begins descending.

"Whoa." I raise my hands and steady myself. "So, we're going down into the pit?"

"Yes."

"And, uh, will I be with someone when I'm riding this dragon? A trained professional?"

"You'll be with me."

"But … you're still learning, aren't you? Clarina said something about … Phillyp being ready for your lesson?"

"That's just what my handmaids have been trained to tell me when Phillyp informs one of them that the coast is clear for me to come here. You know, when there's no one around who might tell my mother they saw the princess on the back of a dragon. I received lessons in the beginning, of course, but they ended a long time ago." She looks at me. "Don't you trust that I know what I'm doing, Em?"

"Uh … I *want* to trust you." I watch the dark earth rising rapidly around us, then raise my eyes to the circular piece of sky growing smaller.

Aurora laughs. "Well, I'm not going to force you, Em. But you *know* you're going to regret being stuck on the ground once you see me soaring through the air."

Somehow, I know this is true.

The magical earthen elevator shudders silently to a halt. Within seconds, a tunnel forms ahead of us, short enough that I can see the lush vegetation on the other side. I follow Aurora through, hesitating at the mouth of the tunnel and looking around for Imperia. Through the trees, I see the shimmering aquamarine and purple scales of one of her legs.

"Hi, Phillyp," Aurora says, walking straight out of the tunnel and to the right.

"Princess," a male voice says. "I'm glad you could come. Imperia hasn't flown for two days. I think she's anxious to properly spread her wings."

After another glance over my shoulder toward Imperia, I hurry after Aurora. She's speaking to a slight man leaning in the doorway of a room built into the side of the pit. His head is shaved completely bare, and the shiny patch of skin on his upper arm looks as though it's been recently burned. "Ooh, ouch," Aurora says, bending closer to look at his arm. "Did Imperia do that?"

"Yes. Totally my fault, though, and you know I'm used to it."

"Yes. And it'll be gone soon, I'm sure," Aurora says as she straightens. "Phillyp, this is Em. My new friend. She's going to ride with me today, so please use the double saddle."

Phillyp pauses for only a moment before inclining his head. "Of course, Your Highness." He turns and disappears into the room.

"He doesn't think it's a good idea," I murmur to Aurora.

"Nonsense. He knows I'm perfectly capable of taking someone else with me. It's just that I brought one of my ladies-in-waiting once, and she screamed the entire time we were in the air. Imperia wasn't impressed, and neither was Phillyp." She snaps her fingers near the back of her skirt, and I notice a brief glow before her spark of magic disappears. "But you don't plan to scream like a little girl, do you, Em?"

I decide not to ask Aurora exactly how she knows Imperia wasn't impressed. "No. Obviously I don't *plan* to scream like a little girl."

A set of stairs, hovering a few inches above the ground, slides out of the room and moves past us toward Imperia. A moment later, Phillyp hurries after it with what I assume is the saddle floating just ahead of him.

"Ah, finally," Aurora says. I turn back to face her as her skirt drops to the ground, revealing form-fitting pants the same color as her corset-like top. "What?" she asks in response to my raised eyebrows. "I can't very well ride a dragon in a dress."

"I guess not. Good thing I'm already wearing pants."

With a wave of her hand, the skirt flies into the room. "You'll want to keep your hair out of your face." Aurora tells me as we head through the trees. She waves a hand near her hair, and her thick purple and black tresses promptly arrange themselves into a neat braid. A silver ribbon appears and ties itself at the end of her hair.

"Lazy bum," I mutter, reaching back to braid my own hair with my hands.

"Not at all," she replies. "You'll soon realize that any spell that saves you time in getting ready and allows you to remain longer in the air on the back of a dragon is a spell worth memorizing." She stops at the edge of a clearing and looks up, her hands on her hips. "I'll teach you later."

My hands still for several moments as I take in the size of the dragon in open-mouthed awe. The set of stairs is just high enough to reach her back, and Phillyp stands at the very top, securing the straps and buckles of the saddle with magic. Imperia lets out a loud snort, emitting smoke through her nostrils.

I swallow. With shaking fingers, I finish securing my braid. All too soon, Phillyp climbs down the steps and Aurora climbs up. She grabs the straps, climbs onto Imperia's back, and swings her leg over the front seat of the saddle. "What are you waiting for?" she asks as she looks down at me. Instead of answering, I lick my lips. "Come on, Em, don't freak out. This will be fun."

"I know." My voice sounds raspy and a little higher in pitch than normal. I clear my throat. "I'm excited. I really am. I just happen to be a tiny bit scared at the same time." *Understatement,* my wildly beating heart shrieks at me. *Gigantic. Freaking. Understatement.*

But that doesn't change the fact that I want to do this. So I force my legs to climb the steps. At the top, I take one last deep breath before placing a hand against Imperia's smooth scales. Beneath my touch, the color ripples and shimmers. I take hold of two of the straps and pull myself up. Thanks to all the walls I've climbed in recent years, my arms are pretty strong. Once I've settled myself in my seat, the steps slide away from the side of Imperia's body.

"Put that strap around your waist," Aurora says, twisting around and pointing to a loose strap dangling from one side of the saddle. I cross it over my body and fasten it through the metal ring on the other side.

Then finally, I look down. We're higher from the ground than I imagined, and we haven't even taken off yet. It's not that I'm afraid of heights, and it's not that I'm afraid of taking risks. Val and I have performed plenty of jumps, somersaults and dives that could easily have landed us in hospital. But I was always in control of my own body then. Now, I'm one hundred percent at the mercy of another creature—and it's terrifying.

Aurora takes hold of the reins. Imperia lifts her wings, and her body rolls one way and then the other as she moves forward a few steps. I inhale sharply and grip the ridge of the saddle that rises between Aurora's seat and mine. Imperia's legs bend slightly. I hold my breath. Then, with a great downward thrust of her wings, she rises into the air. I feel a sickening lurch in the region of my stomach. Dragon wings beat the air, the treetops wave wildly about, and the ground rushes away from us. I imagine plummeting toward it. I almost shout out that I want to get off, but I clamp my mouth shut, cling tighter to the saddle, and tell myself I'm not going to die.

We rise rapidly, the palace growing smaller and the surrounding Unseelie territory coming into view. Imperia's wings slow their flapping. She banks a little to the side, then soars around the edge of the palace grounds. And in mere seconds, my terror gives way to pure exhilaration.

"That was the most amazing thing I have *ever* done," I say to Aurora the moment Imperia's feet touch the ground in her enclosure.

"Told you," she answers with a laugh. The steps arrive a moment later, and we both climb out of our seats. I pause at the bottom and reach up to lay a hand against Imperia's side. "Will I ever get to do this again?"

"Of course," Aurora says. She removes her silver ribbon and pushes her fingers through her hair to free it from the braid. "You can come with me whenever you want. Phillyp can give you lessons, and you'll soon be riding on your own. Then we can take our dragons out together. It'll be perfect."

It would be—if I was planning to stay here. I take a step back and watch wistfully as Imperia trundles away. I wrap my arms around myself and bite my lip. It's scary to admit this to myself, but I think I could actually enjoy living here. Mornings spent lounging in swinging seats, afternoons spent gliding through the sky on the back of a dragon. And with my healthy mother at my side. All I would need to do is look past any horrific acts I happen to witness the Unseelie King committing. And somehow live with the guilt of whatever horrific acts he forces *me* to commit.

No, I whisper silently. *I can't live with that.* "Is it only the royals who have dragons?" I ask Aurora as Phillyp sends the portable stairway back to the storeroom.

"No, but they're awfully expensive, so only the very wealthy are ever in a position to own one."

"Right." So I should take every dragon-riding opportunity I can while I still live here. Once I'm gone, I'll never be able to afford it.

"Fortunately," Aurora continues, "you're about to become a member of an extraordinarily wealthy family. You can have as many dragons as you want."

"If I'd known this was all it took to woo you," a voice says behind us, "I would have brought you here days ago, Emerson."

"Roarke," Aurora says as we turn to face him. "Looking for me?"

"Yes. I thought I might find you here. *You*, however …" He looks at me. "Well, the back of a dragon is *not* where I expected to find you."

"She loved it," Aurora says, clasping her hands together and beaming.

"I heard," Roarke says with an amused smile. "What did you say, exactly?" he asks me. "It was the most amazing thing you've *ever* done?"

"Eavesdropping is rude," I tell him.

"So is keeping secrets from my mother, but I'll continue doing that too, don't worry," he adds as Aurora opens her mouth to protest. "She doesn't need to know about your favorite pastime."

"Where have you been all morning?" I ask as we head back to the edge of the pit. "I thought you might join me for my dance lesson."

"I was … organizing a gift for you, my beloved."

I arch a skeptical eyebrow. "There was way too much hesitation in your voice for that to be true."

"It's true, I promise. I was just considering whether I should tell you or not."

The tunnel materializes ahead of us as we approach the wall. "Okay, if this gift is real, then when will I receive it?"

"As soon as Yokshin is finished with it."

"Yokshin?" I remember that name from somewhere.

"Yes. He calls himself our inventions master. He's the one who was hoping to reproduce your Griffin Ability elixir."

"So … has he managed to succeed?"

"No." We exit the tunnel and step onto the levitating piece of earth. "This is a different gift. You'll have it … soon."

I press my lips together as the ground begins rising. I could ask more questions, but he'll only continue to give me half-answers.

"Why were you looking for me?" Aurora asks her brother.

"Oh, you and I just have a few things we need to see to."

Aurora nods and looks up, saying nothing.

"More secrets you're keeping from your beloved?" I ask.

Roarke gives me his sly smile. "Once you're my wife, all secrets will be revealed."

CHAPTER 8

 and rehearse my story. Tonight is the night Prince Roarke will announce that he's chosen a wife. He'll present me, formerly Princess Aurora's 'strange new friend,' and suddenly everyone will want to know every detail of who I am and where I'm from.

Roarke and his mother tossed around the idea of making up an entirely different past for me—one that didn't involve the human world—but they figured the truth would get out soon enough. And neither of them seemed to trust that I'd be able to keep the details of a made-up history straight, so most of what I've been told to share with people is the truth: I grew up thinking I was human, my magic revealed itself, the Guild got involved so they could imprison me and ensure I never hurt anyone, and then Roarke and his men showed up to rescue me. They took me back to their palace so I could live as a free member of their court. Roarke and I soon fell madly in love with each other, and the king granted our request to form a union. So everything up until the rescue is essentially the truth. After that … well, I somehow have to make these people believe I'm besotted with their prince.

I lean against the balcony railing and stare longingly at the perfect puffy clouds high above me. I'd rather be soaring the skies on Imperia's back instead of preparing myself to face a crowd of Unseelie nobility. Or riding that other dragon Phillyp rode with me yesterday. Bralox, I think his name was. Or dancing simple dances with Dash on the shores of the Griffin rebels' enchanted beach instead of trying to remember every step to every official faerie dance—since my Griffin Ability did nothing to help me in that department.

My door bangs open so loudly I can hear it out on the balcony. I look over my shoulder to see Aurora dancing across the sitting room and out onto the balcony. "It's time!" she sings.

"For what?" She can't be referring to the ball. It's hours away still.

"Time to begin getting dressed, of course. It's a long process involving hair, makeup, jewelry—and of course, we haven't actually chosen your dress yet from the three that were made for you."

"Oh. Okay."

Her face falls. "Why aren't you more excited?"

"I am." I pull on a smile that doesn't feel real. "It's just … parties aren't really my favorite thing. At the last one I attended, my magic exploded out of me and almost killed my best friend."

"Trust me, Em," Aurora says with the kind of smile that makes her eyes sparkle. "This party is going to be like nothing you've ever imagined. And if that doesn't make you feel any better, here's something that will." She removes her hand from behind her back and presents me with a square box a little larger than her palm.

"What's this?" I ask as I take it from her.

"Remember Roarke said he was having a gift made for you?"

"Yes."

"Well, I thought he was just saying that to cover up whatever he was really doing that day—I can usually tell when he's lying—but it turns out he actually did get Yokshin to make something for you."

I remove the lid of the box and find a bracelet sitting upon a small black cushion. Delicate ropes of silver metal twist around one another, with tiny silver leaves and flowers sprouting from the sides. In the middle of the bracelet is a large, clear gem. "It's pretty," I say.

"It's pretty *and* clever," Aurora says. "It's actually kind of like a watch. But it doesn't show the time, it shows the level of your Griffin magic. So in place of a watch face, it has a large ruby. The ruby loses its color once you've used all your Griffin power, and then the color slowly refills at the same rate your magic replenishes. At least, that's how it's supposed to work, and obviously you need to be wearing it."

"Wow, that is clever." I take the bracelet from the box, open the clasp, and place the rigid form around my wrist. The clasp clicks easily into place. As I watch, a fraction of one side of the ruby becomes red. "Huh, I guess that makes sense. It was just before midday that my Griffin Ability turned on, so that was about … two or three hours ago?"

"Yes. So this is supposed to make it easier for you to see when your magic is ready to be used. You know, in case it varies slightly if you're extremely tired, or if you can't always sense it."

"Cool." I lower my arm. "So this was made by … Yokshin? Is that his name?"

"Yes, the inventions master. He experiments with all kinds of magic. Spells, processes, devices." She leans against the railing, flashes a wide smile, and waves at two young men walking below. "It's a fascinating line of work," she continues, turning back to me. "I used to visit him a lot when I was younger, until Mother told me it wasn't appropriate to spend so much time with someone of his station, especially when he sometimes took me to the prison to show me some of his experiments."

"The prison?"

"Yes, just the small one we have here. Anyway, do you like the bracelet?"

"Yes. As you pointed out, it's both pretty and clever." I angle the bracelet this way and that so the mostly colorless gem catches the light. "Has Yokshin made any enchanted jewelry for you?"

"Uh … some." I look up to see her playing with the pendant hanging from a chain around her neck. The silver one with the black stone. I've noticed she wears it more often than her many other pieces of jewelry. "I'll tell you about it another time, though," she adds. "For now, we need to start getting ready."

"Yeah, okay. Um, where's Roarke? Didn't he want to give me this gift himself?"

"He did, but you know men. They don't want to get in the way when ladies are dressing."

"Or he's still avoiding me," I grumble as I walk past her into the sitting room.

"Avoiding you? What nonsense is that?" Aurora follows me inside. "He sees you at least twice a day when he gives you the compulsion potion."

"Yes, that's the *only* time he sees me."

"Well, he's very busy."

Or he's avoiding being around me whenever my Griffin Ability is active—just in case I don't consume all my power on whatever command he's given me and I'm able to use the rest of it to get information out of him. Which is exactly what I would have done if he'd been around. I've been practicing holding my Griffin Ability back. Eventually I have to let some of it go by saying whatever I've been compelled to say, but there've been times when I can sense there's still power left over. I've tried holding onto it until I see Roarke again, but I haven't managed to last that long yet.

"Em?"

"Mm?" I face Aurora, realizing belatedly that she asked me a question.

"I asked if you're actually starting to like Roarke. Is that why you're upset you don't get to see him more often?"

"Oh. Um. Maybe." I guess that's a better reason than *I'm upset because I haven't had a chance to use my Griffin Ability on him.*

She shakes her head and sighs. "You are so bad at lying. Come, let's go to my room. Your dresses arrived earlier and Mother's having them sent up now." She links arms with me. "You can rehearse your epic love story on the way."

The walk to Aurora's suite is long enough for me to recite my 'epic love story' twice. "Well done," she says as we reach her sitting room. "You've got the facts straight. Now you just have to work on sounding as though you actually mean the part about falling passionately in love."

"I'll be sure to do a better job when I'm lying to the elite fae of Unseelie society later."

"Wonderful."

We head into her bedroom, which is far larger than mine and includes a walk-in closet the size of a double garage. "Oh, here's the jewelry Mother selected for you. I meant to show you earlier while we were having breakfast." She lifts a box from her vanity and opens it to show me the contents. "Necklace and earrings. Lovely, aren't they?"

'Lovely' probably isn't the word I would use. Each piece consists entirely of glittering, colorless stones. The earrings are teardrops the size of my thumbnail, and the necklace is a double row of stones that gradually grow larger as they reach a pendant: another large, faceted teardrop. "Are … are they real?" I ask as Aurora removes them from the box.

She steers me toward the seat in front of the vanity before giving me a quizzical look in the mirror. "What do you mean? They're not some kind of illusion that will disappear once the party's over, if that's what you're wondering."

"No, I mean … are they real diamonds?" She seems to want me to sit, so I do. "Or are they fake? Like, glass or crystal or something."

She laughs. "Of course they're real diamonds. Why would we use fake ones?" I remain silent as she fastens the earrings to my ears and places the necklace around my neck. "There. I think they suit you. They'll look gorgeous no matter which dress we choose."

I shake my head at my reflection. I pull the earrings off and remove the necklace. "I don't think I should wear these." I place the sparkling diamonds carefully in Aurora's hand. "Here. You can give them back to your mom."

"What? Why?"

"I can't wear something so valuable. What if the necklace falls off while I'm dancing? What if I misplace the earrings after taking them off, and then—"

"And then what? Don't be so silly, Em. The necklace isn't going to fall off." She opens the box and places the jewelry back on its velvety cushion. "And who cares if it does? Mother certainly won't. This is probably the least valuable jewelry she owns."

I try not to feel ill at her words. "Aurora—"

"Come on, stop making such a big deal out of this."

"But it is a big deal," I snap. She takes a step back, surprised at my anger. "I'm sorry. It's just … well, I wouldn't expect you to understand," I murmur.

She crosses her arms. "And why is that? Because I don't seem to place nearly as much importance on jewelry as you suddenly seem to?"

I roll my eyes. "You know that's not what I mean." I gesture to the box. "That many diamonds are probably worth more than … I don't know. The whole of Stanmeade. I can't bring myself to wear that much wealth on my body, and you wouldn't understand that because we come from such vastly different backgrounds."

"Yes," she says, giving me a look that quite plainly says, *Duh*. "We do. This isn't a brand new revelation, so why is it suddenly a big deal?"

I don't know. I can't tell her why this diamond jewelry has suddenly shone an ever so sparkling light on the difference between my life and hers, or why I'm suddenly comparing my mother to hers. The queen is perfectly sane and in a position to hand out items of immense wealth as if they cost nothing. Mom is lost somewhere inside her own mind and hasn't been able to give me anything except the weight of responsibility for a very long time. "I'm sorry," I murmur, staring at the makeup strewn across the top of the vanity. "I can't wear that jewelry. It just makes me think of everything I've never had. All the things that … that my mom could never give me. And I don't mean the expensive things, I just mean the normal things. And all the things she couldn't *be* to me once she began to lose her mind."

"Em …"

"No, I'm not looking for your pity. I'm just saying …" I don't know what I'm saying anymore. "I just … don't want to wear it, if that's okay?"

She nods. "Okay. Of course. I would never want to make you uncomfortable. Uh …" She turns toward the doors to her closet. "I'm sure I can find you something simpler from my collection."

I stand, beginning to feel even worse now that she's being so understanding. "I'm sorry, Rora. I didn't mean to sound ungrateful. I'm thankful for everything you and your mother have done to help me fit in here. I just don't yet know how to deal with all …" I gesture vaguely with both arms. "All this."

She takes my hand, squeezes it, and smiles. "It's fine. I understand." She walks to her closet, then pauses in the doorway and looks back. "Roarke used to call me Rora when we were younger. Then he grew up and decided it was a silly, childish name. I told him I agreed, but the truth is, I kind of miss hearing him call me Rora."

I wind my hair around my finger. "I ... I don't really know why I said Rora. It just came out that way. I'm sorry. I don't want to make things awkward."

"That isn't what I mean." She smiles again. "You've probably been so focused on the idea of getting a husband you never asked for that you haven't thought about the fact that you're getting a sister too. I know none of this is what you wanted for your life. I know you're only going through it all for your mother. But ... well, I'm happy you're going to be my sister. I hope one day you can be happy too."

She heads into her enormous closet before I can say anything else, and at that moment, the door to the sitting room opens. I peer out of the bedroom door and see the queen, dressed in a robe and slippers, striding across the sitting area with three of her handmaids and an unfamiliar woman following her. Each of the handmaids carries a dress. "Your Majesty," I say to the queen, bowing my head in respect as she comes toward me.

"Emerson, hello." I've never seen her wearing so little makeup and with her hair—black and burgundy like Roarke's—so plain. She leans in and kisses the air on either side of my cheeks. "Ready for the big announcement tonight?"

"Yes," I say with confidence and a wide smile, neither of which are genuine.

"Aurora, love, I've got the dresses," the queen calls out, walking past me. "Ah, there you are," she adds as Aurora exits the walk-in closet.

"Ooh, exciting." Aurora rubs her hands together.

"Put the dresses over there," the queen tells her handmaids, "and then you may go." The handmaids leave the dresses floating in the air above the bed before turning and silently leaving the room. The woman I don't recognize brushes something off the skirt of one dress and plucks a loose thread from another.

I walk slowly around the bed so I can see the three dresses from all angles. The first has a full skirt of deep pink tulle with delicate flowers growing up the back from the waist to the neck. The second is the color of champagne. Its many-layered skirt is covered in gold flowers, and the tight bodice has a sweetheart neckline and no sleeves. The last option is made of rose gold fabric with thousands of tiny crystals glinting in the light as the dress sways gently in the air. The corset top laces up at the back, and though the skirt is kind of scrunched up with a bit of extra fabric over the butt, it isn't as puffy as the other two.

"They're beautiful," I say.

"Aren't they just?" Aurora replies. "And apparently, they're even more gorgeous when you put them on. The pink one changes back and forth between pink and purple, and the petals at the back slowly unfurl as the night goes on. The champagne one comes with a pair of long gloves made of a translucent fabric that looks like champagne bubbles rising up your arms. And the rose gold one has an enchanted shimmery effect that looks like glowing embers."

"Sounds cool."

"They're Raven Rosewood creations," Aurora continues. "Mother and I put the word out to all the top designers that we were looking for something spectacular for a very important event. We hinted at a potential engagement announcement—without using those exact words, of course—which resulted in plenty of rumors flying around. We had *dozens* of designs submitted, and Mother wasn't too keen on you wearing a Rosewood dress, seeing as—"

"Seeing as she's dressed some of the Seelies in the past," the queen fills in. "I did *not* want you wearing one of her dresses. When I saw her name on the outside of the scroll, I almost threw it away without opening it."

"But there was just something about her designs that we kept going back to," Aurora says. "Something that just … captivated us." A dreamy look comes over her face.

"They did turn out quite lovely," the queen admits. "I can see why this Rosewood woman has become popular in recent years."

"Did you send an invitation to her?" Aurora asks. "I want to meet her."

"Of course not, dear. I told you that wasn't appropriate. She has connections to the Guild, and she's designed for the Seelies before. We may have decided to use one of her creations, but I didn't feel comfortable having her here. I asked Lemon to send someone to pick up the dresses, and to be discreet about it."

"Oh, Em, this is Lemon, by the way," Aurora adds, gesturing to the woman who entered with the handmaids. "Our head clothes caster. She probably made most of the clothes you found in your wardrobe."

"Oh. Thank you, Lemon." I try not to snicker at the strange name. "You did a good job."

She nods to me. "Thank you, my lady. And yes, I sent Jefford to fetch the dresses this morning, and I made sure to impress upon him the importance of discreetness. Told him we don't want the embarrassment of anyone knowing we've associated with someone who's worked with Seelies before, even if her work is good."

"So silly," Aurora grumbles. "People are going to find out anyway. We're royalty, for goodness' sake. It's an honor to design for us, so I'm sure Raven Rosewood will tell people."

"Will she?" the queen asks. "I doubt she'd want to risk her reputation with the Seelies."

"She won't say anything," Lemon tells us. "Jefford left the dresses in my room with a note to say the pickup went smoothly. The designer accepted her payment and happily agreed to keep quiet about her involvement."

"And when people ask tonight?" Aurora says. "Because you *know* some of those women are going to want to know who dressed their new princess. All they care about is the latest fashion and trends, and once they see Em in, say, champagne bubble gloves, they'll all be adding the same thing to their new outfits."

"Really?" I ask. "That's so silly."

"That's the kind of influence you have as a princess," Aurora says with a self-satisfied smile as she leans against the vanity. "I once wore live sprites dangling from my ears, and at the next party, I saw at least five other girls wearing the same thing."

"Poor sprites," I murmur, imagining the creatures that look like tiny winged people tied to Aurora's earlobes.

"If anyone asks for the designer's name, tell them it's a secret," the queen says. "Tell them our head clothes caster has an especially inventive new apprentice, and we wish to keep him to ourselves."

Aurora sighs. "Fine. Anyway, we need to decide which one Em will wear so we can all start getting ready."

"Uh, shall I go and ask Roarke what he's decided to wear?" I suggest.

"Yes," the queen answers. "Aurora and I will check that all the adjustments for her new dress have been done correctly, and then she'll meet you in Roarke's suite."

With a glint in her eye, Aurora adds, "Mother doesn't trust you to accurately report what Roarke's outfit looks like without my help."

"Aurora," the queen scolds. Then her expression shifts into an apologetic smile. "Well, I suppose that's true. Sorry, Emerson."

I shrug, then freeze with my shoulders pulled up, remembering the queen doesn't like shrugging. "It's fine. See you there, Rora." I hurry out of the bedroom, waiting until I'm outside the suite before relaxing my shoulders.

The glossy marble floor passes quickly beneath my feet as I head for Roarke's suite. I knock on his door, but after waiting several moments, neither he nor one of his servants has called for me to come in. I knock again and wait, but still nothing.

The absence of guards outside his suite makes me doubt Roarke is inside, but he has mentioned that sometimes his guards patrol further along the hallways just outside this wing of the palace. I crack the door open just enough to stick my head inside. "Roarke?"

No response. Knowing Aurora will be here in a few minutes, I decide to wait in Roarke's sitting room until she joins me. I shut the door and wander slowly around the couches, comparing the suite to Aurora's. Similar furniture fills the space, though in a less delicate style with dark wood and glossy black finishes. I walk to the window and find that I have an excellent view of a sculpture I've never been able to see properly from the ground: a giant snake rearing toward the sky, surrounded by black rose bushes. *Creepy*, I think to myself as I turn away from the window.

From the corner of my eye, I notice movement near the bedroom door. Something dark, like a shadow sliding across the wall. I turn quickly, expecting to see someone there—Roarke or one of his servants—but no one is behind me. I turn on the spot, my eyes traveling over every inch of the room. I look at the wall again, but the shadows created by the furniture and decor are motionless. It must have been something outside. A bird flying past the window, perhaps. Still, this is a palace filled with magic and enchantment, so it's possible I saw the shadow of something that is now hiding in this room with me.

The idea sends a shiver up my neck and into my hair. *Be brave*, I remind myself. *This is your home now. You can't be afraid in your own home.* Forcing my legs to move, I walk around the room again. I bend and look under the furniture. I pull the curtains away from the wall and look behind them. As far as I can tell, I'm alone in this room.

But this isn't the only room in the suite. My eyes slide to the doorway leading to the bedroom. That is, after all, where I saw the movement. I cross the room and peek around the half-open door. I see another window and part of a four-poster bed. No movement or sound, though, so after a moment I push the door open enough to walk into the bedroom. The bedroom that will soon be mine too. The *bed* that will soon be mine.

An image of Roarke and me together in that bed flashes across my mind before I can stop it. I swallow in discomfort and try to push the image away. I've been avoiding thinking about that particular part of our union, but now that I'm staring at the bed that will soon belong to both of us, it's impossible not to think of what will have to happen in it.

I turn away as a shiver whispers across my skin. I still have time, I remind myself. Time to find a way out of this whole arrangement. The engagement announcement will happen tonight, but the actual union ceremony won't take place for another few weeks.

A voice out in the sitting room startles me, but it's only Roarke. "Yes, please close the door, Marvyn," he says. "I'll only be a few minutes." Breathing out and almost laughing at myself for my silly fears, I turn back toward the door. Hopefully Roarke won't be too annoyed after I explain why I'm in his room.

But I stop when I hear a second voice. A female voice.

"Is it still safe to speak in here?" she asks.

"Yes," Roarke answers. "We won't be overheard."

CHAPTER 9

Crap. I cover my mouth with my hand and freeze.

"You're certain?" the woman asks.

"Yes. My father has no control over this suite. My men scour it daily for enchantments and bugs, and they haven't found anything in years."

"Still," the woman says as her footsteps cross the room. "Someone might see us through the window." Her voice sounds familiar, but I can't place it. I've overheard so many ladies of the court since I arrived here. It could be any one of them.

"I doubt it. We're very high up. And if someone does see us, so what? I'm the prince, and I have the right to speak to whomever I please."

My imagination jumps immediately to the worst conclusion. Anger heats my veins at the thought of Roarke cheating on me. Why else would he be meeting a woman privately in his suite? A woman who doesn't want anyone seeing the two of them together? And it's not as though I'm jealous, but he's supposed to be marrying *me* in a few weeks! I reach for the door, about to pull it open fully and demand whether I can expect this kind of thing to continue after our union takes place.

"Okay then," the woman says. "So what are you doing about the ink-shades?"

I stop with my hand raised. *Ink-shades?* I wasn't expecting that.

"You have to get them under control, Roarke. We can't have them terrorizing this world. Or the other world. We can't live there until they've been eradicated completely."

"It's fine. My men are taking care of it."

"Like the guard who showed up dead? Wrinkled and aged?"

Roarke sighs. "You told me you weren't going to get upset about that."

"I've been thinking about it and I've decided I have every right to get upset about something like that. The same thing could happen to us."

I tilt my head toward to the doorway, wishing I could see their body language. Wishing I could figure out the nature of Roarke's relationship to this woman.

"The same thing most certainly will not happen to us," he assures her. "It only happened to that guard because he was stupid enough to let an ink-shade catch him when he wasn't wearing his amulet. And he should have known the right spell to fight back with, but clearly he was too slow. The rest of my men know what they're doing."

"Well they're certainly taking a while to get the job done. All this time wasted. Building has halted. The castle and grounds are just standing there half-formed, and—"

"Relax. It takes time to fill a world."

"Time in which someone else could discover it and claim it as their territory."

"Who's going to claim it? No one else knows about it."

"That isn't true now that you've let other people see it."

"I've told you already," Roarke says. "Neither my father nor Aurora have any interest in claiming that world as their own. He still has the same misbeliefs he had in the beginning, and you know Aurora's far more interested in—"

"I don't mean *them*." There's a pause in which I lean closer to make sure I don't miss her next words. "What about your future *wife*? And the guardian who happened to be with her?" A chill passes through me. I take a silent step backward, as if they might somehow sense my presence if I stand too close to the door.

"Emerson doesn't know what she saw," Roarke says, "and I doubt she even cares. She probably assumed it was part of the fae world. She doesn't know enough about this realm to assume it would be anything else. As for the guardian … well, I doubt he has any clue what he saw either. Guardians are trained to fight, not to think."

"You shouldn't underestimate him," she says darkly.

"And you shouldn't be worrying."

"Okay. Fine. So we're not in a rush. But I'm still worried about the ink-shades. How are they getting through? And is it only here at the palace, or do you think they're able to get through to any part of this world? Or …" She pauses for a moment. "I wonder if they're able to get through to the human world."

"If they can, it'll be the Guild's problem, not ours."

"True."

"And that probably won't happen, because my men are making sure that all the ink-shades will soon be dead."

"Good. Well then, can I get the cloak I came in here for? Marvyn might get suspicious if I walk out without it."

"Marvyn is suspicious already," Roarke says with a chuckle, "but I'll get you the cloak anyway." His footsteps move toward the bedroom. I curse beneath my breath—which sends an image of Dash rushing through my mind for just a second; he wouldn't be impressed with my choice of language. I duck through the only other door and into Roarke's en-suite bathroom. Slipping behind the half-open door, I hold my breath.

And that's when I see what's on the wall to my left.

I clap my hand over my mouth to suppress my startled gasp. A large circle of swirling, sparkling magic takes up most of the wall. Electric blue in color, with dark wispy bits rising from the edges and disappearing, the magic spins lazily in a spiral shape that seems to be sucked inwards at the center.

A portal?

A tiny part of me is curious to know where it leads—if it is indeed a portal—but mostly I'm terrified of what may come charging through from the other side. I lean as far away from it as I can while still remaining hidden behind the bathroom door. Fortunately, Roarke only takes a few moments in his bedroom. The moment I hear him walk out, I tiptoe hurriedly out of the bathroom and hover near the open bedroom doorway.

"… concerned about Marvyn and his suspicions?" the mystery woman asks.

"No, don't worry. He's paid well enough to keep his suspicions to himself."

"Good. Well, I'll leave you to prepare your announcement for tonight. I'm excited that this union will finally be official. Hopefully the ceremony will happen soon."

"It will," Roarke says.

Several moments of quiet follow, in which I begin to feel even more confused than before. This woman wants to hide her meetings with Roarke the way a secret lover would, but she's happy that he'll be marrying me?

I hear the main door to the suite open and close. I wonder if they're both gone, but then I hear Roarke's footfalls—heavier than the woman's—move across the sitting room. Terrified that he might return to his bedroom, I start tiptoeing back toward the bathroom. But the scrape of a chair tells me he's probably sitting now. I crouch down near the bed anyway, just in case I have to slide beneath it quickly for cover.

After several minutes that feel like hours, I hear a knock on the door. Then Aurora's voice once the door is open: "Oh, where's Em?"

Dammit.

"How should I know?" Roarke asks. "I thought she was with you."

Crap, crap, crap.

I do the only thing I can think of: I rush to the nearest window, swing my legs over, and lower myself down on the other side. The tips of my satin ballet-type shoes search out the footholds between the marble bricks. The shoes will be scuffed by the time I make it back inside, but hopefully no one will notice. I descend carefully, pausing as my foot feels the gap of the next window down. I move to the side, climb down another few bricks, and peek in through the side of the window. It looks like a private sitting room. Comfortable chairs, a cabinet full of drinks, a disgustingly ornate gold-framed mirror on one wall, and paintings of half-naked women on the others. But most importantly, there's no one in it.

I step onto the windowsill and hop inside. Seconds later, I'm out in the hallway, walking as quickly as I can without risking attention if I happen to pass someone. I swiftly navigate a few turns until I arrive at the stairway leading up to the royal family's wing. I run up—and almost crash into Aurora at the top.

"Oh, there you are," she says, relief appearing on her face. "What happened? I thought you were going to Roarke's suite." I search her features for any sign of suspicion, but all I see is confusion.

"He isn't there," I tell her. "One of the maids said she saw him near the library, so I went looking for him. Waste of time, though, since he wasn't there either. Are you sure he's finished with whatever important business he was dealing with this morning?"

"Yes, I just saw him in his chambers."

I roll my eyes and laugh. "This is what happens when you live in a home the size of a small city. We could run around all day looking for each other and never pass."

"And that," Aurora says as she takes my arm and turns us back toward her suite, "is why we have servants to do the running around for us. Anyway, I saw Roarke's outfit. I think it will go splendidly with the rose gold dress. Are you happy with that?"

I'm happy with anything that diverts Aurora's attention from the fact that I wasn't where I was supposed to be. Hopefully, if Roarke questions my whereabouts later, he'll believe my story just as easily. "That sounds perfect," I tell her. "The rose gold one is my favorite."

I follow her back into her suite where a flurry of activity has already begun. Hair stylists and makeup artists arrange their tools and spells. Lemon the clothes caster fusses about tiny imperfections in our dresses. The queen's handmaids flit in and out with messages from Aurora's mother about jewelry, hair ornaments, snacks and other trivial matters. And all the while, my mind is full of the conversation I wasn't supposed to hear and the magic I wasn't supposed to see.

CHAPTER 10

Night has fallen, winter has settled, and the ballroom is alive with activity. Women in gorgeous gowns and men in traditional faerie attire—suit pants and high-necked jackets with sharp angled shoulders—mingle on the dance floor at the center of the ballroom. Dozens of round tables encircle the room, each with a dragon ice sculpture forming the heart of the centerpieces. From the glass chandelier at the center of the ceiling, strings of tiny sparkling lights radiate outward. And from the ceiling itself, glittering snowflakes tumble downward, vanishing into nothing before reaching anyone's head.

I stand toward one side of the room with Aurora and two of her ladies-in-waiting who, it seems, have been allowed to return from the holiday Aurora sent them on. They chatter on and on, occasionally sending curious glances my way, while I try to pretend I'm interested in whatever they're talking about. The truth is, my mind couldn't be further away from this party. I can't get the thought of ink-shades out of my head. Roarke and that woman were obviously speaking about the place he and Aurora whisked me away to the day they found me in my old bedroom at Chelsea's house. The place where Dash and I ran from a shapeless shadowy creature—an ink-shade?—and ended up back in the faerie world near the tear in the veil. With everything else occupying my mind, I'd barely thought of that incident until this afternoon.

My gaze travels across the crowd as I wonder which of these ladies was in Roarke's room earlier. It could be any—

"And what brings you to the Unseelie Court, Em?" The question comes from one of Aurora's ladies. Mizza? Some strange name like that.

I take a moment to get my smile in place, but Mizza doesn't seem to notice. "The

Guild wanted to imprison me, but some of the Unseelies—personal guards of Prince Roarke's, actually—rescued me."

She lets out a ladylike gasp and places one hand against her chest. "Oh, how thrilling. Was the prince with them at the time? He is *so* handsome, don't you think?"

"Why did the Guild want to imprison you?" the other young lady asks. Her name has completely escaped me.

"I'm Griffin Gifted, so the Guild thought I deserved to be locked up."

Both ladies' mouths drop open, but I maintain my serene smile. I'm allowed to start sharing the first part of my story now—minus the specifics of my Griffin Ability. By mentioning Roarke's name when speaking of my rescue, I'm hoping people will be more likely to believe him when he stands up later and announces that I'm the love of his life.

"It's a very exciting story," Aurora adds, "and I promise I'll tell you all about it later. But right now, I want to introduce Em to some other people."

"That wasn't too bad, was it?" she asks quietly as she ushers me away.

"Uh … I don't know. I didn't listen to most of what they said."

"Em!" She smacks my arm, but her mock horror soon turns to a smile. "I suppose it is all quite overwhelming for you if you haven't been to an event like this before. So many distractions."

"Yes," I murmur, watching a miniature pegasus fly past. Raising my eyes, I notice there are quite a few of them in the air, each a different pastel shade. As I watch, a woman reaches up, catches one, and bites its head off.

"Oh," I gasp, jerking to a halt. "That's horrible."

"What is?" Aurora follows my gaze and starts laughing. "Oh, Em, it's just a flying cake. They aren't real creatures." She stands on tiptoe and grabs one. It struggles in her grip, but the moment she pulls its wing off, it stops moving. "See? Just cake and icing." She holds the wing out to me, and beneath the pastel pink outer layer, I see caramel-colored cake.

"Um, no thank you," I say when she tries to get me to take the wing part. "That's just disturbing." I look away from the woman sharing the beheaded pegasus with her friend and concentrate on smoothing out my frown. "So, do people know there's a reason they're here other than your mother's birthday?"

"No one knows for certain, but they all suspect an engagement announcement," Aurora says. "I've heard the words 'engagement' and 'union' a number of times while walking around this evening."

"And I'm not supposed to confirm their suspicions yet if anyone asks me?"

"No. Let's keep people wondering for a little while longer. They can spread as many rumors around this ballroom as they like until Roarke makes the announcement. Now, let's see." She touches the choker of black pearls resting at the base of her neck as she looks around. "Who can I introduce you to—Oh. Never mind." The musicians on the raised platform at the far end of the ballroom have stopped playing. Aurora looks toward the massive arched doorway along with everyone else in the room. "My parents have arrived," she whispers to me.

As the Unseelie King and Queen are announced, every guest in the ballroom bows or curtseys. "Welcome," King Savyon shouts out as we all rise. "Thank you for joining us as we celebrate Queen Amrath's birthday. Tonight, you will delight in the grandest of entertainment, feast on the most exotic of dishes, and dance until the sun rises. Let the celebrations begin!"

The chandelier explodes, and the ballroom fills with shrieks and gasps. I duck down and look up, my thoughts floundering to figure out what's going on. An outside attack? The king losing his mind and killing us all? But as the smoke clears, I see hundreds of parachute-like objects floating down toward the crowd. Fearful murmurs turn to whispers of amazement, then to laughter and pointing. Aurora catches two parachutes and hands one to me. A small cube-shaped box hangs from a canopy of petals. As I place the box on my palm, the sides and top disappear, revealing a silver rose within.

"Perfect," Aurora says with a smile. "They turned out exactly how Mother wanted them to."

"What is it?"

"Chocolate." She giggles. "And an enchantment that keeps you from tiring until the sun rises. We'll be partying all night." She pops the rose into her mouth and gestures for me to do the same. I chew the bitter chocolate as I look around at people jumping to catch parachutes, passing them around to their friends, and comparing roses to see if they're all the same. My gaze falls across a man looking at me—and my heart almost stops as I recognize Dash.

Shock slams into me as he looks away and two women jumping for parachutes block him momentarily from view. It can't be him. It's a trick of my imagination, my mind morphing some other young man into the image of Dash. Nevertheless, I blink and peer more closely, some part of me hoping that it might actually be him. But it isn't. His hair is different, and his arm, I notice when he reaches up for one of the falling parachutes, is bare, lacking the markings of a guardian.

"Oh, look!" Aurora grabs my arm and pulls me around. She points upward as the light in the room dims and people in sparkly leotards descend through the air from the ceiling. They slip gracefully between the strings of lights and hang just below them, slowly twirling and somersaulting in coordinated movements to the accompaniment of eerie music. It reminds me somewhat of synchronized swimming, or aerial silks where acrobats perform while hanging from pieces of fabric. Except now, there's no water to float in. There's no fabric to hang from. These performers are suspended in midair by magic.

The evening continues with dancing—which I manage not to mess up—eating, and drinking, interspersed with various outlandish, magical forms of entertainment: jugglers tossing multicolored balls into the air where they transform into rainbow candies that whizz around making popping sounds and shooting star-shaped candies at everyone; a woman blowing bubbles into any shape her audience requests; a pair of centaurs who gallop in and perform a dramatic dance before galloping out; and a man who coaxes his magic into an Imperia-sized dragon made entirely of fire.

My imagination feels like it's on overload from all the fantastical things I've seen in the space of only a few hours when Roarke finally comes up to me. I've seen him from a distance this evening, dressed similarly to most of the other men but with the cuffs and high collar of his jacket made from gold embossed fabric. We agreed a few days ago that we wouldn't speak or dance together until after the announcement. So if he's standing in front of me now, that must mean—

"My lovely Lady Emerson, I believe we have an announcement to make."

I swallow as my stomach lurches. "Oh. Is it that time of the evening already?" I'd hoped to put it off as long as possible. In fact, part of me has been pretending all night that if I refused to think about it, it might never happen.

"Let us not keep our guests waiting any longer." Roarke places his hand against my back and directs me toward the raised platform where the musicians are seated. "I think we've built the suspense long enough. Everyone's enjoying themselves, but by now there isn't a single guest in this room who isn't wondering which pretty lady their prince has chosen for a wife. Let's put all their whispered speculations to rest."

The closer we get to the platform, the quieter the room becomes. Finally, as we climb the three steps leading up the side, silences descends, interrupted only by the occasional whisper and the rustle of skirts. "Remember to show everyone how happy you are," Roarke murmurs, his lips barely moving and his smile still in place.

I'm not sure I can fake happy right now, but I can at least hide my fear. As Roarke faces the crowd and I come to a standstill beside him, I try to mimic the way he holds himself, pushing my shoulders back and tilting my chin up slightly. I force my lips into as much of a smile as I can manage.

Then I make the mistake of looking out at the crowded ballroom. Hundreds of faces stare back at me with expressions ranging from curiosity to outright dislike. *Don't show fear, don't show fear.* I blink and settle my gaze on the far wall, just above the line of people. *Don't fidget, remain poised, keep smiling.* But despite my mask of confidence, a distant roar begins to fill my ears. My heart pounds so wildly I fear I may actually go into cardiac arrest.

Roarke begins speaking, but I hear only scraps of what he's saying: my past in the human realm, my Griffin Gifted status, my rescue from the Guild. I hear the words 'quick courtship' and 'deeply in love,' and then finally, Roarke looks at me, takes my hand in his, and says, "I've never been happier than the moment my father gave us permission to be united." He faces the crowd again, keeping hold of my hand. "And so, my lords and ladies, I present to you the woman I will be uniting with in exactly twelve days: the beautiful, captivating, kind Emerson."

Silence greets the prince's final words. It hovers, expands, presses against my ears, and then finally—it pops. Shouts, cheers and applause fill my ears, and suddenly this union seems all too real. I know I agreed to it, but as long as it wasn't official, I assumed I would find a way out of it. But now that everyone knows, it seems almost impossible. For the first time, it hits me—*really* hits me—that I may have to go through with this. I will marry a prince. This palace and these people will become my life. This will all become my mother's life too. For as long as it takes to figure out how we'll escape.

"Shall we dance now, my love?" Roarke asks me.

Not trusting myself to speak, I simply nod. He leads me down the platform and toward the center of the ballroom as the music starts up again. My legs begin to shake at the thought of an entire ballroom of people watching us dance, but Roarke raises his voice and encourages everyone to join in. With excited chattering, they rush to find partners as Roarke and I face each other and move into the starting position.

I've already danced numerous times this evening, but it's different now. No one cared who I was before. No one paid attention to me. But now, even though they're all dancing too, I feel their eyes on me. It would have been great if my Griffin Ability had been able to give me the skill to perfectly perform every step, but apparently my Griffin Ability didn't know how to do that. So I'm left to concentrate intently on every move, every intricate piece of footwork, every twirl and pivot. Fortunately, with an expert partner like Roarke, it's easy to hide the odd mistake and hesitation.

Partners switch around us as the music changes again and again, but Roarke hangs onto me for a number of dances. He presses a kiss beneath my ear at one point, and I have to work hard to keep from cringing. I tell myself to be grateful he didn't go for my lips. Eventually, he hands me over to another partner, and now I really have to concentrate, my attention split between making polite conversation and following the steps.

Time passes. I continue circling the room, switching to a new partner whenever appropriate. Though I'm entirely out of my comfort zone, the music entices me to continue dancing. Or is it the enchanted chocolate I ate earlier?

Dance, converse, switch partners, repeat. I begin to wonder how long I have to do this before I can excuse myself from the dance floor and take a break from it all. I spin around and into the arms of yet another partner. A man, I realize with my second shocking jolt of the evening, that I do recognize after all.

Dash.

PART II

CHAPTER 11

My feet stumble to a halt. An odd combination of joy and horror rockets through me. Dash's hair is completely different, as I noticed earlier, and several days' worth of well-groomed stubble adds to his disguise. But it's definitely him.

"Don't stop dancing," he says, forcing me to jerkily step back in time with the music. Then, after giving the dancers around him a pleasant and entirely fake smile, he hisses, "What the hell is wrong with you?"

Another shocked second passes before I find my voice. "Me? What is wrong with *you*? How did you even—what did you—do you know what Roarke and Aurora will do if they recognize you?"

"They saw me for all of five seconds that day. They're not about to recognize me now."

"But how did you even—"

"*What are you doing here, Em?* Why are you playing along with this stupid union charade? I expected to find a prisoner, and instead—"

"We are *not* having this discussion here," I tell him through clenched teeth, my smile completely forgotten now. "Meet me outside." I tug free of his grip and twist around. The man I bump into looks startled. He and the woman he's dancing with almost stumble. But fortunately, after two or three fumbling seconds, everyone switches partners, and for anyone watching, it probably appears that the almost-princess accidentally tried to switch a few seconds early. I gladly step into the confused man's arms and continue dancing, trying to keep a serene smile in place while my heart thunders in my chest.

I can still barely believe it. *Dash is here.* Through my anger and terror—because this is exactly the kind of thing I was trying to avoid when I chose to come here, and

273

now he's messing it all up—I'm heart-achingly glad to see him.

"Was it awful growing up in the non-magic realm?" my dance partner asks.

"Uh, well, I didn't know any better, so I didn't know what I was missing out on."

"How thrilling to have discovered you actually belong to this world instead."

"Yes. Magic is ... so wonderful." I'm distracted as I catch a glimpse of Dash with another partner.

When the dance ends, I manage to politely decline the woman who was hoping to be my next partner. I slip past her and weave my way off the dance floor, between the tables and chairs, and toward the arched doorway that leads to the gardens. It's odd looking out and seeing a glittering snow-white landscape while feeling so warm I'm almost sweating. There must be a spell across the open doorway that keeps the freezing winter air outside.

Looking back, I see at least two women making their way toward me with bright eyes and wide smiles, probably hoping to engage me in conversation. Wonderful. Now that everyone knows who I am, I'll never get out of this ballroom unnoticed. I search about for a distraction, and on the nearest table, I spot one of the popping rainbow candies. I discreetly drop it onto the floor, lift my skirt, and kick it to the side. It spins away from me and into the crowd, whizzing and popping and shooting tiny star-shaped candies everywhere. In the commotion, I meet Dash's eyes for a second. Then I turn and slip out into the night.

The cold hits me the moment I pass beneath the archway, but after all that dancing, the icy air is a welcome relief. After hurrying down the stairs, I turn right, step off the path, and wait in the shadow of a tree with silver, snow-dusted apples hanging from its branches. I breathe out long and slow, but my anxiety only increases as the seconds tick by and I wait for Dash.

I tense as hurried footsteps move down the stairs. Dash looks around, catches sight of me, and in a few quick strides he's standing in front of me. "What is wrong with you?" he demands immediately. "Waltzing around like you belong here. Playing along with this union idiocy. You can't possibly be planning to—"

"You want to talk about idiocy?" I snap right back. "*You* are an idiot. Why did you come here? These people are your enemies. Do you know what they'll do to you if they find out what you are and who you work for?"

"They're your enemies too, Em, but somehow you've let them manipulate you into marrying one of them—"

"I haven't been *manipulated* into anything," I counter, still trying to keep my voice to nothing louder than an angry whisper. "I *chose* to be here. Roarke presented an arrangement—marriage in return for healing my mother—gave me time to think about it, and I decided to accept his offer. The only person who wants to force me into anything is the king, but Roarke won't let him. He wants a willing wife. He isn't going to manipulate me into doing anything against my will, despite what you're thinking."

Dash looks like he's about to be sick. "You … you voluntarily came here? Nobody forced you into this?"

"Yes. He offered something I want, and I decided the price was worth it."

"The price is *marriage*, Em! A union! Have you stopped to think how serious that is? We're talking about *the rest of your life*. Unions in this world aren't like the ones in your world. It's a magical bond that isn't easily broken. And royal unions? I've *never* heard of one of those being broken. If you go through with this, it's forever."

I roll my eyes, even as the weight of his words pierce through to my core and leave my skin colder than it was a moment ago. "Now you're being an idiot again. I don't actually intend to go through with this union. I have a Griffin Ability, for goodness' sake. An extremely powerful one. When the moment is right, and when I've learned enough control, I'll get Roarke to tell me everything I need to know to heal my mother, and then I'll escape."

Dash still looks somewhat ill. "Seriously? That's your plan? You really think after all that in there—" he waves in the general direction of the ballroom again "—they're going to let you escape?"

"Okay, first of all, 'escape' implies that I'm not going to ask permission. I'm just going to leave. So it doesn't matter whether they *let* me or not. And secondly …" I slowly suck in a deep breath because I have to admit I'm feeling as sick as Dash looks. "Secondly, I realize that an escape might not be possible. They might catch me and force me to go through with this—"

"You think?"

"—despite everything Roarke says about wanting a willing wife," I continue, speaking over Dash. "And if that's the way it ends up, then so be it. At least I'll get the information I need, and then—"

"That's if Roarke actually follows through with his side of the bargain and tells you what he knows—which is probably *nothing*, by the way. How can he possibly know any more about your mother than the rest of us? But by the time you figure that out, it'll be too late for you." He throws his hands up and looks away as he shakes his head. "This whole plan of yours is utterly pointless."

A chill runs through me. My body has cooled down quickly, and the winter air feels as though it's seeping into my very bones. I run my hands vigorously up and down my arms. "It isn't pointless. Dark magic has trapped my mother in a permanent coma, and Roarke, as a member of the court that uses that kind of magic, knows how to wake her. And, more importantly, he knows what caused her mental illness. It *was* something magical, and he knows how to fix it."

"He's *lying*, Em," Dash says in the kind of tone he would use if talking to a naive child. Absently, he moves his hand in a quick circular motion above my head, and I immediately begin to feel warmer. "Do you really think a pampered prince knows anything about magical mental illnesses? He'd tell you anything to get you to stay and give him full access to your Griffin Ability. Why can't you see that?"

"He isn't lying. He knows far more about my past than anyone else I've come across in this world. He's already proved it to me. He's my best chance for saving Mom."

"But … this is just …" Dash struggles for a moment. He tugs at his hair, which I realize is a wig when it comes away in his hand, revealing his own messy hair underneath. "I know you want your mother to be better," he says, his eyes returning to mine, "but why does her health and happiness have to be solely *your* responsibility? Is she really—" He cuts himself off, breathing heavily. "I know this is going to make me sound like the bad guy. I don't want to ask you if she's worth it, because of course she's—"

"How can you even think that?" I gasp.

"I'm not! That's what I'm saying. Of course she's worth it. She's your mother, and clearly you love her more than anything else in either world, but …" His eyes plead with me. "Would she want you to do this? Would she want you to throw away your entire life in what is probably a futile attempt to save hers?"

"I'm not throwing away my entire life!" I shout. Then I remember myself. I remember Aurora's words—*My father has eyes and ears everywhere*—and I lower my voice again. It's barely a whisper now. My lips hardly move as I speak. "They might force me into a marriage, but that doesn't mean I'll be here forever. My Griffin Ability makes me more powerful than most people in this world. Mom and I *will* escape one day."

"Even if that's possible," Dash says, "how much evil will they force you to commit before then?"

"I … I …" I don't have an answer for that.

"Why do you think they want you, Em? You can make their dirty work easier, that's why." He takes hold of my shoulders and gives me a small shake. "These people are *not good*. Surely you know the kinds of things they're going to make you do?"

I pull myself free of his grasp. "You're wrong. Roarke isn't like that, and neither is Aurora." *But the king is*, a silent voice reminds me. That scene in the king's office—the scene I keep pushing out of my thoughts—appears abruptly at the front of my mind. The king with his hand clenching around the air, and that man's head ripping right off his—

I blink and wince and look away.

"Really?" Dash says. "They're not like that?"

I can tell without meeting his eyes that he knows I'm lying. I breathe in a shuddering breath. "I saw … something." I blink again and shake my head, trying to force the memory away. I focus on Dash's green eyes again, knowing there's no point in trying to convince him with lies I barely believe myself. There's no point in anything but the truth. "What other choice did I have, Dash?" My voice is a desperate whisper now, having lost its defensive edge. "These are the only people who can help me."

"You could have trusted *us*! Me and everyone else at the oasis. We *want* to help you, Em. We've done nothing except try to help you since you got to this world, and that wasn't about to change. I don't understand why you'd just turn your back on all of that and—"

"That's the point, Dash! That's why I had to leave."

He pauses, his eyebrows climbing higher. "Is that supposed to make sense?"

"You and your friends have done nothing but try to help me, and it almost got you *killed*. You were a glass statue. Remember that? You and Violet came so close to dying. *Dying*, Dash!" My voice rises as my chest tightens at the memory of that terrifying day.

"Yeah, but we didn't. It wasn't such a big deal."

"Of course it was a big deal! You almost died *because you tried to help me*. And Chelsea and Georgia actually *were* dead, and they would have stayed that way if my Griffin Ability hadn't made a convenient appearance. So after all that, I decided I didn't want anyone else to be put at risk because of me and my mother."

"Em—"

"Yes, I had everything I could have wanted at the oasis. It's beautiful, it's safe, the people are amazing. But if I'd stayed there, *someone* would have ended up hurt or dead because they tried to help me. This is *my* problem. She's my mother. If there's a price involved in returning her to normal, I'm the one who should pay it. No one else."

Dash is silent for too long before he says, "It's too late for that."

I blink, feeling cold again despite Dash's warmth-producing spell still surrounding me. "What do you mean?"

He shakes his head and looks away. "This … this isn't the way I wanted to tell you. I wanted to get you far away from here first. Back to the oasis."

"Before you tell me what?" I step closer and wrap one cold hand around his arm. "Tell me what, Dash? What happened?"

"Chelsea and Georgia …" He closes his eyes and presses his lips together before continuing. "They both … died."

I drop my hand from his arm as quickly as if his skin just burned me. "What?"

"It happened about two days after the glass incident with Ada."

"But … they can't be dead. My Griffin Ability brought them back to life."

"They were human, Em," he says gently. "Your Griffin Ability may have worked on them, but their bodies couldn't handle the magic. In the end, it killed them."

"But … are you sure they were human? I mean, she's my mother's sister, and my mother's a faerie. And what about all the herbal remedies Chelsea makes? I thought maybe … maybe those were actually magical."

Dash offers no explanations; he merely shakes his head. "I'm so sorry, Em."

"They … they're really dead?" I whisper. "My magic killed them. I thought it saved them, but it killed them."

"Em—"

"I killed my own family."

"It wasn't you who killed them," Dash says, his voice suddenly fierce. "Ada did, with her horrible glass magic. *She* shattered them into thousands of pieces. You did what you could to save them, but it wasn't enough. They were doomed from the moment she first touched them."

My legs can't hold me up. I crumple onto the ground, not giving a second's thought to the expensive dress I'm probably ruining. Quick, shallow breaths consume me as I stare unseeingly into the garden. Dash is still speaking, but I can't hear him anymore. I don't know how I'm supposed to react to this. Chelsea and Georgia didn't love me, and I didn't love them; I can't suddenly pretend otherwise just because they're dead. But they were family. They took me in, even though they constantly made it clear what a burden I was to them. And now they're dead, and I can't figure out what I'm supposed to feel aside from guilty.

"I never wanted any of this," I manage to whisper. I cover my face with my hands, wishing I could blot out this other world and its magic that's sent my life spinning so completely out of my control. "Can't someone just take it all away? Please. I don't want this magic. I don't want a Griffin Ability. I don't want to marry a prince. I just want to go back to that simple life Mom and I had before magic made her crazy and everything started to fall apart."

I feel Dash's arm on my shoulder and sense him crouching beside me. "I wish I could—"

"Emerson?"

I suck in a breath at the sound of Roarke's voice. Slowly, I lower my hands and watch him descend the stairs.

"What's going on? Why are you on the ground?"

Dash rises to face him.

"You," Roarke says slowly, recognition in his eyes. "Well now." His gaze moves to me as his expression becomes unreadable. "Isn't this an interesting situation."

CHAPTER 12

In less than a minute, I find myself back inside the warmth of the palace in a small sitting room somewhere near the ballroom. Despite the turmoil of emotions overwhelming me, I didn't dare disobey Roarke when he uttered "Follow me" in a tone icier than the winter air. Dash hesitated, but he soon caught up to the two of us. Back in the ballroom, no one stopped the prince or his betrothed. No one even looked our way. I suspect Roarke's magic was responsible for that.

The door of the sitting room swings shut of its own accord. Flames spring to life in the fireplace. "What is he doing here?" Roarke demands immediately, gesturing at Dash without looking at him.

"I … I don't …" I run my hands over my face, trying to focus on Roarke's words and seeing only Chelsea and Georgia's lifeless eyes. Their cold bodies. Alone in their beds in their little Stanmeade house. I blink and look into the crackling flames dancing in the fireplace, hoping to sear the bright, warm image into my mind. "I don't know," I say finally, turning away from the fire. "I was as shocked as you are to see him here. This thing is still attached to me—" I touch the coin-sized piece of metal behind my ear "—so no magic should have been able to locate me."

Roarke crosses the room. His fingers wrap around Dash's arm. "Where are your guardian markings?"

Dash tugs his arm away, then lets out a short laugh. "There's this thing girls use. It's called concealer. Works pretty well for covering—"

"And how did you get into my palace?"

Dash takes his time folding his arms over his chest before squarely facing Roarke. "Your mother decided to outsource the design of Em's dress for tonight. When one of your clothes casters came to pick it up, I made sure I was there, ready to take his place. His transport brought me back here. It was all remarkably easy, in fact."

"And how did you know Emerson was here in the first place?"

"An educated guess plus a process of elimination. I figured it was either you, the Seelies or the Guild who got hold of her. I asked around, and the Guild and the Seelies still seemed to be under the impression Em was either dead or missing. You know, since the incident at the cliff." Dash shrugs. "Therefore it had to be you guys."

"So you told your superiors all about your suspicions, and they rewarded you by letting you sneak your way into my home and poke your unwelcome nose around? Doubtful. You don't seem nearly high up enough in the Guild ranks to be trusted with a task as important as retrieving a dangerous and powerful Griffin Gifted faerie like Emerson."

Dash's gaze narrows slightly. "I'm not here on behalf of the Guild."

"Ah." Roarke nods. "I had a feeling it might be something along those lines." He walks to the dresser on the other side of the room and opens a drawer. "You and Emerson seemed to be getting very cozy when Aurora and I found the two of you together in her old bedroom." He closes the drawer and turns to face us again. "*After* she escaped the Guild. When you—a guardian—shouldn't have known anything about her whereabouts." He shakes his head and lets out a quiet laugh. "A traitor to your own kind, I see. How disappointing."

Dash's expression darkens. "Not really. I just happen to disagree with tagging, tracking and imprisoning Griffin Gifted."

"And do *you* have a tag on you, guardian boy? So that someone can summon you or determine your location?"

"I told you I'm not here on behalf of the Guild, so why would I be stupid enough to let someone tag me?"

"Good." Roarke moves toward Dash. "But just in case …" His hand sweeps up and slaps against the side of Dash's neck.

Almost too fast to see, Dash grabs Roarke's arm and twists it, spinning the prince around and trapping his arm behind his back. "What did you just do?" Dash hisses. The sound of a sizzle rushes through the air, and with a yelp, Dash shoves Roarke away from him. "What the—"

Roarke straightens, rolls his shoulders, and adjusts the collar of his jacket. "I don't appreciate being manhandled."

Dash feels the side of his neck. "What is this?" As his hand moves away, I see a small circle of metal just like the one behind my ear.

"A precaution, that's all," Roarke says.

"How dare you—"

"You sneak into *my* home, and you want to know how *I* dare to—"

"Stop!" I shout. My Griffin Ability isn't ready to issue a magical command yet, but my cry is enough to make both Roarke and Dash pause and look my way. "Just … just stop." My voice wavers. "My aunt and cousin are dead, and the two of you are acting like petty children."

A frown tugs at Roarke's eyebrows downward. "Your aunt and cousin? The ones you lived with in the non-magic world?"

I look back into the fire as I nod. "Dash told me. Outside. That's why I was sitting on the ground. I was … I just can't believe it."

"These are the people you didn't particularly care for?" Roarke asks, his tone not unkind, merely curious. "The ones who treated you poorly since you first moved in with them?"

I nod. "But they were still family. Well—I don't know what they were. Mom and Chelsea were sisters, but Mom's a faerie and Chelsea was human, so … they can't have been sisters? I don't know. I don't understand." I press my fingers to my temples again and squeeze my eyes shut. "But I lived with them. For years. I thought they were family, and now they're just *gone.*"

I hear Roarke's quiet footsteps moving closer before he places one hand carefully against the small of my back. "I'm sorry, Emerson. I can't imagine what that feels like. But I can promise you this: you're about to get an entirely new family. And though it may not be obvious from the outside, we *do* care about each other. We'll care for you too. You'll be one of us, and you'll finally belong somewhere. You and your mother."

Across the room, Dash snorts and mutters something under his breath. I almost do the same, because of course Roarke's true motive has nothing to do with a desire to give me a new family and a place to belong. He wants my Griffin Ability. But perhaps there's more to it than that. Perhaps he really does want this union to work out. Perhaps he does plan to care for me for the rest of our lives.

"You'll stay, of course," Roarke says to Dash. "For the ceremony. You're Emerson's friend. I'm sure she'll want you to be here."

"Your ceremony is more than two weeks away," Dash says before I can voice my own opinion. "I can't stay here for that long. I have a job, remember?"

"You also have a desire to stop this union," Roarke points out. "Which means that if I let you leave, you'll tell the Guild exactly what's happening, and they'll attempt to put a halt to our plans and retrieve Emerson. Or kill her."

"Dash wouldn't tell—"

"You don't know that for sure," Roarke says to me. "If you want this union to happen, then we can't take the risk of the Guild getting involved."

"The Guild will wonder where I am," Dash says.

"Let them wonder then. They don't know you're here."

Dash exhales slowly, his bright eyes never leaving Roarke. "I know this doesn't matter to you, but I have important cases—"

"You should have considered that before you broke into my home," Roarke says.

"Fine then." Dash forces his fists behind his back and gives Roarke the most obviously fake smile I've ever seen. "Thank you so much for the invitation, Your Royal Highness. I'd be delighted to stay here and attend your union ceremony."

Roarke nods. "Good. Just make sure your wrist markings remain covered. I can't guarantee your safety if my father discovers what you are."

"Certainly. And I'll keep my lips zipped and ask no questions about any of the laws you Unseelies have broken lately, or about, say, that colorless shadowy place I woke up in after you abducted Em and me."

"Perfect. See to it that you don't forget that promise," Roarke adds in a threatening tone.

"So … is Dash a guest?" I ask. "Or a prisoner?"

Roarke looks at me. "Would you like me to make him a prisoner?"

"Of course not."

"Then he is our guest." He moves closer and tucks a stray curl of hair behind my ear. "I only want to make you happy, Emerson. You've received some shocking news this evening, and I'm sure it will be a comfort to have your friend here."

My frown deepens. "But you don't trust him and you don't want him to leave. So why would you let him wander freely around your palace?"

"Don't worry, he'll be watched wherever he goes. If he steps out of line, I'll make sure the Guild finds out that he knows far more about the Griffin rebels than he's supposed to. I doubt he'll be able to keep his job after that." He looks at Dash. "Sound fair?"

Dash tips his head in the slightest of nods. "Perfectly fair, since I plan to be on my very best behavior, Your Regal Princely-ness."

A muscle in Roarke's jaw twitches, but, fortunately, he decides not to retaliate. "More importantly, my dear Emerson," he continues, turning back to me, "I'd like to show you that I care about your happiness. If that means treating your guardian friend as a guest instead of a prisoner, then I'll do it."

I still don't know whether to believe him, but I guess I'll find out in the coming days. "Okay," I say warily. "Thank you."

"Let's return to the ball now. Push your sorrow aside, my love, and join in the merriment. You'll soon feel better."

I doubt that's true, but I also doubt I have a choice. I don't think my request to leave the party, climb into bed, and pull the covers over my head would go down well. So I follow Roarke out of the room and back toward the party. I breathe in deeply and press my lips together to keep them from shuddering. I take the first drink that's offered to me and down it in one go, hoping the contents are enough to dull my senses for the rest of the night.

When it's close to midnight and my Griffin Ability comes to life, I say the words I've been compelled to say. No one hears me amidst the noise, but everyone oohs and aahs in wonder at the six rainbows that arc one after the other across the room as if marking the twelve points of a giant colorful clock. I wish I could experience a little of their awe at the sight of what my own magic has produced, but it seems the various drinks I've consumed are doing their job: I don't feel much of anything anymore.

CHAPTER 13

When Clarina wakes me the following morning, I feel a little as though someone shoved a stake through my eyeball. And a screwdriver through my other eyeball. Someone must have also turned up the brightness of the sun; I can only peel my eyelids apart for about half a second before having to squeeze them shut again.

"Your lunch is in the sitting room, my lady," Clarina says. "Everyone is eating alone today, as some are still recovering from last night."

"Lunch?" I ask in a croaky voice.

"Yes, it's almost midday, my lady." Her footsteps move closer, and she adds, "The drink beside your bed will ease your headache."

I push myself slowly up and squint at the crystal goblet of clear liquid. I almost ask how she knows about my aching head, but I suppose she's been here long enough to be fully aware of the many hangovers that follow an event like last night's ball.

"Your pool has been filled," she adds.

"Thank you." I swing my legs over the edge of the bed and stare at the floor for a while as my brain runs through the events of the previous night. I remember that Dash is here now. I remember that Chelsea and Georgia are … dead.

I pick up the goblet, and my eyes fall on the outfit Clarina has chosen for me today, hanging on the outside of the wardrobe. A double-breasted coat-dress type thing, aquamarine with floral patterns of white, green and mauve. The queen's birthday celebrations continue with a tea in the gardens this afternoon, so Clarina was obviously told to choose something appropriately festive for me. It's pretty, but it doesn't feel right to wear something so … alive.

"Clarina?" I call, hoping she's still in the next room.

"Yes, Lady Emerson?" She hurries back to the bedroom.

"Would it be okay if you choose a black outfit for me today? Or grey, perhaps, if black is too depressing for the queen's tea party?"

"Uh, certainly, my lady. That should be fine. I believe there's a charcoal-colored item with silver embroidered details. Will that do?"

"Yes, thank you."

I don't feel any kind of deep sorrow for the loss of Chelsea and Georgia. I'm still shocked, barely able to believe they're gone, but I know there was no love lost between us. Still, it feels wrong to simply move on with life and forget about them. I need to do *something*, and if wearing black or grey is the only thing left to me, then that's what I'll do.

The concoction in the goblet works remarkably quickly, and my pounding headache is soon gone. Though I'd like to soak in the pool of purple bubbles for a whole lot longer, I should probably find out where Dash is and make sure he hasn't got himself into any trouble.

After drying and dressing, I do up the buttons of my charcoal outfit and pad barefoot into my sitting room in search of some food. I select the most normal-looking sandwich and head back to my bedroom to choose a pair of shoes.

At the sight of a figure sitting on the edge of my bed, I freeze. He turns his head—and I realize it's Dash.

"Jeez, Dash. Are you trying to give me a heart attack? How did you get in here?"

He gestures over his shoulder to the window where the curtain ripples gently in the warm breeze. "Your window was open. I climbed up to it."

I want to tell him he's as bad as I am, climbing palace walls, but I'm too frightened that someone important might discover he's in my bedroom. "You can't be here," I whisper. "If Roarke or his father find you in my *bedroom*, of all places—"

"No one saw me, don't worry. I didn't leave my room through the door, so anyone watching will assume I'm still inside. And I found your room quite easily. Didn't have to look into too many others."

"Dash!"

"What?"

"What about whoever might be *listening* right now?" I hiss.

Dash frowns. "You're joking, right?"

I shake my head. "There are eyes and ears everywhere."

"Yeah, but in your *bedroom*? That's crossing the line."

I step closer to him and lower my voice further. "After everything you told me about these people, you really want me to believe there are lines they won't cross?"

Dash hesitates. "True."

"I mean, I don't know for sure whether anyone's listening, but Aurora told me to be careful of what I say, no matter where I am."

Dash raises his finger to his lips, indicating that I should remain silent. He begins to walk slowly around the room, looking, listening, even, at times, sniffing. "The only other magic I can sense in this room is coming from your bed," he whispers. "Which is totally inappropriate, if you ask—"

The duvet moves, a shape slides toward the edge, and a black cat lands on the floor.

"Oh," Dash says, his voice no longer a whisper. "Is that Bandit?"

I open my arms and Bandit leaps up, shifting into a bird to help him gain height, and landing in my arms as a cat once more. "Yes." I hug him close to my chest. "I wanted him to stay at the—um, where it was safe. But he must have come with me in a form too small for me to notice."

Dash smiles and comes closer so he can scratch Bandit behind the ears. "Jack will be relieved. He's been so worried about Bandit."

"So you don't think anyone's listening?" I ask.

"I don't, but even if someone is listening, so what? It's not as though I'm acting improperly toward the future princess. You and I are just talking. If you'd prefer, we can do it in your sitting room instead of your bedroom."

I roll my eyes. "As if that makes any difference. You'd still have to explain how you got past the guards outside my door. And climbing in through the window makes you look awfully suspicious."

He heaves a breath and sits on the edge of the bed again. "I just thought you might want to know about … you know. The funeral."

The funeral.

Chelsea and Georgia.

Dead.

"You were there?" I ask.

Dash nods. "Yeah. You may or may not remember that some of the people in Stanmeade were actually my friends. Not true friends, of course, since I could never be fully honest with anyone, but … yeah. I have friends there, and I felt like I should be at the funeral. Just, you know, to support anyone who was friends with Georgia."

I nod and murmur, "Of course. Yeah. I still can't believe she and Chelsea are gone. They were always just *there*, you know? My horrible cousin and aunt that I couldn't wait to get away from. Then I finally did get away, and now …" I shake my head. Now, because Ada was after me, they're both dead. Dash may try to convince me I shouldn't blame myself, but I know I'm responsible. Indirectly, perhaps, but still responsible.

I let Bandit jump out of my arms before walking to the chair in the corner of my room. It's the type of fancy chair that no one actually wants to sit in—an overly embellished wooden frame with cushions too firm to be comfortable. Nevertheless, I perch on the edge of it and clear my throat. "Was it, um, were there lots of people there? At the funeral?"

"Yes. Almost everyone in town was there. I guess Chelsea knew a lot of people, seeing as she ran one of the only hair salons in Stanmeade."

I frown. "She was such a huge fan of gossip and rumor-spreading that I would have thought there'd be a lot of people who didn't like her."

"Well, you don't have to like someone to go to their funeral."

I look across at him. "Did people say horrible things?"

"No. Only good things were said about her. About both of them. It was all very …" He rubs a hand over his face. "Very strange. So tragic, on the one hand, and yet so false hearing all these lovely tributes about two people I personally witnessed being spiteful on multiple occasions. And it seemed *wrong* of me to think those things, but how could I not? I couldn't suddenly turn Chelsea and Georgia into something else in my memory just because they're now dead."

"I … just …" I shake my head. "I don't know what to say or think or feel. What does everyone think the cause of death was?"

"A gas leak."

"I assume the Guild is responsible for that story?"

"Yes. It was the easiest story to go with."

"Do you think … do you know whether …" I hesitate, wondering if I even want to know the answer. "Did they suffer? Did the magic in their bodies cause them to suffer as they were dying?"

"I don't know, Em. I honestly don't know. I hope not."

I lean my elbows on my knees. "Before you told me what happened to them, I was starting to think that all this time Chelsea was also some kind of faerie just like me and Mom, and that the herbal remedies she made were magical. But if they contained magic, they wouldn't have helped anyone in Stanmeade. People would have ended up sick and possibly dead, right?"

"Yeah."

"So Chelsea was definitely human."

"Yes."

"Which means she and my mother can't have been sisters."

Dash shakes his head.

"I wonder if Chelsea knew. I wonder if my mother knows, or if she thinks Chelsea was like her. Someone with magic that couldn't be accessed." I rub my fingers in circular motions against my temples as I stare at the floor. "I have so many questions still. So many gaps in my family history that I need Mom to fill in for me."

"Well, I hope your genius plan works out and you get all the answers you're looking for."

I direct a frown his way. "This isn't just about answers. You know that. Even if Mom knew nothing, I'd still want to wake her and heal her mind."

"Yeah," he says quietly. "I know."

I watch him closely for a while. "Why are you really here? I mean, I've …" I push my embarrassment down as my cheeks heat up. "I've never been nice to you. Surely you don't care enough about me to take the kind of risk required in coming here."

He lets out a short laugh devoid of humor. "It wasn't a question of how much I may or may not care about you. This isn't just about you, Em. It's about what the Unseelie King will make you do. How many lives might be ruined because you're forced to use your Griffin Ability against your will?"

"I … I don't—"

"And I thought you were a prisoner here. I thought I was saving both you *and* all the people you might be forced to hurt in future. I never guessed that you *chose* to come here. That you'd refuse to leave once I found you."

I look away from him. "I'm sorry. Like I said last night, you weren't supposed to find me. You were supposed to stay far away and never get hurt again because of me."

"That was never going to happen, Em. I'm not the kind of person to sit by while the Unseelie King gets his hands on the latest powerful weapon in the fae realm. And I didn't think you were the kind of person to just hand over that power either."

I swallow past my shame. "Well, I guess I am," I say quietly, staring down at the floor. "Like almost everyone else in the world, I'm only looking out for myself and the people I love. I'm not brave or selfless. I'm just doing what I have to do to get by."

From the corner of my eye, I see Dash shake his head. "You can tell yourself that lie all you want, but I know you're more than that. I know what you did in

Stanmeade. You stopped Ada's glass from consuming the entire town. You didn't have to do that. You could have kept your mother's location a secret and let that place splinter apart. But you didn't."

"And what good did my selflessness do then?" I demand. "I gave her what she wanted, but did she stop her attack on the town? No. I had to figure that out myself, and it was a fluke that my Griffin Ability switched on at just the right moment. So what difference will it make now if I refuse to give my power to the king? Nothing. He'll commit the same evil acts he plans to commit. It might just take him a little longer." I feel sick at my own words. I don't *want* to help the king do anything. But really, the world is a sucky place and this is the way it works. This is the way *both* worlds work. Life's a bitch and then you die—just like that old song Chelsea used to listen to sometimes. "Only a few people get to be heroes, Dash," I quietly tell him. "And you may be one of those people, but I'm not. I'm just trying to play the best hand from the cards I've been dealt."

He's quiet for a moment, and all I can see in his eyes is sadness. "At some point, you're going to realize that this"—he gestures around him—"is most certainly not your best hand. I just hope you figure that out sooner rather than later."

"And I hope you get away from here sooner rather than later. There's no need for you to get hurt."

He raises an eyebrow. "You know what I am, right? Getting hurt is part of the job."

And dying? I almost ask. But I don't want to go there. I don't want to talk about death when he's already come so close to it. Not when the deaths of Chelsea and Georgia are still so near.

"Besides," he adds. "I don't think it'll be nearly as easy to leave this palace as it was to get inside."

Bandit jumps back onto my lap. I stroke his sleek black hair and, in an effort to turn the conversation away from such heavy topics, I ask, "Was it true? The story you told Roarke last night. About getting into the palace in place of the clothes caster."

"Yes. Well, mostly. It wasn't supposed to be me who came here."

"Oh." I look up. "Who was it supposed to be?"

Dash gives me a pointed look. "I'd rather not say her name, just in case. But I'm sure you can figure it out, given her particular talent for ... concealment."

Ah. Calla. I nod. "I think I know who you're talking about."

"It would have been much easier for her to blend in. But the clothes caster arrived earlier than expected to pick up the dress from my mother's studio, so—"

"Wait, your mother?"

"Yes. She's the one who designed your dress."

My hand stills on Bandit's back. "Your mother is Raven Rosewood?"

"Yes. I told you she's a fashion designer, didn't I?"

"Yes, but … I never thought … Wait, is your surname Rosewood?" That doesn't seem right, but now I can't remember if I've ever actually known Dash's surname.

"No, it's Blackhallow."

"Oh. Dash Blackhallow," I say slowly, trying out the name.

"Dashiell Blackhallow, if we're going to get technical." He rolls his eyes. "Lots of l's, I know. Anyway, my mother was still a Rosewood when she began designing. That's the name people knew her by, so she kept it."

"So out of all the designers in this world, the queen ended up choosing your mother. That can't have been a coincidence."

Dash smiles. "Of course it wasn't. My mother heard the Unseelie Queen was looking for a particularly special dress. Not for herself, though, and not for her daughter. The rumors suggested that a new young lady had arrived at the Unseelie Palace, and the queen and princess had taken a special interest in her. Normally my mother would stay far away from anything to do with the Unseelies, but she knew you'd gone missing. She told me about the rumors and this unofficial 'competition' to design the best dress. I was almost certain this girl was you, and so I told Mom that one of her dresses *had* to be chosen, no matter what. So we enchanted her designs. A simple spell that made anyone who looked at the pages want to keep coming back to them. And it worked. She was chosen."

My mouth is hanging open by the time he's finished speaking. "It was really that simple?"

"Yes. And then the guy who came to pick up the dress arrived way too early. I was hiding, watching my mother hand the dress over on her own, as she'd been instructed. I hoped she'd keep him talking or something until Ca—um—until our friend arrived, but the clothes caster said he was on a tight schedule. Seemed quite agitated to be there. He kept looking around as though terrified someone might spot him in this upstanding establishment. When he said his carriage was enchanted to turn around and leave in under five minutes, I did the only thing I could think of: knocked him out and took his place."

"So you jumped into his carriage and it all worked out fine?"

"Well, I changed into his clothes first. And Mom found me an appropriately colored wig from her many supplies. And I took his stylus and amber, which was a good thing, since the carriage door wouldn't open until I held his stylus up against it, and I was almost out of time by then. Oh, and there were two guards inside the carriage, but they were disinterested enough that they didn't notice my face wasn't the same as the guy they'd just been traveling with."

"Seriously? No way. No guard is that inattentive to detail. They *must* have noticed a difference."

Dash hesitates, a guilty smile stretching his lips wide. "Ok, so I *might* have discreetly spritzed some contentment potion when I got into the carriage."

"Some what potion?"

"My mother adds it to dresses sometimes, at her clients' request. It's a weird one. Some of these people she designs for are super stressed out and high-strung, and when they go to these fancy events, they just want to relax a bit. Be content and at peace, you know? I was in a rush, and the little spray bottle was right there, so I just grabbed it on my way out."

"And the guards ended up so content they didn't notice you weren't the right guy?"

"Yes. I, uh, may have sprayed a little too much. Fortunately, I put a shield bubble around myself, otherwise I probably would have been so content I'd still be sitting in that carriage."

I blink, not sure what else to say about this half-baked plan that actually worked.

"Look, it wasn't my most elegant undercover operation," Dash admits, "but everything turned out fine. The carriage brought me right into the palace grounds and straight up to one of the doors. It took a bit of work figuring out where to go, but it was nothing I couldn't handle. I pretended to be a little tipsy and confused, complimented one of the girls I found in the kitchen, and she showed me where to go. I dropped off the dress with a note saying the pickup went fine, and then hid until the ball began."

"Wow. I'm amazed that didn't go horribly wrong."

He shrugs. "I'm good with improvising."

My mind backtracks to the beginning of his story. "So they—the people I was staying with—" I don't want to say the words 'Griffin rebels' out loud "—know that you're here?"

"Yes."

I lower my voice and lean forward. "Do you think they'll come here?"

Dash hesitates, then says in a normal voice, "No. They don't know where this place is. That's why one of us needed to come with the clothes caster. The Unseelie and Seelie Courts are hidden, so not many people know where they are." The way he's looking at me though, his eyes boring intently into mine, strongly suggests he's lying. It also suggests he's not entirely convinced someone isn't listening to us.

"Crap," I whisper to myself. The Griffin rebels probably do know how to get to the Unseelie Court, and once they realize Dash isn't on his way back with me, they'll probably come straight here and do everything they can to get us both out. And while I'm sure they're all amazing magical fighters, the chances are high they'll wind up injured, dead or imprisoned.

"Em?" Dash asks after several moments of silence on my side.

"That's, uh, that's good that they won't be able to find this place," I say loudly. Too loudly, probably. I make an effort at sounding normal. "I know they would only be trying to help, but as I said to you last night, I'm not in need of any help."

Dash raises an eyebrow. "If you didn't want anyone's help, you probably should have mentioned that before you ran away. We would have stopped working so hard to figure out the mystery that is your life."

A shard of guilt stabs into my chest and twists. "I'm sorry. But I—"

"You asked for our help, remember? Or at least …" Lines crease his forehead as he frowns. "We offered, and you said yes. Something like that. So you can't exactly blame us for looking into your family history."

"I know, I was only going to say that I assumed you guys would forget about me once I was gone. You have plenty of other people to help, don't you? And—wait, what did you say about my family history?"

He sighs. "We tried to find out about your father. Since your mother isn't awake to shine any light on your strange situation, we figured your father might be able to help—if we could find him. The only thing you mentioned about him was that he paid the medical bills for your mom's hospital, so Chase went there to take a look at the records. He's the only one who knows how to use a computer," Dash adds with a roll of his eyes. "He grew up in your world, in case you didn't know. Anyway, he said your mom's file had some kind of glamour over it. He could see Chelsea's details and all your mom's details, but anything related to the person who first checked her in and was paying for it every month was just … blank. The humans working there would probably see something when looking at it, but Chase couldn't see anything."

"So … no one was actually paying for her?"

"I don't know. The point is, it was a dead end. We couldn't find out anything about your father."

My shoulders sag a little. "It's okay. That's why I'm here, remember? This union is going to lead to Mom's mind being healed, and all the answers hidden inside her will finally be unlocked."

Footsteps cross my sitting room. I clutch Bandit to my chest and stand abruptly—just as Clarina stops in the doorway. "Lady Emerson—Oh!" She stares intently at the floor. "I beg your pardon, my lady."

"This isn't what it looks like," I say immediately. I'm not actually sure what it looks like, but it can't be good.

"I'm sorry, my lady. I knocked on the other door, but—"

"I didn't hear you, I'm sorry."

"I won't say a thing, Lady Emerson."

"There's nothing to say," I assure her with a high, breathy laugh. "We were just talking."

"Of course," she says, bobbing in a brief curtsey and keeping her eyes on the floor. "Please excuse me for interrupting, but Prince Roarke would like to speak with you."

My fingers tense around Bandit's cat form. "Okay. Thank you. Where must I meet him?"

"He's waiting outside your rooms for you, my lady."

"Oh." I look at Dash.

He grins. "Well, I guess I'll be leaving the way I came in, then. Good thing I enjoy climbing."

CHAPTER 14

I swing my door open and find Roarke right outside. "Uh, good morning. Afternoon, I mean. Clarina said you wanted to talk?"

"Hello, my love." He bends forward and kisses my cheek. I freeze and tell myself not to shrink away. "You've recovered from last night's festivities, I see?" he adds.

I step back to let him in. "No need to bother with the 'my love' nonsense. No one else is around to hear you except Clarina."

"Oh, but you are my love." Roarke gives me a sly grin as he walks past me into the room. "Or, at least, I hope you one day will be." He nods briefly to Clarina as she curtsies and leaves the room. He turns slowly on the spot, looking around, and I almost expect him to walk into the bedroom and start looking for Dash. But then he smiles serenely and sits at the table beside my tray of lunch.

And at that moment, Bandit, who I've managed to keep hidden until now, comes bounding out of my bedroom in the form of a bear cub. He shifts into a wolf, jumps onto the divan, and takes a flying leap into my arms, landing in the form of a blue-haired sloth. I remain motionless, but my gaze snaps straight to Roarke. For once, he appears utterly speechless. I bite my lip, waiting for his response.

"Is that—is it … yours?"

"Yes. This is Bandit. He came with when you brought me here, although he must have been in a form too small for either of us to notice."

"So he's been here with you—in your chambers—the whole time?"

"Yeeees." My voice is uncertain, almost questioning. "Well, I wasn't aware he was here for the first two or three days. I think he may have been scared of the unfamiliar surroundings, so he remained hidden for a while."

"I see. How interesting."

Bandit snuggles closer to my chest and tries to burrow his head beneath my arm. "I hope you don't disapprove," I say carefully. "I like having him around. He ... he means quite a lot to me." Instinct tells me I shouldn't reveal to the man I still don't trust that I care about anything. He might choose to use that information against me. But if Roarke cares for my happiness the way he claims to, then he shouldn't mind Bandit's presence here.

"Well, I doubt my mother would approve of animals in bedrooms," Roarke says, his deep reddish-brown gaze fixed on Bandit, "but she doesn't need to know. And if she finds out and has a problem with it, I'll remind her how exceptionally rare and valuable formattra are, and that it's only fitting a princess would have one as her pet."

I nod. "Cool. Thank you." Hopefully Aurora feels the same way and doesn't freak out when she meets Bandit.

"Anything to make you happy, my dear," Roarke says. "Now, why don't you sit here so we can talk?" He gestures to the chair beside him at the table.

"Uh, before we talk, can I ask you something?"

"Of course." He smiles at me. "My soon-to-be wife can ask me anything."

I cross the room to the table and take a seat. I lift my hand and touch the small circular device behind my ear. "I know you put one of these things on Dash, but what if he gets it off? What if the Guild or his friends find out where he is and come after him? I just don't want anyone else interfering, remember?" To be more specific, I don't want anyone ending up in some nasty Unseelie dungeon or, far worse, facing the same fate as that man who was dragged through a cavern into the king's office.

Roarke examines me closely before answering. "You really didn't have anything to do with your friend showing up here, did you."

"What? No, I already told you that. Did you think I was lying?"

"Well, I'd be an idiot to believe that you trust me. Perhaps you arranged for a way out before you even got here."

"I did not. I told you I didn't want anyone—"

"Yes, I know." He leans back. "Still, I wondered if you might just be a very convincing actress."

"But you're not wondering that anymore?"

"You still seem genuinely concerned about the possibility of others discovering you're here. So let me put your mind at ease, Emerson. Even if someone can locate Dash's whereabouts, and even if they come to the very spot they expect to find him, they won't see any palace. Only if that person is in the company of one of our guards will they be able to see and enter the palace grounds."

"Oh. That's … convenient." Kind of like … No, it's gone. I almost had it, an image of the safe place belonging to the Griffin rebels, but it's like trying to hold onto smoke. "Well, I feel better now. I'm glad no one will be able to interfere."

"Good." Roarke waves the fingers of one hand through the air, and a rolled-up piece of paper appears in his loose grip. "Now, we have some preparations to make for the union ceremony."

"We do?" I never expected to be consulted on any wedding-related details. I assumed the queen and Aurora would take care of all of that. As it's been pointed out to me many times already, I have no idea what's appropriate and what isn't for formal events of the faerie world.

"You need to memorize the union vows," Roarke says, placing the paper on the table. "Everything you need to know is on this scroll."

I almost comment on how antiquated the use of a scroll is—I mean, *come on.* Surely folding a piece of paper is simpler and takes up less space—but I'm more concerned about the fact that I have to memorize vows. "So, um, I won't be able to repeat the words after someone?"

"For part of the vows, yes, but the words are in another language, so you need to practice pronouncing them correctly. There's magic involved, so you don't want to get the words wrong."

"Uh—"

"And the other part of the ceremony is the private vows we make to one another without anyone else overhearing. You'll have to memorize those."

"Oh. Why are they private?"

His expression becomes bemused. "Because they're for our ears only." Beneath the table, his hand slides onto my knee. "The special, romantic things we wish to say to one another."

"Oh." I inch a little to the side, moving my leg out of his reach. "But … then why do we need to say them? You and I both know we're not entering into this union for any of the traditional reasons. We don't need to go into detail with anything romantic."

If Roarke is bothered by the fact that I don't want him touching my leg, he doesn't show it. "As I said a moment ago, our vows involve magic. We can't simply skip that part."

My frown deepens. "But … okay. I just … don't quite understand. If those extra words are a standard part of the union magic, then why are they private? Do I really need to memorize them?"

Roarke simply laughs. "Emerson, this is the way the ceremony is done. It's been this way for a very long time. We can't just change it because you don't feel like memorizing words."

"It isn't that I don't *feel* like it." I loop my hair back behind my airs. "I'm just concerned I might forget something or make a mistake. If it's so important to get everything right, then what's wrong with repeating after someone else or reading the words off a page?"

Roarke sighs. "You won't be reading words off a page, Emerson. That's not how it's done."

"Okay, okay." I reach for the scroll and pull it closer. "So, will you explain to me what all the words mean, or am I expected to recite nonsense I don't understand?"

The corner of Roarke's mouth lifts. "It's a good thing I'm the one teaching you these words. Anyone else would be highly offended."

I lean back and unroll the paper, revealing far more foreign words than I'm comfortable with. "Aurora wouldn't be offended."

"True, but Aurora will only learn the private words when it's her turn. It isn't appropriate for her to know them yet."

"Ah, more inappropriateness." I let out a long sigh. "I would ask *why* it's inappropriate, seeing as this is a standard part of every ceremony, but you'll probably just tell me 'this is how it's done.'"

"Yes. That's exactly what I'll tell you." His eyes crinkle at the corners as he smiles. "I'm so pleased to see you're learning."

I lean back in my chair and begin reading the vows out loud, doing the best I can with the unfamiliar combinations of letters. After about three words, I'm aware that I'm probably massacring the faerie language. Roarke waits until I reach the end of the first line before putting me out of my misery. "Okay. I see this is going to take longer than I thought." Another twist of his wrist produces a quill. He hands it to me. "I'll pronounce each word, and you can write it down in whatever way makes sense to you."

We get about halfway through the public portion of the vows before a quick knock interrupts us and my door is thrown open. "Sister, dear!" Aurora calls out to me. "Oh, you're awake." She stands in the doorway and grins. "Look who I found roaming the halls." She reaches back and tugs Dash into view.

"I did tell you I invited him to stay, didn't I?" Roarke says to her.

"Yes, but I haven't seen him since the day we stunned him in Em's bedroom back in the human realm. I didn't get a proper look at him then. He's handsomer than

I remember," she adds with a teasing smile, slipping her arm through Dash's and pulling him closer.

"Thanks." He gives her an equally flirtatious smile. I fold my arms and direct a frown at him, but all he does when he sees my expression is shrug.

"You remember what he is?" Roarke says to Aurora with disapproval in his tone.

"Of course I do. And I remember," she adds in a mock whisper, "that it's a secret."

"We were actually busy with something before you so rudely barged in here," Roarke comments.

"Ooh, yes, memorizing the vows. How romantic. Can I take a peek?"

Roarke swipes the page away from me and promptly rolls it up before Aurora can come any closer. "No, you may not. I wouldn't want to spoil anything for you before it's your turn."

"How thoughtful of you."

Roarke taps my hand with the scroll. "We can try this again later, my dear betrothed—when we have a little more privacy." He spins the scroll on his hand and it disappears.

"The reason I barged in here," Aurora says, "was to suggest we all go down to the tea together. And I wanted to check Em wasn't still fast asleep."

"Oh, is it time already?" I ask. "I thought the tea was later."

"Tea?" Dash asks.

"Yes, at the queen's bower in the garden. Mother's hosting it for those who stayed here after the party."

I push away from the table and stand. "Hang on, I need shoes." Aurora accompanies me into the bedroom to help me select appropriate footwear. I pull the silver slippers on quickly, wanting to give Roarke and Dash as little time as possible in which to wind up fighting.

Once the four of us are out in the hallway—with several guards striding both before and behind us—Roarke asks Aurora if he can speak privately to her. The two of them walk ahead while I fall into step beside Dash. "I wonder how Jewel would feel," I say to him, "if she knew the kind of attention you were receiving from the enchantingly beautiful Princess Aurora."

Dash sighs. "Hopefully she'd understand, given the fact that we had a conversation recently and I told her I don't feel the same way she feels."

"Oh. Um … well done."

"Yeah. It, uh, didn't go the way I hoped it would."

"I'm sorry. That must have been awkward. Was she very upset?"

"Actually, she convinced me to go on a date with her."

I almost trip as I look up at him in surprise. "Really? You said you didn't have romantic feelings for her, and that conversation ended with the two of you going on a date?"

He gives me an amused look. "Is there something wrong with that? Something about the idea of me going on a date with Jewel that upsets you, perhaps?"

"Don't flatter yourself. I'm surprised, that's all. You don't seem like the kind of person who lets conversations get away from you."

"I didn't *let it get away from me*. I simply decided to give her a chance."

"A chance?"

"She asked me to give her one date. I told her I didn't see the point, that I didn't want to lead her on, and that I was sure of my feelings. She asked how I could be sure if I'd never given those feelings a chance. So …" He sighs. "I thought what if—just *what if*—she was right. So I agreed."

"And?"

He cuts a sideways glance at me as we reach the bottom of a staircase. "You seem very interested in the result."

"Only because I'm trying to figure out if you really are the player I always assumed you to be. If you're dating Jewel while also entertaining Aurora's affections … well, that's not cool."

"Entertaining Aurora's affections?" he repeats. "My, you've picked up some fancy lingo since moving in with the Unseelies."

"Oh, just shut up and tell me what happened with the date."

"I don't think I can both shut up *and* tell you something at the same—"

I fold my arms across my chest. "Dash."

"Fine. It was awkward. Seriously weird. I spent the whole evening terrified she was going to try to kiss me at the end of it, and thinking it would be exactly like kissing a—"

"—sister?"

"Yes. And that's just wrong. So before that could happen, I told her—gently—that it wasn't ever going to work out."

"Ok." We reach another grand staircase leading down to yet another vast hallway. "Well, I'm glad you didn't string her along at all."

"Of course I didn't. I'm actually a decent guy, remember?" He lowers his voice. "Unlike the prince you've foolishly chosen to marry."

"I didn't *choose* him. Not like that, anyway. I chose this agreement, and he happens to be part of it. And you don't actually know him. I think he may be more decent than you think."

Dash snorts. "Right. Whatever you say."

I close my eyes a moment and sigh. "Can we please not argue about this any longer?"

"Sure. Tell me this then: what have you been filling your time with the past two and a half weeks? Has it all been parties and teas with the queen and being waited on by your own personal servant?"

"Yes, it's been absolute perfection," I say drily. "I've been waiting my whole life to have someone choose my clothes, run my bath, make my bed, and prepare my food."

Dash squints at me. "Really?"

"No! I can't stand it. I'm perfectly capable of doing all those things myself."

"Look, you had kind of a crappy life at Chelsea's," Dash says, holding his hands up in defense, "so forgive me for thinking you might actually enjoy having someone else do all the hard work."

"I don't. It's weird. And I haven't been spending all my time at parties and teas, actually. Aurora's been teaching me plenty of basic magic, along with some of her hobbies, like archery and dragon riding."

As we reach a wide doorway leading to the sunny outdoors, Dash stops. He looks more closely at me. "Dragon riding?"

"Can you two wait here?" Aurora asks. "Roarke just needs to show me something quickly."

"Yes, okay," I answer.

They disappear down a corridor, and Dash turns to me again. "Did you say *dragon riding*?"

"I did."

"Seriously? So you're a dragon rider now as well as an Unseelie princess-to-be?"

"Not yet, but I'd like to be. Is there something wrong with that?"

"No, it's just …" He shakes his head. "I feel like I don't really know you anymore. You haven't been here that long, and already you've changed."

His words hurt more than I could have imagined possible. "Changed? What do you mean?"

"Well you've … you've learned a lot in a short time. And you look …"

"I look?"

"Like you belong here."

I dismiss his words with a casual wave, hoping he hasn't noticed how deeply they've cut me. "That's just the clothing."

"Is it? The way you carried yourself last night, on the platform and while dancing … you looked every bit the princess people are expecting you to become."

I pull my shoulders back a bit, ignoring the ache in my chest. "Good. At least I know I'm playing my part well."

Dash's expression softens the tiniest bit. "As long as it's only on the outside …"

"Of course it's only on the—"

"Okay, are you ready?" Aurora calls out as she and Roarke reappear. "Let's get to this tea before we upset Mother with our tardiness. And you—" she adds, looking at Dash "—I shall introduce as a friend of mine. Please don't contradict whatever story I decide to go with."

"Oh, uh …" Dash hangs back as Aurora tries to usher us both forward. "I was thinking," he says, "that perhaps it's best if I don't attend this tea thing. If my sleeves roll up too high, and if the makeup rubs off my wrists, your mother might see my markings. She'll know what I am."

"That's possible," Aurora admits, "but if you *don't* come to the tea, you'll almost certainly end up wandering the palace on your own and risk getting up to all sorts of mischief."

He gives her a sly grin. "And what if I promise to stay in my room like a good boy? If anyone asks about me—which I doubt anyone will, since no one knows me—you can say I'm not feeling well."

"If we could trust you to keep your word," Roarke says, "and not sneak out of your room to try and dig up information that might be useful to your Guild, then certainly. That would be fine." Roarke's gaze moves briefly to mine before settling back on Dash. "But we don't trust you. Even if I posted guards at your door, you might climb out of your window instead."

My arms tense at my sides. He can't be hinting that he knows Dash climbed into my room earlier, can he? Unlikely. He would have been angry when he entered my room if he'd just learned that Clarina discovered Dash in my bedroom.

"Climb out the window," Dash says, a thoughtful expression on his face. "Now there's an idea. I may have to try that later after everyone's gone to bed. I hadn't thought about trying to dig up any useful information—Em was the only reason I came here—but now that you mention it, I'm definitely wasting a valuable opportunity by not doing more to find out what kinds of laws you Unseelies are blatantly breaking."

Roarke's placid smile never leaves his face. He steps closer to me and places an arm around my back. "As you said, Emerson is the only reason you came here. If you are indeed a true friend to her, you'll focus on comforting her during this difficult time instead of thinking up ways to bring down her future family." His thumb rubs up and down against my arm, a gesture that's probably supposed to be caring and tender, yet somehow comes across as threatening.

Dash watches Roarke's hand on my arm for a moment before lifting his gaze. Then his eyes narrow as he focuses on something behind me. I look over my shoulder. A woman dressed in dark maroon crosses the hallway with quiet, confident steps. She pauses for a moment to look at us. Perhaps it's the way the shadows fall across her face, but her eyes seem completely black. She tilts her head and sends a knowing smile our way, revealing pointed teeth behind her full, red lips. She turns away and saunters toward the stairs, leaving a cold breath of air in her wake.

CHAPTER 15

"Who was that?" Dash asks immediately. His body has gone rigid, his hands poised at his sides as if ready to grab a pair of glittering guardian weapons from the air.

"Nobody you need concern yourself with," Aurora says. She wraps her arm around his and turns him toward the garden. She leads him down the stairs and into the sun, while Roarke does the same with me, his hand pressing against my back.

"That woman is a witch," Dash says.

A witch. I look over my shoulder again, my mind sifting through everything I've learned in the past few weeks and landing on the memories associated with the word 'witch.' Aurora said she spent her first few years with a witch, before the woman grew tired of her and dumped her here. And Jack, Violet and Ryn's son, said witches killed his sister years before he was born.

"Watch where you're going," Roarke says to me as I almost trip down the next step.

"Yes, she's a witch," Aurora answers. "What of it?"

Dash pulls his arm away from hers as they continue to descend the steps just ahead of us. "You're right. I'm not sure why I'm surprised. You Unseelies have such similar magic to the witches. It makes sense to find you conspiring with them."

"Conspiring," Roarke repeats with a chuckle. "Your friend is far too suspicious for his own good, Emerson."

I don't answer him. I'm wondering instead if this witch might possibly be the woman I overheard in his room. The woman who spoke to him about that shadowy place.

"You don't need to worry about any *conspiring*," Aurora assures Dash. "She is a

304

guest here, and so are you. We don't want our guests fighting."

"Really?" Dash asks lightly. "I imagine that would make for a fascinating new form of entertainment in this court."

"You know, you could be onto something. I'll have to ask Mother about that. Perhaps our next party can incorporate guest fighting."

Beside me, Roarke breathes out sharply through his nose. He removes his arm from around my back and takes hold of my hand instead. "While this kind of flippant banter is amusing, you and I need to get to the tea," he says to me, increasing his pace and pulling me along with him. "Aurora, Dash," he says as we pass them. "We'll see you there."

Roarke and I cross over a little bridge spanning a stream of water that shimmers with translucent rainbow colors. At the sound of a distant roar, I look up. I now know that the indistinct figure high above me is actually a dragon. I stare longingly upward for another few moments before Roarke pulls my attention back down with a squeeze of my hand.

We reach the queen's bower, an area of the garden shaded by enormous overhanging branches laden with thousands of purple and white blossoms. Seats crafted from entwined twigs hang from the branches. Amidst these hanging seats, numerous tables are covered in drinks and delicacies of every shape and size. In such a pretty outdoor setting, I expected pastel colors and flower-painted tea cups, but every item of food is either black or white. The striped tea cups are also black and white, and the champagne flutes are filled with fizzy black liquid.

Many of the guests are wearing colorful outfits, but I'm pleased to see the queen in a form-fitting dress of black, white and gold. At least I don't have to feel too out of place in my charcoal grey outfit. As Roarke and I approach Queen Amrath, she lifts her glass and takes a sip. I watch closely to see if the drink will stain her lips black, but as she lowers the glass, her lips remain a dark, glossy red.

Roarke and I greet his mother, and Roarke introduces me to the friends and cousins who are sitting around her. Dash and Aurora hurry up behind us then, and Aurora introduces Dash as a friend she met several months ago. "Remember when Mizza and I spent a week at her family's home in Nordbrook while we had my suite redecorated?"

"Ah, yes." The queen nods.

"I spent a lot of time with him that week and decided to invite him to your party. Remember I told you about him?"

"I'm so sorry, darling." The queen reaches for Aurora's hand and squeezes it. "It must have slipped my mind. Why don't you get something to eat and drink, and then bring him back to me. Dash, if you're a special friend of Aurora's, I'd love to get to know you better." She gives him the same kind of smile she gave me on my first night here. Polite, but it doesn't quite reach her eyes.

We wander around the tables, selecting delicacies to add to our plates, and Dash eventually ends up at my side. "You should be concerned that there's a witch here," he says in a low voice.

"Should I?" I ask. "I'm sure the addition of a witch can't make this place any more dangerous than it already is."

"Most witches keep their distance from faeries. Faeries of any kind. This one can't be up to any good if she's hanging out here."

I add a square-shaped chocolate cake with black icing and silver sprinkles onto my plate. "Perhaps witches aren't all bad. You can't judge them all for killing your friends' baby."

"What?" Dash frowns. "Do you mean … Did someone tell you about Victoria?"

"If Victoria is the sister Jack mentioned, then yes," I continue. "He said she was killed by witches."

Dash tips a glassful of black liquid down his throat and leaves the glass on the table. "Well, it was something like that. Vi and Ryn believe witch magic was responsible for Victoria's death, even though it was actually a faerie who placed the magic on her. And yes, that's one reason for my intense dislike of witches, but there are many others."

"So what do you want to do? Find this witch and demand to know why she's here? You're supposed to be flying under the radar so you can get out of this place alive, not provoking the enemy." At that moment, a lizard with feathery wings plops onto the table, startling me and almost upsetting a plate of coconut bonbons. The lizard jumps off the table, hits the ground, and scurries away.

"Flying under the radar," Dash repeats, bringing my attention back to him. "I've heard that one enough times in your world to figure out its meaning. And what kind of *guardian*—" he whispers that last word so low I can barely hear it "—do you think I am? Certainly not the kind that goes around demanding information. I never would have graduated that way. No, Em, I'm perfectly capable of flying under this radar you mentioned while also finding out everything I need to know."

"Dashiell, darling," Aurora calls from the other side of nearby table. "My mother wants to chat with you."

Dash frowns for a moment. "Did I tell her my full name?"

I shrug. "Maybe Dash is always short for Dashiell."

"Right. Time to chat up the old ladies."

Since rolling my eyes is considered unladylike, and I've already committed the dreadful act of shrugging my shoulders, I settle for a sigh as Dash heads back to the queen's side. I gather a few more strange-looking treats before searching the gathering for Aurora. She and Roarke are sitting next to the circle that's formed around the queen. Aurora's back is almost against Dash's, and I assume she's paying close attention to whatever he's saying, preparing to intervene if she needs to. I walk around the tables and hover near Dash, close enough to listen, but not quite close enough to be included in the conversation. I assume I'll be forced to join in at some point, but I'll enjoy the snacks until that moment arrives.

"Oh, yes, it's beautiful here," Dash says in answer to one of the queen's questions. "I count myself truly lucky to have been able to visit both your palaces now."

Mild confusion crosses the queen's face. "Both palaces?" she enquires.

"Yes. You have this one that is both summer and winter, for day and night, and the other one that's shrouded in smoky shadows."

I watch as Aurora's smile freezes in place. Her eyes snap across the gathering to settle on Roarke, who's suddenly directing his full attention at Dash. With a puzzled look, the queen says, "I'm not sure what you mean. We have numerous manor houses across the world, but only one palace. Are you referring to one of our past parties, perhaps? We had one a few years ago with the theme of … what was it, dear?" she asks Aurora.

"Obsidian fire," Aurora provides, twisting in her seat to look around. "Is that the one you're thinking of, Mother?"

"Yes, that was it. Every surface was sleek obsidian. We had black fire dancing across the walls, and dark smoke that took on the form of phoenixes. Oh, and everyone dressed in silver, remember? It was magnificent. A stunning effect."

"That sounds enchanting, Your Majesty," Dash says, "but no, I wasn't here for that party. I'm referring to a completely different palace—or perhaps it's more accurate to refer to that one as a castle—with gardens where smoke as black as shadow curls and rises from every tree and plant. Even from the walls themselves." He gives Aurora an innocent smile. "I've never been anywhere like it. It felt almost like … a different world entirely."

Though Aurora's smile is still frozen in place, her eyes contain a barely masked fury. If it were possible to strike a person down simply by looking at them, I have no doubt Dash would be dead right now.

Roarke breaks the silence with a laugh. "Sounds like your friend here ate some of those berries at the last party you invited him to, Aurora. Those green hallucinogenic ones. I had no idea they were so effective. I'll have to try them out for myself sometime."

"Roarke!" the queen says in a horrified tone. "That is hardly appropriate for a prince."

Roarke laughs louder at this, and several people join in. Perhaps it's normal for the queen to admonish her son in front of company. The chatter returns to normal then. Aurora takes Dash's seat and pushes him away from her mother while the queen is looking elsewhere. Roarke returns to his conversation with a slightly rotund man, sending an occasional glance at Dash as he walks toward me.

"What the hell was that about?" I whisper to Dash as he reaches my side.

"Don't you want answers about that place?" he asks. "I've never been anywhere like it. I still can't figure out exactly where or what it was, or how we got there. Or how we got out, for that matter."

"But did you have to ask about it *now*? In front of all these people? That is *not* what I would call 'flying under the radar.'"

"Yes." He glances past me, smiling politely at the person squeezing between me and the table behind me. "I wanted to see their reaction. Now we know that Roarke and Aurora are hiding that place from everyone, even the members of their own court."

"Except …" I look around the gathering as I think of the woman I overheard while I was hiding in Roarke's room. If it wasn't the witch, then it could very well have been one of the ladies at this tea.

"Except?" Dash prompts.

"I overheard Roarke speaking to someone about it," I murmur. "A woman. They called that place another world."

"Really? They actually said that?"

"Yes. And there's at least one other person who knows about it. There was someone else there the day you and I saw that place. We heard a male voice, remember? Someone called out to Roarke and Aurora, and that's when they told us to run, as if they didn't want that person knowing we were there."

"The king?"

"Possibly. I think it was his voice."

Dash's brow furrows. Then, as if remembering where he is, he blinks and pastes on a smile as he looks around. "I need to find out more about that place," he whispers, still smiling unnaturally. "That world, or whatever it was. If the Unseelie King and his children are keeping it a secret from everyone, that can't mean anything good for the rest of our world."

"You can't know that," I say, more to myself than to him. I need to believe the Unseelies aren't as bad as Dash makes out. "It could just be some other private palace they want to keep hidden from everyone except their immediate family."

"And from the queen?"

"I'm sure the Seelies have hidden palaces too," I add, ignoring his interjection.

"It's another *world*, Em," Dash says through smiling, gritted teeth. "At least, that's what it sounds like. And if that's true, it's unlike anything else in … well, in history. There have only ever been two worlds. If it turns out there's a third? That's just … that's huge." He looks around again. "Roarke's right. I should be taking advantage of the fact that I'm here and gathering as much info as I can."

"Sure, if you want to wind up dead."

"I won't. I'll be careful. These Unseelies are hiding something, and I need to find out what it is."

"Why?" Fear begins to unfurl in my chest. "Why does it have to be *you*? Just leave this place with your life intact and let someone else deal with it."

Dash's smile becomes more genuine. His hand wraps around one of mine. "It's nice to know that you care, Em, but I don't run away from dangerous situations." His gaze flicks to someone behind me, and he turns the false brightness of his smile back on. My attention, however, seems oddly drawn to the way his thumb moves against the inside of my wrist. "Looks like people want to speak with their future princess," he whispers, his hand slipping away from mine. "Don't forget to smile."

CHAPTER 16

"You're late," Aurora says the following morning. Her arms remain in position, her eyes fixed firmly on her target, as I hurry toward the area where our archery practice takes place. "I was supposed to give you a lesson before we go to the dragons."

"I know, I'm sorry. I was looking for Dash. He said he'd join me for breakfast this morning but he never showed up. Have you seen him around?"

With a *whoosh* and *thwip*, her arrow strikes the center of the target. She lowers her bow and turns to me with a frown. "Dash left late last night. Didn't he say goodbye to you?"

I blink. "No. I haven't seen him since dinner. Why did he leave? I thought …" I shake my head, this unexpected news making no sense to me. "Roarke was so insistent that he stay. Since, you know, he didn't trust Dash not to bring a whole bunch of guardians back with him."

Aurora's frown deepens. "Didn't Roarke speak to you last night? Later, I mean. Some time after dinner."

"No, I was asleep then." Having to speak to so many people during the queen's tea—which lasted the entire afternoon—left me exhausted, and then Roarke wanted me to practice the union ceremony words again in the early evening. I planned to talk to Dash after dinner, to impress upon him the importance of not sneaking around and getting himself in trouble, but I fell asleep fully clothed and didn't wake until morning.

"My father received news of an attack on a group of guardians. Several of them were killed, along with the family members who were with them. It was that woman who can't keep her glass magic under control."

A shiver chills my blood. "Ada?"

Aurora shrugs. "I don't know what her name is. Anyway, Roarke spoke to me about it, and we decided Dash should know. I mean, it doesn't bother *us* if guardians die. They aren't our allies. But they're Dash's people, so we thought it unfair to keep the information from him."

"You …" I trail off. "I don't understand."

"Why do you still think we're the bad guys, Em? We're not." She nocks another arrow and squints through one eye at the target. "Our ways are just different, that's all. We thought Dash might know some of the guardians who were killed, and it wouldn't be right for him to miss their celebration-of-life ceremony." *Thwip.* Her arrow lands a little left of the mark in the center of the target.

"Wouldn't be right?" Once again, an image of the man who lost his entire head comes to mind. "You just said your ways are different. I thought that included your understanding of right and wrong."

Aurora glares at the arrow before turning to me again. "It does, but not for something like this. It's right to honor the dead and give them a proper farewell. We may not like the fact that Dash is a guardian, but we're not so cruel that we'd want to deprive him of the opportunity to say a final farewell to people he cared for."

"So Roarke just let him leave? That still doesn't make sense to me. Surely Roarke wouldn't put his entire court at risk just to let one guardian attend a funeral."

"He didn't put anyone at risk. He told Dash he could only leave if he allowed an enchantment to be placed upon him."

"What enchantment?"

"He'll become confused whenever he tries to think or speak about the Unseelie Court. Nothing he says will make sense if he tries to tell anyone where it is, and his thoughts will become too muddled for him to bring himself anywhere near here."

That sounds a lot like the protection the Griffin rebels have cast over their hideout. "And he agreed to that?" I ask.

"Yes, apparently. Roarke said Yokshin performed the enchantment. And to be honest, Em," she adds as she crooks a finger for one of the archery assistants, a young boy, to come over, "Dash would have been forced to have this enchantment placed on him no matter when he planned to leave the palace."

I nod slowly. "Makes sense. But I still don't understand why he didn't come and say goodbye to me."

"Well, you said you were asleep." She hands her bow to the boy and takes the glass of water he offers her. "And perhaps he was in a rush. I know he cares about you, Em. He never would have risked coming here if he didn't. But he cares about his guardian comrades too. He would have been desperate to get back to find out who died."

"Yes," I say quietly. "I'm sure he would have."

"Oh, fan please," Aurora adds in a commanding tone as the boy walks away with her bow. He hurries back, makes a few awkward movements in the air with one hand, and an enormous palm leaf appears. He quickly lowers the bow to the ground and grabs hold of the palm with both hands. Aurora tilts her head back and closes her eyes, and I try not to roll my eyeballs right out of my head as the poor boy stands there and fans her. "Okay, that's enough." She waves the boy away after several moments, then raises the glass and drinks all the water. "Right. Dragon time."

"Finally," I mutter.

"Em," she says, cocking her head thoughtfully to the side as we begin walking. "Is there something you haven't told me about Dash?"

"Hmm? What do you mean?"

"Are you in love with him?"

I can't help the laughter that bursts free of me. "No, of course not," I manage to say once I've recovered. "I'm just concerned about him."

"But he loves you."

"Um, nope. I'm pretty sure he doesn't."

"Then why did he risk his life to try to save you from us?"

"Maybe he felt it was his duty. He has that whole guardian ego thing going on, so it's probably hard for him to resist being the hero who rescues the damsel in distress. Or, at least, any damsel he *thinks* is in distress."

"Hmm." She pushes her hair back over her shoulder. "I think he cared about your wellbeing."

"Maybe. A little. In a non-love kinda way."

She gives me a patronizing smile. "Nobody cares that much. Not unless they're motivated by love."

With a sigh I ask, "Have you met many guardians, Aurora? I haven't known them for long, but they all seem to have this crazy desire to fight and protect and rescue, even if it means winding up hurt or dead."

She groans. "I know. They're all so irritatingly selfless. We can't compete, so we don't even try."

All the shame I felt while trying to convince Dash—and myself—that I'm not making life any worse than it already is by giving my Griffin Ability to the Unseelies seeps back into my body. "Yeah, I can't say I identify with the whole guardian thing either," I say quietly.

"Really? Please remind me, my sweet sister, why you agreed to come here in the first place."

I look up. "For my mother."

"Exactly. Now tell me you can't identify with the words 'fight,' 'protect' and 'rescue.'"

"Yes, but she's my mother," I explain. "Possibly my only living family. I love her more than anything. I would fight and die for her, but that doesn't mean I'd do it for people I barely know. I'm not that selfless."

"And that's exactly why you're going to fit in so well with us, Em. We take care of our own. Screw the rest of the world," she adds with a laugh. She wraps one arm around me and gives me a quick sideways hug as we near the enormous shed housing all the carriages.

Aurora's words should make me happy. I've always wanted to belong somewhere, and Chelsea's home was never going to be that place. But her words leave me feeling uncomfortable instead. I've never considered myself to be anything like these people, but what if she's right? What if I'm more Unseelie at heart than I ever imagined? What if—

I smother a gasp as the thought occurs to me.

What if I *am* Unseelie? What if my mother came from this court? What if the cruel magical practices the Unseelies use are part of my history, my blood, my very essence? Is that why I like dragon riding? Is it something *bad* that's associated with the Unseelie Court? No, it can't be. Surely dragons can only be good or evil based on the good or evil things their riders tell them to do. It can't only be the Unseelies who enjoy soaring through the air on the back of a dragon.

As we pass the shed, I stop, momentarily distracted. "Hang on," I say to Aurora. "Just give me a minute." I hurry back and approach the woman busy directing two horseless carriages out of the shed by standing in front of them and motioning with her hands. "Good morning," I say to her. "Were you on duty late last night?"

The woman seems startled to be addressed by me, but she quickly recovers. "No, my lady. It was Henkin. He's off now, but he should be—oh, there he is." She points behind me. "His next shift begins shortly."

"Thank you." I stride quickly toward the man, and after he bows and formally greets me, I ask, "Did you see someone leave the palace late last night? A man—um, faerie. Faerie man. Green in his hair?"

"Yes, my lady. I helped him into a carriage myself. Four guards accompanied him."

I nod slowly. "Okay. And, um … he wasn't tied up or anything? Like a prisoner?"

Lines crease the driver's brow as he frowns. "No, my lady. I assumed he was an honored guest. The prince himself shook his hand and bid farewell to him before he climbed into the carriage."

"Oh. Okay, good. Thank you very much."

I hurry back to Aurora, who's watching me with her hands on her hips. "What was that about?"

"Nothing."

With her usual teasing smile entirely absent from her face, her eyes search mine. "You were checking my story, weren't you? About Dash."

"Yes," I admit. "But you can't blame me, can you? I still don't know if I can completely trust you and Roarke."

"How can you—"

"I trust that you want *me* to be here, but I know how you feel about guardians. And Dash wasn't exactly invited, so maybe you wanted to just get rid of him instead of having him hang around saying inappropriate things like he did at the tea yesterday, or sneaking into places he shouldn't be and sticking his nose where it doesn't belong."

"And now?" she demands. "Do you feel better having spoken to one of the drivers? Did he verify my story?"

"He did. I … I'm sorry I doubted you."

She watches me a moment longer, then smiles. "You're forgiven." She spins around on the spot, and we continue toward the trees.

"But I did notice," I add carefully, "the way you and Roarke reacted to Dash telling your mother about that otherworldly place where everything was shadowy and drained of color."

Aurora's steps falter for a moment, but she carries on walking. When she doesn't answer me, I press further. "What was that place? Was it … another world? Somewhere that isn't the human realm or the fae realm? And why is it a secret?"

Without looking at me, she says, "You'll need to ask Roarke about that."

"Aurora, if you want me to trust you, then—"

"Ask Roarke," she says, looking directly at me, her expression serious. "I don't want to lie to you, and I know Roarke doesn't either. He *will* tell you about it. He's probably just waiting until he knows he can fully trust you."

Several moments of studying her face convinces me she's telling the truth.

"Okay," I say eventually.

We fall into silence as we head through the trees, which is unusual for Aurora. It doesn't feel uncomfortable, though. More like we've both got other things on our minds. As we walk, she absently waves a hand near the back of her head, and her hair quickly braids itself. I lift my hand and concentrate on doing the same thing. After our first ride, I decided she was right about memorizing spells that will help me get ready faster. I don't want to waste a second of the time I can spend in the air.

"Well done," Aurora says, and I realize she's been watching me. "You're getting quicker at it."

"Thanks. That's the plan."

Ten minutes later, we're down in Imperia's enclosure and Phillyp is getting the double saddle ready for us. My heart begins to pound faster, already anticipating the blood-rushing freedom of the skies. Trusting that Imperia knows me well enough now not to chomp me in half, I walk past her front leg and reach up to run one hand along the shimmering scales of her neck. She swings her head slowly around to peer at me through one fiery orange eye. "You might possibly be the best thing about this place," I tell her.

"Hey," Aurora objects from behind me.

"Oh, I mean … aside from you." I face her and add with a smirk, "You're pretty great too."

She laughs and shakes her head. "Thanks, but I was actually thinking of my brother. He might be disappointed to know you don't think *he's* the best thing here."

"Disappointed? Really? I didn't think he cared that much."

"Well, he does. He hasn't confided in me a lot, but I think he hopes that you'll come to care for him and … well, possibly even love him."

"Aurora …" My voice is hesitant as she climbs the stairs up to Imperia's back. "You know my only reason for being here is—"

"—your mother. Yes. I know. But … do you think you could ever mean the words?" She looks down at me from the top of the stairs. "The words you've been practicing. The vows. I know you won't mean them when you actually say them at the ceremony. But, you know … with time … do you think you could?"

Her question leaves me momentarily stunned. "I don't know."

"You must have thought about it," she continues as she climbs onto the front seat of the saddle. "You must have wondered about the future. You'll be together for years. For centuries, most likely. You must wonder if, during that time, you'll come to love him?"

Instead of answering her, I focus on the steps as I climb them. I haven't wondered if I might come to love Roarke because I don't plan on this union being permanent. And that's if it even comes to pass, which I'm hoping it won't. If I get a chance to use my Griffin Ability on Roarke before the ceremony, I'll take it. I reach the top of the stairs and pull myself up and into the seat behind Aurora's.

"Anyway, how's the pronunciation practice going?" Aurora asks, clearly getting the message that I'm not willing to talk about the possibility of loving her brother. "Must be terribly romantic."

"Yes, romantic indeed, being drilled on the precise pronunciation of every single word. I've got the first part down—the public part—but the private vows are harder. The words are more difficult to wrap my tongue around. *Super* foreign."

"Not any more foreign than the first part, surely? It's the same language, after all."

"I don't know. It just seems harder to me. Sola-thuk-ma … uk-na-math-ra … me-la-soni-ra …" I sigh as I secure a strap across my body to keep me from falling out of the saddle. "I sound like a toddler learning how to speak. It's embarrassing."

Aurora twists her head to the side, although not quite enough to look at me. "What other words do you find very difficult?"

"Uh, all of them,' I joke. "Isin-vir-na. Zo-thu-maa. Men-va." I enunciate the words slowly, trying to get each syllable right. "Anyway, I shouldn't be telling you. Supposed to be private and all that."

She faces forward again, her hands wrapped tightly around the reins. "Yes. True." I expect her to urge Imperia into the air then, but her hands remain motionless on the reins.

"Is everything okay?" I ask her. "Why aren't we moving?"

She rolls her shoulders and breathes in deeply. "Yes, everything's fine. I was just thinking we should spend the evening in the library. I need to find more books for you."

"Oh, uh … I haven't actually finished the last set you gave me."

"Well, you need more. So you have the afternoon to finish what I've already given you."

"Okay." I frown at the back of her head, wondering if it's my imagination or if her tone is a little sharp. But she moves the reins then, and I quickly put everything else from my mind. I forget about her acting a little strange, I forget about Dash far away and unable to ever find his way back here, and I prepare to lose myself in the delicious rush of adrenalin.

CHAPTER 17

That evening, snow falls gently outside the palace windows, while inside the library, a crackling fire keeps the room remarkably cozy considering its size. It's the kind of scene that looks perfect from the outside: Aurora paging through books at one of the tables; me curled up in a leather armchair finishing off the final volume from the last collection Aurora gathered for me; mugs of hot spiced chocolate that apparently won't stain anything if we knock them over. Beneath the snug surface, though, my mind is reaching new levels of paranoia. Did Dash return safely to his Guild, or were the guards who accompanied him instructed to harm him once he left the Unseelie Palace? Or perhaps *everyone* is lying to me—Aurora, Roarke, the drivers—and Dash never actually left. The Unseelie King could have killed him already.

Stop! I instruct myself as I turn to the last page of the book. I have no reason for these irrational thoughts other than the fact that Dash showed up out of nowhere and then vanished just as abruptly. If that hadn't happened, I'd be sitting here calmly reading my book and continuing to hope for a chance to use my Griffin Ability on Roarke. *No one is lying to you*, I whisper silently. *That driver didn't even know who you were. Stop. Freaking. Out!*

I breathe out slowly through my mouth and force myself to read the last page of the book. Reaching the end, I snap it shut, having absorbed maybe half of its contents. Half seems good enough to me, though. The book is essentially a list of all the magical creatures inhabiting the Unseelie Court, and it hardly seems necessary to memorize it.

I wrap both hands around my mug and sip the spiced chocolate drink, which does an excellent job at comforting me and putting my paranoid mind at ease. I know there are things that Roarke and Aurora are keeping from me, but I don't think they'd outright lie to me. If Aurora said Dash was sent home, then I choose to believe she's telling the truth.

I move my legs out from beneath me and stand up, pulling my dress straight. Bandit, who was snuggled next to me in some furry form, shifts quickly into a mouse and scampers up my arm to my shoulder. I walk along one of the aisles, reading the spines of the books as I go. "Ooh, magical combat," I say, pulling one of the books off its shelf. "Is this what you were telling me about, Rora? The other skill you wanted to learn, but your mother said only archery was allowed?"

"Hmm?" Aurora looks up with a frown. "Em, you're getting distracted. You're supposed to be finishing those other books."

"All done," I tell her. I flip quickly through the magical combat book, reading snippets about the mental techniques that can make one's mind quicker, and about different fighting stances and ways of throwing magic. Perhaps, if I'm forced to stay in the palace for a while, I can come back to this book. I return it to the shelf and scan some more spines as I wander further down the aisle.

When my eyes slide across a thick, colorful spine with the word *Dragons*, I stop. I pull the heavy book from the shelf and sit cross-legged on the floor to take a closer look at the detailed paintings on each page. "Aren't they beautiful?" I whisper to Bandit. He jumps off my shoulder and sits on my knee. A moment later, he becomes some type of predatory bird, too fluffy to be fully grown. "Oh, that's cool," I say quietly as he cocks his head and peers more closely at the dragon book. "I don't think I've seen that form before, Bandit."

"Make sure he behaves," Aurora whispers loudly. "Unlike the chocolate, if Bandit makes a mess, we will have to clean it up."

Bandit flaps his wings and lands on the floor beside my leg. With a ruffle of his feathers, he shifts form again—and all of a sudden, a dragon sits beside me. "Oh, wow," I say, forgetting to be quiet now. "Bandit, that's amazing." He's nowhere near the size of Imperia—he takes up about as much space as a large dog—but I'm still impressed.

"Em!" Aurora hisses. "I told you he needs to behave if he's going to stay in here."

"He is behaving," I tell her just as Bandit coughs in the direction of the nearest bookshelf. A tiny spark flies from his mouth. "Oh, crap." I jump up, grab the book the spark landed on, and smack it against the floor until only a singed spot remains on the cover.

"You were saying?" Aurora asks drily.

"Okay, Bandit," I whisper to the small dragon after I've replaced the book on its shelf. "While this form is *seriously* awesome, it isn't appropriate in the library. Let's save it for another time, okay?" He blinks, then shifts back into mouse form. "But I want you to know that you make a spectacular dragon," I whisper as I place him into my pocket. I'm wearing a sleeveless dress that seems Japanese-inspired, along with gloves that reach almost to my armpits. The dress has little pockets, but they were so small when I first put this dress on that I could barely fit my hands into them. So I pulled out one of the first spell books Aurora gave to me and almost squealed with delight when I managed to successfully enlarge the pockets so Bandit could climb inside. I just had to be sure to keep my hands in the pockets as I walked to the library this evening so no one noticed the odd lump on my right hip.

With my mind on combat magic once again, I wander over to the nearest window. After looking over my shoulder to make sure Aurora is once again absorbed in a book, I quietly open the window. I raise my hand and wait until I've amassed a small amount of power above it, shivering a little as the chilly air drifts over my bare shoulders. Then I peer outside and choose a tree to aim at. I lean over the windowsill and hurl the magic forward. The glittering sphere strikes the tree, sends a small explosion of snow into the air, and rips one of the branches right off. I clap a hand over my mouth as my lips stretch into a smile. Perhaps I'm not as useless as I thought. I may not be able to shape my magic into anything exiting, but at least I can toss raw power around if I have to fight my way out of here one day.

"Em!" Aurora calls out. "Seriously! What is wrong with you this evening?"

I shut the window quickly and face Aurora, confused by her anger. She doesn't normally mind bending the rules. I half-expected her to join me at the window and start throwing her own magic out into the night. In fact, that's exactly what I was hoping she would do. I might have learned something useful from her. "I'm sorry. I just … thought I'd try it."

"You don't need to try it. Magical combat isn't a necessary skill for either of us."

"Well, neither is dragon riding, but we both want to do that, so—"

"Em!" She gives me an exasperated look.

"What? Why are you so testy tonight?"

"I'm just—" She cuts herself off with a shake of her head. She pushes her hands through her hair. "I'm just looking for something, and you keep distracting me."

"I'm sorry," I repeat quietly. "Uh, maybe Bandit and I should go to bed." And before we get into bed, I can throw some more magic from my balcony without Aurora getting upset.

"What is Bandit doing in the library in the first place?" a voice asks from the library door.

I look around and see Roarke striding in, his footsteps silent on the carpeted floor and his black robe-like coat rippling around his ankles.

"Uh, he's hiding in my pocket," I answer. "And behaving himself. Obviously."

He watches me for a moment before replying. "Good."

"Have you heard from Dash?" I ask. "Did he get back to the Guild safely?"

Roarke folds his arms across his chest. "No, I haven't heard from him, and I don't expect to. It's not as though we exchanged amber IDs."

"But—"

"But my guards did tell me they successfully dropped him off far away from our court where the faerie paths are accessible and he would easily have been able to get himself back to his Guild."

"Okay." I bite my lip before adding, "I suppose he must have returned safely then."

Roarke tilts his head. "Why are you so concerned about him? Were the two of you lovers?"

"What? No!" Heat burns my neck and cheeks.

"You seem to miss him a lot now that he's gone."

"He was my friend. Of course I miss him." More than I expected, actually. In this palace where I'm still not sure who I can trust, Dash was the one person I could be completely honest with.

"But you have Aurora now. She makes a wonderful friend, doesn't she?" Roarke looks across the room at her, then frowns. "Aurora, is everything okay? You look like you might be ill."

She slams the cover of a book shut and swallows as she looks up. "I … I'm sorry." She lets out a breathless laugh. "You know I can't stand some of these history books. They're so horribly gruesome and graphic when they talk about the way people died."

"Then why are you reading them?"

She pushes the book aside and pulls another one closer. "I'm looking for books for Em. She still has so much to learn. Anyway, we can definitely give that one a miss. I'll find something less gruesome." She opens the next book and bends her head over it.

Roarke watches her for a long moment before returning his gaze to me. "I came here to suggest we practice the vows again. Your pronunciation needs to be perfect, Emerson."

Movement catches my eye as Aurora's head snaps up again. I look at her, and she stares back, her expression unreadable. "What?" I ask.

"Are you sure you're all right?" Roarke asks her. "Perhaps you're reading too much."

A smile lifts one side of her mouth. "No such thing, dear brother."

He chuckles. "I suppose not, if you're as fond of books as you are." His eyes find mine, and he tilts his head toward the library door, suggesting we head that way. Though with Roarke, I know it isn't really a suggestion. I allow him to take my arm and place it on his as we leave the library. "She's definitely acting strangely this evening," he muses. "I think perhaps she's jealous of us."

I can't help laughing. "That's ridiculous. Why would she be jealous?"

"You've become a good friend to her in a short space of time. She has her ladies-in-waiting and cousins and other noblewomen to keep her company, of course, but lately she's been spending most of her time with you. I can tell she prefers it that way."

"Really?" As we ascend a stairway, I lift the bottom of my dress to avoid stepping on it and tripping myself. "But I'm so … uneducated and unrefined."

"True, but you don't have anything to hide, and you're not playing games like many of the other ladies. You've been honest from the start about why you're here and what you want. That's refreshing." His words send an uncomfortable shiver up my spine. Thank goodness he doesn't know the truth: that I'm playing a game far more dangerous than any of the other ladies here. They risk gossip and a bad reputation if they fail at their games. I'm probably risking my life if I try—and fail—to escape this union.

I try to shake off my trepidation and convince myself that, as Roarke said, I have nothing to hide. "So you're suggesting," I say to Roarke, "that Aurora's growing jealous because you and I will soon be spending more time together?"

"Yes. I'm taking her new best friend away from her."

"Perhaps she's jealous because *I'm* taking *you* away from her. The two of you have always been close, haven't you? It's probably strange for her to imagine her brother married instead of available to spend his free time with her."

He shakes his head. "I don't think that's it. I've courted other ladies, and Aurora's always made it very obvious when she doesn't like one of them. If that's the way she felt about you, you'd know by now. She would have made your life very unpleasant, and she certainly wouldn't be giving you lessons in magic, archery and dragon riding, or hunting down the best combination of books for you to read."

The guards ahead of us open the door to Roarke's suite. Roarke lowers my arm and gestures for me to walk in ahead of him. "Well, I'm relieved she likes me then," I say as I enter the sitting room. "I'm not sure how I would have survived the past few weeks without her."

I take a seat on the couch while Roarke retrieves the scroll with the vows. "Why don't you recite the vows as you remember them," he says as he sits beside me. He unrolls the scroll but doesn't give it to me. "I'll take note of where you go wrong and let you know what needs to be corrected."

I tilt my head back with a sigh. "This is going to be *so* romantic by the time we say it on the actual day. Such a big surprise."

He gives me an amused look. "I wasn't aware you were looking for romance, Lady Emerson. I can certainly try harder, if that's what you'd like."

I raise an eyebrow. "You really don't need to bother. I was joking. As you've pointed out before, neither of us is in this for the romance."

Roarke shifts closer, discarding the scroll on the floor. "That doesn't mean we shouldn't try," he whispers as he leans toward me. I look away, and he presses a kiss against the side of my neck, sending a shiver along my arms. I silently curse as I shut my eyes. Why the hell did I have to bring up the topic of romance? Although … perhaps Roarke is right. As he drags a trail of kisses along my neck, I wonder if perhaps I should be making an effort with him. Maybe I'll find that I actually like him. Maybe Mom and I will end up staying, and there'll be no need for an escape, and we'll live here happily for the rest of our—

But that image of the king in his cavern and the man with his head bending, bending, bending to the side plays out against the back of my eyelids. I hear Dash's voice in my mind, reminding me why the Unseelie King wants me. *You can make their dirty work easier … These people are* not good.

I open my eyes. "Roarke, I don't know if I—Holy crap!" I gasp and scramble backward on the couch as a dark shape rises up behind Roarke. It spreads in slow motion like a villain's cape ready to settle over his shoulders. Roarke shoves away from me, spins around, mutters a string of words I can't follow, and with a flash of bright light, the dark shape splits apart into a thousand drifting curls of smoke before vanishing.

I press my hand against my chest as my thrashing heart refuses to slow down. "What … the hell … was that?"

CHAPTER 18

Roarke hurries into his bedroom and returns with a necklace in his hands, which he places over my head without hesitation. He steps back and lets out a long breath. "You already know what that was. Or at least, you've seen one before."

I swallow, looking down at the pendant resting against my chest. It's the same as the one I've seen Aurora wearing often. Silver with a black stone at its center. "Some kind of shadow creature," I say in a shaky voice as I look up at Roarke. "From that place you and Aurora took me to."

He nods. "You haven't asked me anything about that day."

"I didn't think of it until … until very recently. There's been so much going on. So many new things to occupy my thoughts."

"That creature," Roarke says as he takes his place beside me on the couch again, "is the same kind of creature that killed a man out in the gardens a couple of weeks ago. It sucked the life out of him. Not just his life, but his magic and his youth as well."

"And it would have done the same to us now," I whisper.

"Not to me. I was protected." He reaches for a chain at his neck, a chain hidden beneath his clothing, and pulls it free. At the end of the chain hangs a pendant very similar to mine. "And now you're protected too," he adds. "The magic embedded in the amulet wards off the ink-shades. I asked Yokshin to make one for you, and he finished it earlier today. I should have given it to you the moment we first walked into this room, but I forgot. I'm so, so sorry, my—"

"You *forgot*? And what about everyone else inside this palace? They should all be wearing these amulets."

"It's fine, Em. The creatures aren't supposed to be in the palace. What happened a

323

few minutes ago—and what happened to the guard—isn't normal and won't happen again. Whoever let this one slip through will be in a great deal of trouble when I find out who—"

"But what if it happens again?"

"It won't."

"And how are they getting here? *What* are they? What was that shadowed place? Why couldn't Dash and I open faerie paths doorways, and why did everything disappear behind us when we found our way back into the magical world—"

Roarke holds one hand up. "Just listen and I'll tell you everything. I've wanted to tell you everything since the day I first took you there, but I had to know I could trust you."

My chest continues to rise and fall with shallow breaths. "How do you know you can trust me now?"

"I don't. Not entirely. But I'm hoping desperately that you're on my side, because I so badly want to show you everything and explain it all to you. Because you and I, Emerson ..." He grips both my hands in his as a smile stretches across his face. "You and I are going to rule that world. I will be its king and you will be my queen. Not just a princess, but a *queen*."

"I ... I don't understand." I try to remember exactly what I overheard while I was hiding in his bedroom, but my memory doesn't include much more than the words 'claim' and 'territory.' "There are already two rulers. Seelie and Unseelie. Are you saying that the shadow place doesn't belong to either court?"

"That's exactly what I'm saying. It's a different world entirely. A world that didn't even exist two decades ago." Roarke shifts closer, and I reach for a cushion and hug it tightly. Bandit squirms against my hip, and it's oddly comforting to remember that he's there. "Do you know what happened back then, Emerson?" Roarke asks. "About eighteen years ago?"

"I've probably been told, but I don't remember."

"Powerful magic ripped through the veil that separates the magic world from the non-magic world. But after the gash appeared in the sky, it didn't stay that way. It wasn't simply an enormous doorway between two worlds. It split further, and the two worlds began to consume one another. An ancient monument managed to stop it, but you know what, Emerson? I always wondered where the pieces of each world ended up. They couldn't have just disappeared, could they?"

I swallow and shake my head. "I don't know. Things stopped making sense the moment I discovered magic."

He tilts his head to the side, watching me for several moments. "You know about the faerie paths, don't you? You know that they're the dark space in between this world and the one you grew up in?"

"Yes."

"Did anyone ever tell you that with the right amount of effort, by refusing to think of anything at all, you can stay inside them for a while?"

"Um … maybe?" Dash might have mentioned something like that, but with all the other revelations bombarding me when I first got here, it's hard to remember exactly.

"Aurora and I did that. Near the monument where the veil was torn over Velazar II—that's the part of the island where the gap is. The Guild split the island in half years ago, so the prison could remain on Velazar I." Roarke stands. "Anyway, I was always so curious about that gap in the air," he continues as he begins pacing from one side of the couch to the other. "I asked so many questions about it during my lessons when I was growing up. And no one ever seemed to have enough answers. So Aurora and I decided to investigate it ourselves. We went back and forth through the tear from the magic world to the non-magic world. We tried to remain concealed, of course, but the guardians stationed by the monument eventually saw us. They tried to come after us, and one of them caught hold of Aurora, so we couldn't simply drop out of the paths into safety. She managed to kick him off while we were inside the paths, but by then they were close enough that they might have been able to follow the trail of our magic.

"So we hid. We focused furiously on nothing, and the guardians soon disappeared. We could no longer hear their voices through the darkness. Aurora said we should leave in case we got stuck inside the paths forever, but that's when I saw it in the distance: grayish light and wisps of smoke as black as shadow. And the edge of two worlds."

If I hadn't seen it myself, and if magic hadn't become an ordinary part of my daily life, I'd be convinced Roarke belonged in the same facility my mother's spent the past five years in. "The edge of two worlds?" I whisper.

"That's what we saw as we moved toward the light. Grassy ground the same as the ground we'd walked across on Velazar Island. Then it ended abruptly and became a field of tall grass surrounded on three sides by a fence. These were two distinctly different pieces of earth, from two entirely different worlds—co-existing in a brand new world. They were muted versions of the originals, as if most of the color had been leeched from them, but they were real. I even bent down and ran my fingers through the grass so I'd know it wasn't an illusion." Roarke ceases his pacing and looks at me. "I finally had my answer, Emerson. I finally knew what had happened to those parts of each world that disappeared. They didn't cease to exist; they were forced into a new world altogether."

"So what did you do?"

Roarke sits on the edge of the couch and stares across the room. "Aurora was afraid. She said we needed to leave. She tried to open a doorway to the faerie paths, but it was no use. That was when she began to think we must be dead. She believed the guardians had killed us, and this was whatever came afterward. Some kind of afterlife. But I didn't believe it. My mind was already rushing to make sense of that world, to piece together how it worked. It seemed to me that the shadow world existed in the same space as the faerie paths. Technically, we were still *inside* the faerie paths, so that's why Aurora couldn't open a doorway."

"How did you get out? When Dash and I were there, we ran until we saw the tear in the veil, and we kept going until we ended up on Velazar Island. We couldn't get out any other way."

"Ah, but there is another way. More than one way, actually." He looks at me. "How would you normally get out of the faerie paths?"

"You focus on where you want to end up, right? It's your thoughts that take you there."

"Yes. And you can leave the shadow world in the same way, but you have to *really* focus. I think it's as if you're so deep inside the faerie paths that it takes concerted effort and intense concentration to get out. An almost meditation-like state."

My thumb runs up and down the edge of the cushion as I process his explanation. "That doesn't seem practical."

"No. It isn't. That's why we linked a faerie paths doorway spell to a traveling candle. It was Aurora's idea. She remembered that that's the way the witches travel. They don't use faerie paths. Instead, they add a traveling spell to a candle. When the candle is lit, the person who holds it can travel to certain places by picturing that place. Very similar to the way faerie paths work."

"Okay, so you would just light one of these special candles, but what about the intense mediation-like concentration part?"

"Oh, the intense concentration is still there. It just has to be employed while creating and applying the spell to the candle." Roarke waves a hand dismissively. "Higher grade magic. You'll get there at some point. Anyway, the candles aren't the easiest method of travel either. They run out, of course, and new candles have to be made. So I went one step further." He stands once more and reaches for my hand. "I created a portal. Right here in my suite, for continual, easy access."

My mind races back to the swirling circle of magic I saw on Roarke's bathroom wall. Without a word, I let him pull me to my feet. He leads me through his bedroom and pushes open the door to his bathroom. I don't have to feign surprise when I see the portal; the fear on my face probably does a good enough job of concealing the fact that I've been here before. "So that's how the shadow creatures are getting through to this world," I say.

"Yes. I have men on the other side guarding the portal from the creatures, although they clearly need to be reminded how to do their jobs properly. We're not sure what the creatures are, but we've been calling them ink-shades. Most of the time, they move slowly, like black ink spreading through water. At other times they blend in so completely with the shadows that it seems they become shadows themselves."

I shudder as I recall hiding alone in here. An ink-shade could have come through at any moment and sucked the life out of me. "So it will happen again," I say in a shaky voice. "Another ink-shade will get through, and if you don't see it and kill it, it will hurt someone."

Roarke rubs my arm, as if that could possibly comfort me. "It won't happen again. I'm going to station guards on this side as well. If an ink-shade does slip into this world, it will be killed before it can get to anyone." He takes a step toward the portal before turning back and holding his hand out to me. "Shall we?"

I shake my head vigorously. "No, thank you. I don't need to go back there."

"But you're safe now. You have an amulet. They can't hurt you."

I frown as I realize something. "I wasn't safe the first time. Neither was Dash. You told us to hide when you heard your father coming, which meant we were on our own in that strange world. Ink-shades could have killed us. One almost did."

Roarke looks down, his expression becoming suitably contrite. "I'm so sorry. We'd had our amulets for a while by then. We'd forgotten there was any need to be afraid."

"You *forgot*? You went on and on about how powerful and valuable my Griffin Ability is, and then you left me alone in a strange world with dangerous creatures that could have sucked my magic and life right out of me?"

"You were supposed to *hide*, not run away. I pointed you in the right direction. If you'd gone that way, you would have seen the door in the hedge that led down into the underground passages."

"We *did* go the way you pointed. I didn't see any—"

"Emerson." He grabs my shoulders and gives me a small shake. "Just stop. I'm sorry, okay? I never meant for any creature to go after you. And now that you're properly protected, you'll be completely fine. You can see this amazing world for what it is."

"Amazing? What is so amazing about shadow creatures and a wispy colorless world?"

"Please," Roarke says. "Please come with me and I'll show you. This is everything I've wanted you to see since we first met. I promise there is nothing scary about this world now that you're wearing that amulet. The ink-shades will simply float right past you."

I wonder if I should refuse, just to see if he'll force me. To see if Dash was right about him. But I'm too afraid to make him angry. So I nod and take his hand, and he leads me into the spiraling magic.

CHAPTER 19

THE PORTAL'S MAGIC SPINS IN CIRCLES AROUND ME, AND I'M ALMOST INSTANTLY dizzy. I shut my eyes, cling to Roarke's hand, and take a few fumbling steps forward. "You can open your eyes," he tells me as the dizziness vanishes. I open them and blink a few times before focusing on the nearly colorless world around me. The grass, the flowers, the trees and hedges—everything is varying tones of bluish grey. The only vibrant color belongs to the four guards who jump to attention at our sudden appearance.

"Would you like to explain to me," Roarke says to them, "why I just killed an ink-shade in my own chambers?"

The nearest guard blinks. "Y-Your Highness?"

I walk slowly away from them as they stammer out apologies and Roarke threatens to feed them to his sister's favorite dragon. I look around, trying to figure out where I was when Roarke and Aurora brought me here the first time, and which way Dash and I ran. Somewhere on the right, I think. I see more artfully clipped hedges that way, and the bench they may have sat on while presenting their offer to me. I walk on a little further and see a castle in the distance. Well, part of a castle, to be more precise. It looks open and unfinished on one side, and oddly hazy due to the wisps of a smoke-like black substance curling into the air here and there. Beyond the castle, the world fades into darkness.

"Incredible, isn't it?" Roarke says, walking up to me.

"You told me you found a piece of land with grass next to a field when you first discovered this world. So where did all of this come from?"

"Aurora and I built it."

I turn my gaze to him. "With magic?"

"Yes, with magic. That's why it's partially built. We can only do so much at a time. It depletes our magic quickly, and then we need to rest before we can do more." He takes my hand and squeezes it as he smiles. "Do you see now, Emerson? Do you see why you are the perfect queen for this world?"

I glance down at my wrist where the ruby on my bracelet is almost completely red. A section of transparent stone on one end indicates that I have about two hours left until power returns to my voice for the second time today. "Because my Griffin Ability can build anything?" I ask, looking up again.

"You can *literally* speak the contents of this world into existence." He reaches out with his free hand and runs his fingers through the silvery grey leaves of the bush we're standing beside. A black, smoke-like tendril curls slowly around his hand and vanishes. "In addition, your magic will make it so much simpler to claim this world as our own."

"What do you mean?"

"This world will be ours, Emerson. Officially. You and I will be its rulers."

I look down at our entwined hands. *And how*, I wonder, *is the woman you were whispering with in your room involved in all this?* There's no way I can actually ask him that, though, so I turn to a different question. "I assume, from what you're suggesting, that becoming the rulers of a world involves more than just sticking a flag in the ground?"

Roarke gives me a bemused look. "That may be the way they do things in the human realm, but in the fae realm, there is magic involved in properly claiming a territory. The magic and the creatures of the land will then be bound to you. It doesn't mean they can't disobey you, it just makes them more inclined to act in your favor. The Unseelie Court and the Seelie Court are territories that were claimed with magic. With your Griffin Ability, we can claim this world for ourselves."

"I don't understand why you need my Griffin Ability, though. People have obviously done this kind of spell before without my specific kind of magic."

"True, but I'm talking about complex magic involving royal blood and sacrifices and many specific words. With your Griffin Ability, we should be able to simply tell the world it belongs to us, and that's all."

"Do you really think it's that simple?"

"We'll soon find out," he murmurs, looking across the land he's already begun to shape.

I bite my lip as I stare at the tower on the completed side of the castle. I probably shouldn't say what I'm about to say, but I need to understand Roarke and his motives.

"Why not just do it now? You've already compelled me this evening—told me what to say when my Griffin Ability replenishes—but you could change that. You could force me with another compulsion potion to tell this world that it belongs to you. If this is what you're really after, then why are you wasting time on a union?"

He faces me fully and takes each of my hands in his. "Firstly, this world isn't all I want. I want to be joined to one of the most powerful faeries I've ever known. *You.* And secondly … don't you understand yet that I'm not like my father? I don't want to *force* anyone to do anything. Yes, I want this world more than anything, and I'll do whatever I can to convince you that our union is a good idea. But if you refuse, I would never force you."

"You'd never *force* me?" I repeat in disbelief. "Roarke, you compel me every day to say exactly what you want me to say each time my Griffin Ability is ready to be used."

"To keep my father happy until the union. I compel you to say what *he* wants you to say. He's the one who doesn't trust you yet."

"So why would he suddenly trust me after the union? He wants my power just as much as you do. He'll never stop compelling me. He would never take the risk that I'd use my magic against him or anyone else in his court."

A smile curves Roarke's lips. "You're getting to know my father, I see."

"So you agree with me?"

"I do. My father will never stop forcing you to speak his will. But once you and I are united and the shadow world is ours, this will be our home. We'll be far away from him and from the land and position he won't allow me to inherit for centuries still. He'll have to declare war on his own son in order to get his hands on you."

"So that's your ultimate plan? To go against your father and take over a new territory?"

"Yes. If I don't do that, it'll be centuries before I can rule over anything."

"And what if your father actually does declare war on you? He has armies. Surely he'd defeat you?"

Roarke lifts his shoulders in a lazy half-shrug. "There are many in the court who are loyal to me. They would follow us here. They'd fight for us. But yes, there's a good chance my father would still defeat me. You, however …" He brushes a strand of hair away from my cheek. "He would never defeat you."

A shiver races across my skin. A whisper of excitement stirs deep within me. In my mind, I begin to see a vague picture of a future I never expected. The promise of power, the promise of finally being in control of my own life. Not just mine, but many others. And Mom would be there too, vibrant and healthy and advising me. This picture of my future is alluring in a way that I recognize is unhealthy. But I was born with this power. Perhaps this brand new world is what I was meant to use it for. "You may be right," I murmur.

"So do you see now?" I hear the enthusiasm in Roarke's voice. "Do you see the endless possibilities of this world and your power within it?"

I nod. Look around. "So the tear in the veil is that way?" I ask, pointing to my right.

"Yes."

"You know the Guild is planning to close it, right?"

"I do know that, yes."

"What do you think will happen to this world then? What if it ceases to exist? All your plans will be for nothing then."

Roarke shakes his head. "I don't think it will disappear. Closing the veil won't restore each world to the way it was before. It will close the gap, that's all. If, however, the veil were to be opened further …"

I frown, following his logic. "Then this world would grow bigger?"

"I believe so. It's limited at the moment. Very small. We've tried to push at the edges, but we end up building into the complete darkness of the faerie paths. We need more space here. We need to extend this world."

"But if you tear the veil open further, you'll destroy more of the human and fae worlds in the process."

With an unconcerned twist of his mouth, Roarke says, "Those worlds are big enough already. They can survive getting a little smaller."

Like a slow chill creeping on as evening falls, my body begins to grow colder. "Parts of those worlds will be gone forever. People will die. Or … or they'll become part of the shadows of this world. I don't know, but either way, we would be killing them."

"Don't be so dramatic," he says with a chuckle. "Besides, your world is overpopulated already. Mine is heading the same way. We would be *helping* those worlds by using them to extend ours." He walks forward in the direction of the castle, pulling me along with him. "I've taken a closer look at that monument on Velazar Island in recent months, and my spies have told me all they know about this veil restoration spell the Guild will soon be implementing. I think we can interrupt it. Shatter it. Blow that gap wide open. We just need to know when it's happening so we can be prepared. And then, my lovely Emerson, we can continue building this world."

The chill that crawls across my skin is no longer a shiver of excitement. I can hardly believe what he plans to do. What he plans for *me* to do. Does he really think I'd be happy with that? Have I painted such a bleak picture of my old world that he thinks I'd gladly destroy parts of it? I look away from him, my heart sinking rapidly. For a few moments, I thought I may have discovered my purpose, my future. The home I've always wanted for Mom and me. But I can't do what he's suggesting. I can't destroy worlds. I can't kill people.

And I can't let Roarke do any of those things either.

But how the hell would I stop him? It would be almost impossible. I'd need to have control over my own Griffin magic, and I'd have to command him and everyone else who answers to him. And this would have to happen *after* he heals Mom; there's no way he'd do anything for her if I first ruined his world domination plans. And Mom and I would have to be ready to escape as soon as I've commanded Roarke not to tear the veil any further.

It's too risky. There are too many things that could go wrong. Who am I to try and stop a prince anyway? I'm nobody. I need to just focus on getting Mom and me the hell out of here once Roarke has healed her. Whatever he does on his own after that will be on his conscience, not mine.

I'm not brave or selfless. I'm just doing what I have to do to get by.

My feet stop moving as my words from yesterday come back to me in a sickening rush, followed immediately by Dash's response: *You can tell yourself that lie all you want, but I know you're more than that.*

"I'm not," I whisper.

"Hmm? You're not what?" Roarke looks back at me. "Not helping those worlds?"

The shadow world comes back into focus around him, and my fleeting aspirations of bravery vanish back into the recesses of my imagination. "Sorry," I say with a forced laugh. "I ended up on my own train of thought there. I only meant that … that I'm not currently making a difference to anyone or anything. I've only ever seen myself as insignificant. But now, with my power and this world, I *can* make a difference." I stare boldly into his eyes, hoping I've covered my blunder well enough. From his smile and the way his gaze roves hungrily across my face, I see I've given him exactly the kind of response he was hoping for.

"I knew you would come to understand. I cannot wait for our union day." He tugs me closer and presses his lips against mine. I'm so shocked I almost shove him back. *RELAX*, I scream silently before I can give myself away. I force my eyelids shut. Entwining my arms tentatively around his neck, I try to meld myself against him.

I try to pretend I'm enjoying the foreign sensation of unknown lips moving against mine.

When I've kept up the kissing act for as long as I can stand, I pull away. My words are appropriately breathless as I say, "I'm excited too. Shall we return to your suite and continue practicing the vows? I want to get them exactly right. I don't want a single thing to go wrong on that day."

Roarke looks at me as though he couldn't have asked for anything better. He puts an arm around me, and we head away from the castle and back toward the portal. "Is there anything you want to ask me? About the shadow world?"

The woman you were speaking with in your room, I want to say. *Who is she? How does she fit into your new world?* "No," I say instead, because I'm not brave enough to risk his anger. "I don't have any other questions yet. I'm just looking forward to trying out my Griffin Ability on something useful, like bringing plants and buildings and creatures into existence."

"So am I. We can try tomorrow. I've already compelled you to say something mundane later tonight when your Griffin Ability returns; may as well leave it at that. You can get some rest, and we'll come back here tomorrow to try something exciting."

After returning through the portal, I spend another half an hour or so practicing the vows with Roarke's assistance. Fortunately, he doesn't try anything more intimate than resting his hand on my knee. When I get back to my own room, I remove Bandit from my pocket. He shifts into a cat in my arms, and I hug him tightly as I stare through a window at the winter night.

Dash's words come back again—*I know you're more than that*—and I wish I could explain myself to him. *I didn't grow up the way you did*, I would say to him. *I've never wanted to save anyone except my own mother. Saving Stanmeade was just a fluke. I'm not a hero, and I can't stop Roarke.*

Before getting into bed, I undress and sink into a hot pool filled with steaming water and silver bubbles. I slide down, letting the water cover my head, hoping it will wash the shame from my body.

CHAPTER 20

Now that I know about the shadow world, Roarke is eager to get me back there. I've barely eaten anything off the tray of breakfast in my sitting room when two of his guards arrive to accompany me to his suite. I stride through the glossy hallways with them, feeling a little better than last night. Probably because I've managed to push my guilt into the far reaches of my mind where I don't have to think about it much.

"Em, I'm so glad you know all about this place now," Aurora says the moment I recover from the dizziness on the other side of the portal. "I've hated keeping it a secret from you." Her smile doesn't quite reach her eyes, though, and I begin to wonder if Roarke may have been right: perhaps she is afraid she'll lose her new friend once the union takes place. But I can't ask her about it now. It would be awkward with Roarke right here.

"Me too," I tell her, forcing a wide smile onto my face. "I can't wait to see what my Griffin Ability can do here."

"Yokshin made more candles," Aurora tells Roarke, removing a bag from her shoulder. She looks past him and holds the bag out toward one of Roarke's guards. "Please go through the castle, and wherever you see a dresser, add some candles to the drawers." The guard responds with a nod and quickly hurries off to do as he was told.

I look around, noting that the light seems to be exactly the same as it was when Roarke and I were here last night. "What time of day is it?" I ask.

"Day and night don't seem to exist here," Roarke says. "We haven't seen a sun or moon, and the same greyish dim light always fills the sky. We don't know the source of the light. Perhaps it's a magical copy of the light that illuminated the original world this land came from."

"That's so strange."

"Yes. We can try to change it, perhaps, but for now, let me show you your future home," Roarke says, putting an arm around me and leading me forward.

As we head for the castle, I can't help comparing it to the palace I've spent the last few weeks living in. Gleaming marble, gold finishes, and an intricate structure make the Unseelie Palace a beautiful and impressive building to behold. Roarke's castle is plainer and appears far more fortified with its stone walls, moat and drawbridge. "It doesn't look particularly welcoming," I comment.

"It isn't meant to be," Roarke says. "I expect someone might try to take this world from us, so I'm prepared to fight for it. You'll notice the castle requires a lot more work still. We've only built about half of it. And so far the moat is in front of the main gate only. We still need to extend it all the way around the castle."

"So you're hoping my magic can help you with this?"

"Yes."

Black smoky tendrils rise from the ground and curl lazily around us as we walk. The dull, indistinct shadow cast by one of the ornamentally clipped bushes becomes darker and more solid. It rises from the ground like a drop of black ink dispersing through water, coalescing roughly into the shape of a stingray with no tail. I stop walking and duck down as the ink-shade comes toward us, but it simply soars overhead and continues on its way.

"You're protected by your amulet, remember?" Roarke says.

"The inside of the castle is also protected," Aurora adds. "Well, most of it. The towers aren't safe yet, but as we build each room, we add the protective enchantments to the interior walls so the ink-shades can't enter."

"We plan to eradicate them all, of course," Roarke continues, "but in case we can't, our home will at least be safe inside."

I look back over my shoulder to make sure there are guards still stationed outside the portal. Not that I'm super confident in their abilities if they've already managed to let two ink-shades slip past them without even noticing. I want to suggest once more that everyone in the palace should have an amulet, but I can see why Roarke isn't interested in that precaution. It would require him or his father to explain why the amulets are necessary—and that won't happen as long as they're keeping this world a secret.

"I assume your father knows about all the building you're doing in this world?" I ask, facing forward again.

"Yes, although he thinks it's for the family. He sees this place as more of a retreat—a holiday destination—and he's been happy for us to fill it in whatever way we want. He has no idea I'll soon be claiming this world as my own. As *our* own," he corrects, taking hold of my hand.

I look to my other side at Aurora. "And you don't mind?"

She keeps her eyes trained forward. "It doesn't bother me that Roarke wants to rule his own territory. I'm not interested in that sort of thing. But I refuse to choose sides if he and Dad end up fighting."

Roarke lets out a low rumble of a laugh. "Hopefully Father will understand."

Having met the Unseelie King, I highly doubt he'll respond reasonably when he discovers his son has taken over this territory and stolen the shiny new Griffin Gifted weapon—me—all for himself. But with any luck, Mom and I will be long gone by the time the king retaliates.

We cross the grey grass and head for the drawbridge. Once inside the castle, Roarke and Aurora spend the next hour or two showing me every single thing they've already built, and discussing exactly what I should try with my Griffin Ability. Roarke keeps glancing at the ruby on my wrist, which, by late morning, is almost completely filled with color.

As my Griffin magic nears the point where it's ready to be used, we walk along the cold, stone hallways toward the unfinished side of the castle. We reach a bare room with only three walls, open on one side where the fourth wall should be. I walk out onto the grass and turn to look up at the partially formed, half-furnished rooms on this side of the castle.

"How much do you want to try building?" Aurora asks. "One room? A suite? An entire wing?"

"I have no idea. I don't know what my magic is capable of."

"Try what we suggested a little earlier," Roarke says. "One complete room with furniture inside."

I blink at him. "Aren't you going to compel me?"

His eyes swing briefly to Aurora before returning to me. "I don't see the need. We trust each other now, don't we? You're not going to turn around and use your magic against us. Are you?" he adds.

"Of course not." But that's exactly where my mind went. This could be my chance. I could command Aurora to stay right here, and command Roarke to leave this world with me. I could leave him somewhere, fetch Mom, and tell him—with whatever Griffin magic I have left—to heal her. And the guards … could I command them to stay here too? Would the magic work if they're all the way back at the portal and can't hear me?

"Emerson?" Roarke frowns at me. "You seem uncertain about something. Would you like to tell me what you're planning for your magic?"

"Sorry, I'm just thinking. I don't always know how best to word these commands." I glance at Aurora, but she's biting her lip and staring at the ground, her mind clearly elsewhere. "Um, I mean … how much detail do you think I need to say? Would it be enough to tell a chair to form itself, and then just picture what it looks like in my head? Or do you think I need to talk about the color of the cushion, and the shape of the chair, and …" I trail off, half my mind still trying to figure out if I can risk using my ability to command all the people in the shadow world instead of doing what Roarke wants me to do.

"I don't know," Roarke says. "It isn't my magic. You need to try it out and see what happens."

Aurora clears her throat, seeming to return from whatever thoughts she was lost in. "Well, from your experience over the past few weeks with all the dull commands Roarke's compelled you to say, we've learned that your intentions and thoughts are almost as important as the words you say out loud. So I don't think you need to speak all the details. Just imagine them, and hopefully your Griffin Ability will do the rest."

Without having to look at the ruby, I sense the moment at which my power is fully topped up and ready to escape me. I decide then that I can't risk commanding Roarke now. I don't have enough control yet, and if I don't say everything perfectly, I could easily wind up a prisoner instead of a bride.

"Oh, and try not to let all your magic go in one command," Aurora adds. "See how much you can hold back."

I look at the empty, three-walled room in front of me and begin speaking. "There is another room here," I say, picturing the room forming around us by adding itself onto the existing one. My voice reverberates in that strange, deep way that still sounds creepy to my ears. "It has a bay window on one side, with a seat beneath the window, and cushions scattered across the seat. Wooden panels cover the walls and floor, curtains hang from the window, and three armchairs sit in the middle of the room."

Magic rushes from me, and I clench my hands into fists, my whole body tensing as I try to hold the flood back. I imagine myself slowly turning a tap, letting out only the required amount of power. And then, all around us, walls begin to rise from the ground. I watch in utter amazement as wooden panels materialize to cover the walls, and a ceiling spreads through the air above us. Where the ceiling meets the walls, ornamental molding forms itself into cornices that look exactly the way I pictured them in my mind.

"Oh, look there!" Aurora exclaims as one of the walls pushes itself outward into a bay window. A seat rises up, and colorful cushions expand into existence on top of it. Curtains the same as the ones in my room at the palace drop down on either side of the window.

"Oh!" I throw my hands out to steady myself as a wooden floor pops up beneath our feet. A grinding, rumbling sensation travels up through my body—the foundation forming beneath the ground?—before disappearing a few seconds later. Then, as three chairs unfold from the air right in front of us, we step hurriedly back. The armchairs expand, their cushions puffing up and their legs molding into that vintage ball-and-claw design I've seen on many of the chairs furnishing the Unseelie Palace. I imagined them as dragon claws in my head, and as the chairs slide into their final positions in the center of the room, the claws lengthen and sharpen into solid wooden versions of Imperia's feet.

Finally, everything becomes still. A wave of tiredness ripples over me, though it isn't nearly enough to dampen the absolute wonder I feel at having created everything inside this room. I raise my hand, lightly touch the wall closest to me to make sure it's real, and then lean my weight more heavily against it.

"Incredible," Roarke murmurs. "We've studied architecture spells, but everything still takes so much time for us to create. Then you come along and complete a whole room in under a minute. It's mind-blowing."

"Absolutely," Aurora breathes, her eyes tracing the contents of the room before finally landing on me. "How do you feel?"

"Quite tired, but I haven't depleted all my power yet. I managed to hold some of it back, though it was difficult. I can feel it struggling to break free." I push away from the wall, part of my attention focused on wrestling my remaining Griffin magic into submission. "Shall I try something else? Something bigger? If it's too much for my magic, then I assume it just … won't happen?"

"I don't know. Maybe. What do you want to try?" she asks.

"Um … something outside?" I realize I haven't created a way out of this room aside from the window, but a simple command results in a door forming between this room and the empty room next to it. We walk through to one of the rooms that's still open on one side, and head out onto the grass. I cast about for something to add to this dull landscape to make it a little prettier. Could I add color? Could I add a sun or moon or stars?

I lift my gaze to the grey sky above and utter a simple command: "There are stars in the sky." It's a relief to let the remainder of my Griffin magic flood out of my body. Far above, pinpricks of light begin to appear. I have a vague memory of how stars are actually formed, but I have no idea if those are real stars way up there, or if they're just balls of magic light floating high above … above …

The light becomes brighter and the world turns white. Sickening dizziness rushes at me. My head tilts back, and I fall, weightless, into nothing. White becomes black. Utter darkness surrounds me.

After an indeterminate amount of time, dim light slowly gathers in my vision. I realize I'm lying on the grass with tendrils of black smoke spiraling lazily into the air on either side of me and a voice faintly calling my name from far away. Aurora's lips move as she leans over me, her features screwed up in concern. "Em? Em!" Her voice is an echo that slowly moves closer, eventually layering itself over the movement of her lips. "Em. Emerson!"

"Mm?"

Roarke appears beside her. "Here, let me give her this. I grabbed it from Yokshin's supplies."

"Are you sure it's the right thing?"

"Yes. I've taken it before." Roarke lifts my upper body and pulls me against his chest. He removes the stopper from a little brown glass bottle that, for a moment, reminds me of Chelsea's herbal remedies. It's so odd to think of her ordinary little salon in her ordinary little house when I'm lying on the ground of a foreign world beneath a sprinkling of stars I created with my own magic. A breathy laugh escapes me, which increases the concern on Aurora's face and makes Roarke pause with the bottle just in front of my lips.

"Em?" Aurora says in a voice that sounds higher than usual. "Why are you laughing?"

Then I remember that Chelsea isn't alive anymore and will never make another herbal remedy, and the breath of laughter dies on my lips.

"I'm going to give it to her, okay?" Roarke says.

"Wait," Aurora says, stopping his hand before he can place the bottle against my lips. "That potion is meant to restore *normal* magic after using too much of it, but Em was using Griffin magic. Her levels of normal magic should be totally fine. That potion isn't going to help her."

"It can't hurt either," Roarke says, tipping some liquid into my mouth.

I've already begun to feel less lightheaded though, even before the unfamiliar liquid burns down the back of my throat. I lick my lips and push my hair away from my face. "Why did I pass out?"

"I think you tried to do too much," Aurora says. "Your Griffin Ability attempted to carry out your command, but you didn't have nearly enough magic to fill an entire sky with stars." Her eyes are still wide as she sits awkwardly on the grass in front of me in her voluminous yellow skirt covered in gold leaves. "You need to learn your limits before trying something so big, Em. You don't want to accidentally kill yourself."

I blink at her. "Do you think that could actually happen?"

"I don't know!" She throws her hands up. "No one else has magic like yours. We're still figuring it out, remember?"

"Why are you angry with me?"

"Because you should have been more careful."

"She's concerned, that's all," Roarke says. He still has one arm around me, but I'm strong enough to sit on my own, so I gently ease myself away from him.

"I'm concerned too," I say. "I didn't realize my Griffin Ability would reach its limit on something so simple. It obviously isn't as powerful as everyone thinks it is."

Roarke laughs. "You created *stars*, Emerson. And not just two or three; dozens of them appeared before you lost consciousness. That's far more powerful than any magic an ordinary faerie possesses. And I think that if you store it up—if you don't use it immediately each time you feel the power coming on—then you can probably do greater things."

"It's dangerous to test these 'greater things,'" Aurora says, her brow furrowed in a deep frown. "You need to be careful."

"Don't worry," Roarke says to her. "I won't let anything happen to Emerson."

She looks directly at him, folding her arms over her chest. "Won't you?"

"Of course not." He looks affronted. "Do you know how fast I ran back through the palace to get that potion? I didn't trust any of my men to get there quicker than I could." He places one hand over mine. "It terrified me to think you might not recover, Emerson. I know that neither of us is in this for love, but I do care for you."

"You care for her Griffin Ability," Aurora mutters.

Roarke pins his dark burgundy gaze on her. "Please don't make scornful remarks under your breath like that. It isn't the kind of behavior that befits a princess. You're better than that, Aurora."

She levels her simmering gaze at him for several moments before looking away. "You're right. I apologize. I only want you and Em to be happy, of course. To take care of one another."

"And that's exactly what we'll do." Roarke fits his arm around me again. His thumb rubs up and down the bare skin just above my elbow in a way that feels uncomfortably intimate. "For the rest of our lives."

Aurora nods and smiles, but her eyes continue to stare off into the distance, and her smile is far from genuine.

342

CHAPTER 21

I don't see Aurora at all the following day, which is odd considering she's had some activity or other planned for the two of us every few hours since the moment I arrived here. She doesn't show up for archery in the morning and, far worse, she doesn't join me in the queen's private parlor in the afternoon for my weekly instruction on etiquette. I've survived two of these etiquette lessons already, but I suspect it was only because Aurora was there to make them bearable by poking fun at her mother—something I'd love to do, but wouldn't dare for fear of receiving some form of horrible magical punishment I've never heard of. So I keep my mouth shut and try not to fall asleep as Queen Amrath drones on.

I assume that perhaps Aurora isn't feeling well, but when Roarke comes to my room in the early evening and I ask how she's doing, he says, "I believe she's in perfect health. I saw her having a picnic this afternoon with her ladies-in-waiting."

"Oh." An unexpected stab of hurt pierces my chest. "So she's gone from being overly friendly and telling me how she looks forward to having me as a sister to ignoring me?"

He sighs. "She's just being moody. I'm sure she'll get over it once the union has taken place. And what does it matter if she doesn't? You'll have me." He tucks my hair behind my ear and drags one finger briefly along my jaw. "It's nothing to worry yourself about."

"Nothing to worry myself about?" I fold my arms over my chest and raise an eyebrow. "Do you plan to continue using this condescending tone once we're married?"

His lips stretch into a smile, his dark eyes glittering with amusement. "Do you plan to continue to be just as feisty once we're married?"

I shrug. "Probably."

"Good. I quite enjoy your feistiness." He lifts my hand and kisses it, which sends a shiver all the way up my arm.

"You think you're being so smooth, don't you," I say with a roll of my eyes.

"Well, it's working, isn't it?"

If you're aiming to make me feel uncomfortable, then yes, I almost say. But it's better if he thinks his attempts at charm are working. He hasn't compelled me to say anything with my Griffin Ability tonight, and if I can get him to hang around until later, I might be able to use my power on him. "Perhaps," I say with what I hope is a sultry half smile. "If you stay and have dinner with me tonight, we can find out."

He chuckles as he lowers my hand. "Oh how I wish I could say yes to that. Unfortunately, I'm going out for a few hours. If Aurora hasn't requested your company this evening, then I assume you'll be eating on your own. I'll tell Clarina to bring your dinner here."

"All right." Disappointment settles over my shoulders, but I won't give up yet. "Perhaps you can stop by when you return later and say goodnight."

"Yes, perhaps. I'll see how late it is."

Something nudges my ankle, and I look down to see Bandit rubbing the length of his grey cat-formed body along my leg. "Looking for attention, huh?" I say to him.

Roarke takes a step back. "Well, have a good evening, my love. If I don't see you later, then—Oh, I almost forgot to give you your second dose of compulsion potion for the day."

The light weight of disappointment on my shoulders becomes a thousand times heavier. I bite back a sigh and give Roarke a polite frown instead. "Do you think that's necessary? It took such a toll on me when I tried to use too much power earlier that I assumed my ability will take longer to replenish. I'm sure I'll be asleep when it happens."

Roarke looks down at the ruby on my arm as he removes a small bottle from a hidden pocket within his coat. "Hmm. Your power may be slightly slower in replenishing itself, but it appears it will still be ready for use sometime later tonight. I'd rather not miss an opportunity for you to use your ability." He holds the bottle of potion out toward me, but I make no move to take it.

"I thought we trusted each other now, Roarke."

"We do." He lowers his voice. "But my father has ways of discovering the things that happen within his palace. If I don't compel you, he'll probably find out. Best to keep him happy, don't you think?"

Of course it's best to keep the king happy, but that means losing out on another opportunity to command Roarke. It's pointless to argue, though, and Roarke might even become suspicious. So I take the bottle from him and sip a small amount.

"Good." He takes the bottle and screws the lid back on. "So, Emerson, when your Griffin Ability next appears, you're going to say the word 'open.'"

"Open? Open what?"

"That's up to you. As Aurora pointed out yesterday, it's becoming clear that your intentions—not only your words—play a role in instructing your Griffin Ability. So I'd like you to give as simple a command as possible—the word 'open'—while deciding in your mind exactly what should open. A window, a drawer, your balcony doors, your wardrobe. Anything."

"Okay." Of course, I'm now wondering if there's any way I can use this to my advantage. Which door can I open that I've never been allowed to open before? And how likely it is that King Savyon might be behind whichever door I choose, ready to take out his wrath on me the moment he discovers me sneaking around?

"Oh, and tomorrow night you'll be having dinner with my family," Roarke says as he opens my sitting room door. "Just the four of us and you. My father would like to see the improvement you've made since he first met you." My fear must be obvious on my face, because Roarke quickly adds, "Don't worry, I'm sure you'll do just fine. Wear an appropriate dress, speak politely about appropriate topics, and make occasional use of basic magic while you're at the table. He just wants to be certain you don't stand out like a human amongst faeries, that's all."

"Right. Of course." I clear my throat. "And, uh, in the morning can we try some more building in the shadow world? I'm excited to see what else my power can do."

Roarke smiles. "Certainly. I look forward to it." Then he walks out and closes the door, leaving me with my heart almost hammering itself right out of my chest.

Tomorrow is the day. Tomorrow I'm going to finally do what I came here to do. Roarke and I will be in the shadow world with hardly any guards around, and when he lets me choose to build whatever I want to build, I'll command him instead.

I walk to the table and sit down amongst the books and papers I've been writing notes on. I can't write down what I plan to use my Griffin Ability for—I can't risk anyone finding out —but I doodle while I think. While I decide what to say to the guards, what to say to Aurora if she's there, and what to say to Roarke.

Tell me every single thing you know about my mother and how to help her.

I repeat the words silently over and over until they're embedded in my brain. Then I begin to wonder just how complicated the magic that's required to heal Mom might be. I probably won't remember everything Roarke tells me. Which means I need to instruct him to write everything down instead. Once he's done that, I'll use whatever Griffin magic I have left to tell the faerie paths to open. If I can manage that, then I don't need to find one of those candles or run all the way to the gap over Velazar Island.

Cold slowly seeps into my bones as the fire on the other side of the room diminishes from burning logs to glowing embers. I reach for my coat hanging over one of the other chairs—a ridiculous thing that looks like something a circus ringmaster might wear. Red with gold-edged lapels, long enough to reach my ankles and billow out behind me as I walk. Clarina paired it with black-and-gold pants and a white shirt with ruffles down the front, and told me the queen would love it. Now that I think of it, Queen Amrath smiled when I walked into her parlor this afternoon, so perhaps Clarina was right.

I stand and walk to the fireplace as I pull the jacket on. Using magic, I manage to lift several pieces of wood from the copper bucket and add them to the fire without being too clumsy. Then I sift through my brain for the right spell to ignite not just one flame, but many. When the fire bursts back into life, I can't help smiling. If I wasn't so anxious about tomorrow, I'd probably clap my hands too.

A loud knock on my door wipes the smile from my face. I turn quickly as the door opens. I haven't uttered a word yet, which means it can only be—

"Em, I have more books for you," Aurora announces as she strides in with a pile of books floating behind her. "I hope you've finished the last lot."

I blink at her. "No, I haven't finished the last lot that you gave me only two days ago."

"Well, these are more important." She directs the pile of books toward the table, and they drop down onto my page of doodles. She stands in front of me and places her hands on her hips. "I'm serious. They contain important historical events from Unseelie history. You need to read them before the union ceremony."

"Before the ceremony? Aurora, I'm not a fast reader like you. You can't ignore me all day, leave me alone to face your mother, and then barge in here to tell me to read a gazillion books in less than two weeks."

She covers her hand with her mouth as she laughs. "Em, don't be silly. I haven't been ignoring you. I had to attend a birthday picnic with one of my ladies. Didn't Noraya bring you my message?"

I cross my arms, but I'm starting to feel silly now. I couldn't help feeling hurt at being excluded from the picnic Roarke mentioned, but if it wasn't Aurora's event—if it was someone else's birthday—then of course it had nothing to do with me. "No, Noraya didn't tell me anything," I say quietly.

"Well, that's very strange. And you know I haven't given you anywhere *near* a gazillion books. You should be able to finish them in a few days. Start tonight. Keep reading late if you have to."

"Aurora, that's—"

"It's important, that's what it is." There is no merriment in her tone, no sparkle of laughter in her eyes. "Our world can be a cold place to those who don't fit in, Em. You want to survive it, don't you?"

"Of course." I lower my hands to my sides. "Why are you being so—"

"Good. If you come across anything you don't understand, I'll happily explain things to you. Perhaps we can go to the spa together tomorrow. I'll have the ladies there prepare some beauty treatments for us. You can tell me all about what you've read."

"Oh. There's a spa here?"

"Yes. We can go in the afternoon. Roarke told me you're visiting the shadow world again in the morning?"

I nod. If all goes well, I won't return to this palace. I won't have any beauty treatments, and I'll probably never see my new friend again. "Uh, yes. We can do the spa thing in the afternoon."

"Great. Unless you change your mind about seeing Roarke. Then we can do the spa in the morning."

I nod again, though I have no intention of changing my plans.

"Well, goodnight then. And happy reading." Aurora spins around, her skirt swishing around her ankles, and strides out with the same haughtiness with which she entered.

I look down at the couch where Bandit is curled up on a cushion, watching me through half-open eyes. "She's still being strange," I say to him. I return to the table and push the pile of books aside. I'll be gone tomorrow, so there's no point in reading any of them. I know what I'm going to say to Roarke tomorrow, but I still need to decide on how to command the guards who'll be in the shadow world with us. I brush the quill feather against my cheek as I ponder different commands. Then I frown as I notice that the book on top of the newest pile is the same book that made Aurora gasp in horror the other night in the library. The book featuring graphic and gruesome deaths of historical figures. She said we'd definitely give this one a miss, but either she changed her mind, or she accidentally included it.

As I draw the book closer, I notice that none of the gold embossed words set into the dark cover are English. Aurora knows I haven't yet learned any foreign fae languages, so it must be an accident that this book is here. I flip it open and turn through the first few age-stained pages, each of which is filled with the same strange combination of letters and unfamiliar symbols.

I shut the book, but as I push it aside, I notice something: the smallest corner of a piece of paper sticking out between the pages. Paper that's newer and whiter than the aged pages above and below it. I slide the book toward me once more and open to the page with the corner of paper sticking out. The paper is a small square with a few hastily scrawled words on it. A scrawl I immediately identify as Aurora's handwriting.

I swear I didn't know about this.

My heart begins to patter again. I push the note aside and take a closer look at the page it was sitting on. Scribbled in between the lines of foreign words, I see partial sentences in English, as if Aurora didn't have time to translate everything properly.

From the ways of the witches … one of the few methods to separate magic from life essence … most subjects survive the spell despite all magic being removed … magic is transferred in its entirety to the recipient … spell relies on complete willingness … cannot under any circumstances be forced … recitation of the following words … used in conjunction with a blood spell, such as the union spell.

With my breaths coming fast now and my fingers shaking, I turn the page—and the words printed across it are words I recognize. Words I've been repeating for days. Words I will be whispering in private to Roarke once we've cut our hands, tattooed marks onto our fingers, and spoken the public words of the union ceremony spell. These are the words—so he's led me to believe—of our private vows. And thanks to Aurora, I can now read what they mean.

I come to you of my own free will,
with a willing heart and a willing mind,
to give you my power,
every part of my magic.
I hand it over in its entirety,
keeping nothing for myself.
My magic is yours.

I blink at the words for several moments, unable to move, barely able to breathe. "Ho-lee crap," I whisper. Then I shove the book away from me and stand so abruptly that my chair falls backwards. *No way*, my brain tells me. *No way, no way, no way.* Roarke wouldn't do something like this. He wants to rule beside me. He wants me to be queen of the shadow world.

Except … he doesn't.

My mind races as I put together the pieces of Roarke's plan. Now I understand why he's always emphasized the fact that he'll never force me into anything: because a *willing* subject is exactly what this spell requires. My hands curl into fists so tight my nails digs into my palms. Everything—*everything*—he's done has been about earning my trust, getting me onto his side. His gifts, his kindness and occasional flirting, even allowing Dash to stay so that I'd have a friend—it's all been part of luring me toward the moment where I *willingly* marry him while *unwittingly* hand over my magic.

Standing there in shocked silence, I arrive abruptly at another realization: Roarke was never going to heal Mom. Once my magic is his, he'll head straight for the shadow world, claim it as his own, and destroy anyone who tries to stop him or take that world away from him. Waking my mother and healing her mind won't come anywhere near his to-do list.

And what about Dash? Roarke would never have let him go. Is he a prisoner? Dead? And Aurora … was she telling the truth about not knowing Roarke's plans to use this spell? Or could she have known all along and suddenly had a change of heart? But Roarke is her brother. Why would she go behind his back and tell me about this spell? Is this information some kind of trap?

Bandit rubs against my legs again, in the form of a ginger cat this time. I bend and pick him up, hugging him so tightly I'm afraid I might hurt him. "I don't know what to do," I whisper into the hair along his back, so quietly that even I can barely hear my own voice.

A loud rap at the door makes me jump. "Emerson, my love?" Roarke's voice calls out.

I press my hand over my mouth to cover my gasp. Bandit tumbles from my arms, shifts into a bird, and swoops onto my shoulder. I look around, lost for a moment with no thought, no plan. Then I quickly return the fallen chair to its usual position, grab the offending book, and shove it under the cushion. "Emerson, are you in there?" Roarke asks. I hurry to the balcony doors. I open and close them as quietly as I can, the cold air hitting me immediately. As Bandit takes off and flies away, I swing my legs over the balustrade and begin climbing down.

PART III

CHAPTER 22
VIOLET

Violet leaned back in the booth, lifted her trumpet-shaped glass of iced night, and took a sip. Ryn did the same with his tankard of ale. The two of them were doing their best to appear at ease, but it was tough in a tavern in the heart of Unseelie territory. Violet pulled her sleeves a little lower, making sure her wrist markings were covered. Things would turn south quickly if the patrons of this tavern discovered two guardians amongst their company, and she doubted anyone would give them a chance to explain their *ex*-guardian status.

Ryn lowered his tankard and leaned forward. "I don't understand why we can't find it," he said in a low voice. "We've been there before. Why is it hidden from us now?"

"It's been a long time since we were there," Violet reminded him. "The Unseelies have obviously upped the security around their palace. Made it invisible to those who shouldn't be there." She tapped her glass with her fingernails. "Calla will get in. You know she will."

"And if the Unseelie Palace has some kind of Griffin Ability detection spell over its entrance like the Guild does?" Ryn asked. "She'll get herself caught while she's following those guards. It won't matter that she's invisible. They'll know someone's there."

Violet slouched a little lower in the booth, attempting to look bored. Beneath the table, she kicked Ryn's foot. He was going to bring attention to himself if he didn't start looking more relaxed. "I very much doubt the Unseelies have that kind of magic over their entrance," she said. "They're not bothered by Griffin Abilities, remember? They *value* them, in fact. They don't just want to use Em's power; they want her to be one of them." News of the Unseelie Prince's betrothal to a Griffin Gifted girl had reached the Guild soon after Dash's impromptu decision to climb into an Unseelie carriage, and Perry had passed the news on to Calla immediately. It confirmed Dash's suspicion that the girl his mother had heard rumors about was indeed Emerson. But it had now been four days since that announcement, and Dash still hadn't returned with Emerson.

Ryn shook his head. "That poor girl. After everything she's been through with her mother and that woman with the glass magic and everyone hunting her for her Griffin Ability, now she's being forced into a union with an Unseelie."

"And she's so young," Violet murmured. "Not even eighteen yet."

"She never should have left the—our safe haven." Ryn's hand clenched around the tankard. "Why was she so foolish? If she'd just stayed with us, we could have kept her safe."

Violet gave Ryn another kick under the table, and he finally leaned back and smoothed out his expression. "What's done is done," she said. "Once we've got Em back to safety, she can explain."

"Dash should have retrieved her by now. Why is it taking him so long?"

"Probably because he doesn't have Calla's ability to cast illusions," Violet pointed out. "He can't simply walk out of there with Em. It's a wonder he got into the palace in the first place."

"*If* he got in," Ryn reminded her. "We still don't know if something happened to him after he got into that Unseelie carriage."

Violet took another slow sip of her drink before answering, needing a few moments to mentally convince herself that nothing terrible had happened to Dash. "He's fine. I'm sure he's fine. He's a good guardian. Calla will get inside, she'll find him and Em, and all three of them will return safely to us."

"We should have gone with her," Ryn said. "Calla could easily have made all three of us invisible."

"Yes, but it would have been harder for her to cast any other illusion at the same time," Violet reminded him. They'd been over this repeatedly yesterday and this morning while planning for Calla to follow the first Unseelie guards she could find. "And we need to be available to respond to any other emergency Ana might inform us of. Now can you please stop being so anxious? I'm going to run out of reassuring things to say."

Across the table, Ryn gave her a small smile. "If *you* could stop being so anxious, I might be able to get past my own worry. But it's tough when I have to feel mine and yours."

Violet began tapping the side of her glass again, feeling guilty—as she always did—when her negative emotions ended up affecting Ryn. "I'm sorry. I thought I was doing a better job convincing myself not to be concerned. But despite my worry—" she reached across the table and placed her hand on his "—I do believe they'll be fine. Dash and Calla have escaped from dangerous situations before; they can do it again, with Em this time."

Ryn nodded. "On a slightly different topic," he said, "have you noticed how insistent Calla's been about staying involved with the search for Em? She was originally supposed to be with Chase today to stop that heist in Paris, but she asked Darius to go in her place."

"Yes. I did notice that," Violet said, leaning back again. "I wondered if maybe she bonded with Em more than I realized while Em was at our safe haven. But … I don't know. Em wasn't with us for very long."

"She's also been more distracted lately," Ryn continued. "And she's been leaving more often than usual without telling us where she's going. I think she's investigating something we don't know about."

"You're probably right. But she doesn't have to tell us everything, does she? Living with family, working with family …" Violet rubbed her finger over a droplet of condensation on the table. "Well, it can be difficult at times when everyone knows everything about you. I don't blame her for keeping some things from us. And she's been talking to Chase, at least. I've seen the two of them whispering together. So whatever's going on, she isn't dealing with it alone."

"True," Ryn said.

A shiver against the side of her leg alerted Violet to a message on her amber. She removed it from her pocket and kept the rectangular device beneath the edge of the table as she tapped its glossy surface. "Message from Perry," she said as her eyes darted across the words. "Hmm. Another glass attack on a group of guardians. Darn that woman. Oh, and this is important. The Guild's finally decided on a date for that big fancy ceremony they want to have while doing their veil restoration spell."

"Idiots," Ryn mutters. "Why are they making such a fuss about it?"

"Well, it is a big deal. It's been, what? Seventeen, eighteen years since it was torn?"

"Yes, but the Guild is practically asking for someone to come along and interfere.

It would have been safer if they'd quietly done it already without any fanfare."

Violet sighed as she put her amber away. "It's happening in four days. Last time we spoke about it, Dash suggested we should be there, and now Perry's saying the same thing. I think they're right. We should hide there and keep watch. Just a few of us—you and me, anyone else who isn't busy at that time. In case your predictions come true and something does go wrong."

Ryn quirked an eyebrow. "You don't think they can handle things without our help?"

Violet rolled her eyes. "I wish they could, but they've been known to mess up before."

"They've been known to *spectacularly* mess up," Ryn said. "I believe that's the word you were looking for."

"I believe you're right," she said with a smile. "So, since we're doing nothing useful right now, we may as well plan how we're going to hide on that tiny piece of island that's left around the monument."

CHAPTER 23

My feet hit the snow-covered ground of a flowerbed far below my balcony. I duck down immediately in case someone walking nearby heard me. With my heart still thrashing in my chest, I look around. I need to run. Not to run *away*—I haven't yet figured out how to escape—but to run the way Val and I used to. As fast as possible, leaping and climbing and somersaulting. Forgetting everything except the ground slamming beneath our feet, the rough sting of bricks and the cold bite of metal against our hands. The exhilaration of successfully making it from point A to point B faster than the previous time.

I can't do that here. These gardens don't contain the right kinds of obstacles, and my long coat would be a bit of a hindrance. But I can at least run. And if someone sees me—if someone catches me—I can tell them a story they'll have to believe: *I'm practicing parkour. You've seen me do it before, right? You've seen me showing Princess Aurora some of the jumps and falls? Why am I doing it in the middle of a freezing winter night, you ask? Well, one needs to train in all conditions, don't you think? You guards train in all conditions, don't you?*

After waiting another few moments to make sure no one's walking nearby, I straighten and take off immediately. My legs race faster and faster. My arms pump at my sides, and my coat whips at the air as it billows out behind me. I swerve between the rose bushes and around the queen's bower. I leap clear across one of the smaller pavilions and keep going. I run further from the palace than I've ever been before.

When my lungs begin to ache and my face is just about numb with cold, I finally come to a stop. Ahead of me is a circular section of paving—uncovered by snow, somehow—with a fountain at its center. Streams of water, flowing from a nymph's hands and mouth into the pool below, are frozen in place. I walk to the edge of the pool as I catch my breath. Bandit, still a bird, flits by and lands on my shoulder. He shifts into something small and furry and climbs down my arm and into the pocket of my coat. I close my eyes for a moment, wracking my muddled brain for the words to a spell that will keep me warm. When I eventually find the words, I hold my hand up over my head, speak the words in a quiet voice, and allow myself to relax a little as warmth blankets my body.

Then I sit beside the pool.

And I try to make sense of my situation.

I can't go through with this union. That much is clear. But how do I get away from here with my life intact? And what about Dash? I recognize now that Roarke wouldn't simply let him leave, which means Dash is either a prisoner somewhere or he's dead. I bury my face in my hands as I shudder. *He can't be dead, he can't be dead,* I silently repeat. It's too awful to imagine him slaughtered in the same way that man in the cavern lost his life.

He isn't dead, I tell myself again, more firmly this time. Roarke may be cruel and hate all guardians, but he likes to take advantage of opportunities when they present themselves. He's aware that Dash knows far more than he should about the Griffin rebels. Roarke could use Dash to try to gain access to the rebels himself if he wants to get his hands on more Griffin Abilities. The more I think about this, the more I manage to convince myself that Dash must be alive. Where, though? I don't know the location of any prisons in this world. Dash could be thousands of miles away.

After sitting quietly for a while, staring across the frozen garden and coming no closer to deciding what to do, I sense my Griffin Ability replenishing. I push my sleeve back and look at the bracelet; the ruby is almost completely red. When my power is ready to be used again, I'll have to tell something to 'open,' which seems a useless command out here where there are no doors. I'll have to tell a frozen rosebud to open or something.

Feeling uncomfortable, I shift my legs into a different position. Bandit wriggles inside my pocket, then crawls out and sits on my knee. "How are we going to get out of here?" I whisper to him. His only response is a twitch of his tiny mouse ear. Then he shifts into a dragonfly-type creature with a tiny humanoid face and glowing wings. "Pretty," I murmur. He shifts again, flashing between several indistinguishable forms before becoming a dragon small enough to fit into my lap. "My new favorite form," I say to him with a smile. "I think it's incredible how you can—" A beat of silence passes as I realize what he's telling me. "A dragon. We can get away on a dragon!" Bandit coughs, and a spark escapes his mouth. "You're so clever," I tell him, running one finger along his smooth, scaly back.

But my excitement fades as I consider all the obstacles I'll need to pass in order to make this dragon plan succeed. I don't know how to open one of those elevators in the ground that would carry me to the bottom of the pit. I don't know how to unlock the room with the saddles and the staircase. I don't know the spell to remove the shield layer preventing each dragon from flying away. And I don't know if Imperia likes me enough to let me climb onto her back without Aurora or Phillyp around.

I check the ruby on my wrist again, then cast my eyes about for something I can open without drawing any attention to this area of the grounds. I wonder if there's any point in being careful, though. I'm so far from the palace now that I doubt anyone would notice if I told a hole to open in the ground, or a tree trunk to—

"Wait a minute," I murmur, interrupting my own thoughts. I can't open any doors out here, but what about door*ways*? Faerie paths doorways, to be more specific. I've heard repeatedly that faerie paths are inaccessible from most parts of this palace and its grounds, but Aurora was always referring to the kind of accessibility one would gain with a stylus. Perhaps, if I turn my thoughts toward the faerie paths when I say the word 'open,' a doorway will form.

Though I've still got another few minutes before I can use my Griffin Ability, I move Bandit off my lap and stand. A thrill sends blood pumping faster through my veins. This might actually work. I might escape the Unseelies tonight. Bandit becomes a tiny lizard and scurries up the edge of my coat. He climbs back into my pocket as I bounce up and down in anticipation.

And it's then that I hear an odd sound. A wail, almost. A person crying out. I stop bouncing and look around, but I don't see anyone. I walk slowly around the fountain, peering into the garden around me, seeing little more than glistening white snow.

Until I almost trip over something.

Looking down, I find a metal circle roughly the size of a manhole cover embedded in the paving. It has a hinge on one side, which is what I almost tripped over, and at its center is a sold metal ring. *A trapdoor?* I crouch down and take a closer look at the symbol stamped into the metal. It's a simple outline of two hands bound together at the wrists. I get onto my knees and lower my ear close to the cold metal. I hear another cry, and as I straighten, I remember something Aurora mentioned in passing. Something about Yokshin showing her his experiments in a prison. *Just the small one we have here*, she'd said.

My thoughts turn immediately to Dash. If he wasn't allowed to leave, and he wasn't killed, then he could very likely be somewhere beneath this trapdoor. I hesitate for a moment, then pull my coat sleeve down over my hand and take hold of the metal ring. I pull gently, then a little harder. But the trapdoor doesn't budge. My survival instincts tell me to stay the hell away from this prison, but my concern for Dash keeps me frozen to the spot. I try the simple unlocking spell Aurora taught me, but that makes no difference either.

A powerful magical command, however, might force it to open.

I begin shaking my head as soon as the thought occurs to me. I stand and take a step away from the trapdoor. I can't use my Griffin Ability for this. I have to open the faerie paths instead. The word 'open'—this one ambiguous compulsion command I've been given—could be my only way out of here.

But what about Dash, my conscience prods. *You know he's probably down there. You can't leave him behind.*

"Dammit," I mutter. And then: "Wait." I blink as something that should have been obvious occurs to me: I can do *both*. It won't take much of my power to open a faerie paths doorway. I'll make sure to hang onto whatever power is left once I've given my 'open' command, and I'll use it to unlock the trapdoor. But then … the faerie paths doorway won't stay open for long. It'll close if I don't have some part of my body keeping it open, which means I can't go beneath the trapdoor to find out if Dash is there. Or … could I tell the doorway to remain open for a long time? For as long as it takes me to get back to it? Perhaps that would work, but if it requires a lot of magic, it might use up all my Griffin power in one go. Then I'll just have to forget about the trapdoor and leave on my own.

And leave Dash behind, my conscience whispers.

But I don't know that for sure. Dash might be back at home, completely fine. I have no way of knowing where he is, and now I'm about to risk imprisoning myself beneath the ground.

No. I won't do it. I'm not a hero; I'm a *survivor*. That's what I've always been, and Dash knows it.

I turn my back on the trapdoor as I sense my Griffin magic simmering beneath the surface of my control. I can't waste this opportunity. I need to get back to Mom. She's always been my priority, and I need to find another way to help her now that the Unseelie plan has fallen through. If it turns out that Dash never made it home, I'll tell the Griffin rebels that he's probably here, and they can come and rescue him.

And you'll be putting even more lives in danger, which is exactly what you were trying to avoid when you came here.

I push my guilt aside and look at the ruby once more. The tiniest sliver—so thin I can barely see it—still needs to be filled. I watch it and wait. And wait. I imagine the faerie paths. I picture myself focusing intently on them as I give my one-word command.

Then I feel the tingling, the magic crawling up my spine, my voice preparing to change. I whip around and point at the trapdoor. "Open," I gasp before the horrible, selfish person that I am at my core can make me change my mind.

With a subdued grinding sound, the trapdoor slowly swings opens.

CHAPTER 24

I SHOULD HAVE CONCENTRATED HARDER, BUT I WAS SO CAUGHT UP IN THE TERRIFYING rush of *doing the right thing* that I completely forgot to rein in my Griffin magic. It escapes me all at once, leaving nothing behind. I shut my eyes for a moment and ball my hands into fists, but there's no point in regretting what I've done. I chose to open the trapdoor. Now I need to find out what's hidden beneath it.

I stare at the dark circle of space and the stairs that lead downward. An icy breeze drifts past the back of my neck, reminding me that I've lost my tenuous hold on the spell that was keeping me warm. I take a steadying breath and place my foot on the first step. There could be a hundred guards waiting at the bottom of these stairs. There could be all kinds of horrifying creatures or threatening magic. I try not to think of the many possibilities as I descend. The white glow of the moon and the snowy landscape filters down through the trapdoor's opening, illuminating the steps ahead of me. But the further down I go, the dimmer the light becomes.

Finally, I reach the bottom. No guards step forward to seize me. No creatures leap out of the darkness to tear me to shreds. No unseen magical force knocks me to the ground. I venture further forward, looking all around. As my eyes become accustomed to the dull light, any lingering doubts I may have had about finding a prison down here vanish. But it's unlike any prison I've ever seen on TV. Large spheres of dark glass fill the vast space ahead of me, each one containing a single prisoner. Some spheres rest on the ground, while others hang in the air at different levels from vine-like ropes. Those on the ground seem to be placed roughly in lines, presumably so guards can patrol the uneven corridors of space between them.

With a shaky breath, I walk forward, the first row of spheres on my right, and the wall—partially covered in creeping vines—on my left. As I near the first prisoner,

I begin to make out more details, like the open section of space on the side of each sphere, and the vertical bars of dark glass lining each open space. A flat surface forms the floor inside each sphere. In the first one, a woman lies on the floor, curled up and sleeping. She doesn't move as my footsteps pass her cell. Even when another howl echoes through the cavernous prison, she remains asleep.

I stride past each sphere as quickly and quietly as I can after checking to make sure I don't see Dash inside any of them. When I notice a male figure with dirty blond hair, I slow down, but as I get closer, I realize the color tangled in with the blond is more turquoise than green. He rolls over as I pass his sphere, confirming for me that he isn't Dash. His eyes meet mine, and he begins laughing. Crazed laughter that should send me scurrying away. But my attention is caught by the markings on his wrists: guardian markings.

"Emerson." My eyes snap back to his, a jolt of adrenalin passing through me at the sound of my own name leaving this stranger's cracked lips. "What a mess we've … got ourselves into," he slurs. "And the irony. The irony!" he calls out before raspy laughter consumes him once more. "I thought I was … doing the right thing for … for once in my life, and look where it got me. Landed me … right back … at the mercy of an Unseelie prince."

"How do you—"

"Em?" It's a different voice this time, from the next sphere over. The voice I've been listening for since I descended the stairs.

"Dash!" I hurry to his cell and drop onto my knees. He's lying on his side, his arm stretched out toward me. Bruises mar both cheeks and one side of his neck, and thick stubble covers his jaw. "Are you okay? I'm so, so sorry. You were right about Roarke. He was never going to help me. And then I realized he would never have let you leave, and that you must be imprisoned somewhere, or … or …" *Or worse,* I whisper silently to myself. I push my hand through the bars, but I can't reach him. "Are you okay? Are you hurt? I mean, aside from the bruises."

"I'm … okay." He pulls himself weakly toward the bars, moving only a few inches before collapsing again. But his hand is close enough now. I can just reach his fingers.

"What did they do to you?"

"I feel … drunk. Sort of."

"What?"

"A potion. A drug. It makes us … weak and disoriented. And my magic. I try to reach for it … and it's almost there … and then it slides from my grasp." His eyelids lower. "Like water … slipping through my fingers."

"Dash. Hey. Wake up." I wrap my fingers around his and shake his hand.

"I'm awake," he mumbles. His eyes open, but he takes a moment to focus on me. "That's the problem. This potion … keeps me drowsy and weak … but it never lets me sleep."

"I'm sorry. That's horrible." He nods but doesn't answer. His eyes close once more. "Dash, what have they done to you? There are bruises all over you. That's … that's not normal for a faerie, right?"

In the next sphere over, the man laughs again. "Not normal," he says. "Definitely not normal. But normal for … for down here."

Dash shifts until he's lying on his back, staring upward. "Sometimes," he says in a weak voice, "they roll the spheres. Or make them swing … back and forth … from a great height." He rolls his head slowly from side to side. "We crash around inside our glass cells. But the glass never breaks. It batters us as our bodies are flung around … but we never die."

"Dash." I squeeze his hand tighter as unshed tears make my throat ache and guilt burns hot in my chest. Isn't this precisely the kind of thing I hoped to avoid when I decided to leave the Griffin rebels' home? "I'm very glad you're not dead. I'm going to get you out of here."

"That would be … a sweet kind of … karma indeed," the man next door murmurs. "I save her, and she saves me."

I frown at him before bending closer to Dash's cell. "Who is that man?" I ask in low tones. "How does he know me?"

"We talk … the two of us … when no one's around. I must have told him about you." With a great effort, Dash pulls himself up and leans against the glass. "His name is Zed."

"Zed," I repeat. "And how long has Zed been down here? Long enough to begin losing his mind?"

"I can hear you, you know," Zed says, rolling over and blinking until his eyes focus on me. "And no, I'm not the one who's … lost my mind. That affliction belongs to … someone else you care about."

I draw even further away from his sphere. Part of me wants to be angry with Dash for telling this stranger about me and my mother, but I can't be. I doubt anyone down here has much control over what they say. And I can't blame Dash for talking to this man when he would otherwise be completely alone. The sphere on his other side, I notice, is empty.

"Dash, we need to plan how we're going to get out of here. I can use my Griffin Ability to open this sphere, but it needs to replenish, and that will only happen tomorrow, late in the morning. And Roarke already knows something isn't right. He came to my room earlier tonight, but I ran before he could see me. He's probably wondering where I am, and if I don't return in the next few hours, he'll send guards out to search for me."

"Everything is … such an effort," Dash says. "Speaking. Moving. Living."

"Hey," I say, louder than I intended, his words disturbing me than I'd like to admit. "Don't say things like that. That's just the potion talking. You do want to live, which is why you need to help me with our escape plan."

With his eyes closed, he nods. "Roarke doesn't know … that you know about his prison. He won't look here first. We'll have … some time."

"Okay. Yes. Hopefully. Then our next problem is that you're drugged and can't use your own magic."

"I can barely even … move," he reminds me.

"True. So how long does it take for this potion to wear off? Because we're going to have to hide somewhere while that happens. And by the time you're able to move easily and use your magic, Roarke will know you're gone too. We're going to have to find a very good hiding place to wait in while my Griffin Ability recharges and your drugs wear off."

"There's lots of … waiting … in this plan," Zed says.

"Well, it isn't your escape plan, so you needn't worry about the details."

"You will … help him too?" Dash says. "Can't leave him here. He's a guardian. He's … my companion."

My first instinct is to reject this idea. It will be harder to escape with three of us than with two. But this man has become Dash's friend. I can't leave him behind. But then … I look around at all the spheres. What about everyone else down here?

No. Stop. You can't go there, I instruct myself severely. I can't save everyone. And many of these people are probably criminals. They must have disobeyed the king in some way in order to have landed up here. If I try to rescue all of them, Dash and I will never get away. "Yes, okay, I'll get Zed out too."

"And what happens," Zed asks, "after all the waiting … and hiding? You know the faerie paths can't … be opened from here … right?"

"Yes, I know that. But my Griffin Ability is more powerful than ordinary magic. I can tell the paths to open a doorway for us, and it should work."

"Don't know … about that," Dash says. "Powerful spells exist … over both royal courts … to prevent access to the paths."

"And you don't think my magic is powerful enough to overcome these spells?"

Dash shrugs. Apparently any more of an answer than that is too much effort in his current state.

"Well, we have to try it," I tell him, "because that's the only escape I can think of. Well, other than stealing a dragon or two and flying out of here, but we're a lot more likely to get caught that way."

Dash nods. "Okay. We'll try … the paths." His eyes slowly close once more. "And what about now?"

"Now …" I wrap my free hand around one of the bars. "I think the best thing for me to do is go back to my room." It's the *last* thing I want to do, but I made my decision when I chose to open the trapdoor instead of the faerie paths. I won't be escaping tonight. "I need to make sure Roarke thinks everything is fine," I continue. "Then I'll sneak away early in the morning before he comes to my room to compel me."

"Don't come until … mid-morning," Zed says. "You'll miss the guards that way."

I frown at him. "How do you have any idea what time of day or night it is down here?"

"I've been here … long enough. The guards talk. I listen. They come … straight after their breakfast."

"Okay. All right." I squeeze Dash's hand, then let go and push myself to my feet. "I'll see you tomorrow." I watch him for another few moments before turning away.

"I'm sorry I … failed you," he says.

I pause, then slowly swivel around to face him. "What do you mean? This is all *my* fault, remember? I chose to come here. I put myself in this mess, which means I put you in this mess too. *I'm* the one who failed, not you."

"It's been my … responsibility … for years. Checking in on you."

"But that assignment—mission—whatever you call it—ended when you brought me to this world. You were done looking out for me." I crouch down and take his hand once more. "Dash, you don't owe me anything. I mean it. I'm the one who owes you. So I'm going to make sure you get out of here alive."

"Does that mean," he asks, "that once this is over … we can put the cliff thing behind us?"

It takes me a few seconds to remember what he's talking about, and then a smile breaks out across my face. "Consider it far behind us already."

He grips my hand with a little more strength than before. "Looks like you might get to be a hero after all."

I shake my head, but my smile is still in place. "I'm not saving the world, Dash. Only you." I stand and cast a glance at Zed. "Well, and your friend. But that's it. I'm not going anywhere near your hero territory."

I stride quietly past the spheres and back up the stairs, pausing near the top and listening before climbing the final few steps up to the frozen pool. I don't take a straight line back to the palace. Instead, I run a little to the right before turning toward the glowing golden lights in the distance. If anyone stops me now, at least it won't look like I'm coming from the direction of the prison. I start running again, faster and faster, partly because I want to get back inside to the warmth of my bedroom as quickly as I can, and partly because I may need to convince someone I was out here practicing my running, climbing and somersaulting.

But I make it back to the palace without anyone stopping me. I consider letting myself in through one of the ground level doors and walking upstairs, but it's faster to climb. I step back and look up to make sure I'm aiming for the correct balcony, then begin my ascent. It's late—past midnight, I'm sure—so most curtains are closed and no one looks outside as I climb past windows. As I step into my sitting room and silently shut the balcony door behind me, I breathe out a long sigh. I remove Bandit from my pocket and set him down on the table amongst the papers and books that appear to have remained untouched in my absence.

"Emerson."

With a barely concealed gasp, I whip around, slapping my hand against my chest where my heart has already leaped into action.

In the doorway to my bedroom, his arms folded tightly over his chest, is Roarke.

CHAPTER 25

"Jeez, Roarke, you nearly gave me a heart attack." I lower my hand to my side, but my heart continues to race along at a panicky pace.

"Where were you?" His expression holds no hint of a smile, and his tone is deadly serious.

"Oh, just doing a little parkour practice." I shrug out of my coat, leave it lying over the back of a chair, and sit down to pull my shoes off. It's easier to appear relaxed and unconcerned if I keep my hands busy. "You know, the stuff I've been showing Aurora. Running and climbing walls and all that."

"In the middle of the night? In winter?"

"Yes." I look up. "My friend and I used to practice at night all the time. Okay, so we didn't do it in winter. It was too cold. But my days here have become so busy. If I want to keep practicing, I need to do it at night." I push my shoes aside and cross one leg over the other. "Besides, it gave me a reason to practice that spell that keeps my body warm. I'm getting better at it."

Roarke walks slowly toward me, each step a silent threat. "Do you expect me to believe that? Do you expect me to believe you weren't snooping around, trying to find something *locked* to use your Griffin Ability on?"

I allow all the hurt and horror I felt when reading the witch spell to become evident in my expression. "Are you serious? I thought you trusted me."

"I'm finding it a little difficult right now after you vanished from the room you're supposed to be in every—"

"Oh, *come on*. You keep going on about how you'd never force me into anything, that this is my home now, and that I'm almost a member of your family—and then you tell me that I'm expected to remain in my bedroom every night like a prisoner?

That makes no sense. And *you're* the one who decided to compel me to say the word 'open.' I didn't ask for that. And I'm far too afraid of your father to go looking for something that's locked and shouldn't be opened."

"Then what did you use your Griffin Ability on tonight? And don't try to tell me it hasn't happened yet." His gaze moves down to my wrist, where the bracelet is peeking out below the edge of my sleeve. "I can see from the ruby that you've used your power already. It has barely any color in it."

"A flower," I tell him, my voice raised in fake anger. "I used it on a flower, okay? I thought I was being clever, actually, since I was outside and there were no doors to open. I thought I'd just end up wasting the power, directing it nowhere, and then I saw a flower. A closed rosebud. So I looked at it and told it to open, and it did."

Several moments of uncomfortable silence pass as Roarke's eyes bore angrily into mine while I stare defiantly back. "A flower?" he says eventually.

"Yes. A flower." I cross my arms over my chest and direct a frown at the floor between us, hoping Roarke can tell just how much he's hurt his betrothed's feelings by accusing her of lying. "I would happily have told you all about it if you'd just asked instead of accusing me of sneaking around."

After another few moments of staring, he turns away from me without responding. I shouldn't be able to see his expression, but he's facing the mirror above the mantelpiece. In the mirror's reflection, for just a moment, I see his face scrunch up with fierce and terrifying fury. He bares his teeth as his fists clench briefly at his sides. Then he closes his eyes, breathes in deeply, and his anger is replaced by a blank expression.

I would have been utterly confused if I'd witnessed this yesterday. Now, I know better. Roarke's patience is nothing but a ruse, and clearly he's having a hard time reining his anger in right now. How frustrating it must be for him to play the kind yet cautious fiancé when all he wants to do is consume my magic and make it his. How difficult—and yet absolutely necessary—if he's hoping for me to come willingly to him.

"I'm so sorry," he says as he turns back to me, his expression soft now. "I messed up."

Damn right, I want to say. *You're supposed to be wooing me into total compliance, and instead you've upset me and made me doubt that you trust me.*

"I just … I couldn't find you," he continues, "and I was worried that … that maybe you'd taken advantage of me. That maybe you've been lying to me all this time. And I've …" He takes in a deep breath, steeling himself to reveal something.

"I've come to care for you more than I thought I would in this short space of time. It hurt to think that you might have betrayed my trust. It hurt a lot more than I expected."

I almost congratulate him on coming up with a great explanation for his anger. If I didn't know the truth, I might almost believe him. "I … I don't really know what to say to that."

"You don't feel the same way?"

It would be easy to say that of course I do, but I can't push this too far or he'll know for sure I'm lying. "I … okay, look. We both know that we're only going through with this union because we'll each get something out of it. Neither of us started out looking for love or anything soppy like that. But … I …" I wish that I could blush on demand. I wish I could look as shy and embarrassed as I'm pretending to be. I glance down, then peek up at him between my lashes. "I do think I actually like you. I expected to hate you, but … but I don't. And the shadow world … I'll admit that it's still a little scary with all the ink-shades, but it's exciting too. I can't wait to see what it will all look like when we've finished building."

Roarke's mouth spreads slowly into a smile. Then, without warning, he closes the distance between us. His hands are gripping my arms, and his lips are pressed to mine, moving hungrily against them. I'm a solid statue, too shocked to move. But I have to give him credit for this. His acting is far better than mine. He seems totally into this kiss, when all I want to do his shove him far away from me. But that isn't the way to play this game. So I try to get into it. I press a little closer to him, place my arms around him, and tell myself to imagine I'm kissing someone else. Someone I might actually enjoy kissing. But it's been a while since I had a crush on anyone, so I can't picture any faces except brief glimpses of hunky celebrities who mean nothing to me. Then Dash's smirking face takes its place at the front of my imagination—which is *super* weird, so I quickly force that thought aside.

"Lady Emerson, are you—Oh, goodness, I'm so sorry."

At the sound of Clarina's voice, I disentangle myself from Roarke. "It's—it's fine," I say with an embarrassed laugh. Fortunately, I'm not the only one feeling awkward in this moment. Clarina's standing in the main doorway to my suite, her gaze pointed firmly away from us and her cheeks turning pink. "We shouldn't—before the union … I mean, it isn't appropriate, is it?" I don't know nearly enough about the customs of this world to know what's appropriate and what isn't, but I'm very much hoping people are more conservative here than in the human world. I might be able to fake a kiss, but I don't think I can fake any more than that.

"Don't worry, my love," Roarke says, taking my hand and running his thumb along my skin. "I don't have any inappropriate intentions."

Right. Except for the intention to steal all my magic. "Okay, well … then I'll see you tomorrow?"

"Yes." He kisses my hand. "I would love it if you'd join me for breakfast in the morning."

"Oh. Um. I was going to have breakfast with Aurora. We have some, uh, girl things to chat about." Hopefully that'll buy me an extra hour or so before anyone comes looking for me.

"Well, I'll see you after breakfast then." He lowers his voice so Clarina can't hear. "We can decide what to build next for our new home."

I watch him brush past Clarina and leave my suite. Without looking at me, she tells me in as few words as possible that she's relieved to see nothing happened to me while I was missing this evening. Then she hurries away before I can ask her how long it took for Roarke to start telling people I was 'missing.'

Finally alone again, I change into pajamas, gather up every spell book I can find in my suite, and climb into bed. I spread the books around me and begin paging through them one at a time. I should be sleeping, but I'm hoping to find some sort of invisibility spell so I can easily hide in the garden tomorrow. I remember Calla concealing us with invisibility when she, Violet and Ryn first rescued me, but she used her Griffin Ability for that, so perhaps invisibility isn't possible with normal magic.

After going through almost all my books and finding nothing, I eventually turn, in desperation, to a book that details some of the less pleasant Unseelie rituals. Among other things, it talks about methods to gain extra power. Certain methods that the Unseelies apparently share with the witches. Finally, I come across a spell that seems useful. It won't make me invisible, but it will help me to be inconspicuous by detecting my surroundings and reflecting them back on me. A form of camouflage, I suppose. I repeat the words over and over in my head until I've memorized them. Then I come to the final instruction, which tells me that I need a 'sacrifice' from my surroundings. This sacrifice will form a bond between me and my environment for as long as I'm holding the spell in my mind.

The word 'sacrifice' makes me feel immediately uncomfortable, as does the word 'living,' which is written in parentheses beside this last instruction. A living sacrifice doesn't sound good at all. I look around, but the only other living thing in my bedroom is Bandit, and there's no way in hell I'm sacrificing him. I wonder if the garden counts as the same environment as my bedroom. How does the spell know if this 'sacrifice' comes from the area I'm in or some other area? Then again, how does my Griffin Ability know exactly who or what I'm referring to when I give an instruction?

Magic makes no sense.

I flop back onto my pillows, about to give up on this camouflage thing. Then I blink at the lights on the ceiling. "Glow-bugs," I whisper. Glow-bugs are living creatures. Perhaps I can use one of them to form this magical bond with my environment. I climb out of bed, stand on the chair in the corner of the room, and unstick a glow-bug from the ceiling. The feeling of its squishy little body between my fingers makes me cringe. I drop it quickly onto the floor and kneel beside it. I can't see a head or legs, only a blob-like body filled with golden light. It's pretty, and I don't want to kill it, but it's essentially just an insect, right? If I was back in the human realm, I'd have no problem swatting a fly or squishing a cockroach. Why is it any different just because this bug has some magic in it?

I remove the heaviest book from the bed. Then I hold my breath and quickly press down on the glow-bug with the book while quietly muttering the spell. When it's done, I stand and look across the room into the mirror inside the open wardrobe door—and suck in a quick breath as I watch my skin and clothing take on the design of the carpet, the edge of the bed, the wall behind me, and a small section of the window.

A small hoot comes from the direction of the bed. Owl-formed Bandit watches me with enormous eyes. "Shh," I tell him. I look at my reflection again and realize the camouflage doesn't cover all of me. Patches of my body still appear normal. I look at the spell book again and re-read the line about the sacrifice. *A sacrifice of adequate size and magical composition.* What exactly does 'adequate' mean? Perhaps a glow-bug isn't big enough. I have no idea what creature I'll use when I'm in the garden tomorrow, but I'll face that hurdle when I get to it.

I release my mental hold on the spell and jump quickly back into bed. I'm torn between elation that I taught myself a new spell and queasiness that I had to kill a creature in the process. *You're going to fit in so well with us,* Aurora said to me only a few days ago. I turn over, ignore the sick feeling in the pit of my stomach, and try to fall asleep.

CHAPTER 26

Sleep manages to evade me for most of the night, and my eyes are open as the first light of dawn peeks below the curtains drawn across my windows. I get up and witness, for the first time, the way winter melts into the ground and gives way to a fresh and vibrant spring morning.

After admiring the one and only sunrise I ever hope to see from this palace, I cross my room to the wardrobe and dig through it in search of an outfit that might possibly be considered comfortable. Something similar to the pants, shirt and ringmaster coat combo Clarina laid out yesterday, since that proved to be easy enough to run in. I'd prefer to go without the coat—in a few hours it'll be far too warm to wear one, and it might get in the way if I need to run—but I'd be conspicuous without it. According to Clarina, this kind of outfit isn't considered formal enough without the coat. She'd put me in a dress if she knew I planned to be outside any later than mid-morning, but a dress is out of the question. I definitely can't climb in one.

After choosing what I deem to be a suitable combination—black pants, a black shirt with gold ruffles down the front, and a bottle green coat with gold detailing—I dress quickly and slide the stylus I stole weeks ago from Aurora into one of the coat pockets. I've asked for my own stylus each time I've been taught a spell that requires one, but apparently Roarke wanted me to wait until he could gift me a special one. A stylus covered in diamonds and sapphires, or something outrageously unnecessary like that. I know it was only an excuse not to give me one before the union.

I pull on flexible pump-like shoes with no heel, then write a note to Clarina telling her I woke early and decided to return some books to the library before going to Aurora's chambers for breakfast. Hopefully she won't check my story with the guards who patrol the hallway outside my room. I wake Bandit, encourage him to shift into something smaller than a cat—he chooses a tiny hamster-type form with blue hair the same color as mine—and let him climb into one of my pockets. *Not* the same pocket as the stylus; I still don't trust that those things don't have residual magic in them, and I don't want Bandit to accidentally get hurt.

I'm about to walk onto the balcony when I remember the book of witch spells hidden beneath a cushion on one of the chairs. If Roarke finds it, he'll realize Aurora was the one who warned me about his plan. I don't know what he'd do to her if he discovered her betrayal, but I'd rather she didn't have to find out. The fire in the sitting room fireplace has long since gone out, but I stride across the room to it, place the book onto the ash, and add another few pieces of wood. I quietly say the spell to light a fire and step back as a single flame ignites the book's cover. I watch it burning for several moments before turning away.

Outside on the balcony, I look down and around to see if anyone's patrolling nearby. Then I swing my legs over the balustrade and begin to climb down. It's early enough that most of the occupants of the bedrooms I pass on my way down will hopefully still be asleep with their curtains drawn.

I hide in one of the flowerbeds while doing the camouflage spell, using a bird that Bandit catches for me while in one of his cat forms. The bird has a tiny crown of gold ridges atop its head, and its wings are almost transparent with flecks of gold. I feel so sick at having to kill this beautiful creature that I almost can't do it. But I remind myself that Dash will remain a tortured prisoner and probably end up dead if I get caught before I reach the prison.

The spell works. I push my nausea aside as my skin and clothes rapidly takes on the appearance of my surroundings. The dark earth, the green bushes and colorful flowers. The strangest part is looking down at myself as I stand and walk out of the flowerbed— my appearance continually changes so that I roughly blend in with whatever's around me.

Since I have to wait until mid-morning so I don't run into the guards, I take my time walking through the gardens. I look down often to make sure I'm still camouflaged, and I try to ignore the constant low-level anxiety twisting my insides into knots. *Everything will work out fine*, I tell myself repeatedly. When I reach the pool with the fountain—no longer frozen—I hide behind a nearby rosebush with blue flowers. I could probably release my hold on the camouflage spell, but I don't want to risk being seen. Besides, it doesn't feel like it's draining too much of my magic.

The longer I wait, the more anxious I become. The people I care about go around and around my head: Mom and Dash and the Griffin rebels who are probably trying to find their way into this court because Dash never returned home. My imagination shows me the worst things that could happen to everyone, and eventually I have to shut my eyes and tell my mind to go as blank as if someone were leading me through the faerie paths.

Except for the camouflage spell. I can't go blank on that. I open my eyes and look down at the pattern of grass across my hand. I'll focus on that instead.

By the time I hear footsteps, my back has begun to ache and my left leg has gone numb. I shrink further down as I peer between the leaves of the rose bush. A line of about ten guards marches toward the fountain. They come to a halt on the far side where the trapdoor is. The guard at the front leans forward with a stylus in his hand, but once he bends down with it, I can't see what he's doing, and I can't hear if he's saying anything.

I slowly roll my shoulders a few times, check the ruby on my wrist, and remind myself to be patient. I have to wait until the guards are gone and my Griffin Ability has fully restored itself. *Unless …* I pause with my shoulders pulled back. What if I sneak down now? Right behind the guards? Then I don't have to use my Griffin Ability to open the trapdoor. I won't have to risk accidentally losing all my power in one command and then having to wait until late tonight before freeing Dash and Zed from their spheres.

I bite my lip as I watch the guards descend the stairs one at a time. How close can I risk getting to them? How well does this camouflage spell work? And what if the guard at the end of the line turns back to close the trapdoor?

But … what if I can't let Dash and Zed out until tonight, and Roarke discovers where I am before then?

I don't give myself another second to think about it. I rise to my feet and tiptoe quietly across the grass. I make it to the pool seconds before the last guard steps down through the trapdoor. With one final glance at my feet to make sure I can't see anything more of them than a faint outline, I step silently through the trapdoor. I pause at the top of the staircase, waiting to see if the guard just ahead of me plans to turn around and close the trapdoor. But he continues descending without a glance behind him.

Holding my breath, I tiptoe down the staircase, shrinking into the shadows on one side when I reach the bottom. I don't dare venture any further into the vast underground chamber while all those guards are still present. They spread out, each heading in a different direction. Here and there, I notice several prison cell spheres slowly descending and disappearing amongst the many other spheres.

In the first row, a guard stops beside the sphere nearest to me. The prisoner inside—the woman who was curled up and sleeping yesterday—scrambles to the other side of her cell. But as the guard flicks his hand, she slides abruptly across the floor and slams against the bars with a groan. The guard crouches down, and I notice he's holding a bottle in one hand. He dips a stylus into the bottle, then reaches through the bars for the woman's arm. He writes a few words across her skin before standing and moving on to the next sphere. Moments later, as the woman slumps against the bars, part of the floor within her sphere shimmers and ripples. A tray of food appears, and after staring at it for a while, she reaches out with a clumsy hand and drags the tray closer.

I wait as the guard performs the same spell on the next prisoner, and then the next. From what I can see down another row of spheres, it looks like the other guards are doing the same thing. By the time the lowered prison orbs rise into the air again and the guards begin marching back toward the stairs, the woman I've been watching has finished eating and her tray has vanished.

I crouch down and keep my head lowered as the guards *clomp, clomp, clomp* their way back up the staircase. Finally, when the trapdoor is closed and I'm certain they're gone, I let go of the camouflage spell I've been hanging onto for hours. I straighten slowly and peer up the stairs once more. Then I tiptoe past the spheres, not wanting to attract the attention of any prisoners in case they start calling out to me and their cries become audible outside the prison.

I run the last few paces toward Dash's cell and crouch down beside his bars. He's lying on his side, his eyes half-closed, one hand wrapped loosely around a bar. "Hey," I whisper to him as I touch his hand. "Ready to get on with this escape thing?"

His gaze shifts to me. He gives me a weak smile. "You made it. No one … saw you?"

"No. I found some sort of camouflage spell in a book last night." I pause, looking hurriedly over my shoulder at the sound of a voice. But it's only a moan from one of the other spheres. "A weird spell that required a sacrifice," I continue, "but I managed to do it."

Dash pushes himself into a sitting position, his eyes widening more than I would have thought possible given his drugged state. "A sacrifice?"

"Just an animal. Not a person, obviously." I push my sleeve back to examine the color of the ruby.

"Em, no," he moans. "You shouldn't have … done that. Especially not here. You don't want to … end up … magically bound … to this court."

"What?" My gaze snaps up. "Is that possible?"

"You're fine," Zed says from the neighboring sphere. I didn't realize he was paying attention to us. "It takes … a lot … to sell one's soul. You're not even … close."

"Still … isn't right," Dash says.

"It was just a bird." Which is what I told myself repeatedly before twisting the poor thing's neck, and it didn't help me feel better at all.

"It isn't *right*, Em," Dash repeats.

"Look, I didn't want to, okay?" I hiss. "It was horrible. But I didn't have many options. I don't have thousands of spells at my fingertips. I'm kinda new to this magic thing, remember? I needed a way to get back to you guys unseen, and that spell was all I could find."

Dash says nothing more. He simply watches me through half-open eyes as he leans against the bars.

I let out a long breath. "I'm sorry. I didn't mean to snap. I just … feel horrible about the bird thing, so it doesn't help when you keep pointing out that it's wrong."

"Sorry," he whispers. He gestures to my bracelet. "How long?"

"Another hour or two." I squint at the ruby. "An hour and a half, maybe. I can't tell exactly. How long until the magic-impairing drug wears off? I assume that's what the guards were doing?" I add. "When they were writing on prisoners' arms?"

"Yes," Zed answers. "They do it … twice a day. So it obviously … doesn't …"

"Doesn't last a full day," I finish for him. I know they can't help it, but I'm finding it difficult not to get frustrated with their slow, slurred speech. "Okay. That's good."

"Some of the others," Zed says, "are wearing metal … that blocks magic. A bangle … a ring …" He leans back against the curved edge of his sphere. "Seems the Unseelies have … run out … of those. This drunken drug thing … is new."

"It's better," Dash adds. "The metal … can't easily be removed."

"Okay. So by this evening, you two should be able to move around and use magic?"

Dash nods, then groans and slowly lowers his head to the floor beside the bars. "It gets worse … now. Straight after … they write … on us."

"Spinning," Zed murmurs. As I watch, he slides slowly to the floor of his cell. "Spinning … spinning …"

"My magic is … so close … yet so far." Dash's hand inches slowly across the floor, as if he's trying to grasp something. "I can't … touch it … can never … touch it."

As disturbing as it is to see him like this, I need to believe that he'll be fine. "Hey, don't worry about it. You'll get your magic back soon. You'll be totally normal by tonight." I scoot closer to his sphere and lean my back against the bars. I pull my knees up, and as Dash and Zed become silent, I prepare myself for yet more waiting. I assure myself once again that everything will be all right in the end. Dash won't remain confused and lethargic forever. We'll both get out of here. We'll return safely to the Griffin rebels. I'll get back to Mom. I'll put this disastrous Unseelie episode behind me and somehow—*somehow*—I'll figure out how to help her.

CHAPTER 27

Some time later, Bandit begins squirming in my pocket. I straighten my legs so he can climb out. In his blue hamster form, he sniffs around on the floor, scurrying further away from me as he explores his strange new surroundings. I have to remind myself—when I start worrying that he might end up lost—that he's successfully followed me across the fae realm numerous times, usually without my knowledge. I don't think I need to be concerned about him.

As I lift my arm to check the ruby, Dash moves and opens his eyes. He holds onto the bars and manages to pull himself up until he's leaning sideways against them. "Hey," I say to him. "I thought maybe you were sleeping." I shift around until I'm also leaning my shoulder against the bars.

He shakes his head. "Can't. I sort of doze, but never sleep."

"Your words sound less slurred now."

"Whispering helps, I think. Takes less effort. My magic is still just out of reach, though."

"Sorry about that. It won't be for much longer, at least."

He nods and closes his eyes for a moment. "I must look terrible, huh?"

"Nah, not too bad." I raise my hand and run my thumb briefly along his stubbled jaw. "You've got that rugged look going on. Some girls dig that. The *smell*, on the other hand …" I pinch my nose before chuckling. "Well, that's another story."

He grimaces. "Yeah. Lack of showers down here. Not impressed with the … quality of this … establishment."

A moment of quiet passes before I ask, "How did you end up in this fine establishment anyway? I was told you were allowed to return home. A guard even saw you saying goodbye to Roarke and climbing into one of the carriages, but that carriage obviously didn't take you home."

"No. Four guards were in the carriage with me. They attacked and stunned me almost immediately. I was completely knocked out until I woke up here. Where are we, exactly?"

"Beneath the gardens. Quite far from the palace. I was running last night. Not trying to get away, just … I needed to run." I look down at my hands in my lap. "I discovered what Roarke plans to do with me, and I just needed to get out of that palace and figure things out. That's when I found the trapdoor and used my Griffin magic to open it."

Dash narrows his eyes. "What does Roarke plan to do with you?"

"He …" I bite my lip, then tell him everything about the witch spell and the words I've been practicing as part of my vows. The words that turned out to have absolutely nothing to do with a union.

"Bastard," Dash breathes when I'm finished.

I look up in surprise. "Bastard? Really? I doubt your mother would approve of that kind of language."

"He wants to *possess your magic*, Em. All of it. I can't even … imagine … how you'll survive that."

I lift one shoulder uncertainly. "Apparently this spell is one of the few ways a person can survive having their magic removed."

"But … your magic is part of … what keeps you alive. What will you be without it? Some kind of … of shell?"

A shiver skitters down my spine. "We don't need to find out, because I'm not going through with the union or the witch spell. So, anyway." I try to brush off my fear. "Did Roarke come to see you? Did he say why he didn't just … kill you? I'm very glad he didn't, obviously," I rush to add. "I'm just wondering why he kept you alive."

Dash's half-open eyes stare past me. "He was here when I woke up. Said he plans to hand me over … to the Guild … and demand compensation for … a guardian getting involved in … Unseelie affairs without authorization. He'll also inform them that … that I know far more than I'm supposed to about … the Griffin rebels. Said he may as well get some entertainment out of … my inconvenient appearance at his court."

"Bastard," I mutter.

Dash hesitates, his green eyes refocusing on me. "Yeah, you're right. My mother wouldn't like that word."

I give him a small smile. "Even if I explain to her that it's appropriately applied in this case?"

"Hmm. She might understand. Just this once." He makes a weak attempt at a laugh, then adds, "You're actually not such a potty mouth anymore. You've improved since arriving in this world."

"You know, I never actually stopped to think about it until you pointed it out." I screw my face up in thought. "I think I remember my mom scolding me years ago when I was little for using bad language, but then I got to Chelsea's, and she didn't seem to care. In fact, she and Georgia used that kind of language all the time, so I ended up speaking that way too." I shrug. "So do most people in my world, I think. It isn't a big deal."

"It isn't a big deal for plenty of people in this world either." His voice is close to a whisper again, which seems to make it easier for him to speak. "My mom's the only reason I don't use bad language."

"The soap spell, yeah. I didn't believe you when you first mentioned it."

"Unfortunately for young fae all around the magic realm, that spell is very real."

I pull my knees up to my chest again and wrap my arms around them. "Your mom must be so worried about you."

He nods. "Probably. But … she's my mom, and I'm a guardian. So she's always worried about me. And I'm sure she knows that Ryn or one of the others is looking for me. That should give her hope."

"Do you think they really are trying to get into the palace grounds? Roarke said no one can see the palace unless they're in the company of an Unseelie guard."

"That doesn't mean they'll stop trying to find a way in. And not just for me, but for you too. They would never leave you in the clutches of the Unseelies once they discovered you were here."

I cover my face with my hands, guilt gnawing at me again. "This wasn't supposed to happen, Dash. They were supposed to give up on me and move on to helping someone else. Because, you know, they hardly know me and I've only caused them trouble since I met them. Now they've wasted their time and resources on me. I can't imagine how angry they'll be when you and I finally get back to them."

"Okay, your first mistake," Dash says, "was assuming they'd give up on you."

I lower my hands and look at him. "You mean my first mistake was assuming everyone's as selfish as I am?"

"Em. If you were as selfish as you think you are, you would have left without me."

I look away from his half-drugged gaze and decide not to tell him I almost did leave without him. That most certainly would have given Ryn, Violet and the others a good enough reason to be angry with me. I doubt they would …

Hang on. My thoughts take a detour as something occurs to me. "Hey, Dash," I say to him. "I thought the protective enchantment on the rebels' safe place kept us from thinking or speaking of it to anyone who doesn't already know about it."

"Yes. Something like that."

"But how do they take anyone new there? How did they take *me* there? How could they think of it when I was with them?"

"The leaders—Ryn and Vi, Chase and Calla, a few of the others—had a different enchanted place on them. They can't speak about the place … and they can't think exactly of it … but they can think of … the area? I don't know the specifics, but they can think of … the surrounding area … and once they get there, they can see the actual place. Something like that."

"Sounds complicated."

"Yeah. I guess it needs to be. To keep everyone safe." His gaze moves down. "How long now? For your Griffin Ability, I mean."

"Soon." I push back my sleeve and squint at the ruby. "Half an hour, maybe."

"Okay."

Another few minutes pass with only the occasional sound of a groan or cry reaching us. Then a few repeated thumps, as if someone's banging against the inside of their sphere, and then the muffled sound of crying. As the crying fades once more to silence, Dash asks, "How are you feeling about Chelsea and Georgia?"

Mild nausea lurches in my stomach the way it always does when I think of my aunt and cousin. No one else has asked about them since I told Roarke what happened, but that doesn't mean they haven't been on my mind. "I still don't really know what I should be feeling," I admit. "Whenever I think of them, it's with regret and guilt. Like I should have made more of an effort with them while they were alive. Maybe I would have discovered they weren't as awful as they always came across. And I should never have let Ada anywhere near their home."

"You didn't exactly have a choice about Ada showing up in Stanmeade. We don't know how she knew you were there."

"Yeah, I know." I nod slowly. "I know it wasn't directly my fault. But still … it all happened because Ada came after me."

Dash hangs onto the bars and pulls himself a little straighter. "Remember I told you about my classmate and mentor who died?"

"Um, yes. I think so."

"Did I tell you it was my fault?"

I hesitate, casting my mind back. "No. I think I'd remember if you mentioned it being your fault."

"It was supposed to be a paired assignment with supervision. Meaning my classmate and I would do it together while a mentor observed. Just in case something went wrong and … we needed help. That's how it works in … the early years of training. Groups, pairs, and a more experienced guardian observing and … getting involved if necessary." He pauses to take in a deep breath. Even whispering, it's clearly still an effort for him to speak. "On the day we were supposed to do this paired assignment, I ended up injured from a training session. My leg hadn't healed yet, so the Guild gave my mentor and classmate a different assignment. Something they thought suitable for one trainee. But it went horribly wrong … and both my classmate and mentor were killed."

"Oh, that's horrible. I'm so sorry." I swallow, then cautiously add, "But surely you can't be telling me you felt like that was your fault? It isn't the same as what happened with Chelsea and Georgia. I basically led Ada to their doorstep. But you couldn't help being injured."

"True. I couldn't. But if we'd all gone on our original assignment together … maybe they would have lived."

"And maybe they wouldn't have. Maybe your paired assignment would have gone wrong too and they would have died anyway."

"And maybe Chelsea and Georgia … would have died anyway. A car accident, or … some other random tragedy."

I look away from him and shake my head. I press my fingers against my temples. "This is a pointless discussion."

"Just like it's pointless blaming yourself for … something you didn't do. I know, because I had to figure that out for myself. So I could move on." He takes hold of my left hand and gently pulls it away from my face. "You'll figure it out too, Em."

"Maybe," I say quietly, lowering my right hand and wrapping it around my legs. My left hand rests on the floor of the sphere between two bars, still in Dash's grip. I don't pull it away. "But not yet. It doesn't feel right yet to just move on."

"Okay," he says. "That's okay."

"Thank you for telling me about your mentor and your friend. It must be difficult to talk about them."

"It's been a few years since … since it happened. It's easier now to speak about them."

I lean my head against the bars as I watch him. "I don't think I ever asked you why you chose to be a guardian."

"Hmm. I don't think I ever wanted to be … anything else. I always liked all the stories my dad told me of the heroic things he did … and the lives he'd saved. I wanted to be just like him. My mother thought … it was a horrible idea. She'd been afraid for years that she might lose him … and now she'd have to be afraid of losing me too. I understood where she was coming from, but … I chose this life anyway. And I've never regretted it. There are lives that might not have been saved if … if I wasn't there to save them."

A few months ago, I would have rolled my eyes at that last comment. But there's no trace of cockiness in Dash's tone. He's simply stating a fact. "And just think," I add with a smile, "of all the pretty young ladies who would have been deprived of swooning over their handsome, heroic rescuer if you hadn't become a guardian."

He manages a quiet laugh. "Exactly. And I wouldn't have met you."

My smile slips away. "Yeah. You wouldn't be locked in a prison right now."

"Ah, well." He looks away as he shrugs. "It's worth it."

Something stirs deep inside me. Something warm and weirdly pleasant. Something I recognize immediately and tell myself it's ridiculous to be feeling right now. "You don't actually mean that, do you?" I say to Dash.

He frowns as he continues staring into the distance. "I wasn't really thinking about what I was saying, but …" He refocuses on me. His hand moves a little over mine, his fingers brushing my skin before becoming still again. "But I think I did mean it. I can't imagine … not knowing you. You've been part of my life for years. A mystery I had no way … of solving, but a mystery I … couldn't stop thinking about. And you looked so beautiful … at the ball. I wish I could have … danced longer with you."

A shiver unrelated to cold or fear races up my arms and neck. I can't help remembering what Aurora said about Dash: *Nobody cares that much. Not unless they're motivated by love.* I argued then that Dash was motivated by his need to be a hero, and I'm still convinced this has nothing to do with love. That drug potion that was written onto his arm earlier probably has a lot to do with what he just said. What it doesn't explain is why *I'm* suddenly feeling like a hundred butterfly wings are fluttering against the inside of my stomach, but that's—

"Hey," Zed groans. He pushes himself up just enough to turn his head and look our way. "Now … is definitely … not the time."

I narrow my eyes at him. "Not the time for—"

"Also … your mother would say … you're too young for a boyfriend, Emerson."

"I—Excuse me?" Fiery flames of embarrassment lick their way up my neck. I pull my hand away from Dash's and wrap it around my legs. "That is *not* what's happening right now. And you have no idea what my mother would say."

"Just trying to … help you avoid distractions," he mumbles. "Don't want this escape attempt going sideways."

I return my gaze to Dash and find him laughing so quietly it's little more than silent shaking. Hopefully he's laughing at himself and the unlikely notion that being locked up in this prison might be 'worth it' because he got to meet me. I clear my throat and look down at the ruby on my wrist. "Oh, hey, it's almost time."

"Good," Zed murmurs. "Guess I'd better … get myself ready." He grips the bars of his cell and pulls himself upright.

"What are you going to say when your power is ready?" Dash asks.

"Um …" I look back at forth between his sphere and Zed's. "Something like, 'Dash's sphere and Zed's sphere, open.' Sounds stupid, but it should work."

Dash nods. "Okay. And what about everyone else?"

With a sigh, I close my eyes. Why did he have to bring that up? I was hoping not to have to think about it again. I don't want to face the moral dilemma I have no answer to. "I don't know if I should do that, Dash. I'm sure some of these people don't deserve to be here, but most of them probably do. How do we distinguish the innocent from the guilty? And I don't know if it's even possible for me to open every sphere. If it requires too much power, I'll end up passing out."

Dash blinks. "Really? Has that happened?"

"Yes. I overexerted myself trying to do too much with one command. I think if I allowed my Griffin Ability to replenish multiple times without using it, I might be capable of doing more, but we don't have time for that now."

"But Em, you … you brought two people back from death. That must have taken … an enormous amount of power. Opening just two spheres shouldn't use … too much. I'm sure you can try to open more."

"And what if I'm freeing criminals?"

"If they're the king's enemies, they're probably on our side."

"True," I admit, "but how do I know who should be freed and who shouldn't?"

"We can't save everyone," Zed says. "It isn't possible. They'll—" He cuts himself off, a look of horror slowing spreading across his face. Then he lets out a bitter laugh, staring wistfully into the distance. "Finally, I understand. If only I'd … understood years ago. I could have … made them understand too. None of this would have happened." He looks at me. "None of it."

I stare back, completely confused. "Um …"

"We can't leave innocent people behind," Dash presses, pulling my attention away from Zed.

"Then you can tell your Guild about it when you're safely back home. They'll fix this. That's their job, isn't it? To right these kinds of wrongs."

Zed laughs again. "All those years ago … they said the same thing. We'll come back for you … they said. And they never did."

"Hey, I thought you were on my side for this one," I tell him. "We can't save everyone, remember?"

He nods. "We can't save everyone."

"Not everyone," Dash agrees, "but some."

"And then what, Dash? Let's say I let a whole bunch of people free. And then let's say it turns out I actually can't open the faerie paths. Like, I run out of power, or it isn't possible to open them with a Griffin Ability, or something like that. Then what happens to all the people I've freed? They can't use their magic, and the guards are going to come rushing down here to lock them away again. Some of them will fight back, and they might end up dead. Which means *more* people I'm indirectly responsible for killing. I don't want that on my conscience, Dash. Maybe you think I'm a selfish coward for not wanting to free anyone else—and that's probably partly true—but I also don't want people to end up dead because we don't have a proper plan for getting everyone out of here. So I'm only freeing the two of you. We'll escape this court, and you can tell the Guild about everyone down here. *They* can come and investigate."

Dash shakes his head. "It doesn't work … that way. The Guild can't simply barge in. There's … a balance. They'd risk starting a war between the courts."

"They don't have to do any barging, okay? They can just ask for details of who's imprisoned and why. Surely they have a right to do that?"

"Maybe, but the Unseelies aren't going to like it."

"Then your precious Guild is just going to have to upset the balance. If loads of people are unjustly imprisoned here, then maybe it's worth starting a war over."

"This …" Zed says, pointing weakly at me. "This is what we needed … all those years ago. Someone willing to start … a war for us. Someone who didn't choose to leave us in prison."

"I'm *agreeing* with you," Dash protests, his breathing even heavier now. "But I'm saying we should … get everyone out *now*."

"I think he's still confused," I tell Dash. "Too drugged to make sense."

"I am making sense," Zed says, his eyes never leaving mine. "You'll see."

I turn back to Dash. "Please just trust me on this. My Griffin Ability has limits. I need to break open both your spheres, tell the drug potion to leave your systems, and then open the faerie paths. I don't think I can do all that *and* free everyone." I don't add that if any Griffin magic remains after those three commands, I should be able to hold onto it. If I do end up with some leftover power, then we can decide what to do with it.

Finally, Dash relents. "Okay. You know your power better than I do. When I'm back … at the Guild … I'll see what I can do about … freeing these people."

I stand as I sense that shiver of power getting ready to radiate up my spine. I don't know how these spheres would normally open, but I picture the unbreakable glass bars cracking apart and falling away. As my power rushes to the surface, I halt it. It struggles to break free, but I manage to release it slowly as I speak. "These two spheres will open," I say, stepping back and looking first at Dash's round prison cell, and then at Zed's. My voice sounds both far away and right inside my head. "The drug potion will leave your bodies, and you'll have full access to your magic. And faerie paths," I add, turning and speaking to the air itself, "open a doorway."

I swing back around to face the spheres as I hear a crack. Then another crack. Dash's bars snap and tumble to the ground with several clangs, followed almost immediately by the bars imprisoning Zed. Dash raises his hand, and sparks jump to life immediately, whizzing around his fingers. With a grin, and his eyes alight with life and energy, he climbs quickly from his prison cell and sweeps me into a brief, tight embrace. A smile stretches my lips as I hug him back, then twist in his grip to look behind me.

The air ripples, distorting my view of the vine-covered wall beyond it. The ripples become waves, undulating repeatedly and violently, as if something is trying to rip through the air itself. My Griffin power begins to drain from my body. I grasp mentally at it, tugging it to a halt as my hands tighten into fists and my body tenses. Success. I can't quantify it, but I sense there's still power simmering beneath the surface of my control.

I relax my limbs and focus on the space in front of me, hopeful that a doorway is about to materialize.

But the seconds tick by, and nothing happens.

CHAPTER 28

"It didn't work," I say, my shoulders drooping as if a weight is slowly crushing them.

"So it isn't possible after all," Dash says quietly.

"I don't understand. I obviously had no way of knowing if it would work, but I really thought my Griffin Ability would be powerful enough to access the paths. I mean, it doesn't take much magic to open a doorway, right?" I turn back to face Dash.

"It doesn't," he says. "Perhaps it would have worked if the faerie paths were here to obey your command. But maybe they don't exist here."

"I thought they existed everywhere."

He shakes his head. "I don't know, Em. Maybe the ancient enchantments keeping them from being accessed in this part of the world are so powerful that even your Griffin Ability can't mess with them."

"Emerson," Zed says. I look at him. He moves closer, but stops a few paces away from me. His gaze is intense as he watches me closely. "Thank you."

I wonder if it's disbelief I'm seeing on his face. Perhaps he doubted I would actually free him. "Um … sure. You're welcome."

"So," he says. "Dragons are the only way out, then?"

"You're free," a woman says from somewhere behind us. "How did you get free?"

I look back and see a woman in the sphere beyond the empty one next to Dash's sphere. She watches us with wide eyes, then scrambles to the front of her cell and grips the bars. "Let me out next, girl."

"I … I can't. I'm so sorry. My magic is finished." Which is a lie, of course, but I know we'll need the rest of my Griffin power to escape this palace. "The, uh, the spell

I used—the ingredients—I only had enough for two cells."

"Liar!" she hisses. "I heard you. All you did was speak. You didn't apply any additional enchantment. If you could open their cells, you can open mine."

I back away, not wanting to face the guilt of leaving everyone else behind. "I can't. I'm so sorry." I glance around and see other faces watching us. Some visible in the gaps between the Dash and Zed's spheres, other hanging higher up. "Let's go," I mutter to Dash and Zed.

"Wait, please," the woman says, one hand reaching through the bars as her expression changes from suspicion to desperation. "I didn't mean to accuse you of anything. I've just been here for so long. Please help me. Please."

I shake my head. "I can't, but I'll be sending someone back for you."

Her face twists suddenly into a mask of rage. "Let. Me. Out," she hisses through her bared teeth. "LET ME OUT!"

I take another step back as fear weaves its way through my insides. "Why isn't she slow and sluggish like the two of you were?"

"I don't think they drugged her," Dash says.

"They didn't," Zed says. "See the metal band on her wrist? It blocks her magic. She can't access it, but she still has her ordinary strength. She isn't experiencing the fatigue we experienced."

"We need to leave before her screaming alerts the guards," I say, turning my back on the woman. We hurry toward the stairs, but her shrieks only grow louder.

"Don't you DARE walk away! I will KILL YOU, you little WHORE!"

"Whore? Jeez." I throw a glance over my shoulder and see her tugging on the bars of her cell, rocking wildly back and forth.

"I'll kill you, I'll kill you, I'll kill you!" she screeches.

"So how far away are the dragons?" Zed asks as we reach the stairs.

"On the other side of the palace."

"Wonderful," Dash mutters.

"But toward the left. So we don't have to get too close to the palace itself. Hopefully we can make it there without being seen."

"That's the challenge," Zed says. "Everything in this place is guarded."

"I still have some Griffin power. I've been practicing holding onto it, and I managed to prevent it all from slipping away when I freed you. Maybe I can use it to mimic that camouflage spell. If I have any power left after I've opened the trapdoor."

"If you don't, then we might just have to hide until it's dark," Dash says. "Which we should perhaps do anyway so that no one sees a dragon flying away when it isn't supposed to."

We're about halfway up the steps when I hear a low rumble. I freeze and look up. Bright light shines down from the trapdoor. "Guards," Dash mutters. He spins around, tugging me with him. The three of us hurtle down the stairs so fast I'm amazed we don't trip and tumble over each other all the way to the bottom.

"There she is!" someone yells behind us.

We jump down the last few steps and take off between the rows of spheres. Bright golden light flares on my right, and then on my left. A hurried glance both ways tells me that both Dash and Zed have guardian blades in their hands. The glittery magical kind that appear from nowhere.

"I doubt there's anywhere else to go down here," Zed says as we duck left beneath a low-hanging sphere and race between another two rows. "They'll soon corner us."

"Then we'll fight them off," Dash answers.

"Did you look behind us as we reached the bottom of the steps?" Zed asks. "There must have been dozens of them rushing through that trapdoor."

"We can handle it," Dash says.

"Have you seen Bandit anywhere?" I ask, suddenly remembering he's no longer in my pocket.

"Little preoccupied here, Em," Dash says, beginning to sound breathless. "But I'm sure he's fine. He's smart. He's probably out of the prison already."

With a wall up ahead, we veer right and turn between another two rows of spheres—and I slam into the back of Dash as he skids to a standstill. At the other end of the row, at least ten guards race toward us. Dash's knives disappear, replaced instantly by a bow. He raises it and—

"Run while we still can!" Zed says, tugging me back between the spheres before I can see where Dash's arrow lands. "Fight when we have no other option."

"I hate running," Dash shouts, but I hear his footsteps pounding the ground just behind us.

"I love running," I mutter.

"Back to the stairs?" Zed calls over his shoulder to Dash. "We'll fight off whatever guards are waiting there for—Aaah!"

Pain crushes my side and the world flips around. My head whacks something solid. I come to an abrupt halt, feeling cold ground along the length of my body. I gasp, my winded lungs desperately seeking air and getting nothing. Scrabbling against the ground, I push myself up and looking wildly around, trying to make sense of things as my lungs cry out for oxygen. I see one of the spheres rolling away from me, knocking into another sphere. All around me, prisoners are screaming.

"Move!" Dash yells. An unseen force shoves me to the side, rolling me over and over into a disoriented heap. I look up in time to see a sphere racing past me at a terrifying speed. It crashes into two more spheres, sending them spinning, which in turn sends more spheres rolling.

"Dammit," I gasp when I can finally get some oxygen. "It's like a giant freaking pool table in here."

Hands grasp beneath my arms and pull me up. I shove backward with my elbow, and my attacker lets out a grunt of pain. "It's just me," groans Zed.

"Crap, sorry."

Dash ducks past a rolling sphere and runs up to me. "You okay?"

"Yeah."

"There are too many to fight," Zed says, twisting around, looking everywhere. Nevertheless, he moves so that his back is against Dash's and raises a glimmering, golden sword in each hand. A crossbow materializes in Dash's grip. I press closer to both of them, my eyes darting around. Everywhere I look, I see men and women in Unseelie uniforms racing toward us between the rolling spheres, weapons raised and magic sparking from their fingers.

"Dammit, dammit," I mutter, wishing I knew how to fight or use combat magic.

"Say something, Em," Dash tells me. "That's the only way we're getting out of here."

"I ... I don't know what to—"

"Anything!"

I allow power to leak into my voice and utter, "The guards can't see us!" before grabbing onto the last wisps of my magic. Dash holds his crossbow in one hand and wraps the other around my arm. He pulls me swiftly sideways between two spheres that are about to knock into each other. Zed darts after us, and we make it through the gap just before the spheres collide and bounce apart. Guards still surround us on every side, but some of them are slowing down now, and others are looking around in confusion as they run. Not a single one is focused directly on us.

"Are we invisible?" Dash whispers.

"I think to them we are." A brief smile stretches my lips. "It worked."

"Damn, your voice is freaky when you're using your Griffin Ability," Zed says.

"Freaky amazing," Dash says. "Now, if we can just sneak past all the guards, we can make it up the stairs and through the trapdoor."

"Quickly," I whisper. "They're not stupid. They'll block our way out soon."

We slip between spheres and past guards, making our way toward the stairs faster than I would have thought possible. Behind us, the guards shout to one another, quickly coming to the conclusion that none of them can see us.

Then someone yells, "Block the stairway!"

We've already made it to the base of the stairs, though. We race upward without pause. Oddly enough, a squirrel leaps from step to step just ahead of us. "Bandit?" I hiss, and the squirrel freezes. Its tail twitches. Then it jumps up as we run past, landing in my arms in cat form.

Once outside, Dash spins around, sweeps his hand through the air, and the trapdoor swings shut. "Do a locking spell," Zed says immediately.

Dash crouches down, then looks up. "I have no stylus."

"Oh. Here." As if he knows I need my hands, Bandit shifts into a smaller form and scurries up the lapel of my coat. I retrieve Aurora's stylus as quickly as I can. Dash swipes it from my hands and bends down—just as something bumps the trapdoor from below.

"Crap." He smacks both hands down on the trapdoor.

Zed drops to his knees and holds both palms just above the trapdoor. I don't see any magic, but his gritted teeth suggest he's exerting some kind of invisible force on the trapdoor. "Quickly!" he says. Dash writes across the trapdoor, then pulls his hand back. Slowly, Zed does the same. Banging and the sound of shouts reach our ears, but the trapdoor remains shut.

"They'll break through the enchantment quickly," Dash says, rising and stepping backward as he returns the jewel-encrusted stylus to me.

We run through the garden, roughly toward the left side of the palace. We skirt around empty pavilions and leap across streams. Only when we reach a pair of silver trees with elaborate carvings in their wide trunks do we come to a stop to reassess our situation. I take a few moments to catch my breath, leaning against the tree trunk with one hand. When my breathing finally slows and adrenalin is no longer pumping through my system, I'm able to sense it: a glimmer of Griffin magic. I managed to hold onto some of it after telling the guards they couldn't see us.

"Do you think your command applied to every Unseelie guard?" Dash asks. "Or only the guards in the prison?"

"No idea." I look back the way we came, but I don't see anyone hunting through the garden for us. If the guards have managed to open the prison trapdoor, then they're looking for us elsewhere right now. "I don't know exactly what I was thinking when I gave them command, and all I said was 'the guards.' I hope it was all of them, but I think that would have taken more power than I had left."

"We'll find out soon enough," Zed says.

"I'd rather not find out," Dash replies. "Em, do you think we can get to the dragon enclosures now without being seen, or should we wait until dark?"

"Uh … now is probably better. Even if we don't try to escape until dark, there's a thicket of trees just before the dragon pits that hardly anyone ever goes through. It'll be safer to hide there than to hide on this side of the palace."

"Okay. So we move now," Zed says.

We continue our stealthy mission through the gardens, passing nothing more threatening that a few small flying and crawling creatures. "Hey, I never asked what Guild you're from," Dash says to Zed at one point as we pause behind a thick bush to scope out our surroundings again.

Zed rubs his neck as he peers through the bush's leafy branches. "It's a long story, but I'm not affiliated with any particular Guild anymore."

"Oh. But your markings—"

"My markings are still active, yes. But it's a story for another time. Let's get out of here alive first."

I happen to agree with Zed. Especially since I've just discovered our first major obstacle. "Hey, I think we have a problem," I say to them. They're both so intently examining the garden on the other side of the bush that they haven't yet noticed what's happening in the distance behind us.

"What's wrong?" Dash asks, turning to face the same way I'm facing. "Ah. I see it. Where the bunting is hanging between those statues?"

"Yes. A picnic lunch is about to take place there. I just saw the last baskets of food being placed around the blankets, and the first few ladies have just arrived. Oh, and there come more people," I add as a small group of colorfully dressed men and women wander toward the picnic area.

"I assume we were planning to walk right through that spot to get to the dragons?" Dash asks.

"Yep. Unfortunately."

"We could backtrack a bit and go around the other side of the palace," Zed suggests.

"It's a lot longer going that way around," I tell him, "and it takes us past the main entrance where all the carriages drive in and out. We'll have to do almost a full loop of the castle."

"Bad idea," Dash says. "Let's just head further to the left and go around the picnic."

"I've never been to that part of the grounds," I tell him, "so I don't know what we might find there. I have a suspicion there are houses that way for some of the fae who work here, but I'm not sure."

"Well we can't go *through* the palace," Dash says, "so going further left is our best option. Besides, most people should be at work during the day, right? So if there are houses that way, hopefully they'll be empty."

"Fine. But I hope you're ready to fight, because you might have to."

"Have you learned any combat magic since arriving here?" Zed asks me as we sneak out from behind the bush.

"No. Not officially. I tried out some magic on my own, but I doubt I could produce it fast enough to use it in an actual fight." We slip behind our next cover— the first of a row of trees clipped into giant birds—and crouch down. And then … an odd sound reaches my ears from somewhere behind us.

"Oh, fudging heck," Dash says. "The guards are out."

I look around. A wave of uniformed men and women is moving through the garden toward us. They stab their swords into bushes, slash at leaves, and wave their blades beside every tree. "Looks like they're not too concerned about stabbing us or chopping off a limb or two," I say.

"We need to keep moving," Dash says, "or it won't be long before they reach us."

Keeping our heads down, we run alongside the row of topiary birds. The back of my coat drags along the grass behind me. I wish I had time to stop, undo the buttons, and shed the smothering garment. I'm beginning to bake inside it. At the other end, we carefully step out into the open again. We're a good distance away from the picnic, so as long as we make no sudden moves, we shouldn't catch the attention of any—

"There she is!"

The distant shout comes from the direction of the picnic. I freeze and look across the garden. I'm too far away to know for sure, but I think it's one of the guards who's been stationed near my room since the day I got here. He launches forward and runs toward us. Another two guards detach from the gathering and join him.

"Well, that answers our question about the other guards seeing us," Zed says as we start running.

My mind races ahead, trying to visualize a way out of this. If we can beat the guards to the dragon pits, we can jump down into one of them. Hopefully we won't break any ankles or legs, or become a snack for Imperia. Then we can get Phillyp to remove the shield over the enclosure and let us fly away—or threaten his life if he doesn't. Not the best way to go about things, especially since I like Phillyp, but it's our only option now.

Until suddenly, our only option vanishes.

Almost straight ahead of us, from the area of the grounds I've never been to before, dozens upon dozens of guards come racing into view. "Crap," I mutter, skidding to a stop along with Dash and Zed. "Go back the other way. The long way around the palace. At least the prison guards can't see us." We take off in the other direction, but the three guards from the picnic are gaining on us. *Run, run, RUN*, I tell myself, easily keeping up with Dash and Zed. They may be elite warriors, but I feel like I've spent my life training for this moment: fleeing a small army's worth of Unseelie guards.

We hurtle past the front of the palace, providing great entertainment for anyone who happens to be in their suites looking out at the garden. I have no idea what we'll do once we get around to the side where all the carriages drive in and out, and dozens more men and women stand guard along the walls. My mind tumbles through half-formed ideas of what I can use the last remaining part of my Griffin power for.

But I never get a chance to make a decision, because around the corner of the palace comes yet another group of uniformed faeries.

CHAPTER 29

"Dammit!" I cry out. I'm running so fast I almost trip over my own feet as I try to stop. Dash grabs onto my arm and tugs me back. "Into the palace," I pant. "We don't have … a choice now. We can hide … somewhere inside."

There are open doors and archways all across the ground floor, and it's far too easy to race into the palace. It's a trap, of course. We're running into an elaborate, lavishly decorated trap. Because once all the doors and windows are sealed off—and I have no doubt the king can do that in a matter of seconds with the aid of magic— we'll have nowhere else to go.

Except …

I stop running halfway across a portrait-lined hallway, and Dash almost collides with me. "What?" he asks. "What's wrong."

"There's a way out."

"Where?" Zed asks.

"It's—wait. Come on." At the sound of running footsteps behind us, we keep moving. I lead the way down another hall, through a small parlor, then take a few turns along increasingly narrow passages, and eventually race past an enormous kitchen. I duck through the first open doorway I see, which turns out to be packed to the ceiling with bags of various kinds of grain.

After peering back out to make sure no one's seen us, Dash quietly shuts the door. He faces me. "Where's this other way out?"

"It's a portal. A gateway into another world." I pause to catch my breath and wipe tiny beads of sweat from my brow. "Not the human world and not this one. The other world Aurora and Roarke took us to. The shadow one."

Deep lines crease Dash's forehead. "That place with barely any color? Where that black shapeless creature chased us?"

"Yes. It isn't a place in this world. It's—"

"Between the worlds," Dash murmurs.

"Yes. Just like you said. There's a portal in Roarke's room that leads straight into that world, and once we're there, we can use the candles to get out."

"Candles?"

"Yes. With—the way the witches—I'll explain later. The point is, we can get out of that world."

"And what about the creatures that rose up from the shadows and wanted to kill us?"

"We can run if we have to. I'm safe, actually." I pull at the chain around my neck and lift the pendant from where it's hiding beneath my shirt. "And you guys know how to fight. So we should be fine. I'd rather take my chances against a bunch of shadows than against an Unseelie army."

"I hope you realize," Zed says, "that whatever the two of you are talking about makes zero sense. A world between worlds? What does that even mean?"

"Now isn't exactly the time to go into detail," I point out, "but it's real. I promise. It came into existence when the veil was torn. And it's the only way I know of to get out of this palace."

Slowly, Zed nods. "Okay. But won't this portal be just as heavily guarded as any other exit?"

"I don't think so. Roarke and his father don't want anyone but their closest guards knowing about the shadow world. And I don't think the king knows about the portal. I'm pretty sure Roarke kept that a secret from him. I know Roarke stationed a few of his men on either side of the portal, but he may not have had a chance to send more guards there yet. If we make it there quickly, and there are only a few guards—"

"We can handle them," Dash says. "Definitely."

"How far to his chambers?" Zed asks.

My enthusiasm wilts a little. It seems impossibly far right now. "Uh … far enough that the chance of being seeing is extremely high."

"The key is to blend in," Dash says. "If we're not running away from anything, we won't catch anyone's attention. We just need to look like your average three nobles wandering around the palace."

"Well, we've already failed then. You guys look awful."

"Thanks," Dash says drily. "But we can't very well shed our clothing. We'll make even more of a spectacle if we wander down the halls without—Oh." His face brightens. "That could work."

"What?"

"Remember where I went when I first got here?"

"Um … no. I wasn't with you when you first got here. You were—Oh, the clothes casters."

"Yes. I had to leave your dress in the chief clothes caster's workroom. And guess where that is?"

I raise an eyebrow. "If the answer isn't 'right next door,' that would be a very sad ending to this story."

Dash smiles. "It's *almost* right next door."

Zed nods. "That's almost as good."

We sneak out of the store room and make it to the clothes caster's workroom without being noticed by anyone. The workroom, by some miracle, is empty, and contains numerous racks of court-appropriate clothing for both men and women. "Perfect," I say. "Too bad we don't have time for you guys to shower. Hopefully the clean clothes will be enough to mask your dirty hair and … you know …"

"The smell?" Zed prompts.

"Yeah."

"No time to shower?" Dash repeats. "Ha. You've heard of magic, right?"

I place my hands on my hips. "Seriously? Faeries have shower spells?"

"Something like that. Not as satisfying as a genuine soak in a hot pool, but it has the same effect."

Ten minutes later, after hiding behind a screen and drenching themselves in water and mint-scented soap that somehow never touches the floor and dries almost immediately, Dash and Zed step out as well-groomed members of the Unseelie Court. They just need to take care to keep their wrists covered.

"Right," Zed says. "Let's do this."

It's difficult to walk slowly when all I want to do is flee, but I manage to keep my pace to a casual stroll beside Dash and Zed. Once we've left the storerooms and workrooms behind us and we're strolling the glossy marble hallways once more, Dash moves a little closer and places my arm over his. "Take her other arm," he tells Zed.

"My, what a lucky lady I am," I drawl, sarcasm coating my words. "A man on each arm."

"You're a lot less likely to be noticed as Prince Roarke's future wife," Dash says, "when you have a man on each arm, don't you think?"

"I guess so." I look down and notice magic swirling around his other hand as it hangs loosely at his side. "Getting ready to fight?"

"To stun, actually. It'll be quicker and cleaner."

"Stunning someone means knocking them unconscious with magic, right?"

"Yes. It isn't a quick spell, though. Enough magic needs to be gathered first. It can take—"

"There!" The shout comes from the top of the staircase at the end of the hall. The staircase we need to ascend. Sparks of magic shoot past us as the guards race down the stairs.

We duck down immediately, Zed swearing beneath his breath. "We're gonna have to fight," Dash says.

"Don't waste your stunner magic if you can help it," Zed tells him. "Save it for—" he dodges to avoid more sparks "—for the portal guards."

"Yeah. And Em—"

"I'll be fine." I focus on the railing that runs along the gallery at the top of the stairs. "See you up there." I launch forward with a burst of speed. The guards—just reaching the base of the staircase—might think I'm aiming directly for them. But I duck beneath their sparks and swerve to the side, heading straight for a bureau with a vase of flowers sitting atop it just to the side of the stairs. I leap up, strike the top of the bureau with one foot, and jump again. My fingers grasp the gallery railing. I pull myself up, swing over the railing, roll across the gallery floor, and spring to my feet. A momentary glance back down to the hall shows me Dash and Zed following the same path I took, with guards right behind them and others racing up the stairs.

I spin around and run. Highly polished floors streak by beneath my feet, and I'm grateful my shoes have enough grip to keep me from slipping onto my backside. I risk a look over my shoulder, and Dash yells, "Don't stop!" I sprint toward the final staircase that will take us to royal family's wing of the palace. But of course, it isn't that easy.

Guards are lined up at the top of the stairs, and they're not running down to meet us. I know nothing will make them leave their posts. Magic spins around their fingers as they raise their hands to attack. As colorful sparks fly toward me, I twist one foot, drop down onto my side, and skid clear across the floor beneath their magic. With no time to worry about the pain shrieking at me from my hip and shoulder striking the floor, I scramble through the nearest doorway. Then I'm up and running again along a new hallway, limping only slightly from the pain. "Keep going!" Dash yells, which tells me he and Zed escaped the magical assault.

My thoughts tumble ahead, planning a new path. The only way to the Roarke's suite is up that staircase—unless you count his balcony and windows, which I do. *Go down a level, double back, sneak through someone else's window, and climb up*, my brain instructs. As the pain in my hip begins to dull, I race forward with a fresh burst of speed. I turn a corner and find the winding staircase I was expecting. With every second counting, I don't bother with the actual stairs. I swing myself easily over the railing beside the top step. *Leap, land, shoulder roll, jump up, keep running*, I mentally recite as I execute the maneuver almost perfectly. Despite the life-threatening circumstances, I can't help doing a mental fist pump. Val would be so proud of me.

I run back along halls and passageways until I reach a large parlor that I judge to be roughly beneath the stairway to the royals' wing. From walking through this room before, I know that the various hallways leading off it will take me to the chambers of extended family members and other lords and ladies who live here. A quick look over my shoulder confirms it's still Dash and Zed who are following right behind me. As they reach the parlor, I hurry along another passage, pass two or three doors, then stop. After listening for a moment, I quietly open the door. Dash and Zed reach my side as I peer into the bedroom and confirm that it's empty. We slip quickly inside, and I shut the door behind us.

"Holy freaking crap, Em," Dash says between gasps for air. "You'd make one hell of a guardian if you knew how to fight."

"Yeah. Knowing how to fight might be useful." I swallow and suck in another deep breath. "But I'd rather not be part of any Guild, thanks very much." I cross the bedroom—not quite as lavishly decorated as mine—and look out the window. "Okay, I think we should move over one more room to the right. Once we're directly in line with the snake sculpture out there, we should be below Roarke's balcony."

"We're climbing into his room?" Zed asks.

"Yes. Easier than fighting all those guards, don't you think?"

We move to the next room, which is also empty. Everyone's probably at the picnic. I swing my legs over the windowsill, turn carefully to face the wall, and begin climbing. I edge a little to the left as I ascend, and before long, I'm level with Roarke's balcony. I grab onto the railing and climb over it. On tiptoe, I move toward the open doorway.

"Is this the right one?" Zed whispers from behind me.

"Yes." I recognize the interior of the sitting room.

"Let me go first," Dash says, stepping past me. "We may need to use magic." I notice that sparks of light still dance around his hand. Seems he's managed to hold onto the stunner magic he was gathering earlier.

He creeps inside. I follow him, ready to duck at the first sign of magic. But the room is empty. "The portal is through there," I say in a low voice, pointing to the door leading into Roarke's bedroom. Dash walks ahead of me into the next room, then looks over his shoulder at me in confusion. "The bathroom," I whisper as Zed and I follow him. He nods. I slip past him and stop beside the bathroom door, which is slightly ajar. I look back at Dash. He raises his magic and nods again. I take a deep breath, then kick the door open. He and Zed rush in—and stop.

"There's no one here," Dash says. "But—holy freaking ferret-whistle." His eyes widen, along with Zed's. "That's a portal."

I stride into the bathroom after him. "Yes. That's it. All we need to do is walk through—"

The bathroom door slams shut. Against the wall, standing in exactly the same spot I stood in when I hid here, is Roarke. "Going somewhere?" he sneers.

CHAPTER 30

The scuffle is so quick, my eyes barely follow what happens: Dash flings his magic; Roarke twists away while hurling a crackling mass of power at me; Zed launches himself in front of me, cries out, and drops to the ground. By the time my useless gasp is out of my mouth, the action is over. Dash now holds a protective layer of magic in front of the two of us, and Roarke's raised hand suggests he's doing the same thing. Zed, who took the full force of the magic Roarke tried to attack me with, lies unmoving at our feet.

"Is … is he—"

"Not dead," Dash says, his eyes trained on Roarke. "Stunned."

"Yes," Roarke says. "And the two of you will soon be in the same position."

"I don't think so," Dash answers. "We have the portal right behind us now, and it'll take you far too much time to gather enough magic for another two stunner spells. We'll be gone long before you can carry out your threats."

Roarke lifts one shoulder in an unconcerned shrug. "You're welcome to go through that portal. My guards are waiting on the other side, ready to knock you out the moment you appear. And unlike you and me, they haven't yet used up the stunner magic they've been gathering."

"Well, thanks for telling me exactly what to expect on the other side. Now that I'm prepared, I have no doubt I can stop them all."

Roarke snorts. "Guardians have always been over-confident. I can only hope it gets you killed."

"My over-confidence has served me well so far." With the hand that isn't holding up the shield, Dash pulls me closer to the portal.

"Emerson," Roarke says, directing his hard gaze at me. "Why don't you tell me what all this silliness is about. I thought you and I had an agreement. We both want something, and our union will get us what we want. If you've changed your mind, you'll never get your mother back the way you want her."

"Em, don't listen to him. He's just wasting time so he can—"

"I'll never get what I want from you anyway," I say to Roarke.

"Oh? Is that a lie your guardian friend has told you?"

"I know what you plan to do. I know the meaning of the words you've been making me memorize, and I know you're planning to take every bit of my magic and make it your own."

Several beats of silence pass as Roarke's cold gaze grows icier. "Interesting," he says, slowly grinding the word out. "However did you discover that?"

I wish I could tell him it was his own sister who shared this information, just so I could see the look on his face. But I won't give Aurora away. Whatever her motives were in going behind her brother's back, she doesn't deserve his wrath. "Everyone's been so insistent that I stuff my head with as much knowledge of this world as I can," I tell him. "Wouldn't want your future wife to be an embarrassment to this court, would you? Well, guess what? In all that reading, I stumbled across the one piece of knowledge I needed more than anything else—the words of a particular witch spell and their meaning."

"A coincidence?" Roarke spits. "You expect me to believe that you stumbled across this spell by *chance*?"

I force a laugh out. "Funny, isn't it? You thought it was silly how much reading I was doing, and yet reading is what ended up saving me."

"Em, we need to—"

"Saving you?" Roarke's quiet laugh chills me. "You think you're going to get away from me? Just like your idiot guardian friend thought he was going to get away from this palace?" He looks at Dash. "You really thought I was going to let you leave in that carriage, didn't you. You *fool*," he hisses. "Did you think you could sneak into my betrothed's bedroom and there'd be no consequences?"

I suck in a breath. "How did you—Wait, you *have* been listening in on me. You disgusting—"

"Of course I've been listening. My father and I make it our business to know exactly what everyone says and does beneath our roof. We have untraceable enchantments almost everywhere." His gaze returns to Dash. "I could hardly allow a filthy guardian to continue sneaking around with my future wife once I knew about it."

"We were *talking*—"

"Em, let's—"

"Ah, but what if talking turned into something else? Something far less appropriate and far more … intimate. I couldn't have someone sullying my bride-to-be."

"We were talking about my family's *funeral,* you sick bastard," I shout, even as my face burns at the thought of what he's implying.

"Yes, and then he was going to sneak around my home and hunt down information he could use against me. Therefore, he needed to be removed from the palace."

"Em!" Dash says, putting more force behind the word this time. At our feet, Zed moans. Clearly there wasn't much magic behind Roarke's stunner spell. "We're leaving now," Dash says. Invisible magic raises the half-conscious Zed into the air, where he flops over Dash's shoulder with a grunt. I look immediately at Roarke to see what he's going to do to stop us.

"I'm not worried, Emerson," he says with a smirk, reading my unspoken thoughts. "My men on the other side of the portal will stop you from getting away."

"They won't," Dash tells him. He takes my hand and pulls me toward the portal. "Get ready to throw some magic as soon as we get through," he whispers to me. "Whatever you can handle. I'll do the rest."

I make my decision then, not giving myself even a second to consider all the things that might go wrong. I tug my arm free, shove Dash and Zed through the portal, and swing back around to face Roarke. He drops his shield of magic, a wicked grin spreading across his face.

But before he can do anything, I open my mouth and speak. I release the final bit of my Griffin Ability, and I say the one thing I've wanted to say since the moment I got here. The words I repeated endlessly the other night: "Tell me every single thing you know about my mother and how to help her!"

Roarke goes rigid. His hands rise to clasp his throat, as if he could possibly stop the words from escaping his lips. Then his mouth twists into an evil smile as a single sentence is ripped magically from him. "I … don't know … anything."

My shock silences me for several moments. "What?" I finally manage to say. How can he lie like that? How is it possible for him to disobey my Griffin Ability? "That isn't true. You *do* know things. You told me things about my mother and her past. You—"

"No." He lowers his hands and rolls his shoulders as he recovers from the magic's effects. "I told you things about the woman who raised you and then lost her mind and ended up in a hospital. I didn't tell you anything about your mother."

I blink.

The full meaning of his words takes its time making its way to my brain, but when it finally gets there, it almost knocks me to my knees. I swallow, shaking my head, refusing to believe him. I've been down this road, and I will *not* travel it again. "She *is* my mother. Everyone thought she was human, but she isn't. We both have magic. We're both faeries, so—"

"Oh, stop," Roarke says in a tone that almost sounds bored. "That's the stupidest logic ever and you know it. Just because you're both faeries she must be your mother? Ha! She could be my mother then, and we both know that isn't true."

"But … then—"

"No, no, silly girl. It's too late now." Roarke takes a step toward me. "You should have asked the right question while you still had some power in your voice. You should have *thought* about what you were asking. You should have mentally focused on *Daniela Clarke* instead of simply blurting out words without putting any true intention behind them." Another step. "Besides, it wouldn't have helped for me to *tell* you how to heal your mother. I have to do it myself. You might have learned the history of Daniela Clarke, but you would not—" one more step "—have learned how to help her yourself."

Crap. My half-formed plan—to get right up to the portal while Roarke was telling me everything I needed to know so I could rush through it the moment he finished speaking—crumbles to imaginary dust around me. I twist around, throwing my body in the direction of the portal as Roarke lunges for me. He catches my arm, tugging me back and sideways, and we crash to the floor just in front of the portal. With my shoulder screaming out in pain, I scramble away from him. His hand lashes out, twisting in my hair and scratching down the side of my neck before grabbing hold of a clump of my hair and yanking me back toward him. I cry out, reaching up to claw at his arms. I slash my fingernails along his skin, and as he yanks one hand back, I squirm around, pull my legs up to my chest, and kick him as hard as I can. Then I scramble onto my hands and knees and dive through the portal.

I roll onto the ground in the shadow world to find the dull landscape illuminated by glittering, colorful magic whizzing through the air in all directions. Three guards lie motionless on the ground while Dash and Zed fight two other men. They kick, spin, punch, and dodge amidst clouds of sand, shrieking bats, and flying needles. Through their grunts of pain and cries of anger, I hear Dash yelling, "*What the hell did you do?*"

I know he's shouting at me.

I scramble to my feet and whip around to face the portal. I need magic. Or a weapon. Roarke will arrive at any second. I look down at the rocky ground I'm standing on, searching for a sharp-edged stone—and wondering briefly why Roarke and Aurora transformed part of the grassy world they found into hard earth covered in pebbles and rocks. I spot a suitably sharp stone and bend quickly to retrieve it—

And pain collides suddenly, shockingly with my abdomen. I'm knocked off my feet and hit the ground hard on my left side. I curl in on myself, sucking uselessly at the air and getting nothing. *Breathe*, I tell myself. *BREATHE!* An invisible force tosses me into the air, and as I come to a halt, suspended somewhere above the ground, I see Roarke beside me. With a flick of his hand, I begin moving back toward the portal as he walks alongside me. I'm still gasping for oxygen, wriggling in the air, horrified at how powerless I am against Roarke's magic, when a wordless cry reaches my ears.

A split second later, a blinding flash of white-green light strikes the portal—and the entire thing explodes into yet more light and sparks and spinning glitter. Roarke and I are thrown backward, though his magic seems to cushion my fall. My ears are ringing. My left side still aches. Somehow, though, breathing is becoming almost a possibility. As the flare of light fades away, I push myself up to see what's left of the portal.

It's gone.

Beside me, Roarke curses loudly. I scramble away from him. I don't have time to find a sharp stone, so I aim for the heaviest rock I think I can lift. Without pause, I hoist it up and hurl it at Roarke's head. It strikes exactly where I intended it to. In horror, I watch as he collapses to the ground. Blood begins to ooze from somewhere amidst his hair. "Oh crap oh crap oh crap," I mutter.

And then, after one last thump, everything becomes quiet except for the sound of labored breathing. All the guards are knocked out, and Dash and Zed—covered in scratches and cuts, their clothes partially torn—gather their breath as they stagger toward me. I look back at Roarke, sickened by what I've done. "I didn't kill him … did I?" I pant.

"No," Zed says. "He'll easily survive that."

"What is wrong with you, Em?" Dash demands. "You were supposed to come with us, not make it easier for Roarke to catch you."

I ignore Dash and keep my eyes fixed on Roarke. "Can we tie him up? And the guards. I don't want them to get away. Roarke knows things. I … I need to question him still."

"Haven't you done that already? Isn't that why you shoved me through the portal without you?" Dash replies. "So you could stay behind and question him?" Despite his frustrated tone, he crouches down beside Roarke as a glittering rope forms in his hands. Zed does the same with one of the guards.

"I did question him. Seems I asked the wrong question."

Dash looks across at me, pausing with the rope partially wrapped around Roarke's wrists. "You didn't ask about your mother?"

"I did." I focus on the ground at Dash's feet. "I used the words 'my mother.' And that, apparently, was a mistake." My eyes rise to meet his as an unbearable ache forms in my chest. "Turns out she isn't my mother after all."

Dash stares at me with the same kind of expression I probably gave Roarke. "Shoot," he murmurs eventually. "I really thought—after she turned out to be magical—that she must be your real mother."

"Yeah. Me too."

"I'm so sorry, Em."

"This world …" Zed says, looking around. "It's an entirely different realm. This is just … crazy."

"It is," Dash agrees.

"Em." Zed walks closer to me. "Where are the candles you spoke about? We need to get out of here. Once we're somewhere safe, we can talk. I have a lot to—"

"Watch out!" I grab his hand and tug him down as a dark shape swoops over him like an undulating blanket with wispy edges. "Crap, I totally forgot about the ink-shades." I press closer to Dash and Zed as ink-black shapes gather around us. I reach for my necklace—my protection—but my stomach drops when my fingers find no chain against my skin. All that remains are the stinging scratches left behind from Roarke's fingernails scraping down the side of my neck. "Dammit. We need to get to the castle."

"But you're protected, aren't you?" Dash says. "If Zed and I stick close to you, we can—"

"My necklace is gone. Roarke must have broken the chain when he attacked me in the bathroom."

"Terrific," Dash mutters. Then, as the ink-shades swoop closer, he adds, "I think it's time to run again!"

I'm on my feet, racing beside Dash and Zed, hoping Roarke is wearing his amulet. If not, he won't last long, and he'll take all his knowledge of Mom with him. I toss a glance over my shoulder, but all I see are dark figures swooping through the air like misshapen bats. "Aim for the castle's main gate!" I shout as I look ahead once more. "The drawbridge is down."

I shriek in fright as a shadow sweeps right past me. Dash and I veer to the left, while Zed, on the other side of the ink-shade, swerves right. Separating themselves from the ground, a dozen more ink-shades join the one that just startled me. And for some reason, they gravitate toward Dash and me, forcing us further left. "Darn, they're quick," Dash pants. "We can't get around them.

"The tower," I answer between breaths. "The moat doesn't … exist there yet … and the windows are low. We can climb up." With an extra burst of speed, we aim for the tower. "Zed!" I yell to him, then wish I hadn't when he almost stumbles as he looks around for us.

"Keep going!" Dash yells at him. "Better for him … to go that way," he adds to me. "He'll make it to the gate."

My feet pound the ground, and my chest begins to burn, but we're going to make it. We're fast, and the castle is less than a hundred yards away now.

And then, in a move that Val most certainly would *not* be proud of, I trip over a clump of grass and land flat on my face. Struggling for air yet again, I manage to turn over. A dark shape swoops down and settles over me, covering me completely. As I scrabble uselessly at the ground, I feel the sensation of cold lips on my neck. All strength drains from my body. My limbs become heavy and cold. My eyelids slide shut as bone-weary tiredness consumes me and a deathly chill pervades my body.

CHAPTER 31

Through the darkness and silence, a sizzling crackle reaches my ears, followed immediately by a piercing shriek. My eyelids spring apart, and I see the dull grey sky far above instead of a cloak-like shape. Adrenalin rushes through me. My exhaustion vanishes. "Come on," Dash says, his hands already around my arms. He pulls me up. "My magic scared it off but didn't kill it. I don't know what spell to use, and—crap, they're already coming back."

We sprint the final distance toward the castle, and though I've always been fond of running, I'm fast approaching the point where I've had enough for one day. I kick off the ground the moment I reach the wall, and my fingers *just* reach the edge of the lowest window. Dash hauls himself up and takes a dive through the window. He jumps to his feet and grabs my wrists, pulling me the final distance. Once I'm through, he reaches up—but there's no window pane for him to pull down. "What the heck? Where's the rest of the window?"

"Not finished," I pant, just as a dark shape separates itself from the wall and rises behind Dash. I tug him forward. "The towers aren't protected yet. Need to get … into a room."

We rush down the stairs, around and around, and almost fall into the sparsely furnished room at the base of the tower. Together we slam the door shut and take a few hasty steps backward. My heel catches on the edge of a rug, and I land on my butt, accidentally pulling Dash down with me. "Are you sure it's safe here?" he asks, his chest rising and falling rapidly.

I nod, only knowing for sure because I've been in this room before. "That thing," I whisper, "was so cold." Dash leans closer and bundles me into his arms, and now that I'm finally still and not running for my life, I realize my whole body is shaking. I wrap my arms tightly around him and don't let go, even when my heart slows and my breathing returns to normal. I finally stop shaking, but still I hold onto his warmth. That creature was *so damn cold*. I don't ever want to be that cold again.

Eventually, just as I'm telling myself I should probably let go of Dash, he asks, "Are you all right?"

I detach myself from him and shift a few inches away. "Yes. I think so. It only got me for a few seconds, right? I felt so cold, so tired, but it was only for a little bit."

Dash nods. "Good. I also meant … about your mother."

Roarke's shocking revelation drops onto my shoulders again. I look away from Dash as I shake my head. I press my hands against my face and rub my eyes. "It feels like I've been on this crazy see-saw of emotion since I discovered magic and the fae world. She wasn't my mother, and then she was my mother, and now she isn't my mother again." I lower my hands. "I suppose I just have to remember all the things I told myself last time. That it doesn't matter how we're related. I still love her the same way. I would still do anything to help her get better. And—Oh! Bandit!" A sudden wriggling against my hip reminds me that I haven't seen him since we escaped the prison. I've hit the ground numerous times, and I haven't heard a squeak from him. What if he's hurt? I gently lift the edge of my pocket and peer inside—and tiny lizard eyes stare back at me. "Bandit," I breathe. "I'm so glad you're okay."

"Wow, he survived a lot," Dash says. "I wonder if he was in your pocket the whole time."

"Yeah, I wonder," I say, my thoughts turning back to Mom again.

"Anyway, we should get back to the oasis. Hey, look at that." He brightens. "I can say the word. *Oasis.*"

The oasis. Surrounded by all these muted tones, I long for the color and warmth of the oasis. Hopefully everyone in charge there will forgive me for whatever trouble I've put them through and allow me to return. "We must be truly alone if we can talk about the oasis. Well, aside from Zed, but I guess he isn't close enough to hear us." I push myself to my feet. "Do you think he made it inside?"

Dash nods as he stands. "Yes. I saw him cross the drawbridge just before we reached the tower."

"If he's found any candles, he's probably gone by now. I wouldn't hang around if I were him."

"Yeah. I'm sure he's got his own life to get back to. I'll have to see if I can find out anything about him once I'm back at work—if I still have a job, that is. It's strange that he still has his markings if he's not working for the Guild anymore. Usually they deactivate those if a guardian leaves the Guild's service."

"Do you know how he ended up locked in an Unseelie prison?"

"No. He kept saying he'd tell me about it when we were less drugged. And we never really got to the point where that was the case." Dash looks around. "So where are these traveling candles you mentioned?"

"Wait. What about Roarke?" I move to the window and look outside, but we're too far from the spot where the portal was for me to be able to see Roarke. "I need him."

"You *need* him?" I look back and see Dash watching me with raised eyebrows.

"You know what I mean. He can heal my mother. Or—you know—the woman I think of as my mother."

"We're not taking him with us, Em. Even if I wanted to, the protective enchantment around the oasis would forbid it. Once we're near him, we won't remember where we're supposed to go."

"Yes, I know. So the only other thing to do," I continue slowly, knowing that Dash won't like this, "is to bring Mom here."

"You realize that's crazy, right? Your mother is safe right now. If we bring her here, she won't be. And neither will we."

"Are you talking about the ink-shades? Because I can command them not to attack any faerie ever again. We only need to wait until tonight for my Griffin Ability to become useful again."

"Not just the—what did you call them? Ink-shades? I mean what about all the people aside from Roarke who know about this world? His sister, his personal guards, his *father*. Em, the Unseelie King himself could show up here at any second."

I lean back against the windowsill and fold my arms over my chest. "The Unseelie King probably thinks we're still hiding in his palace somewhere."

"And when he figures out that we're not? He'll discover that Roarke is missing too, and where is he going to look first?"

"Honestly, I don't think it will be here. He doesn't know Roarke showed me this world. And he won't see the portal because it isn't there anymore. Even if the king does think that I somehow overpowered Roarke with the help of my two prisoner friends, he has no reason to suspect we'd bring him here."

Dash frowns and purses his lips in thought. "I suppose not. So your plan is for us to bring your mother back here, wait until later to command the shadow creatures to leave us alone, then take her to Roarke. I assume you're planning to still have some power in your voice to command him to wake her and heal her?"

"Yes. And we don't necessarily have to wait until we can command the ink-shades. We can look for the underground passages that lead back to the hedges out there near where the portal was. We can get to Roarke that way."

Dash's frown doesn't leave his face. "I'm not sure there's any point in doing that if your Griffin Ability won't be ready to command him."

"Right. That's true." I let my arms fall back to my sides. "Then yes, we'll do as you said: fetch Mom, command the ink-shades, command Roarke. And once he's healed Mom, we'll leave immediately and go straight back to the oasis."

"Where we'll all live happily ever after," Dash finishes.

"Well …" I look away. "Things never work out that simply, so I assume something will go wrong along the way. Someone unexpected will appear out of the blue and try to screw up our plans, and we'll have to fight them off, and *then* we can live happily ever after."

"There's my cynical Em." Dash grins. "I've missed you."

I give him a withering look. "You know I have good reason to be cynical."

"Yes." He moves closer and places his hand on my arm. "But sometimes, Em, things do work out. Hopefully this is your time."

I cover his hand with mine, wishing I could believe him. "Hopefully you're right."

"I am." He rocks forward a little, and for one insane moment I think he means to kiss me. But his hand slides away from my arm and he turns, looking around the room once more. "The candles?" he asks. "Are they around here somewhere?"

"Uh, in the top drawer." I point to the sideboard. It's the only other piece of furniture in this room. Apparently Aurora spent days constructing it while teaching herself the relevant spells. Roarke then added his own personal touch by creating a solid gold snake holding a dagger in its mouth for the top of the sideboard.

Dash crosses the room. "I can't help feeling like this snake is going to come alive and stab me in the hand," he comments.

"Don't worry. I don't think Roarke had time to add delightful enchantments like that to the decorative items in his castle. He was still too busy with the actual architecture."

Dash takes two candles from the top drawer and leaves another few lying on top of the sideboard beside the snake. "In case Zed hasn't found any yet and he comes through here while we're gone." He joins me by the window. "So this is the same way the witch candles work? You light them, think of your destination, and you're taken immediately there?"

"Yes. I think that's how Roarke and Aurora brought us here the first time."

He hesitates. "Perhaps one of us should stay here. Keep watch. Just in case someone unwelcome arrives while we're gone. We don't want any unpleasant surprises when we get back here with your mom."

"Mm. Maybe you're—"

The handle of the door leading to the next room twists. Dash drops the candles. Without thinking, I launch across the room, bring myself to a halt against the sideboard, and yank the dagger free from the snake's mouth. The door swings open.

"Whoa." Zed holds his hands up the moment he sees me brandishing the dagger. "It's just me."

"Sorry." I lower the weapon I would have had no idea what to do with if it hadn't been Zed who walked in. "I assumed you would have found a candle by now and left."

He nods as he heaves a sigh. "I did find some candles. I could have left. I could have vanished and never seen the two of you ever again. But ..." One fist clenches and unclenches as he stares at the ground by my feet. "I owe you, Em."

I focus on that fist for a moment, then again on his face. "You owe me?" My laugh sounds forced. "Because I freed you? I think we're even, Zed. You threw yourself between me and a stunner spell, remember?"

"I wish that made us even. I wish that could come close to making up for the mess of a life you ended up with."

My grip tightens around the dagger's hilt, and from the edge of my vision, I make out something bright and golden blazing in Dash's hands. "Who the hell are you?" I whisper.

"I don't know if this is the best place to talk," Zed says, his gaze shifting back and forth between Dash and me. "Those shadowy creatures are everywhere, and Roarke is still—"

"We're staying exactly where we are," Dash says, his voice low and threatening as he raises a glittering crossbow and points it at Zed.

"How do you know me?" I demand, louder this time.

Zed raises his hands once more. "Almost eighteen years ago," he says slowly, "I was supposed to kill you."

My breathing becomes shallower. My heart pounds harder. But I swallow, steady my voice, and ask, "Why?"

"The people I worked with wanted to hurt your parents."

"Why? Who were my parents? What did they do wrong?"

"It's what they *didn't* do that was the problem. It wasn't their fault, but their inaction led to the pain and suffering of many people—myself included. Years later, those of us who survived couldn't get past it. Some wanted revenge. Some of us …" He shakes his head. "Well, some of us got caught up in finally belonging somewhere and having a purpose again."

I have no words to answer him with. All I can do is stare in horror.

"I was told to kill you," Zed continues, his voice wavering ever so slightly, "but I couldn't do it. I couldn't kill a faerie baby. Especially not a faerie baby who was related to someone who used to be a friend of mine long ago. So I did something else. Something that might be considered even worse."

My heart thunders as I wait for him to continue. "What did you do?" I whisper.

"A changeling spell."

CHAPTER 32

"Ho-lee shovel," Dash whispers.

My gaze snaps toward him, then back to Zed. "What? What is that? What's a changeling spell?"

"Witch magic," Dash says darkly. "Swapping a faerie baby and a human baby. I thought the witches stopped doing that kind of thing more than a century ago."

"The spell changes the appearance of both the human and the faerie," Zed explains, "so that they look like each other. Over time, that part of the magic fades away, leaving the faerie child looking the way he or she would have without the changeling spell. The faerie's magic remains blocked, though, and he or she will grow up as a human in the non-magic realm, knowing nothing of the world they truly belong to. Usually, the faerie's magic remains blocked for the rest of his or her human-length life. But sometimes, the magic breaks out."

"Which is what happened to me," I murmur. It doesn't seem real. It sounds like the story of someone else's life. The kind of thing I might watch in a movie, sitting side by side with Val and munching on popcorn.

"You forgot to mention," Dash growls, "what happens to the human baby. It doesn't live long. With magic running through its tiny human body, it barely survives a few days."

I'm gripping the dagger so tightly now that my hand begins to hurt. "So you couldn't kill me," I say to Zed, "but you could kill a human baby? You're despicable."

"I know," he says. "But somehow I felt less despicable than if I'd killed you."

This is insanity. This is barely believable. I was born in one world and stolen away to another, and—

"Wait." I point the dagger at him. "If you took a human baby away from its mother and replaced it with me, then why isn't my mother—the woman who raised me, Daniela Clarke—human?"

Zed shuts his eyes and releases a long breath before speaking. "That is where things get a lot more complicated."

"*More* complicated?"

"You'd better start explaining," Dash says, the crossbow still aimed at Zed's chest, "because we're not going anywhere until Em gets every single answer she's looking for."

Zed looks between the two of us. "Can I sit?"

"No," Dash and I say at the same time.

"Okay then." He nods. "I guess I should start with the fact that I'm Griffin Gifted. Don't worry," he adds as I inch back slightly. "I won't be using it on either of you. The effects are just as unpleasant for me as they would be for you."

"Forgive me if I don't take you at your word," Dash says. "This crossbow will be staying right where it is."

"I guess I don't blame you." His eyes move to Dash's empty hand, where magic has begun to gather. Then he focuses on me again. "Almost two decades ago, a group of fae formed based on a common interest: getting revenge on the Guild for leaving us at the mercy of a former Unseelie Prince. You might think I should have felt some loyalty toward the Guild, seeing as I was a guardian for years, but I didn't. I hated them for allowing innocent people to suffer. For their imperfect system that essentially allows them to *choose* who to save." His gaze flicks back to Dash for a moment. "You know I'm right. So we attempted to take down the entire Guild system. But we failed. Then we decided to target specific people instead. That's when I was tasked with killing the child of two guardians. And, as far as the leaders of our group knew, I succeeded. This spurred them on to go after others, but that changeling spell disturbed me more than I wanted to admit. I began to lose faith in our cause. It didn't seem like justice anymore. It just seemed like … murder.

"So I ran, and one of my Griffin Gifted friends—Daniela—ran with me. She'd also lost all interest in getting revenge. She no longer cared whether we killed all the guardians. She didn't care if we made people suffer by murdering their children. She was tired of it all. So in the end, because Dani was the only one I trusted, I confided in her and told her what I'd done. I told her about the changeling spell, and that I hadn't actually killed the faerie child. She was glad. She said I'd done the right thing by not killing an innocent baby."

"You did, though," I remind him. "You killed an innocent *human* baby. Does human life mean less to you than faerie life?"

"It shouldn't," he says, so quietly I can barely hear him. "Years ago, I pledged my life to protect both fae and humans. But by the time I was told to murder a baby, I'd been away from the Guild for so many years that I managed to convince myself that one human life didn't matter."

"That's—"

"I know. All the terrible words you can think of, that's what I am. But just like me, Dani didn't seem to mind too much about that part. So the two of us were on the run. We traveled for a while, and then one day, she asked me to show her the changeling. She said we should check that all was well, and that the human mother hadn't noticed anything strange. We should make sure the child's magic was properly blocked. If it revealed itself, she cautioned, and the Guild ended up getting involved, they might trace it back to us. I didn't believe her, but I took her anyway. The whole changeling concept seemed to fascinate her, and I knew she wouldn't let it go until she'd seen one with her own eyes.

"So we watched them. We watched Macy Clarke and her changeling child Emerson. And they were both completely fine. Dani, though …" Zed shakes his head. "She wasn't fine. She saw this simple human life, and she wanted it."

"She wanted to be human?" I confirm.

"Yes. Not just human, though. She wanted Macy's life. She wanted the changeling child, and the lovely little house, and Macy's job, and … everything."

"But that's … just …" I shake my head. "Aside from being totally wrong, that just doesn't make sense. Why would she want to give up her magic, her friends, her own world?"

"If you knew about her past …" Zed says. "It wasn't good. Her life was horrible. She thought getting revenge on the Guild would make her happy, but it left her feeling even more desolate. She wanted a chance to start over. A new world, a new life. New everything. So she asked me to perform a changeling spell on her. I'd never heard of it being done on an adult, but she was so desperate, so miserable, and she was convinced this would make her happy. I had to figure it out."

"You didn't *have* to help her commit murder and steal someone else's life," Dash interjects. The mass of magic swirling above his raised hand flickers.

"I began working on adjusting the spell," Zed continues, ignoring Dash. "Normally, it binds magic forever but changes the baby's appearance for only a short while—about a year or so—before slowly wearing off. In that time, a baby would grow and change anyway, so the difference isn't too noticeable then. But with an adult … well, I couldn't have her look like Macy for only a year and then slowly return to her normal appearance, so I had to figure out how to make it last longer. For the rest of her life."

"Which would now be shortened, I assume," Dash says, "without access to her magic."

"Yes. Once I was convinced I'd correctly altered the spell, we went ahead and did it. And as far as we could both tell, it worked. Her name was now supposed to be Macy Clarke, but she didn't like that, so she had it officially changed to Daniela Clarke. I checked in on her every week or so. In that time, we … well, we started to become more than friends. I fell in love with her. She didn't look the same, but she was still Dani. We had a month or two in which everything was blissful happiness. And then …"

"Then?" Dash motions with the crossbow for Zed to keep talking.

"The changeling spell that I'd altered so drastically had side effects. It blocked all her ordinary magic like it was supposed to, but somehow it didn't block her Griffin Ability. And her mind …" He rubs one hand over his face. "It affected her mind. She started forgetting things. Forgetting she'd ever been magical. Seeing things that weren't actually there. Afraid of imaginary things."

"So it's your fault," I whisper. "You're the one who made her crazy."

"I only did what she asked," he wails. "I only wanted to make her happy."

"Your spell drove her mad."

"And I will live with the guilt forever," he whispers. "In the beginning, it wasn't so bad. She didn't get confused too often. Just like her Griffin Ability didn't happen often. But I wanted to help her. Heal her. I tried to convince her that we should find a way to reverse the changeling magic, but she refused. She ended things between us. Told me she was happy with her human life and that she didn't need me to be part of it anymore. But I kept an eye on her. I watched as her Griffin Ability became … out of control."

"What was it?" I ask. "What could she—"

"But then it stopped," Zed says, ignoring my question. "Her Griffin Ability disappeared just like the rest of her magic. Soon after that, she snapped completely. I didn't witness it—the day she was hauled off in an ambulance—but I heard about it afterwards. I listened in when the doctors and nurses spoke about her. After that, I consulted healers—a select few that I trusted—but they couldn't do anything. I'd properly blocked her magic when I did that changeling spell, and now her Griffin Ability was gone too. They couldn't sense anything in her, and no one wanted to attempt reversing the changeling spell. No one was brave enough to try to fix the mess I'd made. In fact, they told me it was probably impossible. So, since the healers could do nothing for Dani, I had her moved to a private institution. The best I could find in your world. I was happy to pay for it for the rest of her days. And you—"

"I ended up with an aunt who wasn't really my aunt. Someone who didn't want me. Thanks for that."

"Look, I'll be honest with you, Em," Zed says with an apologetic expression. "I never cared all that much for you. It was Dani I loved. You were more of a nuisance than anything else. You were the child she chose over me. So being able to send you off to your aunt was something of a relief for me. Dani loved you, so I didn't want you to end up a homeless orphan, but I didn't care much beyond that."

I grit my teeth together so tightly my jaw begins to ache. I open my mouth, then snap it shut. I've already told him he's despicable, so there's no point in repeating that.

"I checked in on Dani fairly regularly," Zed continues. "Over the years, the hospital tried to release her a couple of times, but, as you know, it never went well. Occasionally I would try some new form of magic I'd come across, but I was never brave enough to try anything drastic. I didn't want to risk killing her. And with her magic blocked—as far as I could tell—she was as weak as a human.

"We went on like this for years. Then one day, your magic finally broke free of the spell I'd placed on you, and your Griffin Ability revealed itself. Suddenly everyone in power in the fae world wanted to get their hands on you. And I, unfortunately, heard the news too late. The Unseelie King told his son to learn everything he could about you. His search led him straight to Tranquil Hills Psychiatric Hospital—where I was trying to retrieve Dani. She'd always been safe there, but now I needed to get her elsewhere. I didn't act quickly enough, though. Prince Roarke showed up while I was in Dani's room. He captured me and took me back to his home, leaving Dani at the hospital as bait for you, Em. With two potions—truth and compulsion—he forced the story out of me. He discovered that you and Dani were both changelings.

"He brought in a witch then. An old witch well-versed in the magic of her people. Crisanta. He made me explain exactly how I'd performed the changeling spell on Dani, and together the three of us figured out how we could heal her."

"Wait." I hold my dagger-free hand up. "Why would Roarke do that? He doesn't care about my mother. He doesn't need her. He was never planning to fulfill his side of the bargain I struck with him, so why would he go to so much trouble to try and fix her?"

"It was his back-up plan. He thought that if all else failed—if you ended up with the Guild or the Seelies and refused to enter into any agreement with him—he would then steal your mother and heal her. Then he'd contact you, present a fully healed Daniela Clarke to you, and only agree to set her free if you handed yourself over to him."

I find myself slowly shaking my head.

"No?" Zed asks. "You don't think you would have agreed to that? I think you would have."

He's right. I'm not shaking my head because I disagree with him. I'm shaking my head because I still can't quite believe all of this. It's so far removed from anything I've ever imagined for my own life. He can't be talking about *me*. He can't be talking about *my mother*. She wouldn't steal someone else's life, would she? But somehow, deep down in that part of me that recognizes I've been utterly out of my depth since the moment the earth ripped itself open at my feet, I know that Zed's story is the truth. It's my story. It's my mother's story.

"Em?" Dash asks, his crossbow still pointed firmly at Zed. The magic he's been gathering over his palm is almost the size of a bowling ball now. "Everything okay?"

It takes me a few moments to find my voice. "I … yeah. But I have a lot of questions. Starting with my mother's Griffin Ability. What is it? What can she do?"

Zed opens his mouth, then pauses before speaking. "It's … complicated. I doubt you've come across a Griffin Ability like it before."

"I've known about magic for only a few weeks, so there are *many* Griffin Abilities I've never come across, Zed. I don't care how complicated this one is. I want to know about it."

"Fine." Zed presses his lips tightly together, then says, "Your mother has … she *is* … a split personality."

I shake my head, his words making little sense to me. "What do you mean? Her mental illness is a Griffin Ability? So she was crazy before you messed her up with changeling magic?"

"No, not like that. Not the way you're thinking of it. There aren't just two personalities living inside her. There are two *people*. And those two people—"

"—can separate," a voice says from behind Zed. He spins around to face the door. Someone pushes it open fully, and there stands a woman in an all too familiar silver cloak and black mask.

Ada.

CHAPTER 33

And those two people can separate. Despite the sudden threat of Ada standing in this very room with us, my brain latches onto those words, racing to put together the pieces of this puzzle.

Two people.

They can separate.

Mom and her 'friend' always arguing.

The friend I heard through the walls but never—

"Thank you for sharing that fascinating story, Zed," Ada says in sickly sweet tones.

A knife appears in Zed's hand. Dash steps to the side and aims his crossbow at Ada. "Adaline," Zed grinds out between his teeth. "How nice to see you again after so many years."

Adaline, my brain repeats. Another puzzle piece. I turn it over and around, desperate to make it fit in somewhere. I *know* it fits somewhere.

"I never liked you," Adaline says to Zed as she reaches for the door handle. "I could never understand what Dani saw in you." Glass begins splintering with alarming speed across the door and down to the floor.

My brain abandons the puzzle. My hand raises the dagger. I'm ready to leap over the glass and stab it right into Ada—

But Zed's hand flashes forward. His glittering knife pierces Ada's stomach an instant later. She cries out and doubles over, her hands pressing against her stomach. Her enchanted glass shards stop inches from Zed's feet. He throws his hand up, and a faint ripple in the air hints at the protective shield he's now holding in place.

Ada looks up, her eyes filled with fury. She tugs the knife free, and after it vanishes from her grip, she presses her hands over the wound. "You know you'll have to do a lot more than that to stop me, Zed."

"Yes," he says. "But in order to stop you, I have to slow you down first."

"Hardly," she mutters. "It won't take long for this wound to heal. You don't know what kind of power I possess now."

"I've heard rumors," Zed growls. "Rumors of witch rituals."

"You can hardly judge me, Zed. Not after the witch magic you used." She presses both hands more firmly against her stomach. "Now, I think it's time you finished your story. You were nearing the end, but I'm afraid I interrupted you before you got to the punchline." Her wicked eyes alight on me. "I don't think Em has quite understood yet. And what a delicious punchline it is indeed."

And those two people can separate. My brain fumbles once again with the puzzle pieces it's gathered as Ada raises one blood-soaked hand, pushes her hood back, and removes her mask.

And suddenly I'm looking into the face of my mother.

The dagger slips from my grasp. The air is sucked from my world. My knees begin to weaken. I'm hot and cold and light and heavy and *finally*, all the pieces click into place. "Line," I whisper. That's the only thing I've ever been able to remember Mom shouting through the walls while she argued with the 'friend' I never met. "But it wasn't 'line,'" I say, my voice coming out as a croak. "It was *Adaline*. It was *you*."

Ada nods, her smile slipping away and her gaze turning more venomous. "I couldn't stand the way she used to say my name whenever we separated and ended up arguing. 'Ada*line*,' she used to say. 'Don't be so stupid, Ada*line*. You can't go after the Guild, Ada*line*. Your Griffin Ability is weak and useless. I'm the strong one. What will you do without me? Bury them alive in glass trinkets and ornaments?'" A bitter laugh escapes Ada's lips. "Well, I showed her, didn't I. Once she was too lost in her own mind to control me, I got out. She wasn't strong enough to pull me back inside, and I was finally free once and for all. The witches taught me how to increase my power, and now look where I am. My glass isn't fit merely for tiny trinkets. It's an unstoppable force. And the moment you drop that shield, while the two of you are wasting time with fancy guardian magic you don't think anyone can beat, my glass will get you. It'll crack through you in seconds."

"I doubt it," Dash mutters.

"Ah, and there's that guardian ego we all know and love to use to our advantage," Ada says with a labored laugh. "What will it be today, young guardian? Razor blades, birds, rocks? Glass shards of your own, perhaps? Are you skilled enough to transform your magic at the speed of thought, or are you one of those unimaginative men that likes to throw raw power around?"

"The latter," Dash says. Zed's hand drops to his side, the shield vanishes, Dash throws his arm forward, and all the power he's been gathering since Zed stepped into this room strikes Ada in the chest. A single second passes. Then her eyes slide shut and she crumples to the ground. "Stunner spell," Dash says. "It's amazing how often people forget that one."

"Takes a while to gather the required amount of power," Zed says, kneeling beside Ada and holding her wrists together. "That's probably why."

"Thanks for being so quick with the shield," Dash says.

"Thanks for being so quick with the stunner spell," Zed replies, his hands rapidly looping golden ropes between and around Ada's wrists.

I drop onto my knees as my legs finally give in. "She's … she's my mother. She's *part* of my mother. She's … they're two people. Inside one? That's the Griffin Ability?" I look at Zed for confirmation.

"Yes."

"That's … just … so …"

"Complicated," Zed says. "Super complicated."

"Did you know? Before you did the changeling spell?"

"Yes. Dani told me some months after we met each other. She said that as long as she could remember, she'd been aware of this other presence in her mind. She was seven, I think, when she first split and this other identical person revealed herself. Her parents named her Adaline. Adaline and Daniela. A little bit like twins, but in a weird, magical, share-one-body-most-of-the-time kinda way. Dani was always the stronger one. Adaline couldn't last long on her own. She'd get tired, and the two of them would meld together and become one again. It was strange. I could talk to both of them, and after a while, I could figure out which one was speaking. But if Dani got annoyed with Ada, she could silence her. That was always the way things were."

"Until you messed with their magic and made Dani weak and insane," I say.

"Yeah," Zed murmurs. Finished with the rope, he pushes himself to his feet. "I don't know why it happened that way. Why it affected Dani's mind and not Ada's. Why Ada's magic wasn't blocked but Dani's was. None of it makes sense."

"Sounds like you messed with the changeling spell too much for any of this to make sense," Dash says quietly.

"It changed both their appearances, though," I point out. "They look exactly the same. It's so weird. If I hadn't seen her glass magic, and if I hadn't heard the way she speaks, I would have said without a doubt that this is Mom."

"Yes. They've always looked identical. That's where the similarities end, though. They've never wanted the same things. It was Ada, rather than Dani, who wanted revenge on the Guild. Dani wanted it too in the beginning—Ada obviously couldn't force her—but she grew tired of it a lot faster. Ada wanted to stay. She tried to convince Dani, but Dani wouldn't listen. After we ran, the two of them didn't split as often anymore. It seemed like Ada was sort of … sulking. Then when Dani asked me to do the changeling spell, Ada was furious. She forced her way out and told Dani how stupid she was being, throwing their magic away for a boring human life. But Dani was still stronger then. She forced Ada back inside. They didn't separate for a long time after the changeling spell, and I began to think that the magic must have blocked Ada. But after Dani began to properly lose her mind, Ada started separating from her again. I saw her a few times, disappearing and only coming back hours later. One day I watched her vanish into the early evening—and I never saw her return."

"So you knew she was out there, then?" I ask. "You knew what she was doing?"

"No. Not for years. I assumed she began a new life in the magic realm, and I was happy to forget about her. I hoped I'd never see her again. But in recent months, I heard rumors about a masked woman who was turning people into glass, and I wondered if it might possibly be Ada. I didn't know for sure until she walked into this room and started speaking. This is …" He gestures to her. "This is the first time I've seen her since she disappeared."

"So … when the two of them are together," I say, "their Griffin Ability is that they can split. But when they separate, Ada has her own Griffin Ability: transforming things into glass just by touching them. So does my mother—does Dani—have her own ability when she's on her own?"

"No. Well, not that I know of. The way she explained it to me, her Griffin magic was the ability to split into two different people. The ability to have this other person become part of her while still maintaining a separate consciousness inside her."

"It's so weird," I say again, shaking my head, not moving from my position on the floor. "So super weird. It's like … I don't know. Maybe they were supposed to be twins, and then one of those Griffin discs affected them before they were born, and they ended up in this weird, messed-up, unconventional twin form with one living inside the other."

"Who knows," Zed says with a shrug. "That might actually be what happened."

"And I don't understand why she didn't reveal her face to me before now. She could have pretended to be my mother. I would have been confused, but I'd have gone anywhere with her."

"I don't think so," Dash says. "You're smarter than that. You know now that shapeshifters and illusions are real. You would have suspected some kind of magic. And she didn't actually want *you*; she wanted your mother. So she was probably trying to avoid questions and explanations."

"Then why is she here now?" I murmur, more to myself than anyone else. Dash and Zed don't know any better than I do why Ada might be here. "Anyway." I swallow and clear my throat and prepare to ask Zed my most important question: "Can you heal Daniela Clarke? After spending time trying to figure it out with Roarke and that witch you mentioned, did you discover a way to make her healthy again?"

"We did," he says, and my insides bloom with warmth and happiness. "At least, we think we did. We obviously haven't tried it yet. And there is one catch."

A dark cloud draws across my elation. "What?"

"The changeling spell was applied to both of them. To Dani and Ada. In order to properly remove it, the two of them need to be one again."

I look down at Ada, considering exactly what this means. "She'll never agree to it, obviously, and it sounds like she's strong enough now to resist, but I can command her to do it. To … reform with Daniela, if that's what you call it." I look back up at Zed. "I assume you know how to wake my mother from whatever spell Ada placed on her? Or I suppose I can just tell Ada to do it. She called it 'irreversible,' but if Roarke was planning to wake Mom, then Ada must have been lying about that part."

"I know how to wake her based on what I overheard from the prince," Zed says. "But perhaps it would be better to command Ada to do it. She's the only one who knows exactly what magic she used."

I glance down at the ruby on my bracelet. "So many things for my Griffin Ability to do." Having recovered from my initial shock—physically, at least, if not emotionally—I climb to my feet. "I'd better go and get Mom so she's here when my ability is ready to be used."

"On your own?" Dash asks, surprise coloring his features.

"Yes. You said one of us should stay here, remember? And that was before Zed ran into the room and then Ada showed up. Now you have to watch both of them, as well as keep a look out for any new dangers. You definitely can't come with me."

"Hey, haven't I proven myself yet?" Zed asks. "I told you the truth. About everything to do with you and Dani and the changeling spell. And I helped stun Ada." He looks at Dash, who is no longer holding a crossbow. His hands are steady at his sides, though, as if he's prepared to grab another weapon at a moment's notice.

"You don't have to worry about guarding me," Zed says to him. "I'll watch Ada if you want to go with Em."

"No," Dash and I say at the same time. "I'm not leaving you alone here," Dash adds. "But Em, maybe you should wait. We can go together later after you've used your Griffin Ability to—"

"No. I don't want to wait any longer. I'll be fine, Dash. No one wants to hurt me where I'm going."

"Okay, but your mom is heavy. How will you carry her?"

I walk to the sideboard and pick up one of the candles. "I'm actually not completely useless with ordinary magic, Dash. I can do this—" I snap my fingers and a flame appears atop the candle "—and I can carry my mom."

As bright light flares around me, I squeeze my eyes shut and picture the only other place I can think of that was safe: Dash's parents' home. When I sense grass beneath my feet, I open my eyes and look around. I expect to find the pretty garden—that's what I was picturing—but I'm standing in front of a tall hedge. "Crap," I murmur. I must be outside the property. I look hurriedly around, but there's no one else here. And now that I'm alone, away from Zed and Ada, the protective enchantment over the Griffin rebels' safe place allows me to once again think of and picture the oasis.

I remove Aurora's stylus from inside my coat and replace it with the candle. The candle might work to get me to the oasis, but I'm not sure. At least I know how the faerie paths work now. I bend down and write on the grass while speaking the words I thankfully haven't forgotten. A thrill rushes through me at the sight of a doorway appearing on the ground at my feet; the novelty of performing magic hasn't yet worn off for me. I sit on the edge of the dark hole and let myself slip into it. I might be falling, but I can't tell. Everything is utterly dark and still as I focus firmly on the desert and the dome layer that shields the oasis.

Then abruptly, my feet strike sand and I stumble forward. Hot air smothers me and bright light almost blinds me. I manage to catch myself before tripping onto my knees. After steadying myself, I squint and twist around until I see the faint outline of a dome and hazy shapes within it. When I left, part of me thought I'd never see this oasis again. I knew I might never return from the Unseelie Court. I hoped I would, of course, but I was willing to go through with that union as an absolute last resort if it meant healing Mom.

Now, the thought of that union makes me want to be sick.

I walk as quickly as I can across the hot sand and slip through the dome layer into the fresh, cool oasis air, hoping desperately that no one sees me. I don't have time to answer questions or explain where I'm taking Mom. And I don't have time to apologize—which I definitely want to do properly once this is all over and Mom is safe and healed.

My eyes scan the oasis as I stride quickly—but not too quickly—toward the tree that contains the house I left Mom in. I lower my head and try to remain inconspicuous, but then I remember I'm wearing completely ridiculous clothing, and that of *course* I'll stand out if someone sees me. But it appears to be the middle of the day here, so I guess everyone's busy.

At the base of the giant tree, I pause and look around again. Two kids sit beneath another tree eating something, but neither of them look my way. In the distance, someone leads a large creature—a gargoyle?—out from behind a clump of shrubs. But he or she is too far away to realize I'm not someone who lives here.

My footsteps are silent on the many stairs winding around the tree. When I reach Ryn and Vi's door, I listen outside for several moments, hearing no movement or voices. They're probably far away on some important mission. They might, I realize with a guilty lurch, be searching for Dash and me. I almost continue upward, but my conscience gets the better of me. I duck into their kitchen, then pause for a moment to breathe in the smell of something freshly baked. I look across the counter tops and find a blank scroll and a pencil that keeps changing colors in my hand. Quickly, I scribble a note: *Dash and I are fine. I've taken my mom. Will be back soon. I'm so sorry I left. Em.*

I leave the paper in the center of the kitchen table and place a vase over it just in case a breeze moves through here. Dash would do more than this. He'd go looking for someone he knows here. He'd explain things. He'd make sure that anyone out searching for us is notified immediately of our safety and our whereabouts. But I don't have time for things like that, and I'm already aware that Dash is a better person than I am.

As I head for the door, my stomach grumbles, and I realize suddenly how hungry I am. Hungry and thirsty. Telling myself it isn't stealing—even though it kind of is—I grab the cloth-wrapped loaf of bread from the top of the stove, along with the contents of the fruit bowl, and drop them all into a backpack hanging from one of the chairs. I cast about for something to drink. Do they have bottles in this world? Something I can take with me? For some reason, I doubt plastic exists here. Then I notice an ornate glass shape with something that might be a cork in the top. After removing the stopper, sniffing the contents, tasting it and confirming that it's water—and then taking a second, large gulp—I add it to the backpack.

And that's when I notice three glass vials lined up along the back of the counter. Vials the same size as the one containing the elixir to stimulate my Griffin Ability. Vials, I realize as I bend closer, that have my name written in tiny letters on them. "Perfect," I whisper, silently thanking Ana for making more elixir for me. I remember her saying she would, but I knew I'd be gone by the time she was done with a new batch.

I slide the vials into a pocket inside the backpack and hurry out of the house. I continue further up, just past the simple little tree house that was mine for the brief period I stayed here. Stopping outside the next room, I experience a sudden, irrational fear that I'm going to step inside and find the room empty. I twist the handle and push the door open—and Mom is exactly where I left her. Relief courses through me as I hurry to her side. Looking down at her unconscious form, I'm almost overcome by everything I've learned in the past hour or so. *You don't really know this woman at all*, a tiny voice reminds me. But I can't focus on that thought. For now, I need to get her out of here.

I take a few steps back, recall the early spells I practiced while at the Unseelie Palace, and mutter the words that will lift Mom from her bed. She slides sideways and rolls clumsily into the air. With fierce concentration, I manage to catch her and keep her floating there. Once I'm certain she isn't going to tumble to the floor, I direct her through the air just ahead of me and walk out of the tree house. I manage to successfully make it all the way down the spiral staircase, though it takes me longer than I would have liked.

I realize, as I reach the bottom, that this is probably the last time I'll see this place. I once secretly dreamed of Mom and me living out the remainder of our days in this magical paradise, but that was before I knew she wasn't just one person. That was before I knew that in order to heal her, she'd have to join with Ada, one of the most dangerous faeries I've met in this world. When the Griffin rebels find out who my mother truly is, I doubt they'll let us return.

I walk across the grass, keeping close to Mom as she floats next to me. As I near the dome layer, a shout reaches my ears. I look over my shoulder to see someone in the distance waving and moving quickly toward me. *No time for that*, I remind myself as I step through the protective layer of magic. Heat slams into me as I place Mom on the sand. I kneel beside her, hold tightly onto one of her hands, raise the black traveling candle between us, and light a flame.

CHAPTER 34

Blinding light blazes around us as I shut my eyes and picture the room at the base of the tower in the shadow world. After a moment, I sense a hard surface beneath my knees, and the light on the other side of my eyelids begins to dim.

"Em. You did it!"

I open my eyes to see Dash in front of me, a bright splash of color against the muted tones of the shadow world. "No need to sound so surprised." I let go of Mom's hand.

"No, I just mean that I thought someone would stop you. I thought someone— at least one person—would come back with you."

"I didn't see anyone I know," I tell him, leaving out the part about someone running toward me as I left. Zed crosses the room, kneels on the other side of Mom, and takes one of her hands in his. "I guess everyone must be busy at the moment. I did leave a note, though." I can't remember where, now that I'm in the company of someone who isn't supposed to know about the Griffin rebels, but I know I left a note somewhere.

"A note?" Dash says. "That's it?"

"Someone will see it soon, I'm sure. And besides, this will be over soon, right? Then you can return, and I'll find somewhere safe for me and Mom. Hopefully once she's a normal, healthy faerie again, she'll be stronger than Ada, and Ada will never be able to get out again. Mom will be in control, and everything will be fine."

Dash and Zed both look at me with doubtful expressions.

"What?" I demand. "It'll all work out, okay?"

Zed nods, returning his gaze to my mother. "It will. I'm just not sure it'll be as easy as you're hoping."

"Don't worry, I'm used to that," I grumble as I look across the room at Ada.

She's lying in the same position I last saw her in, but a semi-opaque spherical shape surrounds her completely. "What's that?"

"I put her in a bubble," Dash says. "A shield. I figured she might wake up quietly without us noticing. She could probably turn her ropes to glass in an instant and shatter them, and if that happens, I want her to remain contained."

"Good thinking." I remove the backpack from my shoulder. "I brought some food. Well, technically I *stole* some food, but hopefully Vi and Ryn won't mind too much. At least we can eat and drink something while we wait for Ada and Mom to wake up."

"Waiting in this world is dangerous," Zed says quietly. "We should go somewhere else. My home, maybe. No one important knows about it. No one would find us there."

"Great idea," Dash says. "If only we knew we could trust you."

Zed looks up with a frown. "You haven't forgotten that I love her, have you?" he says fiercely. "I'm not going to run away from this. I'm here to fix my mistakes."

"Look, this may be a strange world," I say to them, "but it's the safest place for us to be right now. The Guild doesn't know about it. Most of the Unseelies don't know about it. And the one other place that's properly safe is impossible for us to get to as long as Dash and I are not alone. So let's just be patient until Zed can perform the spell, and then we'll get out of here. Dash, you can return to your Guild job—assuming you still have one—Zed, you can get back to your life feeling a little less guilty than before, and Mom and I … we'll find somewhere safe to go."

Zed opens his mouth, probably to tell me where he thinks Mom and I should go, but I silence him with a glare. If he's about to suggest we all live together as a happy family after the things he's done to Mom and me, I might have to hurt him.

I move to sit a little further away from Mom, place the backpack in front of me, and open it. "Look what else I found," I say to Dash, holding up one of the three glass vials.

He sits beside me and takes the vial. "Is this …"

"The stuff that stimulates my Griffin Ability? Yes."

"Awesome." He hands it back. "Now we don't have to wait until tonight."

"Yep. We can get on with things as soon as Ada wakes up." I remove the bread, fruit and oddly shaped bottle from the backpack. My parched throat is desperate for water, but before I can drink any of it, Dash places both hands around the bottle. He concentrates furiously, and gradually the bottle doubles in size. "That's convenient," I say.

We pass the bottle around, each eagerly drinking from it despite the awkward shape and size. In the silence that accompanies us as we snack on chunks of bread, my mind begins churning over every detail of Zed's story. It's still hard to believe that my mother—Dani—decided to leave her own life behind and take over someone else's. And Zed never mentioned exactly what happened to the original Macy Clarke after the changeling spell. She must have died, but … how long did it take? Did it happen in her own home? Did she know what was happening to her? And what did Zed and Dani do with her body afterwards?

It's so horribly morbid to think of, but I can't help it. Macy didn't do anything wrong. Zed randomly chose her, replaced her baby with an imposter, and then essentially killed her too. And Mom is the one who asked him to do it.

I shrink away from that idea, not wanting to think of my mother as a murderer. She must have had a very good reason for taking over Macy's life. Perhaps it was a reason Zed didn't even know about. Something bigger, something that makes more sense. And she'll probably tell me it was a horrible, awful mistake to have caused an innocent human's death, and I'll tell her not to regret it because it brought the two of us together.

Even though I can barely think the words without feeling sick to my stomach.

"Oh, we shouldn't forget about Roarke," Dash adds, interrupting my thoughts. "And his guards. They're probably awake now, tied up with guardian ropes they hopefully have no way of breaking. I assume they're protected from the shadow beings?"

"Uh, yes." I gladly latch onto this distraction from my disturbing thoughts. "Their amulets will protect them from the ink-shades. They should be fine until we can get back to them."

"Unless someone else finds them first," Dash says. "What about Roarke's sister? She knows about this world. She may have rescued him already."

"Yes, that's possible." I tear the chunk of bread in my hands into two smaller pieces. "Or maybe … there's another woman. I didn't see her, but I overheard her talking to Roarke. She knows about this world too. She might already have found him."

Dash's expression darkens. "If that's the case, then she might still be here. Looking for us."

"See?" Zed murmurs. "Staying here is a bad idea."

"Nothing's going to go wrong," I tell him sternly, wondering if I should get the elixir out of the backpack and put some magical power behind that statement.

Dash nudges my knee with the edge of his shoe. "Glad to see my positive vibes are rubbing off on you."

I roll my eyes. "Don't get your hopes up. That's about as positive as I'll be getting."

Dash gives me a sad face, then pulls the oversized bottle closer to drink more water. I pop a piece of bread into my mouth and chew. Since thoughts of my mother are too confusing to face right now, I let my mind turn back to the start of Zed's story. To the guardian couple he was told to steal a baby from. Fear tangles with a whisper of excitement. Do I want to know who they are? Do I want to know who *I* really am? Do I want to know what my name would have been, whether I have any siblings, where I would have lived?

I clear my throat. "You said you're here to fix your mistakes," I say to Zed. "Do you mean your mistakes regarding my mother and the changeling spell? Or do you mean me as well? Because it wasn't just her life you screwed up. You started with mine."

He looks away from me. "I wish I could say I can fix your life too, but—

"But you only care about Dani."

He sighs. "It's true that she's my first priority. But if I could help you too, Em, I would. I just have no idea where your parents are now, or if they're even alive."

I swallow. "What do you know about them?"

"They were excellent guardians. Two of the best, so I heard, although that wasn't what I experienced when I went to their home to take you. They were unprepared, and it was easy enough to stun them both. I don't know what happened to them after I took you. They were related to an old friend of mine, but I never saw her again either.

"The huge battle on Velazar Island took place not long after that. There were prisoners, guardians, witches, and even Lord Draven himself, with his own army of gargoyles. I still don't know how that was possible; he was supposed to have been killed a decade before that. Some said afterwards it was all a lie, but plenty still believe it was actually him who was burned to death after the veil was ripped. Anyway, my point is that your parents were probably there. They might have been captured by the Guild after the head councilor at the time revealed all the Griffin Gifted. Because they must have had Griffin Abilities themselves," he adds as he gestures toward me. "Your own Griffin magic is proof of that. Or they might have been killed in the fighting. I don't know."

"And you never cared to find out," I murmur.

He shakes his head. "No. You can hate me for it, but I didn't care to find out. I didn't ever want to think of them again."

"What were—"

Crack.

My gaze whips toward the bubble. The rope around Ada's wrists is now glittering glass instead of glittering gold. With another crack, she tugs her arms apart, shattering her bonds into hundreds of shards before climbing upright.

CHAPTER 35

Ada's angry cries, only somewhat muted by the bubble surrounding her, greet my ears. She pummels the inside of the shield with glass, hail and stones. "And she mocked *us* for wanting to use fancy magic," Dash says to Zed.

"Dash," I say as I fumble with the pocket inside the backpack, "maybe this shield bubble thing wasn't such a good idea. You should have gathered more magic to stun her a second time."

"And then have to wait another few hours for her to wake again?"

"A *small* stunner spell then! But this? She's going to get free." I wrap my fingers around one of the vials and jump upright.

"She won't," Zed says. Both his hands are raised. Hopefully he's reinforcing whatever magic is surrounding Ada.

"Is that Dani?" Ada demands, pausing briefly in her attack of the shield bubble. "You stupid people. You know she can't wake up, don't you? I put her into an eternal sleep!" She continues flinging her magic around, trying to break free.

"Em, are you ready?" Dash asks. "Tell her what you need to tell her."

"Wait. Will my Griffin Ability work through the shield?"

"I don't know! Why wouldn't it?"

"I'm going to kill you!" Ada screeches, reminding me for a moment of the woman in the Unseelie prison. "I'm going to kill you two useless excuses for guardians. I'll hide Dani in a distant hole no one will ever find, and then I'll take what I came for. You!" she spits at me.

"So you've changed your mind about me?" I ask as I pull the stopper from the vial. "Because back in Stanmeade, you made it sound like you didn't have much use for me. But whatever your reasons are for showing up here, Ada*line*, I'll soon discover them all." I tip at least half the vial's contents down my throat.

Ada goes still. She clenches her fists, shuts her eyes, and lets out a blood-chilling scream. Glass explodes from the floor in a ring around her, slices straight through the shield, and embeds itself in the ceiling.

The shield bubble is gone.

She freezes for one second, a triumphant smile on her face and a terrifying gleam in her eyes. Then she raises her hand toward me. That familiar tingling sensation starts at the base of my spine as my Griffin Ability gets ready to rush to the surface. But it isn't *quite* there yet, and if I can't—

Zed launches across the room and collides with Ada.

"No!" I gasp as the two of them crash to the floor. I expect Zed to turn to glass in an instant. I expect to see all my hopes for Mom shatter to pieces. But the two of them become strangely still as they lie there on the floor. Zed's hand is wrapped around Ada's wrist, but his grip isn't tight, and she isn't fighting him. They're staring at something beyond sight. Twitching, moaning. "No," Ada whimpers, watching something neither Dash nor I can see. "No, please don't. Stop, please."

Frozen in place, without a clue of what to do, I ask, "What's happening?"

"I don't know." Dash inches closer to the two of them.

Then finally, my Griffin magic races to fill my voice with power. Words tumble from my mouth: "Ada, your glass magic has no power in this world." An unexpectedly large amount of magic floods from my body, leaving me a little unsteady. I raise my hands to steady myself. Fortunately, I sense some remaining Griffin magic lingering at the edge of my control. "Ada, you will obey me when I tell you to wake Dani from the enchanted sleep you placed over her," I add quickly. "And Zed, you will answer my questions with the truth, and you'll do everything possible to heal Dani and return her to the way she was before the changeling spell."

My voice has lost its deep resonance for the last few words of my command, but I'm confident I managed to say enough to ensure Zed can't intentionally hurt my mother. Just in case it turns out he's lied about everything so far.

I take a few careful steps closer to Ada and Zed. His hand slips away from her wrist. Her whimpering ends, and they both lie still, trembling slightly. As Ada blinks and looks around, Dash rushes to her, grabs her hands, and forces them behind her back. Zed pushes himself up, wiping moisture from beneath his eyes. "You swore you'd never do that to me," Ada whispers shakily to Zed.

"I swore I'd never do that to Dani," he answers without looking at her. "I didn't swear anything to you."

"What did you do to her?" I ask, my eyes shifting back and forth between them.

He swallows. "My Griffin Ability. I try never to use it. But … desperate times and all that."

I crouch down in front of them. "What does it do?"

"Nightmares. I can make people relive their worst nightmares." He closes his eyes. "The catch is that I have to feel every ounce of terror they're experiencing. So my Griffin Ability tortures me almost as much as it tortures my victims."

An involuntary shiver crawls across my skin. "That's horrible."

Ada yanks suddenly against the bonds that now hold her hands behind her back. "What did you do to me? What did you say?"

"If you've realized you can't use your Griffin Ability anymore, then you can probably guess what I said."

"You little *cow*," she spits. "How dare you take my own magic from me?"

My gaze hardens. "You've killed people. You were about to kill Zed and Dash. You're the reason my aunt and cousin are dead. Forgive me if I can't muster an ounce of pity for you over the fact that you can't use your horrible glass magic."

Her gaze narrows. "You never loved your aunt and cousin. Your friend always told me that. I did you a favor by getting rid of them."

I stand and take a step back. "What friend? What are you talking about?"

Her glare turns into a taunting smile. "I seem to remember telling you I've always had someone watching you. Someone ready to update me every few months when I stopped by Stanmeade to find out if anything interesting had happened to you yet. I'm not going to tell you *who*, of course. I might need to use that person again."

"You won't," I assure her, "because we're going to make sure you're put back exactly where you're supposed to be."

A frown creases her forehead as she looks between the three of us. Then her gaze settles on my unconscious mother—and I watch as understanding finally dawns in her eyes. "No," she says. "You can't. It isn't possible. Dani has to be awake for—"

"She will be awake. *You* are going to wake her up."

She goes still for a moment, her mouth open, probably ready to refuse. But she can't escape my Griffin Ability. A wordless cry of anger finally breaks free as she begins shuffling across the floor toward my mother. Dash takes hold of her arms and helps her along. He deposits her right beside Mom, where she begins thrashing from side to side. "Dash, her arms," I say, moving closer. "I think she needs to use her hands." He bends as a knife forms instantly in his grip. He cuts the ropes binding her wrists, and she brings her hands around to hover over Mom's motionless body.

"Dammit—I don't want—Argh!" She's putting up a good fight against my magical command, but even as her furious cry leaves her mouth, other foreign words begin flying from her tongue. Dash takes a step back and raises a crossbow, pointing it straight at Ada. Zed moves to stand beside him, a short curved blade appearing in each hand. For good measure, I pick up the dagger from the floor and walk to Dash's side.

"We shouldn't need to stop her," Zed says to Dash as the speed of Ada's chanting increases. "I recognize the words. She's saying the right thing."

Dash nods. "Em's voice is hard to resist. But we don't know what she'll try once Dani's awake. Be ready to act."

I tighten my sweaty grip on the dagger's hilt. As Ada chants her spell repeatedly, I sense something different and unnatural pervading the atmosphere. Something that gives me the urge to look over my shoulder to see whether some kind of threatening force is inching closer, about to grab me. I flinch as her chanting reaches a new level of frenzy. She tilts her head back, and an uncomfortable shiver raises the hair at the back of my neck. Dash's hand wraps around mine, and I don't pull away. I want to flee as far as I can from this unnatural magic, but since I can't, it's good to feel the solid, reassuring warmth of someone right beside me.

Suddenly, it's over. Ada lowers her head and stops speaking. Zed drops his knives—which vanish before hitting the floor—and grabs Ada's wrists. She tries to release a few sparks of magic, but he manages to force her arms behind her back without too much difficulty. "Not so dangerous without your glass touch, are you?" he says.

"Why isn't she awake?" I ask, lowering myself onto my knees beside Mom as Zed drags Ada away from her.

"She will be soon," Ada says bitterly.

"How soon?"

She gives me a twisted smile. "You shouldn't be so eager for her to wake up, Em. You know I'm going to tell her what you did once the two of us are joined again. I'm going to make sure she knows all about how you handed her over to me in your weak attempt to save a human town you don't even like. At least I'll get one moment of satisfaction out of this mess: getting to tell Dani that her beloved daughter—the changeling she stole from someone else—betrayed her."

Everything in me longs to lunge at Ada and rip my fingernails down her face, but that would probably give her more satisfaction than it would give me. So I pretend to be perfectly level-headed and sensible, and ask, "Why didn't my Griffin Ability work to wake her?"

Ada shrugs and looks away. "Clearly you're not as powerful as you think you are."

"That has nothing to do with it," Zed says. He looks at me. "People have known about Griffin Abilities for a long time now. Some of the witches figured it out even before Prince Zell began to put the pieces together and started rounding us up for his army. So the witches, who've always been particularly creative with their spells—"

"And particularly evil," Dash adds.

"Creative," Ada repeats with a chuckle. "They certainly are."

"The witches," Zed continues, "came up with a few spells that are resistant to Griffin Abilities. Not many. Just some basic ones they could be certain would resist any kind of magical influence. Like, for example, putting someone into a permanent sleep."

"Which doesn't seem to be that permanent," I breathe, inching closer to Mom as she begins to stir. I'm so happy that for a moment I forget she'll probably still be confused and scared. I have to remind myself that her mind is still as messed up as the day we rescued her from Tranquil Hills. She may not even recognize me.

"Look at you," Ada murmurs in disgust. "So excited over nothing. You won't win this, you know. You won't stop me."

I grit my teeth and continue staring into Mom's face. "I will."

"You won't. You know why? Because you want your mother. And as long as she's alive, so am I. And as long as *I'm* alive, I'll never give up."

"On what?" I demand, looking up again. "What is your goal anyway? To turn as many people into glass statues as you can and kill them? For no reason other than the fact that you enjoy being in control instead of having Dani control you?"

"You honestly think I don't have a better reason than that? I have a *very* good reason, Em. And seeing as how you've been hunted by the Guild just as I was—just as Zed was—you should understand. Zed understood, once upon a time, and then he got scared off by a *baby*. By *you*."

Dash takes a step toward her, moving his crossbow closer to her head. "All the people you've killed have been related to the Guild in some way. Guardians, former guardians, family of guardians. So is that your goal? You're still trying to get revenge on the Guild, even though the rest of your guardian-hating group disbanded years ago?"

"I'm not just *trying*. I'm succeeding." She directs her glare at him. "What else do I have to live for? It was our life's purpose until Dani decided we should leave magic behind and pretend to be human. Of all the disgusting things she ever made me do against my will, that was the worst. Serves her damn right for going crazy. She deserved it."

"Em?" a quiet, raspy voice says.

Everyone falls silent. My gaze drops immediately to Mom's face. Confusion fills her eyes, but *she recognizes me*! Emotion wells up abruptly, cutting off any words I might have been planning to say. Tears fill my eyes so quickly they spill onto my cheeks before I can stop them. "Mom," I manage to choke out. I blink furiously and clear my throat. "You're awake."

Her eyes slide past me and land on Ada. And that's when everything goes wrong. She shuffles weakly away from me. "What ... what's happening? Who are you people?"

"Mom, it's okay." I hold my hands up to show her I mean no harm. "It's just me. It's Em."

"Dani, hey, just calm down," Zed says gently. He takes a step toward her, then stops when she begins scrambling away from him.

She shakes her head. "I don't ... I don't know who ..."

"Yes you do. You know me. You know Zed. And that's Ada." I point across the room to the exact image on Mom. "You know her too. She's ... she's part of you. And we're going to make you one again."

"No, no, no," Mom moans, her terrified eyes fixed on Ada. "She isn't real. I'm seeing things. They keep telling me ... that I see things." Her shallow breaths are shaky. "Why are you all ... in my room?" She shuffles further back, covers her head with her hands, and presses her back against the far wall.

I bite my lip to keep it from shuddering. I wrap my arms around my middle, attempting to hold myself together, and look at Zed. "Can you just do it please? Start the spell. The reversal—whatever. I don't want to see her like this."

He nods and moves toward Mom without pause, as if the only thing he's been waiting for is my permission. He gently takes her arms and speaks quietly to her, encouraging her to lie down. Dash walks to Ada and pulls her to her feet. "Don't struggle," he tells her. "You'll only make things more difficult."

"I'm happy to make things as difficult for you as possible," she says between gritted teeth as she shoves her elbow into his stomach.

"Stop it," he groans, throwing her into the air.

And there she stays, floating. Wriggling, but unable to get away. With one hand raised, Dash directs her through the air and toward my mother. He lowers her to the ground, where she continues squirming. But his magic must be holding her in place, because she doesn't move anywhere. "I'll break free again," she says. "I swear I will. You can't meld me with *her* and expect me to be the weaker one." She twists her head to the side and glares at Dani. "Look at how weak she is. How pathetic. Useless, insane—"

Zed covers Ada's mouth, cutting off her words with one hand and producing a piece of cloth that's just as golden and sparkling as the rest of the guardian weapons I've seen so far. He places it over Ada's mouth, and despite the fact that she writhes around, the cloth successfully ties itself behind her head within seconds.

"Don't worry," Zed says to her. "Dani may be weak now, but I'll help her to become strong again. And until that happens, I'll personally make sure you don't go anywhere." He turns to Mom. "Dani," he says gently. "Dani, love, I need you to do something." Mom is still crying quietly, but Zed manages to gently pry her hands away from her face. "See this woman? She isn't imaginary. She's real and she's your sister. And all you're going to do is touch her arm, okay? Touch her arm, and don't resist." Mom looks wildly uncertain, but she's spent the past few years doing what doctors and nurses tell her what to do, so perhaps that's why she lets Zed take her arm and extend it toward Ada. "Just relax," Zed says to her. "Relax and don't resist."

Mom's hand touches Ada's arm—and the strangest and most unnatural thing I've ever seen takes place. With a stifled shriek, Ada is sucked into Mom's body. It's over in less than a second. If I'd blinked, I would have missed it.

"Sorry," Zed says, looking up at me. "It's freaky if you're not used to it."

I swallow. "Um … yeah. Definitely freaky." What's even freakier is the way Mom's expression keeps alternating between rage and fear. One moment her lips pull into a snarl, and the next her gaze darts fearfully about the room. As if the two personalities inside her are at war. "Is it … will the spell take long?" I ask Zed.

"Yes, it's a quite complex."

"Are you sure you remember it all?"

"Yes. I made sure to memorize every step while the prince, Crisanta and I were crafting this changeling reversal. I knew he only planned to use it as a last resort. That he'd probably never do it. I hoped I'd be able to get away eventually, find Dani, and perform the spell myself."

"Okay," I whisper. "You can start."

With Mom lying down, Zed places a hand on her arm and closes his eyes. As he begins speaking, I imagine I can see magic seeping from his fingers into her body.

Dash moves a little closer and stands beside me. "It's finally happening," he says quietly. "You've wanted this for so long."

I nod, still finding it difficult to speak. "What if … it doesn't work?"

He's quiet for a while before saying, "Then we'll find another way. You're both faeries. You'll both live for many years to come. We've got time to find a solution. Look at the tear in the veil. After it happened, no one had any idea how to fix it. No one knew if it would ever be possible. And now, almost twenty years later, someone found a way to do it."

A hiccup of a sob escapes me, and my next words are stilted as I do my best not to give in to the tears. "I don't want to—wait twenty years. I've waited—so long already."

Carefully, as if he's worried I might shove him away, Dash puts one arm around me. "I know."

We stand like that and watch the spell, and I plead with everything in me for this to work.

After what feels like only a few minutes, Zed stands. "Is that it?" I ask. He made it out to be such a complicated spell that I expected it to take far longer.

"No, that was the first step. I've put her to sleep and initiated the spell. But I need certain ingredients in order to finish it. A few items that are key to the changeling spell, and that Crisanta believed would be necessary in reversing it."

My heart sinks. "You need other ingredients? Why didn't you say anything about that before?"

"Because I knew how that would have sounded. 'Hey, I can heal your mother, but first I need to go home and get some stuff.' You wouldn't have believed me for a second, but I'm telling the truth, Em. I swear I am."

"I know." I let out a resigned sigh. "I commanded you to answer my questions with the truth. And I commanded you to do everything in your power to heal Mom."

He frowns. "You did?"

"Yes. You were lost in a nightmare at the time. You probably didn't hear me."

He sucks in a deep breath. "Okay. That's a little scary."

"Why? Are you planning to hide something from me?"

He answers without pause: "Only things that have nothing to do with you."

I nod. "Seems fair."

He steps closer. "You know I want her to be healed just as badly as you do."

"Yes, I do. But … Zed, what exactly are you hoping to get out of this?" May as well find out what his end goal is. If he's imagining patching things up with his former girlfriend, he'll have to make a new plan.

"I want to finally have peace about all the things I did years ago," he says, not looking away from me. "I hope that Dani will forgive me for driving her mad. I hope you'll forgive me for stealing you from your family. I know I can't expect to get a happily ever after out of this, but hopefully I'll be at peace when I leave the two of you. I'll know that I've done everything I can to fix my mistakes."

I'm glad he doesn't expect to stay with us, to become part of our lives. I suppose Mom could eventually choose that for herself, if she wants, but I hope she doesn't. It's probably selfish on my part, but it messes with the perfect picture I've been working toward all my life.

"Okay," I say to him. "Go and get the things you need. We'll be waiting here."

He nods. "Thank you. And don't touch her. You might disturb the spell."

CHAPTER 36

"You don't have to stay if you don't want to," I say to Dash as we sit against the wall beside Mom. "I know you've got your own life to get back to, and you've helped so much already." I almost laugh at my own words. *Helped so much?* Now there's an understatement.

"Are you kidding? I'm not leaving."

I don't want to admit how relieved I am to hear that, so all I say is, "Thank you."

"I'd never pass up the opportunity to defend a damsel in distress," he continues, "and who knows what other dangers might show up before this spell is over?"

I manage to smile, grateful for his attempts to lighten the heavy atmosphere. "Thanks for the reminder that I'm still essentially useless when it comes to normal magic."

"Hey, you know I was just joking, right? You've never been a damsel in distress. Not back in Stanmeade, not in the fae realm, and not here. I have no doubt you'd put up an excellent fight if someone unpleasant showed up."

"Well, I do have a dagger now. I could probably inflict some damage with it."

"Exactly. And also …" He pulls his knees up and rests his arms across them. "I figured you probably wouldn't want to sit here alone waiting for Zed to get back."

"Yeah. Not really. Although I do have Bandit." I watch Bandit, who crept out of my pocket as a lizard about a minute ago, exploring the room in cat form. He sniffs at the candles Dash dropped on the floor earlier, then kneads a section of the rug. When he notices me watching him, he shifts into dragon form—still no bigger than a large dog—and stretches his wings out. He stops, points his face toward the ceiling, and coughs out a tiny flame. "Well done, Bandit!" I open my arms to him, and he shrinks rapidly back into a cat, crosses the rug, and climbs into my lap.

"You guys are so cute," Dash says as he pulls the backpack closer. "Thank goodness I stopped you from selling him."

"Hey." I cover Bandit's ears with my hands. "You know I didn't mean that. I was just being …"

"Contrary?"

"Well, yes." I stroke one hand along Bandit's back.

"Blueberries?" Dash holds a handful out toward me.

"Thanks." I lean my head back against the wall as I chew. Bandit turns around in my lap at least three times before curling up and closing his eyes. I look across at the window. A dark shape floats slowly by, reminding me that I still need to tell the ink-shades never to attack another faerie. Once the changeling reversal spell is done, I'll drink some more elixir and go outside to command them. "You know, I thought I'd have some power left over after commanding Ada and Zed," I say, "but I spent almost all of it telling Ada not to use her glass magic."

"I guess her Griffin Ability is powerful. Makes sense that it would take a lot of your power to stop her power." He looks at me then, his brow creasing. "What did you say to her, exactly? Your glass magic has no power *in this world?*"

"Uh … I think so."

"What about the other worlds? I assume her magic will still work out there."

"Crap. I suppose it will. I'm sorry, I wasn't thinking clearly. But once this spell is complete, she'll be back to her weakened form inside Mom. She won't be able to do much with her magic."

"Yes." Dash nods. "You're right. This is all going to work out fine."

And though I keep cautioning myself not to be too hopeful, I find that I actually believe him. I'm so close to getting Mom back now that there isn't much room left for anything to go wrong.

I allow myself to relax against the wall. It's impossible to know what time of day or night it is by looking outside, but it feels to me like it must be evening by now at the Unseelie Court. I didn't sleep much last night, and I spent half the morning running away from people, so it's not surprising my eyelids feel so heavy.

"You never got to finish asking about your parents," Dash says, rousing me before my head can droop forward. "He said they were a guardian couple, but he didn't mention anything about which Guild they were at."

"No, he didn't," I murmur, blinking and watching Mom again.

"Do you want to know more about them? Once Zed gives us their names, I can look them up. Find out if they're still working at a Guild, or if … if something else happened to them."

I absent-mindedly run my finger across the soft fur of Bandit's head. "I don't know. Maybe. At the moment, all I can really think about is Mom. But once life gets back to normal—whatever normal ends up being—I think I'll probably be curious. I'll probably want to know more about them."

"Yeah. Well, let me know when you're ready, and I'll see what I can find out. Just imagine," he adds with a grin, "if your parents are alive, how overjoyed they'll be when they find out their daughter is actually … " He trails off, a frown slowly replacing his smile as he stares at the floor. Then he looks at me, his eyes searching my face for something. "I wonder if … no. That can't be what she was talking about."

"What? Who?"

"I overheard … but it was probably something else."

"Overheard what?"

He pulls his head back a little as he examines my face intently. Then he shakes his head. "I can't tell. Your face is too familiar to me now."

"What on earth are you talking about?"

"Nothing. Sorry. Just thinking out loud."

"If you're going to be cryptic and refuse to explain yourself, then perhaps you should keep your thoughts to yourself."

"You're right." He looks away, the shadow of a frown still present on his brow. "I'm sorry."

I nudge his arm with my elbow. "I'm right? Really? That probably isn't something you often say to people," I tease.

He pulls his trademark grin back into place. "I was saving it for you. Since you're so special and all that."

I roll my eyes and shake my head. "Can I please stop being special? It's seriously overrated. I just want to be an average faerie who knows how to use average magic."

"Sorry, Em, but I don't see 'average' anywhere in your future."

"Great," I say with a sigh. "Well if something else exists between 'average' and 'special,' I'd like to aim for that then."

Dash laughs and reaches for the giant water bottle. He hefts it up and offers it to me. I drink a few gulps, then pass it back. "It's probably a weird thing to say, but this—" he gestures vaguely between us with one hand "—feels comfortable. Like, way more comfortable than it would have been a few weeks ago. It's just strange how quickly things can change, I guess."

"Comfortable. Yeah." I nod. "I mean, we're in a world between worlds where shadows rise from the edges of everything while watching my mom, who is actually two people, change back into someone I've never actually met. But … yeah. If this had happened a few weeks ago, we'd definitely be sitting on opposite sides of the room."

"Yep. Mortal enemies and all that," he says in a deadly serious tone, before allowing himself a laugh. He drinks from the bottle, then lowers it.

"Sorry. I was really mean to you over the years."

He shrugs. "It's not like I ever gave you a reason to think I was anything other than a jerk."

"True. But at least I know better now."

"Aah, you think I'm better than a jerk?" He presses one hand over his chest. "Emmy, that's so sweet of you. Fills my heart with warmth."

"Shut up."

"Still not a fan of 'Emmy,' huh?"

I look out the window again. "I guess it's not so bad. It's just … it always felt too familiar when you said it to me. Like a nickname that a close friend or family member might give me. But you weren't close to me, and I didn't want you to be."

"Did your mom call you Emmy?"

"Sometimes. Mostly Em, but sometimes Emmy."

He nods slowly, then smiles again. "Well, we can be close friends now, right? Then I can call you Emmy without you wanting to … what did you say before? Hurt me?"

I turn my head to face him, a strange flush heating my skin as part of the conversation we had in the prison comes to mind. He said it was worth it to wind up locked in a prison because he got to meet me. I wonder if he meant that, or if it was simply the drug potion talking. "Is that what you want to be?" I ask quietly. "A close friend?"

"Um …" He shifts and mirrors my position, the side of his head leaning against the wall as he watches me. "Why do I feel like this might be a trick question?"

"I don't know. It isn't." I don't have time for trick questions. Perhaps I would if I were an ordinary girl back in the human world with nothing more to worry about than school and friends and a boy staring at me the way Dash is staring at me now. I could ask trick questions and play hard to get, and then rehash every single second of the exchange with Val late at night, trying to figure out what he meant and what I meant.

But my world isn't like that. It never really was.

"Hmm, let's see," Dash says. "Do I want to be your close friend?"

"Yes or no," I say simply, though part of me is beginning to think it isn't that simple at all.

"How about yes *and* no?"

I narrow my eyes. "Didn't I already tell you how I feel about you being cryptic?"

He nods slowly. "Yeah. You did. Somehow, I'm finding it difficult not to be."

Without warning, a bright green spark skitters across the floor, transforming into green flames that race from one side of the room to the other. I pull my knees up in fright. Bandit lets out a yowl as he winds up half-squished between my legs and chest. "What the hell is that?"

"Uh … I think that was me."

"You *think*?" I jump to my feet as Bandit leaps away from me. The green flames die down and vanish. "What if it wasn't? What if someone else is here?"

Dash remains seated. "It was me. I'm sorry. Just … some escaping magic. Which is really weird. I thought I'd outgrown that."

After a final look around, I sit again, tiredness already seeping back into my bones. "Outgrown what?"

He examines my face for a while before answering. "I'll explain when you're older."

I muster enough energy to punch his arm half-heartedly. "Idiot."

He laughs. "Fine. You really want to know?"

Bone-weary exhaustion creeps closer. I lean against the wall again. "Mm hmm."

"Well …" He looks down as his hand nudges against mine. After a moment's hesitation in which my heart begins to pump faster and suddenly I don't feel sleepy at all, I let him lace his fingers between mine.

And then, in a blinding flash of light, Zed reappears. I snatch my hand away from Dash's and sit upright. "Did you get everything you need? Did anyone see you? Is everything—"

"Yes, no, and yes, everything is fine. If that's what you were going to ask." I nod as he crouches down beside Mom. He looks around at me. "Can I continue?"

"Of course."

Part of me wants Dash to finish what he was about to say before Zed returned, but I think I already know, and it isn't something either of us would be comfortable talking about with Zed in the room. Besides, the reversal spell is far more important, so I should be paying attention to that instead.

I watch Zed working on his spell for as long as I can, but after the third time my head droops forward and jerks up again, Dash tells me to stop being silly and just lie down and sleep. "I'll watch Zed," he says. "Make sure nothing goes wrong. I'll wake you when it's over."

"Aren't you tired too?" I mumble. "You didn't sleep at all … in that prison."

"Don't worry about me. I've been a faerie a lot longer than you have. I can survive on barely any sleep."

"That's … not …" I slide down and rest my head on the floor. "I've been a faerie … all my life. Just like you."

"You know what I mean. And here, lie on this." He pushes the backpack toward me, and it feels like the greatest effort in the world to raise my head. "Besides, I'm a guardian," he continues. "I'm used to stressful situations. You're not. Stress and terror are exhausting when they're new to you."

"I'm not … a damsel," I manage to mumble, and I think he replies but I'm already drifting away.

CHAPTER 37

It feels as though only minutes have passed when Dash squeezes my hand and says words my brain is too muddled and sleepy to understand. "Mm?" I manage to peel my eyelids apart and squint up at him. "What?"

"The spell is complete."

"So quick?" I push myself up and rub my eyes.

"It's been about an hour."

"Oh." I blink again and crawl toward Mom.

"Yeah, a regular changeling spell doesn't take as long," Zed says, "but I wanted to make sure I correctly undid every single alteration I made to Dani all those years ago."

I reach Mom's side—and a gasp escapes me when I see her face. "She—she doesn't look normal. What's happened to her face?"

"Her appearance has begun to change," Zed says.

I breathe out slowly. "Right. Of course." In the back of my mind, I knew this would happen. She needed to be returned to her original form, and her original form obviously didn't look anything like Macy Clarke. But it's still hard to imagine looking at a stranger and thinking of her as the mother I've always known.

She isn't the mother you've always known, though, I remind myself. *She was hiding so much from you.*

"Don't worry, you'll get used to her appearance over time," Zed assures me. "She's still the same person inside."

"Well, the same two people inside." Which is still completely freaky to imagine. "How long do you think it will be before she wakes up?"

"I'm not sure. There's a lot of magic working through her system right now. It could be an hour. Maybe more, maybe less."

"Should we leave this world now? In case it isn't safe here much longer. If Roarke is still tied up out there, the king will be searching for him. Eventually, he or some of his guards will show up here."

"I agree we should leave as soon as possible," Zed says, "but I'm not sure we should move Dani until the spell is complete. It *should* be fine, but I'm not certain."

"Okay, then we wait." I look back at Mom, and already her face has changed some more. Even her hair looks lighter than it was a few moments ago. And is that … pale pink? I lean forward with my hands on my knees and examine the strands of hair lying across her forehead. "Pink?" I ask Zed.

"Pinky peach, she always called it."

I try to imagine how she'll look when the spell is done. "Pinky peach. Sounds like an odd eye color."

"Where you're from, yes," Zed says. "But I always found her eyes quite pretty."

My own eyes are achingly tired. I rub them as I stand and start pacing. Like an impatient child, I keep wanting to ask Zed how long it will be until she wakes up. But I know he doesn't know. I stop moving, fold my arms, and look across the room at Dash. "You must be exhausted by now."

He leans down and lifts the glass bottle, which contains maybe a quarter of the water it contained after Dash's enlargement spell. "I may have placed a small enchantment on this water. An energizing enchantment." He holds the bottle out toward me. "Want to try it?"

"An energizing enchantment? Okay. May as well." I take the bottle in both hands and tilt it over my mouth. The water that runs over my tongue and down my throat tastes a lot like watermelon. I lower the bottle, and it's remarkable how quickly I begin to feel less weary. I drink a little more before carrying the bottle to the sideboard. I check the ruby on my wrist and realize that its color is almost full, which tells me it must be around about midnight back in the Unseelie part of the fae world.

A murmur draws my attention back to Mom. "I think she's waking up," Zed says.

"Crap, crap, crap." I return to Mom's side. "This is so weird. I have no idea how to act around her. I don't know what to say."

"Tell me about it," Zed mutters.

I kneel down and look into the face of a complete stranger. Her cheekbones are higher, and her lips are thinner. Her hair is almost blonde amidst the strands of peach, and a handful of freckles are sprinkled across her nose. This is my mother. This is the person who chose me. The person who chose the simple life we had together while I was growing up.

This is the woman who stole someone else's life, a quieter voice adds. *She stole* you.

I shove the voice away. Mom and I may not have come together in the conventional way, but that doesn't mean it wasn't somehow meant to be. She is my mother and I am her daughter. That's the only thing that's ever felt right in my world.

I reach for her hand and push away the nagging idea that I'm wrong. That maybe *nothing* has ever felt right in my world.

With my help, Mom slowly pushes herself up into a sitting position. She looks down at her hands, her eyebrows drawing tightly together. She pulls her hair over her shoulder and examines the blonde and peach strands tangled together. Her gaze lifts—and eventually falls on me. "Emmy," she whispers, her eyes dancing across my face. She leans forward, pulls me into her arms, and hugs me as tightly as if she's making up for every hug we've missed out on since the day that ambulance took her away. Tears blur my vision as my arms come up to wrap around her. My body begins to shudder as I finally let myself cry properly.

I don't want to let go of her, but I guess we shouldn't stay on the floor of a half-finished castle in this strange world for much longer. There must be a better place for us to continue our reunion. "I'm so sorry about everything I kept from you," Mom says as we separate. She wipes her thumb across the tears on my cheek and tucks my hair behind my ear. "We have so many things to talk about."

"I know. I have so many things to tell you as well."

"And now we have the rest of our lives."

I nod and smile and try to keep myself from crying more.

We stand, and she looks around the room. "Zed," she says. I watch her face closely as it crumples for a moment, unable to figure out whether she's teetering toward pain or anger. But then her expression smooths into a tentative smile. "You did it. You fixed me."

He blinks away the sheen of moisture in his eyes. "I—I didn't know if you'd want me to."

"I know. For a long time, I didn't. And by the time I regretted my decision and wished I could beg you to change me back, I was already too lost inside my own mind."

"So you … you remember it all?" I ask.

She nods slowly. "I think so. Most of it." Her eyes fall on Dash. "Do I know you?" she asks. "And where are we?"

"You don't know me," he tells her, "but I'm a friend of Em's. I assisted in your rescue from the psych hospital. And I've been helping out since then." He gives her one of his charming smiles, but I know him well enough by now to notice a brief wariness in his expression before that smile takes over. "It's a long story. I'm sure Em can fill you in at some point." He doesn't mention he's a guardian, which is probably best. If Mom spent a large portion of her life hating the Guild, she probably wouldn't warm up to someone currently employed by them.

"And this is a new world," Zed adds. "A different one. A world that came into existence when the veil was torn. Do you remember that?"

Mom nods as she walks to the window and looks out.

"The ink-shades—those dark beings out there—aren't safe," I tell her. "If we stay here longer, I'll tell them not to hurt us, but I think we should probably leave soon."

She looks over her shoulder at me. "Your Griffin Ability is incredible."

"You know about it?"

"Ada does. Which means I now know about it too."

"Is she ... talking to you?" I try not to imagine the weirdness of someone else's voice inside my brain.

Mom's expression becomes thoughtful. "Not really. She's angry with me, I think. Ignoring me. But I'm aware of her memories as if they were mine."

"That's so strange."

"Em?" Dash says. "If you don't need me anymore, I should probably go."

"Right. Yes. Of course."

"Can we ... say goodbye?" He motions with his head toward the door. "Out there?"

"Uh, sure." I smile at Mom. "I won't be long." After a hesitant glance at Zed, I follow Dash into the hallway. We walk to the end of it and into a large room furnished with nothing more than curtains. Dash faces me. He starts speaking, and at the same time, I say, "Thank you so much for everything."

We both stop, and he laughs. "You're welcome, Em." He rolls one of the black candles between his palms as his expression turns serious. "Are you sure you can handle things with your mom now? She seems okay, but what if Ada gets out?"

"I think everything will be fine. We've got Zed. He said he'd make sure Ada remained under control until Dani's strong enough on her own. And my Griffin Ability will help. So yeah, don't worry about us. I know you must be anxious to get back to your own life."

"Me, anxious? Never."

I laugh. "Well, anyway, I hope you're not in too much trouble with the Guild when you get back."

He gives me that cocky grin I've become familiar with over the years. "It'll all be fine. The death penalty was brought back especially for Princess Angelica after she tore through the veil, but the next head councilor outlawed it again. The worst I'll get is a lifetime in the Guild's special prison reserved for the worst guardian traitors."

I blink. "You wouldn't seriously land in prison for this, would you?"

"Nah. You know I can charm my way out of anything."

I cross my arms over my chest. "Yeah, I see that worked out really well for you with Roarke."

"Look, if Roarke were a member of the fairer sex, I could totally have talked my way out of that prison."

"Um. I highly doubt that."

He chuckles, rolls the candle some more, and looks everywhere except directly at me. I wonder if he plans to finish what he was saying earlier, or if he thinks now isn't the right time. "Anyway, where will you and your mom go now? I'll need to know where to find you. You know, just in case you want to hang out some time."

"Hang out some time?" I smile. "Yeah, maybe. I'll check my busy schedule and see if I can fit you in somewhere in the next few centuries. And I'm guessing I don't need to tell you where I'll be going, because as long as you're friends with Violet, you can always find me. I mean, once this is gone." My fingers rise to the back of my ear and touch the small circle of metal still stuck to my skin.

"Oh, yeah." Dash's hand rises to the same spot behind his ear. "I need to get mine removed too. Someone at the Guild will be able to do it."

"That's good. I'll have to figure out something else, since visiting the Guild is out of the question for me."

His eyes finally settle on mine. "I have a feeling that if you just *tell* it to remove itself, it will."

"Oh. Yes. Why didn't I think of that?"

"Uh, all of that—" he gestures over his shoulder with his thumb "—might have been distracting you?"

"Yep. I think you're right."

"Well, anyway. I'll see you soon, Em. You should get an amber so we can stay in touch."

I nod. "Okay. Yeah. Hopefully life will be so pleasantly boring from now on that we'll have nothing to talk about." *Except maybe that thing you were about to say before Zed returned to finish the spell.*

"One can only hope." He takes a few steps back, putting some distance between us, and raises the candle. He hesitates. "Ah, what the hell." He lowers his hand, walks right up to me, and kisses me. His soft lips move against mine as one hand slides into my hair and the other, still gripping the candle, presses against my back.

I'm so startled that by the time I realize I'm enjoying it, it's over. I blink as he takes a step back. "Um …"

"There." He grins, then looks down at the ring of green flames that's mysteriously formed around us. The flames vanish an instant later. "Now we'll have something to talk about next time I see you," he says. "And now I can stop torturing myself wondering what it's like to kiss you. Although …" He rubs the back of his neck. "Now I'm probably going to be tortured wishing I could do it again." He laughs and shakes his head. "Sorry, this is weird. I'm usually way cooler around—"

Without giving myself a moment to think about it, I grab a fistful of his shirt, tug him closer, and kiss him again. His lips are parted this time, and his mouth tastes faintly of watermelon. As he tugs me closer, pressing his fingers into my back, shivers of hot and cold race across my skin, and bright light pops beyond my closed eyelids. I'm probably imagining it, but I think something almost … *electric* zaps across my tongue and lips. I pull away from him, look into his bright eyes, and give myself a moment to catch my breath. "You're cooler when you stop trying to be cool."

He swallows, looking completely ruffled, and I like it way more than the cocky, self-assured Dash. "Right." He clears his throat. "Okay. We definitely have something to talk about next time I see you."

I shrug, feigning indifference. "Maybe. I guess we'll see."

His confident smile returns. He lifts my hand and kisses it, keeping his eyes on mine. "Bye, Emmy. Don't miss me too much."

I shove him playfully away. "Dumbass."

"Save me a kiss." He winks as he steps further back and raises the candle.

I shut my eyes against the bright white light. When it fades, I open my eyes to an empty room. I wonder if I should regret acting without thinking, but I don't. A bubble of laughter escapes me. Maybe that kiss meant something big and maybe it didn't, but so what? Ada's glass magic is basically gone. Mom is healthy. No one's trying to lock us up or hurt us or use us, and soon we'll be hidden far from anyone who might want to do those things. *And* I got to kiss a hot guy. Twice.

All of a sudden, life is good.

Well, except for the part where Roarke wants to tear the veil further open instead of allowing the Guild to close the gap. But I can command him not to before Mom and I leave this world. And if somehow he's already gone, then the Guild can stop him. Mom and I don't have to get involved.

With my joy somewhat dampened, I head back for the room at the base of the tower. "And you're sure she's not struggling to get out right now?" Zed asks Mom as I walk in.

"Yes, I'm sure. I could always tell, remember? I'd get kind of twitchy if I was trying to hold her back and she was trying to get out. Like that night at the Punk and Mouse Face concert, remember? But I'm totally fine now." She holds both hands out and looks at them. "See, no shaking."

A slow smile takes the place of Zed's anxious expression. "I can't explain how strange it is to see you like this again. If I try hard enough, I can almost imagine the past seventeen or so years never happened."

Mom's smile is sad. "But they did. And we've both changed."

"I'm so sorry for everything you went through, Dani."

Looking a little confused, she asks, "Were you expecting me to be angry with you?"

"Yes, of course." Zed's brow furrows. "You ended up going crazy because of a spell I cast over you. You *should* be angry with me."

She shakes her head. "I thought *you* would be angry with *me*. I was the one who insisted you do the changeling spell. You never wanted to do it. I thought you'd be shouting 'I told you so!' right now."

"I would never say that to you, Dani."

I edge a little further into the room. It feels rude to interrupt them, but, selfishly, I want my own time with Mom now. Noticing me near the doorway, Mom waves me over. "Anyway, Zed," she says as I reach her side, "I think you and I should probably part ways now."

"Oh. I thought—maybe—"

"Look, our relationship wasn't healthy. I think you know that. So it probably isn't wise if you're around while I'm trying to figure my new life out. Figure *our* new life out," she corrects, smiling at me. "It would just confuse things," she continues, looking at Zed once more. "Don't you agree?"

"I do," he says carefully, his eyes swinging back and forth between Mom and me, "and I'm not asking for the kind of relationship we had before. I'm just worried about you, and I want to help you get back on your feet. There are so many things you don't know anymore. Our world has changed."

"It can't have changed that much. I'll figure things out. And if I really am lost, I'll come find you. Or perhaps catch up with some old friends."

He frowns. "You don't mean …" He pulls his head back slightly. "That group doesn't exist anymore, Dani."

"Not *them*. I had other friends before I took up with those guardian haters. I had other friends before you, Zed. Things will work out." She puts an arm around my shoulders. "Em and I will make our way in the world together."

I smile at her. I thought she'd wake up from the changeling reversal spell a little confused. Or at least in need of some direction. But she appears fairly certain of her thoughts and feelings. It lifts a weight of responsibility off my shoulders. For so much of my life, I've been trying to figure out how I'd take care of Mom one day. I didn't believe until recently that she'd ever be normal again. And now that she is, it's incredibly freeing to realize she's able to take care of herself. And not just herself, but me too, perhaps. She doesn't *look* anything like the person I remember, but Zed was right. She's the same inside. I recognize the way she speaks, and this is the quiet confidence I remember my mother possessing before she began to lose her mind.

Zed, however, doesn't seem convinced. "But what if … what if Ada gets out?"

"Zed, you've restored things to the way they were before. She's the weaker one now. Yes, she might get out on occasion, but it won't be for long. You remember how things were. She couldn't remain separate from me if I didn't want her to."

"Yes, I remember. I'm still worried, though. I'm not saying I want what you and I had before. I'm not asking you for anything. Why don't you just stay with me for a few weeks until we can be certain you're in control? You'll be safe at my place."

Instead of arguing, Mom turns her gaze to me. "Em, what do you think?"

Surprised to be asked my opinion, I take a few moments to formulate my response. I know Zed isn't lying. I know he's only suggesting we stay with him because he's worried about Mom. But I don't think he has anything to be concerned about. More importantly, he doesn't belong in the picture that I—and Mom, it would seem—have of the future. "I appreciate your concern, Zed, but I think Mom and I are fine without you. You've righted some of your wrongs, and I think that's enough."

With a weary sigh, he nods. "Okay. I suppose you've got your Griffin Ability. If Ada gets out, you can tell her not to hurt you or your mother or anyone else. But you know where to find me if you need help, Dani," he says to Mom. "Orangebrush Grove. In case you've forgotten." He crosses to the sideboard and picks up a candle.

He looks at me. "Orangebrush Grove. Tell the faerie paths, and they'll take you there. If you ever need help."

"Thanks." I hope I'll never need his help again, though. Mom and I wouldn't have needed it in the first place if he hadn't messed with our lives to begin with. "Oh," I say, raising my hand to stop him, remembering suddenly that I never asked him the names of my birth parents. But the candle is already lit, and he's gone in a flash of light.

"Did you need something?" Mom asks me.

I turn to face her and realize that everything I need is right here in front of me. "No. It wasn't important. We'll probably see him again some time, so I'll ask him then."

"Maybe," Mom answers. She tilts her head back, lets her eyes slide shut, and breathes in deeply. Then she laughs and focuses on me again. "I can't wait to spend hours and hours just talking, catching up on everything from the past few years."

A wide smile stretches across my face as I watch her. "Where shall we go? We can go *anywhere*, Mom. Anywhere in any world. Or … do you have a home somewhere? From before?"

"I did, but …" She turns slowly on the spot, looking around. "Why don't we stay here? Make this our home."

"What? But … this is hardly a home. It's a half-formed world. A *tiny* half-formed world. And it isn't safe."

"We can make it safe." Her hands clasp my upper arms as she gazes proudly at me. "*You* can make it safe."

"I suppose I can."

"And we can fill it with life. Your power can create almost anything, and my magic can help. In small amounts," she adds with a laugh. "It doesn't matter that it's a small world. It only needs to be big enough for the two of us—and maybe a few other people over time. And you can *tell* it to belong to us, so no one can ever try to take it away." Her hands slide down to grip mine. She swings our arms back and forth between us the way an excited child would. "This will be our home, Em. Our fresh start. What do you think?"

I don't know if it's reckless or stupid, but suddenly I don't care. Mom's enthusiasm is contagious, and the way she says it, it sounds like a perfect idea. "Yes. Okay. Let's do that."

And so, about fifteen minutes later when the color has filled my ruby completely, Mom and I stand at the window together, looking out at our wispy grey surroundings as power fills my voice. "The shadow world is ours. Yours and mine. The Unseelies will never enter this world. The Guild and its members will never enter this world. Only those we give permission to can enter this world. The ink-shade creatures will never attack anyone here. We will be safe."

In the distance, a ripple of magic races along the horizon as my Griffin power rushes out of me, leaving me weak but happy, knowing the shadow world is about to become our home.

PART IV

CHAPTER 38

DASH

The only place Dash wanted to go was home. First, to reassure his mother he hadn't met a horrible end at the hands of the Unseelies, then to send a message to Ryn, and lastly, to enjoy a proper shower and a good sleep. But he knew that after almost a week of unexplained absence, he needed to report to the Guild first. So, with the traveling candle blazing in his hand, he pictured the inside of the Creepy Hollow Guild's entrance room—and that's exactly where he appeared moments later.

The light faded to reveal two guardians with weapons pointed directly at him, probably due to his unorthodox arrival. "Dash?" one of them said, lowering her sword. "You're not dead."

Dash raised both eyebrows. "Nope."

"Is that a candle?" the guy next to her asked, his knives vanishing as he let go of them.

"Yep. No stylus. I had to improvise." Dash headed through the archway—which would scan his wrist markings to determine he wasn't an imposter, and would detect any other dangerous enchantments that might have been placed on him—and into the main foyer. He hastily made his way upstairs. The sooner he explained himself to a Council member, the sooner he could get home. But he expected his report meeting would take a while, so if he could send a message to his mother first, that would be great.

Reaching the open-plan office area he shared with several other junior guardian teams, he rifled through his desk drawers, searching for an old amber. Or perhaps he

461

had a mirror here somewhere. He could make a quick call while on his way to the Councilors' level.

"Dash!" He looked up and saw Jewel across the room. He expected her to run over and hug him, but her delighted expression soon turned to wary confusion. Guilt stirred uncomfortably in his chest. He'd abandoned his team—including one of his best friends—to go on this unofficial mission. Hopefully they'd understand why he did it, once he explained himself, but he still felt bad about whatever worry he'd caused them.

"Dash?" A different voice uttered his name this time, and he turned to the side to see Councilor Delmore walking through the door, accompanied by several senior guardians. "I'm glad to see you've returned safely," she said, though her eyes lacked their usual warmth. "We need to talk."

"Great timing," he said. "I was just about to come looking for a Council member. I have a lot to report."

"Good," she says. "We have a lot to ask you."

"I'm just calling my parents first," Dash added, his fingers finally locating the edge of a mirror in one of his drawers. "They don't know I've returned."

"We'll get a message to your father," Councilor Delmore said. "He's on duty nearby in the forest. Your debriefing is more important."

Dash hesitated for a moment, then moved to walk beside her. He wondered at the presence of the additional guardians who accompanied her, but he told himself there was no reason to be concerned. He assumed they already knew he'd been with the Unseelies—he'd told his mother not to lie about that part seconds before he climbed into the Unseelie carriage—so they were probably here to ensure there wasn't some form of dangerous magic lingering about him.

But a minute later, as he and Councilor Delmore sat across a table from each other in one of the oval conference rooms and six guardians lined up along the wall, his apprehension returned in full force. There was definitely something different about this debriefing.

"I'll get right to the point, Dash. We received correspondence from the Unseelies this morning regarding your unauthorized presence in their court."

"Okay," Dash said with some uncertainty. "But you were already aware of that, weren't you? Didn't my mother inform you straight after I left her studio for the Unseelie Palace?"

"She did."

"I know it wasn't an authorized mission," Dash hurried to explain, "but I couldn't pass up the opportunity. I'd heard the rumors about a new young lady at the palace and the royal family's interest in her. I strongly suspected it was the Griffin Gifted girl, Emerson. I discovered at the last minute that my mother was handing over a dress to one of the Unseelies, so I had to act immediately. There was no time to alert the Guild or make an alternate plan. I'd hoped to correspond with you from there, but the prince took my amber when he discovered I was a guardian. Oh, and this?" Dash tapped the piece of metal behind his ear. "The prince added this special little touch to make sure you couldn't summon me if I was tagged. And then I was thrown into their prison. Which, I might add, we knew nothing about. I think there are plenty of people imprisoned there who shouldn't be. The Guild needs to get involved."

"Well, we'll be sure to look into that," Councilor Delmore said. "But for now, I'm far more concerned about the part of the letter than implied you have inappropriate connections to the Griffin rebels."

Dash's stomach lurched. After a beat of silence, he said, "What? That's insane."

"The Council has reviewed the letter, and we believe we have sufficient cause to question you under the influence of a truth potion."

Crap, crap, crap. Dash tried to keep the alarm from showing on his face. "Woah, seriously?" He laughed her words off in his usual manner. "You're going to believe the Unseelies over me?"

She sighed, leaning back a little and regarding him with an almost apologetic expression. "Dash, I've known you since you began your training here. I don't believe you'd work against us like this. Not for a second. But it would be remiss of us not to be absolutely certain. And the fact that you've been missing for days …" She lifted her hands from her lap and placed them on the table, revealing a tiny bottle in her grip. "We just need to know what's going on. I don't want any unpleasant surprises further down the road."

Dash swallowed, his eyes on the bottle of truth potion. He couldn't refuse. He could only hope that the protective enchantment would keep him from revealing anything too important, and that any other questions would be vague enough for him to avoid giving away too much information. "Well, let's get this over with then," he said, holding his hand out for the bottle. "We've all got work to get back to." He opened the bottle, allowed a few drops to fall onto his tongue, then passed the bottle back. Behind him, he heard the door open and a few more people walked in.

"Councilors," Councilor Delmore said with a nod, and Dash decided not to look over his shoulder to see who, exactly, had joined them. He needed to appear unconcerned. So he leaned back and loosely folded his arms, giving Councilor Delmore an expectant smile. He would feign innocence as long as he possibly could. Across the table, she laced her fingers together and asked her first question: "Are you keeping information from us about the Griffin rebels?"

Damn. There was no avoiding that one. Dash tried to clamp his mouth shut, but he couldn't. He *couldn't*. His answer left his mouth almost as a grunt. "Yes."

Councilor Delmore blinked. In her eyes, Dash saw not only disappointment, but sadness as well. She shook her head and looked away. "Do you know, I didn't actually believe it until this moment."

He wanted to cry out that he wasn't the traitor she thought he was. The Griffin rebels were *good people*. He was doing the right thing by helping them. But he'd only dig himself into a deeper hole, so he bit his lip and remained silent, waiting for the next question.

"What do you know about the Griffin rebels?"

"I … mmm." He pressed his lips tightly together, breathing out sharply as he struggled against the barrage of information that longed to pour free from his mouth. There was certain information he'd never be able to give away, but there were *so many other things*. It was too much. Far too much for one answer. He wouldn't even know where to start, and that—he realized with relief—was what helped him to fight off the potion's influence.

But Councilor Delmore was smarter than that. "Sorry. That was far too broad." She paused, then asked, "Where are the Griffin rebels based?"

"I don't know."

"Are they planning a move against the Guild?"

"No."

"Are they planning to interfere in the veil restoration ceremony?"

Interfere. Focus on interfere, he instructed himself. They weren't planning to interfere. They were only going to watch. He'd suggested it, and he knew they agreed it was a good idea. They would be back-up. Just in case something went—No! Nothing would go wrong. They wouldn't have to interfere. "Nnnnno," he managed to force out.

Councilor Delmore's eyes narrowed. "You didn't sound like you entirely meant that, Dash."

"They don't plan to interfere," he said, the words tumbling quickly from his lips.

She nodded slowly. "I see." Then she asked, with far more emphasis on each word, "Do they plan to be there?"

Dash squeezed his eyes shut, gripped the chair's arms fiercely, and tried with all his might to force the answer down. But it slipped from his mouth anyway. "Yes."

Footsteps sounded behind him as someone moved around the table. Head Councilor Ashlow, with her stiff posture and her unreadable expression. She nodded as she stopped beside Councilor Delmore. "Good. Now we know who it is. This confirms what the Seers have Seen and filled in the specifics that weren't clear to them." She looked across the table. "Thank you for being so helpful, Dash. We'll question you further at another time."

As glittering handcuffs snapped around his wrists and rough hands tugged him to his feet, Dash shut his eyes and let the horrendous guilt at having betrayed his friends sink into him.

CHAPTER 39

Bandit prances from rock to rock across the pool of water I created earlier, leaping from the last rock into the air and landing in my arms as a cat. Mom laughs at him. "He is very sweet. Where did you say you found him?"

"The forest outside Chevalier House. And it would probably be more accurate to say he found me. He's been following me ever since."

"Lovely," Mom says. She leans back in one of the two beach chairs I spoke into existence earlier and looks out at what we've achieved in our first day together: a river that leads away from the rock pool, clouds that change shape, drift across the sky, and never actually disappear, and a new section of the castle. Plus what isn't currently visible: the two wardrobes of normal, court-inappropriate clothing back inside the castle.

My command to the shadow world late last night sapped me entirely of my Griffin power, but I took one of the elixir vials from the backpack and walked to where the portal used to be, planning to command Roarke not to interfere with the veil. I was then going to light a candle and tell it to take him and his guards back to the Unseelie Palace. But I couldn't find him or his men. Perhaps Aurora or some of the Unseelie guards showed up and took them away while we were hiding inside the castle. Or perhaps it had something to do with the command I gave this world about Unseelies not being able to enter. Either way, Mom and I now seem to be the only ones in this world.

So I returned to the castle, where Mom had chosen two bedrooms near each other that were mostly furnished, and prepared one of the beds for me to climb into. I almost cried when I saw it. I decided to blame my emotional state on exhaustion, but I knew the real reason: my mother was finally here to take care of me.

I slept for so long that my Griffin Ability was almost replenished by the time I woke up. After using it for the big things—the river, the clouds, the castle, and telling the dim light in the sky to mimic the day and night of the Unseelie Court—Mom taught me a few things with ordinary magic. Like changing the patterns on our bedspreads, using an organizational spell for all the food we found in the pantry, and getting a cleaning spell going in the kitchen to take care of the dirty dishes left behind by Roarke's guards. And all the while we chatted endlessly. I decided not to go for any of my big-deal questions yet—like 'How could you allow a human to die so you could take over her life?'—choosing to stick to less serious topics until Mom and I get to know each other a little better.

Now we're sitting by our little rock pool drinking something Mom concocted as the light around us gradually grows dimmer. I'd love to watch a real sunset, but I'll have to make do with the enchanted lighting. Perhaps I can add color to it when my Griffin Ability next refuels itself. Or I could use the elixir, but I'd rather save that for emergencies.

As I sit in my comfy chair with Mom right beside me, Bandit on my lap, and a strange yet tasty drink in my hand, my thoughts turn toward Dash. He may have been joking when he said he'd wind up tortured wishing he could kiss me again, but I'm starting to feel a little tortured myself. It's not as though I've never kissed anyone else, but none of the boys in Stanmeade can quite match up to a guy with magic racing through his veins. I've replayed that kiss over and over in my mind, and each time I remember something else that seems sort of … magical. And not in the corny, figurative sense. I mean *actual magic*. The flashing lights I noticed through my closed eyes, the sensation of sparks on my tongue, the hot-cold shiver that didn't quite feel like a normal shiver. Not to mention the flames that briefly encircled us.

Interesting. Very interesting. Like Dash said, we'll definitely have something to talk about the next time we see each other. I probably shouldn't get too attached to the idea of him, though. He might have already moved on to whatever new guardian girls have arrived at the Guild in his absence. It may feel to me like we've created some kind of bond while surviving life and death together, but he's probably experienced the same thing with plenty of other guardian females. Life and death situations are an everyday occurrence for them, right?

"Everything okay?" Mom asks, and I realize she's watching me.

"Yes. Better than okay. Why?"

"You just had this frown on your face, that's all."

"Oh." I make sure I'm smiling instead. "Sorry, I didn't even realize."

"Do you have more questions?" She shakes her head. "I mean, of course you have questions. But is there something in particular you were wondering about right now?"

"Um …" I suppose I could ask her about the magical side-effects of kissing, but I don't feel entirely comfortable about that. Right now, it still feels like something private that I want to keep between Dash and me. So I decide to ask a different question instead. "You said you have Ada's memories of the years since the two of you separated, right?"

"Yes."

"Can I ask you some things?"

"Of course, honey." She turns a little in her chair to face me. "I've been waiting for you to ask more about my Griffin Ability and Ada. I thought you'd be more curious."

"I am curious, I just didn't know if it was something you'd want to talk about."

"Em, I'm happy to talk about anything with you." Her smile crinkles the skin around her strange peach-colored eyes. "No more secrets, okay? I want everything out in the open."

"Okay. So … how did Ada know about this world? I thought it was just a few of the Unseelies and their guards who knew about it."

Mom pauses for a few moments, perhaps digging through Ada's memories to find the answer. "It seems she discovered it by accident, actually. She wanted to, uh … Ugh, this is horrible. She wanted to kill the guardians stationed by the veil tear. But they saw her coming and chased her with magic. She escaped into the faerie paths, but the guardians were so close behind her, she was worried they might actually be able to follow her through. So she stayed inside the paths. Which, in case you don't know, is a difficult thing to do," Mom adds. "And while she was hiding there, she began to notice light in the distance. She thought that was odd, since the faerie paths are supposed to be completely dark, so she followed the light, and she discovered this world. There was a wall and a door, and once she went through it, she found a half-formed castle, and soldiers or guards in the distance. She didn't stay long, but I can tell from her memories that she's been here a few times since, just to see what's going on."

Suspicion has been growing inside me while Mom's been talking. "That's very weird," I say when she's done. "That's almost exactly how Roarke and Aurora discovered this world."

"Oh." Mom tilts her head to the side. "That is strange. I wonder how many other people have also accidentally stumbled into this world, probably not even realizing what it is. It's a good thing you told this world it belongs to us. Now we don't have to worry about random strangers wandering through our home."

"Yeah …" I say, though there's definitely an edge of doubt to my voice. "Wait, but how did Ada know I was here yesterday? She arrived and basically said she came for me."

"She …" Mom screws her eyes shut, then breathes out sharply as she opens them. "She's keeping certain things from me."

"Is that possible?"

"Yes. If she chooses to deliberately not think of certain things, or cover them up by firmly thinking of other things, then it's difficult for me to access her memories."

"Is she … gaining control?"

"No, no. She's just hiding a few things from me."

"Oh. Okay." Nevertheless, my eyes scan Mom's body for signs of twitching. That's what she said to Zed, right? That she used to twitch when she was struggling to maintain control?

"I'm fine, Em, I swear," Mom says, noticing me watching her closely. "And I'll figure out what Ada's hiding. She won't be able to keep things from me for long."

"Okay." I sip my exotic drink and find my mind turning back to the changeling spell. I want to understand why Mom decided it was okay to steal someone's life. She must have known Macy Clarke wouldn't survive the spell. So it was more than stealing, actually. It was *murder*.

I shove away the image of my mother as a murderer. I know that isn't who she is. She was just confused and lost at the time. And maybe she didn't know what would happen. Surely it isn't possible for every faerie to know every spell that exists, so maybe Mom had never heard of a changeling spell. And maybe Zed left out the part about Macy ending up dead. That seems far more likely to me than Mom agreeing to murder.

Movement catches my eye. I look to the side and see Mom holding her glass toward me. I raise mine and clink it against hers, smiling as I force all my doubts to the back of my mind.

By the end of the second day, when Dash hasn't returned yet, I suddenly remember that I told this world no member of the Guild would ever come here. So before I climb into bed, I drink a tiny bit of the Griffin Ability elixir and listen to my oddly distorted voice saying, "Dash Blackhallow is allowed to enter this world."

Then, since there seems to be a little bit of my Griffin power left over, I look down at my feet and tell them they're wearing unicorn slippers. Fluffy white fabric wraps itself around my feet while filling with some kind of padding. Silver wings pop out the sides, a head bulges over my toes, a mane of fuzzy rainbow hair appears, and a gold horn materializes on top of each unicorn head. Peering down in delight at my latest creation, I clap my hands together and laugh. Then I imagine what Val would say if she saw me wearing *unicorn slippers*, of all things, and I laugh harder.

I hurry down the passage to Mom's room and offer to make a pair of unicorn slippers for her too with the last remaining shred of my power. Once her slippers are done, I climb onto her bed. We stretch out our legs so we can wiggle our feet back and forth in front of us as Mom shares stories from her past. I remember Zed mentioning that her life was horrible, but if that was true, she doesn't speak about it. She tells me only the fun things about her childhood. Faerie school, and getting her first stylus, and the rules she loved to break. I'm happy to sit here and fall asleep to the sound of her voice.

My eyes are half-closed when Mom quietly says, "I wasn't sure if I should bring this up, but I meant it when I said I don't want there to be any secrets between us."

I blink, open my eyes fully, and push myself up a little straighter. "Okay. What is it?"

She looks down at her lap. "I know what happened outside Chelsea's home. When Ada came for you. I know you gave me up."

My stomach plummets instantly, weighted down by guilt. "Mom, I'm so sorry. It wasn't like that—"

"I know, honey."

"She was going to kill my new friends. She was going to wipe out the whole of Stanmeade. And the last thing I wanted to do was tell her where you were." I reach for her hand. "I swear, Mom, if my heart could literally have broken, it would have. But I couldn't—"

"I know, Em, I know." She strokes my hair as if I were a small child. "You couldn't let all those people die. You had to choose them over me."

"It wasn't that I was *choosing* them—"

"Sweetie, I know. I understand." She kisses my forehead. "I forgive you."

It should be a relief to hear those words, but I feel even worse. She shouldn't *have* to forgive me. I should never have done something to her that would require forgiveness.

We say goodnight, and with a heavy heart, I return to my bedroom. I pull Bandit closer and snuggle him against my chest, trying to tell myself not to be silly. Mom forgave me, so I should be able to forgive myself too, right? It was an impossible situation. I *had* to choose to save a whole town of people over saving just one, right? Even if that one person was my own mother …

I sit up and walk to the mirror over the dresser. I haven't tried the spell to call anyone, but I know the words. I touch the mirror, thinking of Dash, then immediately withdraw my hand. I doubt he'd want to hear about my troubles. He's probably busy saving someone else's life right now. A damsel in distress. He wouldn't appreciate the interruption.

The only other person I want to talk to is Val, and that's impossible right now. My best friend would have a heart attack if her mirror started talking to her, and I don't know if the spell would even work on an ordinary mirror in the human world. Or if it would work in the shadow world, for that matter. But that doesn't stop me from longing to tell her every single thing that's happened since that horrible night at the party.

I return to bed without attempting to call her. One day I'll go back to Stanmeade and explain my disappearance as best I can, but now isn't the time. I need to focus on the new life Mom and I are building and shove the past far behind us.

CHAPTER 40

By the end of day three, our world is even fuller. I closed up the side of the castle, added some rose bushes and other flowers alongside the river, and spoke a golf cart into being. Mom thought the golf cart was a bit strange, especially in a world of magic, but I thought it would be fun to drive around our land. She reminded me that we have nowhere to plug it in, and I reminded her that we can make it move with magic. Then I used the last bit of my morning's Griffin power to tell two ink-shades to take on the form of dragons as large as Imperia—just to see if they could.

And they did. I bounced up and down with sheer excitement before climbing onto one of them. After I got past the odd sensation of sitting on a cloud of icy air, I flew around and around our little world, only landing when Mom told me to come down and learn how to transform some pillowcases into curtains for our bedrooms.

I wish I could show Dash everything we've done, but he hasn't returned. Totally understandable, I keep reminding myself. He probably has a ton of work to catch up on after being AWOL for days. Still … I kinda miss him.

I walk into the castle's enormous kitchen to help Mom with dinner. "Can I chop these veggies?" I ask, pointing to the pile on the counter beside the stove.

"Yes. Thanks, sweetie. You remember the chopping spell?"

"I think so." I move a few potatoes, carrots, and something that looks like purple celery to another counter, marveling at the simple fact that I can stand in a kitchen with my own mother while we prepare a meal together. I push the veggies aside to make space for my chopping board—and that's when I notice two perfect glass roses in a vase on the windowsill.

My blood chills instantly. "Mom," I say carefully. "What's this?"

"Hmm? Oh, I wanted to add some flowers to the kitchen, but I didn't feel like walking out to the rose bushes by the river. Don't you think the glass ones are pretty?"

Swallowing, I turn slowly to face her. "Did Ada make them? Did you … give her some control so she could do these?"

"What?" Mom's eyes widen. "No, don't be silly. I made those."

"But she's the one with the ability to—"

"Em, honey, she doesn't have a monopoly on glass magic. She can do far more with it than any ordinary faerie, but the rest of us can still make use of simple spells involving glass. And you know I like glass trinkets as much as she does."

"Yes, but … okay." These roses look far from simple to me, but I suppose that's because I'm still new to most magic. "Sorry, I guess my first response is to freak out when I see something I don't expect that's made of glass."

"Understandable," Mom says with a laugh as she turns back to the stove.

"I guess we'll need to go shopping for more food soon," I say. "I thought we could create a veggie garden here, but then I remembered we don't actually have a sun in this world, so that wouldn't work. Oh, and while we're on the topic of no sun, that isn't exactly healthy, is it? We should probably go back into one of the other two worlds at some point just to get some sun."

"Good idea. And you're right about the fresh food too. It won't last much longer."

"Yeah." I'm starting to think that living in this world isn't a viable long-term option, but I decide not to voice that opinion just yet. Mom seemed really keen on the idea, so I'm happy to stay here for now. Maybe until everyone out in the magic realm forgets about me and I don't have to worry about looking over my shoulder wherever I go.

I get the chopping spell started, then wander into the pantry to check out the state of our supplies. "When do you think we should go?" I call to Mom. "To get more food, I mean. And should we go to the human world or the faerie world? Oh, and what about money?" I walk back into the kitchen. "Crap. That could be a problem."

Mom sets up a spoon to stir the pot by itself before facing me. "Em, I was thinking I should go without you. I know you want to see the fae world, but I don't think that's wise at the moment. It isn't safe out there. People are still looking for you."

"I know, but it won't be for long. And we can go to an area I've never been to before, so there's no risk of anyone recognizing me."

"Em." She gives me an indulgent smile. "You know that isn't a good idea. At least not yet. The Guild has other ways of finding people. Rather wait a bit longer until they've begun to worry about other things."

"Um, okay."

"Hey, come here." I cross the kitchen and she puts her arm around my shoulders. "You know I love you, right? You're the most important thing in the world to me. In any world."

"Of course. I love you too. More than anything and anyone." It's still a little weird to say that to someone who doesn't look like my mother anymore, but I still mean the words.

"Good." She rubs her hand up and down my arm. "Then you know I only want to keep you safe."

"Yes, of course. But … you know I've been looking out for myself for a long time, right? I think I'd probably be fine out there now that I've got a better grasp on my magic."

"I'm sure you could, hon, and I know you can take care of yourself. But I've missed out on so many years of taking care of you. Why don't you let me do it for a little while? Let me make up for all the years I didn't—"

"Mom, you don't have to make up for anything. Seriously."

"Em, please. Just let me do this."

After a moment, I give in with a smile. "Sure. Of course." It seems silly to me, but if this will help her feel like my mom again, then cool. I can handle that for a while.

The silence is awkward for a few minutes as we continue preparing dinner, but soon we begin talking about other things. I don't mention the money problem again, but that doesn't mean I don't think about it. What will we do when we need to buy food? I don't particularly want to create money from nothing with my Griffin Ability. It wouldn't be *stealing*, but somehow the idea doesn't feel right either.

The dining room is empty except for the long table Roarke built in here, but Mom and I dragged a few chairs in yesterday from other rooms. I'll get around to furnishing it properly at some point. For now, Mom and I sit next to each other in mismatching chairs, and Bandit sits on the other end of the table in monkey form with a collection of fruit in front of him.

"Your Griffin Ability is already so impressive," Mom says when we're halfway through dinner, "but I wonder what more it could achieve. I think if you had more power—if your base magic levels were higher—you could probably do even greater things."

"Maybe." I finish another mouthful of food, then add, "I thought if I could save up my Griffin Ability's power instead of using it, then once it's replenished a second time, I'll hopefully have twice as much power."

"But that would take so long," Mom says. "It would be a lot faster to draw magic directly from another source."

"Okay. Like what?"

"You know, the way the witches draw power from other beings." She pauses to sip her faerie wine. "I can see exactly how to do it from Ada's memories. I'm sure that would power-up your Griffin Ability much faster."

I laugh at Mom's crazy suggestion. "We can't do that."

"Of course we can." She returns her glass to the table. "We'll find some people who don't matter. Some humans."

I slowly lower my fork, realizing that she might not be joking. "*All* people matter, Mom. Including humans."

"Not the bad ones. There are humans who've done terrible things. We'll look for those ones. Raid a police station or something."

I stare at her for several moments. She continues eating as if nothing is wrong. As if she hasn't just suggested something horrendous. "You're not serious, are you?"

Confusion colors her expression. "Of course I am."

"We can't do that, Mom. Seriously. It's not happening."

It's her turn to lower her cutlery. "I don't understand what the problem is, Em."

"The problem is that we can't *kill* people just to get power."

"Em, we're talking about people who are going to die anyway. You know, people who've been sentenced to death. Their energy may as well be of some use to us before they die."

"I … I can't …"

"I'm sorry, Em, I didn't realize you'd have such a problem with this." She places her hand over mine, and her thumb rubs back and forth across my skin. "We can wait a bit longer until you're okay with it."

I pull my hand away. "I'll never be okay with it."

Her expression slowly becomes stern. "I don't remember you talking back to me like this before."

"Probably because you never suggested we go out and kill people together."

"Em, I'm your mother. You need to trust that I know better than you about certain things."

"I don't think you do, actually."

"Emerson!" Mom smacks her hand down on the table.

Bandit shifts rapidly into a dragon and snarls at her, letting loose a small stream of flames.

"Down!" Mom shouts, sweeping her arm through the air. A flash of sparks swipes him across the face and knocks him backwards. He tumbles off the table, shrinks into a cat as he hits the floor, and whimpers.

"Bandit!" I jump up and rush to end of the table, dropping onto my knees beside him.

"Em, I'm so sorry," Mom says. Her chair scrapes the floor as she rises. "I'm still getting used to having magic again. I don't know my own strength. I didn't mean to hurt him."

Bandit crawls into my hands as a mouse, where he repeatedly licks his front paws and rubs them over his ears. "I think he's okay," I say quietly. I stand and place him inside my hoodie's front pocket. Then I look at Mom.

"I really am sorry, Em. Please come back to the table and finish dinner."

"Yeah," I say quietly, still trying to make sense of the highly unpleasant turn our discussion has taken. "Okay."

I sit and pick up my fork, and Mom says, "I'm sorry I lost my temper. I'm just trying to do what's best for you, and I don't know why you're fighting me on this."

"Because you're talking about mur—"

"We've had horrible lives, both of us. You lived with that awful human sister of Macy Clarke's. And I suffered with the changeling spell tormenting my mind for years. And then I almost ended up unconscious for the rest of my life because—" She cuts herself off, closing her eyes briefly and biting back the words I imagine she wants to say: Because *I* gave up her location to her dangerous other half.

Sickening guilt twists inside me once again as I press my lips together and stare at my remaining dinner. My hand clenches around my fork.

"My point is, Em, that this is our chance to make everything so much better. So you need to stop questioning me. I'm your mother, and I know what's best for both of us. So we're going to increase your power, okay? I'll give you some time to get used to the idea and to understand that it's a totally normal part of our way of life, but then we're doing it. No more arguments, okay?"

I force myself to look up at her and nod. I even manage a small smile and a resigned sigh. But inside, I can't stop shaking.

CHAPTER 41

After cleaning up, I give Mom what I hope is a cheerful smile and tell her I'm going to relax in the pool in my bathroom for a while, now that I've learned a few spells for changing the scent and color of bubbles. But the moment I'm up the first flight of stairs, I run. My feet don't stop pounding the floor until I reach my room. My hands shake as I pull a jacket on over my hoodie and snatch a candle and stylus from the drawer beside my bed. I double-check to make sure Bandit is still in my pocket.

Then I freeze, completely lost for a moment as to where to go or what to do.

Mom wants me to *kill* people? What the freaking hell?

The picture I have in my head of the perfect life the two of us are supposed to have now has suddenly become as brittle as the glass ornaments Mom and Ada love so much. It's balancing on the edge of knife tip. About to fall. About to shatter.

No. Everything will be fine. This is merely … a hiccup. A misunderstanding. Ada's influence, most likely.

With a snap of my fingers, the candle is alight. I close my eyes and concentrate fiercely on the one place I know we can still be happy: the home I grew up in. Number twenty-nine Phipton Way. Bright light flashes beyond my eyelids. As it slowly fades away, peace begins to soothe the shivering fear in my heart. Soon, I'll be home. Soon, everything will be okay.

When I feel solid ground beneath my feet, I open my eyes. I'm standing outside number twenty-nine in dim light that reminds me all too much of the shadow world. The wet road and the smell of damp earth tells me it recently rained. Pushing the remaining piece of the candle into the front pocket of my jeans, I take a step closer to the wooden fence. It's tangled with bushes, just as it was before. More overgrown now than I remember, but that's okay. My heart thumps uncomfortably against my ribcage as I walk toward the pedestrian gate. The crunch of my shoes against the damp road seems overly loud in this quiet neighborhood.

Bandit twitches, climbs out of my pocket, and scurries up my arm to my shoulder. I reach the gate and find its hinges rusted with age. The number twenty-nine painted onto a block of wood and nailed to the gate is so faded I can barely read it, and the wood itself is split in various places. *Not right*, my mind whispers to me. *It isn't supposed to look like this.*

I swallow the painful lump in my throat before stepping forward and pulling the gate open. It screeches on its rusty hinges. Once inside, I look around as my heart continues to sink lower and lower. "This is all wrong, Bandit," I murmur. The setting sun should cast warm light across the garden instead of being hidden behind grey clouds. The grass should be cut short, not growing wildly out of control. The rose bushes should be neatly pruned, not choked to death by weeds. This nightmare of a garden is nothing like the perfect home from my memories.

But then, with slow and horrible clarity, I begin to realize that it never was.

I push my hands through my hair as the rosy memories begin to crack and darkness appears in the gaps. I remember now that it wasn't always sunny, and Mom wasn't always happy. I'd find her outside at night, brandishing a broomstick or garden shears, shouting at no one. She wouldn't come inside, so then I'd start crying. Eventually she would drop her weapon, tug me inside, and lock every door. We'd huddle together, and sometimes she'd cry too, and she'd swear to protect me from the bad guys. The first few times, I was terrified along with her, but I soon grew to realize there was no one there. The things that frightened her existed only in her mind.

I drop my hands to my sides. As if in a daze, I walk back to the gate. I turn and face the house once more, realizing finally that it was never the safe place I thought it was. And it was never *ours*. This was Macy Clarke's home. This was the home Dani stole. This was the *life* Dani stole. This is where the real Macy Clarke and the real Emerson never got the chance to live their lives. The only thing I see when I look at it now is loss and misery.

And I don't ever want to see it again.

My feet turn me around and carry me out through the gate and into the road. I keep walking, though I have no idea where I'm going. I think I want to cry—I feel like I *need* to cry—but I'm too empty even for that. I walk to the end of the road. Then I place my butt down on the hard wet curb and rest my head in my hands.

I must have been in a dream the past few days. A silly happily-ever-after kind of dream that could never exist in real life. How could I have let myself get caught up in it? I should have known better than to believe it. I drag my hands down the sides of my face and try to picture my future now, but where there used to be a solid goal to work toward, there now exists a void where my life should have been. The life Zed took from me when he stole me from my real parents and my real home.

Zed.

I look up as the tiniest glimmer of hope lights the darkness in my heart. Zed stole my life, which makes him the one person who might be able to give it back to me. He doesn't think he can do anything else to fix the mess he made, but he hasn't told me the one thing that could make a difference: who my real family is.

I have no coherent plan. I don't know what I'll do with the information Zed gives me. I don't know what I'll say to Dani when I get back to the shadow world. I can only think of one step at a time. And the current step is this: find Zed and ask him who my real parents are.

I stand and return Bandit to the shelter of my pocket. My sleeve slides back a little, so I check the ruby. I estimate it's about an hour or two away from being fully colored in. I probably should have brought some elixir with me, just in case I need to get out of a sticky situation before returning to the shadow world, but I wasn't exactly thinking clearly when I left the castle.

I pull Aurora's stylus out and remind myself what Zed told us just before he left. Orangebrush Grove, I think. That was all. No street name, no number. *Well, here goes.* I open a faerie paths doorway on the sidewalk. I don't know what to think of, so I try to think of nothing as I slide into the darkness while repeatedly whispering, "Orangebrush Grove, Orangebrush Grove." It almost becomes a tongue twister, but I don't stop saying the words until the darkness begins to melt away around me.

I find myself on a piece of land containing a few scattered houses amidst tall trees, with rolling hills and horse paddocks in the distance and a setting sun bathing the scene in rose-gold warmth. If I'd had the time to formulate some kind of expectation before getting here, this would not have been it.

I approach the nearest house, looking around as I go and seeing no one else. I avoid the front door; I'm not going to knock when I don't know if this is the right house. Instead, I edge around the side and peer in through a half-open window. An unmade bed stands on one side of the room, and clothes are strewn across the floor, but none of it tells me whether this house belongs to Zed or not. I move to the next window, but the living room furniture doesn't give away much either, aside from the fact that it's worn and outdated. I'm about to move on to the next house when I see it: formal Unseelie clothing draped over the back of an armchair. The clothing Zed was wearing when we escaped from the Unseelie Palace.

Yes! I mentally congratulate myself for finding the right house. Then I head back around to the front door and knock. After waiting a few moments, I knock again. When it becomes clear that Zed isn't home, I walk around to the half-open window, hoist myself up, and swing my body inside. Trespassing isn't cool, I guess, but I'm not waiting outside the front door. Not when I have no idea who else lives around here. And why did Zed leave his window open anyway? I thought magical homes had better security than this. Although, now that I think about it, I have no idea if I'm in the magic or non-magic world.

I walk through the bedroom and into the living area. Still wary of the types of neighbors Zed might have, I choose a chair that can't be seen from the window and sit down.

And I wait.

And I try not to think about my mother, because dammit, I don't know what I'm supposed to think anymore. I spent so many years wanting her back the way she used to be, only to discover that that person never actually existed. It was all a facade. She was a faerie pretending to be human. She was two people pretending to be one. And, worst of all, she was pretending to be my mother.

Crap. This *not thinking about her* thing isn't working out well. I lean forward in the chair and dig my fingers into my hair. "Dammit, dammit, dammit," I mutter. Why did someone have to invent a changeling spell in the first place? What a seriously messed-up idea.

Bump.

My head jolts up. I freeze. I'm sure it's only Zed, though. But I wait a few seconds, and no other sound reaches my ears. No door opening, no footsteps. *Holy crap*, I whisper silently to myself. What if someone else is here? What if Dani was right about the Guild having other ways of tracking me down, and now that I've left the shadow world, they've sent someone after me?

I rise silently from the chair, tiptoe across the room, slip behind a curtain, and flatten myself against the wall. My blood rockets through my veins, and my hand moves to the candle in my pocket. How quickly would I be able to light it if someone came into the room? And could I get away before setting the curtain on fire?

Then I hear the sound of a key in a lock. A door opens and closes. Footsteps cross the wooden floor. Surely this must be Zed? But the person or thing that caused the bump must still be in the house somewhere. Or perhaps it was nothing more than a bird or a squirrel or some other animal on the roof. Or maybe it was one of those noises that old houses make sometimes.

I risk moving my head a few inches to the side so I can peek out beyond the curtain. When I see Zed shrugging out of a jacket and tossing it on top of the Unseelie clothes, I almost wilt with relief.

"Don't. Move."

I freeze.

So does Zed.

"Raise your hands," a woman's voice says from the direction of the bedroom.

Again, I don't move an inch. Zed, however, does as he's told. "Who's there?" he asks, twisting his head to the side as he tries to see over his shoulder.

"You're an exceptionally difficult person to find, Zed," the woman says, stopping in the bedroom doorway with a shadow across her upper body and light illuminating a knife in one hand and a throwing star in the other. "I didn't think I'd have this much trouble locating you." She moves fully into the light of the living room, and finally I see who she is.

"Calla," Zed says, turning to face her.

What the actual heck? I demand silently. Even if I wanted to reveal myself right now, I don't think I could. My body is too shocked to move.

"Don't be too hard on yourself," Zed adds. "I've been hidden recently. Magically hidden. Against my will."

"Yes. At the Unseelie Palace."

"You know about that?"

She narrows her golden eyes at him. "Why are you surprised? You know I can find out pretty much any information I want. All it takes is the right illusion."

He nods as he slowly lowers his hands. "True. I guess I'm not surprised that you know exactly where I've been recently. But I am surprised it took you this long to come looking for me. I thought you'd catch up to me years ago. Or, at least, I thought someone from your family would."

Calla crosses the room in about two seconds. Her knife flashes through the air and comes to rest firmly against Zed's neck. "Someone from my family almost did. Someone from my family wanted to rip you to shreds for what you did. I'd be lying if I said I didn't want to do the same thing."

Zed makes no move to get away or fight back. "Then why haven't you?"

Calla steps back. She spins the knife in her hand before pointing it again at Zed. "What did you do to Victoria?"

"I suspect you already know, or you wouldn't have come looking for me after all this time."

"Tell me what you did!" she shouts.

His exhale of breath is slow. He swallows. "A changeling spell."

I watch as her breathing becomes shallow and she slowly lowers her hands to her sides.

"I took the baby and replaced her with a human one," Zed continues. "Victoria grew up in the human world."

"So it's true," Calla whispers, turning slightly away from Zed. Almost in slow motion, she drops onto her knees. Her weapons clatter to the floor beside her as she stares unseeingly past Zed.

"I'm so sorry," he says, showing emotion for the first time since she appeared. "I'm so, so sorry for what I did. But I can show you—"

"Stop talking." Calla takes another shuddering breath, almost a gasp this time. She runs her hands through her hair, then leans forward and presses her palms flat against the floor. "I can't believe it. When I saw the birthmark, I knew. But I wanted to be sure. I had to be sure. She didn't die. All this time … all this time, and she was actually alive."

As she repeats the same thing over and over, I push the curtain aside and step forward. I'm fairly certain—unless Zed is some kind of serial changeling creator— that the baby they're talking about is me. But they still haven't said enough for me to understand who I am and how Calla knew me back then. "Please explain," I say.

Zed whips around to face me. Calla's response is slower. She freezes, her palms still flat on the floor, before slowly raising her head. She stares at me between the golden strands of her hair, her eyes wide and red, her cheeks tear-stained. Then she stands and rushes toward me. Her arms are wrapped around me before I can move away, and she hugs me tightly, crying into my hair. "You're alive, you're alive, you're alive."

"Um …" I don't know what else to say.

"We saw your note, and Vi tried to find you, but she kept seeing a shadowy place she couldn't get to, and we still haven't heard from Dash, and … holy flip, you're ALIVE."

"I … I am. Yes."

"And *you*!" she hisses, lurching away from me suddenly and advancing on Zed. "How could you DO THAT? How could you KILL A HUMAN CHILD?" Her words are punctuated with sparks of magic that fly from her fingers and tongue, striking Zed.

"Hey, I did what I had to in order to stay alive. I didn't—"

"You didn't *what*?" she spits as magic skitters across the floor all around her. "Have a choice? So you decided to go ahead and ruin two families?"

"I made the best of a bad—"

"You COWARD!"

I don't know who moves first, but suddenly they're fighting. Bare fists and blinding sparks, flying furniture and grunts of anger, dodging and ducking and punching. Calla spins around and lands a kick directly in the center of Zed's abdomen. He crashes to the ground. She grabs a chair, swings it toward him as he tries to get up, and whacks him solidly across the head.

He slumps to the floor and doesn't move.

"I've been wanting to do that for years," she breathes as she lowers the chair. Then she twists around and pulls me into another hug. It only lasts a few seconds, though, before she pulls away from me, wipes at a few stray tears on her cheeks, and smiles. "I'm sorry. You must have so many questions."

"Only one, really," I say in a shaky voice. "Who the hell am I?"

Her smile stretches even wider. "You are Victoria Larkenwood. Violet and Ryn's daughter."

CHAPTER 42

I have to repeat the words several times in my head before they can begin making even the tiniest bit of sense. Calla is saying something, and I'm staring dumbly at her, and still the words are trying to sink their way into my brain.

Victoria Larkenwood. Violet and Ryn's daughter.

I have parents. I have a brother. I have an aunt who's once again hugging me tightly. And the weirdest part is that I've met them all already. I've talked with them, shared meals with them, tried to figure out my past with them, and not once did I ever imagine I might belong to them. I'm probably supposed to be happy. Overjoyed. But I'm too stunned to feel much of anything.

Except … sick?

I pull away from Calla and press one hand against my stomach. "Em?" she says. "What's wrong?"

"I feel … squeezed? I think?" I double over as nausea overwhelms me. Dizziness spins my brain around. I throw my arm out to steady myself against something.

"Em, what is it?" Calla catches hold of my hand. "Oh … shoot."

"Dizzy …" I manage to mumble.

"I think someone's using a summoning spell on you."

"Everything is … pressing in on me."

"Resist," she instructs. "It's a difficult spell to get right. You can resist it. Just be strong. Root your mind and body firmly here. *Resist*, Em!" Her hand tightens around mine.

Then everything goes dark and I'm squished, squeezed, and tossed around through nothingness. The force pressing in on my body is almost unbearable. Just when I think I'm about to explode, the pressure releases. Everything finally stops moving and the nausea begins to ease—but Calla's grip on my hand is gone. She isn't here.

And where is 'here'?

I'm kneeling on the ground, my hands pressed into grey grass. Tendrils of inky blackness rise between my fingers, giving me my answer: I'm back in the shadow world. I pat my front pocket—but Bandit isn't there. "No!" I whisper. If that summoning spell did something to him, I'm going to have to hurt the person who cast it. I push myself to my feet and turn around—and find myself faced with dozens upon dozens of men and women in Unseelie uniforms.

My heart jolts. I take a step back.

Unseelies. In my shadow world. How did they get here?

"Em, I see you decided to take a little trip." My eyes dart to the side at the sound of Dani's voice. "Let's make sure you can't do that again." My hip is tugged forward as the candle flies from my pocket. I steady myself. Then, looking up, I see Dani raise her hand toward me—

Flames fly across the ground, racing to form a blazing circle around me. I shy away from it, but I have nowhere to go. Then a glistening ripple rushes through the air, forming a layer just inside the fire circle. The indistinct ripple spreads upward, enclosing me completely in a hemisphere. She's imprisoning me in magic.

But on the other side of the magic layer and the waist-high flames, Dani looks confused. She narrows her eyes at me. "When did you learn a shield spell?"

I blink at her as something suddenly becomes painfully obvious. "When did Ada become the one in control?"

She cocks her head. "Really, Em? Are you that stupid? I've been in control since the moment I woke up from Zed's reversal spell."

"But … it was my mother—it was Dani who—"

"What, you think I can't act? You think I can't pretend to be exactly like her after sharing my body with her for most of my life?" She stands a few feet away with her hands on her hips and light flickering across her face. In her jeans and shirt, it's difficult to imagine her as the deadly glass faerie in the silver cloak and black mask. But it's her, no matter what she looks like now. "You're an idiot, Em. An idiot for believing Dani would ever be strong enough to take control of our body after we merged again. She's so weak, I can't even hear her. She may as well be dead. And since I'm the one in control now, she'll never be able to use her Griffin Ability again. She'll never be able to force us to split."

"If you're so brilliant at acting like her," I say bitterly, "then perhaps you shouldn't have suggested that our mother-daughter bonding include *killing people.*"

Ada rolls her eyes. "If you knew Dani as well as I do, you'd know that she'd be just as likely to suggest using an insignificant human to gain power. But you don't, Em. You've never known what she's really like."

"But *you* should have known *me*," I tell her. "I grew up in that world. Did you really think I'd be happy killing one of its inhabitants? *You're* the idiot, Ada."

She shrugs. "Yeah. I'm the idiot with an Unseelie army on my side."

I look out at them again, fear tightening my stomach. "It shouldn't be possible," I murmur, trying to fathom how they can be here. "I said they would never enter this world."

"Yes, but you also made the mistake of saying this world belonged to me as much as it does to you. So I gave the Unseelies permission to enter. As easy as that." She twists her hand in the air, and a small sandstorm attacks the shield layer. I duck down, but the shield remains intact. "Impressive," Ada says. "You clearly forgot to mention you learned how to cast a shield."

I say nothing as I straighten. I have no idea where the shield layer came from, but I'm not complaining about it as long as it separates me from Ada and the soldiers behind her—and the heat of the flames. "You should hate the Unseelies, shouldn't you? Zed said you guys were tortured by a former Unseelie Prince. So why would you bring them here?"

"Come on, Em. I can't hold an entire family responsible for one prince who decided to go rogue and build an army to take power for himself. That would be unfair of me. The people I *do* hate, however, are guardians. There are plenty I still need to get rid of, and that kind of thing is easier when you have friends to help you. Ah, and there he is," she adds, looking past me. "One of my newest friends."

"Guardians are gathering at Velazar II," a voice says from behind me. A voice I've come to hate. "They'll be starting the ceremony soon. Ah, you retrieved Emerson. Well done." Roarke strides past the fire circle and stops beside Ada. And with him is—

"Clarina?" I say.

Still in her handmaid's uniform, Clarina folds her arms across her chest and stares directly at me. "I think I'm enjoying this shocked expression I keep seeing on people's faces. Aurora, these men and women behind us, and now you. It almost makes all the years of waiting worth it." Her voice is devoid of its usual respect. I realize abruptly that this is the woman I overheard in Roarke's bedroom.

"Wow," I say, shifting my attention to Roarke. "I didn't take you for someone who'd fall in love with a lady's maid."

Roarke snorts. "Clarina isn't a lady's maid. She's a spy. *My* spy."

"And I am, in fact, of noble birth," Clarina adds.

"Ah, well that makes sense then. A prince of the Unseelies would never shack up with the hired help." I look at her, thinking of all the times she's seen Roarke and me together. Not once did she seem upset, even when she caught us kissing. "You're a good actress. I'll give you that, at least."

"I'm a *very* good actress," she corrects. "And now the pretense is finally paying off."

"Why? What was the point?" I look at Roarke. "Who were you spying on?"

He smiles. "Everyone."

"Where's Aurora?" I ask, suddenly realizing I haven't seen her since the night she warned me about Roarke's plans. "Is she also—"

"It's none of your business, actually," Roarke continues, "and we have more important things to do now than tell stories. I would take you with us, Emerson—I suspect your Griffin Ability might actually be powerful enough to tear the veil open further—but I can't risk losing you to the Guild. I might never get you back, and you'll be worth more to me in the future than you would be today."

"And why bother with Em when you have me?" Ada adds. "I've gathered far more power than she'll probably ever have."

"That's true. For now, at least." Roarke breathes in deeply. "Okay, get rid of that shield of hers," he says to Ada, "then hand her over to Clarina. She knows where to lock her up."

"With pleasure," Ada answers, raising both hands. Behind her, several soldiers do the same. I duck down again as hundreds of stones bombard the shield. Within seconds, the rippling shield magic vanishes with a flash. Heat sears the air around me. I carefully raise my head enough to peer over the top of the flames, already planning my escape route.

"Where the hell is she?" Roarke yells, his eyes sliding past me.

What? I look down, but as far as I can tell, I'm still visible.

"Dammit, where did she go?" he shouts, walking right up to the circle. Is this world protecting me, perhaps? Because I told it I'd be safe here? I don't know, but I'm not wasting this opportunity. Turning away from Roarke, I bend my knees, then kick off the ground with as much force as I can muster. My knees come up to my chest as I sail across the fire circle, clearing the ring of dancing flames. I hit the ground with both feet and straighten immediately. Then, with no candle to get me out of here, I take off in the direction of the wall that conceals the veil tear.

"Find her!" Roarke shouts. "And the rest of you, follow me to Velazar."

Crap. That's the same way I'm going. A glance over my shoulder tells me the soldiers aren't marching slowly; they're running. And Roarke and Ada are rising into the air on the back of my ink-shade dragons!

Anger flashes through my chest. *Those are mine!* I want to shout at them. But I need to get to Velazar before they do, so I force my legs to move as fast as I know they can. Roarke may have forgotten what time of night it is, but I haven't. My Griffin Ability is almost ready to be used, and if Roarke thinks my magic is powerful enough to open the veil further, then it must be powerful enough to close it. All I need to do is hide somewhere and say the right words as soon as I'm able to, and I could save countless lives on both sides of the veil.

An unexpected thrill races through me, along with the terrifying thought that I might be edging near hero territory. If I had enough breath left in my lungs, I'd probably laugh at myself. Does it count as being a hero if you hide while you're saving the world? I don't think so. I think it just counts as doing the right thing.

With ink-shades streaming past me on both sides, I push myself faster than I've ever run before. I slow a little as I reach the wall and veer to the side so I'm running along it. When I reach the door, I tug it open, run through, and slam it shut. Then I face the great big gap in the sky, my lungs burning as I gasp for air. As I stop near the edge of the opening, I see figures in black, some lined up, others walking around. While it's almost midnight in the shadow world—at least, the enchanted version of midnight—it looks like late afternoon over Velazar II Island.

Hoping that I'm still somehow invisible to everyone else, I step quickly onto the monument, swing myself around the trident, and jump to the ground behind it. I crouch down, listening carefully through my heavy breaths. When I don't hear any shouts or hurried footsteps coming my way, I relax a tiny bit.

"Don't scream," a voice says right beside me.

I can't help my involuntary gasp as Calla appears out of thin air right beside me. "What—where did you—"

"I've been with you since you were summoned," she whispers. "I masked myself with invisibility."

"So—the shield was yours? And now, when they couldn't see me ..."

"Yes, that was me. Sorry I didn't conceal you sooner. I needed to find out what was going on, so I shielded you instead, hoping they'd tell you something useful. And they did." She leans a little to the side and looks past the monument. "I need to warn the others."

"Others?"

"Yeah, they're here somewhere, watching. Keeping an eye on things."

"Violet and Ryn are here?"

Calla looks at me. She places her hand on my shoulder and squeezes it. "Yes. And we're all going to get out of this alive. You'll get your family reunion, okay? I'll make sure of it."

"Before we begin," a voice shouts out, "there is an important matter we need to take care of." I lean far enough to the side to catch a glimpse of the person standing in front of the monument addressing everyone. I recognize her as the woman who came to Chevalier House to take me away after I revealed my Griffin Ability to everyone there. Head Councilor Ashlow. She nods toward someone I can't see—

And then the strangest thing floats into view just in front of her: a chair with a man securely tied to it. And though he's facing away from us, I can see enough of the side of his face to recognize him.

Dash.

CHAPTER 43

"Griffin Gifted rebels," Councilor Ashlow shouts in a magically magnified voice, "we know you're hiding here watching us. We know that Dash Blackhallow has been working with you. And if you don't hand yourselves over to us now, we will kill him."

I clap one hand over my mouth. Calla's grip on my shoulder tightens.

"You have two minutes," Councilor Ashlow adds. "Then we will carry out the execution."

"How can they do that?" I demand in a low voice. "Surely that's against the law, even for people who *make* the laws."

"They're desperate," Calla says darkly. "They're so afraid of us that it seems they'll do anything these days to apprehend us." She pulls her head back behind the monument, adding, "Chase needs to be here." She retrieves her amber and stylus, scribbles a few words, then returns both to her pocket. "Okay, I need to help the others. And you need to get away from here. Do you have a stylus?"

"I—yes, I do, actually."

"Open a doorway and get yourself back to safety."

"But I can help—"

"No. I refuse to lose you again, do you understand me? If Ryn and Vi were hiding here with us instead of somewhere else on the island, they'd say the same thing."

"But my Griffin Ability can—"

"No, Em. I mean it. We can stop Roarke and his soldiers without you. His army isn't that big. It's nowhere near the size of the entire Unseelie army. And you are too important to us."

I know there's no time to argue, so I don't. I nod, even though I have no intention of leaving this place. If Roarke tears the veil further open and this island is consumed, the majority of the family I have left will die. There's no way I'm letting that happen when I know I can stop it with only a few words.

"Okay." She gives me a brief hug. "See you when it's over." Then she vanishes. I don't hear her footsteps, but, looking closely at the rocky ground surrounding the monument, I see small pebbles moving here and there as she walks away.

Since I'm not leaving the island, I should probably find a better place to hide than right behind the monument the Unseelies will be targeting the moment they get here—which, now that I think about it, should have happened already. Where are they? Those soldiers were moving almost as fast as I was, and the ink-shades can be quick when they want to be.

I look around. The closest form of cover is a collection of rocks a short distance away. The only problem? I'll almost certainly be spotted as I run toward it.

"Is no one interested in saving the life of this young man?" Councilor Ashlow shouts. She waits another few seconds. "No? Well then. I guess we'll get started with both the execution spell and the veil restoration spell."

Several guardians form a tight ring around Dash while another few climb onto the cylindrical base of the monument. I can no longer see what's happening to Dash, but I tell myself not to panic. Calla won't let anything happen to him. Neither will any of the other Griffin rebels. They must have a plan.

I throw my hands out as the ground suddenly shudders beneath me. I push myself a little further away from the monument and look up. The gap in the veil is difficult to see from this angle, since it's almost directly above me, but I think the edges are beginning to move.

A loud cry makes me look around the side of the monument again. *Not Dash, not Dash*, I plead. But it's Councilor Ashlow, flat on the ground with blood seeping from her shoulder. Guardians rush to her side, while others raise their weapons toward the slowly diminishing gap. And then, with a cacophony of whoops and roars that chills my blood, the Unseelies leap through the tear into this world, brandishing their weapons.

Chaos follows, and in the midst of it, I jump up and run to the rocks, hoping like hell that no one notices me. I drop down behind the rocks and press my back against them. I look up and around, but I don't see any ink-shade dragons. They must have remained in the shadow world. My gaze drops then to the ruby, but its color isn't quite full yet. So I press my hands against my ears, trying to drown out the clash and clang of blades, the roar of wind, the shouts of men and women. *Come on, come on, come on*, I silently urge, as if that might possibly help my Griffin Ability replenish faster.

"Stop her!" Someone's voice rises above the noise. "STOP HER!"

I risk a glance around the side of the rock and see a woman—Ada—racing for the monument with glass slivers streaming from her fingertips. And Ryn, sprinting just behind her, expertly dodging the glass. *No!* I want to scream. *Don't touch her!* He lunges for her, brings her crashing to the ground, and she kicks him in the face and scrambles away—which I'm almost thankful for because it means she hasn't turned him to glass. Ada throws herself forward, grabs hold of the edge of the monument, and the entire thing becomes gleaming, faceted glass. She pulls herself up and gives the monument a good kick accompanied by a flash of magic. A crack zigzags all the way through the monument. Then she dances away from it, glass shards raining down from her fingers and rushing to form a glass wall. I suck in a gasp as Ryn rolls out of the way just in time. He leaps to his feet just as the monument shatters into thousands of glass pieces on the other side of Ada's wall.

I look up. My stomach turns. The gash in the sky is now growing larger instead of smaller. I see the field on the other side, and it seems to roll toward us as both worlds are consumed by the shadow world. I grasp my wrist and look down, but the darn ruby is still missing a fraction of color. "Dammit!" I moan, tears of frustration welling in my eyes. "Just *hurry up!*"

With my hands tugging uselessly at my hair, and almost everyone else on the island still fighting each other, I watch the hole in the sky widening and moving closer. It reaches Ada's glass wall—and it stops. "What the …" I mumble breathlessly. I don't understand why. The monument had ancient power or something, but Ada's glass wall has … what? The power of all the people whose energy she's consumed recently?

My momentary relief vanishes when I realize the human world is still being consumed. Our world is fine, but the other one still seems to be slowly rolling toward us. The field is gone now, and then the road, taking two people with it. Then another field, and a tractor with a man on it, and the side of a building—

I can't look. I pull my head back behind the rock, hating myself for being such a failure. I have *so much power*, yet I can't do a damn thing right now. I grit my teeth and clench my fists and try not to count every second that passes. Time goes on. And on. And on.

Then finally—*finally*—that familiar tingle radiates throughout my body. My eyes close for a moment, forcing tears down my cheeks as I relax for the final few seconds it takes for my power to reach my voice. Then I twist around to look at the veil. I don't shout anything out. I don't move any further away from the rock. I simply focus fully on that rapidly increasing gash in the sky and say, "Stop growing bigger. Start closing instead. Close completely so that the veil is fully restored."

I slump sideways against the rock as my power rushes out of me to do my bidding. All of it in one go. Dizziness wraps around me, but it lasts only a few seconds. The fighting pauses. The island becomes almost quiet. We watch as the edges of the tear move rapidly toward each other. They meet, light flashes in a jagged line, and then it's over, leaving no sign that there was ever any imperfection in the sky.

It's done.

I did it.

I experience a single moment of satisfaction before noise assaults my ears once more. I look further past the rock and realize that despite having succeeded at something so huge, my world is about to shatter anyway. Because everyone is fighting with renewed fervor instead of retreating, and near the edge of the island, Ada's got a circle of glass enclosing Dash. And beside him, standing back to back with glittering weapons raised, are Violet and Ryn.

No no no no no. I press my hands against my cheeks, searching the battle for the other people I know. Where are Calla and Chase? Or any of the other rebels I met? There must be more of them here. But there are so many people, so many weapons, so much magic flying around. How the hell does anyone know what's going on? And why doesn't anyone seem to care that the veil is now *closed*, dammit!

Then I notice the other movement inside Ada's glass circle, and my anxiety ratchets up a notch. *What the heck is that?* They look like the people I've seen Ada transform into glass statues, except they're moving. She must have *animated* her statues instead of shattering them. And I see at least seven—eight—inside the glass circle with Violet, Ryn and Dash. Dash is free of his bonds, so at least he can fight, but the glass statues seem, oddly enough, just as quick as if they were made of flesh. They dodge the glittering weapons and block the magic hurled at them.

Ada pumps her fist in the air, as if she's cheering them on. As if this is a game. Then, because it probably is a game to her, she waves her fingers through the air in a graceful motion. As I watch, the jagged glass circle begins splintering inwards, growing rapidly smaller.

Crapping hell. I'm not hiding any longer. I launch up from behind the rock and bolt past the fighting toward the edge of the island. The glass circle reaches the first statue and crunches it to pieces. The other statues edge closer to the center, where Ryn, Vi and Dash slice through the air with their weapons and spin and throw their magic. They manage to shatter one of the statues, and then another. They could probably knock each one down almost instantly in hand-to-hand combat, but I can tell none of them wants to risk touching Ada's glass.

The circle grows smaller, and Ada's grin grows more twisted, even as she watches another one of her own statues taken down by the encroaching edge of her circle. "Stop!" I scream as I get closer to them. "Ada, stop!" She cocks her head to the side, then turns enough to look at me. Her magic, however, doesn't change. "Ada, please," I gasp, slowing down and hoping to appeal to whatever part of Dani is left inside their body. The only part that might still care about me. "Stop, please!" I shout again. "They're my parents!"

I come to a halt a few paces away from Ada, my chest heaving as I catch my breath, my words still ringing in my ears. In the center of the circle, Violet and Ryn stop fighting. Their eyes lock onto me, and on their faces I see ... blank shock.

A solid glass arm swings toward them. Dash jumps forward, brings his sword down, and slices clear through the statue's arm. At the same time, Ada charges at me. Her magic lashes out, slapping me across the face and knocking me sideways. My knees and palms scream out at me as I land hard on the ground. Hands grip my shoulders and shove me over onto my back. The next thing I know, Ada's leaning over me, both hands around my neck. "Are you kidding me? You tell me that those guardians are your parents, and you expect me to *stop* attacking them? How stupid are you?" She squeezes harder. "Those are the two people who left us to suffer at Prince Marzell's hands. Now I *definitely* want to make them suf—Argh!"

Her hands disappear from around my neck. She twists to the side, and as I cough and gasp for air, I see a glowing arrow protruding from her shoulder. "Damn guardians," Ada hisses, looking behind her. I push myself up and follow her gaze. At the center of the glass circle I see Violet—my mother—with a fierce expression on her face, and her bow and another arrow pointed straight at Ada.

Ada rolls instantly away from me, and I duck down too, just in case Vi lets that arrow go. I'm about to scramble back toward the circle when something grabs onto my ankle and drags me back. "Where do you think you're off to?" Ada asks. The arrow is gone from her shoulder, which means she must have somehow ripped it free herself. "I'm not done with you. And don't—" she adds, grabbing my jaw and forcing me to face her "—worry about your parents. My glass guardians are making sure to inflict as much pain as they can."

I swat her hand away, then swing my arm around and punch her face as hard as I can—which probably hurt me as much as it hurt her, but was worth it to see the look on her face.

"Oh, you little—"

"Get the hell off me!" I yell at her, kicking with both my feet. She slides a little further away from me toward the edge of the island, and by the time she sits up again, I've got the smallest glimmer of magic zapping back and forth between my hands.

She laughs at me, which I suppose is warranted. "What are you going to do with that, Em? Tickle me? Because that's about the only thing such a pathetic amount of magic can achieve."

I imagine digging down deep to wherever my core of magic is, and pulling it free. More and more and more. It doesn't seem to make much difference, but *any* difference is better than none.

"You know what, Em?" Ada says, unconcerned by whatever power I'm gathering between my palms. "I don't particularly care if you survive this battle or not. The prince asked me to retrieve you, so I did. But he isn't watching right now, so I can easily say it was someone else who did it when I bring your dead body back to him in multiple pieces."

"You're sick."

"Nope, just looking out for myself. Something I'm sure you can identify with."

"Not like this." Behind her in the sky, I notice strange ovoid shapes moving toward us. Shapes that look like they have people inside them. *Crap.* Who do we have to fight off now?

"He wants us both to use our powers for him, did you know that?" Ada says. "And while that might be a great idea for him, I don't see that working out so well for me. I wouldn't want to have to compete to be the favorite weapon, you know? So." She stands up and shoots a stream of glass at me. I scoot to the side, and it narrowly misses me. "While I like this kind of game, I think we should probably bring it to a—"

I hurl everything I've got at her. It's pathetic, probably not even enough to stun her, but it knocks her down, spins her over twice—and rolls her clear off the edge of the island.

"Holy crap," I gasp. "Crap, crap, crap." I push myself up and rush to the edge. Far below, I can just make out the white bubbles from the splash where she must have landed. Is she dead? Or is this another thing a faerie can easily survive? And why the hell do I care when *she just tried to kill me*?

I turn and race back toward the only people who matter now: Vi, Ryn and Dash, who are—where? I skid to a halt. A pile of shattered glass sits in the middle of the enclosing circle. Hell, if they're part of that pile of glass, I might have to—

"Em!" Violet shouts my name from the other side of the circle, where she and Ryn are fighting off another three glass statues. I take off toward them—

And I'm knocked to the side by a bright bolt of magic.

Moments later, darkness clears from the edges of my vision. I find myself face-down on the ground, horrendous pain burning my side. I manage to roll over and sit up. My hand comes away from my side covered in blood, but I try not to panic. *Faeries can heal easily*, I remind myself. *This is totally fine.*

"Emerson!" someone screams.

I look around. The ovoid shapes I saw in the air have landed on the island. They remind me a little of the prison cell spheres, although the glass isn't as dark, and there are no bars anywhere. On one side, I notice a gold emblem I might possibly have seen on uniforms at the Guild.

"Em!" someone shouts again. Amidst the chaos of Unseelies and guardians running everywhere, I finally see them: Violet and Ryn, their hands and feet bound, being tossed into one of these ovoids. Dash, similarly restrained, is already inside.

"No," I mumble, managing to get to my feet. I stagger a few paces toward them. "No. Let them go." I raise my voice. "Let them go!"

The side of the ovoid closes up, and it rises a few feet above the ground. "No, stop. Stop!" I shout, pressing one hand against my wound and moving more quickly toward the vehicle. It skims above the ground, gaining speed, and then it's off the island, gliding away from me, and the last I see of my parents is their faces pressed against the glass as they shout words I can't hear.

I drop onto my knees. I strike the ground with one fist and let out a furious cry. "Come back!" I yell. Anger, desperation and a heartbroken sob mingle together, making my voice crack as I scream even louder: "COME BACK!"

Hands grab hold of me, and that voice I hate so much speaks into my ear. "Time to return to our shadow world, my dear. Wouldn't want the guardians getting their grubby hands on you."

"NO!" I thrash against Roarke. Then my head jolts forward abruptly. Sickening pain radiates through my skull, and—

Darkness.

CHAPTER 44

I wake in a room covered entirely in padding. The floor, the walls, even the ceiling. It's probably Roarke's idea of a sick joke, given the type of institution my mother—nope, not my mother. *Dani*—spent the past five years in. Either that or he honestly thinks I'm so depressed about the current state of my life that I'm planning to hurt myself by ramming into walls.

He wouldn't be entirely wrong there.

Not about the wall-ramming part. That would be excessive. But the depressed part isn't far off. The same thoughts have been tormenting me since the moment I woke up. The same images. Vi and Ryn's shock when I shouted, 'They're my parents!' Their bodies pressed against the glass as that oval-shaped vehicle carried them away. Their silent shouts.

I saved the veil, but I couldn't save my own family. That's how messed up my magic is. I have a super powerful Griffin Ability, but when I can't use it, I'm essentially useless. I keep thinking of all the ways things might have ended differently for us if I knew what to do with my own magic. I could have attacked Ada from a distance. I could have helped to fight the glass statues. I could have protected someone with a shield while they fought someone else. I might, at this very moment, have been sitting with my family in the oasis, finally reunited after almost eighteen years.

I also can't help thinking about how things would have turned out if I *hadn't* been there. I wouldn't have distracted Violet and Ryn. They might have fought their way past the glass statues sooner. They wouldn't have been so worried about what was happening to me that they let themselves get caught by the Guild. They'd probably be back at the oasis by now, and hopefully Dash would be with them.

Although, if I hadn't been at Velazar today, what would have happened to the widening gap in the veil?

And of course, there's the continual guilt regarding my mother. Dani. The person who became so weak she's now locked inside the body she has to share. She isn't the innocent person I always believed her to be, but I don't think she's anything like Ada either. If I'd had the chance, I could have commanded them each to have their own bodies. She and I could have had a second chance to get to know each other. Instead I pushed her over the edge of an island floating high up in the sky.

I might possibly have killed her.

And then there's Dash. Dash who only ever wanted to help me. Who ended up in trouble because he braved the Unseelie Court to come and get me out. Who is now a guild prisoner just like my parents. I want to see him almost as badly as I want to see Violet and Ryn.

And Bandit! Where is my Bandit?

I tilt my head back against the padded wall, screw my eyes shut, and let my tears fall. What an absolute mess I've made.

A bang on my cell door interrupts my crying. I wipe my hands quickly across my cheeks and stand. The padded door swings open and Roarke walks in. My hatred of him rears its ugly head instantly. I almost lunge at him, but then I notice the slight shimmer in the air that tells me he's placed a shield between us.

"I trust your wound has healed?" he asks.

I nod. Barely a hint of a scar marked my skin by the time I woke up earlier. Now, two or three hours later, even the faint scar is gone. I sniff and ask, "Where am I?"

"The shadow world, of course. I told you about these underground passages, didn't I? Though I probably chose not to mention the prison cells."

"I wonder why," I say, my voice weighted with sarcasm. "So, what are you doing here in my lovely cell? Got any more marriage proposals for me?"

"No. That plan always hinged on your complete willingness. It would never work now. I'll marry Clarina, which was always my ultimate intention. We needn't wait any longer, now that we've relocated to this world."

"You've relocated? Officially? But this world belongs to me, not you. I claimed it."

Roarke looks almost amused. "You're in a prison cell, and I'm in control. The necessary rituals still need to be performed, but for all intents and purposes, this world is already mine."

I cross my arms. "Your father must be thrilled about that."

"Not particularly. But I'm not here to talk about my family. I'm here to talk about yours."

"Where's Aurora? She said she didn't want to choose sides, but I assume she'll have to now."

Roarke's composure flickers for a second. "More specifically," he continues, ignoring my interruption, "I'm here to talk about what an enormous disappointment it must have been for you to discover what kind of person your mother really is. You—"

"*Is?* So she's still alive?"

Roarke's narrowed eyes tell me he doesn't appreciate being interrupted again. "We'll find out soon enough, I suppose. But either way, you must feel so lost now, when your life's purpose has always been to return your mother to exactly the way you remember her." He takes a few steps closer to the magic layer that divides us. "You need a new purpose, Emerson. And I would love to give you one."

"You can take your new purpose and shove it up your—"

"Let me remind you," he says, speaking over me, "that you have nothing else left."

"I have a family. I have real parents who—"

"Who are probably being executed by the Guild as we speak."

"Liar!" I walk right up to the shield layer and ball my hands into fists as I stare defiantly back at him. "The death penalty doesn't exist anymore."

"True, but the Guild has been known to make exceptions. And, given how they feel about these Griffin Gifted rebels who've evaded them for years, I'm almost certain this will be one of those exceptions." He folds his hands neatly together. "The Guild will kill them. Then they'll find the rest of your Griffin rebel friends and lock them up. You will have no one and nothing. All you will know is the inside of this cell. And when you are finally broken, Emerson, then we can start again. We can build you a new life with a new purpose. One that involves serving me."

"Yeah, and pigs might fly."

He smiles. "Well, there's always compulsion potion if you insist on being difficult. I'll make sure your first compulsion command includes telling pigs to fly." And with that, he walks out of the room.

I return to the wall, slide down against it, and pound the padded floor with my fists a few times. But my anger dissipates quickly, my misery returning to take its place.

"Don't scream."

"Holy CRAP!" I gasp, my heart thundering instantly in my chest. I look across the room at Calla leaning against the wall. "What are you … are you real?" I wouldn't put it past Roarke to play magical mind games with me.

"Of course I'm real," she says in a low voice. "I followed you and Roarke back here from Velazar Island. I've been waiting outside your cell for hours. I came in when he opened the door."

I push myself hurriedly to my feet. With my emotions so close to the surface, I can't help the words that tumble from my mouth: "The Guild took them. They took Ryn and Vi, and I never—I didn't get to speak to them—or … or even touch them. I tried so hard to get Ada away from them, and then they were gone. And Dash said the Guild has a special prison for the worst traitors, but Roarke said sometimes they just execute people instead. And they have Dash, and they know he's been helping the Griffin rebels, and what if the Guild executes all three of—"

"Stop," Calla tells me firmly. She crosses the room and places her hands on my shoulders. "Stop. Breathe. Calm down. We're going to get out of here. Then we're going to get Ryn, Vi and Dash back. And then we're going to kick this prince's Unseelie ass. Okay?"

I breathe out a long and shaky breath. "Okay. That sounds good."

"Oh, and I thought this might help you feel a little better." She unzips her jacket, and nestled against her stomach is a black rabbit.

"Bandit!" He jumps into my arms, and I almost start crying as I hug him close and rub my cheek against his soft hair.

"He leaped away from you after Ada summoned you earlier, but I caught him and concealed him. He was with me the whole time at Velazar."

"Thank you for keeping him safe."

"Of course," she says with a nod. "Now, help me decide on the best illusion to get us out of here."

REBEL FAERIE

PROLOGUE
VIOLET

It was embarrassing. Violet could hardly believe Ada had managed to corner her, Ryn and Dash inside a circle of jagged glass. They were guardians, for goodness' sake. Before the former Head Councilor publicly exposed all guardians with Griffin Abilities, she and Ryn had been two of the best. And she liked to think they'd only got better since then. Fighting Ada should be easy!

But it was her glass statues that were the problem. Ada herself—who turned out to be a wispy woman with blonde and pale pink hair now that she'd removed her mask and hooded cloak—could turn anyone to solid glass with a single touch. Those statues had become animated and were now fighting for Ada, their movements as fast as if they were still made of flesh. What worried Violet the most, though, was whether the touch of these glass soldiers was as lethal as Ada's touch. Violet wasn't sure, but she couldn't take the risk. And that meant she couldn't get close enough to properly fight off these beings.

All around them across the small floating island known as Velazar II, the battle between guardians and Unseelie fae raged on. The veil had somehow resealed itself instead of being torn further, but rather than abandon their cause, this only made the Unseelies fight harder.

Two glass soldiers lunged toward her, drawing her attention away from the outer battle and back inside the circle. She ducked down, rolled to the side, and sprang up again, an arrow materializing at her fingertips. The bow appeared in her other arm, and within a second, her arrow was flying straight at one of the soldiers. He shattered into thousands of glittering shards as the other soldier, closer now, swung at her again. His shoulder almost grazed her arm, but she jerked out of the way just in time. As she spun back around, her bow raised a second time, Ryn's glittering sword came down upon the glass man's head. He broke apart almost instantly.

Then something changed. The dozens of jagged glass pieces forming the circle began tumbling over one another, heading for the center of the circle. Ada's little fighting ring was growing rapidly smaller. Violet tossed yet more magic at the encroaching glass soldiers as she backed up a few steps, closing the space between her, Ryn and Dash. Ryn swung his blade again, and a spray of splinters flew through the air as another soldier went down.

"Stop!"

As Violet ducked to avoid the splinters, she looked to where the shout had come from and noticed someone racing away from the battle and toward Ada. *Emerson?* she wondered, surprise jolting through her. It certainly looked like her, but what was she doing here of all places? The soldiers inched closer, and the glass circle grew smaller, and Em's shouts reached Violet's ears: "Stop! Ada, stop! Ada, please!"

Unable to pause long enough to shout a warning at Em, Violet gripped two guardian knives in her hands and threw them at her nearest glass opponent. With a quick twist to the side, he dodged the one, but the other struck his chest, turning him to a pile of glittering shards.

"Please! They're my parents!"

At first, the words made no sense to Violet. Then she raised her eyes. She looked beyond the glass and saw Em's desperate face looking straight past Ada and into the circle. At her. At Ryn.

And Violet's world came to a standstill.

They're my parents.

Her brain rejected the words immediately. Em obviously didn't mean what it sounded like she meant. This was a trick to get Ada to stop her attack. A trick that made no sense, but still a trick. *It isn't true,* Violet's brain repeated.

But as she looked across the floating island at the girl who'd stumbled so unexpectedly into her life, she saw several things at once: She saw her son's face, full of terror after waking from a nightmare. Younger and more boyish than Em's face, yet undeniably similar in this moment. She saw Calla and Chase whispering together, always out of Violet's earshot. Whispering that had only begun after Em disappeared. She saw Calla's absolute insistence on finding Em and bringing her back at all costs.

She saw—a glass arm sweeping straight toward her face.

A blade flashed through the air, severing the arm from its body. The glass soldier fractured and fell in gleaming pieces to the ground. Violet barely saw it. Her eyes were trained on Em as Ada threw her onto the ground and launched herself at the girl. "No, no, no!" Violet gasped.

Dash shouted something and moved in front of her, blocking her view of Em. His words were an indistinct echo as she tried desperately to see past him. "Vi!" he repeated, grabbing her shoulder and shaking her. "You have to keep fighting!" He whirled around, shoved another glass soldier back with the edge of his crossbow, then shot him. He jumped back quickly, pushing Violet out of the way as glass fell to the ground near their feet.

Violet steadied herself, looking back around immediately to where Ada had Em pinned to the ground. *Don't you dare touch her.* The thought flashed fiercely through her mind as she narrowed her eyes, raised her arms, and took aim the moment the bow and arrow appeared. She let go. A second later, the arrow struck its target.

Ada cried out and looked around at the arrow protruding from her shoulder. Violet wasted no time fitting a second arrow against the glittering bowstring. As Ada rolled out of the way, someone tugged urgently on Violet's arm, causing her arrow to shoot into the sky. "We have to jump!" Ryn shouted at her. "Over the glass. Now!" She looked about and saw that every opponent within the circle was gone—and the encroaching glass shards that had formed the circle were about to reach them. "JUMP!" Ryn yelled.

She hesitated only a moment before bending slightly, then launching away from the ground. She cleared the glass easily, as did Ryn and Dash. "Where is she?" Ryn asked, whipping around immediately and looking back to where Ada and Em had been moments ago.

Violet didn't have time to answer as yet more guardians who'd been turned to glass rushed toward them. She felt oddly detached from the scene as she fought back with weapons and magic, never getting close enough to let anyone touch her. It all became a confused blur as her mind spun in the background, trying to figure out how Em's words could possibly be true. Guardians, glass people, Unseelies, Guild transporter pods.

Transporter pods. Those definitely hadn't been there when this fight began.

After finishing off another animated statue, she looked around, searching for Em again. There! She couldn't see Ada, but Em was running toward what remained of the glass circle. "Em!" Violet yelled. The girl looked up, her eyes searching until she found Violet. She altered direction, kept running, and then—

Violet cried out as a bright bolt of magic collided with Em. She rolled several times before coming to rest face-down on the ground. Violet started running, but someone caught hold of her arm and tugged her back. She barely had time to try and pull her arm free before she was forced to the ground. A man in a Guild uniform loomed over her, and before she could react, something snapped painfully around her wrists. Guardian handcuffs, the golden sparkling kind she'd never be able to get off. As two guardians pulled her roughly to her feet, she heard Ryn yelling, "Emerson!"

Crapping crapping crap, what had he seen? How badly was Em injured? Was she dead? Violet struggled against her captors with all her might, managing to get an elbow in one guardian's face and a foot in the other's groin before a third appeared to assist in subduing her. Within seconds, her ankles were bound as well.

"Em!" she shrieked, craning her neck to see what had happened to the girl. And finally, Violet caught a glimpse of her, sitting up, her hand pressed against her side. Their eyes met for one moment before the world tipped to the side and Violet was tossed into a transporter pod along with Ryn and Dash. Several guardians jumped in after them, and the clear glass pod sealed itself shut. "No, wait!" Violet gasped. She paid no attention to the guardians moving to their positions within the pod, two facing the front, three facing the captives. She rolled onto her side, pushed herself up, and shuffled in a wriggling fashion toward the glass. She pressed her bound hands against it. "Em!" she screamed as the girl clutched her side and stumbled toward them. The pod rose a few feet into the air and began moving away from her.

"Turn this damn thing around!" Ryn yelled from beside Violet.

But the guardians, of course, didn't listen. Em was running after them now, shouting something, but she would never catch up to the pod. She dropped onto her knees at the edge of the island, still shouting. As the pod gained speed and shot away through the air, Em's kneeling form grew smaller and smaller, and Violet's heart was somehow full and broken at the same time.

She let her hands slide away from the glass as she looked at Ryn. "You heard what she said." Her voice came out hoarse. "You heard it. Please tell me you heard."

"I heard it." Though his hands were also tied, Ryn raised them and gripped Violet's arm. His eyes pierced hers. "How ... how could she be ..."

"If someone used a shapeshifter?" Violet suggested. "Like ... like with my father ..."

"But a child, a baby, can't control their shifting. It couldn't have been that."

"Changeling," Dash moaned from several feet away. He had a gash across his forehead and another on his arm just above the handcuffs. He dragged himself toward Violet and Ryn. "There was a man in the Unseelie prison. Zed. He explained everything."

"Zed?" Ryn repeated, his tone sharp.

"Stop talking," one of the guardians snapped at them.

"He told Em she was a changeling," Dash continued, ignoring the guardian as he dragged himself closer. "He told her he stole her from a faerie guardian couple … and replaced her with … a human. He didn't say who her parents were …" he collapsed against the curved glass of the pod "… but she must have found out."

Violet's chest rose and fell rapidly as her breath came in gasps and her eyes filled with tears. "I can't believe it. I can't …" She shook her head as Ryn's fingers slipped away from her arm and he pressed his bound fists hard against his chest.

"It's really true," he uttered.

"Victoria," Violet whispered. "She isn't dead. She didn't die. And she was *there*, with us at the haven, and we let her go—"

"I told you to stop talking!" the guardian repeated.

"And I told you to turn this damn thing around!" Ryn shouted right back. His voice shook. Violet could see the agony on his face, the ache of everyone's heightened emotions assaulting him.

The guardian who'd shouted turned to the others and sighed. "Please tell me you've gathered enough power."

"Just about," one of them answered. Then: "Yeah. Definitely enough for a few hours."

The other one said, "Me too."

The shield separating the rebels from the guardians vanished.

Knowing what was coming, Violet reached quickly for Ryn. She tugged his arm, and he looked around at her. "We'll find her," she said, raising her hands to touch his face. Then the stunner spells flashed across the pod, and Violet knew nothing but darkness.

PART I

CHAPTER 1

Cold perspiration settles on my brow as I follow a golden haired faerie through a busy clearing in the Creepy Hollow forest. We leave the chilly night air behind and enter the stuffiness of a guardian-filled bar. I spot other types of fae here and there—some with scaly skin, some with pointed ears, a woman with horns protruding from her forehead—which makes me feel a fraction better. But far too many men and women with swirling black patterns inked onto their wrists fill this place. I push my hands into the single front pocket of my hoodie, finding Bandit hiding there in his small furry mouse form. I wish I could hide too.

Boisterous laughter pulls my attention to the left. A guardian man and woman fall against each other while listening to someone relate a tale in animated fashion. Behind them, a man sitting alone in a booth reaches casually into the air. A knife appears in his grip, golden enchanted light glinting off its blade. He uses the knife to flip the cap off the bottle of whatever he's about to drink. His eyes catch mine for a moment before he lets go of the knife. It vanishes, and he lifts the bottle to his lips.

"This is madness," I whisper to Calla as we make our way casually toward the bar. "Everyone's going to realize we don't belong here."

"They won't. This place is open to anyone in Creepy Hollow who feels like relaxing after a hard day's work. Sure, it's mainly frequented by guardians, but no one will look twice at the two reptiscillan women who've just walked in."

I swallow and look down at my hands, which appear to be covered in fine blue-green scales. "Are you absolutely sure that's what they can see?" I know that's what *I* can see, but if Calla isn't projecting her illusion far enough, then any of the guardians inside this bar can see exactly who we are. And while they may not recognize Calla—it's been almost twenty years since she fled the Guild—they'll almost certainly recognize me: the Griffin Gifted girl whose enchanted voice can command anything. The girl who caused quite a fuss when she escaped the Guild recently and led numerous guardians into a fight with a bunch of Unseelie faeries at the edge of a cliff.

"Hey." Calla turns to face me. "Are you still doubting my ability? Even after we walked unseen past dozens of Unseelie guards and escaped that strange grey place?"

I raise both eyebrows at the memory of how we came exceptionally close to *not* escaping the shadow world. A guard came along to put a magic-blocking band around my wrist, but Calla tricked him with an illusion. We got out of my cell and made it into the castle under the cover of invisibility. We hunted through almost every room for the black traveling candles before realizing Roarke must have moved them all. Knowing those candles were our best option for escaping the shadow world, I told Calla we had to keep searching. Finally, we found the room Roarke appeared to be using as his operations center. We listened in as he shouted at one of his guards. After he dismissed the man and stormed out, we snuck inside—and found ourselves caught in a spell that flipped us upside down and suspended us in the air in the room's doorway.

Guards came running. Roarke came running. Calla managed to cut us free from the spell that held us in the air. Mayhem ensued as we hunted through drawers while Roarke and his guards—who could follow our movements even though they couldn't see us—tried to hit us with their magic. I found the candles inside Roarke's gigantic desk, and Calla and I escaped with partially singed clothes, a few minor wounds, and our lives intact.

"Well, no," I admit to Calla. "I'm not doubting your ability. But our escape didn't exactly go the way we planned."

Her lips twist into a smile. "No plan ever goes the way it's planned." She looks around. "Ah, there he is. Just stick close to me, Em. I swear I will not let a single person inside this bar see you as anything but a reptiscilla."

As we approach Calla's guardian contact Perry, I do my best to push away the concerns cycling repeatedly through my mind. What has the Guild done to Vi, Ryn and Dash? Did Ada survive after I pushed her from the edge of Velazar Island? Do I still need to be worried about Roarke coming after me? What happened to Aurora after I fled the Unseelie Palace?

Stop, I tell my overworked mind. Vi, Ryn and Dash are the priority, and that's why Calla and I are here inside this bar. As she keeps telling me, we're going to get them back, and everything will be fine. I shove away the tiny voice that tells me that's not the way the world works.

Just ahead of us, Perry is sitting on a stool at the bar, asking for a drink. Calla trips forward, knocks into Perry's shoulder, and catches herself against the bar. "Oh, excuse me," Perry says, turning swiftly. "I'm so sorry."

"No, no, I'm the one who should be apologizing," she says with an easy laugh. "My mind is elsewhere, and I wasn't watching my feet. Oh, hey, don't I know you?" she adds, her smile spreading wider as she leans against the bar beside him. "I'm from the Reptiscillan Protectors Institute. I think we collaborated together on that case with the invisible leprechaun."

Perry's smile freezes. "Calla?" he asks with lips that barely move.

"Don't. Be. Weird," she instructs.

Perry lets out an unnatural laugh.

"You're being weird."

"Hey, so, how are you doing?" A forced smile pulls his lips up. "It's been too long. I've been expecting you to message me for ages." He lowers his voice. "For hours. I've been checking my amber every minute for *hours* after hearing from one of our mutual friends that Em was taken and you followed her and our favorite Unseelie faerie."

"I'm so sorry about that," Calla says lightly, her perfect smile still in place. "I would have messaged if my amber hadn't fallen out of my pocket when I was dangled upside down by said Unseelie faerie. Fortunately, my assignment partner and I"—she places her arm around my shoulders and pulls me against her side— "managed to escape this dangerous mission unharmed."

Perry's eyes move to me. "Em?"

"Yeah. Hi." I lift my hand and give him a small wave.

"Oh, thank goodness." His gaze moves back to Calla. "I've been so worried that—"

"Maybe we should catch up someplace quieter," Calla suggests. "This bar's always been a little too noisy for me."

"Right. Of course."

It takes a good deal of self-control to stroll out of the bar instead of running for my life, which every instinct in my body tells me I should do. I breathe in a cool breath of relief once we're back outside. We stride away without hesitation, and we're soon lost in the bustle of activity in the clearing. Though it's night time, stores are open on either side of the wide walkway. Signs floating above tree doorways announce the names of the stores. Candy Sparkles, Musical Mayhem, and numerous other fascinating places I'd love to explore if my current purpose in life wasn't strictly focused on rescuing the people I just discovered are my family.

We head along the pathway and into the trees, where tiny insects glow in the branches above us and pedestrian activity is minimal. As we come to a stop, Perry makes a series of discreet but complicated movements with his hands while whispering words too quiet for me to hear. Silvery dust appears in the air and floats down onto us. Wary of anything in this world that I don't already know about, I try to swat it away. "Don't," Calla says, catching my hand. "It's to keep anyone from overhearing us."

"So you don't have an amber anymore," Perry says, "but instead of returning to your haven and using someone else's to contact me and arrange a meeting, you decide to walk into the most popular guardian bar in Creepy Hollow?"

"Yes, because I know how to conceal myself, and because Em and I don't want to waste any time. We need to find out what happened to Vi, Ryn and Dash. I know you've probably already passed on whatever you've heard to someone at the haven, but I don't want to hear this information secondhand, and I don't have time for a whole load of questions about where Em and I have been. So please tell me exactly what you know so I can free my family before they're permanently locked up somewhere."

Perry looks at me and hooks his thumb toward Calla. "She's bossy, isn't she."

"Perry!" Calla and I say at the same time.

"Jeez, sorry, I get it. This is important."

"It's more than important," I tell him. "They're my—I mean ..." I cut myself off, not because I want to hide who I am from him, but because we don't have time for explanations of exactly how I turned out to be the supposedly dead Victoria Larkenwood. "Just tell us where they are so we can get them back."

"I don't think I like that 'we,'" Calla mutters, looking at me, "but we can argue about whether you're involved in this plan or not once we know what we're up against."

"Hey, that part is not negotiable," I tell her. "I know I can't fight like you can, but my ability can do amazing things when it's powered up. I closed the veil, remember? And I'm partly responsible for them being captured, so I want to do everything I can to—"

"If the two of you would let me speak," Perry says, "you'd know that your plans to rush into an immediate rescue mission are futile."

"What?" we demand, together once again.

"Okay, not *futile*, exactly, but you can't do anything right now." He swats at a bulbous glowing insect drifting lazily past his face. "Vi and Ryn have already been taken to Noxsom, and Dash is in a holding cell at the Guild, which neither of you can enter unless I sneak into places I'm not supposed to be and spend hours disarming the Griffin Ability alarm."

"Noxsom? Dammit." Calla places her hands on her hips and turns away. "I figured if they were in transit somewhere—like sailing to Velazar—we could intercept them."

I frown. "Why would they be going back to—oh, not the same Velazar where the tear was."

"No, the other one." Perry says. "There are two Velazars. Confusing, I know. The Guild split the island in half so the one part could remain stationary with the gap over it, and the other part with the prison could continue to—"

"Perry?" Calla says. "Not really the time for a history lesson."

"Right. Got it. So, Dash's crimes aren't considered as serious as Vi and Ryn's," Perry continues. "He's being charged with conspiring with Griffin rebels and passing information to them, and he's awaiting trial. Vi and Ryn, however, were taken straight to The Noxsom Facility. No trial, no questions asked."

"What's The Noxsom Facility?" I ask.

Perry's gaze flicks back to Calla for a moment before he answers me. "A prison."

"And they call it a 'facility'? That makes it sound even worse."

"Because it is," Calla mutters. She's pacing now, her hands still on her hips.

"And no trial?" I add. "Can I point out once again that your law-makers don't seem to be particularly law-abiding?"

"You can." Perry sighs. "Where Griffin Gifted fae are concerned, it seems the Guild Councilors will do just about anything to apprehend them."

"But Vi and Ryn definitely aren't being executed, right?"

Perry shakes his head. "No, definitely not. No one's been executed since Princess Angelica and her witch accomplice. And even then, people thought the death penalty was a step too far. The next Head Councilor came up with The Noxsom Facility instead, although some people argue that death is preferable to whatever happens at Noxsom."

"What happens—"

"Okay, so this isn't what I was hoping for," Calla interrupts, "but the good news is that Vi and Ryn are alive. Now we just have to figure out how to free them. And once Dash has been moved from the Guild, we can free him too."

Perry nods, then adds, "If Flint doesn't do something before then."

"What?" Calla stops pacing. "No, Flint mustn't do anything."

My eyes jump back and forth between the two of them. "Who's Flint?"

"Dash's father," Perry answers. "He also works at the Guild."

"And if he does anything to free Dash," Calla says, "the Guild will almost certainly know it's him."

"He's not stupid, Cal. He isn't going to get himself caught. And the Guild has much bigger problems to worry about than Flint and Dash. Much bigger than the Griffin rebels too, which is saying something."

"What do you mean?" Calla asks.

"Do you have any idea of the mess going on in the non-magic realm right now because of the veil tearing further before it was closed? Humans think it's the apocalypse or something."

Calla lets out a grim sigh. "Shoot. Of course. I was so focused on getting Em away from Roarke and then finding Vi and Ryn that I didn't think about the consequences of what happened with the veil."

I look away from both of them, pressing my fingers against my temples as guilt begins to gnaw at me. "I should have been able to stop it in time. I could *see* it happening—the ground being eaten up, and then a house and people—and my stupid Griffin Ability just wasn't *ready*."

"Em, their world would be in a far worse position right now if you hadn't fixed the veil when you did," Calla reminds me. "Your 'stupid Griffin Ability' is amazing, and if every human knew what you did, they'd be eternally grateful to you for keeping the rest of their world intact." She looks at Perry. "I assume this mess is too big for the Guild to cover up? Too many people's memories to alter?"

"Exactly. Videos and photos spread almost instantly. I'd be surprised if there's anyone in their world who *doesn't* know by now. My sister said she saw it on the news. This big hole in the air with people fighting on the other side, and their world slowly being sucked into the hole."

"Holy heck, people could actually *see* that?" Calla asks. "Like, there was no glamour hiding it?"

"No, not once the hole began growing bigger and the guardians casting the glamour ended up fighting Unseelies. The human world has now seen things we've been hiding from them for centuries. The theories are endless. Heaven, hell, parallel universes, magic, time travel."

Calla smacks one hand against her brow. "Ugh, what a disaster."

"Yeah, and on top of that, we have big problems in our own world. The Seelie King is threatening to declare war on the Unseelies because their prince fought a whole bunch of Guild members and stopped their veil restoration spell."

"Flipping heck." Calla slowly lowers her hand. She looks over her shoulder toward the clearing. "Disaster on both sides of the veil, and everyone is just … carrying on with business as usual?"

"Well what else are they supposed to do?" Perry asks. "Your average fae can't help with something like this. So after gossiping about the terrible state of the world for a few hours, then yes, they go back to business as usual. The Guild Council is obviously trying to find out exactly what happened, since the Unseelie King denies having anything to do with stopping the veil restoration spell. He says his son left the Unseelie Court, took half their army with him, and he has no idea of his whereabouts now."

"He knows exactly where Roarke is," I say darkly. "In the shadow world. The world between this one and the non-magic one."

Perry blinks. "The … what?"

I look at Calla. "If we're not racing off somewhere to rescue Vi, Ryn and Dash, then I assume we do have time for explanations?"

"If you're talking about an entirely new *world*, then we definitely have time for explanations. Is that what that place was? The colorless place?"

I try to ignore the urgent prompting that I need to *run! Rescue! Don't waste time!* "Yes. Well, Roarke called it a 'world,' even though I don't think it technically is one. But it's definitely separate from this world and the human world. Roarke thinks it came into existence when the veil was first torn. When the two worlds collided into each other, the bits of each world that everyone thought disappeared actually formed this new world. At least, that's what he thinks happened. It seems to exist in the same space as the faerie paths."

"Insane," Perry murmurs. "It doesn't sound possible. Are you sure you weren't somewhere in the fae realm that you've never been before? There are plenty of weird places in our world."

I arch an eyebrow. "I'm pretty sure Roarke wouldn't have been so excited about it if that were the case. And it just … it looks and feels different. *Very* different."

Perry turns his frown on Calla. "You've been there?"

"Yes. I was holding onto Em when someone summoned her there. And it's … Perry, I've never seen anything like it before. It definitely didn't feel like this world or the other one."

"That's why Roarke wanted to open the veil further instead of closing it," I explain to them. "He wanted to make his new world bigger. Now that we've stopped him, I'm sure he's furious."

Calla groans. "Wonderful. So now we have two worlds in a mess plus a third world with a ticked-off ruler who's probably looking to extend his realm in some other way. And if we went straight to the Guild right now and offered our help, I'm sure they'd still rather lock us up than work with Griffin Gifted fae."

"Or they'd rather sit back, have a drink, and do a fat lot of nothing," I mutter, gesturing over my shoulder toward the bar.

"Hey, if those guardians are in there enjoying a few drinks, it's because they've earned their time off," Perry says, the volume of his voice going up a few notches. "There are Guilds all around the world, which means plenty of guardians to try to fix the mess left behind by that prince you almost married, so we don't *all* have to work on every problem at the same time."

My mouth has dropped open by the time he's finished speaking. "I can't believe you're defending these people who completely disregard their own laws, who talked about killing me if they couldn't keep me away from the Unseelies, who've now imprisoned people we care about, and who'd no doubt turn on *you* in an instant if they knew you helped us!"

"Okay, calm down, Em," Calla says. "And Perry, you're not usually so defensive. What's—"

"I'm defensive because we're not all like that! The wrong people keep getting elected into positions of power, which makes it almost impossible to change things. I'm actively searching for other guardians who don't agree with the Guild policies on Griffin Abilities, but when everyone's afraid of being labeled a Guild traitor, it's a little bit difficult to organize any kind of official opposition."

Several beats of silence pass before Calla says, "Okay. Clearly we're all tense at the moment, so it's easy for us to lose our tempers. We're all worried about the people we love, and Em and I are in desperate need of a bath and a meal. So we should probably head back to the haven, clean up and eat something, and then plan with the rest of the team how we're going to get inside Noxsom."

I heave a deep breath and look down. My clothes are stained with the dirt I rolled across on Velazar, and both my jacket and hoodie are torn down the side where someone's magic struck me. "Yeah. Good idea." I glance up at Perry. "Sorry I snapped at you."

He smiles. "Me too."

"Me three," Calla says. At Perry's questioning look, she adds, "I'm pretty sure I snapped at you earlier. But I really appreciate you and all the risks you take for us."

He rolls his eyes, and it's possible his cheeks turn just the slightest bit pink. "Yeah, yeah. Let's not get mushy now. Here, let me open a doorway for you ladies." He removes both his stylus and amber, but as he raises the stylus to the nearest tree, he pauses, his eyes focused on the amber in his other hand. "Oh no," he murmurs.

Calla steps closer. "What?"

"A Guild-wide memo." He looks up, his expression falling.

"What? What is it?"

His eyes drop to the amber and he reads, "Eight suspected members of the so-called Griffin rebel movement have been captured while trying to rescue known Guild traitors Oryn and Violet Larkenwood."

"No," Calla whispers. "Is Chase—"

"There are no names."

She takes my hand. "We need to get back home immediately." And together, we rush into the faerie paths.

CHAPTER 2

We're already running as a glimmer of light appears ahead of us. I expect hot sand and a blinding sun, but the light is dim and the air that drifts across my skin is almost icy. "Quickly," Calla says, pulling me across the sand beneath a night sky bright with a million stars. Our feet sink with every step, slowing us as we try to run toward the dome of magic that conceals the Griffin rebels' hideout. Calla mutters something, and magic shoves us the final distance, launching us clear through the dome layer. I stumble and run forward a few steps as my feet hit the grass inside the oasis.

The lush landscape is filled with giant trees, bushes laden with flowers, and a river tumbling over rocks in the distance. The breeze is just the right temperature, and a fresh floral scent fills my nose. It's a piece of paradise hidden in the middle of a desert.

The last time I was here, creeping away with Dani's sleeping body, I thought I'd never see this place again. I figured the Griffin rebels would never allow my mother and me back in when they discovered she and Ada—a faerie fond of killing people by turning them into glass—actually belonged inside the same body. Returning here—knowing that I belong here, that my family already lives here—is surreal.

"Em, come on," Calla calls back. She's already hurrying ahead of me. I run to catch up with her, looking up at one of the enormous trees with a stairway spiraling around its trunk and houses built onto the enormous upper branches. A few days ago, Dani was in one of those tiny houses. I picked her up with magic and walked right out of here. Guilt fills me every time I think of how I failed her. Instead of waking her and giving her a happy life, she ended up trapped inside a body that Ada controlled, and then pushed off the side of Velazar.

As we run past the tree, I sense my Griffin Ability—the special magic that lends my voice incredible power—has almost replenished itself. Out of habit, I look down at my wrist to check the level of the ruby's color. But my bracelet is gone, of course. Calla told me to throw it away after we escaped the shadow world. Having been commissioned by a controlling Unseelie prince, she was worried it might have some kind of tracking enchantment on it. "They shouldn't be able to detect it once you're beneath the oasis dome," she said, "but it's better to be careful."

We continue running. Past the hammocks, past the house they call 'the mountain' where meetings are held, and past the orchard. When we finally stop outside one of four little houses in a row, I bend over to catch my breath. Calla walks up the porch steps and knocks. Without waiting, she opens the door and walks inside.

At that moment, my Griffin Ability's magic floods through my body. I concentrate fiercely for several moments, pushing it down so I can use it at another time instead of losing it all in whatever I say next. When I'm confident I've got it under control, I straighten and hurry into the house after Calla.

"Gaius?" she's busy calling. "Gaius, are you awake?"

I try to remember whether I've heard that name before. Thinking back to the many things Vi and Ryn's son Jack—my brother, I remind myself with a startling jolt—told me the day I first got here, I remember he mentioned someone named Gaius. Uncle Gaius, he called him. He said Uncle Gaius was one of the people in charge here, but because he's sick he doesn't come out of his house much.

I follow Calla into a room that's part study, part living room, with plants crawling across almost every surface. A skinny man with hair pointing in every direction turns away from the window to face us. My mind has conjured up an image of someone old and frail, but of course, he looks about the same age as every other adult faerie I've met in this world—thirty-something at most.

"Calla!" he exclaims. "Thank goodness. And—it's Em, right?" he asks, looking at me.

"Have you heard?" Calla asks before I can say anything. "Do you know what's happened?"

"Yes." His expression becomes somber. "Vi and Ryn were captured. We're doing everything we can to—"

"Everyone who went to rescue them has been caught."

Gaius freezes with his mouth half open. His eyes widen further. Then he reaches with a shaky hand for the chair behind his desk. Slowly, he lowers himself into it.

"Who did you send?" Calla asks. "Was Chase there?"

"No. He hasn't returned from Lunar Mountain yet."

Calla breathes out heavily as she nods. "So who are the eight people then?"

"Everyone mission-approved who wasn't already out working on something." Gaius reaches for a scroll of paper and pushes it across the desk toward Calla. "Here's the list."

She takes the paper while I fold my arms over my chest and hover nearby. "Darius, Lumethon, Orange …" Calla murmurs several other names, none of which I recognize. "Crap, even Ana?" she adds. "Ana hates leaving the oasis."

"Yes, and once we get her back, I doubt she'll ever leave again."

Lowering the page, Calla asks, "Why did she go along in the first place?"

Gaius leans forward. "We had a meeting as soon as I received the news from Perry that Vi and Ryn were being taken to The Noxsom Facility. Rather than spend more time planning, we collectively decided the sooner we carried out the rescue the better. From what we know, The Noxsom Facility has several levels of security and it takes some time for prisoners to be processed completely and placed within the torture simulation. So—"

"Torture?" I interrupt, a sick feeling twisting in my stomach.

"Yes, unfortunately," Gaius says, turning his serious expression toward me. "That's the way the Guild has chosen to operate these days when it comes to certain crimes. But as I was saying, the team assumed if they got there as soon as possible, they'd only need to break into the first level. Or, even better, they might arrive at the same time as Vi and Ryn. This was never going to be a mission of stealth. They planned to cause as much havoc as possible and get Vi and Ryn out of there while all the Noxsom employees tried to figure out what was going on. It would seem, unfortunately, that this might have been a trap."

Calla shakes her head. "They should have waited for me. My skills are invaluable in this kind of mission. You *know* that. I could have concealed everyone."

And I could have commanded all the guards with my ability, I think to myself. But it's pointless to mention that now when it's too late.

"How long were they supposed to wait for you, Calla?" Gaius asks. "Of course they wanted you with them, but we had no idea where you were or when you'd return. Darius said you followed the Unseelies away from Velazar, and that was the last he saw of you. And even though the team didn't have your skills, they did have others. They took some of the abilities from the vault."

"What?" Calla's voice is almost a screech. "You're the one who's always told us what a bad idea that is. That we shouldn't touch those abilities unless—"

"Unless in extreme circumstances. Everyone voted, and they determined this situation to be extreme. It's not just about getting Vi and Ryn back. It's about everything they know. An entire community is at risk if our magical fail-safes don't hold."

Calla pushes her hands through her hair and begins pacing the small section of the room not covered by plants, books, scrolls or furniture. "I know that, Gaius. I'm only repeating what you've always told us. And now, not only have we lost all those abilities—"

"What abilities?" I ask, too curious now to remain silent.

"—we've lost almost everyone who can fight," Calla finishes, either not hearing me or choosing not to answer.

"We haven't lost *everyone*," Gaius counters, pushing away from the desk and standing. "Those out on other missions will return soon."

"And how many is that? Four people, right? Chase, Kobe and the Millingjays?"

"Yes. And we can contact others. Elizabeth and Tilly."

"Good luck finding either of them without Vi. And even if we do manage to find them, that makes only seven of us in total."

"Eight," I say, putting my hand up. "What?" I add when they both look at me with doubt. "I have a Griffin Ability. I can help. From the sounds of it, you'll need all the people you can get."

Calla moves a few steps closer to me. "Em, we need people who've done this kind of thing before. The Noxsom guards will be expecting us, so we need to be ready to fight back. As long as Chase and I go, that's more than enough power to get our people out." Her eyebrows pinch together as she looks back at Gaius. "Assuming Chase returns soon. Have you heard anything from him? I sent him a message saying we needed help at Velazar, but he hadn't got back to me yet by the time I lost my amber."

Gaius shakes his head as he moves around to the front of his desk. "No, I've heard nothing. I'm sure he's fine, though. You know he goes silent sometimes in the middle of a mission. And this thing with the Argenti elves at Lunar Mountain is complicated."

Calla sighs. "Yes. I'm sure you're right. He's fine."

"Wait." I catch hold of her arm before she can start pacing again. "Your amber fell out of your pocket back at Roarke's castle. Doesn't that mean he'll be able to read all the messages people send to you before they realize you don't have that amber anymore. Roarke could learn valuable information we don't want him to know."

"Don't worry," she says. "He won't learn enough for it to be useful to him. We have code names for places, and we don't sign our names on messages. And Roarke will probably suspect that we might try to deceive him by sending false information, so I doubt he'll believe everything he reads anyway."

"But what if he replies to someone pretending he's you? What if he manages to trick someone into revealing something important?"

Calla answers my question with a frown. "How would he do that? He can't mimic my handwriting."

"Oh yes. Handwriting. I forgot about that part." I fold my arms over my chest again. "So what do we do now?" I ask, moving swiftly past the part where I tried to sound clever and instead made an idiot of myself.

"We do what Calla isn't particularly good at," Gaius says with a wry smile. "We wait. Once everyone's back—including Chase—we plan properly. Failure is not an option."

"Failure is definitely not an option," Calla murmurs, staring at the floor.

"Okay. So we wait." I bite my lip and stare at the carpet. "And we try not to imagine all the horrible things that are happening to the people we care about. And we try not to worry about what Roarke is planning next, and we try not to think about whether Ada survived that fall from the edge of the island or if … if maybe I killed her." I breathe in deeply, look around for an item of furniture that isn't already occupied by something else, and end up sitting on the edge of an armchair.

Calla pushes a pile of scrolls onto the floor and takes a seat opposite me. "It's hard to kill a faerie, Em, so I'm almost certain she survived. And if she did die … well, you were fighting her in self-defense. You never intended to kill her."

"Yes, but—" I want to explain that it's not just about whether it was an accident or not. It's about the fact that Dani was trapped inside that body with Ada. The woman who raised me for the first twelve years of my life also went off the edge of that cliff. *That's* what I feel terrible about. But I don't want to get into the whole Ada-Dani explanation right now, so I just shake my head.

"As for the other things we should be trying not to worry about," Calla continues. "Yes, I'm sure Roarke is planning something else since he failed to significantly enlarge his world. He was shouting at a guard about the rituals involved in claiming a territory, but he must be planning more than just that." She returns her gaze to Gaius and tells him about the shadow world and how the two of us escaped. As she finishes, I notice movement near the door and look over to see a tray with two glasses gliding into the room. "Oh, thank you," Calla says, reaching for one of the glasses. "I didn't realize how thirsty I was until now."

Neither she nor Gaius seem surprised by the tray's arrival, so I decide not to ask about it. I suppose this kind of thing is normal in faerie homes. Kitchens that automatically know when thirsty guests have arrived … or something like that. I reach over and take the second glass. Gold flecks float in clear liquid. It tastes like plain water, but I assume it contains magical properties of some sort. Before I can ask, Gaius says to Calla, "You mentioned seeing a witch with Prince Roarke in this shadow world?"

"Yes. I only glimpsed her briefly when we were hiding in one of the castle rooms, but she was definitely a witch."

Gaius turns his attention to me. "Do you know anything about the work she was doing for Prince Roarke? That might give us a clue as to what he's planning next."

I take another sip of my drink before shaking my head. "The witch's work didn't have anything to do with helping him extend his territory." I wrap both hands around the glass and prepare myself for the detailed explanation I knew I'd have to give at some point. "She was helping him figure out how to reverse a changeling spell. For Ada. And Daniela. The woman who was staying here before I … well, snuck back in and took her. It was Roarke's back-up bargaining chip in case I wouldn't agree to marry him."

Calla holds up a hand. "Okay wait. I am totally lost now. Daniela Clarke was a changeling? Like you?"

"Like Em?" Gaius repeats. "Since when is Emerson a changeling?"

"Hang on, we'll get back to that," Calla says, waving away his question. "What's this about Daniela and Ada?"

I press one hand over my face. "I wish Zed had explained this entire thing to you before you knocked him out. That would have saved me having to do it."

Calla tilts her head to the side. "Zed knows the woman you thought was your mother?"

"*Thought* was your … she isn't really your mother?" Gaius asks.

"Ugh." I lower my hand, sit back, and explain from the beginning. I start with telling them about Zed's friend Dani who was Griffin Gifted. She could become two separate people: Dani and an identical person named Ada. I continue all the way through the story until the night Zed forced Ada and Dani to rejoin into one body so he could perform the changeling reversal spell. "It was *seriously* weird to watch," I tell Calla and Gaius. "First the part where the two of them were pulled together into one body, and then the part where she began to look different as the changeling spell slowly reversed." I turn to Calla. "The woman you must have thought was Ada— the blonde woman controlling all that glass on Velazar II—that was Ada and Dani together. That's what they really look like."

Calla's mouth hangs open slightly, and she blinks several times before replying. "I—that's just—"

"Almost too strange to believe?"

"Yes. I've never heard of a changeling spell being done on an adult before. And on Velazar … well, I'd never seen Ada without a mask until then, so I didn't think anything of the fact that I didn't recognize her face. And obviously I had *no* idea she was the same person as Daniela."

"Yeah." I look down at my hands twisting together in my lap. "And then my magic pushed her off the edge of that island, and now she might be dead." I swallow as I try to maintain control of my emotions. "I know Dani isn't the person I always believed she was, but she isn't as bad as Ada. She just wanted to live a simple life with me. What she did in order to *get* that life was wrong, but she was still my mother for all those years. And I might have *killed* her."

Calla reaches across the space between us and places her hand over mine. "I doubt it. Faeries are tough, Em. And if Roarke was working with her, he would have ordered someone to retrieve her after she fell. He wouldn't have wanted to lose her Griffin Ability."

Gaius slowly raises his hand, for all the world as if he's requesting permission to ask a question. "This is all extremely complicated and fascinating," he says, "but can I ask again about Em being a changeling? Because that would imply she was stolen from a faerie family as a baby, and I'm just … wondering …" He pushes away from his desk and moves closer to me. He bends a little and squints as he scrutinizes my face. "I don't want to say it, in case I'm wrong, but is it possible … that maybe …"

"It's more than possible," Calla says, a smile spreading across her face for the first time since we walked in here. "It's true. I finally located the one person who could confirm it for me yesterday."

"This … this is …" Gaius looks across his shoulder at her.

She stands and gestures toward me. "Gaius, meet Victoria Larkenwood."

His mouth drops open. He stares at me. Then at Calla. When he finally finds his voice, he says, "That should have been the first thing you said when you ran in here! This is *amazing!*" He hugs Calla, then leans down to hug me. I'm not a fan of strangers getting in my personal space, but I have a feeling I'm going to like this guy, so I gingerly pat his back before he pulls away. "I can't believe you ended up *here*," he adds. "With your family. And no one knew."

"Well of course she ended up with us," Calla says. "She has a powerful Griffin

Ability and was unable to hide it, so she only ever had two options really: caught by the Guild or caught by us. If she *didn't* have a Griffin Ability … well, I'd rather not think about how we'd probably never have known she existed."

"My goodness." Gaius beams at me. "This is all just … beyond belief. How immensely unfortunate that we now have to plan a massive rescue operation instead of planning a celebration."

"Don't worry, we'll have that celebration," Calla says. "Just gotta do the rescue thing first."

"Of course, of course." Gaius nods vigorously. "Well, uh, can I get you some food? I know it's late, but you're probably hungry. We can have a small celebratory meal, if you'd like?"

"Um, actually …" I hesitate, hoping it isn't terribly rude to refuse a meal. "I'm not that hungry."

"Ah, yes, the drink." Gaius gestures to the glass I placed on the floor during my long story about Ada and Dani. "It contains nourishment of some sort."

"Oh. Cool." I open my mouth to ask what the gold flecks are, but I find myself yawning instead.

"I think a bath and a sleep are in order," Calla says. "For both of us."

The word 'sleep' is all it takes for my eyelids to feel as if a weight has been lowered onto them. I don't know how long I was passed out in that underground cell in the shadow world, but it doesn't feel like it was nearly long enough to make up for all the activity that came before it. "Well, if we're not about to rush off somewhere right now …"

"We're not," Calla says. "However much I might wish we could."

I squint at the darkness through the window. "What time is it here anyway? Traveling instantly between time zones is so confusing."

Gaius looks across his desk at a contraption with numbers spinning slowly around miniature planets and pinpricks of light that might be stars. I don't have the first clue how to read it, but with just a glance, Gaius says, "It's a little before midnight."

I blink a few times. "Yeah. Okay. I could definitely sleep."

Gaius accompanies us as we walk to the front door. I push both hands into my hoodie pocket, startled for a moment to find that Bandit is gone. I remind myself not to worry, though. He probably crawled out unnoticed in Gaius's study so he could explore. And with his knack of following me wherever I go, I'm sure he'll find his way back to me.

"Sleep well," Gaius tells us as we head down the porch steps.

"Thanks, I hope so," I answer, my attention already turning inward to the thoughts buzzing around my mind.

"You don't need to hope," Calla says as we walk away. "You're more tired than you think. I'm sure you'll be asleep before you know it."

"Even with everything to worry about?"

"Hey." She reaches for my arm and pulls me to a stop. "This is all going to work out. Sure, the rescue probably won't go exactly according to plan, but it will be a success. I've broken into plenty of places before, including Velazar Prison and both faerie palaces."

"Both? You've been inside the Unseelie Palace?"

"Yes, I was there several days ago. I was too late, though. You'd already escaped. My point," she says as we continue walking, "is that it's not impossible to break into Noxsom and free Ryn and Vi and the others. And that's if they don't free themselves before we get there. Your parents are pretty good at kicking butt when they get the chance."

"And when I'm not distracting them and allowing them to get caught," I mutter.

"Yes." Calla nods, her tone serious. "I'm sure it was entirely your fault the Guild managed to apprehend them. It can't possibly have had anything to do with the fact that they were fighting glass soldiers they had to be careful not to touch in case they turned to glass themselves. Or that we were completely outnumbered because we didn't expect an Unseelie army as well as all the guardians—or the reinforcements that arrived in transporter pods. And that's all on top of the fact that we only ever planned to observe, not get involved in a small battle. None of that could *possibly* have had anything to do with them being captured."

I cross my arms. "Your sarcasm isn't helping."

"Blaming yourself doesn't help either." She looks up through the nearly transparent dome layer at the stars as she lets out a long sigh. "You know what, Em? *Everyone* makes mistakes. And trust me on this: the mistakes you've made don't come close to some of the terrible things the other members of your family have done—including me. But you can't dwell on the things you've done wrong." She places her arm around my shoulders and pulls me against her side as we keep walking. "If you can fix them, then you fix them. If you can't, then you move on."

I watch my feet as my tired legs move me step by step toward one of the giant trees, and I decide then that I will do whatever it takes to fix the things I've done wrong.

CHAPTER 3

"A sword?" I narrow my eyes at the straight-bladed weapon Calla holds out to me after breakfast the following morning. We're in the kitchen, which seems like far too ordinary a setting for the pile of weapons that just sailed through the air from another room and landed on the table. "What do you want me to do with that?" I ask as I reach tentatively for it.

"I'm going to teach you how to use it, along with some basic combat magic."

A snort of laughter escapes me, but I stop when I realize she isn't joining in. "Oh, you're being serious?"

"Of course."

I fit both hands around the hilt, adjusting my grip a few times before gently swinging the sword between us. "But you said you don't want me involved in any rescue plan."

"Yes, that's what I said." She takes the sword from me, places it on the kitchen table, and hands me a different one with a slightly curved blade. "But I know you're not going to listen to me. There's a stubborn streak running through our family, and clearly you haven't escaped it."

I twist the sword this way and that, watching the way the light reveals faint patterns engraved on the blade. "Look, it's not that I'm *stubborn*, it's just that I know my ability can help. If I'd listened to you back on Velazar Island, the veil would probably never have been closed."

"True." She takes the curved sword and gives me one with a shorter, wider blade. "I recognize the value of your ability. I know it can be useful, but I also don't want to risk losing you."

"But I—"

"So maybe we can come up with a way for you to be involved in this rescue plan from a distance. You can say something that will make it easier for us to break in, but I want you to be far enough from the facility that you're not at risk of being caught."

I consider this compromise. "Okay. I suppose that could work if I'm close enough for my magic to reach the outside of the prison. But don't you think you'll need my ability once you get inside?"

"Not enough to risk you getting caught by someone, having your mouth taped shut, and not being able to say a thing to help yourself or anyone else."

I sigh. "And here I was thinking I'd become slightly less useless by being able to control when and how much of my ability I use. But I'd be just as useless if someone got close enough to cover my mouth."

"And that's why you need to learn some other skills. Self-defense, combat magic, a few weapons." Calla replaces the sword in my hands with a metal star. Six deadly blades make up its six points. "I wish I could tell you that you don't *need* to learn to protect yourself, but your life is probably never going to be completely safe. Whenever you leave the oasis, you'll be at risk. Especially if you end up in the same line of work as the rest of your family—which makes me sick with worry to think about, but I'd understand if you want to do that."

I touch my finger to one of the star's sharpened points. "You mean … putting my life at risk to help people I don't even know?"

"Yes, pretty much."

"Hmm. I'm not sure about that." I place the throwing star on the table beside the various swords and knives. "I would have done anything to help my mother—Dani, I mean—but aside from that, my self-preservation instincts are pretty strong. I'm not really in the habit of voluntarily putting my own life at risk. Which, you know …" I shrug. "I think is the kind of response you'd get from most normal people."

"From most normal people, yes. I just thought you might be more on the risk-taking side of normal. You certainly put your life at risk when you decided to stay on Velazar so you could tell the veil to close."

I roll my eyes because that was completely different and she knows it. "Calla, that was two whole *worlds* that were at risk if I didn't do something."

"Yep." She nods. "Two worlds and a whole lot of strangers that meant absolutely nothing to you."

I throw my hands up. "Are you trying to encourage me to follow in my parents' footsteps? I thought you just said the idea makes you sick with worry."

Her laugh is easy, natural. The kind of laugh I don't think I've heard in ages.

"You're right. I shouldn't have said anything more after that." She leans her hip against the edge of the table. "So, shall we go outside where there's more space and play around with some swords?"

"Oh. Uh …" I send a wary glance toward the table's contents.

"Wooden training swords, of course," she adds. "I just got these out to show you how pretty they are."

"Pretty. Uh huh." I cross my arms and bite my lip. "Look, it's not that I'm against this kind of thing. In fact, it would be pretty cool to learn how to use a sword and engage in magical combat. It's just that *right now* feels like the absolute worst time. How can we hang out in this tiny piece of paradise playing with wooden swords when our family is being tortured! Don't you feel like we should be doing something?"

She raises both eyebrows. "Of course I feel that way. Believe me, I'm trying not to tear my hair out I'm so desperate to get out there and free all our people. Why do you think I'm trying to distract myself with things like beginner sword lessons?" She gestures to the table before letting out a long sigh. "But waiting is necessary, Em. If I go to Noxsom alone, it will be almost impossible to get everyone out. As Gaius said, we need to plan this properly. Failure isn't an option."

"But how long will we have to wait before the rest of your friends return to help you? And what exactly is happening to Vi and Ryn in the meantime? Gaius said something about a torture simulation. What did he mean?"

"I …" She looks away. "I'm not completely sure."

"Really? Or are you only saying that because you want to keep the details from me?"

She returns her gaze to me. "Look, I've only heard rumors, and I'm not going to repeat them to you because there's no point in you worrying about things that could very possibly be untrue." She shrugs free of her jacket and leaves it hanging over the back of a chair. "Now, are you going to sit up here on your own and worry about everything, or would you like to pass the time more constructively by learning how not to die when you find yourself in a fight?"

With a sigh and a roll of my eyes, I say, "I guess I'll go with the not dying option."

She smiles. "Always a good choice." She leaves the kitchen, and the pile of weapons rises from the table and dutifully follows her.

Without warning, a section of the tabletop detaches itself from the rest of the table and rises up. I step back with an involuntary gasp, but it's only some form of oversized stick insect, almost the exact color and texture of the table. "Flip," I murmur, placing a hand against my chest. Then the stick insect changes shape, becoming a blue rabbit a moment later. I groan. "Seriously, Bandit? Are you trying to give me a heart attack?" He stands up on his hind legs. One ear twitches. Then he hops off the table, shifting into a black cat before reaching the floor. He slinks away into another room. "Okay then," I say. "Whatever."

"What was that?" Calla asks, returning with two wooden longswords.

"Nothing. Just talking to Bandit. He seems to enjoy sneaking around and surprising me. Oh, hey," I add, noticing her bare arms, "didn't you have more tattoos when I first met you?"

She stretches her arms out and examines them. "Yes, I think I did. They were temporary. Real, but temporary." She lowers her arms and heads for the door that leads outside. "Chase used to be a tattoo artist. He draws new patterns on my arms every few weeks."

"Cool." I follow her outside. "Is that a magical thing?"

"Actually, no. It's the magical ones that are permanent for us. The normal kind—the way you'd get a tattoo in the human world—end up being temporary. Our bodies' magic slowly gets rid of the ink."

"Interesting." I look down to the ground far below as we begin descending the tree's spiral staircase. "So, uh, is Jack around?" I ask, referring to the boy I'm now supposed to think of as my little brother. I never imagined having a sibling, so applying the label 'brother' to anyone is incredibly strange. "I didn't hear anyone inside Vi and Ryn's house when I walked past it this morning, and I assume they wouldn't leave him on his own, would they?"

Calla shakes her head. "Jack and Filigree stay with another family here whenever Vi and Ryn are away at the same time. So he hasn't suspected yet that anything's wrong. We won't tell him unless ..." She hesitates for only a moment before continuing. "We won't tell him at all. We won't need to because Vi and Ryn will be home soon."

"Do you think ... should I tell him who I am? Or should I wait for Vi and Ryn to explain it? Maybe I should wait," I add hastily, before she can suggest otherwise. "It will probably make more sense coming from them."

"Yes, maybe that would be easier. Oh, look, the Millingjays are back." Calla points across the grass to where a man and woman have just entered the oasis. "Now we're only waiting for Chase and Kobe."

As the Millinjays head for the base of one of the other enormous trees, my gaze moves upward and travels over the numerous small houses nestled among the branches. "So the rest of the people here," I say to Calla, "they don't fight? They can't help us?"

"No. They're here because they were hunted by the Guild and we offered them refuge. They asked for safety, not a fight. They're … well, they're just Griffin Gifted, not Griffin rebels."

"Do you guys actually call yourselves that?"

We step onto the grass, and Calla smiles as she hands me my training sword. "We do, actually. At first, I hated it when the Guild labeled us rebels. But after a while, I figured we should go with it. Claim it as a badge of honor. We're rebelling against a system that should change, and as far as I'm concerned, that's something we should be proud of. So yes." She swings her sword back and forth a few times. "I'm a rebel."

I take a few steps back and try to mimic her movements with the sword. "I'm from a family of rebels," I tell myself. "That's actually pretty cool."

"It certainly is. Even my parents—your grandfather and my mother—have rebelled in their own way. They knew I had a Griffin Ability and they chose not to register me on the Griffin List. Not only that, but your grandfather also bribed important people to *keep* my name off the list, since there were several incidents during my childhood that indicated there was something different about me. But the Guild eventually found out, and my parents received some prison time."

"Jeez. Exactly how many people in our family have been to prison?"

"Uh, most of us, now that I think about it," she says with a laugh.

"You too?"

"Yes, although that definitely wasn't the legal type of imprisonment." She looks down, hiding her expression from me before quietly adding, "I'll tell you about it some time."

"And you're going to tell me about everyone else in my family, right? I mean, other than the things you've already told me."

"Of course. Later, though. Right now—" she pokes my chest lightly with the tip of her training sword "—you need to focus on everything I'm about to show you." She places one foot ahead of the other and bends her knees slightly. "You're going to start by standing like this."

As Calla begins by showing me some of the basic footwork, I try to free my mind of every worry that's plagued my thoughts since we escaped the shadow world. Vi and Ryn, Roarke, the Guild, Ada and Dani …

Block it all out, I tell myself. At first, I assume it will be difficult, but I find it's a relief to focus fully on something else. My feet moving backward and forward. The smooth wooden hilt beneath my palm. The weight of the sword. The sound it makes sweeping through the air. The dull *crack* when it meets Calla's sword, and the vibrations that travel up my arms.

Calla demonstrates a basic sequence of movements, which we practice in painful slow motion before speeding things up. When I'm beginning to feel a little more confident, I tell her to show me how fast she can really move. I get ready to do my utmost best to defend myself—and she knocks my sword to the ground and pretend-stabs me in about two seconds.

"Wonderful," I mutter as I rub my wrist. "Learning how not to die isn't going so well."

"Hey, don't get grumpy. You can't expect to be an expert after only half an hour. You're actually doing quite well for your first lesson."

"Thanks. But if an opponent showed up right now, all I'd be able to do is savagely swing and strike and hope for the best."

"Well, that's better than nothing." She bends her knees. "Now get into position and let's try again."

"Fiiiiine." Instead of bending to retrieve my fallen sword, I focus for a moment on letting some of my Griffin Abilty's magic slip out. "Sword, come to my hand," I say in my magically deepened voice. A moment later, it does. "Just practicing control," I tell Calla. "Releasing my power in small amounts at a time instead of losing it all at once."

"Ah. Good idea. If you want to practice more, even after you've run out of power, you can use some of that elixir. The stuff that stimulates your Griffin Ability."

"Oh yes, I forgot about that." I swing the wooden sword a few times before pausing. "Although … when I came back to get Dani so Zed could reverse the changeling spell, I took those three vials that Ana made for me. The ones that were in Vi and Ryn's kitchen. And now they're in a room inside the castle in the shadow world. So there goes that idea."

"Oh." Calla frowns. "I'm pretty sure Vi asked Ana to make more for you. I think you'll find a couple vials if you look in Vi and Ryn's kitchen again."

"Okay, cool. I'll practice a bit later and use some elixir if I happen to run out of power."

"Perhaps use it sparingly, though," she adds. "Ana's the only one who knows how to make it, and she's stuck inside Noxsom at the moment." Calla bends her knees again and brandishes her sword. "Okay, are we just going to stand here chatting, or are we doing this?"

My attention shifts to someone in the distance. "Hey, is that Gaius coming over here?"

She raises an eyebrow. "Are you trying to make me look away so you can disarm me?"

"No, I'm serious." I point with my sword. "I think he's coming this way."

She turns around. "Oh. You're right. Must be something serious if he's left his house." She starts walking toward him.

"Is he sick?" I ask as I catch up to her. "I think I remember Jack saying something about him not going out much."

"He unfortunately isn't very well. His Griffin Ability makes him sick. It never used to, but he's quite old now, and it seems to have taken a toll on him. He can remove others' Griffin Abilities," she adds as I'm about to ask. "Remove them, give them back, transfer them into other objects. He used to do it for people who didn't want to deal with their Griffin Abilities anymore."

"Wow, that sounds really useful for someone like me who's tired of being hunted by the Guild and everyone else."

"Yes. It was very useful. But it began to make him ill. I think having so many different kinds of magic flowing in and out of his body sapped his strength. We didn't realize what was making him ill for a long time, so he kept using his ability and he kept getting worse. By the time we figured out the connection, it was almost too late for him. He managed to recover, but he's a lot weaker now, and I don't think he'll ever be the way he was before."

"Does he still have all the abilities he took before he got sick? Oh, wait, are those the abilities you guys were talking about last night?"

"Yes. He never kept any of the abilities he removed. He always transferred them into inanimate objects for safekeeping, just in case people change their minds and came back for them. So we have a whole bank of these abilities."

I lift my sword and rest it on my shoulder. "Sounds useful."

"It is. Except that sometimes things go wrong when you try to use someone else's Griffin Ability. Hey, Gaius," she says brightly as we reach him. "What's up? Please don't tell me something else has gone wrong."

Gaius's expression gives nothing away. He holds a slim piece of amber out to Calla. "Here's the new amber you asked for. You'll obviously need to give the ID to everyone who needs it. You can start by giving it to Perry when you see him now."

"Now?" She takes the amber from Gaius. "So something has gone wrong?"

Gaius sighs. "I received communication from him a few minutes ago. Things are getting worse on the human side of the veil, and he has news regarding your friend who was detained at the Creepy Hollow Guild."

"Dash," I say.

Gaius nods. "Yes. We try to leave names out of messages whenever possible, but there's no one else he could be referring to. He said he'd like to meet you at the aviary, Calla."

"Of course," she says. "I'll go immediately." I open my mouth to speak, and she adds, "Yes. I know. You want to come with."

"Dash is my friend too. And the human world used to be my home." My mind turns from an image of Dash to an image of Val. I can't help seeing the ground tearing open every time I think of her. I can't help the guilt that always gnaws at me when I remember how I left with no explanation.

My grip tightens on the hilt of the training sword. "Please," I say to Calla. "I need to know what's happening there."

CHAPTER 4

THE AVIARY TURNS OUT TO BE ONE OF PERRY AND CALLA'S PREDETERMINED MEETING points, and it has nothing to do with birds. Instead, when we walk out of the faerie paths, we're in a park in the middle of a city. Even without the surrounding apartment blocks and the cars driving past, I think I'd be able to tell we're no longer on the magical side of the veil. There's something different about the atmosphere here. Something that feels a little bit … lifeless. It's probably always felt this way and I'm only noticing it now because I've spent weeks in a world where magic is woven through everything.

"There he is," Calla says, pointing across the park to a bench. Perry waves at us.

"You're glamoured, I hope?" he says to me as we join him on the bench.

"I think so." I look up at a young man hurrying by with earphones on and two teens in school uniforms running the other way. "No one's looking at me strangely because I'm sitting alone on a bench speaking to myself, so that's a good sign. Hopefully no one comes over and sits on top of us."

Perry grins. "Now that would be awkward."

"If your glamour's working properly, it'll direct people around us," Calla tells me. To Perry, she says. "You're up early. I think. If I'm calculating the time correctly back in Creepy Hollow."

"Yeah. I wanted to do a bit of snooping around before the Guild got too busy. I made sure to get in before the night guards went off duty. The ones in the entrance room are always so bored by the time their shifts end. Always eager to chat."

"And what were they chatting about this morning?"

"Dash Blackhallow, the traitor who was removed from the Guild in the middle of the night after attacking three guards and seriously injuring one of them."

539

"Shoot. Removed to where?" Calla asks.

"No one knows."

"Wait," I say to them. "Would Dash really attack other guardians? Aren't many of them his friends? He doesn't always agree with them, but he wouldn't want to hurt them."

"He was probably provoked," Perry says. "As you know all too well, some guardians have an intense dislike of Griffin Gifted fae. If they discovered one of their own was actually helping the Griffin rebels, they could become extremely unfriendly."

"Or this story could be a lie," Calla says. "An excuse to remove Dash from the Guild. An excuse they can give Flint when he demands to know why his son disappeared when he was supposed to be awaiting trial."

Perry sighs. "I wish I could say that was out of the question, but we know it isn't. If the Councilors think they can use Dash in some way to uncover your rebel community, they'll bend their own rules to get what they want."

"You seriously need a new Council," Calla mutters.

"Don't I know it."

I turn sideways so I'm facing the two of them. "Surely the Council will have to tell Flint where Dash is. I mean, he's Dash's father. Even if he can't do anything about it, he has a right to know what they've done with … Actually, never mind." I shake my head and slump sideways against the back of the bench. "It appears rights don't mean much to these guardian Councilors."

"True," Perry says, "but they'll have to tell Flint *something*. It'll be interesting to see what story they come up with."

"It had better be a good one," Calla says grimly. "Otherwise Flint's going to start an uprising with anyone who'll listen to him, and he'll get himself and a whole lot of other guardians in trouble."

"Maybe that's what needs to happen," Perry says. "This Griffin Gifted persecution has gone on long enough. It's about time some of us stood up to the Guild's leadership."

"I'm not going to disagree with you on that, but is now really the best time?" Calla asks. "Gaius said you told him things are getting worse here. Don't you think you should focus on calming the hysteria in this world before creating a divide within the Guild?"

Perry sighs. "You're right, of course."

I straighten and peer past Calla as I ask, "What did you mean about things getting worse here? What exactly is happening?"

"Well, there's the hysteria going on in the town where the gap in the veil was visible. People are evacuating in droves. Fights have broken out in stores because everyone rushed to stock up on supplies before leaving town or disappearing into their bunkers, and there've been car accidents because of the crazy traffic. And at the same time, the media is flocking in the opposite direction *into* that town."

Calla shakes her head. "Sounds like chaos."

"And then there are the rumors I heard this morning about several other incidents—magical incidents—that have taken place in full view of dozens of humans. Apparently there's reason to believe these incidents are linked to the Unseelies."

"Roarke," I say. "It's far more likely to be him causing trouble in this world than his father."

"Do you know where these other incidents took place?" Calla asks Perry.

"No. I left after I heard about Dash. I assume teams have already been assigned to deal with the incidents. Hopefully they're minor enough to be covered up within a few hours. Rhiningsville, on the other hand ..." He sighs. "That's the town where our world was visible through the gap in the veil. I have no idea how we're going to cover that one up now that the whole world knows about it." He stands. "My team hasn't been told to get involved, but I want to see for myself what's going on, so I'm headed that way now. I figured you'd probably want to come along."

"Definitely," I say at the same time Calla says, "You figured correctly."

We stand, but before either of them opens a doorway, Perry takes Calla's arm and pulls her a short distance away from me. He lowers his voice, but if he was hoping for some actual privacy, he should have moved a lot further away. "This is a little unorthodox, isn't it?" he asks. "Bringing along the newest member of your community to one of our meetings? I would ask if you're training her to become part of the core team, but I know she's barely even been introduced to our world, so she can't possibly be ready to go out on missions with you."

"Perry—"

"It's not that I don't like her," he continues, while I cross my arms, look away, and try to pretend I'm not feeling super awkward. "It's just ... *why*? You don't ever do this. You rescue Griffin Gifted fae, leave them to make a home within your haven, and you get on with the next mission. You don't bring extras along for a field trip or to listen in while I share confidential Guild information."

"I'm sorry this makes you uncomfortable, Perry. But Em is more than just the latest Griffin Gifted person we've rescued."

"Which means what, exactly?"

When Calla says nothing else, I turn just enough to see her looking at me. "What?" I call to her.

She rolls her eyes and motions for me to come closer. "Don't 'what' me. I know you heard everything. Perry's always been louder than he thinks."

"Hey, I can be quiet when I need to be."

"Do you want to tell him?" Calla asks me. "You don't have to if you don't want to. We can leave him in suspense and he can find out when Vi and Ryn are back. But he'll be super excited once he knows. He was one of my only friends back when—when it happened."

Perry's gaze moves back and forth between the two of us. "When what happened? Tell me what?"

"I guess I don't mind him knowing," I say. "Then hopefully we can avoid further discussions about why I'm tagging along for field trips." I push both hand into my pockets as I look at Perry again and decide to go with the shortest explanation possible. "So, uh, you know how Vi and Ryn's daughter died years ago?"

"Yes?"

"Well … she didn't actually die. There was a changeling spell, and she was swapped with a human baby. So … surprise, surprise. Here I am."

Perry blinks. He looks at Calla, then back at me. "Um … what?"

"Crazy, I know," Calla says. "I still can't get over it."

"This is Victoria?" he asks, gesturing at me, his face the picture of disbelief.

"Yes, it is." Calla steps closer and gives me a quick sideways hug. "My little niece, all grown up. She walked right into our lives and we had no idea who she was."

"No way."

"Yes way," Calla answers.

"But … surely the healers would have tested the Victoria who died for something like this. Don't they have spells that would have detected she was a human instead of a faerie?"

"I don't know. The changeling spell was on her, so the healers would have detected magic within her body. And changeling spells have been so rare for so long that it probably didn't cross anyone's mind that that might have been the explanation. And because of the fact that Zed stole her a couple of weeks before that," Calla adds, "everyone assumed her death was caused by a spell he used on her. After all, we knew he had ties to the witches and had used their dark magic before."

Perry blinks several more times. "Wow. Holy heck. Holy *fuzzballs*."

I smile. "Do you and Dash hang out often? 'Cause that sounds like something he'd say."

"We do occasionally, though we try not to make it obvious. Wouldn't want anyone at the Guild wondering how we became good friends. Okay, wait." He holds his hands up. "Do Vi and Ryn know about this? Did you manage to tell them before they were taken?"

Guilt eats at me knowing that my revelation distracted Vi and Ryn enough to get them caught. "I kind of … yelled it out while they were fighting. They heard me. And then guardians got hold of them."

"And now you're desperate to get them back," Perry says, nodding. "Right, I get it. I mean, you'd want to get them back anyway, but now you *really* want to get them back." He tilts his head to the side and frowns at Calla. "I still don't get why you let her come along today, though. Since she's your long-lost niece, doesn't that give you even more reason to want to keep her safely tucked away within your haven?"

"She begged," Calla says simply. "And I kinda feel like she's safer if I don't let her out of my sight."

Perry nods. "Got it. So … are we calling you Victoria now?" he asks me.

I feel my eyes widen. "Uh, nope. I mean, it's a pretty name, but … it doesn't feel like mine."

"That's totally fine," Calla says. "You're Emerson. That's who we know you as, and you're welcome to stay that way."

"Thanks."

"Oh, Perry," Calla adds, reaching for one of her pockets. "Before we go, let me give you my new amber ID. I don't want to forget."

"Cool, okay." He removes his amber from a pocket inside his jacket and taps the edge against Calla's for a moment.

"I should probably get an amber at some point," I say. "Dash was going to get me one, but then … well, he got a little preoccupied with the Guild locking him up."

"You should definitely get one like this," Perry says, placing his sleek, translucent amber on his palm and showing it to me. "See how thin it is? Almost like paper. And man, oh man, the things this baby can do."

"Perry, she doesn't need the latest, greatest amber," Calla says, putting hers away and taking out her stylus.

He sighs. "You've always been so behind in the technology department, Cal."

"*Everyone* is behind you in the technology department, Perry. That's what happens when you buy the newest version of everything before anyone else does."

She writes a doorway spell on the back of the bench, and Perry mutters, "Yes, well … I like toys."

Calla takes hold of my hand and Perry's, and together we walk into the darkness of the faerie paths. "You're directing us, I hope?" Calla says to Perry.

"Yes."

After several moments of walking through nothingness, light appears up ahead. "What did you say is the name of this town?" I ask as we step onto a road between two fields.

"Rhiningsville," Perry says. "Not much happened here until the sky opened up and revealed a parallel world on the other side."

At the sound of voices coming from somewhere behind me, I turn—and that's when I see them all. The vans, the reporters, the tents and caravans. The crowd begins further up the road and extends as far as I can see up the hill. The majority of this town's residents may have evacuated, but plenty of people have arrived to take their place. "So many of them," I murmur.

Beside me, Perry nods. "And with every day that passes, more people arrive. Everyone wants to get a shot of the exact spot where an entire piece of land, along with several houses and families, simply vanished. At least, so I've heard from the Guild gossip. I haven't had a chance to get here until now."

"What exactly are they photographing if the land and houses aren't there anymore?" Calla asks.

Perry shrugs. "I guess we can walk closer and find out."

We weave our way through the vehicles and the crowds. No one looks at me, so I think I'm finally getting the glamour thing right. When we eventually reach the edge of the crowd where barricade tape and police officers are making sure no one pushes forward any further, I see what everyone's photographing, and it sends a shiver across my skin. It's the single wall of a house, with family photos still hanging in frames, and several inches of the ground floor and upper floor jutting out from the wall. There's even a small section of a kitchen counter and the back half of a stove attached to the wall downstairs. Outside, the grass on one side of the wall is different from the grass on the other side of the wall. Because of course, there's a large piece of earth that once existed between those two sections of grass. A piece of earth that vanished into the gap between two worlds and became part of the shadow world.

"Good luck to any scientists trying to explain this," Perry says. "No wonder people are taking about aliens and parallel worlds and the apocalypse."

I swallow and clear my throat before asking, "Do you know if there were people inside this house?"

"Yes. Sadly, there were. Apparently there were people inside all the houses that have vanished."

I breathe deeply against the rising nausea. "If my Griffin Ability had just been ready a few seconds earlier, I could have saved this house, this family. I could have—"

"Don't." Calla grips my arm. "Don't even start that. *You didn't do this.* You stopped it from happening to every other house in this town. Okay?" Though I can't push the nausea down completely, I nod. I know she's right, even though it feels like I should have done more.

I hear a faint hum then, and Perry reaches into his jacket for his state-of-the-art amber. He frowns at it for several moments before writing a quick reply and putting it away.

"What was that about?" Calla asks. "More news?"

"No." He doesn't look at her as he answers. "It was Gemma, actually."

"Oh." Calla nods slowly. "Are you guys …"

"No, don't worry. We're not getting back together *yet again*."

"Okay. Good. I mean, I think that's good? I wouldn't want the two of you to break each other's hearts for … what? The fifth time? Sixth time?"

I turn away from the wall and face the crowd as Perry says, "Fifth."

"Right," Calla says. "So, uh, is she still at the Estra Guild?"

"Yes. She was just asking for the name of our new fish bowl designer. She wants to get in touch with him for some reason. I'm not asking why."

"Okay."

After breathing out slowly once more, I think I've managed to bury the nausea. "Can we find a TV somewhere and see some of the stories that are being reported?" I ask. "Or I guess we could just hang around out here and listen."

"TV's probably the quicker option," Perry says. "We can just go into one of the homes around here and find one."

I look over my shoulder at him. "You want to go *inside* someone's home?"

With a puzzled look, he says, "How else are we supposed to watch the news?"

"Um, I was thinking more like a cafe? You know, so it doesn't feel like breaking and entering?"

"Don't worry, we won't be breaking anything. Faeries do this kind of thing all the time. How are we supposed to save a sleeping human from an enchanted winged serpent that's taken up residence beneath the bed if we're bothered about things like entering private homes?"

I blink. "That's … a joke?"

He laughs, while beside him, Calla pulls her stylus out and looks around. "Nope," Perry says. "That was one of my first solo assignments when I was a trainee. I successfully pulled off the entire operation without waking the human. I would have scored full points for that assignment if I'd been able to capture the serpent instead of letting it get away." He frowns at my open-mouthed expression. "Why are you so shocked? I thought Dash told you all about what guardians do. I mean, when they're not hunting down Griffin Gifted fae."

"He ... he did. He spoke about trainees and assignments and ... stuff. I guess I just didn't think about monsters hiding under people's beds and invisible faeries wandering around homes without permission." My frown deepens as I consider something. "How many faeries hung around inside Chelsea's home watching me before I realized I had magic?"

"Probably just Dash," Perry says. At my raised eyebrows, he quickly adds, "And in case you were wondering, it is absolutely forbidden for us to simply *watch* a human when it's inappropriate to be watching them. If Dash happened to see something he wasn't supposed to see, it would have shown up on his tracker band and his mentor would have severely reprimanded him. Then he would have been replaced with someone—"

"Holy heck, you mean he could have been hanging around when I was *changing* or *showering* or—"

"No! Absolutely not. That's what I'm trying to say—"

"Okay!" Calla says, loudly enough to be heard over both of us. "That house over there." She points past the lone wall. "That's where we're going. I'll open a doorway and direct us. Keep your minds blank."

I think of nothing but the darkness while we're inside the faerie paths. We exit on the other side—and walk straight into a coffee table. Perry grunts in pain as the table screeches against the floor, and Calla and I grab hold of each other to regain our balance. "What was it you said about not breaking anything?" I ask Perry as he bends to rub his shins.

"The table is completely fine," he informs me.

Calla walks across the room and into the next one, saying, "I'm just double-checking no one's home."

I look around at the well-worn couches, the scratched wooden floor, the desk and computer in the corner, and the TV and picture frames on the wall. "It's so weird just walking into someone else's house."

"Do you want to sit?" Perry asks me, gesturing to one of the couches.

"No, of course not. That would be even weirder."

"Looks like we're alone," Calla says, striding back into the living room. "Perry, can you turn the TV on?"

Perry picks up the remote control from where it's sitting on the table we bumped into. "Okay, uh … how exactly do I find the news?" Perry frowns at the remote. "This doesn't look the same as the one my sister has."

"Here, this'll be faster," I tell him, moving to the desk and computer in the corner. "Most people only have streaming services on their TVs these days." I slide into the chair, tap a random key on the keyboard, and wait for the screen to come to life. Fortunately, there's no password required to log in. Instead, I find a browser window displaying an email inbox. "We're totally invading someone's privacy right now," I mutter as I click to open a new tab. In the search bar, I type the name of the first news broadcaster that comes to mind. After clicking through to their website, my eyes dart across the home page, looking for words like 'magic,' 'apocalypse,' and 'end times.' It seems utterly absurd. This is one of the biggest and most reputable news names across the world. They wouldn't sully their home page with words like—

But there it is: a link labeled 'Live Coverage on the Supernatural Attacks.' My heart thunders as I click the link. A video pops up showing a woman with perfectly styled blonde hair standing in a park with tall buildings rising above the treetops in the background. For a moment, it appears there's nothing unusual about this scene—until I notice the bright sparkling light whizzing around the top of the tallest building in the background.

"… in Central Park, where less than an hour ago, the brand new Haverton Tower Hotel was attacked by what many are describing as—" the woman hesitates, her mouth twisting slightly, as if she can't bear to say the word "—supernatural forces. Guests of New York's tallest hotel have been evacuated after three men appeared in the penthouse suite and attacked the occupants with what appeared to be electrical discharges emanating from—from their hands." Her own hand clenches around a section of her purple pencil skirt as she says this. "Dozens of eyewitnesses have reported seeing the same unexplained electrical activity as the men made their way down the upper floors of Haverton Tower, and many claim to have been knocked down by invisible forces. The penthouse suite occupants managed to escape with minimal injuries, though Haverton Tower management declined to confirm their identity. The number of casualties is unknown at this time.

"The three suspects, one of whom has repeatedly been called a 'demon' by eyewitnesses due to his dark red eyes and red and black hair, vanished upon reaching the hotel's foyer. His two accomplices are reported to have hair dyed green. Police are on the lookout for men matching this description and have requested that anyone who happens to see them maintain a safe distance after informing authorities.

"This is the sixth in a series of unexplained incidents that have taken place across the world since the sudden appearance of an opening in the air above Rhiningsville, almost forty-eight hours ago. Cell phone video footage of the event depicts what appears to be a battle between human-like figures on the other side of the opening. The video, which has since gone viral, was initially assumed to be an elaborate hoax. But the disappearance of a section of land containing seven homes and a barn housing livestock, along with five other unexplained events taking place across the world, suggests otherwise."

"Holy fudge," I murmur as the reporter mentions a theory about aliens from a parallel universe while in the background, the sparks of magic move steadily downward, encompassing more and more of the Haverton Tower Hotel. I risk a glance away from the computer screen to check Calla's reaction.

"What is Roarke doing?" she whispers. "What is he *doing*? It must be him, right? And he's breaking, like, the most important rule. *Everyone* plays by this rule, even the Unseelies. What the hell is wrong with him? Doesn't he care that he's exposing us to the entire human realm?"

"Even Draven didn't go that far," Perry says, his tone grim.

"Well, I think he planned to," Calla says. "Eventually. He was just making sure he had the entire fae realm under his control first. But this crazy young prince?" She gestures at the computer screen. "Who knows what his plan is."

"Or if he even has one," I add quietly. "He could just be letting us all know how royally pissed off he is that I ruined his plans to make the shadow world bigger."

"Whatever his reasons," Calla says, "someone has to stop him. I hope the Unseelie King is already on his way to deal with this mess."

"I don't think we can count on that," Perry says.

"Well, the Guild and the Seelies then."

"Not you guys?" I say to her, only half-joking.

She shakes her head. "I'd love to, but this is too big for us. This isn't the kind of thing we do. We operate undercover, helping out where we can. We don't take on armies, even if they're only half-sized armies. Especially when more than half our number is currently in Guild custody."

A crackling sizzle and a scream draw my attention back to the computer screen. Bright light blocks out the image for several moments. When the park comes into view again, it's at an odd angle with grassy ground filling half the screen. The news reporter and her purple skirt are visible in the other half. She manages to push herself up, leaving us with a view of her ankle, one purple high-heeled shoe, and the silvery sparkles of magic drifting around her leg. She lets out another shriek and a string of curse words that would make Dash's mother whip out her soap spell immediately. "Dammit, get *up!*" the reporter shouts at someone. "Leave the camera!"

Her leg disappears as she runs away. The camera remains still. The only movement filling the screen is the dancing and swaying of bright sparkles amidst glowing light.

"Holy frikkin' moly," Perry murmurs. "I didn't think anything could be worse than Lord Draven taking over our world. But this? This is gonna be worse."

CHAPTER 5

"I hope the Guild has sent guardians to monitor every news station in existence," Calla says to Perry as we walk through the media crowd again, listening in on snippets of conversation. "If your Seers aren't Seeing all these things before they happen, then the news is probably the best way to stay up to date on all the trouble Roarke's causing."

"They must have Seen something," Perry says. "But perhaps their visions didn't contain enough details for anyone to stop these incidents. And I guess no one connected them to the Unseelies until after they'd happened." He pulls his amber from his pocket as it hums again. "Aaaaand people are wondering why I'm not at my job right now. I'd better go."

Once Perry's disappeared, Calla says, "We should go too. We can't do anything about what's happened here in Rhiningsville, and we can't help with that huge mess in New York City either. We need to get on with freeing our team, and let's hope the Guild and the Seelie army can do enough to fix all of this." She raises her stylus to the side of a van and writes a doorway spell.

"It kinda feels like there's no way back from this," I say quietly as an opening forms on the side of the van. "Like ... the world has changed forever now."

Calla reaches back and takes my hand. "Maybe it has. Maybe magic will never be a secret again."

We cross the desert sand and head for the oasis. We're barely through the dome layer when I see someone hurrying toward us. "Chase! You're back!" Calla calls out, running to greet him.

I hang back a few steps as Chase pulls her into a tight embrace. "You're okay," he says.

"*I'm* okay? Of course I'm okay. What about you? I never heard back from you after I messaged you from Velazar, and then I lost my amber."

"Yeah, I had a similar problem. Both my amber and mirror ended up cracked after I, uh, landed on a rock. I can't get either of them to work."

"Someone threw you onto a rock?" Calla exclaims. "But the Argenti elves' ruler *asked* you to be there. Didn't he tell everyone you were assisting with the Petran negotiation?"

"We didn't get that far," Chase says as I cross my arms and try not to feel awkward. Should I leave? Should I wait for them to finish talking? "We didn't even reach the meeting point with the Petrans," Chase continues. "Everything went to hell after the Unseelie Prince pulled his stunt at Velazar II. Seems he has supporters among the Argenti. He called on them for help—told them all about what had happened and sent them to attack all the glamour magic around those old elf manor houses in Wales in the non-magic world. Apparently he thinks the humans in that area should know about the fae that have been living in secret alongside them."

"That idiot prince!" Calla hisses.

"So half the Argenti ran off to do his bidding. I followed, of course, hoping to stop them. I could have done with some backup, but I didn't have any means of communication, and I didn't want to waste time coming back here. I couldn't keep them from breaking the glamours, so I set up a storm around the manor houses. Hopefully it'll keep humans away long enough for someone to get the glamours back in place or for the occupants to leave."

"And when did you get back here?"

"About twenty minutes ago. Gaius just told me what happened with Vi and Ryn and everyone else." At that moment, Chase's gaze moves past Calla and comes to rest on me. "Oh. Em. Hi." A smile breaks out across his face. "Welcome to the family."

I blink at him, then take a few steps forward. "You know who I am? But you haven't seen Calla since she found out. Or …" I look at her. "Did you send him a message while you were waiting to sneak into my cell in the shadow world?"

"I did. But Chase knew about my suspicions already."

"And the first time I saw you," Chase adds, "I had the strangest feeling I'd met you before. You reminded me a little bit of Vi when I first met her."

I'm silent for a moment, my mouth hanging open, before I'm able to speak. "Wait, really? Why didn't you say anything?"

"I figured I was imagining things. We all believed Victoria was dead. It never crossed my mind you might actually be her." He laughs. "I'm still having a hard time believing it. It's just … incredible." He gives me a smile that's almost as wide as the one plastered across Gaius's face last night when he heard the news of who I am. But after a moment, it fades to a more serious expression. "I wish there was nothing else wrong in the world right now, and that we could catch up on decades of family history. Unfortunately, we first need to plan how best to break into The Noxsom Facility."

"Does that mean Kobe is back as well?" Calla asks.

"Yes. Gaius said he returned about an hour ago."

A thrill of nervous anticipation rushes through me. This rescue is finally happening. It's *real*. I'm going to get Violet and Ryn back.

As we head away from the dome layer, Calla asks, "Any news from Elizabeth and Tilly?"

"Elizabeth's on her way," Chase says. "She'll be here tonight. But Tilly's in the middle of another expedition. Gaius can't get in touch with her, though he's left her numerous messages."

"Let's assume she won't receive those messages in time. That leaves us with seven people to work with."

"Seven?" Chase asks.

I raise my hand as Calla says, "Em wants to help. From a distance, of course. We won't let her anywhere near the inside of that facility."

For a moment, it looks as though Chase might argue that point. But Calla shoots him a glance, and after another a few seconds of silence, he nods. "Okay. Let's start planning."

Our rescue party is an interesting combination of fae. Calla and Chase are faeries, but their friend Elizabeth turns out to be part siren. She has magical powers of influence, which I suppose will come in handy if a guard needs to be convinced to leave his post. Only after I ask why she's wearing gloves does she mention, with a serene smile upon her face, that her siren abilities include the power to suck the life out of people.

Kobe, a guy with narrow vertical pupils and no hair, tells me he's a drakoni. He doesn't speak much, and if I hadn't been watching closely, I would have missed the fact that his tongue is forked. I'm interested to know whether drakoni are related in some way to actual dragons, but with our conversation focused solely on how to get in and out of The Noxsom Facility, I decide to save that question for another time.

The next two members of the team are Krystal and Carter Millingjay, a faerie couple who fled the Guild at the same time Ryn and Vi did, years ago when someone came up with a way to visually identify Griffin Gifted fae. They were from a different Guild, though, so Vi and Ryn didn't meet up with them until about a year after they all went into hiding. Like Vi and Ryn, the Millingjays' guardian markings were never deactivated, meaning they still have access to their guardian weapons. Krystal's Griffin Ability is something random and unhelpful to do with flowers, and Carter isn't Griffin Gifted. I'm sure they've both got kick-butt fighting skills, though.

And then there's me. A faerie with only one skill to offer: the Griffin Ability I've recently gained tentative control over. It 'recharges' itself twice a day, about twelve hours apart, and if I focus hard enough when it appears, I can reserve that power to use at another time, either in a single command that requires a large amount of power, or in numerous minor commands. It's a power that will definitely be useful to our team—as long as I don't lose focus.

When introducing me to the rest of the team, neither Calla nor Chase mention my connection to their family. "It's too much to explain right now," Calla said earlier. "Let's get Vi and Ryn back first, and they can tell people whatever they want to tell them." So after she explains to everyone that I'm involved in the rescue mission because of my Griffin Ability, we get on with our initial planning.

Over the course of the evening, we discuss different options for exactly how to break into Noxsom. We can't make definite plans until we know the internal layout of the facility—information we'll hopefully get our hands on tomorrow, Calla tells us—but in the meantime, we plan as much as we can, including which powers to borrow from Gaius's Griffin Ability vault and how to magically communicate with each other.

I use the term 'we' loosely, of course, since I keep my own mouth shut most of the time. Partly because I have zero experience in this area, and partly because I'm worried that if I draw too much attention to myself, everyone will decide it would be safer to leave me out of this.

Despite the fact that I should be less agitated now that we're finally doing something to rescue Vi and Ryn, a barrage of thoughts bombard me when I try to fall asleep that night. Front and center is the unsettling reminder that no one has any idea where Dash is now. I try to settle my anxiety by telling myself we need to take one step at a time. First, rescue everyone from Noxsom, then find out where Dash is and do the same for him.

I turn over yet again, hug Bandit against my chest—he's in the form of a half-grown leopard—and finally drift toward asleep.

The following morning, Calla leaves the oasis to meet Perry so he can hand over the Noxsom floor plans he stole during the night. When she returns, we reassemble inside the house everyone calls 'the mountain.'

"You know what?" Elizabeth says as Calla drops the rolled-up drawings onto the oval table at the center of the room. "I'm finding the Guild less and less impressive as the years go by. They don't even know when their own people are stealing from them."

"Architectural plans aren't actually stored at the Guild," Calla tells her, "which made it even riskier for Perry to steal these ones. He had to sneak into a records department he had absolutely no reason to be in and hope they have far fewer surveillance bugs flying around than the Guild has."

Elizabeth takes a seat at the table and crosses one leg over the other. "He should have worn one of those disguises he loves fooling around with so much."

"He did. There was a wig involved. And some form of fake facial hair. But still." Calla leans across the table and spreads the blueprints open. "I worry we're going to land him in serious trouble one day."

"Then we'll do exactly what we're doing right now," Chase says, tilting his head as he examines the plans. "Save him from whatever trouble he finds himself in."

Which won't change the fact that his career will have been ruined, I almost add. But I remind myself that I've decided to say as little as possible during these planning meetings. Besides, it's Perry's choice to help the Griffin rebels. He's obviously decided it's worth the risk.

"Okay." Calla separates the pages, placing six large drawings beside each other. "Six levels. We'll only know once we get there and check the inmate records in this room here—" she taps her forefinger onto one of the blocks on the first page "—exactly which cells our people are in. But let's assume the worst and figure out how we're going to get all the way down to the furthest floor below ground."

"And remember," Carter says, "they'll have a Griffin Ability detector over their entrance."

Chase nods. "So one of you who isn't Griffin Gifted will need to sneak in first and disable the enchantment."

Kobe raises his hand. "Great," Calla says. "Thanks, Kobe. Em will tell the gate to open, so that won't be a problem, and I'll hide outside and imagine you as invisible."

"Or Em could tell *every* lock in the prison to unlock," Carter suggests. "That'll make our lives easier once we're inside."

"And risk some actual criminals escaping?" Calla says. "Probably not a good idea."

Kobe leans forward and asks, "Do we know where the detector enchantment is housed?"

"It'll be in the control room here." Chase points to another part of the plans.

"Once that's disabled," Calla continues, "we can all get inside."

"And the surveillance bugs that will no doubt be flitting around?" Elizabeth asks. "Both inside and outside. They'll see through whatever illusion you're projecting. Kobe might not even make it inside if someone sees him on an orb."

"Tropical storm," Chase says. "It's going to rain so heavily outside The Noxsom Facility that no one will be able to see a thing."

Elizabeth nods. "That works for outside, but what about inside?"

"We can do that explosion thing again?" Kobe suggests. "To cut all the light spells. It worked well at the Maxwood Museum."

Despite my plan to remain quiet, I can't help asking, "Are you sure you guys aren't criminals? Why on earth would you need to break into a museum?"

"Because the curator of that museum stole a valuable family heirloom from someone," Calla explains to me. "The Guild couldn't help her because they couldn't prove anything, so after hearing about us, she asked for our help. We located the heirloom hidden inside the museum and stole it back for her."

"But … what if it wasn't actually hers?" I ask. "What if she'd been lying to you?"

"The family crest engraved on the item was a bit of a giveaway. We assume the curator was planning to remove it, but if so, he hadn't got around to it yet."

"Is it really necessary to tell this story right now?" Elizabeth asks.

Calla sighs and looks at Elizabeth. "Just explaining that we're not actually criminals."

"Or," Krystal says, "that we're the right kind of criminals. That might be more accurate."

"So, back to the explosion," Chase says, looking at Kobe. "Yes, exploding some nightlace should work well. Whoever's hanging out in the control room won't be able to see a thing."

"It'll make it difficult for *us* to see as well," Elizabeth reminds everyone.

"Yes, but it won't be *completely* dark," Calla says, an edge of frustration to her voice. "We'll be fine."

"If it isn't completely dark for us, then it won't be completely dark on the surveillance orbs the guards are watching."

"Elizabeth! It'll be fine. You heard what Kobe said. It worked well at Maxwood."

"It did work well," Kobe adds, nodding.

Elizabeth holds her hands up and sits back. "Okay. Just checking."

Calla turns back to the plans. "Next thing we need to figure out is how to get through the security gate that separates each level from the next one down."

"Well," Carter says, "the logical thing to do is use that Griffin Ability that can unlock anything. You know, the one Gaius transferred into that antique key."

"Isn't that one of the Griffin Abilities we lost when the others went to get Vi and Ryn?" Chase asks.

I clear my throat and lean forward. Nerves flutter in my stomach as I say, "Do you know how much easier all of this would be if you just let me go inside the prison?" Silence greets my suggestion. Everyone looks at me. I elaborate quickly. "If I go into the control room with Kobe, I can tell all the guards on duty there that they can't see any of you. Then I can go to each gate and tell it to open. I can open whatever cells Vi and Ryn are locked in. Every step of the way, I can simply *say* something, and it will happen."

Another beat of silence passes. Then: "Out of the question," Calla says.

"Why? It would be so much easier that way."

"Does your Griffin Ability have enough power for that many commands?" Krystal asks.

"Well, I told the veil to close. And it did. I assume that would have required a rather large amount of magic?"

Carter's mouth drops open. "Wow. Okay. Yeah, I think you can handle a bunch of locks and surveillance enchantments."

"Still out of the question," Calla repeats.

"Why?" Krystal asks. "If her magic can do all these things, then why make this rescue operation harder than it has to be?"

"Em is brand new here," Calla reminds everyone. "We can't ask her to do something this dangerous."

"You're not asking me," I remind her. "I'm offering."

"Ryn and Vi wouldn't want you to do this. You're—" But she cuts herself off before finishing, which makes me wonder if she was about to tell everyone that I'm actually Vi and Ryn's presumed-to-be-dead daughter. Would it make a difference to anyone's decision to let me inside the prison if they knew? I don't get the chance to find out, though, because Calla says, "Yes, Em's ability can do all these things. Which is exactly why we can't risk the Guild getting her in their clutches again."

"But if we don't use her magic," Krystal says, "chances are high that we'll fail to rescue our people. We could all end up imprisoned as well."

Calla looks at Chase, a question in her gaze. He's quiet for several moments before saying, "You can stay with her the whole way. Keep her concealed. And I'll remain close by so I can fight off anyone who happens to see the two of you."

Calla's face is full of uncertainty. "Chase …"

"I know," he says. "But we need to get everyone back, and this is the best way. We'll make sure Em doesn't get caught in the process."

Calla looks at me. Her voice is pained as she says, "I don't want to lose you again."

Carter turns to Krystal and whispers, "Is there something else going on here I don't know about?"

"No idea," she whispers in response.

"I know," I say to Calla. "But you won't. I can do this. I have more control now. You know I've been practicing. We'll all come out the other side of this just fine."

I guess I sound more confident than I feel, because eventually, Calla gives in and agrees. But as we sit down to decide on the exact words I should say at each point in the operation, I can't help remembering what she said after we very nearly messed up our escape from the shadow world: *No plan ever goes the way it's planned.*

CHAPTER 6

We wait until late in the evening before leaving the oasis so we don't have to hide too long near Noxsom before my Griffin Ability's magic is ready to be used. Technically, we should be able to go at any time; I'm fairly confident that I can hold onto my Griffin power and release it at will later on. But Chase and Calla decided it would be better to wait. "This way," Calla said, "you'll have whatever power you've reserved from this morning, plus the additional power you'll receive when your ability replenishes again tonight."

We gather in the living room of the mountain and Chase goes around the group, writing a quick spell onto each person's arm with his stylus. We discussed numerous communication options last night, including tiny devices the Guild recently developed—a few of which Gaius somehow got hold of—but this enchantment is apparently the easiest option. "Just don't try any other spell that requires writing on your skin while you've still got this one on," Chase tells me. "It'll interfere with communication."

"That shouldn't be a problem," I assure him. "I don't know any spells that involve writing on my skin."

"We may not even need to use this spell," he adds, "but if we have to split up inside Noxsom and you want to talk to the rest of us, just touch the words on your arm to activate the spell and then speak normally. "

Elizabeth rises from the couch and sets her amber tablet aside. "The news is everywhere," she says as she holds her arm out to receive her communication spell. "The Guild can't stop crowing about their success at having sent a whole bunch of Griffin rebels straight to Noxsom."

"Yes, I saw that," Krystal says. "And I noticed that those who've always been the most outspoken about the controversial methods The Noxsom Facility employs are keeping strangely quiet."

"Of course. I mean, torture's totally acceptable when you're doing it to Griffin Gifted fae, right?"

I'm about to ask someone to explain the kind of torture methods Noxsom employs, but Chase speaks before me. "Look, it's horrible that it's splashed all over the news, but at least we know we're heading to the right place."

"Do you think they've jacked up security there?" Elizabeth asks. "You know they feel totally threatened by any Griffin Gifted fae. They've probably added another hundred guards because they're so afraid our friends are somehow going to escape."

"Surely Noxsom is secure enough as it is?" Calla says, rolling her sleeves down once her communication spell is done. "If the rumors are true, then most of the prisoners are asleep. Besides, Perry would have reported it to me if he'd heard anything about extra security around Noxsom."

"Look, Perry's great," Elizabeth says, "but he doesn't know everything. He's part of one small department inside one Guild. He has nothing to do with the security at Noxsom."

Chase raises his voice above the chatter and says, "I think we can safely assume the Guild hasn't sent an extra hundred guards to Noxsom. You know why? Because the Guild is facing the one thing no one else in the history of our world has ever faced: the entire human realm suddenly becoming aware of our existence. That's massive. And since Prince Roarke began openly attacking humans, things have got even worse. With all of that going on, the Guild isn't going to waste extra guardians on a facility that's already highly secure."

"True," Elizabeth says. "You're probably right."

"Let's hope so." Chase pats his jacket and the belt slung around his hips, probably to check that all his various weapons are still in place. "Okay. Everyone ready to break into a prison?"

"Absolutely," Krystal and Carter say at the same time, before laughing at one another.

"Hey, it's nothing we haven't done before, right?" Elizabeth says, pulling her gloves a little tighter. "Should be a piece of cake."

"Em?" Chase looks at me.

"Yep. All good." What I really want to say is, *Am I the only one who feels like throwing up?* Probably, since I'm the only one who hasn't done something like this before. I try to push aside my doubt and the nagging reminder that pretty much nothing in my life ever goes right. Instead, I silently repeat, *This will all work out.*

"Hey, Em?" I look up and find Calla in the doorway looking back at me. It seems everyone else has left the room already. "Are you sure you're okay?" she asks.

"Yes." My voice sounds odd, so I clear my throat and try again as I walk toward her. "Yes, I'm fine."

"Are you having second thoughts about—"

"No. I'm fine, don't worry. I know I can do this. It's just *speaking*, right? It's easy."

She grips my upper arm and gives me an encouraging squeeze. "I'll be with you the whole time. I won't let anything happen to you."

Outside the dome layer, in the cool desert night, the seven of us hold hands and walk into the faerie paths together. If I weren't so nervous, I'd probably want to laugh at how strange we look. Instead, as the darkness closes around us, I focus on trying to keep my heart from leaping right out of my chest.

The faerie paths bring us to a wooded area bathed in pale beams of moonlight. The air is warmer, balmy like a summer night. Looking up through the trees, I notice that the moon isn't as high as it was by the oasis. *Early evening*, I think to myself. Noting the position of the moon or sun wasn't something I ever did in the non-magic world. But that was back when I had a cell phone to tell me the time, and when I didn't switch time zones so often—or ever, for that matter.

"It's this way," Chase says, leading us through the trees. We don't have to walk far before we reach the edge of the forest. Up ahead, surrounded by the kind of shield layer that shimmers just enough to be seen, is a plain, rectangular, single-story building. The Noxsom Facility. It doesn't look too bad from the outside, but I don't let the boring exterior fool me. All kinds of horrific torture could be taking place on the five additional levels hidden beneath this one.

"How long until your magic is ready, Em?" Chase asks.

"Uh …" I focus my attention on my magic for a moment. "Probably less than fifteen minutes. I can sense that it's almost ready."

We spread out as we wait, each of us remaining pressed against a tree to blend in with the forest so Calla doesn't have to conceal us yet. True to her word, she sticks right beside me, her back against the same tree I'm peering around. "I assume we can't use the faerie paths to get to the other side of that shield layer," I say.

"Nope. No access to the faerie paths beyond this forest. At least, that's what Perry said when he was explaining how to get here. We have a complicated series of enchantments we generally use to disable shield magic—including a few spells no one outside the Guild is supposed to know—but hopefully your Griffin Ability can save us the hassle."

"Yeah. I think it should work." I lean back against the tree and fan my face with my hand. It's warmer here than I expected, and my nerves are starting to make me sweat.

"I could cool you down with magic," Calla says, "but it might interfere with the communication spell."

I let my hand flop down against my leg. "It's okay. I'll probably cool down if I just stand here calmly and stop fanning myself."

"Probably," she says.

But I find it impossible to keep still. My hands end up twisting together. One heel taps repeatedly against the grass.

"You're nervous," Calla says, stating the obvious.

"I'm fine," I reply, though we both know I'm lying.

"You're scared this isn't going to work."

"Actually, I'm scared of the opposite. I mean—" I shake my head. "Sorry, that didn't sound right. I'm scared of seeing them again—Violet and Ryn—not because I don't want to, but because …" I swallow, and my heel tapping begins again. "Because … what if they don't want me as their daughter?"

Calla turns her head to look at me. "What?"

"I mean, what if I'm a huge disappointment to them? They've probably spent years building Victoria up in their minds, this perfect daughter they would have had if she'd never died. She'd be just like them, brave and selfless and totally kick-ass. And now I come along and I'm just … me. I'm the girl with the totally average human-world upbringing. I'm the girl who ran away from everything they offered me without explaining myself. I'm the girl who trusted the Unseelies instead of trusting them. There's no way they're *not* going to be disappointed by that girl."

"Look at me," Calla says. When I do, I find her bright golden eyes staring fiercely back at me. "Don't you dare let yourself believe lies like that. I can promise you, Em, that disappointment is the *last* thing they're feeling. You are their *daughter*. They will love you no matter what kind of person you are or what you've done. Okay?"

I breathe out slowly, letting go of some of my anxiety. "Okay." I tilt my head back against the tree, shut my eyes, and remain like that until the moment my Griffin Ability's magic rushes to the surface. I hold on tightly to it, imagining it as a living thing I'm wrestling into submission. Each time I do it, it gets a little easier. When I'm certain I've got it under control and it isn't about to escape me in a single flood, I open my eyes. "I'm ready," I tell Calla.

"Great." She raises her voice so the others can hear her and says, "I'm picturing us all as invisible now."

"Alrighty," Carter says from the next tree over. "It's all on you, Em. No pressure."

I manage a breathy laugh. "Yeah. No pressure at all."

Holy. Freaking. Fudge nut.

I breathe out slowly through my mouth and try not to throw up. Then I remind myself that I volunteered for this—that somewhere deep inside me, I still *want* to do this—and I walk forward with the rest of the team.

We leave the trees behind us and walk at a steady pace toward the facility. On the other side of the shield surrounding the building, rain begins to fall. It seems Chase is keeping his storm confined for now. I'm not sure what will happen once the shield is gone, but hopefully someone here knows how to keep us from getting drenched.

When we're a few paces away from the shield, we stop. No one says anything, but I know they're waiting for me. Like turning a faucet, I let some of my power leak out. My voice is rich and resonant, both far away and deep inside my chest, as I tell the shield around The Noxsom Facility that it no longer exists.

Then I wait. For a moment, I'm convinced it isn't going to work. I'm going to disappoint my team before we've even begun. But then the shield ripples and vanishes with a faint *pop*. And the dull roar of the rain reaches us.

"Nice," Kobe says as Elizabeth quickly raises her hand, forming an invisible umbrella over us.

"Awesome," Carter adds.

I manage a smile. "Thanks." This successful first step gives me a tiny boost in confidence. *I can do this.*

We head forward through the storm. The wind pummels us, but not a single drop of rain strikes my body. We reach the imposing main gate outside Noxsom, and unlocking it proves to be just as easy as removing the shield. Telling the Griffin Ability-detecting charm that it no longer works goes smoothly as well. Next, I unlock the door into the building itself, and finally—we're inside.

Chase quietly shuts the door behind us, and as I face the bright, sterile interior, my next command is for any surveillance bugs in this corridor. I can't see them, but I don't doubt they're here. "Surveillance bugs," I say, imagining tiny enchanted insects, "you can't see us." After a pause, I add in my normal voice, "I hope that worked if I can't actually see them and don't know where to direct my intentions."

"Well, let's move quickly," Chase says. "The sooner we get to the control room, the better. This way." He walks ahead of us, and we follow as quietly and quickly as we can along the bare and brightly lit corridors. With no visible hint of magic, this building is the closest I've seen to something that looks like it could belong in the human world.

Every few steps, I look around and repeat my command to the surveillance bugs I can't see. "Be careful not to use up all your magic," Calla says.

"I know, I'm just trying to keep us out of sight until we reach the control room."

"Almost there," Chase says. We turn a corner into the next corridor, where we have only two doors to choose from.

We come to a stop outside the first door, and Carter whispers, "Inmate records? In the room next door, right?"

Chase nods. "Yes, you can take a look at those. Make sure you find all ten of our people. Calla and Em, we're going into the control room. Kobe, Krystal, Elizabeth, you're out here to stop anyone from coming into either room." He reaches for the first door.

"Wait," Calla whispers. "Sorry, just let me focus. We're opening the door, but I need them to see a door that stays closed. And wherever we're standing, they need to see empty space." She pauses. "Okay, got it."

"Em?" Chase asks. I nod, but my heart patters painfully fast as he reaches for the door handle. The door barely makes a sound as he opens it. We step silently into the room. The four guards—two men and two women—seated in the center of the room watching at least a dozen orbs floating in rows in front of them don't turn their heads. If they did, they wouldn't see us. Calla's making sure of that with her illusion. My job now is to make sure they won't see us in their orbs as we steal along every corridor from here down to the bottom of this facility.

"Don't panic" is the first command I give them. Then, as they all look around at the sound of my voice, I add, "Stay seated. When you look at your orbs again, you won't be able to see any of us, no matter where we are inside The Noxsom Facility." I follow that command with another one that names us each individually, just in case the first command wasn't explicit enough. Finally, I add, "Forget that someone was in this room speaking to you."

The guards' faces take on blank expressions for a moment, then confusion. One man looks at the other. "What?" the second man asks.

"Nothing. Just … looking around."

They return to watching the orbs then. Calla raises a finger to her lips, and we quietly back away. The moment the door is closed behind us, giddy exhilaration rushes through me. "This is working," I whisper to Calla. "This is actually working."

"Well done," she answers. "Just don't get cocky now. We still have a lot to get through."

"I know, I know. This is just really cool, that's all."

Carter slips out of the room next door. "Found them," he says. "They're all on the third floor down."

"Good," Elizabeth says. "Not too far to go."

"All fine in there?" Carter asks, pointing to the control room door.

Chase gives him a thumbs up, then says, "Okay, let's get moving. Cal, you're still projecting that invisibility illusion?"

"Yes. In case we pass other people out here."

"Great."

The seven of us slip silently along the corridors with Chase leading the way. We're nearing the gate that separates this level from the next one down when we begin passing rooms with glass windows that allow us to look in. Calla and I pause briefly beside an occupied room to take a better look. A narrow bed stands in the center of the room. Its occupant, dressed in white overalls, is asleep. A funnel hangs from the ceiling, and from its open end, faint sparkling wisps of something drift down over the prisoner's head.

"That's so weird," I murmur. "What's coming out of the funnel?"

Calla shakes her head. "I don't know."

"I thought you said people are tortured in this prison."

"They are." She pauses before adding, "From what I've heard, the torture takes place inside their minds."

A chill creeps over me. My thoughts can't help turning to the kinds of nightmares this seemingly peaceful prisoner might be enduring right now.

"Calla, Emerson, come on," Elizabeth says. "We don't have time to waste staring at sleeping prisoners."

We hurry after the rest of our team. "Vi and Ryn and the others must be asleep too," I say. "Do you think we'll be able to wake them?"

"If we can't," Elizabeth says, "we're going to have to direct ten sleeping bodies through the air all the way out of this facility. That's going to take some coordination."

"Yeah," Chase says grimly. "Not an ideal situation, but we can make it work. Calla needs to focus on her ability, and so does Em. That leaves five of us to direct ten bodies. We should easily be able to manage two each."

Cartner nods. "Cool. I like it when you use the word 'easy.'"

"Or," I say to them, "I can *tell* our people to wake up and hope it works."

"Even better," Carter says.

We continue on, soon reaching the gate that blocks our access to the stairway leading down. But all I have to do is tell the gate to unlock itself, and it does. With each command I'm able to successfully give, my confidence rises. The next two gates open easily, and by the time we get to the correct level, I'm starting to think we might actually pull this off without anything going wrong. But I tell myself not to get too excited yet. We still need to get everyone out of here, and if for some reason I can't wake them, we'll have to levitate them. And directing ten sleeping bodies through the air doesn't sound like it's going to be as easy as everyone believes it will be.

"Okay, this is it," Chase says, stopping as we turn into a long passageway lined with doors. Instead of being closed, each one is slightly ajar.

"Weird," Calla says. "But I guess the doors don't need to be locked when the prisoners on the other side of them are unconscious."

"Were any of the rooms we passed on previous levels also open?" Krystal asks. "I can't remember now."

"Yes, I think some of them were," Elizabeth answers.

"So we're hoping this is normal?" I ask. At that moment, something crawls up the top of my arm. In fright, I inhale sharply and smack at my shoulder. But the crawling insect has morphed into a bird and narrowly misses my hand as it flits away. "Holy crap," I breathe. "Bandit, you have got to stop following me everywhere."

"You brought your shapeshifter pet with?" Elizabeth asks, arching one unimpressed eyebrow.

"Of course not," I hiss. "He likes to shift into tiny forms and hide in my pockets without my knowledge." Bandit lands on my shoulder and becomes a lizard. I grab hold of him and push him into my jacket pocket. Then I bend my head forward and whisper, "Please stay there."

"Ready, Em?" Chase asks. "Are you going to try to wake them?"

"Yes."

He looks behind us, then ahead once more. "I'll stay here at the end of the passage in case I need to keep anyone away while the rest of you are freeing our people. Calla and Em, check the first room." He looks at the other four. "You can move on to the next rooms."

As I walk toward the first door, my heart begins to race again. Who will I find in this room? Will it be Violet or Ryn? Then, as I reach out and push the door open, a sense of déjà vu overwhelms me. I remember being at Tranquil Hills Psychiatric Hospital several weeks ago, pushing open a door to see Dani. I remember the alarm that suddenly screamed through the quiet.

I cross the threshold into this room—and no alarm goes off. Calla follows quickly. I can't see the occupant of this bed because a thin grey blanket covers him or her completely. Which seems … strange? Calla must be thinking the same thing because she's now frowning at the bed. She edges closer, slowly takes hold of a section of the blanket, and yanks it back.

The bed is empty. Whatever formed the shape of a person beneath the blanket is gone.

"Crap!" Calla gasps as something darts out of the wall and catches hold of her arm. I jump backward as another something—a metal arm?—extends in my direction. Behind us, the door bangs shut. She shouts, "Don't go into the—" But her words are abruptly cut off as something like an electric current flashes across the room, burning into us. For a moment, intense pain paralyzes me. Then everything goes dark.

CHAPTER 7

I HAVE NO IDEA HOW MUCH TIME HAS PASSED WHEN I PEEL MY EYELIDS APART AND blink into the darkness. I give myself a few moments to recall what happened before I fell asleep. No, before I passed out. Before magic knocked me unconscious.

Before I became a prisoner.

I try to sit up, and that's when I realize my arms are bound behind my back and that something—dark fabric of some sort—covers my face. I start to panic then. It's too close—way too close—right up against my mouth, suffocating me—

The fabric is tugged upward, revealing an unfamiliar bearded man standing in front of me. He steps back, dropping the blue-black material—a pillowcase, judging by its shape—onto the floor. A hurried glance around me as I suck in a few deep breaths reveals a nondescript room. Fairly dark. No windows. Several plain chairs around an equally plain table, all pushed to one side of the room.

And five or six guardians.

Beside me, Calla jumps to her feet faster than should be possible for someone whose hands are tied together behind her back. "My magic may be blocked," she says, "but that won't stop me from fighting my way past all six of you."

Blocked magic? My eyes dart across Calla's body until they fall on the metal band clamped tightly around her right wrist. Is that was flashed out of the wall earlier? I don't know if my Griffin Ability can remove it, but I'm sure I can help with the ropes. As Calla takes a few menacing steps toward the guardians, I tell both her ropes and mine to break apart.

"Thanks," she says as her bonds drop to the floor. As she raises her fists, she adds. "Maybe you could try that with the—"

"Hey, there's no need for violence," the bearded man says. He holds one hand up as he takes a step back. "We're trying to help you."

Calla lets out a bitter laugh. "Is that so? Forgive me. I must be imagining the guardian markings I can see on every single one of you. Em?" Without looking away from the guardians, she shakes her right hand in my direction.

"That metal band is no longer attached to your wrist," I say quickly, letting some of my power flood into my voice. Everyone stares as the metal band expands and slips off Calla's hand. One or two guardians even flinch as it strikes the ground.

After another moment's pause, the bearded man speaks again. "Yes, we're guardians. That doesn't mean we agree with the Guild's policies regarding Griffin Gifted. We just want to set you free, that's all."

"Uh huh," Calla says. "That's why there are six of you all looking like you're ready to attack the moment I move."

"We're ready to defend ourselves," a redheaded woman says, "because we figured you wouldn't trust us. And there's a lot more than six of us, by the way."

"That sounds like a threat, not help."

The bearded man frowns at the redhead before turning back to us. "She didn't mean that as a threat. She means there are plenty more guardians who don't think it's right the way the Guild handles Griffin Abilities. You don't really believe every single guardian is against you, do you?"

"Kinda seems like it to me," I say.

"Look, I don't know exactly who you both are or what the Guild—whichever one you've had the misfortune of coming into contact with—has done to you," he says, "but I promise we're not all like that. Now there's a door back there—" he gestures with his thumb over his shoulder "—and you're welcome to leave through it. But we first need to tell you a few things so you don't get yourselves into more trouble."

Calla's still standing with her fists up, ready to fight. If I had the first clue what I was doing in the fighting department, I would have assumed the same stance by now. "A whole bunch of guardians ready to help us?" she says. "Sounds too good to be true. And that door you just pointed out sounds like a convenient trap."

"Why would we need to trap you?" the woman asks, throwing both hands up in exasperation. "You were already trapped inside a cell back at Noxsom. Every room in that corridor was a trap for you and the rest of your rebel friends. We could have left you there if we weren't on your side. Or, if we'd known about the trap sooner, we could have done something about it. Instead, Harryd risked everything to get you both out. And he opened the staff elevator so your friends could get back up to ground level and escape. They would have been trapped otherwise when every level went into complete lockdown."

"There was no elevator," Calla says immediately.

"It was hidden, of course. The door can't be accessed by anyone but a Noxsom guard."

I watch Calla's gaze dart toward the door before returning to the bearded man, Harryd. "If this *isn't* some kind of trap," she says, "then your fellow guards would have stopped you before you got out of Noxsom with us. You would have had to get us all the way back up to the entrance. No way could you have done that undetected."

"Those of us who work there have other ways of getting in and out of the facility. We know where the faerie paths can be opened. But yes, someone will have seen me by now in one of the surveillance orbs." He takes a deep breath. "I guess I'll be going into hiding now like you guys. Either that or turn myself in."

"We'll make sure you and your family are well hidden," someone else says.

I'm already shaking my head, still highly suspicious of these people. "So you gave up your job—your safety, your *everything*—just to get the two of us out of Noxsom?"

Harryd looks around at his fellow guardians. Then he laughs. It sounds the tiniest bit hysterical. "Yeah. It seems I did." He scratches his ear. "It was a spur-of-the-moment decision. Hopefully my wife doesn't kill me. But we've been talking about taking action for a long time, so it's not as though I've never considered doing something like this before."

Two or three guardians behind him nod. One says, "Nah, Lucilla will understand."

Harryd smiles, then adds, "We still don't know if we have the numbers to make a stand against the Guild's current leadership. We were trying to figure out if it might be possible to free the other rebels without revealing ourselves, but we hadn't made a concrete plan yet before the Head Councilor herself arrived at Noxsom earlier today and took the other rebels away. I've been working there for years, and nothing like that's happened before. She just showed up—no prior notification whatsoever— spoke to the warden, and then took the rebels. And after that, all the news reports kept saying the rebels were still at Noxsom. By the time I figured out the Councilor was setting a trap for you, it was too late to do anything about it. And then the two of you appeared in that cell after the spark stunned you, and at that point, it seemed like rescuing you was the only thing I could do, seeing as how we failed to get the other rebels out."

Calla doesn't move. "You're very convincing," she says. "I wish I could believe you."

The redhead turns away from us. "Just stun them and dump them out in the forest somewhere. We've done what we can for them. They're on their own now anyway, whether they trust us or not."

Magic ignites around Calla's fingertips. "Em, get ready to—"

"Whoa, hey!" Harryd raises his hands again. "Nobody's stunning anyone. Let's all just step back and let the two ladies leave the room."

"So you can stun us while our backs are turned?" I ask.

Harryd shows us his empty palms. "Look, no magic."

"And yet," Calla says, "I still don't believe you."

The redhead groans. "Is this what Perry meant when he spoke about the major challenges involved in helping the Griffin Gifted?"

Harryd sighs. Calla tilts her head ever so slightly. "Wait, who did you just mention?"

A small frown creases Harryd's brow. "Perry. You know him?"

This could also be a trick, I want to say to her. *Maybe they suspect Perry. They want us to confirm his involvement with the Griffin rebels.*

Instead of giving him away, Calla asks, "Perry who?"

"I don't know," Harryd answers. "He only used his first name. He's the one who wrote the original letter that's been circulating in secret, passed along by those of us who don't agree with the Guild's policies. It talks about all the things so many of us have been thinking but have been too afraid to put into action. Forming a united front. Going public with our beliefs and concerns. Challenging the Guild's policies and calling for new leadership. But it all depends on how many are willing to take the risk and stand up for what we know is right. This guy—Perry—has been gathering names. Well, numbers really, since none of us have added our full names to the letter. He just wants to know if we have enough people to make a difference."

The expression on Calla's face tells me she knows nothing about this letter. But a recent memory nudges the edge of my mind. A memory of Perry saying something about actively searching for other guardians who disagree with the Guild. It was a comment he made in passing, probably sandwiched in between the news about which prison Vi and Ryn landed up in and the memo he received about eight more Griffin rebels being captured.

"Sorry," Calla says to Harryd. "I don't think I know this Perry you're talking about."

Which is what I was hoping she would say. If these guardians do have a letter from Perry, it doesn't prove they're on our side. They could very easily have confiscated the letter from someone. Or they could be lying about it.

"Well, hopefully you will one day," Harryd says. "Now, if you'd like to leave—"

"Wait," someone else says. "You need to warn them about the tracking, remember? And your suspicions about where they took the other guy. Blackhallow."

Dash, I whisper silently.

"I'm not listening to any more of your lies," Calla says, and I know she's right even though I long to hear more about Dash. She raises both hands, magic crackling dangerously around her fingers. I swallow, open my mouth, get ready to use my Griffin Ability—

"Hey, hey, wait," Harryd says. "The Guild's tracking you now!" I pause with my mouth open, wondering if perhaps we should listen to him for just a little bit longer on the off chance that he's telling the truth. "You can't go back to wherever you've been hiding," he continues. "They'll find you there. They'll find you anywhere."

Calla pauses with her hands still raised and ready to attack. "Em," she says without looking back at me. "I hope you're ready to say something in case things are about to turn south."

Irritated mutters reach my ears as I answer, "I am."

"Then tell me, Harryd," Calla continues, "why we should be so worried about this tracking spell when no one has ever been able to track us before."

"It's the newest kind of enchantment," Harryd explains hastily. "I thought it was still in the experimentation phase, but the Head Councilor ordered it to be put in the funnels in all the Griffin rebels' cells when she arrived. You breathed it in as soon as you went in that room. It's slower than some other tracking or summoning spells, but it's far more accurate than anything else we've ever used. But it only works as long as you remain in one place. As soon as you travel any considerable distance, they have to restart their location spell."

"Let's say you're telling the truth," Calla says. "How long do we have until we're found?"

"The longest it's taken the Guild to locate someone is twenty-three and a half hours."

"And the quickest?"

"Sixteen hours."

She hesitates, then nods. "And how long until it wears off?"

"The fastest they've seen is three weeks. In some cases, it's lasted up to two months."

"Right. And what information do you have about Dash Blackhallow?"

"I overheard part of a conversation in which both Dashiell Blackhallow and Reinhold were mentioned. The two could be unrelated, but if not, that could be where they're holding him."

"Reinhold?"

"An off-site research station. I've heard the name only a few times over the past few years. I don't even know where it is."

"I see. Em? I think it's time for—"

"Every guardian in the room will become motionless for the next ten minutes." My words reverberate around the room. The guardians have only a second to direct their fearful glances my way before they become frozen to the spot. I launch myself toward the door after Calla, and together we run.

CHAPTER 8

NO GUARDIAN ARMY WAITS ON THE OTHER SIDE OF THE DOOR TO ATTACK US. A tunnel with rough rock walls extends left and right. Calla picks left. "Only ten minutes?" she comments as we race along the tunnel. "How generous of you."

"Yeah, well. I figured there's a possibility they were actually telling the truth. No need to keep them frozen for longer than necessary." We come to a halt, and I add, "Are we trying the faerie paths? Hopefully they're accessible from here. Wherever 'here' is."

"Yes." Calla's stylus is already in her hand. She scribbles quickly against the wall, and I hold my breath for a moment before a dark doorway materializes. As we rush into the faerie paths, she says, "I wanted to believe them. I really did. I just couldn't take the chance."

"I know," I answer as the darkness closes around us. Moments later, we rush into a forested area faintly illuminated by a moon far above us. Not the same forest as the one outside Noxsom, I realize. It feels colder and more overgrown. "Where are we?" I ask.

"Random part of Creepy Hollow."

I tip my head back and take in the spindly branches scraping lazily at the night sky. "It definitely seems creepy."

"Yes. This part is." She pushes her sleeve up and looks at her arm. "Communication spell's gone," she mutters, then reaches into a pocket and removes a small mirror. "That woman said something about Harryd opening an elevator so the rest of the team could get out. Let's hope that wasn't a lie." She draws a quick pattern across the mirror's surface with her finger before holding the mirror up in front of the two of us. For several endless seconds, all I see is the reflection of our pale faces. Then the glass surface ripples, and suddenly we're looking at Chase instead. "Did you get out?" Calla asks immediately.

"Calla! Where are you?"

"We're fine. Creepy Hollow. Did you get out of Noxsom?"

"Yes, we're hiding nearby trying to figure out how to get back in to retrieve you guys, but I'm guessing that's no longer necessary."

"No." Calla briefly explains what happened while I look around in all directions to make sure we're not about to be attacked by some ferocious magical beast.

"You were probably right not to trust them," Chase says when Calla's finished speaking, "though I sure hope they were telling the truth about being on our side."

"I know. It would be amazing if a whole bunch of guardians finally stood up for us." She switches the mirror from one hand to the other. "Chase, can we meet at blue two? Oh, and please bring supplies. Weapons, potions kit, all of that. I'll explain when you get here."

"Uh, okay. I'll be there as soon as I can. Ten minutes, tops."

Calla taps the mirror to end the call. "Blue two?" I ask. "Is that code for something?"

"Yes." She looks around, then quickly opens another doorway to the faerie paths. The ground we step onto on the other side is hard, covered in frost, and illuminated by starlight. I see no trees, no life, only a vast, still lake stretching out before us, and a snow-capped mountain beyond it. An icy breeze lifts my hair, raising a shiver across the back of my neck. Bandit, still in the form of a lizard, climbs out of my pocket, scurries down my leg, and begins exploring.

"Before we decide on anything else," Calla says, "we need to talk about the tracking spell they mentioned."

I pull my jacket tighter around my body as I face her. "You think it's real?"

"It could be. And if it is, we can't risk going back to the oasis. We can't have guardians pouring in there if it turns out this spell is as accurate as they say it is."

"Sixteen hours. That's the fastest they've found someone."

"Yes. Which means we need to keep moving every fifteen hours to be safe."

"They also said this spell could last for two months."

"Yes."

I breathe out a heavy sigh. "So we have to keep moving every fifteen hours for *two months*?"

"We'll find a way to get rid of it before then. Like your Griffin Ability, for example. Perhaps you can tell the enchantment to leave us."

A brief humorless laugh escapes me. "Knowing my luck, it'll be one of those special witchy spells that's immune to Griffin Abilities."

She frowns. "Special witchy spells?"

I tell her what Zed said about witches being aware of Griffin Abilities long before anyone else, so they crafted a few spells that would be resistant to any kind of Griffin magic. "It makes sense," I add, "that the Guild would use magic that can't be tampered with by Griffin Abilities if Griffin Gifted fae are the ones they're trying to track down. Even if it means they have to consult with witches."

Calla rolls her eyes. "Yeah. At this point, I wouldn't put it past certain Guild Council members to work with witches if it served their purposes." Her gaze shifts past me. "It's hard to imagine I was once so desperate to be part of that world."

"Well," I say quietly, "from what Perry says—and if we can believe the people who freed us from Noxsom—not all guardians are like that. Hopefully plenty of them exist who wish the Guild was the same kind of place you wanted to join all those years ago."

She smiles as her eyes refocus on me. "That's probably the most optimistic thing I've ever heard you say."

Her words bring to mind all the things I'm *not* feeling optimistic about—like how are we ever going to find Violet and Ryn now that the Head Councilor's taken them from Noxsom? *One problem at a time*, I remind myself. "Okay, let's continue with the optimistic streak then." I feel for my Griffin power. It's tough to tell how much is left, but hopefully it's enough to get rid of whatever magic we breathed in while we were inside that Noxsom cell. "What exactly shall I say to get rid of the tracking enchantment?"

Calla thinks for a moment, then gives me a few suggestions. Once we've decided on the best words, I let go of my hold on my Griffin power and speak. "The Guild's tracking enchantment will leave our bodies now." I touch Calla's arm. "Your body contains no magic that will allow anyone to track you or find you. My body contains no magic that will allow anyone to track me or find me." I pause, sensing the rush of power as it leaves my body. I don't try to hang onto any of it, just in case every last bit of it is needed for my command. "I really hope that worked," I say after a few moments.

"We'll find out tomorrow. And if it didn't work, then we'll just keep moving around. It won't be that bad, I promise."

"I guess." I look around for Bandit, just to make sure he hasn't wandered too far, and find him in cat form scratching at the frozen ground. "I'm starting to wish

I hadn't removed that small metal thing Roarke stuck behind my ear," I say. "It kept Violet from finding me while I was with the Unseelies, so hopefully it would have kept the Guild from finding me too—although we'd still have to worry about them finding you. Oh—" I look up as something occurs to me. "Crap. What if the Guild forces Vi to use her ability to find us? Then it won't matter if this tracking spell is still on us or not."

"Don't worry about that," Calla says with a shake of her head. "They don't know what she can do. They know she's Griffin Gifted, but that's it."

"Won't they try to find out, though?"

"Probably, but they won't be able to. Like the location of the oasis, there's certain information we've made sure is wrapped up in our protective enchantment. And we've all been trained in resisting compulsion potions and truth potions. The Guild will be lucky if they can get anything useful out of our people."

I look at Bandit again and think of all the movies I've seen that include interrogation scenes. I think of how the interrogators often threaten the life of someone else—a family member, friend, partner—in order to make a person talk. My mind can't help taking the next step and imagining Violet being tortured in order to make Ryn talk—or vice versa. The chill in the air seems to sink through my clothing and into my bones. I rub my hands up and down my arms, but the action does little to warm me. "I don't think I can be as hopeful as you," I quietly tell Calla. "I think if the Guild wants information, they'll get it in whatever way they can."

"Hey, what happened to that optimism from a few moments ago?" she asks. "This will all work out. We'll get our happy ending."

I shake my head and let my hands fall to my sides. "You don't know that, though. You guys think you're all, like, superheroes or something, but it isn't possible for you to save the day *every single time*. Maybe this time, there is no happy ending. Maybe this will never work out, and we'll never be a family."

Calla's expression becomes as fierce as when I told her Vi and Ryn would be disappointed to have me as a daughter. "That is not an option. We *will* get them back. Somehow, no matter how many wrong steps we take along the way, we will rescue Vi and Ryn and everyone else." She breathes out a shaky breath as she looks away. "After you died—after we *thought* you died—it almost tore our family apart. It was … I can't explain to you how horrible it was. And now, when we've been given the chance to be a whole family again, something else is threatening to divide us again." She swallows. "Most people don't get a chance to fix their mistakes. They have to deal with the consequences and move on. So that's what we did all those years ago.

But for whatever reason, I've now been given that chance. And I refuse to mess it up."

I let her words sink in before asking, "What mistake?"

She pulls her head back slightly. "Zed didn't tell you? He didn't mention that he was a prisoner in the Guild and I allowed him to escape when he should have remained locked up? That if I hadn't let him go free, he never would have been able to conspire with witches and place a changeling spell upon you?"

I shake my head. "No. He didn't say anything about that. So … you're saying … setting him free was your mistake? And because of that, you blame yourself for what he ended up doing to me?"

"I'm saying I recognize the part I played. For a long time, I tried to make up for what I'd done, until I realized it was impossible. I could either hate myself forever or forgive myself and move on. So moving on is what I did. Now, though, I have a real chance to make things right. That's why I did everything in my power to get you back from the Unseelies, and that's why I will do whatever it takes to get Vi and Ryn back."

I swallow against the emotion tightening my throat. "Thank you. And also … I don't hold you responsible for the mess Zed made of our lives. That's all on him."

She gives me a small smile. "That means more to me than you can imagine."

A faint ripple in the air nearby catches my attention. A second later, a doorway opens and Chase steps through. Before either of us can say a word, he pulls us both into a tight embrace. I'm not the hugging type when it comes to people I don't know well, but I barely have time to be startled before he steps back. "What else happened?" he asks immediately. "Why can't you return to the oasis?"

"The Guild is apparently tracking us now," Calla says. "It was something we breathed in while we were in that empty room. Did any of our team go into the other rooms?"

"No. They didn't get a chance before your door slammed shut."

"Good." Calla explains to Chase how we're going to have to keep moving, possibly for the next two months.

"Well," I say when she's finished, "we could return to the oasis for a few hours in between each move. But then …" I shake my head. "No, I guess that's too much of a risk."

"Definitely too much of a risk," Chase says. "What if the Guild's tracking techniques improve?"

"Look, who knows if this whole tracking spell thing is even true," Calla says, "but until we know for sure, we're not going back to the oasis. Em's told the spell to vanish from our bodies, but we won't know until tomorrow if her magic was successful."

"Why wouldn't it be?" Chase asks. "Her ability seems pretty amazing so far."

"Thanks," I say, "but Zed told me certain witch spells are immune to Griffin Abilities. If the Guild knows about that kind of magic, then I'm sure they'd try to take advantage of it."

Chase sighs. "Wonderful. Well, in case you need it, here's your bag." He hands Calla a leather backpack. "Weapons, a full potions kit, some money. You'll need to buy food."

"And a change of clothes, perhaps." She gives me a watered-down smile. "This is going to be fun, right?"

I lift my shoulders against the cold and start shifting from foot to foot while eyeing the backpack with skepticism. "Small weapons only, I assume?"

"Some of them," Chase says. "But most of them are small because I shrank them. You'll have to make them bigger before you can use them."

"Oh. I didn't know that was possible." I shake my head at myself for being so silly. "But of course it's possible. Everything's possible in this world, right?"

"Almost." He frowns as I continue to shuffle from foot to foot, then waves his hand briefly above my head. "Sorry, I didn't realize you don't know how to warm yourself."

"Oh, thanks," I say as the sensation of warmth slowly envelops me.

Calla pulls the backpack onto her shoulders. "Ugh, I just can't believe they tricked us like that," she groans. "For the second time! First they used Ryn and Vi as bait to draw some of us there, and then tonight the rest of us walked into the exact same trap."

"We were far better prepared tonight," Chase reminds her. "We could have pulled it off if our people had actually been there."

"Which leads us to the next problem," I say. "Where are they now?"

"I'm going to find out," Chase assures me. "I'd like to travel around with the two of you, make sure you're both safe, but—"

"No, you need to find our family," Calla says. "Oh, and see if you can find out anything about a place called Reinhold. It's a research station, apparently, and there's a chance Dash might be there. If this Reinhold place exists, that is."

"Reinhold. Okay. What will the two of you do? Vacation in a different spot every day?"

"I was thinking more along the lines of following Roarke's mess around and cleaning it up. Discreetly, of course."

Chase bends to scratch Bandit behind his cat ears as the shapeshifter comes close enough to sniff his shoes. "Good idea. Stay in touch with Perry. He'll know about things before they become public. And the Seers will See some things before they happen. If the Guild discards any of those visions, you can take care of them."

Calla nods. "So, it's pretty much business as usual then. Except I'll be doing it with Em." She looks at me. "You don't have to be involved. Or you can assist from a distance. We can assess each situation as it comes."

"Bandit will need to travel around with you as well," Chase says as Bandit purrs contentedly. "He must have breathed in the same spell you two breathed in."

"That won't be a problem," I say, "considering he follows me everywhere already." Bandit opens his eyes and looks at me, as if he knows I'm talking about him. "Okay, so you promise you'll do everything you can to find Vi, Ryn and Dash?" I ask Chase. "And you'll tell us the moment you know anything? I know both worlds are falling apart around us, so this is probably a selfish thing to say, but they're kind of a priority to me."

"Don't worry, they're our priority too," Chase says, straightening and producing his stylus. "The Guild and the Seelies are dealing with the worlds-falling-apart problem." As he opens a doorway to the paths, he adds, "I'll stay with you for the night, then return to the oasis. You two can sleep, and I'll keep watch in case Em's command didn't work and guardians happen to show up earlier than expected." He looks back at us. "Any suggestions for where you want to spend the night?"

"As long as it's not on this cold, hard ground, I'm happy," I tell him.

"How about orange three?" Calla says, stepping forward and taking Chase's hand.

"Orange," I say. "Sounds warm."

She smiles as she reaches for my hand. "It is."

I follow her into the faerie paths, choosing to be optimistic for now. My Griffin Ability command has worked, I tell myself. The tracking spell is gone. We'll confirm it tomorrow, and then we'll return to the oasis to focus on what really matters: finding Violet and Ryn.

The following morning, after Chase leaves us, Calla and I remain in the small seaside town where we spent the night. We hang around the busy marketplace in the town square, concealed by an illusion of invisibility and ready to escape through the faerie paths at a moment's notice. The afternoon passes slowly by, and eventually it's been fifteen hours since we arrived here last night. My heart pounds as we wait in silence, watching people go about their business. As we approach sixteen hours, I begin to feel sick. It's not that I'm afraid we'll get caught; it's the anticipation I hate so much. The *doing nothing*.

But the sixteenth hour passes us by, and nothing happens. I know we need to wait until twenty-three and a half hours, just to be certain, but already I begin to feel hopeful. I remember the optimism I chose last night as I walked into the faerie paths.

But my optimism is short-lived. At about half an hour after the sixteen-hour mark, the guardians show up. I thought a horde of them would suddenly appear—if they arrived at all—but they're subtle about it. I don't know how long they've been there when Calla nudges my arm and points out several pairs of faeries who don't quite seem to fit in with everyone else. Their eyes dart around too much, never settling on one person for more than a moment. Clearly they're not interested in any of the items for sale at the stalls set up in the square.

For several moments, disappointment threatens to overwhelm me. I want to scream out, *Why is everything so hard?* Why is there always another obstacle between me and the happiness I've been trying to get to my *whole freaking life*? But I breathe deeply, push my disappointment down, and swallow back my angry tears.

I'm a survivor.

I've never given up on anything before, and I'm not about to start now.

And I'm not facing any of this alone.

I take Calla's hand and follow her into the faerie paths, and so begins our nomadic life.

CHAPTER 9
VIOLET

Time was a concept that didn't seem to exist in the ever-changing landscape Violet wandered through. It was a place full of shadows and memories and the dark, fading edges of a vignette. It was a place of terrors, of pain. It was a place she might have lived in for a day or a year, or perhaps a hundred years. She couldn't tell how many times she'd relived the nightmares.

The only thing she knew was that none of it was real.

She looked around at the distant echo of a cry. The others—the friends who'd tried to rescue her—were here somewhere, trapped in this world of waking nightmares. They came close sometimes. Close enough that she could almost touch them before they were yanked away.

Seeing no one, Violet turned and hurried in the opposite direction. She was in the Guild's foyer now. The old Guild, the one that had been destroyed. An ache twisted in her chest at the memory of her beloved Guild lying shattered and broken across the forest floor. She ran for the stairs, hoping to leave the memory behind. Hoping to outrun what always came next.

But suddenly she was no longer running. Instead, she found herself on her knees among leaves and twigs, acrid smoke burning the back of her throat. Without having to look, she knew the devastation that filled the scene: a mound of debris, a forest in ruins, and a body crushed beneath a fallen tree. Tora's body.

Tora had been a mentor first, then a friend, and eventually, she'd felt almost like a sister. And now she was lying dead in front of Violet. And though none of this was real, it hurt just as much as when it had happened. It was a knife stabbing into Violet's chest, through her heart and through her lungs, so that she couldn't breathe and the pain radiated from her heart to fill every inch of her being.

She fled from the memory of Tora's death and found herself in a nursery. A nursery with a crib and a baby that didn't move.

Another Victoria.

Another death.

Pain and absolute bone-chilling horror.

She couldn't bear to look, but the nightmare wouldn't have it any other way. The crib was right in front of her and the baby inside was unnaturally pale, completely still.

But this wasn't right, Violet reminded herself, finally managing to tear her gaze away. A spark of hope ignited inside her as she remembered the heart-stopping words Em had shouted on Velazar Island. *They're my parents!* How could Violet have forgotten those words? How could this nightmare have extinguished a light as bright and warm as the news that her own child was still alive? She shut her eyes, blotting out the image of the crib and the tiny lifeless body within it, trying with all her might to hang onto an image of Emerson.

But the nightmare wouldn't let Violet go that easily. A heavy weight bore down on her, and when she opened her eyes, she was leaning over the crib. Her hand reached out, and one finger touched the cold skin of the baby's cheek. That moment—that exact moment when she realized her baby was no longer living—hit Violet square in the chest. She sucked in a desperate breath as her heart shattered and the echoes of her own heartrending scream from that night assaulted her ears over and over again.

She pushed herself away and ran. Into the night. Into the forest. She'd been here before, and here she would stay forever. Running from her father's death, running from Nate's betrayal, running from Victoria's lifeless body. "It isn't real," she kept repeating. "It isn't real. It isn't real." But the pain was real. The heartache was real. And try as she might, she couldn't outrun it.

"Vi!"

She stumbled to a halt at the sound of someone shouting her name. She swung around and saw him coming through the trees toward her. Ryn. She ran for him, reached for him, but as always, she couldn't get close enough. He was always just a little too far away.

"Are you okay?" he asked.

She nodded, though an echo of her pain still pulsed through her body. "I keep seeing … the crib."

"Me too." He swallowed. "I keep reminding myself that she's actually alive, but it does nothing to remove the pain every time I have to relive that moment."

Violet nodded, looking up at the tangled branches above as she blinked away tears.

"They'll pull us out of this nightmare eventually," Ryn said as the forest around them shifted and changed. They were in a different part of it now, where the ancient gargan tree they'd loved as children lay fallen.

"I know," she said, "but when? I've heard they pull people out every few days, but I have no concept of how much time has passed. Sometimes I think I've been stuck in here for years."

Ryn shut his eyes and breathed out a shaky breath. "Soon. It has to be soon, or else … I don't know how many more times I can go through this."

Violet's heart broke for him as much as for everything she'd endured in this nightmare. "You have to, though. We both have to. When they pull us out, they'll question us. They'll demand information. And when we refuse to give it to them, they'll toss us back into this nightmare. They'll do it over and over again until we give in."

He opened his eyes. "I'll never give in. I'll never give up the people we love."

"Neither will I."

"And we'll be tortured for eternity because of it," Ryn added quietly. "We'll never know Victoria. Emerson. We'll never find her."

"We will." Violet reached across the space that seemed so small and yet utterly infinite at the same time. "We'll find a way out of this," she said, desperate inner strength finding its way into her voice. "I swear to you we will."

PART II

CHAPTER 10

"Seriously? I thought I'd got it by now."

"Almost." She walks closer and adjusts the position of my fingers around the knife's handle. "There." She steps back. "Try again."

I face the tree and the round frisbee-sized target Calla transformed from a stick. I repeat her instructions in my head yet again, trying to turn the steps into one fluid motion. Then I raise the knife, swing my arm forward, and let go. The knife spins through the air, whacking the target a second later. The blade strikes first—which is a lot less embarrassing than the handle striking first—but the angle's off, and the knife bounces away and lands on the ground beside the other knives that have failed to impale the target. I stare at it for a moment before muttering, "I suck."

"You don't suck," Calla says. "You've already improved. And considering you'd never thrown a knife before yesterday, you're doing pretty well."

It's our third day on the run from the Guild's tracking spell, and most of our spare time has been spent playing with weapons or throwing various forms of magic at one another—while Calla protects each of us with a bubble of shield magic, of course. The continued activity helps keep us distracted from the frustration of not being able to find or save Vi, Ryn, Dash and the others. They're constantly at the back of my mind, though, no matter how busy we keep ourselves.

Perhaps it's Calla's preference, or perhaps this world is covered in far more trees than the human world, but each time we move, we end up in another forested area. This one's my favorite so far. The trees, bushes, flowers, and even the creatures form a continuous palette of autumn colors. Orange, gold, reddish brown and bronze. Bandit seems to love it too. He's been scurrying around exploring all day.

"Can we go back to the sword fighting lessons?" I ask as I fetch the fallen knives and the one that managed to land vertically in a tree root. The root heals itself as I pull the knife free. "I think I'm better with a weapon that doesn't have to leave my hand. Arrows and knives and throwing stars have much greater potential for missing their target."

"Yes, but arrows, knives and throwing stars mean you're further away from your attacker. I don't plan for you to get close enough to an enemy to use a sword."

"You know you can't really control that kind of thing, right?"

"Yes, I know," she says with a sigh. "We can play around with swords again later. For now, try again with—" A lighthearted melody plays briefly behind us, then stops. Calla turns to face the two amber tablets and the mirror suspended in the air a few paces away. "Hmm. Was that someone trying to call us?" She moves closer to the mirror and frowns at its glossy surface. We have the mirror for communication, the one tablet for general news, and the other tablet for Guild Seer visions. The news spell was an easy one, apparently. The kind of spell anyone can apply to any amber device in order to read the latest news. The Seer visions feed, however, was more complicated to get hold of.

Violet mentioned Seers to me when I first arrived at the oasis, but Calla explained again how they see glimpses of the future. They report their visions of things going wrong to the Guild, and the Guild sends guardians to stop certain things before they go wrong. Thanks to Dash's father Flint, Calla and I now have access to some of these Seer visions. He went into the Seer department at the Creepy Hollow Guild and managed to illegally duplicate one of the vision lists. Specifically, the visions related to incidents of unglamoured magic in the human realm—incidents that Roarke and his followers will most likely be responsible for.

"If it *was* someone trying to call us," Calla says, still squinting at the levitating mirror, "they obviously decided they have better things to do." She takes a step to the side and peers at the tablet with the list of Seer visions. Having gathered all the fallen knives, I join her side.

"No important news from Chase yet, I see. Oh, and that vision still hasn't been assigned to anyone." I point the tip of a knife at a vision involving two Unseelie faeries and a movie theater. "It's been there for hours. Time's going to run out if they don't send someone to deal with that problem soon."

"Yes, but we can't do anything about it unless we know for sure the Guild's not handling it. We don't want to get in some guardian's way."

I heave a resigned sigh as I nod. All visions remain on the list until a trainee or guardian team is assigned to deal with the impending problem. If a Council member decides a vision isn't important enough to be dealt with, tiny letters appear in brackets beside it: *alternate*. Calla said the Seers believe those visions are taken care of in some other way they're not aware of. But thanks to Perry's sneaking around and eavesdropping, the Griffin rebels have known better for years. Any visions labeled 'alternate' are considered too minor for the Guild, with their limited number of guardians and trainees, to get involved with. So those visions are discarded. They're the visions Perry's spent years secretly gathering up every few days and sending to the Griffin rebels.

Calla and I have prevented two of these 'minor' incidents from taking place, and this morning we cleaned up the mess left behind from a third incident, since we arrived too late to prevent an Unseelie royal guard from appearing at a school swimming lesson and turning the pool water into sand. Calla planned to go around from child to child—while glamoured, of course—and apply some kind of charm to make them confused and forgetful about what they'd witnessed. But I had some Griffin Ability power stored up, so I told the whole class and the teachers to forget what they'd seen.

And it worked.

"Okay, try again with the knives," Calla says, turning away from the tablets. "We can check the visions again in about ten minutes." She glances to the side at the glowing numbers hanging in the air that are counting down toward zero. "And we'll need to leave in just over an hour."

I nod as I turn back to face the tree and drop all the knives except one onto the grass beside me. It was a little disconcerting at first to be followed around by an enchanted timer, but I've become used to the glowing numbers suspended beside the tablets and mirror. It's a useful reminder of exactly when we need to open a doorway to the faerie paths and move somewhere else. Calla resets it for fifteen hours every time we move, which gives us a cushion of about an hour to gather our things, open a doorway, and move to a new part of the world.

"Okay," I sigh. "Let's see if I can hit the target at least once before we have to leave. Too bad I can't command myself to be expertly skilled at knife throwing."

"Now that's an idea," Calla says. "Maybe that would work."

"I doubt it. When I was at the Unseelie Palace, I told myself I knew how to dance every traditional faerie dance. Unfortunately, it didn't work." I raise the knife, but at the back of my mind I'm still wondering if I might actually be able to use my Griffin Ability for this. Part of the way my power seems to work is by knowing my intentions. The magic needs to know what I *mean* as well as what I'm saying. Obviously I didn't know what I meant when I told myself I knew how to dance because I didn't have the first clue what the steps were for any of the dances I hadn't yet learned. But throwing a knife is different. I know what I'm *supposed* to do. I know how the knife should strike the tree. I just don't seem to be able to physically do it myself.

"Em?" Calla says from behind me. "Everything okay?"

I realize I've been standing still with the knife raised for several moments. "Yes, I'm just … thinking." I look at the target once more, then relax my hold on my Griffin Ability and say to the knife, "When I let go, you'll fly toward the tree and your blade will strike the center of the target." Then I swing my arm forward and let go.

I watch the knife spin and land with the same expert precision it possessed when Calla demonstrated the maneuver. A smile spreads slowly across my face.

"Aha," Calla says with glee. "It does work after all."

I look over my shoulder at her. "Do you think it's cheating?"

"No, it's just a different skill you're using. If the point of the exercise is to get the knife to hit the target, then it doesn't matter how you get it done."

"Cool. Maybe I can do it faster. Maybe I can do it with other weapons. Maybe one day I'll be able to fight as well as you, but using words instead of my own physical strength."

Calla smiles. "I don't see why not. But you wouldn't be able to completely replace actual physical fighting, because as I said before—"

"What if someone prevents me from speaking," I finish. "I know. So we can carry on with the lessons you were giving me, but maybe I should practice fighting this way as well. I mean, if I've got the ability, then I may as well use it. You fight with yours, right?"

"Yes. I use it to distract and confuse."

"Well it'll certainly be distracting and confusing when I start talking to my weapons in the middle of a fight," I say with a laugh.

I try again with our collection of knives, and each time, the blade strikes exactly where I tell it to. I practice saying the words faster and faster, then test out my speed by placing several knives on my palm and telling them to fly through the air one after the other. Calla walks back and forth behind me, checking the Seer visions tablet and giving me the occasional suggestion. "Tell the knife to return to you after it reaches its target," or "Tell the knife to stab the target several times after striking it once."

Eventually, when my brain feels like it needs a break, I bend over and lean my hands on my knees. "Whew, this is exhausting. You wouldn't think the only thing I was doing was speaking."

"Well, you were using magic too, and that gets tiring." Calla crouches down by the backpack and searches inside. "Do you want a chocolate apple?"

"Sounds amazing. Oh, hey, Bandit," I add as Bandit transforms from a cat into a small dragon covered in silver scales. "That's, what, the fourth time today you've decided to be a dragon?"

"He seems to really like the dragon form," Calla says, standing and walking to my side.

"Yeah, probably because he knows how much I loved riding the dragons at the Unseelie Court."

"Here you go." Calla hands me a small apple-shaped chocolate, dark and covered in gold dust, then focuses on Bandit again. "I don't know if you know this, but he won't easily be able to shift into a dragon for much longer. As he gets older, he'll assume the shape of the older version of whatever animal he's shifting into. Problem is, an adult dragon is enormous, so that would take a huge amount of a formattra's magic to achieve."

"Oh." I pop the tiny chocolate into my mouth and bend to pat Bandit's silver-scaled head. "Sorry, Bandit," I say around the chocolate. "Oh, but—" I finish chewing and straighten. "I'm sure Jack told me Filigree became a dragon once. Was that when he was little?"

"No, he was fully grown then. It's not that it's impossible, it just requires more magic and makes them extremely tired. I'd never seen Filigree as a dragon before, but a witch was about to kill Violet, so I think Fili got a little overprotective. After he shifted back into something smaller, he barely moved for days. Vi wasn't sure he'd ever shift again, but he recovered eventually."

"Okay, so if Bandit is really desperate, he can at least—" I look around as the mirror's melody interrupts me.

"Okay, someone's definitely calling this time," Calla says, heading back to the mirror. "Oh, finally. It's Perry." As I reach her side, she taps the mirror's surface where an image of a wide-eyed Perry has appeared.

"Hey!" he exclaims. "Finally. I tried a few minutes ago and had to abort when I realized someone in the shop was watching me." He pushes his hair out of his face and continues before Calla can say anything. "I'm *so* sorry about what happened at Noxsom. No one had any idea the Council was using that as a trap for you guys. And I'm sorry I haven't got back to you until now. I've been working all hours, and I feel like everyone's looking over my shoulder, even when I'm not at the Guild. Everyone's suspicious of everyone else now. I had to dig up this old mirror just in case the one I normally use has been tampered with. Flip, it's getting more and more dangerous trying to do the right thing."

Calla folds her arms across her chest. "You didn't exactly help your situation when you decided to send a letter around the various Guilds gathering support for your anti-Guild vendetta and sign your actual *name* on it, you idiot."

Perry pauses, his mouth half open. He blinks, shuts his mouth, then says, "I don't remember telling you about that."

"You didn't. The Guild members who rescued Em and me from Noxsom were trying to use it as proof that they're on the Griffin rebels' side. I'm still not sure if that was all an elaborate trick to get us to reveal who we're communicating with inside the Guild."

A grin spreads across Perry's face. "The people who got you out of Noxsom were Guild members? That's fantastic! Did they say how many supporters have been added to my letter? I haven't seen it since I first sent it out."

"Perry!" Calla exclaims. "Are you trying to land yourself in a prison of eternal torture for being a Guild traitor? Why would you put your name on that thing?"

"Look, to be fair, it was only my first name. And I've heard of at least one other Perry in the Guild system."

"That was still a huge risk. I know you want to change the way things are, and that's extremely admirable, and … I actually really want to hug you for doing something like that for us, but at the same time, you're no use to anyone if you land yourself in a prison cell for being a Guild traitor. So be careful, for goodness' sake!"

"Aah." He gives her a big goofy grin. "This is like when your mom gets super mad at you for nearly getting yourself killed by crossing the street just as a carriage is about to land, and then a second later she hugs you and tells you how much she loves you."

I tilt my head a little closer to the mirror and say, "Yes, I think it's exactly like that. And we're both very grateful you're taking a risk for people like us."

"Of course I'm grateful," Calla mutters. "I'm just hoping it doesn't get you arrested."

"Hey, I was very careful," he tells us. "I gave the letter to someone I was almost certain agreed with me. All he had to do after indicating his support on the letter was find one other person he believed to be on our side and pass the letter on."

Calla heaves a sigh and drops her hands to her sides. "Okay. Well thank you."

"So, I know you just said you've been busy," I say to him, "but have you been able to find out anything more about where Vi and Ryn and the others are being kept?"

"No. I haven't had time to do any snooping, and the Council members don't exactly hang out in corridors chatting loudly about their private plans so everyone can overhear them."

"And did Chase tell you we need information on a place called Reinhold?" Calla adds. "It's possible Dash might be there, and if Dash is there, the other rebels might have been taken there as well."

"Reinhold? I've never heard of it. But—" He cuts himself off, his expression turning thoughtful. "I wonder if that could be …"

"Could be what?" Calla prompts.

"Remember those experiments you stumbled across years ago when you were sneaking around the lower levels of the Guild? Those rooms where they were experimenting on Griffin Gifted fae? Well those rooms disappeared about four or five years ago. I figured they couldn't be gone completely. They must have simply moved, right? I tried to ask around, but no one seemed to know much."

"And then?" she asks. "You didn't try to look into it any further?"

"Calla, I have so much to keep up with already. And right now, I've barely even—oh, crumbs, gotta go." Perry vanishes from view as he lowers his mirror.

"Wait!" Calla calls. "Please can you try to find—" The mirror goes blank for a moment, then shows us our own perplexed faces reflected back at us. Calla shuts her eyes, exhaling sharply. "I know the Guild needs every guardian available right now to keep both sides of the veil from falling apart, but this is a seriously inconvenient time for Perry to suddenly become too busy to spy for us."

"Tell me about it," I mutter.

"Anyway, we should probably pack up and get moving soon. I'll shrink the weapons."

As she turns away, my eyes are drawn to the tablet listing the Seer visions. The one about the movie theater has vanished, so hopefully someone took care of that. But a new one has popped up at the top of the list. Like most of the other visions, the details are incomplete. Several pieces of a puzzle that show only part of the finished picture. But all I care about is that one word at the end. That one word that sends ice traveling down my spine.

A magical eruption inside a restaurant with pink shutters. Uniforms with insignia of the Unseelie royal guard. Shadow length and quality of light suggest late afternoon. Town name: Stanmeade.

"Stanmeade," I say out loud. "That—that must be my Stanmeade. Unless there's more than one? But the pink shutters—that's Bloomberry Cafe. It has to be." I turn around. "Calla, we have to go there."

Calla drops a handful of tiny weapons into the backpack before standing. "Roarke knows you used to live there, doesn't he? Didn't he abduct you from Chelsea's home the first time you met him? This may be a trap for you."

"Why would he do it this way, though? He doesn't know you and I are following the Seer visions. And how would he know if this would even show up in a Seer's vision. If he wanted to get me to Stanmeade, this would definitely not be the best way to go about it."

"I suppose so, but then don't you think it's a very big coincidence that something's happening in Stanmeade of all places?"

"No. I'm sure he is doing it intentionally. But not because he wants to draw me there. Probably just because he hopes I'll hear about it at some point and it'll seriously piss me off." I pull both tablets and the mirror from the air. "We have to go there. We have to stop it."

"Em, slow down. The Guild is probably going to send someone. We need to wait."

"We can't wait!" I crouch down and shove the tablets and mirror into the backpack. I pull my jacket out, and Bandit scurries into one of the pockets in the form of a mouse. "What if they decide to label it 'alternate' and then it's too late for us to do anything? We have no idea what time it is there right now." I stand and pull my jacket on, then close the backpack. "At the very least, we need to go there and see what time it is. If the Guild sends someone, then fine. We can watch and make sure they do their job properly. But I'm not going to sit around somewhere far away and hope it all works out."

"Em, it isn't safe. We can't just—"

"I have friends there!" I shout. "My best friend. She's … I haven't seen her since my magic almost killed her. If she happens to be nearby when that magical eruption takes place, and she ends up—" I cut myself off and shake my head. I hoist the backpack onto one shoulder. "I can't let her get hurt again."

A beat of silence passes. "Okay. I understand." Calla closes her hand in the air near the floating countdown numbers, hiding them for now. "Let's go. You're directing the faerie paths."

CHAPTER 11

We step out of the faerie paths into the alley between Tygo's Diner and the abandoned library. The intense familiarity of it—the graffiti on the walls, the stench of garbage, the damp, gritty ground beneath my shoes—is disorienting. For a moment, it feels as though I never left. It could have been yesterday that I stood here selling one of Chelsea's homemade herbal remedies to Slade Murphy after my shift in the diner's kitchen. Yet at the same time, it feels as if a lifetime has passed between then and now.

"Em? Come on."

I blink, shake my head, and follow Calla to the end of the alley, pulling the backpack's second strap onto my other shoulder as I go. It's brighter out in the main street, but still difficult to tell what time of day it is. Clouds gather in the sky, darker along the horizon and lighter directly above us, along with that odd greenish tinge that signals a storm is brewing. "You know," I say, "it would be great if amber devices could automatically update to reflect whatever time zone we're in, the same way cell phones do."

"Some ambers have that capability as part of their enchantment set," Calla says. "As Perry pointed out to you, mine's a little simpler than that. The one we bought you yesterday probably can't do it either."

I turn onto the sidewalk and walk to the diner's nearest window. "We should be able to see the clock inside." I squint through the dirty window at the clock on the wall behind the counter. "It's ten past four. I hope we're not too late."

"Where's Bloomberry Cafe?"

"This way," I answer as I turn and hurry along the street. It isn't far. We reach the corner, turn left, and the cafe is across the street on the right. I can tell before we reach it that it's unusually busy. The tall stools lining the counter tops along the windows are full, and as we cross the street, a bunch of kids run past us and straight into the cafe. I don't understand it until I notice the writing on the large chalkboard standing outside the door. The board tells everyone that Bloomberry Cafe is celebrating its fifth birthday with 'un-blooming-believable discounts' on everything. "Well, at least we're not too late. If something had already gone wrong, this place would be a disaster zone, right?"

"Right." We pause outside the cafe, and Calla glances up and down the street.

I peer in through the window, my eyes traveling across the patrons seated at tables and the kids crowded around the ice cream counter choosing flavors. I'm relieved when I don't see Val anywhere. I turn back to Calla and ask, "Are we going in? Or are we hoping to stop this Unseelie guard—or guards—before they get inside the cafe?"

"We don't actually know where they're going to appear, but yes, that's the idea. If we can keep them from getting inside the cafe, then none of the occupants of this town need ever know anything was wrong. We can stun them, tie them up, and take them through the faerie paths to somewhere near the Guild. Which reminds me, I need to start gathering stunner magic." She turns her right hand palm up. "And I'll only be able to stun one of them. We'll have to take the others down in a different way."

"Right. Okay. I'll be ready to say whatever's necessary to stop them."

"Do you still have Griffin power left after all those commands you gave the weapons?" she asks.

"Yes. I don't know how much, but it doesn't feel like it's about to run out. It didn't take much magic to direct the weapons. Just a lot of concentration."

"Okay." She watches the cafe door as a woman walks out. "You need to keep your distance, though. I don't want one of the Unseelies grabbing hold of you and vanishing through the paths before I can stop him or her."

"How will they see me, though? Aren't you going to make us appear invisible?"

"Yes, but I'd rather not have you anywhere near the action. Although," she adds with a frown, "I don't want you out of my reach either. Anyone could show up and abduct you—including a guardian, since we don't know if the Guild assigned someone to deal with this situation."

"But—"

"And I know you think you can handle these things because your voice has more power than anyone else's," she adds sternly, "but I don't think you understand how quickly things can get out of hand."

"Hey, I successfully helped you with the other three incidents we've got involved in, remember? I'm not as useless as I once was, so you don't need to get all overprotective now."

"Those weren't Unseelie guards we were dealing with," Calla argues. "They were random Unseelie fae that Roarke was using to cause mischief. But if the details of this afternoon's vision are correct, then several Unseelie guards—trained to fight, to kill, to abduct—could appear at any moment. I think my overprotectiveness is justified."

I doubt I'm going to get anywhere by arguing with her, so I give in with a sigh. I hook both thumbs beneath the backpack's straps and ask, "Okay, then what do you want to do?"

She pauses for a moment before continuing. "We'll go with an invisibility illusion, and you can stay here on the sidewalk with me. But keep your glamour in place in case I have to stop projecting the illusion. That will at least keep the humans from seeing you."

I nod as I consciously probe at my glamour magic to make sure it's there. I'm never entirely sure I'm doing the glamour thing correctly, but I think I can sense an extra layer of magic hovering just above my skin.

Behind us, the sun peeks through a gap in the clouds, sending shafts of orange light through the cafe windows. The table and chair legs cast long shadows across the checkered floor. A chill creeps up my spine at the memory of the Seer's words: *Shadow length and quality of light suggest late afternoon.* I'm about to mention it to Calla when I notice tiny spots of water marking the pavement. I feel a few on my hands and cheeks. Casting my gaze beyond the nearest building, I notice the way the heavy purple-grey clouds are drawing in around that one spot where the sun refuses to be blotted out. "The perfect dramatic backdrop," I say to Calla.

She smiles, though her gaze remains trained on the pavement in front of the cafe. "I have a certain fondness for storms. Even the dangerous magical ones."

I look at the sky once more with a frown. "I thought this was just a normal storm."

"Oh, it is."

"What's the difference between a normal storm and—"

"Em, someone's here," she whispers.

My gaze darts back down in time to see a uniformed man step out of a doorway in the air. The two young boys walking out of the cafe stumble back against the door in fright, one of them losing his ice cream cone in the process. "Crap, no glamour?" I murmur.

"Obviously not," Calla replies as a second Unseelie guard exits the faerie paths. And behind him—a brownish green creature roughly the size of a person, with bulging orange eyes, hairy arms, and long, pointed ears.

"Holy heck," I whisper. "What *is* that?"

"That," Calla says, "is a goblin." As the two men and the goblin move toward the cafe door, she adds, "Quickly. I'll stun one of the Unseelies. You stop the other two." She hurls her magic forward without pause. My mind races, almost causing me to stumble over my command, but as the first guard falls unconscious to the pavement, I manage to successfully tell the other guard to drop down and stay there. The goblin swings around, his orange eyes searching for any sign of a threat. "Goblin, you—"

Screams erupt from inside the cafe. "Shoot, there are two more guards inside," Calla says. "They must have come through another doorway." I rush to the window and peer inside, forgetting the goblin for a moment. The people in the cafe are more important. I have only a moment to see the man and woman in Unseelie guard uniforms before every table and chair explodes into the air. Screaming people fall to the ground, crashing into those who were already standing or rushing for the door. The furniture breaks apart in the air, and splintered chair and table legs fly around. As the two guards vanish into the faerie paths and uninjured people race for the door, the goblin moves into the doorway and spreads his hairy arms, blocking the way.

"Stop!" I shout out, but my thoughts are so scattered that my Griffin Ability has no idea what I'm yelling at. "Tables and chairs, stop moving and remain in the air," I say. Every item of furniture freezes. At the same time, Calla throws a handful of sparks at the goblin's back, then kicks him so hard he stumbles forward into the cafe. As people shriek and scramble out of his way, she draws a knife from each boot.

"No human is injured," I say. "They can all stand up and leave the cafe." They obey my command almost instantly, standing, hurrying for the door, and climbing over the two Unseelie guards. The goblin turns and lurches after them. Calla throws a knife above the heads of the escaping humans just as I say, "The goblin is—Oh!" I gasp as someone grabs my arm and spins me around.

"Who are you and what are you doing?" the unfamiliar man demands. It takes only a second for me to notice the dark patterns on his wrists marking him as a guardian. *Crap, crap, crap.* Calla must have lost hold of her illusion. "Get off me!" I shout, already looking away from him and at the large hairy creature rushing out of the cafe. "The goblin is unconscious!" I yell, finally getting my command out. An invisible force knocks the guardian away from me just as the goblin falls forward across the two Unseelie guards.

"Well, look at that," a voice says behind me. "Some guardians have come along to ruin our fun." I spin around and find the Unseelie man and woman who were inside the cafe standing in the middle of the road.

"I'm the only guardian here," the guardian says, jumping up from where my magic threw him onto the pavement. He brandishes two glittering swords, pointing one at Calla and the other at the two Unseelies.

"The Unseelie man and woman can't move," I say immediately, hoping I still have enough Griffin power left. They freeze in place a second later, and the guardian whips his head around to look at me. I think he might be about to say something, but at that moment, wild whooping and calling and the sound of hooves beating against the ground reach my ears. From around the corner on the other side of the Unseelies, dozens of horses—no, centaurs?—come racing down the street. The startled guardian points both swords at the centaurs as they gallop past the motionless Unseelie man and woman.

With absolutely no idea what I can say to stop this stampede, or if I *should* stop it, all I can do is stare. Calla grabs my hand and pulls me further along the pavement, away from the guardian, the Unseelies and the centaurs. Together, we slip around the side of the building at the end of the block. When we're out of sight, Calla stops and looks back. After the last centaur disappears around a corner at the end of the street, she quietly says, "I just want to make sure the guardian can handle all those Unseelies and the goblin."

"What on *earth*?" I gasp. "Centaurs? Freaking centaurs? In Stanmeade?"

"Illusion," Calla answers. "Distraction. You can't believe everything you see around me, remember?"

All I can do is gape at her.

"He's tying them up," Calla says, looking around the edge of the building again. "He should be able to get them all into the faerie paths if he ties them together."

"I—you—" I shake my head, still trying to come to terms with the fact that the centaur stampede never existed. I suddenly become aware of the fact that rain is pattering down on us, and probably has been throughout the whole encounter. "Um, can the Unseelies move at all?" I ask, wiping my hand over my face and peering carefully around her. "Or do you think my magic's going to keep them frozen forever? Maybe I should say something else. If I have any power left, that is. I think my it's almost depleted."

"Yes, okay, just let the guardian finish tying them all up. And the goblin."

Once the guardian is done with his glittering rope, I say another command telling the four Unseelie guards and the goblin they can move again. "That's gonna give the poor guardian a fright," I say, "but at least he's—"

"Em?"

I whip around at the sound of the voice, accidentally knocking the backpack into Calla. I mentally grasp for the glamour magic that's supposed to be concealing me from human sight—and realize abruptly that I completely forgot to keep that magic in place.

"Is it really you?" asks the girl standing in front of me. Dark frizzy hair frames a face as familiar as my own, and her eyes are as wide and scared as the last time I saw her, when my magic almost sucked her into the ground.

"Val!" I hesitate for only the briefest of moments before flinging my arms around her. I'm sure she's mad at me for leaving, but she can shout as much as she wants once I've hugged her. I forget about Calla standing behind me, about the goblin and centaurs, about the terrified humans whose memories will now have to be altered, and simply cling to my best friend.

But after several moments in which Val stands almost as still as the Unseelie man and woman I magically paralyzed just minutes ago, I pull away and take a step back. She blinks at me. "I just—saw—what did you just do?" she stammers.

Words tumble from my mouth. "I can explain everything. I promise. And I'm so, so, *so* sorry about that night at the Masons' farm. I know you think I ran away after that, but I swear I didn't. I'm going to tell you the truth. I'm going to tell you everything."

"Actually, we need to go," Calla says from behind me. "If either the guardian or the Unseelies recognized you, this place will be swarming with Guild members within the next few minutes."

"She's ... *gold*," Val whispers, staring at Calla.

I turn back and find that Calla's already raising her stylus to the wall. "The guardian didn't recognize me, and I don't think the Unseelies did either. They thought you and I were guardians at first."

"That doesn't change the fact that we need to go." A doorway opens up, causing Val's mouth to drop open even further.

"No," I tell Calla. "I'm not going anywhere. I need to explain things to Val."

"Em—"

"I have to!" My gaze flashes once toward Val, standing completely still with her wide-eyed gaze stuck on the faerie paths doorway, before returning to Calla. "You know what happened that night my magic broke out," I continue, my voice lower now. "How would you feel if you'd done something like that to your best friend and then vanished with no explanation?" Calla's expression softens a little, and her gaze moves to Val. "Please!" I add, seeing her wavering now. "Remember what you said about past mistakes and fixing them if I can? Well I need to fix this. I need to make things right with Val."

After another moment's hesitation, she gives in with a nod. "Okay. Val?" she says, but Val's eyes are still trained on the gaping hole in the side of the wall.

"Val," I say, gently placing my hand on her shoulder. Finally, she looks at me.

"You need to go straight back to your house," Calla tells her. "Em and I will go a different way. We'll meet you there. And don't tell anyone what you've seen or that we're coming."

I squeeze Val's shoulder. "Are you okay? Can you get back home?"

She breathes in deeply, blinks a few times, and starts looking a bit more like the self-assured Val I remember. "Yes. I'm fine. It's all just … a bit shocking."

Calla looks over her shoulder again. "Seriously, Em. We need to go." Without waiting for an answer, she takes my arm and pulls me into the faerie paths.

"I'll see you at your place," I call back to Val. "Run!"

CHAPTER 12

I picture Val's backyard, a small patch of ground with a swing set that broke years ago, and the faerie paths deposit us there moments later. Calla brushes her hand absentmindedly through the air, which causes the rain to divert itself around us. My gaze moves up to a window on the second floor before returning to Calla. "I'll be up there." I shrug free of the backpack and hand it to her. "Are you going to hide down here?"

"Yes. Wait, Em," she says before I can move. "I know you've known this girl for a long time, so you're probably going to be offended by this, but are you sure you can trust her? She isn't going to … I don't know, try to sell your story to the tabloids or something?"

A few weeks ago, that kind of statement about my best friend definitely would have offended me. But almost everyone I've trusted in the fae realm has, at some point, tried to kill me, incarcerate me, or take advantage of my power, so I understand where Calla's coming from. "Yes, I'm certain I can trust her. There's no way she'd try to cash in on my situation like that—even though her family could definitely do with the money." I gesture at the broken swing set that some of Val's younger siblings would no doubt love to use. "And even if she does happen to tell her mom or some of our friends about me, well …" I shrug. "So what? It's not like magic is a huge secret anymore."

Calla raises an eyebrow. "You know we're hoping to change that, right? We're hoping to make it secret once again."

"I know, I know, but how long is that going to take? Even if it can be done, it'll be months or years before the Guild figures out how to make the whole world forget. But right now, my best friend is confused, and I need to tell her the truth. That's all there is to it."

"I understand. I really do. I just want you to be careful, that's all. So ... I don't know, maybe keep your glamour on until you get up to Val's room. It'll just make things more complicated if you have to explain yourself to her family as well."

I nod. "Probably a good idea."

From inside the house, I hear Val shouting, "Mom, I'm home. I just need to finish some homework, then I'll help with dinner."

"Wow, that was quick," Calla comments. "Is the cafe close?"

"Not that close." I head for the back door. "But she's fast. Like me."

After quietly opening and closing the back door, I pass through the kitchen and living room, experiencing again that intense familiarity overlaid with the jarring sense that *everything* has changed. After all, I'm walking right past three of Val's siblings fighting over a cell phone, and not one of them can see me. I can barely believe it, despite the many magical wonders I've witnessed in recent weeks.

I cross a hallway, hurry toward the stairs, and ascend as quietly as I can. Halfway up, I stop and pause, instinct suggesting something isn't right. Is that *magic* I can feel? In a place where magic shouldn't exist? A shiver whispers across the back of my neck. I look down the stairs, then up again, but I see nothing suspicious. Slowly, I draw a knife from one of the custom-made pockets inside my jacket. I tiptoe the rest of the way up the stairs, the knife gripped tightly in my hand, words like 'get away from me' ready to fly from my tongue.

Could it be the guardian who showed up outside Bloomberry Cafe? Perhaps he saw us speaking to Val and followed her back here. Perhaps he's hiding somewhere upstairs, waiting to rush into the room once he knows I'm here. Or perhaps I'm overdoing it with the glamour thing, and it's my own magic I'm sensing.

I peek into the bathroom and two other bedrooms before reaching Val's half-open door, but I don't find anyone. Slowly, I push her door open. Her back is to me as she leans over her dresser. My eyes dart about, but I don't see anyone else—until a furry orange shape leaps at me from the bed. I shriek in fright, and Tibs the cat streaks out of the room. Val spins around, clutching at the dresser before swearing loudly and slapping one hand to her chest. "Are you trying to give me a heart attack?"

"I'm sorry, I'm sorry! I just thought ..." I look back over my shoulder. "I had this weird sense that someone else—or some*thing* else—might be up here. But I can't feel it anymore. I think I'm just imagining stuff because it's so weird to be back here." I face Val again and find her gaze fixed on my hand. I realize belatedly that I'm still holding a knife. "Oh. Sorry. I should probably stop waving that around." I bend and push it into the side of my boot before straightening.

"Is that ... did you just put a *knife* into your *shoe?*"

"Uh ... yes?" I look down again at my brand new ankle-high boots, purchased after our first night on the run when Calla and I stopped to buy a change of clothes and some food. After spending days wearing the ballet pump-type shoes I escaped the Unseelie Palace in, I would have been happy with anything that looked like regular sneakers. But Calla insisted boots would be better. "Weird, I know," I say to Val, "but it's actually quite a convenient location for a knife. More comfortable than the ones inside my jacket."

"You have knives inside your *jacket?*"

"Yes. Um ... Calla—the woman you met near the cafe—created these little pockets inside the jacket on each side so I have somewhere to keep my ... uh ... knives." I trail off as Val's eyes continue to widen. "Okay look. I know it's weird, and we always thought that only creeps with strange obsessions carry knives around with them, but when almost everyone you meet in a foreign world wants you dead or imprisoned, you learn to carry weapons around so you can defend yourself."

Val blinks.

I sigh.

And the awkward moment is interrupted by a dull light pulsing from within the half-open top drawer of Val's dresser. She shoves the drawer shut. "Sorry. Cell phone. Now is *so* not the time to answer it."

I almost laugh. "I guess not." Then, as I push my hand through my hair, I ask, "Can I start at the beginning?"

She nods slowly. "Please do."

We sit on Val's bed and I tell her everything that's happened since the moment I said those horrible words that came to life: *Then let the earth split open and swallow you whole.* I tell her about the special magic I possess, about the Griffin rebels who are just like me, about living at the Unseelie Palace for a while, about discovering who I really am and why I grew up in the human world, and about the changeling mother who isn't really my mother. Val watches me with a frown the entire time, her mouth dropping open when I tell her that Dash is actually from the magical world too. When I tell her about Dani, she finally interrupts.

"Wait, she's—say that again. She's actually two people? Inside one? Daniela, the person you always visited in the hospital, and—what did you say the other one's name is?"

"Ada. Adaline. She was always the weaker one, but since Zed forced the two of them back into one body and reversed the changeling spell, she's now the one in control."

Val's frown deepens as she looks away. "That's so freaking weird," she whispers.

"Yeah. Tell me about it." I finish off by explaining everything that's happened since I escaped Roarke and the shadow world. "Technically, I'm not supposed to tell you any of this," I add when I'm done. "The magical world and all the beings who inhabit it are supposed to be a secret. But that isn't exactly the case anymore, judging by what I've seen on the news."

Val looks at me again. "The things they're reporting are just insane, Em. I didn't believe the news at first. I mean, who would? It looks like special effects movie stuff. But then more and more stories were reported from all over the world—by, like, reputable news people—and I started to think it must be true. I kept saying to my mom, 'Is it really that impossible? People used to believe in magic and paranormal stuff centuries ago, and there must have been a reason for it.' And then … what happened at Bloomberry Cafe …" She inhales deeply. "I can't exactly deny all this magic stuff now that I've seen it with my own eyes."

"Yeah. So, um …" I reach for one of her pillows and hug it to my chest as I finally voice the thought that's been plaguing me every time I've thought of Val over the past few weeks. "I thought you'd be furious with me for leaving Stanmeade. For running away without telling you, since that's the story the guardians said they spread. But you don't seem mad at all." That last statement comes out sounding more like a question.

"Of course I'm not mad, Em. I was just seriously worried about you. If you did run away without explaining anything to me, then I knew there must have been a damn good reason for it. I was more concerned about what that reason might be than about the fact that you didn't explain anything."

"Okay." I nod, relieved. "And you're sure you don't remember anything about that night at the Masons' place? About getting sucked into the ground?"

She swallows and shakes her head. "It sounds … terrifying."

"So what did you think the next day when you woke up?"

"Um … my mind was a little hazy. I thought I'd drunk a bit too much. And then I heard from my uncle that you'd run away. I was shocked, obviously. It was so unexpected. I thought maybe something happened to you at the party. I tried to get hold of you, but none of my messages were delivered, and whenever I called, it just went straight to your voicemail. Like your phone was dead."

"I'm sorry." I hug the pillow more tightly. "As soon as that Councilor told me they'd cooked up some story about me running away, I wanted to come back here and set the record straight. But she wouldn't let me. And then it was just one thing after the next, and even though I was constantly battling to try to figure a way out of it all, it was like I got sucked further and further into that world until I realized I actually …" I breathe in slowly and push my hand through my hair as I think again of the changeling spell and the moment in Zed's home where I discovered exactly who I am and who my family are. I can't help the small smile lifting one side of my lips. "I realized I actually belong there."

Val's smile is wider than mine. "It's weird how you ended up with your own family and you didn't even know it at first. But I guess, like you said, if they search for people who have special magic, and you're one of those people, then the chances were always good that they'd find you."

"Yeah." My smile slips away as I try not to imagine the horrors Vi and Ryn might be going through right now.

"You found your *family*, Em!" Val says, wrapping her hand around my arm and squeezing. "That's *incredible*! And I know you're worried about the situation your parents are in right now, but they sound like they're super kick-ass. I'm sure they'll be just fine."

I nod and clear my throat. "So, uh, how's everything been here? How's your family?"

She rolls her eyes. "Are you kidding? You want to talk about my boring family that hasn't changed since you left? Tell me about *your* family."

I laugh and stop hugging the pillow so tightly. Placing it on my lap, I say, "Okay, well, the woman who was with me outside Bloomberry is my aunt. She's the one who first figured out who I am."

"She's beautiful," Val says. "I was going to ask if she's wearing contact lenses made of actual gold, but I assume that's … just … the way she is?"

"Yes. And the gold bits in her hair are natural too. Anyway, while I've been traveling around with her, she's been telling me about everyone else in my family. I mean, we've been doing a lot of other stuff—like learning self-defense and combat magic—but at night before one of us falls asleep and the other stays awake to keep watch, she tells me all about them. I swear, it's almost like a soap opera, Val."

Her curls bounce as she leans to the side and laughs, and when she says, "Okay, now you *have* to tell me more," it almost feels, for a moment, as if this evening is the same as any other evening sitting on her bed chatting about anything and everything.

"So, three of my four grandparents are still alive," I tell her, deciding to give in to the nostalgia and pretend everything's normal for just another few minutes, "which is apparently quite something considering they were all guardians. Vi's mother died when Vi was very young, and then her father died when she a teenager—although he didn't *actually* die. It was all part of a major undercover operation he was working on for the queen—"

"The *queen*?"

"I know, right? It was this elaborate cover-up because faking his death would ensure his daughter's safety. Ryn's parents divorced after Ryn's older brother died. His father remarried and had Calla, so she's, like, my half-aunt? And then some years after that, Ryn's mother and Vi's dad—who'd been friends for years—ended up having a brief relationship after Vi and Ryn got together."

"What? Oh my gosh, *super* awkward."

"Yeah, it must have been," I agree with a laugh. "I can't wait to ask them more about it. Oh, and this was all after Vi and Ryn spent years hating each other because Ryn blamed Vi for his brother's death."

Val shakes her head. "You're right. Definitely soap opera-worthy. And the part about Dash? I mean, who would ever have guessed he was actually from another world? And then you *kissed* him!"

I roll my eyes. "Yep. That was definitely one of the, uh, nicer things that's happened in recent weeks." The laugh I hear then is the silly, girly, giggly type I never thought would leave my own lips. I clear my throat and continue quickly. "I'm not really sure how I feel about him—aside from, like, really missing having him around all the time—but now doesn't feel like the most appropriate time to be figuring out romantic entanglements." I take in a deep breath and let it out slowly. "So, anyway, it's a bit strange wrapping my head around all of this. And at the back of my mind, I can't stop thinking about Ada and Dani. This woman I always thought was my mother, and now doesn't even *look* like my mother, and how maybe … maybe I killed her. Them? How do you even refer to someone like that?"

"I … I don't know."

"I just feel super guilty every time I think of her." I press one fist into the pillow on my lap. "Then I have to remind myself that she wanted to kill me, but that doesn't really make me feel any better."

"She wanted to *kill* you?"

"Yes. I think I became too much of pain in the ass and more trouble than I was worth." I'm pressing both fists into the pillow now. "And Prince Roarke wanted to use us both as a weapon, and she didn't want to compete to be the favorite. Something like that. The words every child wants to hear their own mother say."

"Em … she isn't really—"

"I know, I know."

"And it would have been Ada who said that, right? Not Daniela."

"Yeah, I know." I relax my shoulders and stop squashing the pillow. "Still. It sucks when the evil half of your ex-mother wants to kill you."

"But … you can fight her off now, right?" Val asks. "You're carrying all these weapons around with you, and you said you know something about self-defense and … combat magic? Is that what you called it?"

"Yes, but I doubt I could actually fight her off. I'd have to use my Griffin Ability and say exactly the right thing before her glass gets me. That is, if she's still alive."

Val looks down at her hands twisting together in her lap and mutters several expletives. I consider telling her about Dash's creative alternatives to curse words, but that doesn't seem important right now, so instead I simply say, "Yeah. Exactly."

She looks up at me. "We should go for a walk."

"You know what? I was actually about to suggest the same thing." I push against the edge of the bed and stand. "There's something I need to do. I want to go to— the cemetery." It sounds odd saying it out loud. "I assume Chelsea and Georgia are buried there? I remember Chelsea saying she didn't want to be cremated when she died because the idea of her body burning freaked her out."

"Yes, they were both buried," Val says as she climbs off the bed.

"So, I know it probably sounds stupid, seeing as how I didn't really love them and they didn't really love me, and now it turns out they're not even my real family, but … I feel like I need to say goodbye."

"That doesn't sound stupid at all."

"Okay. Good."

Val's gaze moves to the window. "It looks like it might start raining again soon. We should go now."

I look past her and take in the heavy clouds darkening the sky outside her window. I shrug. "Getting soaked is pretty low on my list of problems these days."

She points at her head. "You know what happens to this frizz in the rain, don't you?"

I smile. "The frizz gets frizzier. We should definitely get moving before the rain comes back."

Val opens her wardrobe doors and grabs a jacket with a hood. "I should have been wearing this earlier. This frizz is already getting out of control."

As she pulls the jacket on, I say, "So, uh, don't be surprised when we're walking downstairs and I suddenly go invisible. It's this type of magic—a glamour—that hides me from humans. I just don't want your brothers and sisters or your mom to see me. It's easier than having to explain everything to them."

Val's expression suggests she's on the verge of being freaked out, but, to her credit, she does her best to shrug it off. "Sure. That doesn't sound weird at all. Um, I'll see you outside then?"

I nod, and she goes downstairs ahead of me. I follow her a few moments later, pausing when I reach the living room to make sure no one's noticed me. I'm about to walk quickly across the room when I see Calla standing on the other side, also entirely unnoticed by Val's siblings, one of whom is playing a game on a phone while the other two hover over her, watching.

"Em," Calla says quietly. "Come here. Have you seen this?" She nods to the TV where running soldiers and flashes of gunfire light up the screen while a 'breaking news' banner scrolls across the bottom. My first thought is that I've never seen anyone in Val's house watching the news. Calla must have changed channels without anyone noticing. My second thought is that the blood-splattered person currently being wrestled to the ground on screen looks distinctly inhuman.

"What's going on?" I ask. "There's no TV upstairs. I haven't seen any of this."

"I don't know how, but a group of human soldiers has discovered one of the natural openings into the fae realm. This channel's just reported on the first expedition into the Other World, as they're currently calling it. They've got guns and other horrible weapons, and I saw … I saw several fae bodies. Dead. And this reporter is using words like 'experimentation' and 'aliens.' It's just … horrifying."

"Crap," I breathe. "Stupid freaking Roarke. These people would never have come looking for our world if not for him. He's going to end up starting a war between our worlds."

"I've never wanted to kill," Calla says between her teeth. "Justice without death has always been important to me. But right now?" She shuts her eyes and exhales sharply. "Right now I could kill Roarke if no one was there to stop me."

I press my lips together as the camera catches a glimpse of trees with rainbow leaves and softly pulsing dots of light hovering in the air just beyond the ordinary green and brown trees of this world. Then an explosion obliterates our view of the rainbow side of the image as the camera shudders and the reporter babbles on.

Unexpected anger flashes hotly through my body. That's my home now. That's *my world*. And it's being destroyed.

"I need to get the mirror out and talk to Chase," Calla says, looking down at her backpack sitting in the corner of the room. "We obviously don't want to get in the way of whatever the Guild's planning to do, but I feel like we need to help somehow. At the very least, I want to know what the Guild's doing about this."

I shove my anger deep down and say, "I was … well, I was planning to go to the cemetery with Val. To see—to say goodbye—to Chelsea and Georgia. I know it isn't important in comparison to what's going on in the magical world, but—"

"Em, of course that's important." Calla shakes her head. "I'm sorry, I've been so consumed with what's happening out there, in this world and the fae world, that I didn't even think about your—about Chelsea and Georgia. But of course you'd want to go to their graves." She bends and lifts her backpack. "I'll go with you. I can contact Chase once we're at the cemetery."

We cross the living room, and though I tell myself not to look, I can't help one last glance back at the news. My stomach twists at the sight of a blue-green scaled hand sticking out from beneath a sheet covering a motionless body. "I can't believe they're showing things like that on TV," I growl as we leave. "That's the kind of horrible behind-the-scenes footage that the government usually tries to keep hidden from the public."

"I think it's impossible to hide anything to do with the discovery of the 'Other World,'" Calla says, curling her fingers into air quotes for those last two words. "I'm sure almost every reporter in the world is looking for a story related to it."

"Not just reporters," I mutter. "There must be tons of amateur footage spreading across the Internet every second."

"Yes. Meaning it's less and less likely that we'll be able to make the whole world forget what's happened," she mutters grimly.

"Hey, there you are," Val says when we reach the pavement outside her house. "I told my mom I need to go get some study notes from Sherry. Since my education is more important than me helping with supper and making sure Lincoln and Lissa bath, she didn't mind too much. Oh, hi," she adds, looking at Calla. "You're … gold." She clears her throat. "Sorry. I mean … you're Em's aunt, right?"

"Yes." Calla smiles as she holds her hand out to shake Val's. "It's good to meet you, Val, even though it isn't under the best of circumstances."

"Yeah, you're right about that." Val looks up. "Come on, let's get moving."

I follow her gaze to the stormy sky above. When I lower my eyes, she's pulling her hood up and over her head. "Good idea," Calla says as we start walking. "Em, remember the hood we added to the inside of your jacket? You should put that on. We don't need anyone recognizing you between here and the cemetery."

"Yeah, yeah." I reach back, tug the hood free, and pull it over my head.

As I tuck a few stray strands of blue hair beneath the hood, Val says, "Did I tell you your hair is totally awesome?"

"I don't think so. Did I tell you I was born this way?"

"What?" she stops walking. "Shut the front door. Are you serious?"

"I am. All faeries are born like this. You know, like the gold in Calla's hair, and the green in Dash's hair."

"Dash's hair?" Val walks forward again, confusion pulling at her features. "I've never seen any green in Dash's hair."

"Oh. Huh. He must have been using a glamour all these years."

We turn off the main road and head around the side of the high school so we can cut across the school field. "We probably shouldn't go back to my house after this," Val says. "In case someone saw you go there with me. They might be waiting for you there."

"Yes, I suppose it would be safer not to return."

"Do you think you'll ever be safe?" Val asks. "Or will you be running from people forever?"

"Probably forever."

Calla nods. "Yes. Well, unless we stage a dramatic scene in which everyone watching believes they've witnessed your death."

I pause, waiting for her to laugh, but she doesn't. "Uh, that's a joke, right?"

She glances sideways at me, smiling. "Actually, no." She taps her forehead. "The entire thing would be an illusion obviously. I've done it once before. To save—someone. I knew the Guild would never stop hunting him if they believed him to be alive."

"Wow," Val says. "That is one serious con."

"It was." We continue past the school wall and onto the field. "If the right situation presented itself, I'd do the same thing for you, Em. The Guild would stop looking for you if they thought you were dead."

"Yes, but … wouldn't they want proof? Like a dead body? If you did an illusion of some sort and we escaped, then we'd leave nothing behind. No bodies. Surely they'd know it's a trick?"

"That's why it would have to be the right kind of situation."

"And how exactly—"

But I never get to ask how we would provide bodies for the 'right kind of situation,' because racing toward me across the field is a stream of glass shards. And on the other side of the glass stands a woman.

Ada.

She's alive.

CHAPTER 13

"Run!" I shove Val to the side, and though I didn't plan it, a burst of magic escapes my hand, propelling her a lot further than I intended. I don't have time to see if she lands okay, but I trust she'll perform an expert shoulder roll and be up and running within seconds. My gaze darts back to where Calla hurled a small fireball of magic to stop the glass racing toward us. I look at Ada and reach for my remaining Griffin power. "Your glass—"

Ada twists her hand, and something zooms through the air and slaps itself over my mouth. It's white and sticky, and though I claw at it, I can't remove the damn thing. I scratch more desperately at it, telling myself not to panic.

And then I vanish completely.

I stop struggling for a moment and look around. Calla's gone too, and so is Val, so this must be one of Calla's illusions. "How interesting," Ada calls to us as she walks closer. "This is a Griffin Ability, I assume? The power to make people invisible?"

"Don't make a sound," Calla whispers from somewhere nearby. "I'll try to open a doorway and keep it invisible. Though I'm not sure how I'll know it's actually there …"

As Ada moves closer, my thoughts race to catch up with what's happening. *She's alive!* That means Dani's alive. And that means there's still a chance I can separate Dani from the body she's forced to share with Ada. Also, how the heck did Ada find me here?

"Aah!" Calla groans out loud at the same time horrendous pain shoots through my head. A moment later, we both become visible again. I know I should be worried about Ada and her glass and the thing stuck over my mouth, but I can't think of much beyond the pain. I press both hands against my forehead and bend over.

"That doesn't feel so good, does it?" Ada says. "Hard to concentrate on your magic when you've got an ear-splitting headache."

The sound of splintering glass reaches my ears. I force my eyes to focus for long enough to see Ada's glass racing around us to form a circle. I don't see Val anywhere, which makes me hopeful she got away. "You like to … enclose people … in circles," Calla manages to say.

"I do," Ada says. "I guess I'm unimaginative that way."

I rub my fingers against my temples and mumble against the white stuff.

"Sorry, Em, I didn't quite catch that?" Ada says, her tone taunting. I manage to raise my eyes enough to see her twisted smile before she adds, "Dani says hi."

I feel a sick lurch in the pit of my stomach. Despite the pain ricocheting through my head, I try to yell at her, but of course, I can only make muffled sounds. Calla breathes deeply before answering for me. "No she doesn't."

"You're right. She doesn't," Ada replies. Her eyes return to mine. "She's screaming at me to leave you alone. She's wailing, tormented and trapped, all because you decided to force the two of us back into one body."

I grit my teeth as Calla says, "Stop lying. Daniela lost her mind … a very long time ago … and we all know that Em … had nothing to do with it. Aargh, dammit!" She presses one hand against her head.

I wish I could believe Calla, but what if she's wrong? What if Dani has been perfectly sane ever since the changeling reversal spell, except now she's trapped and screaming inside the body she can no longer control? What if—*ugh, what if this damn headache splits my entire being in half?*

My body vanishes for a moment, then flickers in and out of view, before finally remaining visible as Calla groans beside me. Ada laughs. "Can't handle the pain, huh? You guys are pathetic."

"What are you … doing?" Calla asks her. "Do you like to … play with your food … before you eat it?"

The small part of me that can still pay attention to my surroundings notices Ada pacing slowly in front of her glass circle. "Oh, I'm not going to eat you. Or, you know, kill you. I assume that's what you meant. Well, *you* I might kill," she says to Calla. "I'm still trying to work out whether Roarke would appreciate it or not if I brought you back to him. But Em I'm definitely not killing, unfortunately. Roarke specifically asked for her, and if I'm hoping for him to keep his side of our agreement, I'm going to have to bring her back alive."

"What … agreement?" Calla asks, leaning forward on her knees and breathing heavily.

"Hmm, let's see. How did that initial conversation go? 'Ada, I see you've got one hell of a powerful Griffin Ability there. Killing people with glass left, right and center. How about you work for me? You can be part of my group of elite personal guards. Come to my aid whenever I call you. In return, I'll give you whatever you want.'" Ada swings her arm lazily back and forth, letting tiny glass shards sprinkle onto the ground at her feet. "It sounded like a great offer, so what did I say? 'I want the Guild brought down. Completely. That's always been my goal, and it remains my goal to this day.' And he responded with, 'How interesting. That sounds like a goal that aligns perfectly with my own plans. And hey? Wanna ruin some human lives too?' To which I said, 'Yeah!'" Ada pumps her fist, releasing a small spray of glass into the air. It rains down over her, seeming to have no effect on her whatsoever. "Pretty simple agreement," she says. "And no, it doesn't bother me that I'm telling you all about it. It's not as though you didn't already know my ultimate goal. I've always been after the Guild. Guardians and their families are the ones I've been turning into glass since I began my little crusade."

"You're so … full of yourself," Calla mutters.

"Yes. I am. And now I need to decide whether—"

Calla throws both arms forward, magic flying from her fingers and words leaving her lips as a groan. A burst of flames shoot straight at Ada, and as she throws both hands up to form a shield, the splitting headache finally releases its hold on me. "Thanks for monologuing," Calla says. "I needed a bit of time to gather my strength."

With the flames having vanished, Ada drops her shield and hurls magic forward without pause. Calla diverts the continuous assault of what appear to be glowing stones flying at us one after the other.

Then suddenly, we're invisible again. But Ada continues her attack, shouting, "I know you're still inside my circle."

I mumble incoherently, infuriated by the magical gag I still can't unstick from my face. "Fine then," Calla mutters as she continues fighting off Ada's magic. "We'll go with something different." A grating snarl reaches my ears, and in the air behind Ada, a winged beast with curved, ridged horns and fangs protruding from its overly wide mouth appears. A gargoyle, I realize as it hovers jerkily above Ada and grasps at her with its clawed hind legs. She ducks down, unaware that the gargoyle isn't real, and flings a handful of glass at it. She doesn't stop her attack on us, though, and glowing stones continue to fly from her other hand.

I try again to pry the sticky, white substance from my face while Calla throws up a shield and keeps the gargoyle illusion going. "Can you open a doorway?" she says to me through gritted teeth. "Quickly. I can't—damn, this woman has stolen power from somewhere. Her magic's definitely stronger than it should be. She's going to—argh! I can't hold this up much longer on my own!"

I reach with one hand inside my jacket, fumbling among the various weapons for my stylus. With my other hand, I direct a spark of magic at the white stuff, hope desperately that I'm not about to burn a hole into my face. Instead, I hear a sizzle as my magic eats into the sticky gag. Abandoning the stylus search for a moment, I tear at the substance again, ripping through it and *finally* managing to pull the horrible stuff off my face.

And right then is when a dragon swoops down and hovers above us. Blue-green with the occasional shimmer of purple, along with giant red spikes running along part of her back and tail. I would have assumed it was part of Calla's illusion if not for the girl sitting atop the dragon in a dress far dirtier than anything I've ever seen her wear. Aurora leans down and beckons.

"What the—where did you come from?"

"I've been waiting for you," she shouts. "Come on. I'll explain, but we should probably get out of here first."

"Who are you?" Calla gasps as she throws all her effort into maintaining the shield and the gargoyle that Ada's still trying to fight off.

"Roarke's sister," I hastily tell Calla. "She's the one who warned me about what Roarke was planning to do to me."

"Sister? And you trust her?"

"Yes. I think so." Wiping my sticky hands on my pants, I add, "You climb up first. I need to say something to stop—"

Imperia roars and sends a blazing inferno straight through Calla's shield. Ada abandons her offensive magic and throws up a shield of her own. "Or Imperia could just burn her to a crisp," Aurora says, a hint of pride in her voice. "Now hurry up!" she adds, looking at us again.

"No, a doorway will be better," Calla says, reaching into her jacket.

I shake my head, then bend my knees, push against the ground with an extra spurt of magic, and leap free of the glass circle.

"Em—"

"I have to find Val," I tell her.

"*What?*"

"I need to make sure she's okay."

"She's fine. She was running toward the school. I'm sure she's far away by now."

"I have to, Calla!" I call back to her, already moving away from the circle. "You said you understood."

She groans loudly, as if trying to protect me is fast becoming the bane of her existence. "Fine," she shouts above the sound of Imperia's roaring flames. "I'll project something. An image of you climbing onto the dragon with me. We'll lead Ada away. Get Val to safety, and we'll meet you at her house. And if you're not there, I swear I'll—"

"I'll be there," I shout, racing away and trusting Calla's ability to keep me hidden from Ada. I head for the wall surrounding the school's staff parking lot, my arms pumping back and forth and my feet slamming against the grass. I launch myself at the wall, momentum helping me to pull myself up. After swinging my legs over, I drop down on the other side, bending slightly before straightening and running forward. It's a maneuver I've performed many times, usually with Val at my side. I take the same route now that we've always taken together. Past the squash courts, up the stairs outside the IT building, onto the railing, one foot on a windowsill, and finally up onto the ridge of the roof. We used to come up here to watch the rest of the town below us and the main road into and out of Stanmeade. Sitting together in one of the shallow window wells set into the roof, we'd talk about all the people wasting their lives in this dead-end town, and we'd dream of the day we could finally leave.

For a moment, as I pull myself onto the highest point of the slightly sloped roof, I wonder why on earth I let my feet carry me up here. Val wouldn't hide in a place that's mostly exposed. She's probably inside a dark closet somewhere in the school where neither Ada nor I will ever find her.

But there she is, huddled in the same spot we've sat in so many times. "Val!" I call out to her as I pick my way across the roof ridge. "Val, I'm so relieved you're okay." I climb around the side of the window and onto the flat part in front of the glass. After lowering myself beside her, I wrap my arms around her shaking body. "It's okay. You're okay. I'm so, so sorry I brought this nightmare here, but you're okay."

She shakes her head and sobs harder—which is highly disconcerting. I've only seen Val cry once or twice before. She's tough. She's a survivor. She is *not* a crier. She leans away from me, and it's then that I notice the glowing light leaking out between the fingers of her clenched fists. "Val," I say carefully, a silent warning already knocking at the edges of my mind. "What are you holding?"

She shakes her head and stutters. "I—I'm sorry."

I reach for her hand and manage to loosen her fingers. She spreads them apart, like the petals of a flower opening to reveal—a stone. A glowing stone. My breathing quickens. I swallow. "Val. Is this … something magical?"

She nods and whispers, "Yes."

"Where did you get it? How long have you had it?"

She sniffs. "About … about five years."

Cold drenches my body. "*Five years?*"

"Yes."

At the back of my mind, I'm already beginning to guess the answer to the question I'm about to ask. But I have to ask it anyway: "What does it do?"

"It communicates with someone."

"With *someone*," I repeat, my words almost too quiet for me to hear. I remember returning to Chelsea's backyard with Dash a few weeks ago after taking an unintended trip to the shadow world with Roarke and Aurora. Not long after we got back, Ada appeared—and that was after Dash heard someone on the other side of the fence. I think of the glowing light I saw in Val's dresser drawer earlier—too bright to be a cell phone screen lighting up—and how Ada arrived here in Stanmeade not long afterward. I remember what Ada herself said to me some time ago: *I've always had someone watching you.*

"Ada," I whisper. "You were communicating with Ada. You told her I was here."

"Em, I am so, so—"

I pull away from her. "I don't understand. How could you do that? I … I just told you *everything*. You know she tried to kill me, and you still called her here?"

"I didn't know she tried to *kill* you, Em." Val's eyes are wide, desperate. "I used the stone before you got back to my house. Before you explained everything to me."

"*Why?*" I grab her shoulders and give her a good shake. "Why the hell would you do that? How do you even know her?"

She pushes my hands away and shouts, "I knew her before I knew you!"

"What?"

"I …" She rubs the tears from her face and sniffs. "Dammit, I never asked for any of this."

"Any of *what*, Val?"

"She appeared out of the blue years ago, okay? She showed me things that should have been impossible. *Magic* things. And she told me about a new girl who'd just moved to town. A new girl who was like her. *Magical.* But this new girl didn't know she could do magical things, and she might never know she could do magical things. But this woman—Ada—told me I had to befriend you. She said I had to know everything that happened in your life so I could report it back to her when she came to check on things every month or so. She promised me that if I did this until you either moved away one day or until you managed to access your magic, then she would make sure my family would never want for anything else ever again. She said she'd fabricate some kind of inheritance and make it seem legit. I wouldn't need to ever worry about my brothers and sisters and my mom."

"I can't believe you'd say yes to someone like—"

"Then she showed me what else her magic could do. How it could hurt and kill. And she asked if I would ever want anything like that to happen to my siblings or my mom. So what was I supposed to do, Em? Choose you—someone I'd never even met—over my own family? Of course not. No one would do that. You wouldn't have done that."

Perhaps she's right, but I don't want to try to understand her position when I can barely see past the shocking revelation that the most important friendship I've ever had was based on a lie. "I can't believe this," I whisper, staring past her. "You've been spying on me throughout our entire friendship. This is why you weren't mad at me for leaving." I look at her. "You should have been mad, Val. That's what I was expecting. We did *everything* together. We told each other *everything*. And then one day I ran away and didn't answer your calls or return your messages, and you should have been *furious* with me. That's how I would have felt if you'd abandoned me with no explanation."

"Em …"

"But you weren't mad. You had your own guilt to deal with instead."

"Yes! I did. Doesn't it mean anything to you that I felt guilty about what I had to do?"

I don't answer her. I push myself to my feet. From among the many straps and pockets attached to the inside of my jacket, I finally find my stylus.

"Wait, Em, where are you going?"

Still, I say nothing as I bend and write on the roof.

"Em, I'm sorry. Don't you understand? I had to keep my family safe. What other choice did I have?" She grabs my wrist, but I twist my arm out of her grip. It's difficult with my mind so distracted and my emotions tugging me in every direction, but I manage to open a doorway to the faerie paths. Without looking back at Val, I climb hastily into the darkness. I have to remind myself to think of a destination. I remember at the last second that I'm supposed to meet Calla and Aurora back at Val's house, but before that thought, there was an image of the cemetery that flashed through my mind.

Dull light materializes around me. I'm disoriented as I step back into the human world, unsure for a moment where I'll find myself.

The cemetery.

That's where the faerie paths brought me.

I take a few steps forward, my stylus still clutched in my hand. I try to shove Val and her betrayal from my mind and replace her with an image of Chelsea and Georgia. I wanted to say goodbye to them, so I may as well do it now that I'm here. As rain begins to patter lightly onto my head, I scan the dozens of headstones around me. I don't know where to begin looking for them. I have no idea which section they've been buried in. I squeeze my eyes shut—*Go away, Val, go away, Val, go away, Val*—and though I know they can't hear me, I mutter, "Goodbye, Chelsea. Goodbye, Georgia. I'm sorry for … for …" *I'm sorry for leading Ada here.*

The same Ada who threatened Val's family. The same Ada who definitely would have followed through on her threats if Val had disobeyed her. I squeeze my hand around the stylus and let out a wordless cry. I'm supposed to be here for Chelsea and Georgia, but my mind can't focus on them. They're gone. But Val … Val is still alive. Val is my best friend. Val is sitting alone on a rooftop hating herself for the very thing I've spent my whole life focused on: looking out for the person I love most.

I clench my jaw. "Dammit," I hiss, raising the stylus. I turn, looking for something to write on, and see the pillar on one side of the cemetery gate. I hurry to it and raise my stylus. Moments later, a doorway yawns before me. I walk into the darkness, picturing the school roof. On the other side, as I step carefully onto the ridge of the roof with one arm reaching back to keep the doorway open, Val is still there. She's standing now, her arms wrapped tightly around her body as rain runs down her body.

"Em!" she cries out when she sees me. "You—you came back. I …"

"I want to be mad at you. I do. I *am* mad at you, dammit!" I suck in a breath between my teeth, willing myself not to cry. "But I know that … that I would have done the same thing if I'd been in your position. I would have done anything for my mother, and if someone came along five years ago and offered me everything we could ever possibly need in exchange for befriending you and reporting information about you, I would have said yes. And then, after we became friends, I …" I shake my head and sniff. "I don't know, Val. I like to think I would have refused at some point. I like to think our friendship would have meant too much for me to continue going behind your back like that, but I don't know. I probably would have kept lying to you. Because no one ever meant as much to me as my own mother." I bite my bottom lip to keep it from wobbling, but my voice is a whisper now, barely audible above the pattering of rain on the school roof. "And then she turned out to be the biggest liar of all."

"Em, I'm so, so sorry." Val moves as if to climb around the window toward me, but she stops when I hold my hand up.

"I know." I swallow. "And I just wanted to say that I understand." With that, I turn and walk back into the darkness.

CHAPTER 14

"There you are," Calla says the moment I show up on the pavement in front of Val's house. Imperia's wing sweeps past the edge of my vision, and I realize as I look up that she's hovering just above the houses with Aurora on her back. "Where's Val?" Calla asks.

"She's … she's the one who called Ada."

Calla pulls her head back. "What?"

"She's fine. Let's go." I look up again, my gaze focusing on the section of Imperia's back behind Aurora. "Are we using the faerie paths to get up there?"

"Em, what do you—"

"Let's just go, okay? I'm sorry. I thought I could trust Val. But apparently Ada got to her years ago before she and I were even friends. So, you know … I can't really blame her. And I don't want to talk about it." I spin around. "Where is Ada anyway?"

Calla looks beyond me, her eyes focusing somewhere in the distance. "Ada and her glass weapons are following my illusion to the edge of town. I can't project the illusion much further, though, so it'll soon disappear and she'll realize we've tricked her. So if you're sure you're ready to go, then—"

"I'm ready."

"We can leave on our own," Calla adds, her voice lower now. Looking down, I see that her stylus is already gripped in her hand. "We don't need to go with this Unseelie princess. You and I are safer on our own, and we have things to deal with that she doesn't need to be involved in."

I catch Calla's hand before she can write a doorway spell. "Aurora said she was waiting here for me. I don't want to just leave without—"

"What if she was waiting here to take you back to the Unseelies?" Calla hisses in a frustrated whisper. "You've already had one friend show you this evening that she can't be trusted. What if Aurora can't be trusted either?"

Her words sting, but I can't deny them. Especially since Aurora's lied to me before. She gave me a nonsense story about being a witch slave and tried to get me to run away from Chevalier House with her. But that was before I shared a home with her. That was before we became friends. Would she really try to trick me again now?

"Hey!" Aurora shouts down to us. "What's that at the end of the street?"

I twist around and see a figure at the other end of the road stepping out of the faerie paths. Glittering glass shards race ahead of her, splitting the road into chunks of tar as they go.

"Crap, crap, crap," I mutter. Of course Ada would come here to look for me. She saw us with Val on the field, and she knows exactly where Val lives.

Calla wraps her hand around mine. "I'm opening a door—"

"Grab onto Imperia!" Aurora shouts just as the dragon's tail slams into me, knocking the breath from my lungs and sweeping me off my feet. I gasp for air and cling tightly to the slippery scales, one arm wrapped beneath Imperia's tail and the other wedged between two reddish pink spikes. It's more than a little awkward, and I wonder how long I can hang on before the sweeping motion of her tail causes me to lose my grip.

"Use the spikes to climb up!" Aurora shouts as Imperia's wings beat the air and the ground recedes beneath us. "Just—Oh, crap, watch out!"

Imperia swerves to the side to avoid a spray of glass pieces shooting directly into the air. Her tail swings around, causing me to shriek and shut my eyes and hope I'm not about to plummet to my death.

"Try to climb up now," Calla shouts above the sound of wind and rain rushing past us. I open my eyes and twist my head to the side until I can see her. She doesn't look nearly as terrified as I feel. Then again, she's probably used to doing crazy life-threatening things like hanging onto dragon tails. "If you fall, I'll catch you with magic," she adds. "Go on. Get to the saddle."

"Okay," I answer, the word sounding more like a breathless grunt. As I wrap my hands around spike after spike, dragging myself along the side of Imperia's tail and up her back, I'm thankful for every wall I've ever pulled myself up. Looking back, I see Calla following me.

Finally, with rain stinging my skin and cold wind tearing at my hair, I manage to pull myself onto the top of Imperia's back. I cling to the raised edge of the saddle Aurora's sitting in, shut my eyes, and breathe out. Exhilaration battles its way through my fear as we soar through the sky, leaving Stanmeade, Val and Ada far behind.

When Imperia's flown a good distance away from Stanmeade, she circles around and lands on an open field. I expect we're about to climb down, but instead, I watch as Aurora's stylus leaves her hand and flies through the air on its own. I wonder how her magic will flow out of her and into the stylus until I notice the glowing thread of magic linking the stylus to her hand. She speaks the spell, and after waiting a little longer than we normally would, an extra-large doorway to the faerie paths opens. "I'm directing," Aurora says as she flicks her hand and her stylus shoots back toward her. "So don't think of anything."

Imperia lumbers forward into the darkness. I cling more tightly to the back of the saddle and try to think only of the blackness that surrounds us. Slowly, an opening materializes up ahead, and Imperia carries us into a misty valley bathed in a pinky purple hue. Hills and mountains surround us, and the faintest hint of magic drifts across my skin on the breeze.

"Nobody will find us here," Aurora says. She removes the straps securing her to the saddle and slides down Imperia's side. She lands on the dragon's bent knee, then jumps to the ground. I wipe the moisture from my face and follow her, despite the fact that I sense Calla's about to say something. The moment my feet strike the ground, Aurora rushes at me and swings her arms around my shoulders. "I'm so glad you're okay." Then she steps back, her smile vanishing. "You idiot!"

I blink, confused by her rapid shift in mood. "Excuse me?"

"You were supposed to come to me for help, not run off on your own and wind up with half the palace guards chasing after you."

My eyebrows rise a little higher. "Oh, is *that* what I was supposed to do? Because you didn't exactly give me instructions. In fact, you couldn't have been more cryptic if you'd tried."

"I wrote out the translation for the whole spell!" she exclaims, throwing her hands up as Calla strides past us and stops a few paces away, making intricate movements in the air with her fingers. "It explained exactly what Roarke was planning to do."

"True, but ..." I trail off for a moment, distracted by Calla digging in the backpack. She's been so insistent that we head off on our own, but it seems she's given up on that idea for now. She removes the mirror from her backpack and holds it up. I turn back to Aurora, trying to remember what I was saying. "But ... but you didn't *tell* me about Roarke's plan. You didn't even write a proper note and give it to me. You handed me a pile of books and expected me to open the right one and turn to the right page. That was a serious shot in the dark. I almost missed it. I definitely would have missed it if it hadn't been for the tiny corner of your I-swear-I-didn't-know-about-this note that was sticking out."

"It wasn't supposed to be a tiny corner," she answers, frowning at me as if this is my fault. "There was supposed to be at least an inch of that note sticking out."

I roll my eyes. "Aside from the fact that I might never have seen the note, I still didn't know if I could trust you after that. It might have been some kind of test. Another game you and Roarke were playing with me."

Her purple eyes widen. "Are you *kidding*? A game? Do you know what I risked in order to give you that information? My *life*, Em! Roarke wanted to kill me when he found out what I'd done."

"He—really?"

"YES REALLY! Holy flip, Em. I had NO idea what he was planning to do with your magic. Oh, and the whole Clarina thing? What the hell? A *spy* in my service, and I had no idea!" She's pacing by now, literally spitting angry sparks of magic. "So I ran for my life, straight to Imperia's enclosure, and got both of us out of there."

I fold my arms across my chest. "But … when Roarke caught up to me by the portal in his room, he seemed confused that I knew all about his plan. He couldn't have known that you'd told me."

"Well of course he didn't know *then*. He hadn't had time yet to figure it out. He'd only just discovered that you were missing and had freed two of his prisoners. It was only after that—after you got away through the shadow world—that he put the pieces together. And he didn't have proof, of course, but I was unprepared when he confronted me, and I guess I'm not as good a liar as he is."

"I don't know about that," I mutter. "You seemed pretty convincing when I first met you."

Aurora stops pacing and looks at me. Mist shifts lazily around her as her angry expression softens. "Please believe me, Em. I know I lied to you in the beginning, back at Chevalier House, but that was just to get you on our side. Ever since then, I've only ever told you what I believed to be the truth. I had no idea my own brother was lying to me. I didn't know he made a secret agreement with that glass woman. I didn't know he locked Dash away in our prison. In fact, I never would have suspected a thing if you hadn't mentioned some of the vows you were memorizing."

"The vows? But you weren't supposed to know …" A memory of Aurora asking me how my pronunciation practice was going comes suddenly to mind. "Oh yes. I did tell you some of the words."

She nods. "They were supposed to be words from the old faerie language, but they most certainly were not. I recognized them from … well, from long ago. From the witch. That in itself would have been suspicious enough, but the actual words you told me … something about giving up your magic …" She shivers. "I had to check it out. I had to look for the spell. Which is why I said we needed to go to the library after that. And then Roarke was *there* when I finally found the right spell! I was too damn terrified to say anything about it. And the next day, even if we'd had a moment alone, I wouldn't have dared say anything. I know Roarke and my father can hear what's going on in most of the rooms if they choose to listen. The only thing I could think of was writing a note and giving you the book itself. And I'm sorry the note was so …" She waves her hand as she searches for the right words.

"Lacking in instructions and additional information?" I ask.

"Yes. It took me a while to translate the whole spell—I wanted to be sure of what it all meant—and I had to keep hiding what I was doing. I was so flustered. By the time I'd finished the translation, I just wanted to get the book out of my hands and into yours."

"I assume you didn't even let your handmaids see what you were doing? If Clarina had figured out you were translating Roarke's spell, she would have gone straight to him."

"Clarina. Ugh!" Aurora clenches her fists and begins pacing again. "That conniving little snake."

"How did you find out about her?"

Aurora lets out a dramatic sigh. "So let me fill you in on everything that went down after you ran away."

I glance at Calla again, now deep in conversation with Chase via the mirror. "Okay," I say, returning my attention to Aurora. Then I let the last remaining bit of my Griffin power leak into my voice and say the thing I should have said the moment we got here: "Don't lie to me."

Aurora opens her mouth, then blinks, clearly taking a few seconds to realize what I've done. Then: "You just commanded me. You used your power on me."

I give her a half-smile laced with guilt. "Don't be mad. You know I had to. I have to be sure you're not trying to trick me again."

She glares at me for another few moments before sighing. "I suppose I understand. And in case you were wondering," she adds, "nothing I've said so far was a lie."

"Good to know."

"So, can I carry on now?"

I nod and lean back against Imperia's side, crossing my arms over my chest.

"Okay, so Roarke returned from the shadow world late that night. He told us—Mom and Dad and me—that it was that woman with the glass Griffin Ability who'd found him in the shadow world and freed him from the bonds he'd been tied up with." Aurora frowns, looking past me. "It sounded as though he'd been working with her for a while. Like they had some kind of prearranged way for him to signal her to come to his aid. He didn't go into detail about it, though, so I couldn't tell if Dad already knew about that arrangement. Anyway, Roarke said he'd sent her to look for you and not to return to his side until she had you."

"So that's how she found the shadow world," I say. "She told me she accidentally discovered it the same way you and Roarke did, which seemed like a weird coincidence to me. But it must have been Roarke who showed her that world. And I guess it wasn't too hard for her to find me after Roarke told her to. She probably searched the castle first, and that's where I was."

"Wait, you were still there? Why didn't you get out? And if she found you, then how come you're—"

I hold up my hand to silence her questions. "How about you finish your story first?"

She lowers her shoulders. "Fine. Okay, so Dad and Roarke went off together to have a private meeting that apparently Mom and I didn't need to be a part of—presumably so Roarke could tell Dad more lies and Dad would never know that Roarke was planning to, like, ruin the whole human world. I was kinda freaking out, wondering if I'd wake up to find you being dragged back into our palace. And I was also terrified Roarke would discover I was the one who tipped you off about the spell.

"The next morning, he summoned me to his room and told me to bring Clarina with me. I thought perhaps he just wanted to question her about you, since she'd been serving you for the duration of your stay with us. But then I got to his room, and the very first thing he said to me was, 'So, you went sneaking around behind my back, discovered I planned to take Emerson's magic, and told her all about it.' I was too shocked to say anything for a few moments, and I'm sure the truth must have been obvious on my face. I didn't even get to deny it before he carried on, saying that he wasn't the only one keeping secrets from me. That Clarina had a secret too, and now was the time to share it. And then she walked over to his side and *he put his arm around her*." Aurora stares at me with wide eyes. "I swear, a sprite could have knocked me over I was so shocked."

"Did he explain what that was all about? The only thing he said to me was something about her being a spy and of noble birth."

"Roarke didn't seem interested in sharing the story, but Clarina obviously wanted to tell me." Aurora walks over to Imperia and sits on her bent knee before continuing. "Several years ago, Roarke was pledged to marry someone. A girl from a noble family far away. It was part of some kind of agreement that was obviously beneficial to both parties. But then someone broke the alliance. I never did find out if it was my father or the other family. Anyway, that ended the engagement. But Roarke had already met this girl and fallen for her. Not that I can imagine him ever falling for anyone," she adds, rolling her eyes. "And this girl—Clarina—loved him too."

"I'll bet the idea of possibly being queen one day didn't hurt either," I mutter.

"I'm sure. And Roarke wanted to be king but didn't want to wait centuries for Dad to give up the throne or die. So Roarke and Clarina decided she would come to the palace. Nobody knew her there, so she could easily masquerade as the princess's handmaid and learn whatever she could from the royal family members. Eventually, she and Roarke would figure out a way to rule together."

"And then you guys discovered the shadow world, and Roarke obviously thought that was the perfect opportunity."

"Yes. But what I couldn't figure out when they were telling me this was why they'd kept it secret from *me*. I knew about Roarke's plan to make the shadow world his behind our father's back. He trusted me with that information. So why didn't he tell me about Clarina as well? So I asked him, and he said ..." She trails off as she looks away, her eyes focusing on distant, hazy mountains.

"What did he say?"

"He said ... 'You've never been my real sister.'"

The hurt is evident in her voice. "Rora ..." I say gently, though I have no idea what to add that might possibly comfort her.

"He reminded me that it was a witch who left me at the palace years ago. That I might be part of some elaborate long-term plan for a witch to gain access to the Unseelie crown. Which is completely ludicrous, and I told him that, but clearly that didn't matter to him because at that moment he told his men to seize me and—and get rid of me."

"Jeez," I murmur. "How did you escape? It's a long way from your room to the dragon enclosure."

"Noraya was there too," Aurora says, referring to her other handmaid, "so she helped me. She struck someone with her magic—which clearly no one expected—so we were both able to get out of the room. Then we used the hidden passages within the walls. I know them well. I played in them for hours when I was a child. I knew if I could just get to my father, he'd protect me. I could tell him everything Roarke was planning, and he'd make sure my brother never got his hands on me.

"But Roarke knows the passages too. He cut me off, and I couldn't get to Dad, and Noraya and I ended up separated. I found myself near the kitchen, and I knew my only escape would be to get outside to the dragon enclosures. And Noraya …" She brushes one hand over her face. "I don't know what happened to her. I know I'm the most awful person in the world for not going back to look for her, but I couldn't! Roarke's men would have caught me. And in those dark passages …" She shakes her head. "No one would have known what happened. They could have hidden my body, pretended I ran away or something. So I—I left Noraya. I ran all the way to the dragon enclosure and flew away on Imperia."

I wrap my arms more tightly around myself as I start to shiver in my wet clothing. "Maybe … maybe she got away. She's been working at the palace for a long time, hasn't she? She must have friends there. Maybe one of the guards or carriage drivers smuggled her out."

"Maybe," Aurora says quietly, though she doesn't sound convinced.

Not too far from us, Calla says goodbye to Chase and walks toward us. Behind her, the mirror remains suspended in the air, its glossy surface having returned to normal. "Forgive me," she says to Aurora, "but I'm still not sure we can trust you."

"We can," I say to Calla. "I'm sure this time. I told her not to lie. You know, with my Griffin Ability."

Calla looks between the two of us, nodding slowly. "Okay. Good. Well done. But it's probably still best if we go our separate ways," she says to Aurora. "Em and I have things to take care of, and you—"

"No, no, no." Aurora looks horrified. "Please. You don't understand. I have *no one*. I can't go back home because even though Roarke's left the palace, I know he has other spies there. Spies who could make me disappear when no one's looking. And my father would protect me, but he isn't always there. Especially now, with all this mess going on, he's probably meeting with important people, making it known that he doesn't condone Roarke's actions. I can't go back home until this is all over." Her pleading gaze moves back and forth between Calla and me. "Please don't leave me on my own. It makes sense for me to stay with you. We want the same thing. We both want to stop Roarke."

"You really want to fight your own brother?" Calla asks. "That might seem like it's not such a big deal, but when you're face to face with him and a lifetime of shared memories floods your mind, I doubt you'll find it easy."

Aurora pauses. "Well, I … I don't know about face-to-face fighting, but I certainly want to help stop him. You must know the Unseelie Court doesn't agree with what he's doing, right? We were happy with the way things were. *I* was happy. And now Roarke's actions have threatened to take away everything we care about. So whatever you're planning to do to stop him, I want to help. I can tell you things about him. Give you information you might be able to use against him."

Calla narrows her eyes. "What makes you think *I'm* planning to do anything about Roarke?"

Confusion flickers across Aurora's face. "You're part of the Griffin rebel movement, aren't you?"

Calla doesn't respond, but neither does she deny it.

"Yeah, so obviously you'll want to stop Roarke," Aurora continues. "I've heard about some of the things you guys do. Not the Guild stories." She rolls her eyes. "Every Unseelie fae knows the Guild is full of tall tales when they're talking about any organization other than their own. I'm talking about the other stories. The stories about how you help people—off the record. You're almost as irritatingly noble as the guardians themselves, but, you know, since you're breaking the law to do it, that makes you way cooler."

Calla raises her eyebrows and looks at me. "When you told her not to lie, was that only to you, or to both of us?"

"Hey, I'm not lying to you," Aurora exclaims. She looks at me. "I am not lying to her. I want to help. I want my old life back, and the only way that's ever going to happen is if Roarke is stopped."

Calla sighs and mutters something about possibly regretting this, but what she says is, "Okay. You can stay."

CHAPTER 15

WE MOVE AGAIN, CALLA DIRECTING THE FAERIE PATHS THIS TIME AND NOT TELLING us where we are when we get there. Instead of a valley, we're at the top of a hill this time. It's one of many rolling hills stretching as far into the distance as I can see. Which is quite far, thanks to the bright moon above us. What's strange about these rolling hills, though, is that the grass they're covered in is blue. The trees and bushes dotted across the landscape have blue leaves, and the flowers blooming near the spot Calla's chosen for our campsite are blue too.

Imperia sits, folds her gigantic wings neatly around her body, and lowers her head to the ground, clearly deciding she's had enough activity for today. Bandit finally leaves the safety of my pocket, shifts into the largest cat form he can manage, and hesitantly sniffs Imperia.

I leave him to explore our new surroundings and remove the tablets and mirror from the backpack so I can suspend them in the air. The spell is so simple, it's barely a spell at all. More like nudging magic toward the items to surround them and hold them in position. I've just left them lined up in the air when Aurora comes to my side and says, "The middle of nowhere? Seriously? Calla definitely doesn't trust me."

"She's just taking precautions," I say, looking over my shoulder to where Calla is walking around us in a wide circle, weaving her fingers through the air like she did at the last location and repeating the words to a protective enchantment. "She doesn't know if there might be some spell on you that relays everything you hear or think back to someone else." I pause and turn back to Aurora. "I assume a spell like that must exist? There seem to be spells for just about everything else."

Aurora shrugs. "I guess. Maybe. But she could take us back to wherever you guys live and I'd have no clue where it is. I don't understand why we have to camp out a billion miles away from civilization."

I ignore her exaggeration and explain that because we tried to rescue several Griffin Gifted rebels from a Guild facility and ended up breathing in a tracking spell, we're now constantly on the move.

"Oh. That's unfortunate," she grumbles as I crouch down again beside the backpack. "I was hoping to sleep in a real bed tonight." I look up at her, and she hastily adds, "But I'm still grateful you let me come with you, of course. And the possibility of a bed was certainly not the only reason I said I want to help stop Roarke."

"Good." I tilt my head. "Where exactly have you been sleeping since you ran away?"

She seats herself on the grass beside me and says, "Uh, in a field a short distance outside Stanmeade. I slept right up against Imperia so she could protect me if a threat showed up during the night."

"Sounds like a far cry from the palace luxury you're accustomed to."

She runs both hands down her dirty, crumpled skirt. "It was. But I was hoping you'd come back to Stanmeade at some point. I didn't know how else to contact you. I hoped you'd do something magical and I'd somehow know you were there. Then I saw fire and glass shooting into the air earlier and figured I should check it out."

"I'm glad you did. Oh, hey, you must be hungry." I rummage inside the backpack and add, "I wonder if we still have any food in here."

"Um, actually …" Aurora hesitates, then says, "I probably shouldn't tell you I stole food and a few blankets from someone's home."

I shrug and continue removing items from the backpack. "You had to survive somehow. As long as you didn't hurt anyone, I'm not going to judge you."

"Of course I didn't hurt anyone." She cocks her head and points at the soft, pill-shaped object in my hand. "What is that?"

"A sleeping bag. A miniature version." I shake the backpack, and what tumbles free looks almost like the contents of a doll house. Aside from all the miniature weapons, we've also got sleeping bags, pillows, a first-aid potions kit, empty bottles to collect water when we do our water-drawing spells, a notebook, and even a tiny pouch of toiletries. "We have quite a few things to carry around with us," I explain, "so it's easier if most of them are small. We didn't shrink our clothes, though," I add, pulling out a few crumpled items of clothing. "We don't have many outfit options, so we didn't think it necessary to shrink them. And they provide cushioning for all the miniature items."

"Do you think I could perhaps borrow some of those clothes? You may have figured out I've been wearing this dress for a number of days. And, uh …" She scratches her arm and mumbles, "I was obviously never taught any cleaning spells. Or clothes casting spells. So I can't even transform this dress into something more suitable for riding around on a dragon. I know a basic shower spell, thank goodness," she adds hastily. "So at least I'm semi-clean. But showering the dress doesn't seem to get grass stains out."

I laugh. "We'll make a plan. You won't have to wear a dirty dress for much longer."

She pokes through our collection of miniature belongings and picks up a tiny sword to examine it more closely. "Cute. But you know you're using up magical energy every time you shrink and enlarge these things, right?"

"Yes. But it's separate from my Griffin Ability magic, so at least I'm not wasting that. Besides, I don't know how to do much with my normal magic yet, so I can't exactly help in other areas, like casting protective enchantments and hurling combat spells at anyone who wants to fight us. I'm learning, of course, but since Calla's the expert, she can do that stuff and I usually do the daily shrinking and enlarging of everything we have to carry around with us." When Aurora doesn't answer, I glance up and find her watching me with a smile I can't decipher. "What?"

"You've learned so much since we first met at Chevalier. Do you remember how you could barely create a flame during that first lesson we had together?"

"You mean the *only* lesson we had together?" I ask with a wry smile. "Yes. I remember. It was so flipping frustrating."

"And now look at you. Opening doorways, shrinking and enlarging things, plus all the things I taught you while you lived at the palace. And I'm guessing you're a lot closer to mastering your Griffin Ability now, seeing as how you were able to command me at will earlier." Her gaze slips down. "And you don't have the bracelet anymore."

"No. I got rid of it after I escaped the shadow world," I explain as Bandit pads closer, shrinks into a rabbit, and hops onto my lap. "Calla thought Roarke might be able to use it to track me."

Aurora frowns. "I don't know. Perhaps he could have. Although … if he could track you, then he wouldn't have needed to tell his glass faerie friend to go looking for you. Or perhaps that was another lie." Her shoulders slump as she leans back. "It's hard to know what the truth was now that I know how many things he's lied about."

"Yeah." I enlarge one of the sleeping bags and roll it out. "But yes, to answer your question, I definitely have more control over my Griffin Ability now. I can hold onto it, using only little bits when I need it, which usually means I have enough to keep me going until it replenishes again. Although now that I'm using it for fighting, it probably won't last nearly as long."

"You're using it for fighting?" Aurora asks. "How?"

I smile and reach for another sleeping bag. "I'll show you tomorrow."

"Okay, I think we should be safe here," Calla says, walking over and taking a seat opposite us on the ground. She crosses her legs. "Thanks for doing the sleeping bags."

"No problem. I just need to do one more. Good thing Chase threw a few spares in here." I find another sleeping bag among the items spread out on the ground in front of me and enlarge it.

"Hey, uh, sorry to interrupt," Aurora says, "but is that something we should be worried about?" She points past the mirror and tablets hanging in the air to where familiar gold numbers are counting down the time until we need to leave.

"Remember I told you we're constantly on the move now?" I say. "The countdown reminds us when to leave."

"Ah. Clever."

I turn to Calla. "So what's going on? What did Chase say when you spoke to him at the last stop?"

"It sounds like there's going to be a meeting with the Guild Council, the Seelie King, the Unseelie King, and their respective advisors. A summit."

"Seriously?" Aurora sits forward. "My father's meeting with the Seelies and the Guild? That's ... I don't think that's ever happened before. At least, not since I've been living at the palace."

"It is kind of historic," Calla says, nodding. "It's been proposed that the most important thing now is restoring the divide between the two worlds. Magic that has spilled into the human world must be removed, and those human soldiers who found their way into this world must be sent back. Seelies and Unseelies need to put aside their differences to accomplish both those goals. Afterwards, they can go back to their separate territories and hate each other from a distance."

"I assume someone said that in more politically correct terms?" I ask.

"Hopefully," Calla says with a laugh. "Anyway, Chase will get back to me when he knows more details about the summit. In the meantime—" she turns to Aurora. "—why don't you tell us more about your brother? And I'll see what food we have left in here." She lifts the backpack and looks inside.

"I've already checked," I say, pushing a small box toward her. "Our options are limited. Grapes, a few chocolate apples, and those dinner pop things."

"Dinner pops?" Aurora repeats, referring to the bite-sized spheres that apparently contain a full meal's worth of nutrition while managing to taste like nothing. "Wow, I don't think I've ever been in a position where I've been forced to eat a dinner pop," she says. Calla arches an eyebrow and looks at her, and Aurora hastens to add, "Right, sorry, talk about Roarke." She sucks in a deep breath. "Uh … let's see. Well, he's always been very ambitious. I thought that was normal for someone who was born to be a king one day, so I didn't realize the full extent of his ambition until he started talking about claiming the shadow world without our father's consent so he could rule it. I suppose that makes him impatient too. He never wanted to wait until Dad stepped down or … or died."

Calla nods as she passes each of us a dinner pop. She balances a few grapes on my knee in front of Bandit and asks, "So he's always been desperate to rule, to be in control?"

"Yes. And he always admired our Uncle Marzell. His life's work, at least. Obviously we never met him. It always irritated my father whenever Roarke went on and on about the amazing things Uncle Zell could have achieved if Lord Draven hadn't got in the way."

"Interesting," Calla murmurs.

I finishing chewing my tasteless dinner pop and lean forward. "Was this guy Marzell your father's brother?"

Aurora nods. "You've probably heard about Lord Draven, the guy who almost conquered our entire realm. Covered most of the world in perpetual winter and brainwashed everyone. Well, it actually all started with my uncle. He was in search of a famous dead halfling's power so he could consume it and become more powerful. He also figured out that some faeries had extra magic—this was before the Guild discovered them and called them Griffin Gifted—and he was hunting them down so he could make an army of them. Draven was one of these Gifted—also a halfling with a buttload of power—and after my uncle found the hidden power from the dead halfling, Draven killed him and took the power for himself. Roarke always said how unfortunate it was that it happened that way. If Draven had never got involved, it would have been our uncle who took that power. The Unseelies might have ruled the entire world by now. Or both worlds, actually."

"Or whoever killed Draven would have killed your uncle. Someone did kill Draven, right? I think I remember that from one of the few lessons I had at Chevalier House."

"Well, yes, but it's complicated," Aurora says. "Everyone *thought* he was killed. And he totally deserved it, the brainwashing bastard." Calla coughs, interrupting Aurora's next words, which is probably exactly what Dash would have done if he were here. Aurora gives us a guilty smile before continuing. "Sorry. Language. I know. Anyway, everyone thought Draven was dead, but then it turned out he'd survived somehow, and he ended up in the Seelie Queen's custody. And then when that whole Velazar veil thing happened, he was consumed in an enchanted fire. So yes, he's dead now. But if it had been my uncle in his position, he might have survived all that. He might still be ruling today, and that's what Roarke always liked to point out to my father."

"No offense to your family," I say, "but I'm glad that didn't happen." I look at Calla to see her response to this information, but she's staring past Aurora with her eyes partially glazed over. "Calla?" I ask. "Are you still listening?"

She blinks. "Yes. Sorry. Just thinking of—the past." She focuses on Aurora once more. "So your father didn't like the idea of the Unseelies ruling an entire world—or *two* entire worlds, since that was Draven's eventual aim—instead of just their own territory?"

"Well …" Aurora's expression becomes thoughtful. "To be honest, I think he might have liked that idea if he'd been the one to come up with it. But since it was Uncle Zell's secret plan, and he totally failed at it, Dad always said it was stupid. That Uncle Zell reached too far and it got him killed. But, you know …" She pushes her purple and dark brown tresses over her shoulder. "I'm pretty sure he wishes he'd come up with the idea first."

Calla's nodding again. "I see. And Roarke has always admired that idea, so maybe that's what he's trying to do now. Except he can't have our world because he'd have to fight both the Seelies and the Unseelies, and he can't have the shadow world because it's tiny—and let's be honest, it isn't even a real world—so he's left with trying to take over the non-magic world instead."

"So the Haverton Tower Hotel and all the other incidents aren't just part of some massive magical temper tantrum then," I say. "They're part of a last-minute disorganized attempt to take over the human world?"

"Maybe it's not last-minute," Aurora says. "Maybe he always planned to do this eventually. I don't know."

"Or maybe we're completely wrong," Calla says, "and Roarke's just throwing his anger around the human realm because he has nothing better to do."

I push my hands through my hair. "Someone had better stop him soon before he ruins both worlds."

"Do you think they'll kill him?" Aurora asks in a small voice. "The Guild or the Seelie soldiers or whoever catches up to him first?"

Calla is quiet before answering, long enough for me to remember what she said as we watched human soldiers marching into the fae ream with guns and explosives: *I've never wanted to kill … But right now? Right now I could kill Roarke if no one was there to stop me.* "I don't know," she says eventually. "I hope not. I hope he'll be justly punished instead. But it will be up to the Unseelies to determine his punishment."

Aurora looks down at her hands. "Oh," she says, picking up the dinner pop between her thumb and forefinger. "I forgot about this." She places it carefully in her mouth and starts chewing, an unimpressed expression on her face.

I look away from her with a small smile on my lips. I'm glad she got away from the Unseelie Palace and managed to find me. Who knows what will happen at the end of all this, but hopefully, when the Seelies and Unseelies go back to hating each other and Calla and I finally get back to our home, Aurora and I will still be friends.

As the bright moon continues to rise above us, illuminating our enchanted blue surroundings, I say, "Sitting here, it all seems so far away. The Haverton Tower Hotel, and those human soldiers crashing through our world. Almost as if it could never touch us."

"I know," Calla answers. "But it will. Those humans might not possess magic, but their weapons are powerful. Their bombs will rip through immense parts of our world if someone doesn't send them back to where they belong."

"I'm sure it will all be okay in the end," Aurora says, though she sounds far from certain. "We stop Roarke, we push the humans out of our world, and everything goes back to normal."

"Well, that isn't all of it," I tell her. "We have other things to worry about. The Guild has Dash, and they've imprisoned my parents somewhere as well. Until we find them and rescue them, nothing will be normal for us."

"Wait, did you say *parents*? Plural?" Aurora sits forward. "Did you find out who your father is?"

I sigh. "Roarke seriously didn't tell you anything, did he."

"Yeah, I think we've already established that. What's this about your parents?"

I look at Calla. "I'm starting to think I should have recorded this whole story about Ada and Zed and changeling magic and Violet and Ryn being my parents. How many times have I told it now?"

"Hey." Aurora pokes my leg with her foot. "Just tell me the story."

I sigh and launch into my explanation once again. By the time I reach the end, Aurora's listening raptly with wide eyes. "You're a changeling. And you found your family. That's amazing! And Dash ..." Her face falls. "Darn, Roarke must have sent that letter he kept threatening to send to the Guild. The one tipping them off about Dash working with Griffin rebels. Why else would they suddenly have become suspicious of him?"

"Well, he did disappear to the Unseelie Palace for several days without permission and with very little explanation," Calla says.

"Hmm, I suppose that would invite some suspicion," Aurora admits.

"So that's the whole story," I say, leaning back, moving Bandit aside, and uncrossing my legs so I can stretch them out. "I finally find my family, and then they end up in a torture prison—or wherever it is the Guild is hiding them now. I mean, they could still be in the same prison, for all we know. Just hidden in a different part of it."

"That's a possibility," Calla says. She sighs and looks around at the floating timer. "We should get some rest. Who knows what magical mess we may have to deal with tomorrow."

"Or if we'll suddenly find out where the rest of our family is being held captive and have to launch another rescue mission," I say.

She smiles. "We can always hope." As we spread the sleeping bags out, she adds, "I'll take the first watch. You can do the second half of the night, and we can give Aurora her first night off."

"Keep watch?" Aurora asks. "Are you serious?"

"Hey, you wanted to stick with us," I remind her.

"Yes, but—"

"We can argue about this tomorrow night," Calla says. "For tonight, enjoy your sleep."

After some grumbling from Aurora, I hand her a set of clean clothes, and she walks to the other side of Imperia to make use of a shower spell. Bandit climbs into my sleeping bag and shuffles all the way to the bottom, and Imperia, already asleep, sends puffs of steam into the air as she snores.

My eyes slide shut as my head reaches my pillow, but as always, thoughts of Vi, Ryn and Dash begin to wander through my mind. Eventually, at some point after my Griffin Ability has replenished and after my imagination plays through a multitude of things that might possibly go wrong in both worlds tomorrow, I slip into dreamland.

When Calla shakes my shoulder some time later, I feel as though I haven't been asleep for nearly long enough. At first I assume it's my turn to keep watch, but she doesn't normally wake me so vigorously. "Whaswrong?" I mumble, blinking several times and trying to focus on her.

She crouches beside me. "I'm leaving for a little while, Em. I need to go to Central Park. Roarke's magic is spreading quickly, taking over the whole area. I think we were right about him. I think he wants the human world."

CHAPTER 16

I PUSH MYSELF TO MY FEET AS QUICKLY AS MY SLEEPY BODY WILL ALLOW. "WHAT? *THE* Central Park?" I realize as I'm speaking that of course she's talking about *the* Central Park. It's right next to the huge hotel Roarke attacked a few days ago.

"Yes." She attaches a weapons belt around her hips and secures it. "Chase was just here, updating me on everything he knows. The entire area has been consumed by an enchanted forest. Humans are trapped inside and can't find their way out. He's gone straight there, and I'm going to join him."

I blink a few more times and rub my eyes, wishing I could have had a bit more sleep before confronting a new problem. "Has the Guild not sent any guardians to rescue those people?"

"That's the thing," she says, turning and heading to the amber tablets. I follow behind her. "I can see all these vision reports popping up—way too late, I might add—but hardly any of them are being assigned. So many guardians have been dispatched to deal with the advancing human soldiers, and others are attending the summit with the Seelies and Unseelies, which doesn't leave many to deal with all the incidents taking place across the human realm."

"So that summit thing is definitely happening?" Aurora asks. I look back and see her climbing out of her sleeping bag.

"Yes," Calla answers. "Later today. In a location that obviously hasn't been made public, but Perry and Flint have done well with their eavesdropping and information gathering. Chase and Elizabeth are going along to listen in so we know what's discussed and what decisions they come to, because I can guarantee they won't make everything public afterwards. And I need to go with to make sure they're properly concealed."

As Aurora reaches my side, rubbing her eyes and yawning, I say, "Wait, so … did you say you're going to Central Park without us?"

"Yes." Calla opens one side of her jacket—revealing an array of small, gleaming weapons—and removes her stylus.

"But if it's just you and a few other Griffin rebels—and maybe a handful of guardians—then won't you need more help? I can—"

"Em, that whole area—the Haverton Tower Hotel and the park and some of the smaller surrounding buildings—are under Roarke's control now. I don't want you anywhere near there. He could easily get his hands on you."

"How could he *easily* get his hands on me?" I argue. "He won't know I'm there, especially if you're imagining us as invisible."

"True, but I don't want to risk your safety. Not when I know he's nearby."

I throw my hands up. "You can travel anywhere in the world within seconds. *Everywhere* is nearby."

She steps closer to me. "You know how important you are to me, to our family. I'm only trying to keep you—"

"Keep me safe. I know."

"Then why are you arguing with me?"

I press my lips together, holding back my frustration. Blurting out 'I don't like being told what to do' would sound incredibly childish, but that's essentially what this is about. Though I wouldn't give up the family I've just discovered for *anything*, part of me misses being in control of my own life. Chelsea didn't particularly care what I did with my time. I had the freedom to go anywhere I could afford to go— which, sadly, didn't include much beyond Stanmeade. But it was still freedom. Now … well, now I have to do whatever Calla tells me to do.

I take a deep breath and try to sound reasonable. "I'm not saying I want to run into the midst of danger and be reckless. I don't *want* Roarke to find me. All I want is to help you save everyone who's stuck inside Roarke's enchanted forest."

She shakes her head, turns away, and raises her stylus. She writes on the air itself, and a moment later, a doorway appears. She's about to step through it, but she stops. She sighs, looks back at me, and asks, "Why? Why do you want to save them?"

"Because … I don't know. Because I can. And it's the right thing to do."

It's hard to tell through the semi-darkness, but I think she might almost be smiling. "Fine," she says. "But you have to do whatever I tell you."

A thrill rushes through me. I reach down beside my sleeping bag and grab my jacket. "Of course. I wouldn't think of doing anything else."

"Are you happy to stay here on your own?" Calla asks Aurora. "Not that you have a choice. I'm not taking both you and Em."

Aurora points her thumb over her shoulder. "Have you seen my dragon? I'm not exactly alone."

"Good point," Calla says.

"And take care of Bandit please," I add.

"You are coming back, aren't you?" Aurora asks. "This isn't a ruse of some sort to get rid of me?"

"We're definitely coming back," Calla assures her. "I only have an hour, and then I need to leave for the summit. And you're definitely *not* coming along for that," she adds, looking at me. "The only thing we'll be doing is listening."

I finish pulling my jacket on. "Okay."

"Right, let's stop wasting time." She loops her arm through mine and steps into the faerie paths.

"Bye," Aurora says. I look back and see her giving us a small wave. "Imperia and I will guard all your stuff. Please don't die."

Calla hesitates, which I'm sure has far more to do with leaving all our belongings behind than the possibility that we might die. "It's fine," I murmur as the edges of the doorway begin to move toward each other. "We can trust her. And it's just stuff, anyway."

We step into a street near Central Park where it's eerily quiet and a lot darker than I expected. A single light flickers, a siren wails in the distance, and the dark night presses around me. My heart beats a little too quickly as we walk toward the end of the block—then begins racing properly at the sight of the scene awaiting us from the next street onward.

It's the stuff of post-apocalyptic nightmares. Crumbling buildings, bent and twisted lamp posts, the occasional spark from exposed wiring, and trees, vines and enchanted oversized flowers strangling everything. "Ho-lee crap," I whisper. "I know you made it sound bad, but this is *bad*."

"It's like … like our world has erupted into this one and is trying to consume it," Calla says. "And with those human soldiers advancing further and further into the fae realm, everything's just becoming so mixed up. It was never supposed to be this way. This is all so …"

"Wrong?" a voice says behind us. We turn and see Chase walking out of the faerie paths toward us. "Thanks for coming," he says to Calla. "I didn't realize you were bringing Em with."

"Neither did I," Calla answers. "But she was quite insistent."

Chase laughs quietly and says, "Just as stubborn as your parents, I see."

"So I've heard," I tell him.

Calla's expression turns serious again. "How did this forest—this *jungle*—happen so quickly? Surely Roarke doesn't have the kind of magic to create something so large in so short a time?"

"Apparently he has half the Unseelie army on his side," I remind her. "They must have helped."

"Yes, I suppose so." She looks at Chase. "Have you been able to save anyone from this tangled mess?"

"Five so far; two couples and a guy on his own. And I'm not bothering with a glamour. I find people, free them from whatever plant they're twisted up in, lead them out as quickly as possible, then search for more. I have no idea how many are in there, though, and we have limited time if we're hoping to get to the summit."

"Well, we can only do as much as we can," Calla says, already moving toward the ruins. "Whichever guardians are around—plus Carter, Krystal and Kobe—will have to do the rest."

"Wait," I say. "We may as well use my ability since I'm here. Maybe I can tell the whole forest it doesn't exist anymore. Then everyone can get away from the park."

Chase hesitates, then says, "I suppose you may as well try. Your ability seems to obey almost everything else you say."

I move a few steps closer to the overgrown wreckage, stopping when I reach a fallen lamp post. I exhale deeply, thinking of the size of Central Park—and then mentally adding on more area for the surrounding streets and buildings that have been consumed. Basically, this forest is freaking enormous.

As if she can hear my thoughts, Calla asks, "Are you sure you'll be okay if you try this? It seems so … big."

I look over my shoulder at her. "My power is pretty big too, isn't it? That's why everyone else wants it."

She nods slowly. "True. I guess you did close the veil. That was big."

I turn back and focus my attention on the forest spreading out before me. If I imagine the entire thing—if that's where my intention is directed—then this should work, right?

"Hey!"

My gaze snaps up in the direction of the shout. Through the darkness, I see a group of people—ten, perhaps, though I don't have time to count them—leaping over the ruins with magical ease. "Get out of here!" one of them shouts. Sparks of magic fly our way, morphing into flapping, screeching crows. Chase is suddenly beside me, sweeping one hand through the air and tossing the crows aside with a powerful gust of wind.

With barely a thought for what I'm doing, I clench my fists and yell, "Don't attack! Don't come a step closer!"

And every one of the advancing faeries slams up against an invisible wall. An unexpected thrill races through me as I realize I could tell these people absolutely anything and they'd have no choice but to obey me. But I barely have time to enjoy the feeling before Calla tugs me sideways into the faerie paths. Chase dives in after me, catching hold of my arm.

We stumble out of the faerie paths into an almost identical scene of overgrown destruction, near some other part of the park. The road beneath our feet has buckled from the pressure of giant roots spreading beneath it, and water gushes up from beneath the cracks in the tar. Calla whips around, no doubt searching for any sign of a new threat. "Maybe conceal us?" Chase suggests. "Roarke's guys are probably everywhere."

"I am," she answers. "Invisibility."

"That was quick thinking, Em," Chase says to me. "Well done. Now try commanding the forest." He looks back over his shoulder. "Quickly, if you can. I think people are approaching from back there."

I nod, pushing aside the disturbing exhilaration of having so easily commanded a group of people. I shut my eyes and picture the entirety of Central Park covered in a magical forest that shouldn't be there. Then I release the control I'm holding over my Griffin Ability's power and speak. "This enchanted forest—the forest created by Prince Roarke and his followers—no longer exists. Every plant of magical origin is gone, and every human trapped among the plants is now free to move about. Return the park … the park and …" I want to add more. I want to tell the park and surrounding roads and buildings to return to their former state. I want to tell the damage and destruction to vanish along with the forest. But all my power is already flooding from my body. My head is spinning. Spots of light fill my vision as my body becomes weightless.

"Em? Em!"

I blink a few times and lift my head. As my surroundings come back into focus, I realize I'm sitting on a sidewalk propped up between Calla and Chase. "Are you okay?" Calla asks. Her hand is against my cheek, turning my face toward hers.

"Yes, just …" I blink again. "I didn't … have enough."

"It's working," Chase says.

Calla turns her head, and I struggle to look past her. It happens quickly. I barely have time to see the vines, trees and other plants being sucked into the ground like a time-lapse movie clip in reverse before they're all completely gone. The damage, of course, is still there. Cracked roads, broken pipes, half-destroyed buildings. It looks like a war zone.

"Incredible," Calla murmurs. "I wonder if your command reached the entire forest."

Chase stands. "It's impossible to tell from here."

"I don't … think so," I tell them. "I wouldn't have passed out if I had enough power for the whole forest."

"I can see a whole bunch of Roarke's followers now," Chase adds. "Those are definitely Unseelie uniforms. Doesn't look like they're too happy about suddenly being exposed." He turns at the sound of hurried footsteps coming from the other direction down the street. "Now what? More Unseelies?"

Calla takes my arm and pulls me behind a taxi. "Aren't we concealed?" I ask.

"Yes. Just taking extra precautions." She peers around the edge of the car.

I rub my fingers against my temples, still trying to clear my head, and ask, "Who is it?"

"Human armed forces," she answers. "Loads of them."

"Not good," Chase mutters. "They have no idea what they're facing."

"Kind of expected, though," I say. "Obviously humans are gonna fight back. And they don't mind making a mess if it means getting rid of the enemy. They'll probably blow up the whole park if they have to."

"Let's hope they evacuate their own kind from the park before resorting to such extreme measures," Calla says, twisting around and raising her stylus against the taxi's front door. "I'm opening a doorway. We need to get away from—"

Bright light pulses outward, and a shudder ripples through the ground. I throw my hands out to steady myself and squeeze my eyes shut against the blinding light. The air is filled with shouts and the sounds of heavy thumps against the road. As the light dims, I lower my hand. Chase is climbing to his feet, and Calla is grabbing onto my arm. "Are you okay?" she asks Chase. "What was that?"

"Timed magic," he says. "Must have been. They all released magic at the same moment and those armed forces went flying."

Groans and more shouting reach my ears. "We're leaving," Calla says immediately. She raises her stylus again, and this time, nothing interrupts her doorway spell.

"I'm staying a little longer," Chase says. "Just keeping an eye on this situation. Get Em away from here. I'll meet you and Elizabeth at the lake house within the next half hour."

Calla nods as she pulls me into the faerie paths. Darkness surrounds us, and I blink into it, my thoughts still stumbling to catch up with everything that's happened.

CHAPTER 17

 surrounded on all sides by peaceful blue scenery. It's almost surreal compared to the cracked and broken city we just ran from.

Aurora climbs quickly to her feet and asks, "What happened there?"

"Em took down the forest," Calla tells her. "Or some of it, at least." She turns to me and asks, "Are you okay now?"

"Yes. My legs are a little weak, but I'm fine. It's just …" I look over my shoulder, as if I could see through the disappearing doorway and back to the scene we left behind. "All those people who were just attacked—the soldiers—we just left them there. What if Roarke's army is about to kill them all?"

"Chase is still there. He won't let that happen."

"But how could he possibly stop them all?"

Calla walks to the tablets and mirror and pulls them from the air. "With a storm."

"But—"

"A storm like you've never seen." She looks back at me. "Trust me, Em. He can handle it."

I shut my eyes for a moment, then say, "Okay. I'm sure you're right."

"We need to pack up," Calla continues. "I know it's still night here, and you still have time, but I'd prefer to move you both to a new location and restart the countdown before I go to the summit. You'll probably need to move again before I return, though. Possibly more than once."

"Do you think the summit will take that long?" Aurora asks.

"I doubt the summit itself will last more than a day—and if it does, I'll have to leave early in case any guardians are still tracking the spell that's stuck on me—but it's the traveling that will take some time. It's in a region inaccessible through the faerie paths, so it'll take us hours to get there instead of seconds."

"Wow, that must be frustrating for a faerie," I say as I crouch down at the foot of my sleeping bag and start rolling it up.

"Yes. Not a limitation we have to deal with often."

"How will you find us when you return?" Aurora asks. "Em, do you have an amber? I didn't have mine on me when I fled the palace."

"Oh yes, I do have one. We bought it the other day. It should be in the backpack."

Bandit hops out the end of my sleeping bag before I finish rolling it. Aurora crouches down and rolls hers up while I move on to Calla's. Then I add the pillows to the pile, shrink everything, and drop it all into the backpack.

"Okay, I think that's all our stuff," Calla says, her eyes scanning the area. "Aurora, do you want to open an extra-large doorway so your dragon can fit through?"

We make it through the faerie paths together, each of us holding on to some part of Imperia's body. I head out of the darkness and find that we're on another hill, though this one is a lot rockier and it's already morning here. Ahead of us, I see more hills and more rocks. Behind us, not too far away, a sheer cliff face reaches ridiculously high into the sky. "Not as pretty as the last spot, but it'll do just fine," Calla says. "There's a little town just over that hill." She points to the right. "You can buy food there if you need it. Just—"

"Be careful," I say. "We know."

Calla smiles. "I was actually going to say, 'Just make sure to leave Imperia here when you go into town so no one sees her.'"

"Oh. Of course," Aurora says. "I guess it would raise suspicion if she showed up in a town not normally frequented by dragons."

"Indeed," Calla answers. "That's the case for most towns, even in a world of magic."

Aurora takes the backpack from me and asks, "Do you mind if I hide between the rocks and use a shower spell? I, uh, usually like to bathe when I wake up in the morning, so if there's nothing else urgent to be done …"

"Oh, sure, go ahead," I tell her. "Enjoy." As she walks away, I turn to Calla. "I know you said I shouldn't go with you to the summit—"

"You're definitely not coming."

"Just listen to me please. You guys don't want to live in hiding forever, do you? And you want the Guild to let you help them. Well, my Griffin Ability can make that possible. I could tell the entire gathering of guardians, Seelies and Unseelies not to be afraid of Griffin Gifted. I can tell them they don't see us as a threat anymore. I can make them believe they should work *with* Griffin Gifted instead of locking us up, and they won't have a choice but to obey me. It's the perfect opportunity, with so many leaders gathered together."

"Em," Calla says slowly, "you can't take away their free will. That isn't right."

"But I'd be making them do the right thing!"

"But that isn't—" she sighs. "If that's not what they truly believe, then it isn't right to force them into it. Surely you understand that?"

I shut my eyes for a moment, breathing out slowly. "Yes. I guess I do. It's just … I have a chance to make a real difference. Some good could actually come out of this situation."

"I know. But we can't change people who don't want to be changed. At least, not like this. This isn't the way we get things done. This is who the Guild *thinks* we are, but we have to prove them wrong."

"What if they don't even know? What if I make them believe that they came to this decision themselves?"

She shakes her head. "It would never remain a secret, Em. The truth about how you forced non-Griffin Gifted fae into doing something against their will would eventually get out. In the end, it would probably have more of a negative impact than a positive one."

I stuff my hands into my pockets and look away. "Yeah. I guess you're right."

After several moments of silence, Calla says, "Okay, so …" She looks around. "You should be fine, right? You've got the backpack. You can keep the mirror and the tablets. *Don't* act on any of the visions you might see, even if they look important and no one from the Guild has been assigned to prevent them."

"Yeah, yeah," I answer. "Don't do anything dangerous. Got it."

"If you need to keep busy," Calla adds, "you're welcome to continue practicing all the things we've been working on together. Especially—Oh, that's what I was forgetting." She walks to the backpack and digs through the contents. "You should take a look at this." She hands me a thick scroll of papers. "Chase left it with me when he came to tell me about Central Park. It's everything Perry's dug up on a place called Reinhold Research Station. Turns out it's real. Lots of reading, which I don't have time for at the moment. You can give me a summary when I get back."

"Oh, cool." I take the scroll from her. "I thought Perry said he'd never heard of this place. And that he has, like, zero time at the moment to privately investigate anything extra."

Calla smiles. "That's one of the great things about Perry. He always comes through for us, no matter how busy he is." After hugging me tightly, she opens a doorway and waves as she steps into the faerie paths. I try to convince myself, as the darkness closes around her, that everything's going to be fine while she's gone.

After Calla leaves, I set aside the Reinhold scroll to look at later and start practicing some of the things I've learned in recent days. What I really want to do is practice using my Griffin Ability for fighting, but it won't be replenished for another few hours. Instead, Aurora and I come up with various commands I could use during a battle, if I ever find myself in the midst of one.

All guardians, drop your weapons.

Fall down and slide to the edge of the room.

Arrow, strike the Unseelie guard's shoulder.

Sword, chop off everyone's hands.

That last one was Aurora's suggestion. Apparently mine were getting too boring.

When we're tired of commands, we try throwing our own magic around. Plain old sparks are the easiest and quickest, of course, so we stretch ourselves by trying to shape our magic into different forms. Sand, hail, wind, bats, razor blades. It takes me far too long before I can hurl anything interesting at Aurora, but it's fun to try.

Then, after doing a quick spell to draw water from the ground so we're no longer panting with thirst, we set up makeshift targets and move back to real weapons. Aurora goes straight for the bow, since archery is her favorite. I practice throwing knives and various star-shaped pieces of metal—which I mostly still suck at without the use of magic. When I pick up two training swords and try to hand one to Aurora, she refuses. Apparently a princess has to draw the line somewhere. So I practice some of the footwork and different strikes Calla showed me, ignoring Aurora when she tells me how stupid I look doing a slow-motion dance around a non-existent opponent while swinging a wooden stick.

Eventually I'm too tired for further practice, so we sit against Imperia's side and, despite Aurora's complaints about the lack of flavor, we each eat a dinner pop. My Griffin Ability replenishes as I finish chewing, filling my body with an invigorating rush of power. I focus on holding onto it, but it doesn't take too much effort anymore.

I tilt my head back against Imperia's slippery scales, and for a little while, I let myself enjoy a conversation that includes entirely random topics unrelated to the world ending or half the people I care about being imprisoned. Like the fact that Aurora likes to sing in the bathroom—"Hell, no. I don't sing *at all* if I can help it"—and the story of how she came to be adopted by the Unseelie royal family—"So that witch just *left* you there? And they never found her?"—and the strange admission that she's always envied human teenagers.

"Now *that* can't possibly be true," I say when we reach the teenager topic. "Surely nobody has *ever* envied human teens? It's such an awkward phase of life. I *still* feel super awkward half the time, and I'm nearing the end of my teenage years."

"Faerie teens are awkward too," Aurora assures me, "but at least human teens don't have to deal with all that embarrassing magic. If a girl likes a boy, the whole world doesn't have to know about it."

I raise an eyebrow. "I have no idea what you're talking about."

"You know, like when you're attracted to someone and magic escapes you and does weird, random things, and *everyone knows why.*"

"Um ... nope?" But as I say this, I think back to the night Dash and I sat on the floor inside the shadow world castle, waiting for the changeling spell on Dani and Ada to begin working. Sparks and flames appeared from nowhere, and Dash told me it was his magic. Then he said he thought he'd outgrown something. Something he didn't particularly want to explain to me ... "Oh," I say. "*Oh.* Never mind. I think I do know what you're talking about."

"You see? You've been embarrassing yourself and you didn't even know it."

"Actually, it was Dash's magic that escaped, not mine."

A slow smile lights up Aurora's face. "I told you," she crows. "I *told* you he loves you!"

"Whoa, hey, nobody said anything about *love.*" I look around, searching for a change in topic, and see Imperia's back leg beside me. "Hey, uh ... how safe do you think it would be for us to take Imperia for a ride?" I run my hand across her smooth, shimmering scales. "I seriously miss dragon riding."

"I'm guessing dragon riding is on Calla's 'Definitely Don't Do That' list."

I let out a groan. "I think you're right. We probably don't want to draw attention to ourselves." I stretch my legs out in front of me as Bandit wanders closer in cat form. He sits neatly in front of me, then shifts into a small version of Imperia.

Aurora laughs and claps her hands. "So clever, Bandit!"

"Does he know what we're saying?" I ask her. "I've often wondered how much he understands, but I've never actually asked anyone."

"I've heard that formattra are quite intelligent," she says. "I'm sure he doesn't understand *everything*, but I guess he understands enough to know we're talking about dragons."

I lean forward and pat Bandit's scaled snout. "Calla says it won't be easy for him to transform into a dragon for much longer. Something about him getting bigger and it requiring a lot of magic."

Aurora nods. "I think I've heard something like that."

I tilt my head as an idea begins to form. "My Griffin Ability is super powerful, right?"

Aurora looks at me as if that might be a trick question. "Uh, yes?"

"When I say things, they usually happen."

"Again, that would be a 'yes.'"

"So …" I lean forward and focus on my shapeshifting pet. My magical voice echoes around us as I say, "Bandit, you have enough power to transform into a dragon the size of Imperia whenever you want to, no matter how old you are."

I sit back as all my Griffin power drains from my body in one go. I'm left feeling dizzy, but not as light-headed as I did at Central Park. I blink a few times and watch Bandit. Beside me, Aurora leans forward. A shiver courses through Bandit's body. His eyes widen a little, looking for all the world as if he's startled.

Then he begins to grow. I stare in open-mouthed amazement as his body becomes larger and larger, filling the space in front of us. "Oh crap," I mutter, realizing the problem we're about to have at the same time Aurora figures it out. We both jump to our feet, and Aurora smacks Imperia's side.

"Move, move, move," she shouts. Imperia rises as quickly as she can for a creature of her size, lurching a few giant steps away and saving us from being squished between her and Bandit. Finally, when he's about the same size as Imperia, he stops growing. He looks down at me with gigantic fiery orange eyes, and all I can say is, "Wow."

Then, as we watch, he lumbers a few steps backward and begins to change again. Not into a smaller form, but into a different dragon, just as enormous. Black scales line his body, and the forked tongue that darts out of his mouth is bright red.

"That. Is. Awesome," Aurora says.

I walk closer, run my hand along Bandit's leg, and gaze up at him. "You are seriously the coolest pet ever."

It isn't yet evening in this part of the world, but since we didn't sleep much last night, and we need to move to our next location in just over eight hours, I suggest we pretend it's nighttime and go to bed. "And we need to take turns keeping watch, remember?"

As I expected, Aurora's not impressed with this idea. "Is that really necessary when we have Imperia? And Bandit? They'll wake us if something goes wrong."

"And what if Imperia and Bandit fall asleep too? Don't tell me haven't heard Imperia snoring. She was really loud last night."

Aurora rolls her eyes. "Fine. We can do the keeping watch thing. But can I sleep first? I'm super exhausted after using so much magic earlier."

"Sure thing, princess. Whatever you want. Hey! Was that a training sword you just threw at me?"

"More like a pencil," she says with a snort. "It doesn't deserve to be called a sword when it's shorter than my finger.

I return the miniature sword to the backpack and say, "In case you were wondering, your four hours have already started."

"Ugh, that is so not enough sleep for me. And *don't* give me another 'princess' comment," she adds as I open my mouth. "Four hours isn't enough for anyone."

"Actually, Calla told me faeries can last longer without sleep than humans can," I tell her. "That's why I haven't been as tired as I thought I'd be."

"Yeah, well … whatever." Aurora climbs into her sleeping bag. "I'd prefer a lot more."

As she shuffles further down into her sleeping bag, I retrieve the scroll containing all the information Perry found regarding Reinhold Research Station. I settle against Imperia's front leg and start scanning through the pages. It starts with some boring details about all the people involved in designing and building the station, which I quickly move on from once I realize none of the names mean anything to me.

But the details on the next page get straight to the point of Reinhold: to experiment on Griffin Gifted fae. My stomach turns as I read about the various Griffin Abilities the researchers at Reinhold have tried to extract and make use of. Most of these experiments have failed, but this report mentions two that have been successful. One is a healing ability that's so quick it's almost instant. The healing magic has been mixed with other factors to form a liquid that's currently—at least, current at the time this report was written—in the final phase of testing.

The other successful experiment mentioned is first referred to as a 'mental prison.' This Griffin Ability, belonging to a woman named Shyla, can confine people within their own minds. And it's this Griffin Ability, the next page tells me, that made The Noxsom Facility possible.

At the sight of the word 'Noxsom,' my heart thumps faster. I swallow and continue to read about how Reinhold researchers combined this particular Griffin Ability with a tiny amount of poison extracted from a creature called a rememoraith. This creature is apparently a close relative of something called a morioraith—which researchers experimented on first and were unable to extract poison from—but the document doesn't tell me what the poison from either of these two creatures actually does. The section ends with a small picture of Shyla and one last line saying that she remains in custody at Reinhold while further uses for her ability are being determined.

The last two pages talk about plans for future experiments, along with a section about funding, which obviously isn't helpful. I roll the pages back together and place the scroll on the ground beside me, feeling ill. I'm not sure about Dash, but the more I think about it, the more convinced I am that Vi, Ryn and the rest of the Griffin rebels have been taken to Reinhold. They don't all have Griffin Abilities, but most of them do, and if the Guild wants to take advantage of those abilities, this is the perfect way to do it.

Feeling the need to occupy myself with something else, I pick up the knives I haven't shrunk yet and walk a short distance away to where our makeshift targets still stand. I practice for a long time, enjoying the way I don't have to think about anything else when I'm focusing on trying to throw a weapon correctly. As the sun goes down, I manage to form a glowing orb and leave it floating nearby while I continue.

When it's almost time to wake Aurora, I pack away most of our things so we'll be ready to leave when she wakes me. The tablets, the mirror, my jacket containing knives in hidden pockets, any other weapons still lying around. I dismantle the targets, fail to transform them back into branches, and decided to just leave them. Then I unroll my sleeping bag and shake Aurora's shoulder as I climb into it.

She grumbles something about having been asleep for only a few minutes, but she rubs her eyes and crawls out onto the ground.

"Walk around for a bit," I tell her as Bandit sneaks past my arm into the sleeping bag as a cat. "That should help wake you up."

"Mm," she says. As my head hits the pillow, she asks, "Can I read this?"

I look up and see her holding the scroll. "Sure. I should warn you, though," I add as I turn over. "It's kinda depressing."

I wake with a jolt as someone shoves me roughly. For a moment, I'm back on the blue hillside, expecting Calla to tell me about Central Park. We'll get up and race off to the city so I can tell the forest to vanish. But the sleepiness clears from my mind, and I remember that that's already happened.

"Em!" Aurora hisses. "*Get up!*"

"What?" I sit up, pushing my hair out of my face. "What's wrong?" It's still dark, but faint light moves somewhere behind Aurora.

"Guardians!" she says. "It was the light that woke me. I got up and saw them down there." She points over her shoulder. "They're dressed all in black, and I'm sure I saw guardian weapons. They're coming up the hill, Em. Fast."

CHAPTER 18

THE WORLD SPINS AS I SCRAMBLE HASTILY TO MY FEET. "WHAT THE ... HOW DID they ..." My gaze falls on the golden digits hanging in the air. They're all zeros. "Aurora! Dammit, how long have we been asleep?"

Not an important question, I remind myself as she stammers out apologies, since the answer is clearly 'Too long.' I focus on the approaching guardians making their way swiftly up the hill toward us with orbs of light bobbing above them. I can see three figures so far, but there must be more behind them. My immediate thought is to say something, to command them all to freeze, but I remember then that I used all my Griffin magic on granting Bandit the power to become a full-sized dragon. Which, it appears, might actually save us. Because the Bandit who was curled against my chest moments ago is no longer a cat. He's now a sleek black dragon with burning red eyes.

Imperia and Bandit breathe flames at the oncoming guardians, but they shield themselves with magic and continue advancing. I should be running, grabbing a stylus, throwing magic at those guardians—*anything* except standing motionless as my brain tries to decides which will be faster: opening a doorway wide enough to fit dragons through, or climbing onto those dragons and flying away. All while a single thought batters at the edge of my mind: Calla will be so disappointed in me when she finds out I couldn't get this one simple thing right.

"Em, come on!" Aurora yells, spinning around and aiming for Imperia's leg. I'm about to race after her when the orbs bob lower over the guardians and I notice something unexpected about the woman in the middle. Something ... familiar.

"Violet?" I whisper out loud. It is her. And on either side of her are Ryn and Dash. For several confusing moments, I wonder if I might still be asleep. Then

Bandit lets loose another stream of flames, and I know I can't possibly be dreaming the scorching heat. "Wait, stop!" I shout, rushing back a few paces and smacking Bandit's side. "Bandit, stop!" He pauses his attack, but Imperia tosses her head and breathes more flames. I look back to where Aurora's scrambling up Imperia's leg. "Make her stop, please! Those are my parents. And Dash is with them. They must have escaped together." And Vi must have used her Griffin Ability to find me. I launch forward and run toward them. Despite having had days to think about it, I have absolutely no idea what I'm going to say to them. All I know is that they're my family, and they're finally safe.

But why …

Why aren't they …

I slow down as I realize they're not smiling. They're not excited. In fact, their faces seem to be devoid of any expression. And their eyes … Now that they're close enough for me to make out the details of their faces, I can see that something isn't right. A chill skitters across my skin when I realize exactly what it is: their eyes are almost completely white. Glazed over. Staring at nothing. They must be able to see *something*, though, because they continue marching forward with unwavering purpose.

"Crapcrapcrap," I mutter, backtracking hastily. "Something isn't right," I shout to Aurora.

"You think?" she shouts back in the kind of tone that says, *Duh.*

"They're like … zombies. We need to run. We need to fly." As I pass the backpack, I reach down and grab it. "Bandit, shrink!" I yell at him, pulling the backpack onto my shoulders. Seconds later, Bandit swoops through the air in bird form and flutters around me as I scramble up Imperia's side. Above me, Aurora reaches the saddle. She tosses one of the straps down, then yells out a command. As I grab onto the trailing piece of leather, Imperia launches into the air, her wings beating past me with powerful force. Sliding against the side of her body, I hang onto the strap with every ounce of strength I possess. "Quickly!" I yell. "Go!"

Bandit swoops past my head and lands on my shoulder—just as bright magic burns across my right arm. I cry out and almost lose my grip on the leather strap, but I clench my teeth and cling tighter and tell myself *not* to look at the wound.

I expect Imperia to veer upward, but instead, she aims straight ahead at the cliff face. Aurora's stylus zooms ahead of us. It smacks against the sheer rocky surface, skids down, then rises up again. Clumsily, it writes against the rock—and nothing happens. Over the sound of air rushing past my ears, I can just make out Aurora's curse of frustration. The stylus moves again, and this time, a dark space begins to form.

Imperia tucks her wings flat against her body, and we shoot straight into the faerie paths.

The moment we land, Imperia roars and twists around, snapping at her tail.

"What's wrong?" Aurora shouts.

I look back, my heart leaping at the sight of the thing that's causing Imperia's distress. "Dash!" I yell at him. "Get off! You're going to end up flattened!" I doubt he can hear me—and who knows if my words would even make sense to him in his zombie-like state—but he lets go of Imperia's tail and drops to the ground. A second later, Imperia's tail slams down on top of him.

"No!" I gasp. Without pause, I let go of the strap and slide down Imperia's side. As my feet strike the ground, Aurora yells a single word at Imperia, saving Dash's motionless body from being walloped a second time. I race toward him, muttering, "You stupid, stupid boy. What the hell were you thinking?" I drop onto my knees beside him. My eyes dart across his body, searching for puncture wounds from the mastic spikes on Imperia's tail. I can't see any blood, though. It must have been the lower surface of her tail that struck him. Still, I wouldn't be surprised if half the bones in his body have been fractured.

"Don't touch him," Aurora says, running up to my side. "You might injure him further."

"I know, I know." But my hands hover near him nonetheless. "What do we do? What if he has broken bones? We can't take him anywhere."

"I don't think Imperia hit him *that* hard. Hopefully he's just unconscious."

"You don't think she hit him *that hard?*" I repeat, incredulous. "Did you see her tail coming down on top of him?"

"I know it might have looked bad, but she's been trained not to deliver a lethal blow."

"Okay, but this was a threatening situation in an unfamiliar environment, and Imperia knew it wasn't you hanging on to her tail. I think she would have been a little rougher than normal."

"Yes, okay, but ... I'm sure he'll be fine." She leans further over Dash as Bandit, in mouse form, creeps toward Dash's face and gently pokes his cheek with one paw. "He may have a few fractured ribs," Aurora says, "but faerie magic doesn't take too long to heal that kind of thing." As if to prove her point, a groan escapes Dash's lips at that moment. "See?" she says. "He's going to be fine."

Relief floods my body, but it's overshadowed a moment later by the reminder that Dash isn't himself right now. He's still a danger to us. "Crap, we need to tie him up." I shrug free of the backpack and pull it open. Dash groans again, louder this time, and I see his face crumple in an expression of intense pain as I glance up. "Is this what you meant by 'fine?'" I ask Aurora as I continue to rummage through the dozens of miniature supplies.

"Look, obviously he's going to feel some pain. Maybe a lot of pain. But he will be fine. And can you hurry up? He's going to be properly awake any second."

"I know, I know, I'm trying to—ah, there it is." I place the tiny coil of rope on the ground and enlarge it as quickly as I can. Aurora's magic slices it in half, and while I wind my piece around Dash's wrists, her magic directs the other piece around his ankles. "Oh, wait, fluffing hell."

"Excuse me?"

"His guardian weapons will be able to cut through a normal rope. That's what Calla said." I shove my hand back into the backpack and pull out a small notebook. "We have to add … a small enchantment …" I page swiftly past the first few spells Calla wrote down for me. "There!" I touch the rope around Dash's wrists and read out the words, then do the same thing for his ankles. I've barely finished when he begins struggling against his bonds.

"That was close," Aurora says. "Maybe you should memorize that spell—and any other in-the-moment kinda spell where you wouldn't have time to look it up."

"Hey, keep still," I tell Dash as he continues to struggle. "You're only going to hurt yourself more." I lean over him, trying to pin his shoulders down, while Aurora does the same with his legs. Dash grits his teeth against whatever pain he's feeling, his creepy clouded eyes darting everywhere. "Dash!" I say, louder this time. "Stop it, okay? Stop struggling. Hey, can you even hear me?"

Finally, his body goes limp. I slowly let go of his shoulders and sit back. Dash tilts his head to the side and blinks at me. "You must be captured," he says in a voice devoid of emotion. "If you cannot be captured, you must be killed."

A chill raises goosebumps across my arms. "Killed?" I exhale a shaky breath of a laugh. "That seems a little drastic. You like me, Dash. You don't want to kill me."

"You must be captured," he repeats. "If you cannot be captured, you must be killed."

I shake my head and whisper, "What have they done to you?" I can't help remembering the last time I saw him. His cocky grin was in place and his green eyes sparkled as he told me not to miss him too much. *Save me a kiss* was the last thing he said. I hadn't doubted then that I'd see him again soon. I *always* saw him again soon. That seemed to be the way things worked once I reached the fae realm. He was always just … there. Until suddenly he wasn't, and I had no idea why, and I missed him far more than I expected.

"You must be captured," he says once more. "If you cannot be captured, you must be killed."

"Okay, that is going to get annoying really quickly," Aurora says. "We may need to gag him."

I look away from his creepy gaze. "Yes. I'd rather not hear any more about how I must be killed." As I wrap my arms around myself, I become abruptly aware of the stinging pain I forgot all about when I saw Dash had come with us through the faerie paths. I lift my arm to get a better look at the wound, then lower it quickly. The sight of the blood that's oozed down my arm makes me feel a little dizzy.

"Oh, ouch," Aurora says, leaning forward to peer at my arm. "When did that happen?"

"As we were escaping. Just after Imperia took off." I breathe in deeply and try to think of things that have nothing to do with my own blood. Looking around at the palm trees, the tall grass, and the strip of blue sea in the distance, I ask, "Where are we, anyway? Somewhere deserted, I hope?"

"Um … well, my mind wasn't exactly clear when I finally got that doorway open," she admits. "I was trying to think of places I know that are far from any dwellings. I think …" She looks around. "Yes, this is the area I was thinking of. Our coastal manor house is nearby. You know, for holidays."

My mouth drops open. "You brought us somewhere near one of your family's houses? And you thought that would be *safe*?"

"It's fine, Em. The area's deserted aside from our estate. And no one will be there now. Do you really think it's the appropriate time for the rest of my family to take a vacation?"

I exhale slowly. "I guess when you put it that way …"

Dash makes a half-hearted effort at pulling his hands free of the ropes. "You must be killed," he says.

I turn my attention back to him, searching his clouded eyes for any spark of life or recognition. Any hint that the Dash I know still exists beneath the layers of enchantment controlling him. "Do you think he's still in there?" I ask Aurora. "Or do you think the state he's in now is … permanent?"

She gives me a helpless look. "I don't know, Em. I haven't seen anyone in this kind of state before. It sounds a little bit like the brainwashing spell Lord Draven put on people to get them to follow him. But as far as I know, that spell didn't have this sort of … lifeless side effect. Those people appeared completely normal, except for the part where they wholeheartedly believed they needed to serve Lord Draven."

I tilt my head as I watch Dash. "I wonder if my Griffin Ability might work on him. Maybe I can say something that will free him of this enchantment."

"Oh. Yes." Aurora's voice lights up. "That could work. When will your Griffin Ability be replenished?"

"Another few hours, I think." I look up at the position of the sun, but it doesn't help much when I have no clue what time zone we're in.

"Okay, well, whenever it happens, you can try commanding Dash to be normal." She sounds so certain, as if there's no way my Griffin Ability won't work. I, on the other hand, am not so sure.

"Remember I tried to wake Dani—the woman I thought was my mother— when she was in that enchanted coma?" I say. "It didn't work."

Aurora hesitates, chewing on her lip. "True. But you may as well try with Dash, right?"

"Yes, I may as well." Bandit scampers over to me and climbs onto my knee. "The reason I couldn't wake Dani was because the sleeping spell had something to do with witch magic. It was one of the anti-Griffin Gifted spells they crafted. Hopefully whatever's affecting Dash has nothing to do with witch magic. Maybe it's—Oh, maybe it's something they developed at Reinhold," I say, thinking back to all the experimentation Perry's document mentioned. "Did you read any of those pages last night before you fell asleep?"

"Hey, look, I didn't *intend* to fall asleep," Aurora says, crossing her arms. "It was an accident. And that countdown timer should really have a noise enchantment added to it. If it had sung us a song when it reached zero, we would have woken up and left in time."

Dash chooses that moment to punctuate our conversation with a lifeless "You must be killed."

We both ignore him. "Whoa, no need to get so defensive," I say. "That's not what I meant. I was legitimately asking if you read any of the information about Reinhold Research Station."

"Oh. Sorry." She unfolds her arms and looks down at her hands. "And I'm sorry

I fell asleep when I shouldn't have. I really didn't intend to."

"I know. And thanks for the reminder about the timer, actually." I move Bandit onto the ground before standing. Then I walk a few steps away and perform the spell that restarts the golden numbers counting down from fifteen hours. I've only done it once before, so it takes a few attempts for me to get it right, but fortunately, Aurora doesn't comment on this.

"And yes, I did read some of those pages," she says as I return to her side. "Do you think that's where they did this to Dash?"

"Yes, maybe. I was starting to doubt it, since that report spoke mainly about experimenting on Griffin Abilities and Dash doesn't have one. But someone said he might be there, and then he turns up acting like he's under the influence of some weird zombie robot enchantment. It seems like too much of a coincidence, right? That must be where this happened to him."

Aurora nods. "Definitely seems possible."

"And if Dash came from Reinhold, then Violet and Ryn obviously came from there too. And since they didn't catch us, that's where they'd return to, right?"

Aurora lifts her shoulders in a hesitant shrug. "I don't know, Em. We can't assume that."

"Where else would they go?"

"Well, there are many Guilds throughout the world, and any one of them could be imprisoning Griffin Gifted within their walls and carrying out experiments on them. This—" she gestures at Dash "—could have happened anywhere. Your friends—your parents—could be anywhere."

I look at Dash again, and my voice is quiet when I say, "I hope you're wrong, because I'm tired of not knowing where they are. But I also kinda hope you're right, because Reinhold seems like one seriously awful place to be locked up." I stick my hand into the backpack again and fish around for the Reinhold scroll. Eventually, when my fingers can't locate it, I peer inside. A chill settles over me when I realize it isn't there. "Aurora," I say carefully, "what did you do with the Reinhold papers after you read them?"

Without saying anything, she lifts the bottom of her T-shirt, revealing a wad of roughly folded papers flattened against her stomach. "I didn't leave them behind for your brainwashed Griffin rebel friends to find, if that's what you're asking."

I breathe out and take the papers from her. "Thank goodness. It would *not* be good if the Reinhold researchers knew to expect us." I unfold the pages and place them on the ground in front of us. "Okay, did it say anywhere in here where this place actually is?"

"I think I saw a town name somewhere." Aurora shuffles through the pages. "It was on the first page, where they were talking about designing and building the place. It said something about how they planned to keep their work hidden from the locals, and they mentioned a town there. Yes, here it is." She lifts one of the pages. "Hellirstad."

"Do you know where that is?"

She lowers the page. "Normally I'd give you some snarky comment about how I have better things to do than memorize the locations of small random towns. But Hellirstad is, like, the *only* town in the whole of Soriss. So yeah, I've heard of it."

"Soriss?" I ask. "Should I know what that is?"

"It's the southernmost continent of our world. It's completely covered in ice, so even with magic, it isn't the most pleasant place to live."

"So, like, Antarctica?"

"Uh, I think so? My knowledge of the human world is sketchy at best."

"Okay. Great." I gather the papers together and roll them up. "We're going to Hellirstad."

"You must be killed," Dash intones.

I roll my eyes. "Yeah. Thanks. I heard you the first few times."

"You really want to go to this place?" Aurora asks.

"Yes. I'm tired of running. I'm tired of waiting. I'm tired of being *useless*. I want to go to Reinhold Research Station and get everyone back." I clench both hands around the scroll, crumpling the pages further. "You don't know what it's like, day after day, knowing that your family is being tortured somewhere and not being able to do a thing about it. Now that we finally know something, I want to act on it."

Aurora nods slowly as she looks at Dash. "I understand. I still think it's extremely dangerous. And ... well ... Violet and Ryn didn't seem to be tortured in any way while they were marching toward us, so that's a good thing."

"True, but we don't know what will happen to them when they get back to Reinhold."

"*If* that's where they're being held," Aurora reminds me.

"So what do you want to do?" I snap. "More *nothing*?"

"Not nothing!" she exclaims. "But, Em, what if you're wrong? What if they're not there? What if you and I end up trapped inside this research station?"

I pull my head back, narrowing my eyes at her, remembering that she's the reason we were almost caught earlier, and what if ... just maybe ... it wasn't an accident? "Are you trying to stop me from rescuing the rebels for some reason?"

She gives me an are-you-stupid look. "Not for *some* reason. The reason is that I kinda like being alive, and I don't particularly want that to end. I figured you'd feel the same way." Her brow creases further. "What other reason might there be?"

I shut my eyes, feeling terrible for having suspected her, if only for a moment. My brief suspicion didn't even make sense. If she *did* want me to be caught, it would be by her own people, not by the Guild. I press my hand against my brow. "Sorry, I …" *I have difficulty trusting people after everything that's happened recently.* That's what I would say if I finished that sentence. Instead, I lower my hand and open my eyes. "We don't have to get caught or lose our lives. I'll wait for my Griffin Ability to recharge, and then I just need to tell the researchers to set all the Griffin rebels free and not to come after any of them as they walk out. Or something like that. I'll refine the words before I say them, obviously."

"And if you can't remove the magic that's turned them all into—this?" Aurora gestures at Dash. "I'm just saying we need to be sensible, Em. At the very least, we need to know your people are definitely there before we go charging in. And we should probably wait for Calla. We shouldn't do something this big on our own. Especially since I have, like, zero experience in the rescue operation department."

I sigh. "And the only experience I have is one failed attempt."

"You must be killed."

"Shut up!" Aurora and I shout at the same time. "Jeez," she adds. She looks me. "Don't you have something in that backpack of a zillion wonders that we can shove in his mouth to keep him quiet?"

"I'm sure I can find something." I dig inside the backpack for the third time, searching for a small article of clothing. I look up after retrieving a sock and find Aurora leaning over Dash, peering closely at his face. "Uh, what are you doing?"

"Just wondering what's going on behind those creepy eyes. Maybe he's fully aware of everything we're saying, but he can't say anything back to us except what he's been instructed to say. Or maybe he's asleep. Or at least … not aware."

"I don't know, but can you please lengthen this so I can fit it around his head?" I hand her the sock. "I'm sure you can do it faster than I can."

She takes the sock, barely concentrating on the lengthening spell as she continues speaking. "If he's not aware of us, then I wonder if he's dreaming." She passes the extra-long sock back to me. "Dreaming would be good."

"It would?" I ask as I lean over Dash.

"Yes. Communication is possible through dreams."

I sit back, the sock still in my hands. "Really?"

"Yes. I've performed the spell a few times. One of my ladies-in-waiting wanted to get inside the dreams of a guy she liked. You know, to try to influence him in the right direction."

"But … okay." I decide not to point out everything that's wrong with that story. "Is that some kind of weird Unseelie magic? Like, do I have to sacrifice something or draw magic from another person?"

"I don't think there are any laws against it, aside from the laws of social etiquette, which obviously say it's rude to invade someone's dreams without their permission." She pauses, her frown deepening. "Yeah, okay, it's probably against the Guild's laws too, seeing as how it's subconscious influence, and the actual spell can be dangerous if not administered properly. But it doesn't seem like a super serious law." She gives me a knowing smile. "I'm sure Dash wouldn't mind if you invaded his dreams."

"This is serious, Rora."

"Right. I know. Sorry. So … do you want to try it? If he is actually dreaming and you're able to talk to him, you can ask him if the other rebels are definitely at Reinhold."

"That's definitely a more sensible option than rushing off without knowing if they're actually there. Calla might even approve of that option if she were here." I bite my lip. "It still sounds weird, though. Potentially being inside someone's dream."

Aurora shrugs. "You don't have to do it. You can always wait another few hours and see if your Griffin Ability works."

I heave a resigned sigh. "I think I've already told you how I feel about waiting."

"You're tired of it?"

"Exactly."

"Okay then. Time to put you to sleep."

CHAPTER 19

Thanks to the magic-laced lullaby Aurora sings, I fall asleep in less than a minute. It's a different kind of sleep. Sleep filled with an awareness I've never experienced before. I walk across a shadowed landscape of continually changing scenery—roads, corridors, forests—feeling very much awake while also being certain that I'm dreaming. It's fascinating, this dream world. I want to explore it. I reach with one hand toward the tree I'm about to walk past, wondering if bark feels the same in a dream as it does in real life. Beneath my palm, I sense the same rough texture as I drag my hand slowly across the tree trunk.

But all of a sudden, as if the change happened so fast I didn't even see it, I'm standing in a living room near a floor-to-ceiling window. For some reason, the view beyond the window is hazy, but I can make out enough bright lights to know that there's a city full of high-rise buildings out there.

I turn slowly, noticing that the edges of the room are also unclear. The pictures on the walls are blurred, and the staircase melts into a dark brown smudge about halfway up. But I can only seem to look at these things from the edges of my vision, so perhaps they're not really blurry. Perhaps it's just that something is keeping me from seeing properly. "Weird," I murmur.

I keep turning—and my heart almost leaps from my chest when I see the creature in the center of the living room. Draped partially across the coffee table amid upturned furniture is a giant serpent. Its head hangs over one side of the coffee table, eyes glazed over and mouth open just enough to reveal impossibly large fangs. On the floor nearby lie the bodies of a boy in his teens and a man. And beside them, another boy, kneeling on the floor, his hands over his face and his body shuddering as he cries.

The green in his hair reminds me abruptly that I'm here for a reason. Somehow, I'd completely forgotten. "Dash?" I ask quietly.

He freezes. Slowly, he lowers his hands and looks around at me. I can't tell how old he is—younger than present-day Dash—but it's definitely him. He stands, and in less than a blink, he becomes the Dash I know now. "Em?" he asks. "How ... how are you here? You're not part of my nightmare."

It's him. It's really him. The living room melts away as I race across it and throw my arms around him. But I almost fall forward as I end up hugging air. I look again and realize he's just a little further away. I move forward as he opens his arms to me, but still I can't seem to hug him. My arms move through him—or rather, past him.

"Em?"

"What's going on?" I ask, surprised by how desperately I long to feel his arms around me. "Why can't I touch you?"

"I don't know. Maybe because it's a dream. A nightmare."

"You know you're dreaming?"

Trees race past us, then melt away to reveal an empty room. "Yes. I feel like I've been dreaming forever. But why—*how* are you here?"

"It's a spell Aurora did. You ... you're not exactly yourself at the moment. I mean, out there in the waking world. We got you away from whoever it is that did this to you, but they're controlling your actions somehow. You keep saying the same thing over and over. Aurora said I'd be able to communicate with you properly if you were dreaming. Which you obviously are."

"What is this spell? I've never heard of it."

"Probably because it's not the kind of thing the Guild would approve of. Wandering into people's dreams without their permission, and all that."

He nods, then blinks and shakes his head. "That isn't important. You're here. You're *here*, Emmy. And you're okay." He pauses. "Are you okay? It's hard to remember what happened before this. There were pods, and we were flying, and then a prison cell, and a funnel hanging above me ..." He squints at the ground. "It's a lethal dose. You're going to die, Dash."

A shiver chills my skin. "Dash, you're not dying. None of this is real."

"Wouldn't want to kill you all at once ..."

"What are you talking about?"

"I don't know. I can't remember anything clearly. It's like a dream I can't properly recall."

"Dash," I say carefully. "*This* is the dream."

"No," he whispers, still looking at the ground. "This is the nightmare. This is the torture prison."

The chill sinks further, right into my bones. "W-What?"

I realize that the room we're in is no longer empty. It isn't small either. Without me noticing, it grew into an enormous gym. Behind Dash, I see various types of exercise equipment, a climbing wall, ropes hanging from the ceiling, and other unfamiliar items I don't know the purpose of.

The floor between Dash and me expands rapidly, pulling him to the other side of the room in seconds. I start running toward him, watching as a woman walks up to him. I slow down as I near the two of them. "They didn't make it," I hear her say. "The poison spread too quickly. They're both dead."

Dash's body seems to crumple in on itself. He drops onto his knees. "They're … dead?" he repeats.

"They're dead." The woman steps away from him, walking backward as she repeats her words, louder and louder. The words become a screaming echo, tripping and tumbling over themselves as they claw their way into my ears.

They're dead … dead … ed … ed …

… dead … they're dead … they're …

… dead … ed … ed …

I press my hands over my ears as the screams become unbearably loud. Dash is standing right in front of me again, though I'm pretty sure he didn't move. His eyes are red, his face twisted in pain. He reaches for my hand, but his arm sweeps past me instead.

The echoes of the scream vanish, so I lower my hands. "What the hell was that about?"

He clears his throat before speaking. "Don't you understand what this is yet? I'm caged inside my own mind. These are my memories … the worst experiences of my life. I'm forced to relive them over and over. Warped, twisted versions, even worse than the first time around. I tell myself none of this is real, but it makes no difference. It hurts every time. It hurts *all* the time."

"So this … this is what the torture at The Noxsom Facility is all about? They lock you inside your mind and torture you with your own painful memories?"

"Yes."

"Which means the others are still going through this torture as well," I say quietly, something twisting painfully inside me. "Vi and Ryn, and the other rebels who were caught."

"Yes." Dash looks at me more intently then. "Violet and Ryn ..." he murmurs. "Your parents." He smiles, and if it wasn't for the dark skin beneath his red-rimmed eyes, he would look almost like his normal, happy self. "Your *parents*. I remember now. That's what you shouted out. And it made so much sense then, after everything Zed explained about you being a changeling. And yet absolutely *crazy* at the same time. Crazy that you found your way to your family without even realizing it. Damn, I *wish* I could hug you right now. I'm so happy for you. I'm so ..." He makes a half-hearted attempt at a laugh. "Look at that. I'm still inside my nightmare, and I'm actually feeling happiness instead of heartache."

Tears prick my lower eyelids. I blink them away. "Dash, do you know where you were when they did this to you? This nightmare spell, and the other magic that's controlling you. If you remember where it is, then I can stop whatever spell this is. You can be happy all the time again, and you can hug me as much as you want."

He raises one eyebrow. "Careful. I'm gonna hold you to that."

"I know. I don't care. I want you to hug me all the time." His eyebrows jump a little higher, and I race quickly past that admission before he can comment on it. "Just tell me: was it Reinhold? Reinhold Research Station?"

"That sounds familiar," he says with a frown. "I think I heard someone say Reinhold."

"You have to be sure, Dash. I can't risk breaking into another high-security facility unless I know it's definitely the right place."

"It's just ... everything from the real world seems so fuzzy. So disjointed. I know I've heard someone talking about Reinhold, and about using the powers of certain Griffin Gifted fae, and something about a woman named Shyla ... but what if it was a conversation I overheard before I was captured? What if it has nothing to do with me?"

"Shyla," I repeat. "Yes. Her name was in the report. Her Griffin Ability was used at The Noxsom Facility. She can—yes, okay, it makes sense now. They called her Griffin Ability a mental prison. Which is obviously where we are right now. But how is that related to the way you're being controlled now?"

Dash is frowning, trying to follow what I'm saying. "I ... I don't know, Em. Maybe I heard about her ages ago, or—"

"Or maybe you did hear someone speak about her now. The report said she's still at Reinhold because they're trying to determine further uses for her ability—"

"*Emerson!*"

I pause. The gym has become a forest of tall, skinny trees reaching high into the smudged grey sky. The tips of their spindly branches blur into the background. "Did you hear that?"

Dash's eyes, suddenly wide and afraid, dart behind and around me. "Hear what? A hiss? Was it the serpent?"

"No, it sounded like my name."

"*Em!*"

I spin around, my eyes searching between the trees. "There, did you hear it?"

"Yes." He breathes out slowly. "If they know your name, then it's one of us."

"One of us? You mean …" I look again. The spindly trees melt into trees that are larger, more gnarled, tangled. And between crisscrossing branches, I see a woman running toward me.

"It's as if we're all trapped together inside the same nightmarish world," Dash says quietly.

"*They're dead!*" someone screams behind us, but I'm already moving forward because I know who it is that's racing through the trees toward me. A flash of her purple hair, another shout of my name, and I know for sure that it's her.

Of all the ways I've imagined finally being reunited with one or both of my parents, this wasn't one of them. An ever-shifting nightmare landscape never crossed my mind. I race as fast as I can, but the trees don't get any closer. Looking down, I find that my feet aren't actually moving. "Stupid nightmare!" I mutter between gritted teeth. I wrap my hands around my right thigh and manage to pull my foot up. The ground stretches, becomes elastic, and part of it remains attached to the sole of my shoe. When I can no longer hold my leg up, the elastic ground tugs my foot back down. "Oh, *come on*!" I shout at no one in particular. "This isn't even my nightmare!"

"Em!" I look up at the sound of Violet's voice. She's close now, the sticky elastic ground appearing to have no effect on her. She's almost in front of me, and this is supposed to be an amazing moment as I'm finally reunited with my real mother, and this stupid nightmare is ruining it!

As she reaches me, I manage to launch myself forward with a great effort. But we're like the mismatched ends of two magnets. Our arms move past each other, unable to ever touch. "Are you real?" she asks, her eyes searching my face. "Please be real. Please tell me you're not part of someone's nightmare."

"I'm not. I'm—"

The ground expands between us, and we're no longer in a forest. We're in a bedroom. There's a rocking chair behind Violet—and between us stands a crib. I know immediately what this nightmare is, and all I want to do is shove myself far away from what must be lying in that crib. But I can't move. And the crib seems to be growing larger. Or I'm slowing falling toward it. I can't tell.

"You're not real," Vi whispers. "This is still the nightmare. Just another version of it."

I am real, I want to cry out. But just as I can't pull my feet from the ground, I can't pull my eyes from the crib. My body leans over it, as if some sick, twisted part of me is in control now, forcing me to *look*. Finally, with my stomach churning, I see the tiny, motionless body lying within the crib.

The floor opens up beneath my feet. I let out a yelp as I drop through the hole and—

CHAPTER 20

I JERK AS I WAKE UP. MY EYES ARE HEAVY, MY MOUTH IS DRY. "WHAT ... WHYAMIAWAKE?" I mumble, pushing myself up into a sitting position. Bandit rolls down my chest with a squeak and transforms into something blue and sparkly with wings as he launches into the air.

"Oh, hey." Aurora sits up, looking sleepy. "Did you manage to speak to Dash?"

I blink. "Yes, but—why did I wake up? I wasn't finished there."

"The spell only lasts a certain amount of time. It must have reached its end."

"But I need to go back. Can't you do the spell again?"

She shakes her head. "It isn't good for you. You need to wait at least a day."

"But—"

"Why do you need to go back? Weren't you able to ask Dash about Reinhold? You were there for—" she glances sideways at our floating numbers "—almost three hours."

"Three hours? It felt like only minutes."

She arches an eyebrow and gives me another one of her *duh* looks. "Yes, well, dreams tend to feel like that."

"I ... I did ask him about Reinhold. It sounds like the Griffin rebels are there. But I need to go back into the dream for another reason. Let me just drink some water—I'm so thirsty—and then you can do the spell again." I stand—

—and the world spins so violently around me that I have no idea for several moments which way is up or down. When everything settles, I find myself lying on the ground, squinting past Aurora at the bright sky and the palm leaves waving across them. "Sorry," she says. "I forgot to mention the intense dizziness side effect."

I want to sit up but decide to give myself another few moments to recover. "Is that the only thing that's bad for me? Because if it is, I can handle it."

"Em—"

"Violet was there. Which means Ryn must have been somewhere there too. I just want to talk to them and—"

"I can't send you back, Em. The dizziness is just the beginning. If your mind doesn't have a break between dream communication sessions, the spell will begin to leave permanent damage. And even if that wasn't the case, I can't put you in someone else's dream world if that someone isn't here."

I slowly push myself up, trying not to bring on any further dizziness. "But … I saw Violet."

"She was obviously part of Dash's dream."

"That's not what Dash said. He said it's like they're all inside one nightmarish world."

Aurora lifts her shoulders. "I don't know, okay? If they're all inside the same dream, then that's some other magic I don't know about."

I pull one knee up against my chest and wrap my arm around it. "It must be the torture prison magic."

"You mean Noxsom? I thought you said they're at Reinhold."

"Yes, I think they are. But they're still under the influence of whatever torture magic was administered to them at The Noxsom Facility. I don't know what's affecting their bodies now, but their minds are still locked up in a mental prison."

"Okay, so if you're sure they're at Reinhold, then let's go rescue them. You can talk to them once they're free, and you can stop pestering me about putting you back into dream contact with them."

Beside us, Dash mumbles around the sock. I'm fairly certain he's trying to say, "You must be killed."

"Oh. My Griffin Ability. I can feel it." A rush of joy accompanies the surge of magic. I shut my eyes and concentrate on making sure none of it escapes me yet.

"Cool," Aurora says. "Now you can try to wake Dash."

I open my eyes and look at him. His unseeing gaze stares past the palm fronds waving lazily in the breeze. I place my hand on his arm, desperate to free him from his horrendous nightmares and see his green eyes alight with life and humor once again. "But … wait. I don't know exactly what's wrong with him, so I don't know what to say to fix it."

"So then just say a whole bunch of things," Aurora says. "Say everything you can think of that might be wrong with him."

"What if that ends up hurting him?"

"Don't be silly, Em. Why would that hurt him? If you say to someone, 'You no longer have scaled knuckle disease,' it's not going to make any difference to them if they don't have scaled knuckle disease to start off with."

"Okay. I guess so." I don't add the real reason for my hesitation: that I care more about Dash than I realized and I don't want to screw this up. I let my breath out slowly. "This is going to work," I quietly tell myself. "This is going to work. Crap, this isn't going to work."

Aurora's hand rests against my back. "Em, your Griffin Ability is probably the most powerful I've ever come across. Why would this *not* work?"

Because, I answer silently, *when you want something so badly you can actually feel it hurt, life never lets you have it.* But out loud, I say, "Okay. I'm gonna try now." My eyes slide shut as I let go of my power and speak. "Dash, no external magic is controlling your actions. No external magic is controlling your mind. The only magic within you and affecting you is your own." I trail off then and open my eyes, unsure of what else to say.

"I think something's happening," Aurora whispers.

I watch closely as a shiver ripples through Dash's body. He blinks, then blinks again. Slowly, the white cloudiness vanishes from his eyes. At the sight of that vibrant green I've missed so much, hope breaks free from the careful hold I have over it, exploding with warmth throughout me. I lean forward and tug the sock away from Dash's mouth. I don't touch the ropes, though. *It may not have worked properly,* I remind myself, tempering my excitement so the disappointment—when it inevitably comes—doesn't crush me.

He looks around, his eyes traveling across the bright, colorful landscape, so different from the dark nightmare world he's been locked in. "I'm … awake," he says, sounding utterly confused. His voice—no longer robotic—sends another wave of warmth through my body. I dare for a moment to believe that perhaps this time, disappointment isn't coming.

Finally, Dash's eyes settle on me. "Em. You were there. Inside the nightmare. Is this … am I really awake now?" Then his gaze falls to the ropes around his wrists and ankles. His chest rises and falls more rapidly. "Holy fluff cakes. What did I do to you? Please tell me I didn't hurt you."

I almost laugh at the words 'fluff cakes.' As I rush to untie the knots at his wrists, my words tumble happily from my mouth. "Oh my goodness, it actually worked." My fingers fumble with the knots, and whenever my skin brushes against his, heat burns inside me and sparks zip around our hands. I remember Aurora's explanation about magical manifestations of attraction, but I can't find it in myself to be embarrassed.

"Emmy, did I hurt you?" Dash asks, his voice pained.

I laugh and shake my head. "You should be more worried about what Imperia did to you than what you might have done to us." I pull repeatedly at the ropes, and the stupid things are so stubborn, and then Aurora's leaning beside me, pushing my hands out the way so she can use magic instead. And then Dash is tugging his hands free, and finally, *finally* his arms are wrapped tightly around me and I'm sinking against him.

"Thank you," he says into my hair. "You saved me."

I shake my head against his neck. "My Griffin Ability … I didn't really know what to say. My command seemed so simple, but it worked." I want to hold onto him forever, but eventually I have to let go and pull away from him. I want to talk about the last time I saw him. I want to kiss him the way I did then. But now hardly seems like the appropriate time for things as frivolous as kisses.

"Aurora," Dash says, looking past me. "Hi."

"Hey," she answers, giving him an awkward wave.

"You're … on our side?"

"You know I saved Em from losing all her magic to my brother, right? So yes. I'm on your side."

"Okay …" Dash sounds uncertain, but he doesn't argue. Then his eyes are on me again, and he reaches up with both hands to cup my face. "Your parents … your family … I'm still stunned. You're *Victoria*. You have a brother and grandparents and an aunt and uncle. I met you when we were both babies. How crazy is that? It's all I want to talk about, and yet now is just …"

"So not the right time?" Aurora says, echoing my own thoughts.

Dash's eyes remain trained on mine as he says, "Yeah. Exactly." He withdraws his hands, leaving my skin cold.

I clear my throat. "What's, um, what's the last thing you remember? Do you know what happened to you after the Guild took you from Velazar?"

Slowly, he nods. "Things are coming back to me. They're clearer now. So much clearer than when I was dreaming." His eyes take on a haunted look as he focuses on the ground. "The nightmare … consumed me. It became everything. I couldn't imagine anything existing beyond it."

I place my hand gently over his. "It's over now."

"Yes," he says in a tone that suggests he doesn't completely believe me. Then he gives his head a small shake and focuses his bright gaze on me again. "They took me to the Guild first. The detainment center. They told me they sent Vi and Ryn straight to Noxsom, but that I'd be receiving a fair trial. And I actually believed them." He lets out a bitter laugh. "Then one of the Councilors came to my cell with three other guardians. They beat me up and dragged me out, telling me just before I passed out that it was completely unacceptable how I'd attacked these three men. Seeing as how dangerous I was, they'd need to remove me to a more secure facility."

"I knew that story was a lie," I mutter, then add, "Perry told us," when Dash gives me a questioning look.

"I woke up at Reinhold," he continues. "I'd never heard of the place before, but the men and women around me were talking when I woke. I thought they were healers at first. Boy, was I wrong. I remember them mentioning that we were at Reinhold, and they kept referring to someone named Shyla. They spoke about how she was already controlling several people, but she was definitely capable of handling more. And then they dragged me off to administer the nightmare essence."

"Nightmare essence?" I ask. "They actually called it that?"

"Those were the words they used."

"Freaking creepazoids," I murmur.

"They took me to a room with a funnel hanging from the ceiling over a bed."

"That sounds like the cells in The Noxsom Facility," I say.

"Well this nightmare essence must be what they use at Noxsom to torture the inmates," he says. "They probably developed it at Reinhold."

"Yes, that's what those papers said," Aurora chimes in.

Dash is frowning now, his eyes darting back and forth as if watching the scene play back across his eyelids. "They forced me onto the bed and pulled the funnel down so it was closer to my face. The serum came out like a vapor, and no matter which way I twisted my head, I couldn't help breathing it in. And then ..."

"And then what?" I ask.

"I remember it all now. Everything the researcher woman said. Like she was gloating. As if she enjoyed the fact that I knew what was going to happen and could do nothing about it." He looks up. His hand grabs my wrist, and his words become more urgent. "She said I would be a brainless soldier for them. That my friends and I would all be soldiers. While our minds were locked up inside in a nightmare, Shyla would direct our bodies. They'd recently realized her ability could do that too: take control over bodies while imprisoning minds. They planned to send us out in twos or threes, and I didn't know what that meant because I thought they'd only captured two of my friends—Ryn and Violet. But then she told me about the others. She said we would be used to round up the rest of the rebels. Because the rebels would trust us. And by the time they realized something was wrong, it would be too late."

"It almost was too late," Aurora mutters. "Fortunately, we got away on—"

"That's not all she said," Dash interrupts. He stands, sways for a moment, then steadies himself. "Stylus," he says to me, holding his hand out.

"What?" But I stick my hand into my jacket and find my stylus anyway. "Dash, what's going on?" I ask as I hand it to him.

"In order for us to leave the research station but still remain inside the nightmare—" he pauses for a moment to utter the words of a doorway spell "—they would have to give us an extra-large dose of nightmare essence. A lethal-sized dose. That's what she told me, just before I drifted into the nightmare. 'And that's why we're only going to send you out in twos or threes,' she said. 'Wouldn't want to kill you all at once.'"

"Wouldn't want to kill you all at …" I jump to my feet as a doorway opens beside Dash. "But you're fine. The serum didn't kill you."

"Because you stopped it. Your Griffin Ability got me out before it was too late. But whoever else was with me will still have a lethal dose of serum running through their bodies."

I suck in a breath. "Vi and Ryn."

He reaches for my hand. "Come on, we've wasted enough time already."

"Wait, my jacket!" I add, shoving one hand into the backpack and tugging my jacket free.

"Wait!" Aurora cries. "What do I do? I can't leave Imperia—"

"Stay here," Dash tells her, pulling me into the paths. "We'll return to this spot."

"Watch Bandit for me!"

"What if you don't—"

But her protests are lost as the darkness seals itself up behind us.

CHAPTER 21

We hurry out of the faerie paths into an icy white landscape of endless slopes and snow-dusted trees. The first thing Dash says is, "Wait, you didn't use up your Griffin power on me, did you?"

Sick with worry, I manage to stutter, "I—no, I've still got some." I pull my jacket on and zip it all the way up. My eyes sweep across our frozen surroundings, eventually settling on a grey building just beyond the curve of a small hill. "Dammit, Dash, why did they have to choose the three of you first? I know it's incredibly selfish to wish they'd picked someone else, but … *argh!*" I let out an agonized cry. "Why the people I care about the most? *Why?*"

"Hey!" He grabs my shoulders, almost stabbing me with the stylus he's still holding, and gives me a small shake. "Stop freaking out. We're not too late. We'll get to them in time." He takes my hand and pulls me forward.

"You don't know that. We probably are too late. Because the universe freaking hates me, and the only thing it's ever done is kick me in the face when I'm down."

"The universe has nothing to do with this. Those researchers in there picked Vi, Ryn and me because today, you were their target, and since they know you have a connection to the three of us, we're the ones you're most likely to trust."

"How the hell do random people in a research station know who I have connections to?"

Dash sighs. "Because they receive their instructions from Guild Councilors, and there were several of them present on Velazar II when you yelled, 'They're my parents.' Plus they know I'm the one who first brought you to this world."

I press my lips together before muttering, "I hate the Guild."

"Yeah, I'm not exactly the biggest fan of the whole guardian system right now either. Just remember it's only a few of them who are responsible for things like this." He gestures to the building we're heading for. Which reminds me that anyone looking out will easily see the two figures in black hurrying toward the station.

Using the deeper, magical version of my voice, I say, "Any surveillance bugs flying around outside Reinhold Research Station can't see us."

Dash almost halts beside me, then quickly moves forward again. "Good. Okay." He sounds somewhat surprised. "Hopefully that worked."

"It should. It worked at Noxsom. At least, I think it worked there. We were caught, but that's because they knew we were coming. I think those rooms were set to detect us the moment we walked in, regardless of whether the guards could actually see us."

"You've been inside Noxsom? Sounds like you've got a lot to catch me up on once this is over."

An image of the ruined streets and buildings around Central Park comes to mind. "Yes," I say grimly. "A *lot*."

Unlike The Noxsom Facility, Reinhold isn't surrounded by a shield. We march right up to the imposing metal door without anything stopping us. Dash raises my stylus. "They've probably got a locking enchantment on here, but I can try—"

"Open," I tell the door. After the sound of three clicks, the door groans quietly as it swings open.

Dash blinks. "Right. I need to remember that you can actually do stuff now."

"Wait." I catch his arm before he can walk forward. Then I focus on the building and say, "No surveillance bugs or devices or enchantments inside Reinhold can see or detect us. Oh, and no researchers or guardians or other Guild members inside Reinhold can see or hear us."

Dash looks at me with a small frown. "Do you have enough power for all these commands you're throwing around?"

"I have a *lot* of power, Dash. The things I'm saying aren't, like, big deal things. I'm sure I have at least half my power left." *I hope*, I add silently. Perhaps I need to be more careful.

"Okay, if you're sure. But I'm still gonna gather some magic for a stunner spell. Just in case." We step inside and find ourselves in a reception area. White desk, white chairs, a white carpet on the floor. Green plants in green pots in each corner, and pictures of random green scenery on the walls. Fortunately, though, we're the only people in the room.

"Do you remember any of this?" I ask, hurrying forward and looking down the corridors on either side of the room.

"No. If I was brought in this way, I don't think I was conscious."

"Dammit, we don't have time to go hunting for people," I mutter, heading straight for the desk. Numerous scrolls and piles of paper cover its surface. I start shuffling through pages and unrolling random scrolls, but it's pointless, of course. There's far too much information mixed up here. "Ugh, seriously? What kind of filing system is this?"

"Em, let's just go and look—"

I smack my palms down on the desk and glare at it. "Show me where the Griffin rebels are!"

From beneath the desk itself—where I never would have looked—a scroll emerges. It comes to rest on top of the desk as it unfurls, revealing a plan of the inside of Reinhold Research Station. Bright gold dots appear inside four rooms next to each other. "There," I say, pointing at the drawing as my face flushes with the thrill of just how *easy* that was. "They're in these rooms."

Dash holds his stunner magic above hand and grabs the drawing with the other. He turns it, looks both ways, then says, "Left."

We run as quickly as we can while figuring out which turns to take and which stairs to run up. When we almost crash into a woman dressed in a lab coat, we freeze and barely breathe as we wait. But she shows no sign of having seen us as she strides past. After that, we don't bother stopping when we see anyone else. We slow down to keep our footsteps quiet, but that's it.

And then, in almost no time, we've reached the first door. "Every door in this corridor is unlocked," I command, before pushing my way into the first room and looking hurriedly around. Four people, asleep, sitting in partially reclined chairs that make me think for one disorienting moment of the dentist. None of them are Violet or Ryn. Two seem familiar, though, so these must be Griffin rebels.

"Wait, who's that?" Dash asks, pointing at the woman with deep bronze skin and orange-highlighted black hair. "She isn't one of the rebels."

"But she—oh, wait. I think that's Shyla. I saw a picture in one of the reports Perry found. I can tell her to—No, crap, I have to find Vi and Ryn first!" I spin around without waiting for Dash's response. I charge into the next room—

—and there they are. Violet and Ryn. Still alive, and still with clouded, unseeing gazes. But something's changed since they came marching up the hillside for me. They're lurching aimlessly around the room, bumping into the two reclining chairs, turning, and then bumping into the walls. Even more disturbing, their heads keep twitching. Fear clenches around my heart at the thought that I might be too late to save them. I step into the room and focus on Violet first. "Violet, the nightmare essence is—"

She lunges for me, her hands stretching toward my throat. I'm so startled, I don't have time to get out of the way. Together, we crash against the door, her fingers squeezing my neck and my hands and elbows trying uselessly to shove her away. I try to gasp a command, but I can't get any words out. Over Vi's shoulder, I see Ryn throwing himself after her. He lands across half her body, squashing me even further in the process.

Then above me, I see Dash, his hands wrapping around the stunner magic he's been gathering and pulling it into two halves. He throws both at the same time, one at Vi and one at Ryn. And they both collapse on top of me.

Dash tugs their stunned bodies off me as I gasp for breath. I push myself up, coughing and clutching my neck. The moment I'm able to speak, I give my command: "Violet and Ryn, there is no more nightmare essence in your body. Shyla is no longer controlling your mind or your actions." I slump back against the door, sucking in another deep breath as the remainder of my Griffin power leaves my body. The same shiver that passed through Dash's body earlier ripples through Vi and Ryn.

"Are you okay?" Dash asks, his hand on my shoulder.

"Yeah, I … I'm fine." I crawl closer to Vi and Ryn. When neither of them move, I carefully lift one of Violet's eyelids to see if her eyes are still clouded and white. "Normal," I say when I see part of her purple-blue iris. I check Ryn's eyes, and he's normal too. "Dash, why aren't they waking up? It happened almost instantly with you."

"I don't know. Maybe … maybe they're still stunned? You didn't say anything about getting rid of the effects of my stunner spell, did you?"

I groan out a "No" as I sit back. "I was so worried about getting the nightmare essence out of them and stopping Shyla's control, and then my Griffin Ability finished, so it's not like I could have added anything after that anyway."

"It's finished? Are you serious? You're saying we have to get ten unconscious people out of here without the use of your Griffin Ability?"

I look up at him. "Yes."

"Freaking fluff hat," he mutters as I get to my feet. "Okay, we're going to tie everyone together, get them all into the air, and direct their floating bodies out of here."

"Can you handle that with normal magic?"

"It'll be a bit of a strain levitating that many people, but I'm sure I can manage."

"I can try to help," I tell him as he crouches down with a piece of sparkling guardian rope in his hands. He ties one end around Vi's wrist and the other around Ryn's ankle.

"If you think you can lift them," Dash says, "then get them into the corridor. I'll tie up the rest of the rebels from the other three rooms."

In the time it takes me to magically lift Vi and Ryn's bodies and direct them through the door and into the corridor, Dash has been into each of the other three rooms and tied the remaining Griffin rebels together. Then he stands back with an expression of fierce concentration, and slowly they all float out to join us in the corridor.

"Shyla as well?" I ask, spotting her vibrant orange and black hair.

"Yeah, well, I'm sure she didn't ask to be here. She can—" He swings his head around as an echo of hurried footsteps reaches us. "Shoot. I guess someone heard you and Vi crashing around."

"Crap, and even though they can't see you and me, they'll see everyone else floating in the air."

Dash rushes to tie each of the smaller groups of people together, so that we end up with a single line of eleven floating people. "Can you do shield magic?" he asks.

"What? No!"

"Okay, well can you at least help to keep some of these people in the air? The back three or four? Then I can divert some of my magic into a—shield!" That last word comes out as a startled shout. Magic flashes around us. I run to the end of the corridor where the last person is floating, noticing a slight ripple in the air around me. Dash's shield, I hope.

By the time I reach the end of the line, the last three levitating bodies have slowly begun to drop. I push my magic out toward them, imagining it forming a layer beneath them so it can hold those three people up.

Sparks ricochet against our shield and off the walls as the line of floating bodies is tugged forward. As we hurry along corridors and down the stairs, several men and women in lab cots chase us, trying with both their magic and their hands to get through our shield. When a few more appear ahead of us, hoping to block our way forward, the shield knocks them aside. Which is fortunate, because if we had to stop, all these unconscious bodies would fly into each other.

I keep wondering why there are no guardians. Surely a place like this requires a little more security than just a locked front door? But we make it to the white and green reception area without encountering a single person with marked wrists and glittering weapons. The front door—which we left unlocked, of course—flies open when a green spark strikes it. Which must mean Dash dropped the shield for a moment. I throw a glance over my shoulder—and suck in a breath at the sight of the rocks hurtling toward me. The air shimmers, the rocks rebound off the shield and strike the walls, and then I'm running outside onto the snow.

"Em!" Dash yells, and I look forward again. "Run ahead of me and open a doorway!"

I abandon the magic I've been focusing on and run faster. The last few Griffin rebels immediately start drifting downward. As I pass them, sparks and tiny blades fly overhead. I look back again, and finally, there are those guardians I've been expecting. I guess, in a place as uneventful as this, it takes guardians a bit longer to get moving than somewhere like Noxsom.

Though it's hard work in the snow, I push forward with an extra burst of speed. "Hurry!" Dash shouts. "I'm really … struggling here." I notice then that it's not just the last few Griffin rebels descending. The whole line of levitating bodies is slowly heading for the snow. And the shield—

"Aah!" I cry out as something burns the back of my right leg. I tell myself to ignore the pain and *RUN*! Because clearly Dash's shield is gone, and if I don't get in front of all these floating bodies as quickly as possible, those guardians are going to tear through us with their magic.

I finally reach the front of the line. I pass Dash, snatching the stylus from his hand as I go. Run, run, RUN, dammit! And suddenly, I remember Calla's magic sending us flying several feet across the desert sand and through the oasis dome. I don't know what I'm doing, but I imagine sending my magic out and pushing it hard against the ground. With my next step, I'm launched into the air.

One, two, three, four—

I land, stumble, and fall onto my knees in the snow. But my shaking hand is already writing across the white, wet substance. A doorway begins to open. "Faster, faster," I urge. I look back once more, and Dash is barely a second away. "Grab onto someone!" he shouts as he leaps past me and into the darkness of the faerie paths, pulling eleven almost-touching-the-ground people behind him.

Magic, bright and burning, flashes toward me from the guardians who are way too close now. I duck down, almost smacking my face into the snow. Then I shuffle closer to the doorway, and as the rebels are about to disappear, I reach out, grab onto someone's leg, and let their momentum yank me into the darkness.

Seconds later, I drop out of the paths and land clumsily amid the collection of unconscious bodies. "Flip, that was exhausting," Dash gasps.

I push myself up and look around, already imagining Aurora's shocked expression at the sight of all these bodies falling out of the faerie paths. But the image that greets me is nothing like the one in my imagination.

Imperia—motionless on the ground.

Bandit—nowhere to be seen.

Aurora—standing frozen with a dagger against her neck. A dagger held by Ada.

CHAPTER 22

"My GOODNESS," Ada exclaims, her eyes traveling over the unmoving bodies spread across the grass.

"Ada," I gasp. "Don't hurt—" One hand whips forward, and that sticky white substance she gagged me with before flies at my face. This time, I manage to duck out of the way. "Ada—"

"Try to use your voice on me," she hisses, "and I'll slice through this girl's throat long before you've finished speaking."

Aurora whimpers and squeezes her eyes shut. I don't tell Ada she has nothing to worry about. That my Griffin Ability won't be able to command a single thing for hours still.

"How did you find this spot?" Dash asks. His hands are steady at his sides, but I notice his fingers nudge ever so slightly at the air. No doubt he's ready to grab guardian weapons the second he gets a chance.

Ada smiles. "No remarkable feat of tracking magic, if that's what you're wondering. Servants at the manor house saw a dragon fly past. One of them thought he recognized it as one of the palace dragons. He notified the palace. Prince Roarke received the news not too long after that. Then he contacted me and sent me to retrieve his treasonous sister. So here I am." She directs her gaze at me and adds, "He didn't realize you'd be here too. That's a bonus. Although, at this point, I'm thinking of just getting rid of you. It's becoming far too much of a pain trying to bring you in."

"I think we're going to have a problem then," Dash says, "since I won't be letting you kill Em *or* take—" He breaks off, his head turning to the side as something moves in the air several paces away. A doorway opens, and out step three guardians.

"Are you kidding me?" I mutter, my eyes taking in the woman and two men. It appears we do have a problem, though not the type Dash was referring to.

"Well, isn't this interesting," says one of them, a man with flaming ginger hair tempered with a few blond streaks. "It looks exactly like the scene the Seers predicted."

The Seers. Crap. I'd totally forgotten about them. My hand clenches around the stylus I'm still holding. My gaze swings to Dash, my eyes asking, *How the hell do we get out of this?*

"Well, except for the three dead bodies they Saw," the ginger guardian adds. "Clearly that hasn't happened yet."

My eyes dart away from Dash and across the bodies lying around us. Icy fear wraps around my heart. Which of these people are supposed to die?

"Three bodies?" Ada asks politely. "Looks like you've got more than three here."

"Nah," he answers casually, looking around. "These aren't the bodies they Saw. There were definitely weapons and blood involved. These people are just stunned, right? Did you do this?" His tone suggests he's only mildly interested in the answer, but as he looks at Ada, I notice the hardness in his eyes. I feel the tension underlying this casual exchange. I see the way his hands are poised, just like Dash's, ready to grab weapons or throw magic. This is the calm before the storm. The final moments before everything goes to hell.

And suddenly it all seems so pointless compared to what's going on in the rest of this world and the human one. A waste of time, magic, effort. Anger burns abruptly through my fear. After everything we've been through—breaking into Noxsom, our narrow escape from Reinhold, the torture these rebels have endured, the constant effort of having to stay one step ahead of the Guild—I want to yell, *Don't we all deserve a freaking break?*

"You're here because some Seers predicted this?" I snap, taking a step forward. Three pairs of glittering weapons point my way a second later, but I don't even flinch. "Wow. Well-flipping-done. Just imagine what you guys could achieve if your Seers actually Saw something *useful*. Like, I don't know, an Unseelie Prince taking over the whole of freaking Central Park!"

The guardian on the left, a white-haired man, advances slowly, his gold arrow trained on me. "Don't you dare yell about things you don't understand. You have no idea of the many visions that came just before the prince attacked Haverton Tower, or about the hundreds of guardians who worked tirelessly to put together the pieces of a giant, incomplete puzzle as they tried to figure out exactly where this massive assault was going to take place."

"Hey, Rendyll?" the third guardian says. "I think we just scored big time. These unconscious guys?" She nods to the nearest body. "They're Griffin rebels. The ones who were at Noxsom and then the Head moved somewhere else."

"Must've escaped again," the ginger guardian says.

"And *you*," the white-haired man growls at Dash. "I recognize you, *traitor*."

"Hey! What the hell is that?" The woman jumps out of the way of something. Glass.

I look around, seeing shards of it everywhere, quietly spreading through the grass. Ada's lips quirk into an amused smile. Her blade presses harder against Aurora's neck. "The glass faerie," Ginger says. His eyes lock onto Ada. "Get her!"

And the storm hits.

Flashes of magic, explosions of glass, the shimmering of shields appearing here and there. Ada tosses Aurora aside and throws all her effort into attacking the nearest guardian. And it's all happening right here among the unconscious rebels. "Get down!" Dash yells at me, his hand sweeping through the air. An invisible force knocks me onto my knees as a glittering knife flies over my head.

I need to use my hands, so I shove my stylus as far as it will go into the front pocket of my pants. Everywhere I look, I see the glinting of glass. "No—dammit—stop!" I gasp, focusing furiously on drawing raw magic out of myself and throwing it at any glass that gets too close to the rebels. I'm not exactly quick, but at least my magic manages to halt and melt each trail of splinters it hits. The melted glass glows for a few moments before vanishing. Ada doesn't seem to be sending any more glass this way while she's fighting two guardians, but somehow there's still plenty of her glass moving around from her sneaky attack before the fighting began.

"Em, I told you to—argh, stay down!" Dash grunts. Metal clangs against metal as his sword meets the two crossed daggers the guardian woman is fighting with.

"I'm stopping the glass!" I shout back. I crawl a short distance away from him so I'm not in his way. I'm close to Vi and Ryn now, making sure *nothing* gets anywhere near them. My eyes dart everywhere, searching for glass my magic has melted yet. Concentrating intently on pulling magic from my core, I manage to stop another few splinter trails. I start to think that I've finally got it all—when I see the glass on the other side of Violet's body, heading straight for her outstretched arm.

"No, no, no, stop!" I gasp, throwing myself across her in my effort to stop the glass before it reaches her. My hand is inches from the splinters when my magic finally flashes out, striking the glass and melting it. "You're okay," I say to Violet, though it's really myself I'm reassuring. "You're okay. You're both okay."

"Em!" Aurora shouts.

I look up, see the glittering arrow, and then feel myself yanked roughly to the side. Aurora's magic drags me closer to Imperia. She pulls me over the dragon's back foot and into the gap between her leg and her belly. "What are you doing in the middle of all the fighting?" she demands.

"Trying to help," I tell her, pushing myself up and looking over Imperia's leg to see where the arrow landed.

"Dammit, Rora, there's an arrow in Ryn's leg now!"

"Better than it being in your chest," she answers. "You're welcome."

"I'm sorry, I'm just …" I push both hands into my hair and grip the sides of my head. "I'm freaking out. I finally got them back—Vi and Ryn—and now—"

"Hey, it's gonna be fine. Why haven't you used your ability, though? Is it finished?"

"I used it all up at Reinhold." I look up at the blue-green scales above me. "Is Imperia …"

"She's okay, just stunned. This Ada woman must have gathered an enormous amount of power before she arrived here."

"Then hopefully she isn't quite as strong as she usually is. Those two guardians seem to be keeping her busy. At least Dash only has to fight one person. But we can help him."

"What?" Aurora shakes her head. "Em, we can't fight. Not like these people."

"We can throw magic from here. Nothing fancy, just the basic stuff. Or— where's the backpack? You can shoot arrows. You're really good. You can take out those guardians from here."

"It's—I don't know …" She rises a little and looks around. "It's on the other side of Imperia's leg." With a wave of her hand, the backpack comes sailing over and lands in my lap. I tug it open immediately and turn it upside down. "There's the bow. And the quiver must be here somewhere. I've got knives in my jacket, and—yeah, I'll enlarge a sword. Just in case anyone tries to get too close to us." I pick up the first sword I see and point it up into the air as I enlarge it, so it doesn't stab either of us in this small space we're huddled in.

"Quickly, quickly, quickly," Aurora mutters as the bow expands in her hand.

I lower the sword to the ground as she enlarges the quiver of arrows. Then I pull a knife from inside my jacket and look over Imperia's leg again. "What am I thinking?" I mutter to myself as I watch the guardians, Dash, and Ada lunge back and forth amid sparks and other forms of magic. "I'll never hit a moving target with a knife."

"Use your magic instead," Aurora says as she fits an arrow against the bowstring. She aims over Imperia's leg and whispers, "I can do this. I can do this." But she doesn't let the arrow go. After another few moments, as I'm about to ask what's taking so long, she releases the arrow.

It soars past everyone and strikes a palm tree. We duck down immediately. "That's exactly what I was hoping would *not* happen," she mutters. "Don't want to irritate the guardians and bring them running over here."

I risk a glance over the top of Imperia's leg. "Dammit, one of them's coming this way now. The guy with the white hair."

"Seriously?"

"Crap, no, why is he stopping by Vi and Ryn?" I scramble to my feet, but Aurora tugs me back down.

"Don't be stupid!" she hisses.

"Get another arrow! Be ready to stop him if—"

"These are the leaders, aren't they?" the white-haired guardian shouts, pointing his sword at Violet at Ryn. "They're the ones who were caught first. The ones who used to be guardians." He makes a disgusting sound at the back of his threat and spits on Ryn.

I drop my knife, grab the sword, and try to launch myself over Imperia's leg. "You filthy piece of—"

"Em!" Aurora clings tightly to my arm, holding me back.

"Leave them!" the ginger guardian shouts to the white-haired one.

"Why?" he demands. "These rebels are a gigantic pain in everyone's ass. It's time to get rid of them for good. We'll all be better off."

"Lockson, don't!" Ginger shouts.

"No!" I gasp, finally tugging free of Aurora's grip and swinging myself over Imperia's leg. But it's too late. Lockson lifts his sword, point down—

—and plunges it straight into Ryn's chest where his heart is.

My gasp is stuck in my throat. I can't move. I can barely breathe. Dash tackles Lockson before the guardian can hurt anyone else. Just behind them, Ada catches hold of Ginger's wrist—and he turns to glass a moment later. Then her eyes meet mine. Without looking away, she bends and picks up her dagger. A smile twists her lips as she takes a step forward.

I lunge away from Imperia, but I'm too far away, and as Ada drives the dagger down into Violet's chest, I finally find my voice and scream. I scream and scream, and my throat is raw, and somehow I can't hear any of it. Sound is gone. Time has slowed down. And I can't look away from the horrific sight.

Violet and Ryn. Dead. The gleaming blades protruding from their chests.

My parents. Whom I'll never get to know.

My family. Shattered.

Abruptly, time speeds up. Aurora is beside me, trying to pull me somewhere. Ada is crossing the grass toward me. Behind her, Dash yells something as he swings a glittering blade at both remaining guardians. And somehow, in my shocked state, none of it quite makes sense.

And then Ada's right in front of us, grabbing hold of Aurora. She tugs her away from me and brings a blade flashing down toward Aurora's throat. "No!" I yell, my limbs coming to life. I kick Aurora as hard as I can, sending her flying out of the way. Ada's blade sweeps harmlessly through the air. "You little troll," she hisses at me.

"You MONSTER!" I scream at her.

She raises both fists, and glass shards spin in deadly circles around them. "You should never have told me they were your parents." She pulls one fist back—

But I raise my sword over my shoulder and swing it down with all my might. The blade slices through air, through flesh, through the person I've loved my whole life—

"Em!"

I ignore the voice. I watch Ada's body drop to the ground, her head barely still attached to her body. And blood. So. Much. Blood. It's a hideous, horror movie moment that doesn't feel real. Open mouth, unblinking eyes, blood, blood, and more blood.

It's hard to kill a faerie. That's what everyone says. But Ada didn't survive this. I can see already that she's gone. And I can't help thinking it wasn't that hard at all.

Then the reality strikes me.

I killed someone.

I killed Ada. Dani. The woman I believed for years was my mother.

"EM!" someone shouts.

Finally, I look up. I see Calla on the other side of the fighting and the unconscious bodies, running toward me. I don't know how much she saw. I don't know how she knew to come here. But I don't care. All I know is that she'll stop me from what I want to do next.

And I'm done with her stopping me.

Single-minded rage consumes me as I pull my stylus from my front pocket. I walk to the closest palm tree. With shaking fingers, I write a doorway spell against it. Then I walk into the darkness and don't look back.

PART III

CHAPTER 23

I need power. I need my Griffin Ability. And there's only one way I can think of right now to get it. My hands shake and unshed tears sting behind my eyes as I stride out of the faerie paths and into the desert heat. I walk forward, gripping my stylus and sword more tightly as I try to stop the shaking. My throat hurts from forcing the tears back. The ache in my chest is so real, I think my body might actually cave in on itself.

Don't think. Just move.

I force my body into autopilot mode: Through the dome layer, across the grass, aim for the tree, up and up and up all the stairs, past Vi and Ryn's house—

Don't think don't think don't think.

But it's nearly impossible not to think of them. I almost break down completely as I look at their house built across two huge branches. The home they'll never come back to. But I force myself to carry on, further up the tree. I walk into my own little house. I head for the bedside table, open the drawer, and find the two full vials of elixir. I never actually needed any of it when practicing control over my ability, so of course, I forgot all about it.

Holding my stylus and sword together in one hand, I lift a vial, flick the stopper off, and pour the whole lot down my throat. It takes until I reach the door for the effects of that much elixir hit me. My Griffin Ability races through my body with sudden, unexpected speed. The usual ripple up my spine is now a shiver that shudders through my whole body. Dizziness tips me against the wall beside the door, and I press one hand against it, gritting my teeth and clinging to my power so I don't lose it.

As the room stops spinning, I breathe in deeply. I sense my Griffin magic humming just below the surface of my control, longing to be set free. Perhaps I shouldn't have drunk that much elixir. Perhaps it was dangerous. But as long as it worked, I can't bring myself to care.

I walk past their house again—*don't think of them*—out of the oasis, and back into the scorching heat. I tell myself I'm not falling apart, but as I open a doorway, a shuddering breath rips through me. I bite down on my lip as I hurry into the paths and picture a forest I've been in before.

Pain weights me down as I stagger out of the darkness and onto the dappled forest floor of Creepy Hollow. I have no idea if I'm anywhere near the Guild, but it doesn't matter. When I'm ready, the faerie paths will take me straight there. What I need right now is to keep myself from breaking apart. I need to focus on the rage instead of the agony and horror. But it's almost impossible. No matter where I look, I can't escape the image of a dead Ryn and a dead Violet. A dead Ada with her head almost completely detached.

I turn my face toward the sky and open my mouth. The cry I let loose comes from somewhere deep inside me, carrying with it every aching emotion threatening to crush me. I scream until I have no breath left. Until my chest is so tight I almost can't feel the pain anymore. Almost.

It's only when I finally stop, gasp for air, and lower my gaze that I discover I'm not alone. A winged creature about the size of my hand hovers in front of me. Its small green body is human-like, and its wings are transparent and delicate, mostly silver with a few bright spots of neon green. Before I can say a word, the creature changes. It expands, drops through the air, and on the ground stands a dragon small enough to fit in the space between the trees. An instant later, it shifts again, becoming what looks like a large dog. Shaggy hair in tones of russet and copper covers its body.

"Bandit," I whisper, knowing it's him without having to ask. In a wobbly voice, I add, "You follow me everywhere." I don't know if he understood what happened to Vi and Ryn and Ada, but it seems to me that his beautiful gold-flecked eyes are sadder than any eyes I've ever looked into. He walks over and nudges his head against my hand, and that one simple gesture almost breaks me completely. I long to sink against his warm body and cry my heart out. But I refuse to give in to the pain. I won't cry. I won't break. I won't let go of the anger driving me forward. If I let go of it, I might change my mind.

And that is the last thing I want to do.

So I breathe in deeply and tighten my grip on the sword. I don't bother telling Bandit what to do or where to go, because he'll stay with me anyway, in some tiny form I can't see. I raise my stylus and lean my hand against a tree trunk as I write across it. Then I grit my teeth and step into the faerie paths.

Standing at the edge of the darkness, a heartbeat away from embracing the hatred that's built up inside me, I pause. For one brief moment, I hear Calla's voice in the back of my mind: *You can't take away their free will. That isn't right.* I mentally stamp her voice down. To hell with what's right and what isn't. The Guild clearly doesn't care about what's *right*. How many Griffin Gifted lives have they ruined? How many families? *Too many*, I answer myself. *And mine will be the last.*

With that thought, I march forward into the black emptiness of the paths, shoving the stylus back into my jacket. My mind is trained firmly on an image of that small, nondescript room through which people arrive at the Guild. I walk forward, seeing nothing, hearing nothing. Then, up ahead of me, dim light appears in the darkness. I head straight for it.

I step into the room, where one guard sits behind a desk and another stands beside the doorway leading to the grand and impressive main foyer. At first the two men seem almost bored. Then, as their eyes land on the sword in my hand, they frown. I suppose if I belonged here, I'd have no need for real weapons. I would use only the sparkly gold type that appear and disappear at will. The guard behind the desk stands. "Markings or pendant?" he asks. "I need to scan you before—"

"Get down, stay down, and don't make a sound," I command them, my magically enhanced voice resounding throughout the small room. Both guards are knocked instantly to the floor. And there they lie—not dead, not even passed out—but silent and frozen as their eyes dart about.

I lift the sword, rest the blade on my shoulder, and walk beneath the doorway to face the people who've been screwing with my life since the moment I got to this world. An alarm goes off immediately. The alarm indicating that someone with a Griffin Ability has just entered this Guild. I don't give a damn. It's not like I was planning to sneak in unnoticed. But the noise is almost deafening, so I tell it to shut the hell up.

Guardians going about their daily tasks spring into action all around me. As they rush toward me, I raise my voice and unleash all my fury as I yell my command: "Every single person inside this Guild, get down on the floor and STAY THERE!" My voice echoes throughout the enormous circular room as men, women, and a few younger trainees drop to the floor all around me. Their panicked voices fill the air, so I add, "And keep quiet!"

I stalk past them and up the grand stairway, where two guardians have collapsed about halfway up the stairs. At the top, I turn and look down. I should be seeing the men and women sprawled across the floor, but my mind overlays the scene with another image. An image of two bodies, each pinned to the earth with a blade. Tears squeeze from my eyes as I scream, "You will never, *ever* hurt a single Griffin Gifted fae again! You will not lock them up, you will not tag them, you will not force them to add their names to a public registry, and you most definitely will *not* experiment on them. And you will repeat these words to any other guardian you come across."

When I'm done, I don't move. I grip the carved wooden banister with one hand and stand there, my breathing ragged. I've done what I came here to do. I don't know what I expected to feel at this point, but I don't think I wanted to feel … worse. My gaze travels from person to person, refusing to think about whether any of them might actually be against the Guild's policy on Griffin Abilities. I need to hate them all. If I can't, then I'll end up thinking of how much I hate myself instead. I'll think of the blood spilling from Ada's neck. From Dani's neck. She was an unwillingly participant in everything Ada did, and she died for it.

I killed her.

And now I'll never know if it might have been possible to free her from their body. I'll never get the chance to fix the mistake I made in forcing Ada and Dani to rejoin. I'll never really know the woman I called 'Mom' for so many years.

Slowly, I lower myself onto the top step, feeling more tears coming. I place the sword on the floor beside me—and notice suddenly that partially dried blood still coats the blade. Horrified, I kick the sword away from me. Why the hell did I even bring it with? Probably because it was in my hand when I ran away from … from …

I turn my head to the side, blinking tears away as I try not to see their dead bodies yet again. Ryn, Vi, Dani.

I don't know how long I sit there, holding the baluster and watching the foyer as tears stream silently down my cheeks. Hours, I think. Whenever anyone else enters the Guild, I tell them the same thing—get down on the floor, don't move, and don't make a sound. At this point, I have no other plan. I know I'll have to leave soon, though, before the other Guilds find out what's happened here and storm in with too many guardians for me to command. And I don't want them withdrawing guardians who are busy fighting Roarke in the human world or the human soldiers in this world. That's not why I came here.

But right now, I can't bring myself to move. I can't bring myself to think about where I should go. I doubt I'll be welcome at the Griffin rebels' safe haven. The remainder of my family will never forgive me for what I've done to these guardians.

This isn't the way we get things done, Calla said. *This is who the Guild* thinks *we are, but we have to prove them wrong.* Well, I definitely screwed that up. It was worth it, though. The Guild might hate us forever, but at least they'll get rid of their Griffin registry and their tagging system and their experiments. And I suppose I can throw in a command about them liking Griffin Gifted instead of hating them on my way out.

And then … then I'll go after Roarke. If I can bring an entire Guild to its knees, I should be able to stop an Unseelie prince. And now I don't have anyone holding me back telling me how dangerous it is.

Eventually, I pull myself to my feet. Beneath the ache in my chest, I feel empty. There's nothing there. The hope I've been clinging to, the promise of a happy future with a family that isn't broken has vanished into a black hole. I don't know why I'm so shocked. Haven't I always known that this is the way the world works? Life's a bitch and then you die. I just haven't got to the dying part yet.

I plod downstairs, one step at a time, staring at my dirty boots with eyes burning and raw. I don't want to look at anyone. I don't want to see their fear or hatred and end up drowning in my own guilt. These people *deserve* this, I remind myself. The way they treated Griffin Gifted fae was unacceptable. They destroyed my family. They've probably destroyed countless other families.

I stop then, about halfway down the stairs, hearing something … odd. Something like the crackle of electricity. The air feels different all of a sudden, like the charged quiet before a storm. I take another step, and that's when I see a man standing in the doorway to the foyer. A man I recognize.

Chase.

CHAPTER 24

Chase steps through the doorway, and that damn siren goes off again. I tell it to break. I tell it to never make a noise again. In the eerie silence that follows, I let out a bitter laugh. "Have you been sent to bring me in? Is Calla so disgusted by what I did that she can't face me herself?"

His eyes travel across the foyer. "What have you done, Em?"

My heart breaks just a little bit more at the sight of the shock on his face. I knew he and Calla wouldn't condone this, but it's worse seeing his reaction in real life. "No more than they deserve," I tell him.

He looks at me, and his eyes are as sad as Bandit's were out in the forest earlier. Then suddenly, inexplicably, it begins to snow. Within seconds, there's so much snow, I can hardly see the stairs in front of me. I realize it's Chase who's doing this, but the next thing I know, my feet are leaving the stairs and I'm flying through endless white. Wind whips at my face. I try to speak, to command something, but the wind snatches my air away so quickly I can barely breathe. Suddenly, darkness surrounds me. But it only lasts seconds before the white storm tosses me through the air again.

Then my feet are on solid ground. The wind dies down, the snow vanishes, and I stumble across the forest floor, breathing heavily. "What the ... the hell?" With one hand pressed against my chest, I turn and find Chase behind me. "Was that—a blizzard?"

He grabs hold of both my shoulders and looks directly into my eyes. "We're out here because we need to have a private conversation without a hundred frozen guardians listening in. Em, you cannot use your power on people like this."

I shove his hands away. "You gigantic hypocrite. You just used your power on me."

"Emerson, this is serious," he exclaims, his eyes wide. "You need to go back there and undo whatever you've done."

"Oh, so you can tell me what to do, but I can't tell them what to do?"

"Because what you're doing is *wrong*!"

"What *they've* been doing is wrong!" I yell back, jabbing my hand toward the right, though I have absolutely no idea which direction the Guild is actually in.

"That doesn't matter. You're not in charge of anyone else's actions. You control your own, and that's it."

I do my best to swallow my anger so I can sound reasonable. "Chase, they are going to track down people like us forever. You *know* that because you've been part of this world far longer than I have. That stuff at Reinhold? That's going to keep happening unless someone stops them."

"No, it's going to keep happening unless they decide for themselves that they need to stop."

"And what's going to make them decide something like that simply out of the blue?" I demand, throwing my hands up.

"Change is coming. It's slow, but it's coming. Those guardians who rescued you from—"

"It's *coming*? Well guess what. It's too damn late for us, isn't it." My voice breaks halfway through and my last few words come out sounding like a gasp as I struggle to hold back tears. "And even if we don't count today, they tried to *kill me* when I first arrived in this world. Do you remember that? I know you weren't there, but someone must have told you. Do you have any idea what that's like?"

"Actually, yes."

"Oh, fantastic. Is this the part where you tell me that you *understand me*? That making rainbows and snow and wind somehow compares to the kind of power I was trying to figure out when I first discovered my magic?"

"Yes. That is what I'm telling you. I came from the human world too. I also I had no idea what I was. And then I discovered I had incredible power. More power than any normal faerie. Power that people are afraid of. You and I, Em, are a lot more alike than you know."

"I don't have to listen to this," I mutter, turning away. I should be somewhere far from here, mourning Vi, Ryn and Dani, or planning how to get close to Roarke, not discussing Chase's silly little weather ability and arguing about the things I've done. The things I refuse to regret.

"The only difference, Em," Chase calls after me, "is that you have a group of people—a family—that will do anything for you. You're not alone like I was, and hopefully, that will keep you from choosing the wrong path the way I did."

The fact that he's mentioning family—our broken family that will never be whole again—makes me want to hit him. I spin back around to face him. "I killed someone today!" I yell. "So I'm sorry to have to tell you, but I think I'm on the wrong path already. And it wasn't just anyone that I killed. It was someone I've loved my whole life. Someone I should have been able to save. Is that anything like the wrong path *you* chose?"

"No," he says quietly. "What I did was far, far worse than that."

I shake my head, turn around, and start walking. I'm not interested in this discussion anymore.

"And if you keep doing the kind of thing you did at the Guild today," Chase continues, "you're going to end up exactly where I was nearly thirty years ago. And that is *not* a position you want to be in."

I don't look back. I don't care what position he was in. I don't care about anything anymore.

"Emerson," he calls after me. "Have you heard of Lord Draven?"

I almost don't respond, but in the end I stop. I look over my shoulder and say, "Of course I've heard of him. What the hell does a dead overlord have to do with anything?"

A beat of silence passes before he says, "You're looking at him."

I blink. Few things could distract me from the deaths of the people I care about, but this is one of them. I turn to face him fully as a shiver of uncertainty, of fear, passes through me. "You're lying. Lord Draven died years ago."

"No." Chase walks slowly toward me. "Calla projected an illusion onto an island full of people, and everyone believed I died." As he speaks, I remember Calla saying something about an illusion she did in order to stage someone's death. Someone the Guild would never stop hunting. But I can't bring myself to believe that it was *Lord Draven* she was talking about.

"Calla wouldn't do that," I say, a slight tremor to my voice. "She's honorable and decent and … *good*." All the things I'm turning out not to be. "She would never save an evil dictator responsible for loads of death and destruction. Someone who brainwashed thousands and covered the world in … in …" *In winter*, I realize. That's Chase's Griffin Ability. Control over the weather. Only I never knew just how powerful it was. I never connected it to the terrifying magical storms people mention when they speak of Lord Draven.

"You're right," Chase says, and he's close enough now for me to see the infinite sadness in his eyes. "Calla wouldn't have saved that person. Good thing I stopped being him a long time before she met me."

I take a shaky step back, my boot snapping twigs and brushing against leaves. The sound is too loud all of a sudden, as if the rest of the forest has become quiet enough to listen in on our conversation. As if all the creatures here can sense Chase's power. As if they're bracing themselves for whatever comes next.

"I'm trying to help you understand the seriousness of your situation, Em," Chase says. He stops a few paces away and doesn't come any closer. "You only controlled a single Guild today, but what about next time? What happens next time you believe you're right and another group of people is wrong, and you control them too? What if you get to the point where you decide you need to control every Guild? You know you'll need to control the Seelies then too, right? And then you may as well control the Unseelies as well. After all, the things they do are wrong. And you want to stop the things in the world that are wrong."

"No—"

"Do you see where I'm going with this, Em?"

"No, I … I would never go that far. I'm nothing like you. You—you're *evil*."

"I'm not. I've done terrible things, but I'm not that person anymore. I haven't been that person for a very long time. And way back in the beginning, I wasn't Lord Draven then either. But it all has to start somewhere. For you, Em, it could be starting right now. Or you could undo what you've done. You could choose differently."

I take another fumbling step back. If he really is who he says he is, then I need to get far away from him. I clench my fists, open my mouth, and let power flood into my voice. "Don't follow—"

His hand twitches. A powerful gust of air almost knocks me down, sucking my words away from me as it goes by. "Please don't do this," he says. "I don't want to fight you—"

"Get down!" I shout at him, and as he hits the ground, birds screech and take flight from the trees above us. "Tell me the truth," I command him. "Are you Lord Draven?"

"I was," he grunts as he struggles to lift himself from the ground. "I'm not anymore."

"You will not—"

A second blast of wind rushes by, and this one lifts me off my feet. Icy white flakes whip around me, spinning and spinning, tossing me in circles before I land on my hands and knees on the ground. "How dare you?" I gasp, my fingers digging into the leaves and dirt.

"Emerson—"

"You will never leave this forest. Your magic will not—"

Lightning strikes right beside me. I shriek and cover my head. The ground shudders, and the crackling boom that rips through the air at the same moment almost deafens me. "I'm not your enemy!" Chase yells through gritted teeth as the echo of thunder fades away and rain beats down around us. "Stop fighting me."

"You cannot use your Griffin Ability," I command shakily as I climb to my feet. "You can't use any magic. You can't even *speak*! You can't use your hands or your feet or your mind. You can't do *anything*!"

Finally, he stops struggling and collapses onto his back as the rain stops. His limbs lie useless at his sides. His mouth is open and slack, and his chest twitches. This is Lord Draven, and yet ... he's *not* Lord Draven anymore.

You can't do anything.

My words play back at me as I stand there with shaking hands and shuddering breath. Has my command made it so he can't even breathe? Does it mean his heart can't beat? Has he become brain-dead? His chest twitches less regularly. He's almost completely still now. My heart whacks painfully against my ribcage as I consider the fact that he might be dying. And I'm just standing here watching. I'm about to kill a second person.

What the freaking hell is wrong with me?

"I'm sorry," I gasp, shoving my hands into my hair and tugging at it. "Stop. Stop everything I said to Chase. He can breathe, he can use magic, he's normal and healthy and alive."

For several horrifying moments, he doesn't move at all.

Then his chest slowly rises. His eyes blink, and he moves his head to look at me.

And at that point, everything—*everything*—crushes down on me with an unbearable weight. I drop to my knees, my heart finally cracking open entirely. A great sob wrenches free of me as my vision becomes so blurred I can hardly see a thing. Leftover rain drips from the leaves above. It falls onto my cheeks, mingling with my tears.

A few feet away, Chase sits up.

"I just ... never wanted ... any of this," I sob. I press my hands over my face, but it doesn't stop the tears. "All I wanted was ... a family. And to be ... happy. And now they're ... they're dead."

He pulls himself closer to me. "What do you mean by 'they'? I thought it was only … only Daniela."

I lower my hands and stare at him in disbelief. "Violet and Ryn. *Violet and Ryn.* They're dead! They were murdered!"

Chase shakes his head, his eyes wide. "No, they're not. They were both stabbed, but they're faeries. They can survive a great deal."

"They were stabbed straight through their *hearts*! Are you telling me they can survive that?"

"Yes," he says simply, as if I should know this.

I scramble away from him, shaking my head and sniffing. "Stop it. Stop lying. I saw them. They weren't breathing at all. They were—they were dead."

"I know it might have looked that way, but as long as those blades were removed before all magic vanished from their bodies, then their magic would be able to heal them."

I stare at him, hardly daring to believe his words. "That's … actually … possible?"

"Yes. That's the way it works. Magic assists in the body's healing process, so if some object is in the way—like a sword or an arrow through the heart—then the magic keeps trying until eventually it's completely depleted. The more injuries a person has, the less time it will take to deplete their magic. But Vi and Ryn had minimal injuries aside from the blades through their hearts, so they'll be fine. I was with them before I came here. Violet is the one who told me where to find you."

"She's … she's okay?" I'm still not sure it's safe to believe him.

"Yes, and so is Ryn. They're both quite weak, what with all their magic being directed at healing their wounds, so we've put them into an enchanted sleep while they finish recovering. A temporary sleep, don't worry."

I launch forward and hug Chase tightly. "I can't believe it, I can't believe it," I whisper. Then I lurch back and hit his shoulder. "How the hell was I supposed to know that? Why didn't you say anything when you first arrived at the Guild? *I needed to know that!*"

"I—I'm sorry. I didn't realize. I thought you'd learned a lot in the time you've been in this world."

"People have said, 'It's hard to kill a faerie.' They didn't exactly elaborate on all the different situations in which that statement might or might not apply."

"Okay. I'm sorry."

"And the others? All the other rebels who were unconscious? Do—do they need my Griffin Ability in order to get them out of the nightmare?" At this point, I'm hesitant to use my Griffin Ability on any other person. The memory of what I did to Chase is horrifying.

"No, they're okay. They woke up once that magic—the nightmare essence—had worked its way out of their bodies. None of them had been given lethal doses yet."

"Okay. Good. And … the Guild." I press my hands over my face. "I shouldn't have done that. I shouldn't have controlled them. They must think I'm a monster. But the things I said—they were *good* things—and I'm still so angry about the way they've treated us—but …" I slowly lower my hands to my lap. "But I still shouldn't have done that. I need to undo the things I said."

Chase stands and holds his hand out to me. "Shall we go now and do that? Then I can fill you in on how we're all going to bring Roarke down."

"Okay. That sounds good." Then I pause as I look at his outstretched hand. "You were really … *the* Lord Draven?"

"Yes. It's a long story. I can tell you all of it—if you want—when we have time."

"So Calla knows? And everyone else at the oasis?"

"Not everyone, but all the people I work with and everyone in our family—aside from Jack—are aware of my history."

After one last moment of hesitation, I reach for his hand and let him pull me up. He finds a stylus somewhere inside his jacket and opens a doorway. Then we walk into the darkness and head back to the Guild to fix my mess.

CHAPTER 25

After going back to the Guild with Chase and telling every person there that they can disregard all the commands I gave them—and then making a hasty escape—we walk out of the faerie paths into a stylishly furnished living room. I'm reminded for a moment of the scene I walked into inside Dash's nightmare: a high-rise apartment with blurred city lights beyond the floor-to-ceiling windows. But this is definitely a different apartment—the floating gold timer in the corner is a giveaway—so as I walk forward, I push the disturbing memory aside.

I see the back of a couch, and a golden head resting on a cushion. But as our footsteps sound against the glossy floor, Calla looks around. She jumps up, rushes around the side of the couch, and pulls me immediately into a hug. "Are you okay?" she asks, her arms remaining tightly around me. Images of blood and Dani's head come to mind, and I find I can't answer.

Calla whispers something to Chase, and his reply is just as quiet. Then Chase says, "She thought Vi and Ryn were … were dead."

Calla pulls away from me. "I was afraid of that."

"You probably should have mentioned your concern to me before I went to find her," Chase says. "Our, uh, conversation—" he looks at me with a small smile "—would have been a lot shorter if I'd started with the fact that Vi and Ryn survived."

"I can hardly believe it," I say. "Blades through the heart, and they survived?"

Calla leads me out of the living room and along a passageway. Quietly, she pushes open a door. Inside the bedroom, both Vi and Ryn are asleep on the bed. "See?" Calla whispers. "They're fine. Or at least, they will be soon."

I walk quietly to the bed. I don't touch either of them, but I watch for long enough to make sure I see their chests rise and fall. Then I return to Calla's side. As

I pause in the doorway and look back, a startling idea appears suddenly in my head. An idea I must have been too shocked and heartbroken to think of earlier. Blood pounds through my veins as I consider it: If Vi and Ryn had died—*truly died*—could my Griffin Ability have brought them back to life? It worked for Chelsea and Georgia.

Or did it?

They died for real soon after my Griffin Ability reversed Ada's glass power, and Dash said it was because they were human and their bodies couldn't handle magic. But what if that wasn't it? What if it was because no one can truly be brought back from the dead? I never saw them again after it happened, but maybe they weren't normal anymore. Maybe they had become …

My stomach turns as I think of certain supernatural horror movies I've seen. I struggle to push the images from my mind.

Ada, Dani … If I could somehow find out what the Guild did with her body and—it sickens me even further to think it—her head, could I undo her death? But there would be no magic to undo this time. It was my actions that killed her. Could I undo those? Could I tell time to reverse?

I press my hand against my brow, my disturbing thoughts making my head spin.

"Em?" Calla asks, and I realize I'm still standing in the doorway of Vi and Ryn's room.

"Yeah. Sorry." I turn away, and she closes the door.

It all has to start somewhere, Chase warned me earlier. *For you, Em, it could be starting right now.*

No. I'm not starting anything. I'm not going down that path. I won't experiment with time and death.

"Are you sure you're okay?" Calla asks.

"Yes." I give my head a small shake. "Um, what about Dash?" I ask as we walk back to the living room. "I assume he's okay too, or Chase would have said something."

"Yes. Dash is also asleep. He was quite weak after using so much magic—carrying so many people out of Reinhold, and then fighting those guardians—and he had a few wounds that needed to heal, but he's fine. He should wake soon." We sit on the long couch facing the window, and Calla adds, "Aurora's here too. And Imperia's on top of the building."

"And everyone else?"

"All over the place. Some of them are resting in the other rooms here, or they're out somewhere else in the world taking care of personal matters. Chase and I told them to be as brief as possible if they need to go to the oasis. We assume they've all been tagged with the same tracking spell you and I have."

I play with the tassels along the edge of one of the cushions. "So we'll all have to leave this apartment soon then. Whose place is this anyway?"

"A friend of Chase's. He's out of town at the moment—as are many people who live in this area, considering how close we are to Central Park. But we'd be leaving this place soon anyway. Things are happening quickly now that the summit is over."

Before I can ask about the summit, Chase walks back into the room holding two glasses. "Nothing fancy, I'm afraid," he says as he hands us each a glass. "Just water. But I'm going out now to find something to eat."

"Bagels?" Calla asks.

He smiles. "Yeah. Hopefully. Then once Dash is awake, we can tell him and Em what's happening next."

"Cool," Calla says. I'm too busy downing my glass of water to respond. I didn't realize until Chase put it in front of me just how thirsty I am.

"Looks like you need some more of that," he says.

"Yes, thank you." I'm about to hand him my glass when I see that it's already refilled itself. "Oh. Thanks."

He opens a doorway against the large window and disappears through it. Calla drinks her water, and we're quiet for a few moments. Though I've been distracted by our conversation, I can't stop the horrifying images that come rushing back to fill my head now that my mind has a chance to wander. I lean forward and stare into my glass. I take a shaky breath and say, "I ... I killed someone."

She's quiet for a moment before answering. "I know."

"When I think back on it, I don't know how it happened. It just ... did. She was coming toward me, and I had a sword in my hands, and then ... it was done."

"It was self-defense. I saw it, Em. At that moment, it was either you or her."

"Yes, I needed to defend myself. But did I need to *kill* her? Surely I could have stopped her in some other way?"

Calla puts one arm around me and pulls me closer. "Don't do that to yourself. It won't help."

"And the part that makes me really sick is that ... in that moment ... I *wanted* to kill her."

"Well, you definitely wouldn't be the first person to have felt that way about someone who's murdered loads of innocent people."

"It's just … I don't know how to feel about any of it except sickened and horrified and guilty."

"So, uh, one of the many people who've joined the oasis over the years is an elf with a background in counseling."

I pull away and look at her with one raised eyebrow. "Counseling?"

"Yeah, I know, I figured you'd look at me like that. But I think, when this is over and we get back to the oasis, that maybe you should talk to her."

I sigh and push myself to the edge of the couch. "I guess. Maybe. As long as she's nothing like the counselors at Tranquil Hills Psychiatric Hospital, I should be okay with that."

"She's cool. I think you'll like her."

I stand and walk to the window. Dim light in the lower part of the sky suggests it's early morning, but the city is still a sea of tiny lights. Except, I realize as my eyes travel across the cityscape, for the large area consumed by twisted vegetation. "Holy flip," I murmur. "There's so much of it. What happened?"

"It's apparently all across Central Park again," Calla says, joining me at the window. "And it's spread even further on this side. Roots and vines and things have been pushing through buildings, destroying them. In most cases, people have been able to get away in time. The enchanted plants don't move *that* quickly. But there have been wide-scale evacuations, so hopefully this city won't see too many more casualties before the Guild kicks Roarke's ass out of here. Human soldiers have been trying to get into the enchanted area, of course, but there's a shield around it. I heard a news report about bullets rebounding off an invisible layer around the forest." As she speaks, I see a bright orange-white flash over part of the forested area. "Clearly that hasn't stopped them from trying with various forms of explosives," Calla adds. "So, yeah. Roarke's making sure the armed forces from this world can't stop him. And the Guild's going to have to fight through that shield too when they get here. Chase said he couldn't get to the other side through the faerie paths."

I swallow, still stunned by what I can see from here. "Sometimes I wonder if I've been inside an endless dream since the moment I spoke to the ground and it tore open at my feet. The things I've seen are just beyond belief. I mean … this?" I gesture toward the enchanted overgrown disaster zone. "I never, ever imagined anything like this would happen in my world."

"I know. Every time I look out there, I can barely believe it. It's no less shocking than the sun suddenly choosing not to rise, or the sky and the ground flipping the other way around. It's a fundamental part of life: the two worlds have always been separate. That's just the way it is. So to see so much of one world spilling into the other is just … almost too much to comprehend."

"Em?"

I look behind me and see Dash walking out of the passage where the bedrooms are. Warmth floods my chest. "Hey, you're okay." I cross the room, and the moment I'm close enough, he pulls me into his arms. I bring mine up around his back and hold on tightly to him. He doesn't say anything else, and neither do I, and we simply stand like that for a long time. Long enough for Calla to leave the room. Long enough for me to wonder if it would be acceptable for me to fall asleep against Dash.

Eventually, he says, "You told me that once I got out of my nightmare, I could hug you all the time. I took you seriously."

I laugh against his shoulder. "Does that mean you're planning to never let go?"

"I guess I can let go. For short periods at a time." As if to demonstrate, he gently pulls away from me.

"Are you okay?" I ask. "I mean, really okay? Since the nightmare."

"I think I am." He scrubs one hand through his hair. "I was afraid to fall asleep earlier. I was convinced I'd end up back there. But I was so tired, I don't think I dreamed of anything. And now, being awake, it's getting easier to push those memories to the back of my mind where they belong. But what about you. Are *you* okay?" He shakes his head before I can answer. "Sorry, stupid question. Of course you're not okay. I saw what happened. Before you left."

I swallow and say, "I killed Ada. Which means I killed Dani."

Dash doesn't say anything else. Instead, he wraps his arms around me and we stand in another hug for a while. "Is it okay," I say eventually, "if we don't talk about her?"

"Sure. Whatever you want."

We walk to the window, and Dash says, "I assume you know that Vi and Ryn are going to be fine?"

"Yes. I'm still a little shocked about that. Shocked in the best possible way, of course."

"Yeah. Faerie healing magic is pretty amazing."

We stare out the window together. His fingers find mine and slowly intertwine with them. "So," he says after a while. "Victoria, huh?"

"I know. Weird, right?"

"It's crazy. I suspected, you know. When Zed told us about the changeling spell and that your parents were a talented guardian couple, I thought of Vi and Ryn and their little girl who died. But it seemed way too far-fetched."

"It is far-fetched. It just happens to be true as well."

"You know, if things had been different, you and I would have grown up knowing each other. We might have been very good friends. We might have been …"

"Exactly where we are now?"

"Yes. Well, without all the other … stuff. Stanmeade, Ada, Zed, you almost winding up married to an Unseelie prince. But we might still have been standing here together, preparing to fight Roarke—because he would have tried to tear the veil open further with or without you—and feeling semi-awkward because we kissed each other before both worlds got turned upside down, and now we really want to kiss each other again but it's so not the appropriate time."

I press my lips together, but my laugh escapes me anyway. "Oh, is that what we're feeling?"

"Yes." He gives me an innocent look. "Isn't that what you're feeling?"

I rest my head against his shoulder as I continue to smile. "It's actually a crazy kind of comforting to think of it that way. You know, that we're meant to be here right now, in this moment."

"Yeah." He presses a brief kiss against the top of my head. "It is."

CHAPTER 26

quickly before sitting around the dining room table to discuss what was decided at the summit.

"Why is no one else here for this meeting?" I ask before Chase begins.

"I've already reported back on the summit to everyone else," he says. "They know what their next step is. You were at the Guild, Em. And Dash was asleep."

"I prefer the term 'recovering from extreme exhaustion and overuse of magic,'" Dash says. "Makes me sound less lazy."

Calla rolls her eyes. Chase says, "Okay, let's get through this quickly. Cal and I need to leave in about twenty minutes."

"Leave for where?" Dash asks.

Calla tells him to be quiet. Chase opens his mouth to speak again, and at that point, a spider scurries across the table, transforming into a mouse before it reaches me. Bandit runs up my arm and onto my shoulder. "Sorry," I say to Chase. "You can carry on now."

"Right, here's what's happening. The fae world's army of joined forces will be marching on Roarke and his followers this afternoon."

"So soon?" Dash asks.

"The situation is urgent. No one wants to waste any more time. And Roarke's army is small. It's half the Unseelie army, if that. So if we take the other half, plus the Seelie army, plus all the guardians, it should be easy enough to defeat Roarke. Once that's done, the Unseelies will deal with Roarke and the Unseelie defectors.

"Next, a small force of guardians will remain behind to remove the enchanted forest, while the rest of the guardians and Seelie soldiers will split between the three areas of the fae world where humans have invaded. Guardians have tried repeatedly over the past few days to push the human forces back, but the humans keep returning with more weapons. However, with additional Seelie support, the Guild thinks they'll be successful now. Once the humans are back in their own world, guardians will reinforce the glamours and add additional protection to those three openings into the fae realm so they're properly hidden.

"Lastly, as soon as the previous goal has been achieved, every single guardian who can be spared will be sent to locations all across the human world to spread a vaporized potion the Guild has been working on for the past week. It contains a memory-altering enchantment with all the specific details of the story the Guild would like the human world to believe. This enchantment will be spread by magical winds, and the Guild and other leaders are hopeful that the majority of people will breathe it in. Once they've all forgotten that our world actually exists, the Guild will then send out smaller teams over the next few weeks to fix up areas of damage and alter specific memories related to those areas of damage."

"I can see some serious flaws in that plan," I mutter.

"What is this story they're hoping the humans will believe?" Dash asks. "I didn't think it would be possible to make everyone forget our existence, given the amount of destruction Roarke has caused."

Chase sighs. "The story sounds rather implausible to me, but all the leaders agreed on it. They want the humans to believe that a whole host of natural disasters across the world are responsible for all the damage that's actually been caused by Roarke and his followers."

"They want to blame this all on natural disasters?" I repeat. "Seriously? You think people are going to believe that a gigantic forest growing in the space of a few days and pushing its way through buildings and roads is a *natural disaster*?"

"I think they'll find it easier to believe that," Calla says, "than to believe in the existence of a magic parallel world."

"And the forest itself will be gone by then," Chase adds. "Only the damage will remain."

"And Rhiningsville? Can they blame the disappearance of an entire section of land on a natural disaster?"

"A special team has been assigned to Rhiningsville," Chase tells me. "That's part of the long-term plan."

"But what about all the news footage and the photos and videos?" Dash asks. "Surely those aren't going anywhere?"

"The enchantment includes the belief that those videos were all hoaxes put together by a special effects team as part of a publicity stunt leading up to a major film releasing later this year."

I tap my fingers on the table and say, "You know what? That might actually work. Calla's right that people would choose to believe *any* explanation other than a magical or supernatural one."

Dash leans back and folds his arms over his chest. "What about all the people who don't breathe in the memory-altering enchantment?"

"They'll be the minority," Chase says, "and they probably won't say anything once they realize the rest of the world believes a completely different story. And it's not as though it's a new thing for there to be *some* humans who know about our existence. It's always been that way."

"And the natural openings between the worlds?" Dash asks, pointing out yet another problem. "Those who don't forget will come looking for them. And even if they can't see the openings, they know exactly where they are now, so they'll come right back through them."

"Possibly," Chase says. "And while that's a risk the Guild and everyone else is willing to take—mainly because they have no other option—it isn't a risk *we're* willing to take." He looks at Calla. She turns to me.

"We were kind of hoping you could close the openings," she says.

"Oh. Yes. I can do that." I sit forward and place my arms on the table, a small thrill racing through me at the idea that I'm being allowed to make a meaningful difference with my magic. "And I can do other stuff too. Like telling all the humans to go back to their own world. That would keep the Guild and Seelies from having to do a whole load of fighting. And if Roarke still has a shield up around his enchanted forest by the time everyone wants to invade this afternoon, I can tell it to come down. That'll save the guardians and everyone else from trying to break through it with magic."

Concern fills Calla's expression, but she doesn't say no. "All these things would require quite a lot of power from you, Em."

"That's okay. I drank some of that elixir before I went to the Guild, and I still have power left over from that. And my ability will replenish again before this afternoon, so that will be additional power. Plus, I can go back to the oasis and get the other vial. Then if I do run out of power, that will stimulate more. I should be fine."

She still doesn't look entirely convinced. "Em, have you seen the size of the area Roarke's magic has spread across? Because that's the size of the shield he and his followers have created. It's far bigger than the one that was around Noxsom. And there are a *lot* of human soldiers who've now made their way into the fae realm. That's a lot of people to control. And on top of that, closing three gaps in the veil is going to take a huge amount of power. Even with the elixir, I'm worried you're going to run out."

"Okay, then I won't worry about commanding the humans. I'll bring down the shield so everyone can get through to Roarke and his army, and then I'll go close the gaps after all the humans have been pushed back into this world."

Calla says, "Okay. I guess bringing down the shield is important too."

"Wait," Dash says. "One more problem. How do we know the Seers aren't going to See that Em's planning to close these openings? If they do, they might send a few guardians to capture her. That's what happened after we got away from Reinhold with the rest of the rebels."

"Ah, I wondered how those guardians found you," Calla says.

"How did *you* find us?" I ask, tilting my head to the side. "Did Aurora tell you where we were?"

"Yes. She used your amber to send me a message telling me her location. She explained that you and Dash had gone to Reinhold to rescue the others and were planning to return to her."

"Okay, back to Dash's question about the Seers," Chase says. "Hopefully they won't interfere if they See a vision of you closing the gaps, Em. You'll be helping the Guild. They'd close the gaps themselves if they knew how to."

"And what," a new voice asks, "if these natural gaps are not supposed to be closed?"

"Aurora," I say, looking up. I push my chair back and stand.

She places her hands on her hips as she looks at me. "You kicked me."

"I did. I'm sorry. But at least Ada didn't slice your throat open."

She rushes around the table and wraps her arms tightly around me. "Thank you. I mean, you could've used magic to shove me out of the way, but I understand that magic still isn't automatic for you. Kicking clearly comes more easily." I roll my eyes as I pull away from her. "Can I stay for the rest of this meeting?" she asks. "I think my question is valid."

"Uh, sure," Chase says. I return to my chair, and Aurora takes the empty seat on my left. "Your question definitely is valid," he continues, "and no one knows if the natural openings in the veil exist for a reason or not. But we do know there are more than just three, so we hope that closing only those three won't have any negative impact on either world."

"Okay," Aurora says. "And I suppose the negative impact of not closing them would be worse."

Dash leans forward. "So you've told us what the Guild, Seelies and Unseelies will be doing, but you haven't said what you guys and the rest of your team of rebels will be up to. I assume you'll be involved somehow? You wouldn't stay away from something this important."

Calla smiles as she looks at Chase. "He knows us so well, doesn't he."

"There are plenty of people who will be facing Roarke," Chase tells us, "but until they've defeated him, no one will be holding back the human forces in those three parts of the fae realm, other than the local fae who've already been fighting for days."

"Some of whom have no idea how to fight," Calla adds.

"So that's where we'll be," Chase continues. "We've split our team—our full team minus Vi and Ryn—into three groups. That isn't much, but we have Griffin Abilities, which puts us at a major advantage."

"Including a whole bunch of abilities from Gaius's vault," Calla says, "which he's finally allowing us to use."

"Is that where everyone else is right now?" Dash asks. "Back in our world fighting humans?"

"Not yet," Chase says. "I gave them a couple of hours off to sort their lives out. Take care of personal or family matters, or whatever. After all, half our team just spent a week locked inside their own minds. I figured they needed a few hours off before launching into the next battle."

"A few hours," Aurora mutters, her tone suggesting that number isn't nearly enough. And I guess she's right, but with our worlds in the state they're currently in, I guess Chase couldn't give them much more than that.

"So that's where Calla and I are off to now," Chase tells us. "To meet everyone else before we split into three groups. Dash, you'll stay with Em near Roarke's enchanted forest so Em can remove the shield surrounding it when our army shows up. Then you'll go with her to close the gaps. These are the locations." He slides his amber across the table toward Dash.

"And don't you *dare* let anything happen to her," Calla says.

"Hey, she's actually not too bad at taking care of herself," Dash says, pulling the amber closer.

"If my Griffin Ability doesn't run out. Which it won't," I add at the sight of Calla's raised eyebrows. "Because I'm going to pick up the rest of the elixir before we leave for this little mission."

"Good." Chase stands. He looks at Calla. "Then I guess you and I need to go battle some human soldiers and their not particularly nice weapons."

I stand as well, suddenly anxious about the fact that they'll be fighting against bullets and explosives. "What is it you guys say to each other sometimes? Stay alive?"

"Yeah," Dash says. "That's the one."

"Stay alive," I say, looking first at Calla and then at Chase. "I mean it."

CHAPTER 27

"You know I'm going with you and Dash, right?" Aurora says to me that afternoon when I return from the oasis with the remaining vial of elixir.

"Aurora," I say patiently. "You need to stay here with Vi and Ryn. If the countdown timer reaches zero and they're still asleep, you need to move them somewhere else."

"Firstly," she answers, "I think every guardian in existence has more important things to do right now than track down Griffin rebels. And secondly, if we're gone that long, I'll just come back here at the right time and move them. It's not like someone has to be with them at all times. Calla said she put, like, a bazillion protective enchantments around this apartment to lock out anyone who isn't us."

"I know, but I think guardians can eventually get through those because they're not the super complex kind, and …" I sigh. "I would just feel a whole lot better if I knew someone was here with Vi and Ryn. Also, if they happen to wake up while we're all still gone, you can tell them what's going on."

Aurora groans. It looks for a moment like she might even stamp her foot, but then she calmly places that foot back on the floor and says, "Okay. If this is what you need me to do, then I'll do it."

"And can you make sure Bandit doesn't follow me when Dash and I leave?" Bandit, curled up on the couch in the form of a cat, looks up at me. "See?" I say. "He's already plotting how to get out of here without me noticing."

"Hey, Em, are you ready to go?" Dash asks, turning away from the window. "I can see them from here. The fae army. At least, the part that's coming down this road. I assume they'll be approaching from all sides."

I move to the window and look out at the lines of marching people down below. "That's so freaking weird. I wonder if they're glamoured or if any human who hasn't evacuated the area can see them too."

"Well, if they can," Dash says, pulling his jacket on, "they'll forget about it once the battle's over and the Guild has spread their memory-altering enchantment."

"True. Okay then." Noticing that there's no longer a cat lying on the couch, I look around for Bandit and find him sneaking up my leg in the spider form he used on the table earlier. "You know, Bandit, this is not a particularly safe form," I tell him as I carefully detach him from my pants and place him back on the couch. "You're in danger of being squished by every spider-hating person in the world."

"In both worlds," Aurora says with a shiver. Bandit shifts back into a cat, and Aurora adds, "That's better. I like cats." She sits on the couch and tucks Bandit beneath her arm.

"Ready, Em?" Dash asks. I turn and find that he's already opened a doorway beside the window.

Suddenly, I feel ridiculously nervous. As nervous as I was before we broke into Noxsom. "This is going to be fine, right?" I say to Dash, allowing some of my fear to peek through.

"Of course." He gives me that cocky grin of his. The one I used to hate. The one I haven't seen in far too long. "I'm with you, that's why."

I almost kiss him. If I wasn't feeling like I might throw up at any moment, I'd definitely tug him closer and press my lips against his. Instead, I take his hand and step into the faerie paths. "Don't do anything silly," Aurora calls after us. "Stay out of danger. Shoot, I think I'm channeling Calla right now." Then the darkness swallows us up, and Aurora's voice is gone.

We walk out of the paths onto a cracked road and find ourselves between an upturned doughnut van and half a bench. The crackling sound of magic reaches my ears. I duck down immediately, tugging Dash with me. We look around, getting our bearings. We're right at the edge of Roarke's forest. A few roots have pushed their way through the road, and slim vines have wrapped around some of the vehicles left behind, but that's about the worst of it right here on the edge.

"I see them," Dash says. "The army. They've reached the edge of the forest."

I lean past him to get a better view. Between two cars, I catch a glimpse of the fae army. Flashes of magic light up the air just ahead of them. "Looks like they're trying to get through the shield already. I guess it's time to help them." I sit back against the van, remind myself that I have nothing to be nervous about, and then say one simple sentence: "The shield around Prince Roarke's enchanted forest no longer exists."

Power rushes out of me. A large amount, but not everything. I have more than the normal amount, thanks to all that elixir I swallowed before charging into the Guild. I hear a roar from the fae army, and I know it must have worked. "Well done," Dash says, reaching for my arm and squeezing it. "You did it."

I sit up and look past him again. Doorways are opening up all along the perimeter of the forest, and faeries are disappearing into them. "I wonder if they know where they're going," I say. "I wonder if Roarke's army is spread out, hiding in the forest and waiting to attack, or if they're all lined up somewhere. Like, maybe Haverton Tower is his new palace, and his army is guarding it."

"I don't know, but we don't need to worry about that. We need to get to our first location inside the fae realm and wait to close the gap."

I sigh. "Seems like it might be useful to try to hunt down Roarke and command him and his army to stop all of this, but that's—"

"Definitely not happening," Dash says. "It's unlikely we'll get close enough for your voice to have any influence over him, and it's way too dangerous."

"Hmm, that is actually a good question," I say, sitting back. "How close to a person do I need to be in order to command them?"

"I hate to be the boring one," Dash says, "since that's not usually my role, but now's not the time to find out." He opens a doorway against the side of the van, takes my hand, and we crawl into the darkness.

A boom almost deafens me the moment we reach the other side. Something— sand?—sprays through the air nearby. One of the tall, spindly trees cracks right down the middle, and the two halves begin falling to either side. I hear a rapid *puh-puh-puh* before something wraps around my arm and tugs me into the darkness once more.

"Sorry, sorry, sorry," Dash says the moment we tumble out of the paths a second time. We're surrounded by the same spindly trees, but they're blackened and smoking, and ash covers the ground everywhere I look. The sounds of explosions and gunfire are in the distance now. "Are you okay?" Dash asks. "I'm sorry, that was too close. I took us too close."

"I—yes—I'm fine." I cough as smoke catches in my throat.

"Fuzzbucket. That's what needs to end before you can tell the gap to close. In three different places."

"Dash, I think …" I turn and look in the direction of the distant booms. "I think I need to stop that. Surely that's more important than waiting for other people to stop it—for more people to get hurt or killed—and then closing the gap behind them?"

He nods slowly. "Yeah. I think you're right. Maybe Calla and Chase didn't realize how bad it's become. Or maybe they thought it would be easier for them to stop it."

I push one hand through my hair. "Crap, I hope they're okay."

"They have shield magic, don't worry."

"So should I do this?" I ask, dropping my hand to my side. "Should I tell the human forces to leave? Ugh, but there's so much noise, and they can't hear me, and—"

"Em, that doesn't matter. Do you think the reception desk inside Reinhold could hear you when you told it to show you where all the Griffin rebels were? No. It didn't have ears."

A small and somewhat hysterical laugh escapes me. "You're right. Of course you're right. Sorry, I wasn't thinking for a moment."

Dash takes hold of my shoulders, and his intense green gaze locks onto me. "I think you should stop them. And hopefully it won't take as much power as stopping a magical army would. It's not as though you have to halt actual magic. You're just telling them to stop, turn around, leave, and not come back."

"Yes. Okay, yes." I bite my lip, then add, "Calla and Chase are going to be so mad when they realize what I've done."

"You know what? If they're in the middle of that—" he points toward the noise "—I don't think they're going to be too mad." He opens a doorway once again. "I'll try to get close, but not *too* close. Be ready to use your power."

The noise sounds shockingly near when the faerie paths open on the other side. I should speak immediately, but I hesitate, questioning what I'm about to say after the confrontation I had with Chase. But deep down, when I really think about it, I know this is the right thing to do. This isn't like controlling the Guild. This is a battle and both sides are fighting with whatever skills they possess. This just happens to be my skill.

"Every single human in this area will stop fighting, turn back toward the gap between this world and the non-magical world, walk through that gap, and never return."

Dash grasps my hand. I open my eyes.

And I watch my command come to life.

As the humans file dutifully out of our world, Dash takes me closer to where the actual opening in the veil is. It doesn't look like the artificial tear that was once above

Velazar II Island. If I hadn't known this one was here, I wouldn't have seen it. There's nothing at all to see. The humans march along between the trees, and then at some point, they simply … vanish.

Once they've all walked through, I drink about a third of the elixir. I don't want to risk running out of power before this command is complete. Then I focus on that patch of air where everyone disappeared, and I tell the gap between the worlds to close. It uses almost all my power, leaving only a little bit behind. "I hope it worked," I say to Dash. "It's hard to know when I can't see anything different."

We duck quickly behind a tree as several guardians race up to the spot where the last human disappeared. They try various forms of magic and move their hands in different formations, but nothing happens when they try to walk *through* something.

"Yep," Dash says. "I think it worked."

We move to the second location, and after drinking another third of the elixir, I repeat my commands. The humans are gone, the veil is closed, and we move on to our final spot.

And this one, it seems, is the worst. More yelling, more gunfire, more flashes of magic and lightning. Rain slams at my face, and wind almost knocks me over. I lean closer to Dash's ear and say, "Something tells me that Chase might be at this location."

Then I swallow the last remaining elixir and shut my eyes as my power rushes through my body once more. "Every single human in this area will stop fighting, turn back toward the gap between this world and the non-magical world, walk through that gap, and—" I suck in a breath as dizziness rockets through me.

"Em?" Dash catches me before I fall. Everything becomes disjointed.

When the dizziness finally subsides and I find myself lying on the ground, I mumble, "Dammit."

"Your power's depleted, isn't it."

"Yes," I say as I push myself up to sit beside him.

"It's okay. You got most of the command out. They're all leaving."

"But that last part is important, Dash. The part about them not returning. Because if they have enough weapons, then maybe they can force their way back in before that enchantment spreads everywhere and they forget there's another world here."

"The Guild didn't seem to think that was likely."

"The Guild didn't have a better option! They were probably planning to sacrifice more guardians in order to keep all the humans out until that enchantment spreads."

"Okay, so we wait here until your Griffin Ability replenishes."

"That's too long," I mutter, staring past him. "How many people could die in that time?"

"I know, Em. I get it. But if there's nothing we can do, then—"

"Wait," I say, my eyes returning to him as I grab his arm. "There is more elixir. The vials I left at the castle in the shadow world." I swallow. "We can go and get those."

He groans. "Seriously?"

"Yes. Calla still has part of the traveling candle we used to get out of the shadow world. It's in her house at the oasis. We can fetch it, go to the shadow world, get the elixir, and come back here. It'll be quick."

Dash hesitates before saying, "Yeah. Okay. I guess it's not like Roarke's going to be there if he's in the middle of a battle in New York City."

A shiver ripples through me as we arrive inside the castle in the shadow world. Has it only been a week or so since Calla and I escaped? It feels like far too many things have happened—far too many things have gone wrong—since then. But everything looks the same here. The empty passageways are varying shades of gray, and tendrils of smoke-like blackness rise here and there. They shift lazily through the air as we hurry along the corridor to the room that was mine for the few days I lived here with Dani.

Dani. Dead. Her head almost detached.

I take a steadying breath and shove the images from my mind. "Have you been back here since the whole Velazar thing?" Dash asks.

"Briefly. Roarke actually captured me after the Guild took you guys. But Calla got me out."

"Flip, thank goodness for Calla. That sounds like another story you'll have to catch me up on when we're done with all this."

"Yeah." We turn a corner and continue along the corridor. "It was weird, though. For a few days after we escaped, I kept feeling this strange sort of … pull. As if part of me wanted to return to this world. It was only during the first day Calla and I were traveling alone together that I realized what was going on. She said something about 'home,' and my automatic first thought was the shadow world. And then I remembered that when Dani and I decided to stay here, I used my Griffin Ability to tell this world it was our home. Clearly my magic took me seriously when I said that.

It kinda freaked me out, so I used my ability again and told myself the opposite. That seemed to do the trick."

"Good," Dash says. "'Cause it's disturbing to think of this world having some kind of pull on you."

"I know. Okay, this is the one," I say, pushing a bedroom door open. I step inside—and the room is bare except for a bed frame and a wardrobe standing open and empty. "Shoot," I mutter, my heart sinking. "He cleared out my stuff."

Beside me, Dash sighs heavily. "I guess it makes sense."

"I know, I just figured he wouldn't be bothered with looking through all the rooms. I thought maybe he'd abandoned this castle—this whole world—since starting to take over the human world. But maybe ..." I spin around and head back down the corridor. "Maybe he kept them," I say to Dash as he catches up to me. "Maybe the vials are in his office." We hurry back downstairs, turn along another few corridors, and enter the study Roarke was using as his center of operations when I was last here.

"Good thing no one's around to stop us," Dash says, heading for a chest of drawers while I aim for the desk.

"It makes sense. Roarke's followers are all fighting for him at Central Park. There's probably no one left in this—Oh! I found it! There's one vial here." I remove the tiny glass container from beside a collection of black candles in the top left drawer.

"Are you sure it's the right thing?" Dash asks, hurrying to my side.

"It's got my name on it, and it's the same handwriting, so yes." I push the vial into the front pocket of my pants—

—and voices sound from outside the room.

Dash grabs hold of me and pulls me down behind the desk. I press one hand over my mouth and another against my chest, where my heart thunders way too loudly. "Yes, all fighting has ceased and two of the gaps have been closed now," Roarke says as his footsteps move into the room. "He informed me just moments ago. It's a nuisance that the Guild's figured out how to close off those areas, but I can always give the humans more locations. They can get through to our world in other places and continue their attacks."

"And you're certain they don't know who you are?" a second man asks. A man with a deeper voice. A man who sounds very much like ...

Unseelie King? Dash mouths.

I nod. Then I point to his jacket and mouth, *Candle.*

Wait, he responds, but he slowly reaches for the candle anyway.

"No, I'm just another faerie to them," Roarke says. "A faerie they can't stand dealing with. But they'll continue to pay me for the information they want." He snickers. "They have no idea I'm the one they've been trying so hard to remove from Haverton Tower and the surrounding area."

"Your Majesty?" a third voice enquires. "The army's finally made it into the Haverton Tower Hotel."

"Good," the king says. "Let's go and surprise them."

What the hell? Dash mouths.

A door creaks as it swings open. I lower my head closer to the floor and peer beneath the lower front edge of the desk. It looks as though the door that was opened belongs to a wardrobe on the other side of the room. And within it I see swirling, sparkling magic. Electric blue in the center, with darker bits detaching from the edges and vanishing. A portal just like the one Roarke had in his bathroom back in the Unseelie palace.

"Send the ink-shades through in ten minutes, Marvyn," the king says. "Our army will have turned by then, and Roarke and I will be safely out of the way." And with that, the Unseelie King and his son step into the portal's swirling magic and disappear.

The moment they're gone, Dash rises to his feet. A glittering bow and arrow are in his hands a second later. Marvyn swings around—but the arrow is already flying at him. It strikes his chest, and he stumbles back against the wall before a second arrow pierces him. He slides down to the floor.

I jump to my feet, my shaking fingers already retrieving the vial from my pocket. "We can't let the ink-shades through. I'm closing the portal." I take a sip of the elixir, swallow, and in my next breath I say, "That portal no longer exists." It pulls my power from me immediately, and a moment later, the portal fizzles away into nothing. But we've only solved half the problem.

"We have to warn everyone that the Unseelies are about to turn on them," Dash says.

"Yes. And I have to close that gap. We can do both." From the desk drawer that's still open, I grab another traveling candle. "You go to Haverton Tower and warn them. I'll close the gap in the veil."

CHAPTER 28

I RACE OUT OF THE FAERIE PATHS AND INTO CHASE'S FRIEND'S APARTMENT SHOUTING, "Where's Bandit? I need a dragon. I need to get to the top of Haverton Tower Hotel, and the faerie paths won't take me there. I've already tried."

"What the *heck*?" Aurora asks, getting up from the couch where she's been reading a magazine. "I thought you and Dash were—"

"Done. Closed all the gaps. New emergency." I turn on the spot, my eyes combing the room for Bandit. "Oh, wait, Imperia's on the roof." I come to a stop. "Will she let me ride her without you?"

"What is going on?" Aurora demands.

"We were in the shadow world. I heard your father and Roarke. They're on the same side. The Unseelies are about to turn on everyone, and they wanted to let the ink-shades through, but I closed the portal, and I closed the third gap, and now I have power left over and I need to stop the Unseelies."

Aurora gapes at me as I finally take a breath.

"I'm going now," I say, spinning around and lifting my stylus to the wall. "I'm taking Imperia. She knows me. It'll be fine."

"I'm coming with you," Aurora says before I can write a doorway spell.

"Aurora, you—"

"You said my father's there. My *father*. That he and Roarke are in on this together. The same Roarke who wanted to *kill* me."

"Rora—"

"I want to be there!" she shouts. "I need to talk to him—to ask him—I don't know. It's just … now he's ruining everything alongside Roarke, and I need to understand why, because I thought our life was pretty awesome the way it was."

I breathe out. "Violet and Ryn," I say. "If they wake up, and—"

"I wrote them a note. In case I had to leave. Which is exactly what's happening right now," she adds as she turns back to the coffee table and grabs her stylus. She hurries back to the wall and writes the spell for a doorway. Moments later, we're running out of the paths and onto the roof toward Imperia, who seems to be napping in the late afternoon sun. It doesn't take us long to scramble up her side. Within minutes, we're clinging to the saddle on her back as she launches off the top of the building and into the sky.

I wish I could enjoy the rush of being in the air again, but that'll have to wait for another time. "You can't miss it," I say to Aurora. "It's the tallest hotel."

She leans forward and shouts a few commands to direct Imperia. Soon we're soaring toward the building that, from the air at least, appears to be the nerve center of the entire enchanted area. Plants protrude from every window, magic crackles around it like electricity, and the entire building appears to glow a faint green. I half expect someone to begin shooting magic at us as we swoop toward the roof, but I guess they're all further down fighting the invading fae army.

Imperia lands, and we waste no time sliding down onto the roof. The plants have made their way up here too. Creeping vines and thorny bushes and blood-red flowers. "Do you know where we're going?" Aurora asks as we hurry between the plants toward the large glass room at the center of the roof. There's a swimming pool inside, and dozens of loungers. No people, of course. I don't hang out on the tops of hotels very often, but I'm assuming there's a way to get down into the building from inside that glass room.

"I think we're going to the penthouse," I say to Aurora. "But I could be wrong."

"And we can't open a doorway from here into the building?"

"I don't think so. I saw faeries opening doorways down by the park, but it didn't work when I tried to get up here through—Oh, flip!" I try to duck down as first Roarke and then his father walk around the side of a particularly tall thorn bush. But of course, all the plants surrounding me are short, so there's nothing to hide behind. I stand straight and shout, "Stop what you're—

That sticky white substance. AGAIN! It flattens itself over my mouth and spreads all the way around my head. I try a spark of magic, but this stuff is too thick. Thicker than when Ada threw it at me. I tear at the upper edge to keep it away from my nose, trying to push away the fear that I'm about to be suffocated. Aurora's hands fly to my face. Her magic burns brightly and heats my skin. I jerk away instinctively.

"Well, this is a surprise," King Savyon says, pulling Aurora's attention away from me. "A little family reunion."

"And she brought Emerson," Roarke adds. "How convenient."

Aurora lowers her hands. They clench into fists as she faces her father. "Are you hiding up here while your soldiers do your dirty work?"

"Not hiding," the king answers. He rests his hand on the hilt of a sword at his hip. "I'd call it waiting. The Unseelie soldiers who came in here fighting with the Guild and the Seelies have now switched sides. All Unseelies are now fighting together again. For us." He gestures to Roarke and himself.

"So the two of you are—what? Back on the same side again?"

I'm happy for Aurora to keep her family talking while I try to get the magical gag off my face. With any luck, they'll still be talking by the time I succeed and command Roarke and his father to stop all of this. I risk using a few more sparks, despite the fact that I'm afraid of burning my face, but they don't do enough for me to tear through the white substance.

"We've always been on the same side," Roarke says to Aurora. Then, in what must surely be a coincidence, he assumes the same stance as his father: hand on sword hilt, one foot slightly forward. It would be comical if the situation weren't so dire. "Father and I have been planning this for years. Waiting for the time when someone decided to tamper with the veil again. Waiting for the moment we could begin to take over two worlds. One for me; one for Father."

"What about wanting the shadow world to increase? And stealing Em's power so you could use it to claim that world? I thought that's what you wanted."

"Firstly," Roarke says, "I wanted Emerson's power for a lot of reasons. Claiming that world was only part of it. We would then expand the shadow world at the expense of the human world. We always planned to have someone powerful enough to stop it from consuming the faerie world, of course. That's what Ada's wall of glass was for, to protect our side of the veil. But then Emerson messed things up." His hard gaze shifts to me, and I pause in my struggling, alert for any attack that might be about to come my way.

"Perhaps you should strengthen that gag she's struggling with," the king suggests.

"Perhaps," Roarke answers. He raises his hand, makes a squeezing motion in the air, and I sense the white substance tightening around my face. "She's fairly useless with ordinary magic, though. I doubt that gag's going anywhere. But as I was saying, Emerson—" he returns his hand to the pommel of his sword "—you ruined things with the veil, but I've actually been meaning to thank you for it. You helped me see that the shadow world was never going to be a perfect world. It was never a world at all, in fact, and there was only so much I could do with magic to change that. But the human world … well, it's a real world. It has an atmosphere, it has earth and vegetation and water. The only thing that's wrong with it is that it's full of humans. But I'm working on that problem."

"And you're making a mess of both worlds in the process," Aurora says bitterly.

"Yes," the king says. "The mess is part of the plan. We get fae and humans to fight each other. They do the hard work, drastically reducing the population on both sides of the veil. And when they're done, each world will be far easier to rule than before."

"That's … just …"

"A wonderful plan?" the king asks.

Behind the gag, I move on to a different tactic. I try with all my might to pull my lips far enough apart to murmur a command. But the stupid white stuff is pressed so firmly against them, it seems impossible.

"Dear Aurora," the king says, though there's nothing loving in his gaze, "now that you know our plan, would you like to join us on our side? We can give you anything you want, you know."

I shake my head furiously at her while trying uselessly to shout no. She doesn't think he would actually share anything with her, does she? He'll probably kill her as soon as she gets anywhere near him, and then they'll tie me up until they figure out how to use me. I want to hurl my magic at him. I want to take every knife from inside my jacket and throw them at him. But I know he'll attack right back, with far more strength and skill, and *I need to get this damn gag off before that happens.*

"No," Aurora says, to my relief. "I don't want any part of your plans. I don't want a ruined world. The only thing I want is this." She tilts her chin up a little before continuing. "I want to know who I really am. I want to know who that witch was. The one who stole me, started raising me, and then left me at the Unseelie palace. I want to ask her about my real family."

"The witch?" The king chuckles. "You can't ask her anything. She's dead."

Silence follows before Aurora manages to say, "What? How?"

"I killed her myself when her job was done."

"You—so—she never actually abandoned me there?"

"No. We bought you from her. You were a vessel. You carried an immense amount of power that your mother and I paid her to gather for us. She dropped you off, we handed over her payment, and then we killed her. Discreetly, of course. We removed all the power we needed from you, slowly over the course of several weeks as the witch had advised. Someone was supposed to kill you once your purpose was fulfilled, but your mother intervened. She felt sorry for you. She'd come to love you, in fact. I thought it was absolutely preposterous to adopt you as our own. Who knew what kind of lineage you might have come from. But Amrath was quite insistent." He sighs. "One has to choose one's battles, and I decided this one wasn't worth it. Amrath wanted you, so I let her have you."

Aurora looks stunned, and even I've stopped struggling so intently as I listen with half my attention to this awful story.

"So … everything you've always told me," Aurora says, "about a witch coming to work with Yokshin for a while and then abandoning me there—that was all a complete lie? You never actually wanted me?"

"Me?" The king seems surprised. "No, I didn't want to muddy our royal lineage. If we didn't already have Roarke, I most certainly would have said no. But …" He shrugs. "You were a sweet child. Amusing. As long as you played by our rules and kept your mother happy, I didn't particularly mind having you around. You were like a pet who just happened to have the label of 'daughter.'"

I look at Aurora and see tears welling in her eyes. "If you've kept this from me my whole life, then why bother telling me now?"

"Because, my dear, you stopped playing by the rules. You leaked your brother's plans, stole one of my dragons, and joined my enemies. And do you know what happens to those who stop playing by my rules?"

A tear rolls down her cheek. Her lips shudder as she answers, "You kill them."

"I'm glad to see you've learned something in your time with us."

I hear the word 'kill,' and I decide I'm done with trying to get this gag off. I know my skills are seriously lacking when it comes to combat magic, but if there's no other way out of this, then I may as well try. I pull magic from inside of me as quickly as I can. It coalesces above my hand, and I hurl it at the king. Clearly he wasn't expecting that, because he doesn't get out of the way in time. My sparks singe through the top half of his left arm, causing him to cry out. Bolstered by the fact that I've actually managed to achieve something with my magic, I reach into my jacket for a knife.

But Roarke is way ahead of me. Not bothering with magic, he races across the roof and slams into both of us. Aurora screams as we go down, and Imperia, who I'd somehow forgotten about, roars behind us. I barely have time to wonder why she hasn't done anything until now—perhaps because she didn't see Roarke and the king as threats?—before Roarke slams his fist down on my arm, knocking the knife from my grip.

The rooftop shudders from Imperia's movement. Scorching heat rips through the air as her flames head for Roarke. He pulls away from me and hastily raises a shield of magic above us. Somewhere behind him, the king yells out an angry command in a foreign tongue. The top of the roof shudders again, and Imperia lets loose a grating, wailing sound. The flames stop, Roarke knocks Aurora down again with his fist, and I fumble for another knife. Seeing my hand in my jacket, Roarke lunges for me again—

But something catlike pounces from the edge of my vision and lands on him. A small tiger. Then a panther. Then a blue cat with orange spots. It yowls and screeches and tears at Roarke's chest. He strikes out with a bolt of bright red magic, throwing the cat through the air above me. *Bandit!* I shriek inside my head. I twist around to see where he landed and try to scramble toward him.

He begins growing, changing, shifting into my favorite form. Seconds later, a dragon with sleek black scales and burning red eyes stands beside Imperia. And unlike her, Bandit is free to attack anyone he wants on this rooftop. An ear-splitting roar issues from his mouth, followed by a stream of flames. The king darts forward, diverts the flames with a shield, then flings magic right back at Bandit. The magic transforms into glowing arrowheads, and every single one of them pierces through Bandit's scales.

"Mm-mm!" I shriek from behind the gag. Then something wraps around my ankle and drags me backward. I grab onto vines and roots, but Roarke is stronger, and the plants tear through my fingers. I see the knife he twisted from my hand. I grab hold of it. As he flips me over, I drive the knife toward him. But he catches my wrist, squeezes impossibly hard, then tugs the knife from my grasp.

Aurora, who must have got to her feet while I was scrambling after Bandit, flings herself at Roarke with a wild scream. He shoves her back onto the ground, raises my knife, and brings it swiftly down.

Straight into his sister's abdomen.

Aurora gasps. I scream behind my gag. Imperia releases a wailing cry.

And then Roarke is tugged roughly away from us. Black and purple hair whips past. A gold arrow zings through the air. I lift myself up in time to see Violet spin and kick, swing a punch, then drive an arrow directly into Roarke's chest, the words "Not. My. Daughter!" punctuating each move.

Across the roof, Ryn is fighting the king. They're circling each other amid a swirling blaze of magic. Beside me, Aurora is trying to drag herself away from the fight and closer to Imperia. I move toward her—

And suddenly Violet is crouching in front of me, her wild purple eyes dancing across my face. A glittering blade appears in one hand. She raises it to the sticky substance covering my mouth. "I found you, I found you," she gasps. "Finally, I found you." Her guardian blade slices through the gag. I suck in air and—

Roarke looms behind Violet, an arrow still protruding from his chest and his own sword gripped in his hand. He strikes downward.

"FREEZE!" I yell at him, my magically enhanced voice echoing inside my head. And then: "Every Unseelie faerie in and around the Haverton Tower, stop fighting, stop using magic, drop to the ground, and stay there!"

Power races to escape my body. The force of it knocks me forward onto my hands. Then everything becomes still. I raise my head in time to see Roarke's sword slip from his hands and clatter to the rooftop as he topples down among the plants. Across the roof, the Unseelie King goes the same way.

A beat of silence follows.

Then Vi is pulling me toward her and Ryn is racing across the rooftop, and soon the three of us are kneeling, crying in each other's arms while Vi repeats, "I can't believe we found you," over and over again.

Then another pair of arms squeezes around us, and I catch a glimpse of golden hair. I pull my head back enough to see Calla, and then Chase standing behind her, his hand on her shoulder. And then into the picture crashes Dash, almost knocking Chase over as he swings his arm around him. Then the two of them are laughing, and I'm crying, and tears blur my vision as my family wraps itself around me.

Eventually, I pull away enough to sniff and ask, "Aurora and Bandit? Are they okay?"

"That's Bandit?" Calla asks.

"Ah, I see the arrowheads in his chest," Chase says. "He'll be okay as long as he doesn't shrink yet. I'll remove them quickly."

He hurries toward Bandit as Calla asks, "Did you say Aurora was here too?"

"Yes. Roarke stabbed her in the stomach. And Imperia was here. But ..." As I lean to the side to see past Bandit, I realize there's definitely no other dragon on this rooftop. And if Imperia's gone, then ... "Aurora must have left."

"I'm sure she'll be fine," Calla says. "Faeries can survive stab wounds, remember?"

I turn back to face her. I look at Violet, then at Ryn, truly examining their faces for the first time. Their red-rimmed eyes and tear-stained cheeks. Their beaming smiles. These are the faces of my parents.

"Everybody, freeze."

Ice forces its way into the warmth saturating my heart. Despite being told to freeze, we climb slowly to our feet to face the owner of the voice. Head Councilor Ashlow, with her bow raised, takes slow steps out of the glass room housing the swimming pool. Guardians spill out behind her, two of them raising bows and pointing arrows at us. "Isn't it nice that we can bag up all the Unseelies and a bunch of Griffin rebels in one afternoon?" Councilor Ashlow says.

"No," someone answers loudly. From the crowd of guardians behind her, a man steps forward. Perry. And then another—Harryd—the man who rescued us from Noxsom. They walk forward before turning to face their fellow guardians.

"This won't be happening anymore," Perry says in a loud voice. "It's time the persecution of Griffin Gifted fae came to an end."

"Get out of the way, Perry, before we take you down too," Councilor Ashlow snaps.

"Then you'll have to take me down."

"And me," Harryd says.

"And me," someone else adds.

Other guardians walk forward, and soon there's a large enough group of them facing Councilor Ashlow that she appears to reconsider. She lowers her weapon slightly, then says, "Obviously none of you were at the Creepy Hollow Guild when *that one* walked in." She points at me. "She is beyond dangerous and should not be allowed to go free."

"Oh for goodness' sake," Perry says. "She only did that because of the way you've treated her and her family. And the way you've treated others like her for years! You can hardly blame her or any of the others for wanting to protect themselves. And she just *saved us*, I might add. Or did you think all these Unseelies suddenly decided to stop fighting and lie down because it's nap time? No. So you'd damn well better let that girl and her family go."

Councilor Ashlow lowers her weapon. It disappears as she lets go of it. The guardians behind her who have arrows trained on us do the same. "Fine," Councilor Ashlow says, her jaw jutting forward slightly. "They're free to go. For now. But this isn't over yet."

"No," Perry says. "It certainly isn't." He starts to walk away, but then he backtracks. "One other thing. That tracking enchantment they breathed in? The one that's forcing some of them to keep moving every few hours so you don't find them? It needs to go."

Councilor Ashlow's mouth presses into a thin line. "You do not get to issue commands to the Head of the—"

"He's right," one of her henchman guardians says. Moments ago, he had an arrow pointed at us, but now I watch as he breathes out a long sigh and walks past Councilor Ashlow. He stops just in front of her. "I know how to remove the tracking enchantment." He looks past Perry and focuses on us. "I can give one of you the removal spell before you leave."

"Cool," Perry says. "All sorted." He strides back into the crowd of guardians, and with that, they all begin to disperse.

With half-smiles and stunned expressions, my family groups together again. Ryn pulls me against his side for another hug. Violet takes my face between her hands and kisses my forehead. "Come on," she says, reaching for my hand. "Let's go home."

EPILOGUE

Wind streams through my hair and blood races in my veins as Bandit soars through the air above the oasis. From way up here, I've got a great view of every part of the Griffin rebels' home: the giant trees with houses cradled in their branches; the pavilion and hammocks and the various buildings on the ground; the orchard and the playground; the river and the enchanted beach.

A tiny part of me is still waiting for someone to tell me there's been a terrible mistake. That these people aren't my family, and that I should be tossed out into the fae world to fend for myself. But the rest of me is daring to accept that I've finally found the place where I belong. The rest of me is daring to be happy.

We near the edge of the dome layer, and Bandit banks, then takes a nosedive toward the ground. My heart pounds, and my shriek is lost in the wind. At the last moment, when it seems as though he may crash into the three people waiting for us below, he slows, pulls up, and does another small circle—narrowly avoiding knocking out the pavilion with one wing—before coming around to land.

"That was *amazing,*" Jack exclaims, clapping his hands as Bandit comes to a stop and I undo the straps of the saddle Chase found for me. "Can I have a turn now?" He looks up at Ryn. "Please, please, please, please, please!"

"Nope, sorry," Ryn says. "When you're a little older."

"But my *sister* can take me. She'd never let me fall." He beams at me as I slide down Bandit's side. I try not to laugh at the way he keeps saying that—my *sister*. If I were younger, I'd probably keep saying 'my *brother*.' As it is, I keep looking at him, searching for any similarities in the way we look. His hair is different— dark brown streaked with an orange-yellow that he apparently gets from one of our grandfathers—but I wonder if perhaps our noses are the same shape.

Chase walks to Bandit's side and runs his hand along his smooth black scales as Ryn says, "Okay, I'll think about the possibility of you riding *with* someone, but you're definitely not riding alone until you're older. And we'll need to find a saddle that can take two people."

"Uncle Chase said he has one of those."

Chase looks around, a guilty expression on his face. I suppress a laugh as Ryn narrows his eyes and says, "Did he, now?"

"I don't know," Chase answers in an innocent tone. "Did I really say that, Jack?"

"Yes you did!"

"How about you climb onto Bandit's back and sit in the saddle?" Ryn suggests. "That's all I'm allowing at this point."

As Bandit bends a little lower and Ryn helps Jack get up into the saddle, Chase asks me, "Are you finding the dome high enough? If not, we can take Bandit somewhere else to really spread his dragon wings."

"Yeah, we didn't seem to have a problem, so I think there's enough space here. Well, for now, anyway. When Bandit gets more adventurous, we can try somewhere new."

"Perhaps he'd like to meet some of our dragons sometime."

I hesitate for a moment, wondering if I've heard correctly. "Wait. You guys have dragons?"

"Not here," he adds with a laugh. "Back at the mountain. The *real* mountain, not our little operations center here inside the oasis. There's a huge cavern inside the mountain, and that's where our dragons, nascryls and gargoyles live. Other than the gargoyles that now live here. They fend for themselves, and they're wilder now than they used to be, but most of the dragons and gargoyles still answer to me."

"Why didn't you tell me about these dragons when I first came here?"

Chase shrugs. "I guess you didn't tell us you liked dragon riding. In fact," he adds, "I'm not sure you even knew you liked dragon riding back then. You first rode dragons when you were with the Unseelies, didn't you?"

"Yeah. That's true." I watch Jack patting Bandit's back as my thoughts turn for a moment to Aurora and Imperia. I haven't heard anything from Aurora since she vanished from the top of Haverton Tower Hotel two days ago, and Perry says the Guild knows nothing about her either. But I'm convinced she's alive and well. I think she enjoyed her freedom more than she expected, and she decided to disappear before anyone could take it away from her.

"Hey, Em." I look to the side as Violet comes toward us. "I saw you up in the sky a few minutes ago," she says as she puts an arm around my shoulders. "So the dizziness has definitely passed now?"

"Yes, thank goodness." I loop my arm around Vi's back and give her a sideways hug, resting my head on her shoulder. When we returned to the oasis after leaving Haverton Tower, dizziness hit me. According to Ana, it was due to overuse of the elixir that stimulated my Griffin Ability. It came in waves, each one not quite as bad as the one before it, and by this morning, it felt like it might finally be gone for good. "If I can sweep through the air and plummet toward the ground and still feel great by the end of it," I say, "then I think the dizziness is definitely gone."

"Fantastic. Flying on Bandit looked like amazing fun. Do you think he'd mind if I took him for a ride sometime?"

"No, I'm sure he'd love it." I lift my head from her shoulder. "So you like dragon riding too?" In the same way that I keep examining Jack and the rest of my family members for any physical resemblance between us, I keep looking for other things we might have in common. Similar likes or dislikes or skills.

"Yes, I'm definitely a fan of soaring the skies on the back of a dragon," Violet says. "Remind me to tell you about Arthur at some point. He was seriously cool."

"The list of stories I'm supposed to remind you about is getting longer and longer."

Her beautiful purple eyes sparkle as she laughs. "Just wait until we get to our other celebrations outside the oasis when you meet your grandparents. *Loads* more stories are going to come up."

My smile feels impossibly wide as I say, "I can't wait. Oh, and speaking of celebrations, do you need help with any picnic stuff?"

"Thanks, that would be great. We just need to get all the food down to the beach." She leaves her arm around my shoulders as we head for the tree houses. "Ryn said he and Chase will move the chairs, blankets, games and all that. Calla was going to help me with the food, but she's gone to fetch Perry."

"Fetch him? Has he never been here before?"

"No, he actually hasn't. It's never been necessary for him to come here, so we decided it was safer if he didn't know anything about our haven."

"But now?" I ask. "Do you really think things are safer now?"

"Honestly, I think it would always have been safe for him to know the location of this place. The protection we have on the oasis is pretty much unbreakable. But I guess things do feel a little safer now. The real reason he's finally coming here, though, is because we really wanted him to join our celebration. He knew about you back when we all thought you died, so he's obviously excited about that. And he's busy doing so much to help make this world safer for Griffin Gifted fae. Not to mention all the risks he's taken for us over the years. I feel like we have a lot to celebrate with him."

I nod as we reach the spiral staircase leading up and around the tree. And then, since Ryn taught me yesterday how to launch myself up these stairs with magical super speed, Vi and I decide to race each other all the way up to her house. We're neck and neck the whole way, until I smack my hand against her front door split seconds before she does. Then I turn, gasping for breath, and ask, "You didn't *let* me win, did you?"

"Let you win? Emerson." Vi places her hands on her hips as she catches her breath. "Clearly you have no idea yet how competitive I am."

I grin. "Awesome. You know what? We should go into a city sometime and race each other, parkour style, like Val and I used to do." At the thought of Val, though, my smile slips. I turn away and push the door open into Vi and Ryn's kitchen, wondering when I should go and visit her. I haven't seen her since the night I discovered her connection to Ada, but I meant it when I told her I understand why she did it. And she's the closest friend I've ever had, so we should probably try to make amends. I have no idea how much she'll remember about magic and the world I now live in, given that the Guild's memory-altering enchantment has finished spreading. Everything that came before the tear in the veil, I hope.

"Oh, hey, here's your chocolate unicorn," Vi says as she reaches the kitchen counter. "You left if here after lunch."

"Ah, yes." I catch the small unicorn-shaped chocolate in one hand. "My reward for enduring a counseling session this morning."

She chuckles as her magic begins sending all the food that's lined up on the table into three large picnic baskets on the floor. "It wasn't that bad, was it?"

"It wasn't *bad*. It was just ..."

When I can't seem to come up with a word, Vi says, "I know what you mean. At the Guild, whenever a trainee ends up killing someone during an assignment, that trainee has to go for counseling afterward. I always hated it. I never wanted to rehash what happened and how it affected me. But looking back, I know it was a good thing."

"Yeah, I know," I say with a sigh. "And Meira's nice. I like her. Turns out we have quite a few things to talk about. It's just ... not easy." The ache that surfaces whenever Dani comes to mind tightens now around my chest. The thought of her induces so many conflicting emotions inside me. Disgust, because she stole someone else's life and didn't care that that someone would die because of her. Anger, because she never told me the truth about her background or mine. Regret, because I never got the chance to ask her about any of this. Sadness, because I also kind of miss the mother she was to me when I was little.

"Hey," Ryn says, interrupting my thoughts as he walks into the house, "are those picnic blankets still in the top Jack's closet? Oh, Em, are you—" He cuts himself off before he can finish. "Sorry. Doing it again."

"It's okay," I say to him. "Don't worry about it." This has happened several times in the past two days. Ryn senses the intense emotions flooding through me, asks me if I'm okay, and then apologizes for invading my privacy by unintentionally feeling my feelings. I felt a bit weird about it the first time, but I'm getting used to it already.

"The blankets," Vi says. "Yes, they should be in Jack's closet above his clothes."

"Great. And the exploding frisbee?"

"That sounds dangerous," I comment.

"It's actually lots of fun," Vi says, then adds, "Um, I don't know where it is. I'm going to have to look." As Ryn leaves to get the blankets, Vi walks around the table and says, "Em, can you continue putting all the food in the baskets? You don't have to use magic if you don't feel comfortable doing that."

She goes off to search for the exploding frisbee, and I consider whether I should risk trying to move food with magic. But at the sound of footsteps coming toward the front door, I turn around.

"Hey," Dash says, leaning against the doorframe while holding something behind his back.

"Hey!" A smile spreads across my face. "You're here." I haven't seen Dash since we left Haverton Tower. After we walked down from the roof, someone pointed out that the blond-and-green haired man in our company was not a Griffin Gifted rebel. He was a Guild employee who'd recently been arrested and was supposed to be awaiting his trial in a cell somewhere. There was a bit of commotion then, and Dash's father— who'd been reunited with his missing son when Dash arrived to warn everyone about the Unseelies—got extremely angry. In the end, Councilor Ashlow agreed to release Dash into his parents' custody and told him to report to the Guild the next morning to sort out his situation. But of course, she'd been too busy to deal with Dash yesterday, so he had to return to the Guild again today. "Did they make a decision about you? I thought the Head Councilor was going to let this drag on forever."

"Nah, they all got tired of me and dismissed the whole case."

"Really?"

"Well, not exactly. I demanded a truth potion and explained how a Councilor and three guardians beat me up and took me off to a secret research station where tests are run on Griffin Gifted and certain other fae. I didn't even get to the end of my story when Councilor Ashlow rushed in and said she'd decided to dismiss the case and I was free to leave immediately while they dealt with more important issues."

"Like trying to keep half the Guild from turning against her?"

"Yeah, pretty much. But everyone was very interested to hear about Reinhold Research Station. That's all going to be out in the open soon. And Councilor Ashlow certainly isn't going to be Head for much longer, I can tell you that. I think we're going to be voting in an entirely new Council soon."

"That's great," I say. And it is great, but I'm also wondering why he's still standing in the doorway and leaving all this space between us.

He grins. "You missed me, didn't you, Emmy."

"Oh, shut up." I fold my arms. "I didn't miss you nearly as much as you missed me."

He looks down before peering up at me between his lashes. "You're right. I missed you terribly. That's why I got you flowers. Well, not flowers. They're actually leaves. But they're prettier than most flowers out there, and I wanted to give you something I could be sure you've never seen before." He pushes away from the doorframe and steps closer. Then he removes his hand from behind his back and produces a bunch of slender branches with dozens of leaves still attached. Each leaf cycles through a seemingly endless palette of colors. But it isn't just the colors that are amazing. It's the way they glow like burning embers as each leaf shifts from one color to the next.

I carefully take the bunch from him, just in case the leaves are as hot as they look. "Don't worry," Dash says. "I know they look like burning coals, but they're not hot. You can touch them." I raise one finger and run it along the edge of a leaf. It glows a little more brightly wherever I touch it.

"They're beautiful, Dash. Thank you." I look up at him and add, "Okay, maybe I lied. I definitely missed you as much as you missed—"

I don't get to finish my sentence because his lips are already on mine. With the bunch of leaves still in my hand, I wrap my arms around his neck and press myself closer. His hands slide into my hair, then down my back. Sparks zap across my lips and tongue, then down my spine and over my arms. I mold myself against him as his fingers press deeper into my back and something softer than sparks rains down onto my arms. I pull my lips away from his and take a moment to catch my breath. Then I look to the side and see what's drifting down through the air around us: tiny star-shaped yellow flowers. I laugh in amazement. "Did those come from us?"

"Yeah, I'm pretty sure they did," Dash says, and I can hear the smile in his voice. As I watch them, the flowers slowly disappear. Dash presses his lips against my forehead. Then he pulls back and says. "Oh. Oops."

I look up and find his gaze pointing behind me. I spin around. Vi and Ryn are standing in the doorway, Vi with a frisbee in her hand and Ryn holding a pile of blankets. "Well," Ryn says, his eyebrows raised. "That was unexpected."

"Oh, crap, this is embarrassing." I press my free hand against my burning face.

"You know we're gonna have to have a talk about this," Ryn says to Dash.

"Right."

"About your intentions."

"Of course," Dash says. I sense him standing a little straighter behind me. "I have only the most honorable of intentions."

"Uh huh," Violet says, crossing her arms and eyeing him with a doubtful look.

"So, uh, should we head down to the beach?" I ask loudly, waving my bunch of leaves in the direction of the door. "After we finish packing the baskets. Which I'm going to do right now."

I avoid everyone's gaze as I place the leaves on the table and hastily finish packing food into the baskets by hand.

"Yuro leaves?" Vi asks, taking a closer look at the bunch.

"Yes," Dash says. "From Creepy Hollow. Picked them myself."

"Nice."

Once the baskets are packed and the blankets and games have been gathered, Vi and Ryn lift everything into the air and direct it out of the house and down the stairs. Dash and I walk behind them, our hands clasped together, and I'm pretty sure my cheeks burn the whole way down. By the time we reach the ground, I'm starting to recover—until Dash kisses my cheek and whispers, "You're pretty when you blush."

I roll my eyes, but I don't let go of his hand, and I don't stop smiling. I know Vi and Ryn are still close enough to overhear us, and when I can no longer stand the awkward—to me, at least—silence between the four of us, I say, "So, uh, tell me ... about ... the Unseelies. What's happening with the Unseelies?"

"Oh, flipping flip. The Unseelie Court is one gigantic mess," Dash says. "I have *no* idea what's going on there. The only thing I know is that Roarke and the former king will spend the rest of their lives in prison."

"A Guild prison?" I ask. When Dash nods, I say, "I thought the Guild couldn't really mess too much with Unseelie matters."

"Yeah, but this wasn't just an Unseelie matter. They exposed our entire world.

And they tried to take over the human world. That affects everyone. They'll probably end up in Noxsom for what they did."

Ahead of us, Vi and Ryn slow down slightly until they're walking beside us. The blankets and picnic baskets continue to glide through the air. "I almost wish for their sakes," Vi says, "that the death penalty still existed. I wouldn't want to be tortured for life. A few days was long enough for me."

"Perhaps," Dash says, "with an entirely new Council being voted in, they'll take another look at how Noxsom is run."

I look ahead as we near the beach and see Chase and Jack already there. It looks like Chase is giving Jack a lesson in how to move chairs around with magic.

"Oh, I do know one other thing about the Unseelies," Dash says. "Remember that prison I was in? Beneath their palace grounds? I told the Guild about it when they first questioned me about the Griffin rebels. I thought they might conveniently forget about it, but now it sounds like they're demanding to know exactly who's being imprisoned there and why. And now is a good time to ask, what with so much upheaval going on in their court. They won't be able to cover things up easily."

"Oh, that's great." I squeeze his hand. "I think I might actually end up liking this new Guild that's coming together."

"Well that would be cool," Dash says, "seeing as how I currently still work there. Hey," he says to Vi and Ryn. "If the Guild decides that Griffin Gifted faeries are totally awesome and should be guardians, will you come and work at the Guild again?"

Ryn laughs, and Vi raises her eyebrows. "Look, I'm not going to say 'never,'" she says, "since I've got a few centuries ahead of me still. But right now, I think I'll go with 'no.'"

"That would be a 'no' from me too," Ryn says. "For now, at least."

We reach the enchanted beach and find that Bandit and Filigree are there too. Filigree is sitting on a chair in the form of a miniature pig, watching dog-shaped Bandit play around in the sand.

With the help of a bit of magic, we soon have our picnic blankets, chairs and bean bags arranged. Ryn, Chase and Jack move further down the beach to play with the exploding frisbee, which apparently makes a bang and sends colorful smoke into the air if anyone holds onto it for too long before throwing it to the next person.

"Hey!" someone shouts from behind us. "Don't start the party without us!"

I look over my shoulder to see Calla and Perry coming toward us. Calla hurries down the sand and swings her arms around me, squeezing tight as she says, "My favorite rebel."

"Hey, what about me?" Dash complains.

"And what about Chase?" I ask with a laugh. "Shouldn't he be your favorite rebel?"

Before Calla can answer, Perry reaches us and says, "You guys have got an awesome place here. Seriously, I love it."

"Thank you," Vi says. "We've worked hard over the years to make our oasis what it is."

"Just think," he adds. "If the Guild's policies regarding Griffin Abilities change and you no longer have to live in hiding, you won't need all the serious protective magic you've got around here."

She sighs. "As nice as it would be to not worry about keeping this place hidden, I don't think we'll ever get rid of all the protective magic. We wouldn't want to invite any rogue Griffin haters to our doorstep to ruin everything we've built."

"Yeah, I guess not," Perry says. Then he looks at me, reaches into his back pocket, and says, "I have something for you, Em."

"Me?" I ask in surprise.

"Yes. An envelope arrived at our Guild this morning addressed to me, and inside it was a small scroll with your name on it."

"Oh." I take the rolled up paper from him. "That's weird."

"I guess the sender didn't know how else to get it to you."

I walk a few paces away to open the scroll and read it, fairly certain before looking at the name at the bottom that I know who this note is from.

Em,

I thought I should probably let you know I'm okay. I couldn't go home, and I couldn't go with you, so I figured I'd head off on my own. Well, not entirely on my own. Imperia's with me. She couldn't wait to get away from Dad.

I know it was probably one of the worst decisions you ever made, but I'm so glad you showed up at our palace. I had fun getting to know you and teaching you magic. Though I would never wish upon you the kind of fate Roarke planned for you as his wife, I still kinda wish we could have been sisters.

Anyway, maybe one day we'll meet again. For now, I'm off to see the rest of the worlds. Both of them.

xx Rora

A small smile pulls at my lips as I lower the note. I was almost completely sure she was fine, but it's good to know for certain.

"Good news?" Vi asks as I return to the picnic.

"Yes. Aurora's fine. She's exploring the world with her dragon."

"That sounds amazing."

"It does sound like a lot of fun," I say. "Maybe Bandit and I can do some exploration together. After all, most of this world is new to me."

"You know who you should meet?" Vi says at the same time Calla says, "Oh, you have *got* to meet Vi's explorer friend."

They look at each other and say, "Tilly." After laughing, Vi adds, "When Tilly eventually finishes whatever exciting expedition she's currently on, I'll make sure to introduce you to her, Em."

"Cool. Hey, Bandit, do you want to go exploring with me?" I call to the black cat currently swiping at the sand where Dash has buried his feet. Bandit looks up and cocks his head a little to the side. "I'll take that as a 'yes,'" I say as I sit at the edge of the blanket beside Dash.

As the last part of the afternoon passes, other members of the oasis community come onto the beach to join us. Gaius, Kobe, several others I've met once or twice, and some I only know because I helped get their unconscious bodies out of Reinhold. Even Elizabeth arrives at some point.

When the sun has disappeared completely and stars glitter in the blue-black sky above us, everyone gathers on their towels, blankets or chairs while Chase and Ryn walk a little further down the beach. I lean my head on Dash's shoulder, watching Chase and Ryn gathering magic for a few minutes. "Not too much longer," Vi says from beside me. "They should be ready soon." And it looks like they are. I lift my head from Dash's shoulder as Ryn and Chase stand apart and raise their hands. I hold my breath, waiting.

Suddenly, fireworks explode above us. Every color imaginable, spinning and darting through the sky before slowly falling, only to be joined by more light and more colors whirling high above us. With Dash's hand wrapped around mine, and Vi sitting on my other side, I watch the display in wonder until every last spark has drifted down toward the enchanted ocean. Then, as Bandit climbs into my lap, I breathe out a sigh of absolute contentment. I raise my face to the stars, close my eyes, and smile.

I am finally home.

Thank you for reading *Emerson's Story*.

For additional bonus scenes from the Creepy Hollow series,
as well as companion novellas, visit creepyhollowbooks.com.

Begin a new story set in the same fictional world …

Two years ago, the Guild of Guardians killed my parents
for a crime they didn't commit. They tried to kill me too,
but I got away.

I buried the past and made a new life for myself, hidden in a world
not my own. The human world, where faeries belong
in stories and magic is unknown.

But now the Guild has found me. *He's* found me.

~~The boy I once loved.~~ The boy who tried to kill me.

And this time … he wants my help.

. . .

Look out for From Storm and Shadow, *the first book in
the Stormfae series!*

Rachel Morgan spent a good deal of her childhood
living in a fantasy land of her own making, crafting endless
stories of make-believe and occasionally writing some of them down.
After completing a degree in genetics and discovering she still
wasn't grown-up enough for a 'real' job, she decided to return to
those story worlds still spinning around her imagination.
These days days she spends much of her time immersed
in fantasy land once more, writing fiction for
young adults and those young at heart.

www.rachel-morgan.com